2006

Guide to Literary Agents®

Kathryn S. Brogan, Editor
Robert Lee Brewer & Joanna Masterson, Assistant Editors

WRITER'S DIGEST BOOKS
CINCINNATI, OH

Managing Editor, Writer's Digest Market Books: Alice Pope
Supervisory Editor, Writer's Digest Market Books: Donna Poehner

Writer's Market website: www.writersmarket.com
Writer's Digest website: www.writersdigest.com

Published by F+W Publications, 4700 East Galbraith Road, Cincinnati, Ohio 45236. Printed and bound in the United States of America.

International Standard Serial Number 1078-6945
International Standard Book Number 1-58297-399-7

Cover design by Kelly Kofron
Interior design by Clare Finney
Production coordinated by Robin Richie

Attention Booksellers: This is an annual directory of F+W Publications.
Return deadline for this edition is December 31, 2006.

Contents

CONTACTING AGENTS

BEFORE YOU SIGN

LITERARY AGENTS

SCRIPT AGENTS

PRODUCTION COMPANIES

SCRIPT CONTESTS

INDEPENDENT PUBLICISTS

RESOURCES

INDEXES

From the Editor

For the first time ever, I'm writing this letter nearly three months before this book goes to the printer. Why am I not putting it off like I usually do? Because I'm working ahead to prepare for (to borrow a phrase from another editor) the ultimate deadline—my "due date." During one of many sleepless nights, it occurred to me that pregnancy has a lot in common with finding an agent.

Don't believe there's a connection? Well, how about those long, sleepless nights (a common occurrence during pregnancy)? I bet the same thing happens to many writers after they submit their manuscripts to an agent. I bet it's safe to say they lie awake wondering: "Did the agent like my manuscript? Why hasn't he contacted me? It's been three months—did my manuscript get lost in the mail? Did I forget to include my contact information?"

Still not convinced? Okay, think about the listings in this book. There's information on more than 600 agents—each has qualities that appeal to certain kinds of writers, and most have a history of impressive sales. Reading about all of these agents can leave writers feeling very confused, and asking: "There are at least 35 agents who represent science fiction, which is right for me? How do I know I'm not getting scammed?" The same kinds of questions raced through my mind as I registered for baby items: "There are at least 15 different strollers to choose from, which is best? Each product has a different manufacturer, how do I know who is legitimate and who isn't?"

Fortunately we each have good resources to help us navigate our journey. We both have online tools, advice from our friends and family, and a variety of other resources at our disposal, but you have one thing I don't—this book. Yes, there are hundreds of books on pregnancy and parenting, but unlike *Guide to Literary Agents*, there's not one, definitive resource I can turn to. This book, however, is, undeniably, the industry's definitive resource in researching, choosing, and contacting agents. Whether you're looking for answers to your questions, the mailing addresses of agents, or how to format your manuscript, you'll find it in this book.

Use this tool on your journey and, before you know it, you'll have gotten exactly what you've been working and preparing for (and losing sleep over!), your baby—your published book.

Kathryn Struckel Brogan

Kathryn Struckel Brogan
Editor, *Guide to Literary Agents*
literaryagent@fwpubs.com

Getting Started

How to Use Guide to Literary Agents

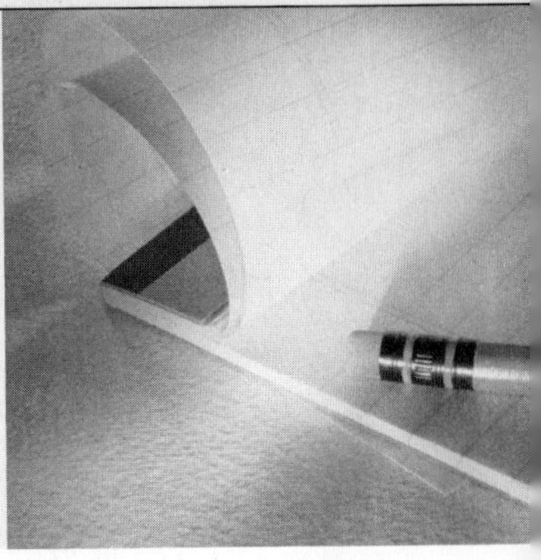

Starting a search for a literary agent can seem overwhelming, whether you've just finished your first book or you have several publishing credits on your résumé. You are more than likely eager to start pursuing agents and anxious to see your name on the spine of a book. But before you go directly to the listings of agencies in this book, take a few minutes to familiarize yourself with the way agents work and how you should approach them. By doing so, you will be more prepared for your search and ultimately save yourself time and unnecessary grief.

Read the articles

This book begins with feature articles that give advice on the best strategies for contacting agents and provide perspectives on the author/agent relationship. The articles are organized into four sections appropriate for each stage of the search process: **Before You Start**, **Narrowing Your List**, **Contacting Agents**, and **Before You Sign**. You may want to start by reading through each article, and then refer back to relevant articles during each stage of your search for an agent.

Since there are many ways to make that initial contact with an agent, we've also provided a section of **Personal Views**. These personalized interviews with agents offer both information and inspiration for any writer hoping to find representation.

Decide what you're looking for

An independent publicist can promote your work—before or after an agent or publisher has taken an interest in it. If you're looking for a publicist, we offer a section of **Independent Publicists.** Often publicists can drum up media time for their clients and help them get the exposure they need to make a sale or increase the number of copies sold.

A literary or script agent will present your work directly to editors or producers. It's his job to get his client's work published or sold and to negotiate a fair contract. In the **Literary Agents** and **Script Agents** sections, we list each agent's contact information and explain what type of work the agency represents and how to submit your work for consideration.

For face-to-face contact, many writers prefer to meet agents at conferences. By doing so, writers can assess an agent's personality, attend workshops, and have the chance to get more feedback on their work than they get by mailing submissions and waiting for a response. The section for **Writers' Conferences** is divided into regions and lists only those conferences where agents will be in attendance. In many cases, private consultations can be arranged, and agents attend with the hope of finding new clients to represent.

Frequently Asked Questions

1 **Why do you include agents who are not seeking new clients?** We provide contact information for agents who are members of the Association of Authors' Representatives who have not answered our request for information. Because of these agents' reputations, we feel the book would be incomplete without an acknowledgement of their companies. Some agents even ask that their listings indicate they are currently closed to new clients.

2 **Why do you exclude fee-charging agents?** There is a great debate in the publishing industry about whether literary agents should charge writers a reading or critiquing fee. There are fee-charging agents who make sales to prominent publishers. However, we have received a number of complaints in the past regarding fees, and therefore we've chosen to list only those agents who do not charge fees to writers.

3 **Why are some agents not listed in *Guide to Literary Agents?*** Some agents may not have returned our request for information. We have taken others out of the book because we received very serious complaints about their agencies. Refer to the General Index in the back of the book to see why an agency isn't listed in this edition.

4 **Do I need more than one agent if I write in different genres?** More than likely, no. If you have written in one genre and want to switch to a new style of writing, ask your agent if he is willing to represent you in your new endeavor. Most agents will continue to represent clients no matter what genre they choose to write. Occasionally, an agent may feel he has no knowledge of a certain genre and will recommend an appropriate agent to his client. Regardless, you should always talk to your agent about any potential career move.

5 **Why don't you list more foreign agents?** Most U.S. agents have relationships with "foreign co-agents" in other countries. It is more common for a U.S. agent to work with a co-agent to sell a client's book abroad than for a writer to work directly with a foreign agent. We do, however, list agents in England and Canada who sell to both U.S. and foreign publishers.

6 **Do agents ever contact a writer who is self-published?** Occasionally. If a self-published author attracts the attention of the media, or if her book sells extremely well, an agent might approach the author in hopes of representing her.

7 **Why won't the agent I queried return my material?** An agent may not answer your query or return your manuscript for several reasons. Perhaps you did not include a self-addressed, stamped envelope (SASE). Many agents will throw away a submission without a SASE. Or the agent may have moved. To avoid using expired addresses, use the most current edition of *Guide to Literary Agents*, or access the information online at www.writersmarket.com. Another possibility is that the agent is swamped with submissions. Agents can be overwhelmed with queries, especially if the agent has recently spoken at a conference or has been featured in an article or book.

For script writers, we have sections of **Script Contests** and **Production Companies**. Winning a contest can help you gain recognition in the film industry, land an internship, or impress an agent. Or, you can use the producers section to market your work directly to independent production companies. Once you have some experience in the industry, you'll make important connections, find additional work, and have the credentials to impress an agent who will help you with your long-term career goals.

BEFORE YOU START

Writing the Story

Work Smarter Instead of Harder

by Candy Davis

Screenwriters often come off like desperadoes—they compete in the rodeo arena of a crazy industry where they have to practically lie, cheat, and steal their way to success. They're expected to create an entire story in 12 weeks—a brutal deadline. How long does it take your average novelist to lasso the same story? Two years if she's lucky, 20 if she's not.

Screenwriters who survive have learned the shortcuts of chasing down a story, roping it, and wrestling it to the ground. If you intend to gallop into a writing career, you need to become a desperado, just like a screenwriter. Obvious tricks like cutting weak characters and sloppy verbs are just the beginning. Below are three tips, stolen from the screenwriters' saddlebag of tricks, to help you work smarter instead of harder.

1. Get a life—a story life, that is.

From the beginning of time, stories that reliably capture an audience are variations on three themes:

- A worthy character fights to overcome the elements.
- A worthy character fights to overcome her nemesis.
- A worthy character fights to overcome her internal flaws.

You would think developing a story would be simple since you only have three themes from which to choose—yet millions of writers get ambushed in this pass, or they quit when they find themselves going around in circles.

I'll let you in on a secret: There's nothing wrong with a little cheating when it comes to rounding up a herd of ideas and heading them in the right direction. Aspiring writers often shoot themselves in the foot when they set their sights on creating a story "that has never been done before."

Each story is a gate opening on the same arena—it's how you ride your story out that counts. Good stories are everywhere, but they're hard to catch. You may find the story fragments peacefully grazing in your mind often frustrate you. For once, you'd like to find a story that works, and that means developing a compelling and admirable main character

---

CANDY DAVIS, freelance editor and founder of Ink Dance Literary Services (www.inkdance.biz), writes award-winning novels, short stories, and screenplays, two of which have been sold and one produced. She is best known for her edgy fiction dealing with complex and sensitive themes.

with an intriguing problem complex enough to entertain an audience for hours. The answer? Follow the great writers who've already blazed the trails for you.

You can do this by picking a tried and true story that's survived the test of time, and make it your own. Shakespeare wasn't the first to put his brand on stories rustled from old sources. He swiped *Romeo and Juliet* from an ancient Italian, Masuccio di Salerno, who stole it from an ancient Greek named Xenophon Ephesius, who stole it from someone else. You may not recognize it at first, but the same story shows up in thousands of modern films, miniseries, sitcoms, novels, short stories, musicals, and countless other forms (i.e., *Romeo Must Die*, *West Side Story*, *It's All Relative*). We never get tired of replaying this ancient drama because it speaks to our basic humanity.

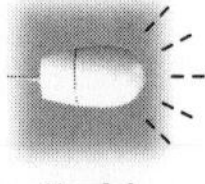

Useful Websites

Where do you dig up usable skeletons like this? You'll find loads of writer's resources, from Joseph Campbell's massive academic tome, *The Hero With a Thousand Faces* (Mythos Books), to the one-liners in *TV Guide*. Start your story-rustlin' project with Ronald B. Tobias' *20 Master Plots and How To Build Them* (Writer's Digest Books). If you prefer to use the Internet, The Internet Movie Database (www.imdb.com) is a quick-stop spot to shop for plots, and you can arrange your search by subject. Still want to do it yourself? Dip into mythology, history, or your favorite family legends—even the Bible is packed with compelling stories begging for a modern remake.

Work Smarter Instead of Harder

Tip

Screenwriters save themselves the effort of developing their own theme, characters, and plots by shamelessly ripping off the bones of a great archetypal story of greed, lust, or revenge. For example, Amy Heckerling's *Clueless* started out as "Jane Austen's *Emma* meets *Beverly Hills 90210*."

2. Promise me anything, but give me the end.

When your story sets out for uptown Los Angeles, but ends up broke and hungry at the rail yards in Amarillo, you need a new trail map to get you (in a straight line!) from "Once upon a time . . ." to THE END.

On the first page of any story you've got to show your readers an admirable, intriguing character with one compelling and attainable goal, and then promise to take them to that goal. By the last page, you'd better make good on your promise, but in a way that's a surprise to both the character and the reader. For example, the movie *The Bourne Identity* centers on Jason Bourne, an amnesiac in search of his own identity. Screenwriter Tony Gilroy knew the beginning and endpoint of this story, so he chose an opening metaphor full of mystery and danger (that evokes the character's single goal): A nameless man lost at sea—in a storm. Unconscious. The end is classic—Bourne learns his own identity, but more importantly that knowledge poses an even bigger question: Can Bourne live with who he is?

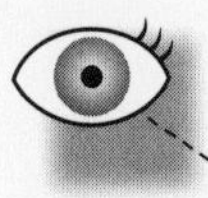

See Also

A good, one-page synopsis is another step to get you from "Once upon a time . . ." to THE END. The synopsis helps you separate the bones of the story (what happens *inside* the character, i.e., her need to accomplish a specific outcome and the emotional process that inspires her to perform actions that change the story direction) from glitzy plot decorations (plot is what happens *outside*: where the character works, what she's wearing, etc.). Throw out unnecessary plot details until you have pure story on one page. (For more information on writing a synopsis, see The Art of the Synopsis on page 60.)

Start writing your synopsis by corralling the beginning (Bourne has no identity), ending (Bourne discovers his identity), climax (Bourne defeats the CIA), and the major turning points in between. In Gilroy's second act, Bourne finds love, an astounding pile of money, and a talent for martial arts. He also discovers someone's hunting him, and the game turns tough. From this point, the story barrels toward the third-act climax, in which the hero meets and defeats the CIA. Fill in the space between these major plot points with the character's reactions and emotions.

Work Smarter Instead of Harder

Try writing a one-page, single-spaced synopsis or outline before you sit down to write your manuscript. Every time the story bucks you off, throw the synopsis out and draft a new one to help you understand how the latest developments will affect your story. Limiting the synopsis to a single page will test your patience, but it will also reveal the heart of your novel or screenplay—and you can use it as a foundation to expand your story to 3, 5, or even 50 pages of narrative.

3. Pitch it!

Before you throw yourself in front of an oncoming agent or editor, test your story the way professional screenwriters do—pitch it to everyone you meet. Write a pitch that sums up the entire story in four sentences. If you can make it shorter, even better, but be sure the references are easy for the listener to understand. The pitch that sold Peter Hyams' *Outland* was "*High Noon* in outer space."

The first sentence of a pitch illustrates the character and his problem. The second sentence introduces the opposition. In the third sentence, illuminate the internal process that leads your character to the goal. The last sentence suggests the ending. A test pitch for *The Bourne Identity* might read something like this:

> An amnesiac is a man of mystery, even to himself. With only sketchy clues to his name and a shady past, he learns an efficient network of killers is on his trail. As he pieces his identity together, he must face the awful realization he was once one of them. Recalling the deadly skills the killers taught him, he puts his life on the line to stop their double assassination plot intended to redistribute the global balance of power.

Screenwriters pitch their stories before they write. You, too, should make rehearsing your pitch part of your daily routine. Give yourself a leg up by first memorizing your pitch—it's easy to sound natural while making eye contact with your listener rather than reading from a page. Then, try your pitch on everyone you meet. If their eyes glaze over as they listen, rewrite your pitch. You'll know it's right when you're still in the saddle eight seconds later and they want more details.

Work Smarter Instead of Harder

It may seem like a struggle to get down to the heart of your story in four sentences, but if you've already lassoed your beginning and end, and hog-tied your synopsis, the pitch will practically write itself.

BEFORE YOU START

Screenwriting 101

Understanding the Basics

by Mark Sevi

So you want to write a script? Great. Let's get down to it. If you're not already a movie fan, start haunting the local video store and begin watching as many films as you can. Then go online and download some scripts and read them (www.script-o-rama.com). This is an essential first step that should become a habit in your scriptwriting life.

Find a writing group or class

Formatting a script is easy. You don't need to know anything about camera direction or technical jargon, but there are a few simple rules about where things go in a script (like dialogue). What you really need is a support system to help you identify problems, offer suggestions, and share information. Go to a community (junior) college, look in your local community center guide, call a college and talk to a professor—anything to help you find a class where you can learn the art of scriptwriting in a supportive environment.

WHAT'S YOUR CONCEPT?

Important

Identify the reasons you're writing a script—is it for personal satisfaction, a learning tool, or something to sell? You need to know your reason for writing a script because you're going to need to define and refine your concept based on your goal. If you're writing for personal satisfaction or as a learning tool, then anything you come up with is fine. If you're going to try and sell your script, you need to figure out the market for which you're aiming. If it's a commercial market, then your concept has to be so interesting it alone could sell the work.

Once you've identified why you're writing your script, you need to define and refine your concept. What makes what you're writing unique? Does that *Die-Hard*-in-a-Spaceship concept you just can't shake have a twist that will elevate it above the other 3,000 *Die Hard* concepts? Isn't *Die Hard*-in-a-spaceship sort of like *Alien*? How would yours be different from either movie?

If you discover your idea is similar to another, and you still want to continue working on it, make sure you have or can find a different slant. Compare *Double Indemnity* and *Body Heat*. Both have similar themes, structure, and movement. The difference between the two is Lawrence Kasdan (*Body Heat*) made his male protagonist an attorney instead of an insurance adjuster. Kasdan used Ned Racine's expertise (or lack of it) as a central element in Matty

---

MARK SEVI (www.plotpoints.com) is a professional screenwriter who lives in Southern California. He has 16 films to his credit and two in preproduction for the SciFi Channel. He also teaches and writes articles about screenwriting.

Walker's plot to kill the husband, blame it on Racine, and reap the financial benefits. It's one minor change that allowed the film to gain favorable comparisons to the Billy Wilder classic without being accused of copying from it.

Also, do some research and see if you can find any scripts similar to your concept (www.scriptsales.com). Scriptsales.com and similar sites provide you with a sense of what Hollywood is buying. You can spot trends, understand what types of films sell, and get a sense of how to shape your script so it has a better chance of getting someone's attention in a real-world film market.

Important

Keep in mind, it's best to check with a lawyer if you're adapting something (i.e., a book), telling a true story, or using characters that are real, because you may have to secure the movie rights. You don't have to do this when you're writing the script, but once your script is complete, know that no industry professional will read or represent your script unless you can deliver the rights.

Once you have an idea of your script's concept, move on to the next step. Don't worry if your concept's not tight yet—you'll refine it more as you work on the script. Plus, the more you think about it as you write, the clearer the concept will become.

NECESSARY ELEMENTS

Tone

Setting the proper tone is key. Will your script be straight horror like *The Grudge*, farce like *Scary Story*, or a combination of the two like *Shaun of the Dead*? Are you funny enough to carry off a romantic comedy, or would you be better served to stick to drama in telling the story of two people who fall in love? Does your story about religion have an irreverent tone like *Saved*, or would you rather move people deeply like *The Passion of the Christ*? When writing your script, you need to decide what tone best gets your message and story across, and best fits your style.

Ending first

You really can't write a successful script unless you know where your story is going. Imagine taking a trip without a clear destination. You can, of course, have a general destination in mind, say Colorado, and then refine your goal as you drive there, Telluride. It's the same with a script. You know it's going to end with the boy getting the girl but having to jump in the water in order to do it (take a "leap of faith" like in *Splash*). Given that ending, what set of characters and circumstances are going to have the most impact? How will the emotional context of the scenes that come before it contribute to the ending? Knowing in what direction the script is heading can only be determined from reverse. Ending first.

But why not create your characters before you write the ending? Any ending can serve dozens of characters. In the movie *Saw*, the killer wants people to start appreciating life. He sets two men to suffer through an emotional turmoil in order to force them to that point. Who are these two men? They could have been anyone, really. What's important is *how* they move through the adventure.

Characters

Several types of characters are going to be necessary depending on what you're writing. If you're writing a romantic comedy, you need a boy and a girl (or some variation). You need supporting characters, like friends, parents, etc. If you're writing an actioneer, then a hero-type and villain-type are required with a sidekick, partner, etc. If you want a good idea of the archetypes that go into most stories, pick up Christopher Vogler's *The Writer's Journey* (Michael Wiese Productions). He describes the various types of characters in solid detail.

When creating characters, choose the villain first and then the main character. Why?

Before the hero can do anything heroic, the villain has to be moving behind the scenes. In the movie *The Incredibles*, Syndrome's (the villain) plan to kill superheroes is in play long before Bob Parr (the hero) becomes aware of him. The villain's plan determines the hero's initial and subsequent movements.

A ghost

Every successful hero-type has a ghost—something from his past that haunts him, a deed he did, something that was done to him, etc. The ghost sits in the back, driving the main story, but is not necessarily a direct part of the story. A ghost can work toward the theme of the story, the "why" of it, or the plot, the "how" of it. In good scripts a ghost does both.

Stakes

What's at stake? Without fail, the answer to this question always needs to be: life and death. It might be physical (real) or it might be emotional (symbolic), but it's always life and death. Stakes don't work unless they are life and death. What happens if Indiana Jones doesn't find the Ark? Nazis will take over the world (physical life and death). What happens if Harry doesn't find true, mature love with Erica in *Something's Gotta Give*? He'll be a lonely and unfulfilled man (emotional death).

Remember: Stakes need a time frame. If I tell someone they're going to die in 50 years, that's not such a stressful thing. But, if I say they only have a weekend to live, that's exponentially more intense. Solving the crime, saving the world, or finding love, all work better if there's a limited time frame that ratchets up the suspense.

Theme

Theme is important because it's the "why" of what happens in a story. It doesn't have to be terribly deep philosophically, but it should be clear enough to you and the audience throughout the movement of the story and contribute to the way the story ends. For example, what does the movie *The Incredibles* say about life? We should value what's around us, like family. How about *The Wonder Boys*? Don't be a coward. *The Aviator*? Believe in yourself even if others don't. Those are the overarching themes that give movies a place to go besides the plot. Theme gives a story an envelope in which to sit so the audience can participate on a deeper level than the events of the story allow. Once a film is finished, you want your audience to feel something more has been imparted than just entertainment.

IT'S ALL AN ACT

For More Info

Once you have most of the above elements in place you should begin thinking about structure. Modern film employs a three-act structure. This article is too limited to go into much detail, but Syd Field's seminal book, *The Screenwriter's Workbook* (Dell), covers structure in an easy-to-understand format.

For the purpose of this article, however, use the following technique to figure out the Acts in your script. Imagine you're telling your friend a simple story about your job. You start with something like, "Well, I got to work, logged onto my computer, and read an e-mail from Julia. It was very cryptic. It said, 'Meet me in the break room in five minutes.' When I went into the break room, she was in tears. She had just been fired, but wouldn't tell me why." That's Act I. Next, go on to tell your friend how you responded, what you did to help Julia through the firing, the confrontation she had later with her ex-boss about their affair, and how he associated her embarrassing scream-fest with you. That's Act II. Finally, tell your friend how you calmed both Julia and her boss, what impact it had on everyone, and what lesson you learned from it. That's Act III.

We write stories the same way we tell stories—there's a beginning, middle, and an end.

If you break your story into those major sections, you're well on your way to understanding structure. Again, I'm not a huge proponent of knowing too much about your story before you write. Not knowing all of it is okay because it forces you to rely on your subconscious. Figure out your ending, your characters, and your first act to get started—the rest will come naturally.

COMMITMENT IS REQUIRED

Imagine you want to learn how to play the piano. How do you do that if you never touch a piano or only practice once in a while? Just like playing the piano, writing is a skill. If you don't find time to write, you can't write. Talent only carries you so far. Beyond that, you need to make a commitment to writing every day. It'll be hard at first, like doing exercise, but it will also be fun. Eventually, though, the newness and excitement will wear a bit and you'll be stuck on a part. You'll put the script aside thinking you'll get to it tomorrow. I've been writing and teaching writing for many years. Trust me—the "next day" never comes.

Scripts are approximately 110 pages. If you break it down and write five good pages a week, it'll probably take you a few months to finish a first draft—then you'll need a second draft (and maybe a third). The entire process might take a year (or years) depending on how meticulous you are in your writing. Writing a script requires a true commitment to the process despite the circumstances that might conspire to prevent you from writing.

Once you've made the commitment to your writing, you also have to teach the people around you about this commitment, help them understand it, and make sure they make allowances for the time you need. You can't let other people drag you aside or distract you when you're writing because, as I said before, the "next day" never comes.

No matter if you write at night or in the morning, or plan during the week and write on the weekends, you need a system of writing that gives you enough time and space to relax and explore the world you're creating.

Writers' Conferences

Getting the Most Bang for Your Buck

by Paula Eykelhof

As a writer—whether you're aspiring, in the beginning stages of your career, or well published—what you're doing is essentially solitary work. Yes, you probably talk to people in the course of doing research. You might escape solitude by belonging to a writers' organization or a critique group where you can discuss your passion with other like-minded souls. But, let's face it: If you're a writer, for the most part, you're on your own.

That's where conferences come in. Attending carefully chosen writers' conferences every year might be one of the best things you can do for yourself and your career. (For an up-to-date list of writers' conferences, see **Writers' Conferences** on page 245.)

There are three important reasons for attending a writers' conference:

1. A good writers' conference is an opportunity to learn about your market and about the craft of writing.
2. It's a chance to make contact with editors, agents, and other writers.
3. It allows you to socialize with people who care about the same things you do in a genuinely inspiring (and enjoyable) environment.

DO YOUR HOMEWORK

The opportunities to learn at conferences take many different forms, and you should try to benefit from all of them. Once you've chosen a conference to attend, thoroughly study your conference agenda and create a personal schedule. If at all possible, make sure it's flexible enough to allow for networking opportunities, chance encounters, and time for visiting with friends (both old and new).

Market-oriented sessions

As you begin studying the conference agenda, identify the sessions and panels concerning the markets in which you're interested. They can include sessions that spotlight various publishers, and discussions with authors published by houses or magazines where you'd like to be published. Many writers' conferences include panels featuring agents and editors—both of whom can give you a good, current overview of the industry. A word of advice: At any workshop or panel involving publishing professionals, take the opportunity to ask questions.

PAULA EYKELHOF is an executive editor at Harlequin Books. She works primarily on single-title, women's fiction but has been involved with series romance for many years. She has also written for magazines, worked as a television researcher and writer, and was—briefly—a puppeteer.

Information sessions of this kind should probably be the first ones you slot into your personal schedule.

Writing-related sessions

Once you've added all the relevant and/or interesting market-oriented sessions to your schedule, go through the specific writing-related panels and workshops in the conference agenda, and choose those that fill a gap in your knowledge or address a weakness in your writing. These sessions are generally lectures or panel discussions, although some conferences offer more extensive workshops, which generally last several hours or more. If you attend one of these longer sessions, be prepared to complete various hands-on exercises and activities.

Writing-related workshops can usually be divided into three groups:

1. **Technical and craft-oriented sessions.** Topics in these sessions are generally related to characterization, style, setting, query letters, etc.
2. **Business of writing sessions.** Topics in this group include financial and tax planning, approaching editors and agents, achieving an appropriate work-life balance, finding inspiration, etc.
3. **Research sessions.** Many fiction conferences, especially those covering a number of genres, offer talks by experts in a variety of areas (a detective or forensic specialist, a historian, a doctor, etc.). If the topic offered is relevant to something you're working on (or hope to work on), or even if it's simply a subject you're interested in, try to make time to attend these sessions because they could lead to valuable ideas and reliable contacts.

NETWORK, NETWORK, NETWORK

Aside from giving you the chance to gather information about the craft and the business of writing, conferences can give you another important benefit: You can meet, speak with, and often socialize with editors, agents, and other writers. Take advantage of the opportunity to talk at meals, in the bar, at publishers' parties, standing in line—wherever you find yourself. Make introductions. Chat with everyone you meet who seems approachable. Pay attention to the names on badges (and wear yours).

Many conferences host formal appointments with editors and agents providing attendees the opportunity to pitch an idea. If these appointments are available and you have an idea to pitch, sign up. If, however, the individual appointments are filled or only for people who have a complete manuscript, check and see if the conference is hosting group appointments. If group appointments are available, sign up because you'll be able to ask questions, and, sometimes, you'll be able to make an informal pitch.

Pitching your idea

So, if you sign up for a one-on-one appointment with an editor or agent, what's the best way to pitch a book idea? Understandably, many writers are nervous. Start by remembering editors and agents are human, and they have as much invested in finding a great new writer as you have in being that writer. But, at the same time, remember they're busy professionals.

When you pitch an idea, you need to be clear, precise, and prepared. I suggest you avoid simply reading a summary of your story or idea. If you don't trust your memory and feel you need the aid of index cards, that's okay, but as you use the cards, try to look up a few times, and make eye contact with the editor or agent. As you pitch, make sure you outline the premise, and, if your work is fiction, say something about the characters—who and what they are, how the plot begins and ends, and the conflict. If it's nonfiction, talk about the subject, your unique slant on it, your research, and your qualifications.

Conference Tips

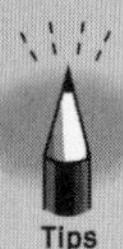

Here are 10 things to do when you prepare for and attend a conference:

1. **Set goals.** What you get out of a conference is entirely up to you. Set goals to stay on track and get everything you need from the conference.

2. **Plan ahead.** Review the conference agenda and create a schedule of the sessions you want to attend. Take time to read the bios of the speakers at the conference in case you are given an opportunity to network with them.

3. **Be prepared.** Take your business cards, résumé, and writing samples so you're prepared when it comes time to network.

4. **Be polite.** Once you're ensconced in a session and the doors are closed, don't walk out of the session unless it's for a legitimate reason (i.e., it's the wrong session, you have an appointment with an agent, medical emergency, etc.).

5. **Gather handouts.** Most speakers will provide handouts during their session. Make sure you take all the handouts that are available—the speaker wouldn't have brought them if they weren't useful.

6. **Listen.** The speakers at the conference are there for a reason—they know something you don't. Make sure you listen carefully, especially when the speaker is an editor or an agent—he will usually tell you exactly what he's looking for in a submission, and how he'd like you to submit to him.

7. **Participate.** If the speaker asks questions during his session, feel free to participate in the discussion, or if you have a question about something the speaker said, don't hesitate to ask.

8. **Be sensitive, but don't monopolize.** While most speakers are more than happy to chat with you after a session, they don't have the time to carry on a lengthy conversation. If you have a question requiring a detailed explanation, ask the speaker if you can contact him after the conference is over.

9. **Network.** Whether you're standing in line, eating dinner, or attending a cocktail party, take advantage of the opportunity to talk to other writers and conference presenters.

10. **Follow up.** You will make many connections at a conference. Bring an envelope with you to collect business cards, and take the time to jot a note on the back of the card about the person who gave you the card and whether you intend to follow up after the conference.

In either case, be as succinct as you can. Mention the market or audience you have in mind. Ask any questions you might have—and give the editor or agent a chance to ask you questions. Enquire politely whether he is willing to see your work; chances are, the answer will be yes.

GET INSPIRED

So, you've scheduled the sessions you want to attend and the appointments with agents and editors, but when does inspiration enter your schedule?

In addition to offering a variety of informative sessions on the craft and the business of writing, most conferences include keynote speakers, often best-selling authors or other well-respected industry professionals, whose primary role is to offer inspiration and personal insight. They might do it by sharing their own experiences breaking into the writing profession or onto *The New York Times* bestseller list, or they might make suggestions or give advice for dealing with the difficulties and discouragement often encountered in publishing.

Attending a conference can be both informational and inspirational thanks to the atmosphere of anticipation and excitement, the people you meet, and the things you learn. And what, after all, is more inspiring for a writer than being invited to submit your manuscript to an editor or agent for further review? Who knows, that may just be the editor or agent who's going to buy or sell your book!

BEFORE YOU START

Do I Need an Agent?

If you have a book ready to be published, you may be wondering if you need a literary agent. If you're not sure whether you want to work with an agent, consider the following factors.

WHAT CAN AN AGENT DO FOR YOU?

An agent will believe in your writing and know an audience interested in what you write. As the representative for your work, your agent will tell editors your manuscript is the best thing to land on her desk this year. But beyond being enthusiastic about your manuscript, there are a lot of benefits to using an agent.

For starters, today's competitive marketplace can be difficult to break into, especially for unpublished writers. Many larger publishing houses will only look at manuscripts from agents. In fact, approximately 80 percent of books published by the major houses are acquired through agents.

But an agent's job isn't just getting your book through a publisher's door. That's only a small part of what an agent can do for you. The sections below describe the various jobs agents do for their clients, many of which would be difficult for a writer to do without outside help.

Agents know editors' tastes and needs

An agent possesses information on a complex web of publishing houses and a multitude of editors to make sure her clients' manuscripts are placed in the right hands. This knowledge is gathered through relationships she cultivates with acquisition editors—the people who decide which books to present to their publisher for possible publication. Through her industry connections, an agent becomes aware of the specializations of publishing houses and their imprints, knowing that one publisher only wants contemporary romances while another is interested solely in nonfiction books about the military. By networking with editors over lunch, an agent also learns more specialized information—which editor is looking for a crafty Agatha Christie-style mystery for the fall catalog, for example.

Agents track changes in publishing

Being attentive to constant market changes and shifting trends is also a major requirement of an agent's job. An agent understands what it may mean for clients when publisher A merges with publisher B and when an editor from house C moves to house D. Or what it means when readers—and therefore editors—are no longer interested in westerns, but instead can't get their hands on enough Stephen King-style suspense novels.

Agents get your manuscript read faster

Although it may seem like an extra step to send your manuscript to an agent instead of directly to a publishing house, the truth is an agent can prevent writers from wasting months sending manuscripts that end up in the wrong place or buried in someone's slush pile. Editors rely on agents to save them time as well. With little time to sift through the hundreds of unsolicited submissions arriving weekly in the mail, an editor is naturally going to prefer a work already approved by a qualified reader (i.e., the agent) and from a reader who knows the editor's preferences. For this reason, many of the larger publishers only accept agented submissions.

Agents understand contracts

When publishers write contracts, they are primarily interested in their own bottom line rather than the best interests of the author. Writers unfamiliar with contractual language may find themselves bound to a publisher with whom they no longer want to work. Or, they might find themselves tied to a publisher who prevented them from getting royalties on their first book until subsequent books were written. Agents use their experience to negotiate a contract that benefits the writer while still respecting the publisher's needs.

Agents negotiate—and exploit—subsidiary rights

Beyond publication, a savvy agent keeps in mind other opportunities for your manuscript. If your agent believes your book will also be successful as an audio book, a Book-of-the-Month Club selection, or even a blockbuster movie, these options will be considered when the agent shops your manuscript. These additional opportunities for your writing are called "subsidiary rights." Part of an agent's job is to keep track of the strengths and weaknesses of different publishers' subsidiary rights offices to determine the deposition of these rights to your work. After the contract is negotiated, an agent will seek additional money-making opportunities for the rights she kept for her client.

Agents get escalators

An escalator is a bonus that an agent can negotiate as part of the book contract. It is commonly given when a book appears on a best-seller list or if a client appears on a popular television show. For example, a publisher might give a writer a $50,000 bonus if she is picked for a book club. Both the agent and the editor know such media attention will sell more books, and the agent negotiates an escalator to ensure the writer benefits from this increase in sales.

Agents track payments

Since an agent only receives payment when the publisher pays the writer, it's in the agent's best interest to make sure the writer is paid on schedule. Some publishing houses are notorious for late payments. Having an agent distances you from any conflict over payment and allows you to spend your time writing instead of making phone calls.

Agents are strong advocates

Besides standing up for your right to be paid on time, agents can ensure your book gets more attention from the publisher's marketing department—a better cover design, or other benefits you may not know to ask for during the publishing process. An agent can also provide advice during each step of this process, as well as guidance about your long-term writing career.

WHEN YOU MIGHT NOT NEED AN AGENT

Although there are many reasons to work with an agent, an author can benefit from submitting his own work. For example, if your writing focuses on a very specific area, you may want to work with a small or specialized publisher. These houses are usually open to receiving material directly from writers. Smaller houses can often give more attention to a writer than a large house can, providing editorial help, marketing expertise, and other advice directly to the writer.

Some writers use a lawyer or entertainment attorney instead of an agent. If a lawyer specializes in intellectual property, he can help a writer with contract negotiations. Instead of giving the lawyer a commission, the lawyer is paid for his time only.

And, of course, some people prefer working independently instead of relying on others to do their work. If you are one of these people, it is probably better to shop your own work instead of constantly butting heads with an agent. And despite the benefits of working with an agent, it is possible to sell your work directly to a publisher—people do it all the time!

BEFORE YOU START

FAQs About Agents

Compiled by Robert Lee Brewer

Literary agents are the gatekeepers of the publishing industry, which means they know what works and what doesn't for writers trying to get published. Here eight respected agents share their knowledge and answer common questions about agents and agenting. You can find these, and other frequently asked questions, at WritersMarket.com.

Loretta Barrett established Loretta Barrett Books, Inc., which handles both nonfiction and fiction, in 1990. Prior to becoming an agent, she was vice president and executive editor at Doubleday, and editor-in-chief of Anchor Books.

Kimberley Cameron has been partners with Dorris Halsey of the Reece Halsey North Literary Agency since 1993. Before becoming an agent, Cameron worked for several years at MGM where she developed books for motion pictures.

Ethan Ellenberg is president and founder of the Ethan Ellenberg Literary Agency, established in 1983. The agency currently represents approximately 80 nonfiction and fiction clients. Before setting up shop, Ellenberg was contracts manager for Berkley/Jove and associate contracts manager for Bantam.

Michelle Grajkowski is an agent with 3 Seas Literary Agency, founded in 2000. Prior to becoming an agent, Grajkowski worked in sales and in purchasing for a medical facility. While 3 Seas Literary Agency accepts nonfiction books, its current focus is on romance novels.

Harvey Klinger began his publishing career at Doubleday, expecting to become a life-long editor. However, he soon began working for a literary agent and created his own operation in 1977.

Donald Maass founded the Donald Maass Literary Agency in 1980. He represents more than 100 fiction writers and sells more than 100 novels per year to top publishers in America and overseas. Maass is also the author of 14 pseudonymous novels and several books on writing and publishing, including *Writing the Breakout Novel* (Writer's Digest Books).

Madeleine Morel founded 2M Communications, Inc., in 1982 after working for Angus & Robertson Publishing Company in England, and Delilah Books in Manhattan. Her agency specializes in nonfiction books and is currently looking for new clients.

Gail Ross is a lawyer, publishing consultant, and literary agent. Ross writes and frequently lectures on publishing issues, and negotiates with major publishers and producers in the sales and distribution of literary properties and their subsidiary rights.

ROBERT LEE BREWER is an assistant editor of *Guide to Literary Agents*, *Writer's Market*, and *Writer's Market Deluxe Edition*, and the online editor of WritersMarket.com. He can be contacted via e-mail at robert.brewer@fwpubs.com.

Even though I've recently published my first nonfiction book and am very happy with my publishers, should I still consider getting an agent?

Klinger: Any honest editor or publisher will tell you an author always gets a better publishing deal when a reputable agent negotiates it. Publishers who negotiate directly with an author generally reserve all publishing rights for themselves to make the most of their investment. The publisher might control everything from foreign rights to film, and you'd basically be out in the cold waiting for your share of those rights to trickle in with your semiannual royalty statements.

Harvey Klinger

The other major reason to get an agent is this: The relationship between an author and editor is intended to be a creative one, not a fiduciary one. I've always thought an author who has to split his author-editor relationship between the editorial and the financial invariably sacrifices something on one side of the fence or the other. Keep your relationship with your editor strictly editorial, and you'll both be a lot happier with the final result.

An agent who's interested in my work is asking for $750 to help underwrite his expenses. Is that normal?

Maass: There is no law saying agents cannot charge up-front fees; however, the track record of fee-charging agents is thought to be far inferior to commission-charging agents, who only get compensated when they actually license a work to a paying publisher.

Photo by Rachel Vater

Donald Maass

Important

The gold standard for literary agents is membership in the Association of Authors' Representatives (AAR). To become a member of AAR, an agent must have proven experience negotiating contracts, be recommended by other members, and must adhere to AAR's strict Canon of Ethics. Virtually no AAR agents charge up-front fees. Many professional writers' organizations consider the charging of up-front fees flatly unethical. Authors looking for representation need to be smart consumers.

Here's my advice: Don't pay fees. If you can't get an AAR agent to take you on, keep working on your writing until you can. You'll be better off in the long run.

Does an author usually work with an agent in his or her city/state? Would it be uncommon for me to work with a New York agent and live in Seattle?

Ellenberg: Geography plays a very tiny role in agent selection. The most important considerations are that the agent is professional, successful, and a good match for you. It doesn't matter where that agent physically resides. Having an agent close by is helpful to some authors, and if the agent does meet with you and work closely with you, that's an advantage. But geography is not a barrier to working closely with an agent and should not dictate your agent search or decision-making. I enjoy very close relationships with out-of-state authors.

I self-published a nonfiction book that sold 1,000 copies, but I found I didn't have the time or contacts to promote the book in the media. I'm now considering looking for an agent. Should I mention I'm a self-published author? Will this hurt my chances of being accepted by an agent or a publisher?

Barrett: Certainly mention to an agent that you've self-published a book, and you've been able to sell 1,000 copies. However, I fear it's not a sufficient number to really be helpful to the agent. Now, if the sales figures were up to 5,000 or 6,000, those numbers would have much more of an impact on getting you a publisher. It will not hurt your chances at being accepted by an agent or a publisher.

Loretta Barrett

What the agent needs to know about the self-published book is: When did you self-publish it? Over what period of time did you sell 1,000 copies? How many copies did you print? How did you distribute them? It's hard to assess what you've accomplished if you just mention you sold 1,000 copies. Also, you need to tell the agent why you self-published the book. Did you try to get an agent or a publisher the first time around? All of this information will be essential for an agent in making a decision to represent you.

If a publisher offers a contract directly to the writer, will the advance and royalties be different than if an agent secured the contract?

Ross: As a general rule, an agent will improve the advance/royalties offered by a publisher. An agent's involvement lets the publisher know the project might be shopped around to others to garner more competition. Therefore, the publisher will try to offer more money. Typically, an agent can negotiate a contract more effectively than an author, and an agent also has the benefit of knowing the marketplace and is able to assess a fair package.

An agent asked me to send my full manuscript, and it has now been with the agent for 10 weeks (his guidelines state he responds in 6 to 8 weeks). What is an appropriate amount of time to check on the status of my manuscript, and what is the preferred method of contact?

Cameron: Literary agents try to respond in a timely manner, but sometimes we are traveling and it's difficult to read and respond quickly. My suggestion is this: If an agent asks to see an entire manuscript on an exclusive basis, you have the right to determine the amount of time the agent has to reach a decision. If it's not an exclusive read (meaning only the agent who requested the manuscript can be reading it at any given time), it can take longer—sometimes months.

Photo by Lisa Keating

Kimberley Cameron

I have a few on my "reading pile," screaming for my time, but my current clients' needs must come first. In any event, a friendly e-mail or polite telephone call is welcome, but I wouldn't call more than once a month. Agents are constantly fighting deadlines and always feel a certain amount of responsibility resting on our shoulders. If you don't hear from an agent quickly, don't take it personally—chances are we're still reading the manuscript and will respond as soon as possible. I strongly feel writers should make simultaneous submissions until asked for an exclusive read—it's only fair you're not wasting time waiting for us.

When I send a manuscript, do I need to be concerned about protecting my legal rights to the manuscript? That is, could the book be stolen, and if so, how do I prevent this?

Madeleine Morel

Photo by Doron Hanoch

Morel: If a proposal is great, why steal the idea and find someone else to execute it? That doesn't make sense. Many times, an agent will suggest getting a foreword from a well-known figure to make the proposal more commercial, but stealing is not something that happens or something authors need to worry about. If you're really concerned, you can copyright your manuscript with the U.S. Copyright Office (www.copyright.gov), but publishers and agents are all pretty honest. No one is interested in plagiarizing.

Useful Websites

I've just finished the first novel in a series I plan to write. Should I pitch it as a novel or as a series?

Michelle Grajkowski

Photo by Michelle Grajkowski

Grajkowski: I'm interested in representing an author from a career standpoint. So, I prefer the author tell me upfront what future projects she has in mind. Goal setting and career planning is a very important part of my business. I help authors set realistic goals, and we do everything we can to meet them. So knowing an author's plans in the query letter helps me to determine if we would have a good working relationship.

Editors, on the other hand, are more interested in looking at one project at a time. While it's important you have a series in mind, most editors will just want to hear about the book you're currently pitching. If an editor expresses interest in that project, then it's good to mention it's part of a series.

NARROWING YOUR LIST

How to Find the Right Agent

A writer's job is to write. A literary agent's job is to find publishers for her clients' books. Any writer who has attempted to attract the attention of a publishing house knows it's no easy task. But beyond selling manuscripts, an agent must keep track of the ever-changing industry, writers' royalty statements, and fluctuating reading habits. And the list continues.

Because publishing houses receive more unsolicited manuscripts each year, securing an agent is becoming increasingly necessary. Nevertheless, finding an eager *and* reputable agent is a difficult task. Even the most patient writer can become frustrated, even disillusioned. Therefore, as a writer seeking agent representation, you should prepare yourself before starting your search. By learning effective strategies for approaching agents, as well as what to expect from an author/agent relationship, you will save yourself time—and, quite possibly, some heartache. This article provides the basic information on literary agents and how to find one who will best benefit your writing career.

Make sure you are ready for an agent

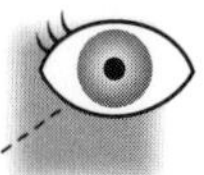

With an agent's job in mind, you should ask yourself if you and your work are at a stage where you need an agent. Look at the ten-step checklists (provided both for nonfiction and fiction writers) on pages 26 and 27, and judge how prepared you are for contacting an agent. Have you spent enough time researching or polishing your manuscript? Sending an agent an incomplete project not only wastes your time, but also may turn the agent off in the process. Literary agents are not magicians. An agent cannot sell an unsalable property or solve your personal problems. An agent will not be your banker, CPA, social secretary, or therapist. Instead, an agent will endeavor to sell your book because that is how she earns her living.

Moreover, your material may not be appropriate for an agent. Most agents do not represent poetry, magazine articles, short stories, or material suitable for academic or small presses; the agents' commission earned does not justify spending time submitting these types of works. Those agents who do take on such material generally represent authors on larger projects first, and then represent these smaller items as a favor to their clients.

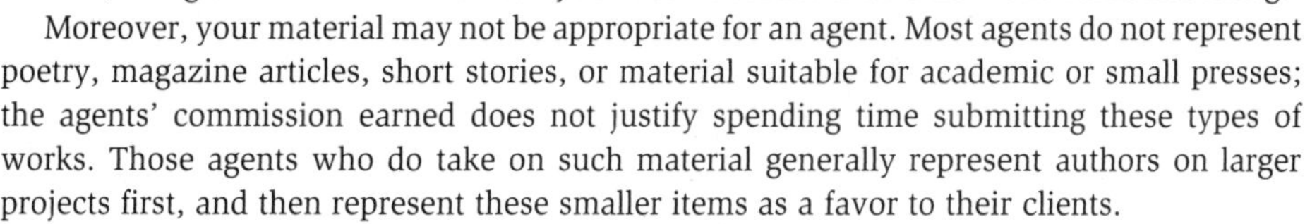

If you strongly believe your work is ready to be placed with an agent, make sure you are personally ready to be represented. In other words, before you contact an agent, consider the direction in which your writing career is headed. Besides skillful writers, agencies want clients with the ability to produce more than one book. Most agents will say they represent careers, not books. So as you compose your query letter—your initial contact with an agent—briefly mention your potential. Let an agent know if you've already started drafting your second novel—let her know that your writing is more than a half-hearted hobby.

The importance of research

Most people would not buy a used car without at least checking the odometer, and the savvy shopper would consult the blue books, take a test drive, and even ask for a mechanic's opinion. Much like the savvy car shopper, you want to obtain the best possible agent for your writing, so you should do some research on the business of agents before sending out query letters. Understanding how agents operate will help you find an agent appropriate for your work, as well as alert you to the types of agents to avoid.

We often receive complaints from writers regarding agents *after* they have already lost money or their work is tied into a contract with an ineffective agent. If writers put the same amount of effort into researching agents as they did writing their manuscripts, they would save themselves unnecessary grief.

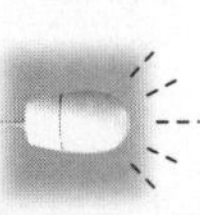

Useful Websites

The best way to educate yourself is to read all you can about agents and other authors. The articles in this book will give you insight not only on how to contact an agent, but also on how the author/agent relationship works. Organizations such as the Association of Authors' Representatives (AAR), the National Writers Union (NWU), American Society of Journalists and Authors (ASJA), and Poets & Writers, Inc., all have informational material on finding and working with an agent. (These, along with other helpful organizations, are listed in the back of this book beginning on page 273.) *Publishers Weekly* (www.publishersweekly.com) covers publishing news affecting agents and others in the publishing industry; discusses specific events in the "Hot Deals" and "Behind the Bestsellers" columns; and occasionally lists individual author's agents in the "Forecasts" section.

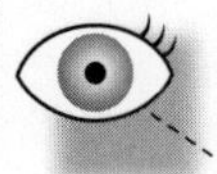

See Also

Even the Internet has a wide range of sites devoted to agents. Through the different forums provided on the Web, you can learn basic information about preparing for your initial contact or more specific material about individual agents. Keep in mind, however, that not everything printed on the Web is a solid fact; you may come across the site of a writer who is bitter because an agent rejected his manuscript. Your best bet is to use the Internet to supplement your other research. For particularly useful sites, refer to **Websites of Interest** on page 275.

Through your research, you'll discover the need to be wary of some agents. Anybody can go to the neighborhood copy center and order business cards that say she is a literary agent, but that title does not mean she can sell your book. She may ask for a large sum of money, then disappear from society. Becoming knowledgeable about the different types of fees agents may charge is a *crucial* step to take before contacting any agent. Before paying any type of fee, read Understanding Agents' Fees—What Writers Need to Know on page 34.

An agent also may not have any connections with others in the publishing industry. An agent's reputation with editors can be a major strength or weakness. While it's true that even top agents are not able to sell every book they represent, an inexperienced agent who submits too many inappropriate submissions will quickly lose her standing with editors. It's acceptable to ask an agent for recent sales before she agrees to represent you, but keep in mind some agents consider this information confidential. If an agent does give you a list of recent sales, you can call the publishers' contracts departments to ensure the sale was actually made by that agent.

The importance of location

For years, the major editors and agents were located in New York City. If a writer wanted to be published with a big-name house, he had to contact a New York agency. But this has changed over time for many reasons. For starters, publishing companies are appearing all over the country—San Francisco, Seattle, Chicago, Minneapolis—and, naturally, agents are moving closer to these smaller publishing hubs.

Advances in technology have also had an impact on the importance of location. Thanks to fax machines, the Internet, e-mail, express mail, and inexpensive long-distance telephone rates, an agent no longer needs to work (or be) in New York to work closely with a New York publisher. Besides, if a manuscript is truly excellent, a smart editor will not care where the agent is located.

Nevertheless, there are simply more opportunities for agents located in New York to network with editors. They are able to meet face-to-face over lunch. The editor can share his specific needs, and the agent can promote her newest talent. As long as New York remains the publishing capital of the world, the majority of agents will be found there, too.

Contacting agents

Once your manuscript is prepared and you have a solid understanding of how literary agents work, the time is right to contact an agent. Your initial contact is the first impression you make on an agent; therefore, you want to be professional and brief.

Because approaching agents is an important topic, we've included several articles on contacting agents in this book: How Do I Contact Agents? on page 49; How to Write a Query Letter on page 51; The Perfect Pitch on page 58; The Art of the Synopsis on page 60; and Professional Proposals—Creating a Nonfiction Proposal on page 65.

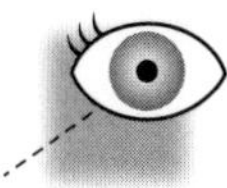

See Also

Again, research plays an important role in getting an agent's attention. You'll want to show the agent you've done your homework. Read the listings in this book to learn agents' areas of interest, check agents' websites to learn more about how they operate their businesses, and find out the names of some of their clients. If there is an author whose book is similar to yours, call the author's publisher. Someone in the contracts department can tell you the name of the agent who sold the title, provided an agent was used. Contact that agent, and impress her with your knowledge of her agency.

Evaluate any offer

Once you've received an offer of representation, you must determine if the agent is right for you. As flattering as any offer may be, you need to be confident that you're going to work well with this agent and that this agent is going to work hard to sell your manuscript.

You need to know what to expect once you enter into a business relationship. You should know how much editorial input to expect from your agent; how often your agent gives updates about where your manuscript has been and who has seen it; and what subsidiary rights the agent represents.

More importantly, you should know when you will be paid. The publisher will send your advance and any subsequent royalty checks directly to the agent. After deducting her commission—usually 10 to 15 percent—your agent will send you the remaining balance. Most agents charge a higher commission of 20 to 25 percent when using a co-agent for foreign, dramatic, or other specialized rights. As you enter into a relationship with an agent, have the agent explain her specific commission rates and payment policy.

As your potential partner, you have the right to ask an agent for information that convinces you she knows what she's doing. Be reasonable about what you ask, however. Asking for recent sales is OK; asking for the average size of clients' advances is not. Remember, agents are very busy. Often asking a general question like, "How do you work?," or requesting a sample contract can quickly answer your concerns. If you're polite and the agent responds with anger or contempt, that signals something you need to know about this potential relationship.

Evaluate the agent's level of experience. Agents who have been in the business awhile have a larger number of contacts, but new agents may be hungrier, as well as more open to unpublished writers. Talk to other writers about their interactions with specific agents. Writers' organizations, such as the National Writers Association (NWA), the American Society of Journalists and Authors (ASJA), and the National Writers Union (NWU), maintain files

A Checklist for Nonfiction Writers

1. **Formulate a concrete idea** for your book. Sketch a brief outline making sure you have enough material for an entire book-length manuscript.
2. **Research** works on similar topics to understand the competition and determine how yours is unique.
3. **Compose sample chapters.** This step should indicate how much time you will need to finish and if your writing needs editorial help.
4. **Publish** completed chapters in journals. This validates your work to agents and provides writing samples for later in the process.
5. **Polish your outline** so you can refer to it while drafting a query letter and so you can avoid wasting time when agents contact you.
6. **Brainstorm** three to four subject categories that best describe your material.
7. **Use the indexes in the back of this book** to find agents who are interested in at least two of your subject areas and who are looking for new clients.
8. **Rank your list.** Narrow your list further by reading the listings of agencies you found in the indexes, and organize the list according to your preferences.
9. **Write your query.** Professionally and succinctly describe your premise and your experience to give an agent an excellent first impression.
10. **Read about the business** of agents so you are knowledgeable and prepared to act on any offer.

on agents with whom their members have dealt, and can share this information by written request or through their membership newsletters.

Understand any contract before you sign

Some agents offer written contracts; some do not. If your prospective agent does not, at least ask for a "memorandum of understanding" that details the basic relationship of expenses and commissions. If your agent does offer a contract, be sure to read it carefully, and keep a copy for yourself. Because contracts can be confusing, you may want to have a lawyer or knowledgeable writer friend check it out before signing anything.

See Also

The National Writers Union (NWU) has drafted a Preferred Literary Agent Agreement and a pamphlet, *Understand the Author-Agent Relationship,* which is available to members. (Membership is based on your annual writing income and open to all writers actively pursuing a writing career. See **Professional Organizations** on page 273 in the back of the book for the NWU's address.) The NWU suggests clauses that delineate such issues as:

- the scope of representation (One work? One work with the right of refusal on the next? All work completed in the coming year? All work completed until the agreement is terminated?)

A Checklist for Fiction Writers

1. **Finish your novel** or short story collection. An agent can do nothing for fiction without a finished product.
2. **Revise your novel.** Have other writers offer criticism to ensure your manuscript is as polished as you believe possible.
3. **Proofread.** Don't ruin a potential relationship with an agent by submitting work that contains typos or poor grammar.
4. **Publish** short stories or novel excerpts in literary journals, proving to potential agents that editors see quality in your writing.
5. **Research** to find the agents of writers you admire or whose work is similar to your own.
6. **Use the indexes in the back of this book** to construct a list of agents who are open to new writers and who are looking for your type of fiction (i.e., literary, romance, mystery).
7. **Rank your list.** Use the listings in this book to determine the agents most suitable for you and your work and to eliminate inappropriate agencies.
8. **Write your synopsis.** Completing this step early will help you write your query letter and save you time later when agents contact you.
9. **Compose your query letter.** As an agent's first impression of you, this brief letter should be polished and to the point.
10. **Read about the business** of agents so you are knowledgeable and prepared to act on any offer.

- the extension of authority to the agent to negotiate on behalf of the author
- compensation for the agent, and any co-agent, if used
- manner and time frame for forwarding monies received by the agent on behalf of the client
- termination clause, allowing client to give about 30 days to terminate the agreement
- the effect of termination on concluded agreements as well as ongoing negotiations
- arbitration in the event of a dispute between agent and client.

If things don't work out

Because this is a business relationship, a time may come when it is beneficial for you and your agent to part ways. Unlike a marriage, you don't need to go through counseling to keep the relationship together. Instead, you end it professionally on terms upon which you both agree.

First, check to see if your written agreement spells out any specific procedures. If not, write a brief, businesslike letter, stating that you no longer think the relationship is advantageous and you wish to terminate it. Instruct the agent not to make any new submissions and give her a 30- to 60-day limit to continue as representative on submissions already under consideration. You can ask for a list of all publishers who have rejected your unsold work, as well as a list of those who are currently considering it. If your agent charges for office expenses, you will have to reimburse your agent upon terminating the contract. For this reason, you may want to ask for a cap on expenses when you originally enter into an agency agreement. If your agent has made sales for you, she will continue to receive those monies from the publisher, deduct her commission and remit the balance to you. A statement and your share of the money should be sent to you within 30 days. You can also ask that all manuscripts in your agent's possession be returned to you.

NARROWING YOUR LIST

Researching an Agency's Website

by Robert Lee Brewer

Successful writers have the uncanny ability to take advantage of resources, especially when it comes to research. It's no coincidence many successful writers have embraced the Internet. In an hour of online clicking and reading, a writer can become a semiexpert on almost any topic.

It's ironic, however, how many talented writers don't have the first clue how to navigate a literary agency's website and use the information on the site to help them secure an appropriate agent. "Ultimately, as an author, my goal would be to find the right agent who would find me the right editor at the right publishing house," says Stephanie Lee, an agent with Manus & Associates (www.manuslit.com). "If I stumbled upon an agent's website and thought, 'My book would be perfect for this agent,' then I could incorporate that information into a great query letter. The agent would immediately know I'd done my research and there was a specific reason I contacted her. Moreover, it would help me shape my submission into the perfect package."

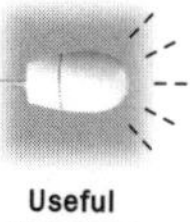

Useful Websites

Just like the agents within a literary agency, every agency's website is a little different. In general, though, most sites contain the same basic information, including writer's guidelines, agent profiles, and recent sales. The primary differences being in how the information is presented and how often it's updated.

Writer's guidelines

Before you submit to an agent, you'll want to look at the writer's (or submission) guidelines on the agency's website. These guidelines explain what you should and shouldn't do with your submission. In general, guidelines outline how an agency likes to be contacted (via e-mail, through traditional mail, or some other means); whether it prefers queries, proposals, or full manuscripts; how to format those submissions; and what response time to expect. Writer's guidelines also tell you whether an agency is accepting new clients or if it prefers to work with established writers, and whether it's accepting submissions.

According to Rachel Vater, an agent with the Donald Maass Literary Agency (www.maassagency.com), "It's frustrating when a query letter intrigues us with a story idea, but the writer has no previous writing credits and hasn't included a sample of his work. Requesting a sample of the writer's work is risky for us because we aren't sure if the writer has the skills

ROBERT LEE BREWER is an assistant editor of *Guide to Literary Agents*, *Writer's Market*, and *Writer's Market Deluxe Edition*, and the online editor of WritersMarket.com. He can be contacted via e-mail at robert.brewer@fwpubs.com.

Contacting a Agent

Each agent has his or her preference as to how to be contacted. For me, I accept e-mail queries (but no attachments) and queries via the postal service. I don't accept phone queries.

In the query, tell me briefly the genre you're writing in, what your manuscript is about (just a paragraph or two, please), what makes it unique, why you feel confident your manuscript will find an audience, who that audience is, how you can help to market you manuscript, and what your writing experience is. It's also helpful to know why you chose to contact me (especially if someone recommended you do so) and if you're contacting other agents.

If I'm interested in seeing your work, I'll ask you for the following: For a novel (including young adult novels):

- a synopsis (5-6 pages double-spaced) in which you tell me the basic plot and introduce me to your main characters.
- the first three chapters (approximately 50 pages of the work).
- your biography, with an emphasis on your qualifications for writing the manuscript and how you can help to market it.

For a nonfiction adult manuscript:

- a proposal, detailing the audience for your work, why you believe the work will attract significant readership, a chapter outline in which you write a paragraph description of each chapter, your biography, how you can help to market the book, any ideas on how a series could be developed.
- the first three chapters (approximately 50 pages of the work).

For a children's book:

- the entire manuscript.
- your biography.
- if you see the possibility of a series, and what the series would consist of.

When you send the manuscript, please include a self-addressed, stamped envelope with sufficient postage to either pay to have the entire package sent back to you or to pay the postage for me to write a letter with my response.

I do not return material or reply to submissions that don't include the postage and an envelope.

Use agency websites, such as janetgrant.com, to double check submission guidelines.

to pull off the story in a compelling, polished way. If no sample pages are included, we often turn down the writer because we choose not to take the gamble."

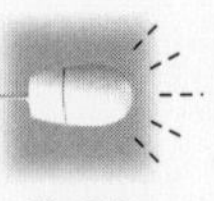
Useful Websites

This may seem heartless, but agents aren't working for potential clients, they're working for those they already represent. As a result, they have to manage their time wisely.

"It's tough for a writer to win over an agent when the first contact isn't made the way the agent has asked for it," explains Janet Kobobel Grant of Books & Such Literary Agency (janetgrant.com). "For instance, I don't like to receive phone calls in which a person gives me a pitch. Honestly, I wasn't sitting at my desk hoping my phone would ring with a writer making a pitch. If I don't control the flow of queries, I can spend the entire day focusing only on pitches rather than doing the work of placing manuscripts and negotiating contracts."

Usually, writer's guidelines aren't complicated, and it's in your best interest to follow them. If you ignore the information found in the guidelines, you could doom your submission to the rejection pile before you even get a chance to make a case for your book.

Agent profiles

Another useful element on an agency's website is the agent profiles (or about us) section. It's important you tell the agent about you and your manuscript, but it's equally important to find out information about the agent—the person with whom you're looking to build your writing career.

"Unlike looking for a dentist or a doctor, word of mouth might be tough to come by as far as agent-hunting," says Lee. "Agent profiles will help you get a feel for who your publishing partner might be for the long run. After all, your agent will be your best friend through the publishing process, so it's nice to feel a personal connection. Plus, it's always handy to know your agent's credentials, background, and affiliations."

Finding an agent who shares the same vision as you is vital to having a healthy author/agent relationship. You can improve your chances of finding the right agent by looking at the subject interests usually contained in agent profiles. Let's say you've written a romance novel and researched two agents who have very similar practices and experiences, and you decide to look at their profiles to see what subjects they represent—Agent A represents romance and Agent B represents true crime. You immediately know, based on the information you learned in the profile, you should contact Agent A.

"We each have different tastes in what we'd like to handle," says Vater. "We've also had some staff changes. So, if writers don't check our website for updates on who we are and

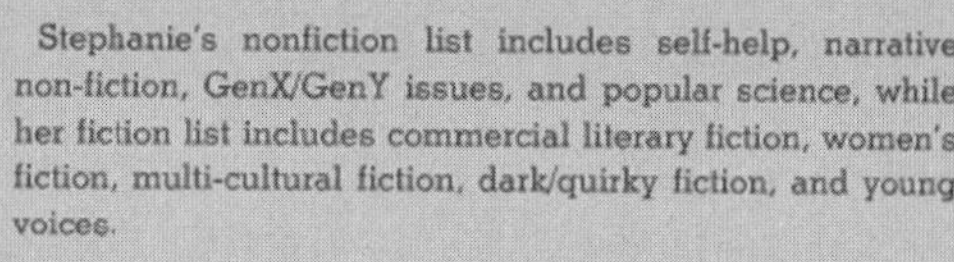

Use agency websites, such as www.manuslit.com, to learn more about individual agents and their interests.

what we're looking for, they may address their query to an agent who no longer works here, and it doesn't get the same priority specifically addressed queries do.''

A quick check of agent profiles can also help you find a new agent who may be more receptive to new clients. Either way, agent profiles will give you a better understanding of the agent you're querying.

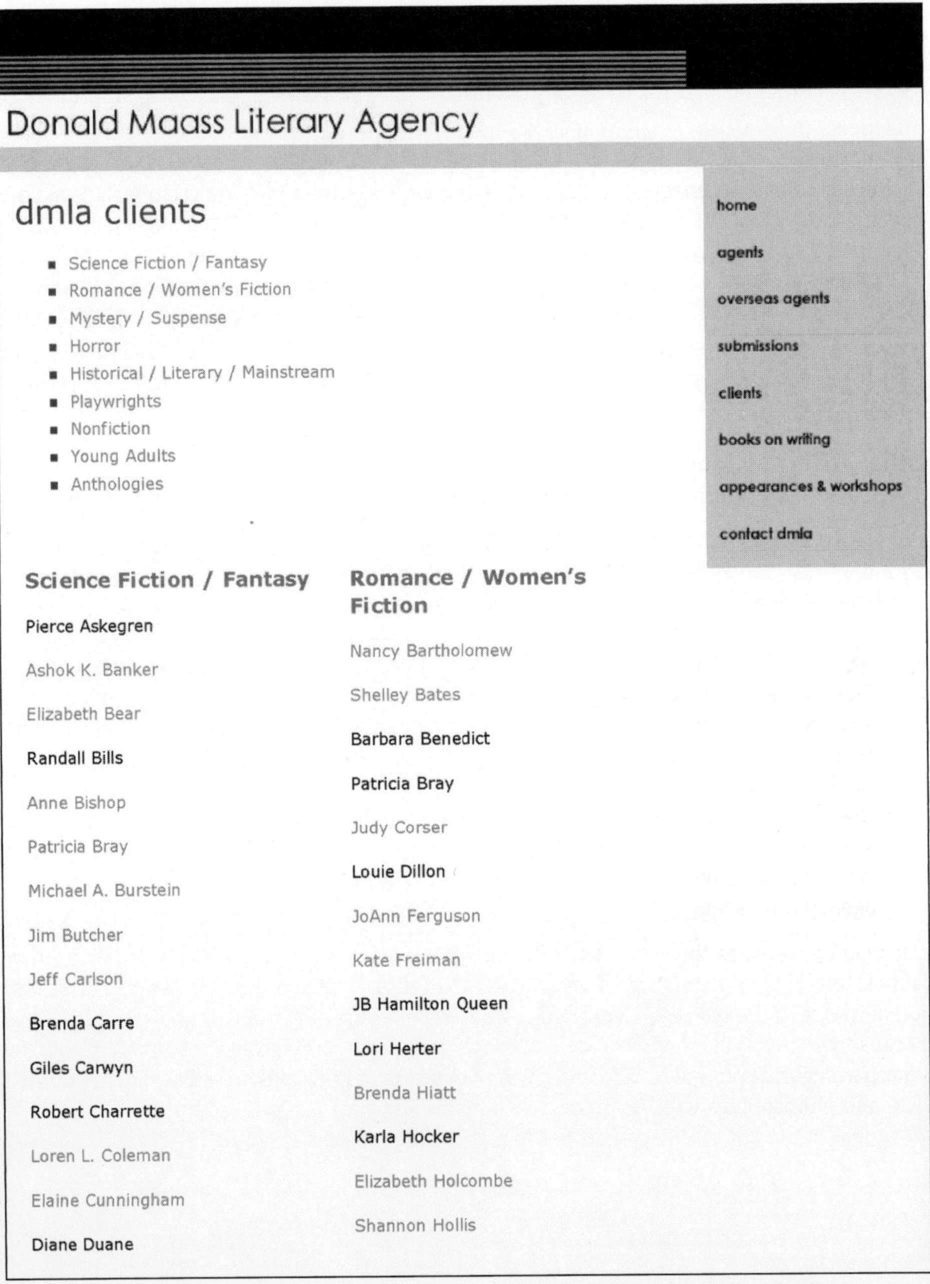

Use agency websites, such as www.maassagency.com, to research client lists and recent sales.

Recent sales

Most agency sites like to show off their recent sales and the clients they represent. Not only is it good PR for the agency, it's also an important clue for prospective clients looking to piece together an agency's interests and effectiveness. "Represented projects are extremely important," says Jenny Bent, an agent with Trident Media Group (www.tridentmediagroup.com). "Writers should know what I'm representing, and if their work fits in well with my list. If they're writing a medical textbook or legal thriller, they should look at the books I represent and realize I'm simply not a good fit for them as an agent."

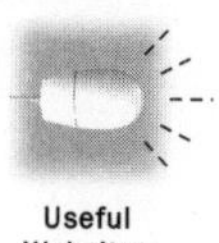

Useful Websites

For writers who wish to write in more than one genre, the recent sales portion of an agency's website can take on added importance—if you want to write nonfiction parenting books and children's fiction, then you know you need to find an agent or agency who can effectively juggle both, something you can easily find out by looking at the agency's list of recent sales.

Recent sales also enable authors to connect with agents who have relationships with a specific publisher. "If sales have been made to some of the publishers you'd like to be identified with, you can be more confident this is the type of agent you want," says Grant.

Another important clue provided by an agency's recent sales: Studying this section could help you earn bonus points in your initial contact with an agent. Vater says, "It's not necessary for writers who query us to be fans of our existing clients, but if they happen to recognize a name on our client list and favorably compare their own work to our clients' work, it lets us know they've taken the time to research us and learn about our tastes."

Other things to look for

There are other things you should pay attention to when you research an agency's website:

- **Frequency of updates.** Check when the site was most recently updated. If a website looks old, outdated, and lists its last update as more than a year ago, you should approach the information with caution. If a site doesn't look like it's being updated on a regular basis (daily, weekly, or even monthly), you could be working with inaccurate information, which could disrupt your search for the most appropriate agent.
- **The "News" section.** This section shows recent book sales, subsidiary rights sales, and the writers' conferences the agent/agency is scheduled to attend. (For more information on writers' conferences, see Writers' Conferences: Getting the Most Bang for Your Buck on page 12.)
- **Useful links.** Some agency websites also include links to resources and/or other writers' websites. Links to resources help you learn more about how the publishing industry works, while links to other writers' websites help you learn more about the writers the agency represents.

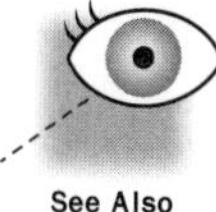

See Also

Use agency websites the same way you use other resources: Figure out which information is most useful to you and discard what's not. "Publishing can be such a mysterious industry for newcomers," says Lee. "Being well informed in choosing your agent is so important because you must take into consideration your long-term writing career. Your agent will be your partner and your guide, so getting a feel for agents' reputations, likes, dislikes, personalities, and philosophies will be a good start to planning your career."

Understanding Agents' Fees

What Writers Need to Know

Before starting your search for an agent, it is extremely important to have an understanding of the various fees some agencies charge. Most agents make their living from the commissions they receive after selling their clients' books, and these are the agents we've listed. Charging writers for office expenses incurred on their behalf is standard, though there are agents who do not charge for this service. Agents also typically make 15 percent commission on sales. The editors of *Guide to Literary Agents* discourage the payment of any other fees to agents.

Office expenses

Many agents—both those who do and do not charge additional fees—ask the author to pay for photocopying, postage, and long-distance phone calls. An agent should only ask for office expenses after agreeing to represent the writer. These expenses should be discussed up front, and the writer should receive a statement accounting for them. This money is sometimes returned to the author upon sale of the manuscript. Be wary if there is an up-front fee amounting to hundreds of dollars, which is excessive.

Reading fees

Agents who do not charge reading fees earn their money from commissions. Agencies that do charge reading fees often do so to cover the cost of additional readers or the time spent reading that could have been spent selling. This practice can save the agent time, open the agency to a larger number of submissions, and may allow the agent time to consider each manuscript more extensively. Whether such promises are kept depends upon the honesty of the agency. You may pay a fee and never receive a response from the agent, or you may pay someone who will not submit your manuscript to publishers. In this book, we have not included those literary agents who charge reading fees.

Important

Reading fees vary from $25 to $500 or more. The fee is usually nonrefundable, but sometimes agents agree to refund the money if they take a writer on as a client, or if they sell the writer's manuscript. Keep in mind, however, that payment of a reading fee does not ensure representation. If you find that a literary agent listed in this book charges a reading fee, please contact the editor.

Officially, the Association of Authors' Representatives (AAR) in its Canon of Ethics prohibits members from directly or indirectly charging a reading fee, and the Writers Guild of America (WGA) does not allow WGA signatory agencies to charge a reading fee to WGA members, as stated in the WGA's Artists' Manager Basic Agreement. A signatory may charge you a fee if you are not a member, but most signatory agencies do not charge a reading fee as an across-the-board policy.

Critique fees

Sometimes a manuscript will interest an agent, but the agent will point out areas still requiring development. Some agencies offer criticism services for an additional fee. Like reading fees, payment of a critique fee does not ensure representation. When deciding if you will benefit from having someone critique your manuscript, keep in mind that the quality and quantity of comments vary widely. The critique's usefulness will depend on the agent's knowledge of the market. Also be aware that an agent who spends a significant portion of his time commenting on manuscripts will have less time to actively market work he currently represents. We strongly advise writers not to use critiquing services offered through an agency. Instead, we recommend hiring a freelance editor or joining a writer's group until your work is ready to be submitted to agents who do not charge fees.

PERSONAL VIEWS

Agents Share Their Secrets

by Joanna Masterson

When agents send a manuscript to a publishing house, they don't do so haphazardly. Instead, they spend a lot of time talking and meeting with editors to determine who is most interested in the manuscript and, more importantly, who is best able to meet the needs of the writer and the manuscript.

There's no better way to find out what agents want than hearing advice directly from the professionals' mouths. The following roundtable interview features four very successful and well-respected literary agents who discuss several basic topics that can help writers find the best agent to represent them and their manuscript.

Elaine English is the managing partner of Graybill & English, which functions as both a literary agency and a legal firm. English only sells commercial fiction—particularly mysteries, thrillers, and women's fiction, including romances.

Donald Maass is a fiction specialist at the Donald Maass Literary Agency in New York. He is a former president of the Association of Authors' Representatives (AAR) and has written 14 pseudonymous novels.

Evan Marshall is the president of The Evan Marshall Agency, which is dedicated to representing novels. Marshall is also the best-selling author of the Marshall Plan series of writing guides (Writer's Digest Books).

Ann Rittenberg started the Ann Rittenberg Literary Agency in 1992, representing literary fiction, upmarket thrillers, and serious narrative nonfiction. Rittenberg works in New York, where she also serves on the board of the AAR.

What do you look for in new/potential clients?

English: I look for someone with an engaging, marketable project who is savvy about the business and/or willing to learn quickly.

Maass: Whatever the genre or type of novel, my agency is looking for writers who are working on a "breakout" level—well-developed characters, layered plots, and everything else that makes a novel feel big.

Marshall: I look for three main things. The first is quality writing: Does this person have a mastery of the conventions of fiction writing? I also look for fresh, new ideas. Are this writer's story ideas original and compelling, or simply derivative? Last is professionalism: Does this person behave in a reasonable and businesslike manner?

JOANNA MASTERSON is an assistant editor of *Guide to Literary Agents, Writer's Market, Writer's Market Deluxe Edition*, and WritersMarket.com.

Rittenberg: First comes the work—I have to be 100 percent enthusiastic about it. Once I love the book, I look for a sense of the writer's passionate commitment to his/her work. I look at the writer's willingness and ability to rewrite. I look for an indication that the writer has a sense of personal responsibility.

We know what agents can do for writers, but what can writers do for agents to increase their chances of representation?

English: Write the best possible book they can.

Maass: In the fiction game it's all about the manuscript. Write a great story, that's it.

Marshall: A writer can educate herself about the protocol of submitting to an agent and then scrupulously follow those rules. It's also important to master the query letter and synopsis.

Rittenberg: These days, many agents have their own websites, many are listed on other websites, and many are profiled in other ways on the Web, so there really should not be any excuses for mis-targeting your query letter. (For more information on agents' websites, see Researching an Agency's Website on page 29.) Once you've determined there could be a match, make sure you follow any submission instructions the agent may have published. Work on your query letter to make it come to life. Spell the agent's name right, get the address right, and never, under any circumstances, use the phrase "fictional novel."

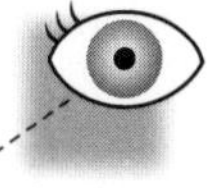

See Also

How much time should a writer give his agent to sell a manuscript?

English: Recently, the market has really slowed, so authors need to be patient. There's no magic time frame, so long as the author feels the agent is continuing to make good faith efforts to sell his work.

Maass: I've sold books overnight, and I've sold books after five years of marketing—you just can't tell. For writers, I'd say as long as the manuscript is circulating and responses are coming in . . . that's good.

Marshall: I think a year is reasonable in light of current editor response times. During this year, the agent should be busy submitting—simultaneously, if necessary.

Rittenberg: As long as the writer feels comfortable. Every agent has stories of selling a book in a day, and every agent has stories of selling a book after 30, 50, even 80 rejections. There is no formula because every book is different—which is why we love them so much.

The publishing industry can be intimidating for first-time writers. What can newcomers expect from the agenting process?

English: First and foremost, they need to find an agent who loves their material as much as they do and who sees it in the same way. Most agents will work with an author to polish the material to make it as marketable as possible. Then an agent will market rights in the project to editors and others. Once there are offers, the agent will negotiate to get the best deal. Once sold, the agent will handle all the contracts, royalty statements, payments, etc., associated with the project.

Maass: Professional editorial feedback, followed by a logical marketing plan for selling the work, and (hopefully) realistic negotiation of any offers received.

Photo by Rachel Vater

Donald Maass

Marshall: Newcomers should expect a first sale to take time. While the agent is submitting, the writer should keep writing, not obsess about the agent's progress. Constant calls and e-mails requesting status reports are not welcome; agents routinely send clients copies of editors' letters. Newcomers should also expect a modest advance at the beginning—often under $10,000. A writer has a right to expect guidance from his agent. Finally, a writer should expect honesty and professionalism from her agent. Inordinately delayed checks, intimidating conversations, and evasive answers to simple questions about submissions are all good reasons to consider finding new representation.

Rittenberg: Newcomers can expect that once an agent takes on your book with evident enthusiasm, he or she is going to go to work on it in different ways, some apparent and some not. Some agents will keep you thoroughly informed about who your book's been submitted to and why, while others will not call you frequently but will be pitching you and your work at lunches and meetings with editors. The thing newcomers shouldn't expect is a miracle. Nor should they expect that once they've handed the manuscript or proposal over to their agent, their work is done.

Ann Rittenberg

Should writers follow trends in publishing? Do trends make a book easier to sell?

English: It's a good idea to be aware of trends. For example, if the market has gone "dark" and you're writing sweet, light stories, you may have difficulty selling your material right away. But you shouldn't be overly influenced by the trends. Trying to force your voice into a mold that doesn't fit generally is not a good way to succeed.

Maass: Forget trends. By the time you identify them, you're already far behind the curve. Write your own unique story as strongly as you can. Become your own brand name.

Marshall: Yes, it's easier for an agent to sell a book that fits into a trend, but a writer should never undertake a book in a trendy genre unless it really appeals to her. A book written solely to grab a quick buck is never as good as a sincere effort, and agents and editors can smell these insincere efforts a mile away.

Rittenberg: No. If something is a trend, that means it's current and could very well be over by the time the writer writes the book or proposal, finds an agent and a publisher, and gets the book published. Don't follow trends—follow your passions.

Personal Views

What are the two most important things you look for in the perfect pitch/query letter?

Important

English: I look for a concise summary of a great concept novel.

Maass: Brevity and the one thing that makes the story different from any other like it.

Marshall: I look first for professionalism in the actual format and writing of the letter. Then I look to see if the book the author is pitching is based on a fresh, compelling idea.

Rittenberg: I look for a natural, conversational tone and an ability to get to the point.

What are your thoughts on simultaneous submissions and exclusive reads on manuscripts?

English: I rarely ask for exclusives because I find I'm hard pressed to guarantee a time frame for reading. I think it's unfair for an agent to keep a manuscript locked up on an exclusive for months on end.

Maass: Some agents ask for exclusive submissions. If agreed to, some time limit ought to be stipulated. For example, the agent agrees to get back to you within 30 days. My agency does not ask for exclusives. We feel we can compete, favorable, with anyone out there.

Marshall: I see nothing wrong with submitting a manuscript to several agents at a time, as long as the writer lets the agents know she is doing this. Sometimes, as with editors, a book may seem perfect for a particular agent. In these cases, a writer should try that agent alone, but should consider submitting to additional agents if the first agent doesn't reply within three or four months.

Rittenberg: I have nothing against simultaneous submissions as long as the writer clearly states it's a simultaneous submission. I do ask for exclusives from time to time, but when I do, I feel it's important for me to hold up my end of the bargain and get back to the writer within a specified time limit. In either case, I ask the writer to contact me before accepting representation elsewhere.

When is the best time for a writer to get an agent?

English: When they have completed and polished a manuscript they genuinely believe is marketable. Preferably they also have had it critiqued by someone other than their family and close friends before they contact the agent.

Maass: After the manuscript is complete, revised, and altogether as perfect as you can make it.

Marshall: The best time for a writer to get an agent is when she has a book-length manuscript completed and polished to the best of her ability, and is writing in an area in which an agent is required.

Photo by Biggs Photography

Evan Marshall

Rittenberg: A great number of the query letters I get are from writers who want to know if what they've written is any good, if they should go on, if they have a chance at all of being published. That's really the worst time to try to get an agent, because if the book isn't in great shape, you've lost your shot with that agent. Get other people to read your book, workshop it, and put it away for a while before revising it.

PERSONAL VIEWS

Sharlene Martin

Agent Embraces "Considerate Literary Management"

Photo by a. Karmo portraiture

by Kathryn S. Brogan

In 1983, Sharlene Martin founded Helping Hands, the country's first American Nanny Agency, and in 1987 she went on to win Entrepreneur of the Year from *Entrepreneur* magazine. Who would have known 21 years later, Martin would secure a major deal with Crown Books for *You'll Never Nanny in this Town Again*, by Suzanne Hansen, the "Hollywood Nanny"?

Interestingly, in 1992, Martin came to Hollywood and worked in the entertainment industry as a talent agent, a manager, an associate casting director, and an independent producer. Then, in 2002, she left the entertainment industry and founded her own literary agency, Martin Literary Management (www.martinliterarymanagement.com), where she currently represents 30 authors.

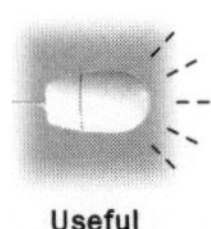

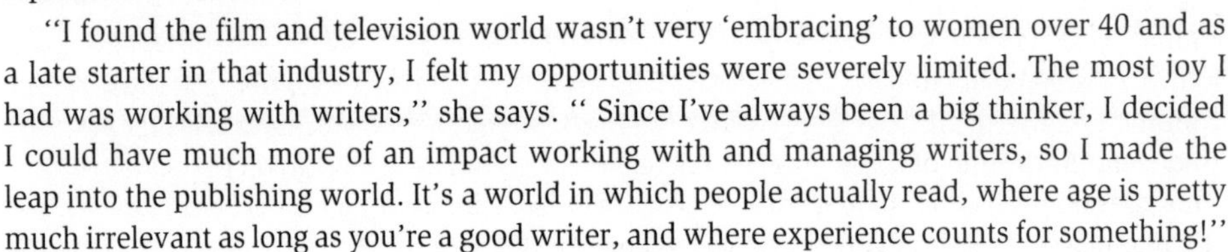

"I found the film and television world wasn't very 'embracing' to women over 40 and as a late starter in that industry, I felt my opportunities were severely limited. The most joy I had was working with writers," she says. " Since I've always been a big thinker, I decided I could have much more of an impact working with and managing writers, so I made the leap into the publishing world. It's a world in which people actually read, where age is pretty much irrelevant as long as you're a good writer, and where experience counts for something!"

In the following interview, Martin talks about why, even after a seasoned career in the entertainment industry, she won't represent screenplays, as well as what happens when a book, like *You'll Never Nanny in this Town Again*, goes to auction.

In a letter on your website, you say, "I hope to establish myself as a leader in 'considerate literary management' for the 21st century." What does that statement mean?

When I coined the term "considerate literary management" I meant I would treat writers, editors, and publishers in a way that perhaps they weren't always used to being treated—in a considerate, thoughtful way. The way I would want to be treated if someone was judging my hard work. That means promptly acknowledging calls, e-mails, and letters, giving constructive responses in a positive manner, and creating healthy, functional relationships with the people who honor me with their work.

KATHRYN S. BROGAN is the editor of *Guide to Literary Agents*, *Writer's Market*, and *Writer's Market Deluxe Edition*.

You also mention on your website you're not interested in representing screenplays. Given your background, do you think you'll ever consider representing them?
I have purposely developed a business that only deals with nonfiction books. I'm a firm believer in creating a niche and then becoming the best you can be in that area. Screenplays are different animals—they have a different thought process, a different structure, and a different buyer. For now, I'll continue to represent books with high adaptability opportunities for film, as I love the world of film, but that will be the extent of my direct representation. There are plenty of screenplay agents out there to handle those writers, and frankly, it's apples and oranges.

Did you ever expect *You'll Never Nanny in this Town Again*, originally self-published, would be such a "hot" property it would garner an auction and a deal with one of the major New York players?
I knew that the "Hollywood Nanny" would capture a large amount of interest. Initially, Suzanne queried editors and had over 40 requests for her book. When she realized she was in over her head, she sent out queries looking for an agent [and found me] . . . Given my background, I knew the subject matter well, but I also knew how interesting this kind of nonfiction memoir would be to people outside of Hollywood. I think that gave me the edge in landing her as a client. Once we had signed contracts, I went back to the editors [who originally requested the book] and, based on the interest, decided to go straight to auction.

Can you explain auctions: What factors determine whether a book will go up for auction, and what happens at an auction?
An auction is usually held when you have several editors from different publishing houses all seriously interested in making an offer on a book. Usually, if you've got an offer, you can use that offer to establish a "floor" or the opening bid of the auction. Then, it's done in rounds, with very specific rules spelled out to each of the bidders. Those rules include how many rounds the auction will go, opening and closing times, how the offer is to be conveyed (phone, fax, or e-mail), which rights are available (world or North American), hardcover or trade, etc. At the end of round one, you reveal the high bid, and then go on to the next round. This goes on until either bidders drop out or are outbid, and a winner is declared. Logistically, it's like juggling, and, of course, I don't exhale until it's all over!

If a book goes up for auction, how much control/input does the author have in the auction?
My authors will tell you I'm in constant touch with them throughout the auction process. Sometimes we even IM (instant messenge) each other so I can keep them abreast of the progress of the auction. But, the author always has final say about which offer to take. I merely guide them in making a well-informed decision. I imagine it's a nerve-wracking experience for most authors who are fortunate enough to have their work go to auction, but ultimately highly satisfying to know numerous publishers want their work.

Approximately 75 percent of your clients are new or unpublished writers. If you could offer advice to new/unpublished writers about submitting to agents, what would it be?
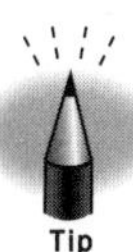

Write the best query letter you can. Take a class, buy a book, learn the essential elements of a good query. The same goes for a book proposal. You only get one chance to make an impression on an agent—take the time to get it right. Be open to constructive criticism on how to make your work better.

PERSONAL VIEWS

Finding the Best Agent

Which Agent Is Right for You?

by Will Allison

When it comes to choosing an agent, which is better for a new author—a seasoned veteran, or a hungry rookie?

Conventional wisdom says a seasoned agent has the connections, the clout, and the experience to sell your book. But the conventional wisdom also says a seasoned agent has less time and energy to devote to individual clients—especially new authors who haven't proven themselves in the marketplace. In which case, perhaps, a first-time author is better served by a less-seasoned, but more ambitious, agent who represents fewer clients.

Of course, the conventional wisdom oversimplifies the difference between rookie and veteran agents. It fails to make a distinction, for instance, between a "rookie" agent who's coming off a 20-year editing career at Random House versus one who has little publishing experience. Likewise, "rookie" and "veteran" are relative terms. Is an agent still a rookie after her first book sale? Her fifth? Her 20th?

It's also important to remember an agent's level of experience is only one of many factors a prospective client must consider. As one veteran agent put it, "The decision made by a prospective client is a very personal one, and while I understand the issue [of rookies versus veterans], I believe this decision is one that is made for so many different reasons that it is more appropriate not to address this as a specific question."

Nevertheless, the four agents in the following interview—two longtime agents and two newer agents—did just that in an effort to give writers a more nuanced understanding of the choices they face in the search for the agent that's right for them and their manuscript. We asked each agent to talk about their agenting process while answering the question: What are the potential benefits and drawbacks of signing with a less-experienced agent versus a more established agent?

Photo by Barry Glassner

Betsy Amster

Betsy Amster, president
Betsy Amster Literary Enterprises

Before opening her agency in 1992, Betsy Amster spent 10 years as an editor at Pantheon and Vintage, two divisions of

WILL ALLISON (www.willallison.com) is a staff member at the Squaw Valley Community of Writers and teaches creative writing at Indiana University-Purdue University at Indianapolis. His short stories have appeared in *Zoetrope: All-Story*, *Kenyon Review*, *One Story*, *Shenandoah*, *American Short Fiction*, *Atlanta*, and other magazines.

Random House. A frequent instructor in the UCLA Extension's Writers Program, Amster also runs publishing workshops at The Loft, the acclaimed literary center in Minneapolis, and at the Squaw Valley Community of Writers. Her clients include best-selling writers María Amparo Escandón, author of *Gonzalez & Daughter Trucking Co.* (Crown); Joy Nicholson, author of *The Road to Esmeralda* (St. Martin's); Phil Doran, author of *The Reluctant Tuscan* (Gotham); Wendy Mogel, author of *The Blessing of a Skinned Knee* (Penguin); and Dr. Elaine Aron, author of *The Highly Sensitive Person* and *The Highly Sensitive Child* (Broadway).

"Most of my clients come to me by referral from magazine and book editors I've known for years or from existing clients, but every year I do take on a few clients I've found in my slush pile or at conferences. What I'm looking for is someone who makes a smart approach. A snappy cover letter is helpful. So is a well-thought-out proposal (for nonfiction) or prior publication in literary magazines (for fiction). I pay particular attention to the writer's credentials and love to work with journalists, experts, and M.F.A. graduates.

"[As a more established agent] I still enjoy taking risks, but the risks I take are more calculated now. Publishers see nearly every category as 'crowded.' Certain books you know you're going to sell—the author has a national platform, a movie of her novel in the works, or has sold 100,000 copies of her previous book. But lots of other books are dicier—mysteries by new writers, humor, memoirs, coming-of-age novels, literary fiction in general. The key here is knowing when (and where) you stand a chance—that knowledge comes from staying in close touch with editors and having made lots and lots of submissions [to editors].

"I've found the longer I'm in the business, the more I can rely on 'the love factor'—if I love something to pieces, particularly fiction, generally I'm going to prevail, even if the project looks like a hard sell from the outside. I've sold very unconventional novels that have gone on to get starred *Kirkus* or *Publishers Weekly* reviews. Persistence is key here—I've submitted novels I'm crazy about to as many as 40 publishers.

"The longer I've been an agent, the more colleagues I've seen elevated to positions of power in publishing houses. This is useful not only when it comes to selling projects but also when it becomes necessary to be an advocate for your clients. You encounter all sorts of wrinkles in this business—editors leave, clients need extensions, occasionally you need to move a project to a new house. The more good will you have built up, the more you can smooth things for your clients.

"How long an agent has been in the business is only one variable for writers to consider, though. The size of the agency also influences the way an agent works. A few years ago I was written up in *Poets & Writers* magazine as an example of a 'boutique agent.' That's a lovely name for a small agency run by a single agent with the help of one or two assistants. Inevitably, I become involved in every stage of the process, including editing proposals and manuscripts, negotiating contracts, and running interference with publishers."

Loretta Barrett, president
Loretta Barrett Books, Inc.

Loretta Barrett

In 1990, Loretta Barrett founded Loretta Barrett Books, Inc., in New York. Prior to that she was editor-in-chief of Anchor Books and vice president and executive editor at Doubleday & Co. Barrett's areas of nonfiction interest include political, social, and religious writing, as well as pop-culture commentary. She represents authors who write on a wide range of topics, from cultural history, to psychology, to women's issues. Nonfiction clients include Raymond Kurzweil, George Weigel, James Martin, Ann Douglas, Michael Novak, and Wayne Muller. Her fiction preferences are largely mainstream and contemporary. She enjoys mystery/suspense and thriller; also, she is particularly drawn to women's fiction and ethnic fiction. Clients on her current fiction list include Dr. Gary Birken, Maria Stewart, M.J. Rose, Laura Van Wormer, and Carol Goodman.

"The most important word in this question is 'experience.' It can mean so many different things. I established my agency 15 years ago. Was I an inexperienced agent? I had been editor-in-chief of Anchor Books, and executive editor and vice president of Doubleday for over 20 years. There was little I didn't know about the inside of a publishing house, including contracts, which was enormously helpful. However, agenting was new to me, and there was much to learn. My closest friends in the business were agents who owned their own agencies, so I was most fortunate to have expert advice at my fingertips from lifelong colleagues.

Important

"Whomever you go with should know publishing from one perspective or another. Less experience should not be a euphemism for not knowing publishing. The advantage of going with a new agent is she is building a list and has the time to give a client that someone else who is long established might not.

"The drawbacks of signing with a newer agent could range from the agent not having a track record in certain areas (so their projects don't get the attention more established agents get from publishers) to the agent not having foreign representation. A newer agent also might not have the necessary resources needed to provide the many services provided by a more established agency (i.e., editing, publicity, etc.).

Tip

"My main question would be: How well does an agent know publishing and publishers? The advantage of going with a more established agent is that they are known—they have a track record. Other advantages include: membership in the Association of Authors Representatives (AAR); editors know their work, and they have constant contact with a number of editors; their list of clients is pretty indicative of their tastes; they have foreign representation and attend foreign book fairs; they've had years of experience in helping put together book proposals and marketing plans.

"What are the disadvantages? Established agents may be too busy to take on many new clients, and they may not have the time to do the development work with a new client that a less established agent might be willing to do. The writer might be passed on to a junior agent in the agency who also might be less experienced. It is a difficult decision and one that should be given great thought, but one criterion should always be that a writer chooses an agent who loves the writer's work."

Kate Garrick, agent
DeFiore and Company

After two years as an agent at PMA Literary and Film Management, Kate Garrick joined DeFiore and Company in 2002. She entered publishing directly after earning her M.A. in English and American literature from New York University and her B.A. (also in literature) from Florida State University. She has worked with Stephen Graham Jones, author of *The Bird Is Gone* (FC2) and *Bleed Into Me: Stories* (University of Nebraska Press, 2005); David Goodwillie, author of *The New York Years* (Algonquin Books, 2005); Stacy Gueraseva, author of *Def Jam, Inc.: Russell Simmons, Rick Rubin, and the Extraordinary Story of the World's Most Influential Hip Hop Label* (Ballantine, 2005); and Stephanie Lessing, author of *She's Got Issues* (Avon, 2005).

"There's no easy answer to the question of new agent versus established agent because of the variety of factors that can influence the author/agent relationship, the most important of which is that both parties share a vision for the writer's work and career. Having said that, once this criterion has been met, it's certainly wise to consider an agent's level of experience before entering into a working relationship with her.

"I'd have to say the biggest advantage of signing with a less-experienced agent, whether she's new to publishing or not, is she'll be eager to build her client list, and thus she may be more likely to invest a little extra effort in the projects she takes on. For a first-time writer, in particular, this may prove an enormous benefit, particularly if the agent makes a point of developing and editing her clients' projects before submitting them to publishers, something more established agents may not always have time to do. A less-experienced agent may also be more willing than her more seasoned colleagues to see a project through several rounds of submissions, something that's often necessary when placing first-time writers' books. Of course, I can think of any number of agents who've been in the business for years who regularly do both of these things, though they may not be as open to writers who don't already have a platform or track record.

"The biggest drawback to signing with a relatively inexperienced agent is, well, inexperience. To balance this, I think it's hugely important authors confirm that agents, and particularly those with budding track records, have established support systems to which they can turn for advice on the book-selling process—from creating the submission list and pitch letter to the nuts and bolts of holding an auction and negotiating a contract. In this way, even an agent who's never sold a book can reap the benefits of her colleagues' experience and provide the best possible representation to her clients.

"At the end of the day, though, the best agent for a project is the one who's the most passionate about it, no matter what her background."

Anna Stein, associate agent
Donadio & Olson

Anna Stein represents such writers as Melissa P., the author of *100 Strokes of the Brush Before Bed* (Grove Press, Black Cat); Yoko Ogawa, *Hotel Iris* (Picador, 2006); and NK Shapiro, *You Won't Be Happy Anyway* (Thomas Dunne Books, 2006).

"It seems to me the conventional wisdom—veterans can offer the benefit of experience, while young agents have the benefit of time/energy—is about half true.

"Since older agents have many clients, they tend to farm out the nuts-and-bolts work of submissions, contracts, rights, etc., to their assistants, or to younger colleagues in the agency. For this reason, it's rarely true younger agents have more time for each individual client. Most of us handle the clients of our older colleagues, as well as doing the lion's share of subsidiary rights, contracts, etc., in exchange for the opportunity to grow our own lists.

Reminder

"But we do tend to be hungrier—much more motivated, ambitious, and thorough than our veteran bosses. Young agents will take the time to read and re-read manuscripts, give editorial feedback (and in some cases stand in as editors), pursue a lead, fix a snafu, and think creatively about where to send work and promote an author.

"Of course, veteran agents are more likely to have the contacts—and clout—to sell a manuscript, so an author should look for one of two combinations: a responsive, well-connected veteran with a smart, careful, and competent assistant (or junior agent) to get the scut work done, or a smart, attentive rookie with the full support of her agency and the energy to chase down every last publisher in town."

PERSONAL VIEWS

Jeff Kleinman

Representing Passionate Writers With Professional Attitudes

by Kathryn S. Brogan

What's the biggest mistake a writer can make when submitting to an agent? Many agents say sending inappropriate materials or addressing a query to the wrong person, but not Jeff Kleinman. For Kleinman, the biggest mistake a writer can make when submitting to him is: "*Not* sending candy." Kleinman is kidding, of course—for him, professionalism on the part of the writer is paramount. Kleinman has been agenting for six years and is one of five agents with The Graybill & English Literary Agency (www.graybillandenglish.com) where he represents a very eclectic range of books ranging from narrative and prescriptive nonfiction to commercial and literary fiction.

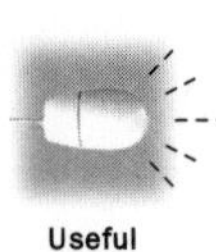

Useful Websites

Prior to becoming an agent, Kleinman was a practicing attorney; however, he says, "At this point in my career, I'm doing almost 100 percent agenting—I'll review contracts and do some other tasks as an attorney, but my first love is agenting, and that's what I spend the vast majority of my time doing." He does admit, though, he's found his legal background very helpful in his career as an agent because it's taught him how to think logically, and it's given him industry knowledge (i.e., copyright, libel, rights of publicity, etc.) that "enhances" the services he provides for his clients.

Kleinman's made many sales in his career, but his most recent was to Harcourt for *The Starmakers*, a popular culture nonfiction title by Jane Jenkins and Janet Hirshenson (casting directors for *A Beautiful Mind, Harry Potter,* and *The Da Vinci Code*, among a hundred others). Below, Kleinman discusses everything from the publishing process and whether writers should follow trends, to what it means to have an agent ask for an exclusive read.

On your agency's website, you say: "The process of getting your book published doesn't end when you type 'The End'; that's where it starts." What do you mean by this? Do you think many new writers tend to think this way?

I tend to think of the book publishing process in three stages.

First, of course, you've got to write the thing. Keep in mind nonfiction and fiction are different animals—nonfiction can often be sold from a "proposal," which is an outline, a sample chapter (or two), and some other basic information about the book and the market; fiction is usually sold from an entire manuscript—but in either case, you'll probably have to write *something* in order for the publisher to buy it. I know most writers feel that's the end of the game, but it isn't.

Step By Step

Second, you have to "sell" the proposal—to an agent, perhaps, if your project is the kind

---

KATHRYN S. BROGAN is the editor of *Guide to Literary Agents, Writer's Market,* and *Writer's Market Deluxe Edition.*

of project that agents represent; and, more importantly, to a publisher. Agents will work to make your project as salable as possible, and may actually do the selling of the project, but I tend to think of the process more in terms of getting the project off the writer's desk and into an excited publisher's hands.

Third, you start dealing with the actual publication process itself. You'll have to interact with your publisher, work with them to make your manuscript as polished and as strong as it can be. Once the book is actually published (and probably a few months before), you'll want to think about how you can really reach your target audience—this is the dreaded "marketing" stuff that writers often hear about. I know from experience that writers who have struggled with Step 1 and are euphoric after Step 2, tend to not to want to even *look* at Step 3—after all, they've spent *so* much time putting the project together, why can't the publisher handle all the marketing? Well, if you're one of a handful of authors, they will; but if you're not, the publisher hopes you'll be an enthusiastic and willing partner in promoting the book to the best of your ability.

There are many qualities a writer must possess in order to be a successfully published author. What quality do you find most important?

Besides wonderful writing and storytelling abilities, I really hope to find authors that realize all of us—the agent, editor, marketing folk, copyeditors, etc.—are all on the writer's side: We all want to create a great book, and we all want to find the next book we can fall head-over-heels-in-love with. It's that helpfulness, that willingness, that sure-I'll-go-the-extra-mile, that can really make a difference.

Given the obvious differences between fiction and nonfiction, how do you balance your representation of both?

Simple: It's what I fall in love with. Like so many other agents (and editors), my first love is fiction; but it's very difficult to find novels that are as dazzling as I hope they'll be. Narrative and prescriptive nonfiction are perhaps a bit easier to sell, but even with those I only choose the topics and the projects I feel very passionate about.

Writers often think it's in their best interest to follow publishing trends. Do you think it's wise for writers to do this?

No, absolutely not. Trying to anticipate a trend will always happen too late—by the time the trend happens, and the writer becomes aware of it and tries to follow it, it's already old news. Assume two years will pass before the writer's book idea is in print, so by then the trend is long over, and the reading public's zoomed onto something else. What writers need to do is write what they're passionate about, write what they love, and write about their subject with skill and precision. I didn't go out to sell *The Starmakers* because I thought a pop culture book would sell—I wanted to sell it because these authors had a compelling, fascinating, extraordinary story to tell.

If an agent is interested in a manuscript, he'll sometimes ask for an exclusive read. What does an exclusive read mean for both the agent and the writer? Under what circumstances might an agent request an exclusive read?

Agents assume, in this marketplace, the writer has simultaneously contacted an unknown number of other agents. That said, when some agents want to read your project, they want to be able to read it and know they're the only person reading it—i.e., that another agent won't be able to swoop in and sign the author without the first agent having had a chance to read and consider the work. So, the first agent will ask for an "exclusive" read.

I think an exclusive's a fine thing, if that's what the agent needs, but the writer needs to be aware he is giving something up by giving that agent an exclusive read—so, the agent should provide something in exchange, perhaps the assurance he will read it quickly. Think of it like a bargain: "I (the writer) am giving you (the agent) a certain time with my manuscript, and you won't have to worry about someone else competing for it. In exchange, you agree to read it quickly because other agents are also interested in reading it." What's "quickly"? It depends on the agent. I think, though, about two months for a novel and about three weeks for a proposal is fair.

What's the biggest mistake a writer can make when he submits to you?

The biggest mistake is not acting professionally enough. Writers need to keep in mind as soon as they enter the publishing business that they need to treat it as a business. Treat it as a job interview. Handle your interview like a professional: be courteous, concise, helpful, and provide the kind of information the guy on the other side of the desk needs to have. Desperation (i.e., "Oh, *please* give me this job! I'm *so* hungry!") rarely works; your potential boss might run the other way. Discourtesy (i.e., writing "Dear Agent:" or "Dear Sir or Madam:") may make it seem you haven't bothered to do your homework.

How Do I Contact Agents?

Once you and your manuscript are thoroughly prepared, the time is right to contact an agent. Finding an agent can often be as difficult as finding a publisher. Nevertheless, there are four ways to maximize your chances of finding the right agent: Obtain a referral from someone who knows the agent; meet the agent in person at a writers' conference; submit a query letter or proposal; or attract the agent's attention with your own published writing.

Referrals

The best way to get your foot in an agent's door is to be referred by one of her clients or by an editor or another agent she has worked with in the past. Because an agent trusts her clients, she'll usually read referred work before over-the-transom submissions. If you are friends with anyone in the publishing business who has connections with agents, ask politely for a referral. However, don't be offended if another writer will not share the name of his agent.

If you don't have a wide network of publishing professionals, use the resources you do have to get an agent's attention.

Conferences

Going to a conference is your best bet for meeting an agent in person. Many conferences invite agents to give a speech or simply be available for meetings with authors, and agents view conferences as a way to find writers. Agents often set aside time for one-on-one discussions with writers, and occasionally they may even look at material writers bring to the conference. If an agent is impressed with you and your work, the agent may ask for writing samples after the conference. When you send your query, be sure to mention the specific conference where you met the agent and that she asked to see your work.

Because this is an effective way to connect with agents, we've asked agents to indicate in their listings which conferences they regularly attend. We've also included a section of **Writers' Conferences**, starting on page 245, where you can find more information about a particular conference.

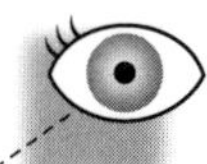

See Also

Submissions

The most common way to contact an agent is through a query letter or a proposal package. Most agents will accept unsolicited queries. Some will also look at outlines and sample chapters. Almost none want unsolicited complete manuscripts. Check the **How to Contact** subhead in each listing to learn exactly how an agent prefers to be solicited. Never call; let the writing in your query letter speak for itself.

Because a query letter is your first impression on an agent, it should be professional and to the point. As a brief introduction to your manuscript, a query letter should only be one page in length.

Step By Step

- The first paragraph should quickly state your purpose: You want representation.
- In the second paragraph, mention why you've chosen to query that specific agent. Perhaps the agent specializes in your areas of interest or represents authors you admire. Show the agent you have done your homework.
- In the next paragraph or two, describe the project, the proposed audience, why your book will sell, etc. Be sure to mention the approximate length and any special features of your book.
- Then discuss why you are the perfect person to write this book, listing your professional credentials or relative experience.
- Close your query with an offer to send an outline, sample chapters, or the complete manuscript—depending on your type of book.

Agents agree to be listed in directories such as *Guide to Literary Agents* to indicate to writers what they want to see and how they wish to receive submissions. As you start to query agents, make sure you follow their individual submission directions. This, too, shows an agent you've done your research.

Like publishers, agencies have specialties. Some are only interested in novel-length works. Others are open to a wide variety of subjects and may actually have member agents within the agency who specialize in only a handful of the topics covered by the entire agency.

Before querying any agent, first consult the **Agent Specialties Indexes** in the back of this book for your manuscript's subject and identify those agents who handle what you write. Then, read the agents' listings to see which are appropriate for you and for your work.

Publishing credits

Some agents read magazines or journals to find writers to represent. If you have had an outstanding piece published in a periodical, you may be contacted by an agent wishing to represent you. In such cases, make sure the agent has read your work. Some agents send form letters to writers, and such agents often make their living entirely from charging reading fees, not from commissions on sales.

However, many reputable and respected agents do contact potential clients in this way. For them, you already possess attributes of a good client: You have publishing credits, and an editor has validated your work. To receive a letter from a reputable agent who has read your material and wants to represent you is an honor.

Occasionally, writers who have self-published or who have had their work published electronically may attract an agent's attention, especially if the self-published book has sold well or received a lot of positive reviews.

Recently, writers have been posting their work on the Internet with the hope of attracting an agent's eye. With all the submissions agents receive, they probably have little time to peruse writers' websites. Nevertheless, there are agents who do consider the Internet a resource for finding fresh voices.

How to Write a Query Letter

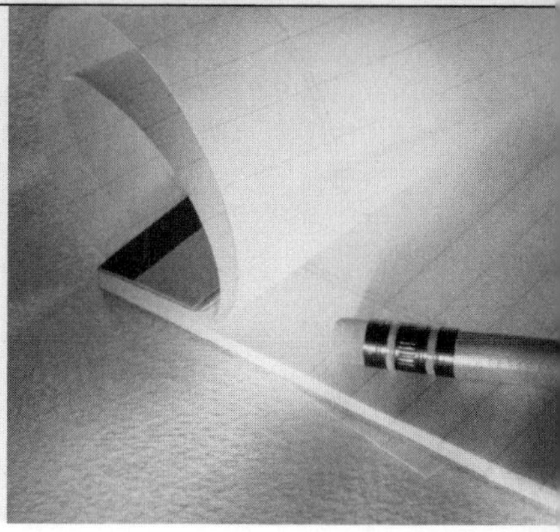

by Kathryn S. Brogan

The query letter is the catalyst in the chemical reaction of publishing. Overall, writing a query letter is a fairly simple process that serves one purpose—getting an agent or editor to read your manuscript. A query letter is the tool that sells you and your book using brief, attention-getting text.

Generally speaking, a query letter has basic elements that are shared when pitching both novels and nonfiction books, but there are some differences you should consider depending on whether you have written fiction or nonfiction.

Query letters for novels

A general rule of thumb when querying an agent for a fiction manuscript: Do not query the agent about your novel until the entire manuscript is written and ready to be sent.

A query letter for a work of fiction generally follows a short, six-paragraph structure that contains the following elements.

- **The hook.** Usually, your first paragraph should be written to "hook" the agent, and get her to request a few chapters or the whole manuscript. The hook usually is a special plot detail or a unique element that's going to grab the agent's attention.
- **About the book.** It is important you provide the agent with the "technical" statistics about your book: title, genre, and word count. Evan Marshall, an agent and the author of *The Marshall Plan for Getting Your Novel Published* (Writer's Digest Books), says that an easy way to estimate your manuscript's word count is to multiply the number of manuscript pages by 250 and then round that number to the nearest 10,000.

- **The story.** This is the part of your letter where you provide a summary of your plot, introduce your main characters, and hint at the main conflict that drives the story. Be careful not to go overboard here (both in content and length): Only provide the agent with the basic elements needed to make a decision about your manuscript.
- **The audience.** You need to be able to tell the agent who the intended audience is for your novel. Many writers find it helpful to tell the agent the theme of their novel, which then, in turn, signifies the intended audience and to whom the novel will appeal.
- **About you.** Tell the agent who you are and how you came to write your novel. In this paragraph, you should only provide those qualifications that are relevant to your novel. List any special qualities you have for writing a book in your genre. Also, list any writing

KATHRYN S. BROGAN is the editor of *Guide to Literary Agents*, *Writer's Market*, and *Writer's Market Deluxe Edition.*

groups to which you belong, publishing credentials, awards won, etc. Remember, though, if you don't have any of the above credits, don't stress your inexperience or dwell on what you haven't done.

- **The closing.** Make sure you end your query on a positive and optimistic note. That means you should thank the agent for her time and offer to send more information (a synopsis, sample chapters, or the complete manuscript), upon the agent's request. Be sure to mention you've enclosed a self-addressed, stamped envelope (SASE) for the agent's convenience.

Query letters for nonfiction books

Unlike fiction manuscripts, it is OK to query an agent about a nonfiction book before the manuscript is complete.

Generally, a query letter for a nonfiction book contains many of the same elements found in a query for a novel.

- **The referral.** Why are you contacting this particular agent? On a recommendation from an author she currently represents? Due to an acknowledgement in a book she has represented? Because the agent has a strong track record of selling books on the subject about which you're writing? No matter the answer, knowing what type of work the agent represents shows her you're a professional.
- **The hook.** The hook is usually a special detail or a unique element that's going to grab the agent's attention and pull her in. Often, nonfiction writers use statistics or survey results, especially if the results are astoundingly unique, to reel in the agent.
- **About the book.** It's important to provide the agent with the "technical" statistics about your book, including the title and "sales handle." The "handle" is a short, one-line statement that explains the primary goal of your book. Agent Michael Larsen, in his book *How to Write a Book Proposal, 3rd Edition* (Writer's Digest Books), says that a book's handle "may be its thematic or stylistic resemblance to one or two successful books or authors," for example "*Fast Food Nation* meets fashion." Essentially, the handle helps the agent decide whether your book is a project she can sell.

Step By Step

- **Markets.** Tell the agent who will buy your book (i.e., the audience) and where people will buy it. Research potential markets according to various demographics (including age, gender, income, profession, etc.), and then use the information to find solid, concrete figures that verify your book's audience is significant enough to convince the agent that your book should be published—and she should represent it! The more you know about the potential markets for your book (usually the top three or four markets), the more professional you appear.
- **About you.** Tell the agent who you are, and why you are the best person to write this book. In this paragraph, you should only provide qualifications that are relevant to your book, including your profession, academic background, publication credentials (as they relate to the subject of your book), etc.
- **The closing.** Make sure you end your query on a positive and optimistic note. That means you should thank the agent for her time, and tell her what items you have ready to submit (mini-proposal, proposal, sample chapters, complete manuscript, etc.), upon her request. Also mention that you've enclosed a SASE or postcard for the agent's convenience.

Formatting a query letter

There are no hard-and-fast rules when it comes to formatting your query letter, but there are some general, widely accepted guidelines like those listed below, which are adapted from

Formatting & Submitting Your Manuscript, by Jack and Glenda Neff, and Don Prues (Writer's Digest Books), that cross industry lines. (Editor's Note: See *Formatting & Submitting Your Manuscript Edition 2*, by Cynthia Laufenberg and the Editors of Writer's Digest Books for more information.)

- Use a standard font or typeface (avoid bold, script, or italics, except for publication titles), like 12-point Times New Roman.
- Your name, address, and phone number (plus e-mail address and fax, if possible) should appear in the top right corner or on your letterhead. If you would like, you can create your own letterhead so you appear professional. Simply type the same information listed above (name, address, etc.), center it at the top of the page, and print or photocopy it on quality paper.

Reminder

- Use a 1-inch margin on all sides.
- Address the query to a specific agent. Note: The listings in *Guide to Literary Agents* provide a contact name for all submissions.
- Keep the letter to one page.
- Include a SASE or postcard for reply, and state in the letter you have done so, preferably in your closing paragraph.
- Use block format (no indentations, extra space between paragraphs).
- Single-space the body of the letter and double-space between paragraphs.
- Thank the agent for considering your query letter.

Query Letter Mistakes to Avoid

For More Info

- **DON'T** use any "cute," attention-getting devices like colored stationery or odd fonts.
- **DON'T** send any unnecessary enclosures, such as a picture of you or your family pet.
- **DON'T** waste time telling the agent you're writing to her in the hopes that she will represent your book. Get immediately to the heart of the matter—your book.
- **DON'T** try to "sell" the agent by telling her how great your book is or comparing it to those written by best-selling authors.
- **DON'T** mention that your family, friends, or "readers" loved it.
- **DON'T** send sample chapters that are not consecutive chapters.

Good Nonfiction Book Query

Roger McCallister
445 W. Fifth St.
Denver, CO 80012
(313)555-1234
rogerme@email.com

July 5, 2004

Always address a specific agent.

Sabrina Smith
Smith & Smith Literary Agency
222 Forty-Ninth St.
New York, NY 10111

Dear Ms. Smith:

The hook.

When was the last time you tried selling an idea? Probably it was the last time you had a conversation.

Single-spaced text.

In today's economy, regardless of your career, selling ideas is what you really do. Companies sell to customers, but they also sell ideas to suppliers. Employees pitch ideas to their bosses, and vice versa. In the modern, team-filled corporation, you may be simultaneously selling your ideas to a wide array of peers, bosses, and subordinates. Until now, however, there was no definitive book on how to sell ideas.

1″ margin.

Differentiates this book from the competition.

That's about to change. I'm preparing a book, *Selling Your Ideas: The Career Survival Strategy of the 21st Century*, to fill the void. Hundreds of highly successful books have addressed sales tactics for salespeople, and dozens of highly successful books address persuasion skills for everyone else. But no one has addressed a book to cover the one sales job in which everyone in corporate America engages—selling ideas. Unlike other sales and persuasion books, *Selling Your Ideas* addresses everyone in business on a department-by-department, function-by-function basis. Because virtually anyone at any walk of corporate life will be reflected in this book, the appeal is considerably wider than any previous work of its kind.

Explains why he should write this book.

Included will be dozens of real-life case studies drawn from my 20 years as a corporate executive, trainer, marketing consultant, and columnist for management publications. I am also an adjunct professor in the business department of the University of Denver and a past president of and consultant for the Business Executives Council.

A polite offer.

I would be interested in sharing my detailed proposal with you at your convenience.

Sincerely,

Roger McCallister

Bad Nonfiction Book Query

Karen Badquery
93 Try Again Lane
Notgood, NE 68501
KarenBad@email.com

March 3, 2004

Smith & Smith Literary Agency
222 Forty-Ninth St.
New York, NY 10111

To Whom It May Concern:

I hope you are interested in nonfiction books about birds, because that is the type of book I have written. I would like to sell it to a publisher, which of course means I need an agent.

The subject of birds is a big one, but I know my book stands out from all the others. People all over the country love to read interesting stories about these fascinating creatures, so the book will appeal to just about anyone who loves birds—they don't even have to be birdwatchers or nature enthusiasts. I've attached the first four chapters of my book and will send the rest at your request.

I had such a good time writing about this, my favorite subject, over the past ten years. I am a bird enthusiast and even met my husband while on a birding expedition in the mountains of New England in 1999.

This is my first attempt at writing a book. I have written many articles that were never published on the subject so I thought it would be a good idea to put them all together in one book. I think with the right editor's expertise and input this book has the potential to be a huge bestseller.

Thanks,

Karen Badquery

Always address your query to a specific agent.

Do your homework—know what kinds of books an agent works with before sending a copy.

Don't be obvious—an agent knows why writers need agents.

This tells the agent nothing about the book. Explain how your book differs from others currently on the market.

Don't send book chapters unless asked by the agent. This is just a query.

Keep your information focused on the book itself. Don't waste time with anecdotes having nothing to do with the book.

Don't point out your (and the book's) shortcomings. If it needs editorial help, get some before you send it to an agent.

Good Fiction Book Query

Always address your query to a specific agent.

Always state your novel's genre, title, and word count.

Briefly tell what the novel is about.

If you think your novel is similar to and will appeal to a specific author's audience, tell the agent.

Provide relevant information about yourself, including pertinent background information, special training, publishing credentials, etc.

Deborah Price
1317 Magnolia Lane
Shreveport, LA 71115
(318)555-6321

September 15, 1998

Mr. Evan Marshall
The Evan Marshall Agency
Six Tristam Place
Pine Brook, New Jersey 07058-9445

Dear Mr. Marshall:

I have just completed a 120,000-word thriller entitled *Under Suspicion*. It's the story of Sara Bradford, a police chief in a small Louisiana town, who is married to a state senator. Sara's happy marriage is overshadowed by distrust when she learns her husband may be living a dark secret life—as a member of the Ku Klux Klan. Sara must learn the truth before it's too late.

I think my novel will appeal to fans of John Grisham and Steve Martini, who have had a strong influence on my work.

I'm a native of Louisiana and, until my retirement, practiced law as a partner in a small firm in New Orleans. I've based much of my novel on my experiences.

Over the past year, *Southern Suspense Journal* has published two of my short stories.

May I send you *Under Suspicion*?

I look forward to hearing from you.

Sincerely,

Deborah Price

Bad Fiction Book Query

The author's name, phone number, and e-mail address are missing—include all pertinent contact information.

Always address your query to a specific agent.

Never mention you're a first-time writer or you've never been published—it singles you out as an amateur.

Don't ask an agent for advice or criticism.

This is vague and tells the agent very little about the book.

Don't draw attention to your lack of experience as a writer, and don't mention anything about yourself that's not pertinent to the novel.

Don't mention copyright information or payment expectations.

839 Wrong Way Dr.
Unpublished, OH 40511

July 24, 2004

Big Time Literary Agency
200 W. Broadway
New York, NY 10125

Dear Agent:

I've just completed my first novel and would like to sell it to a publisher. I've never had a book published, but I know this novel will be a bestseller. I'm looking for an agent to help me. I would really appreciate it if you could read over the enclosed chapters, and give me some advice on whether you think this a good novel and if it needs any extra work to make it a bestseller.

The Subject of Susan is about 60,000 words and is geared toward an adult audience. It's about a headstrong woman named Susan and her trials and tribulations throughout the 1950s and beyond as she makes her way in the legal world after graduating from law school as the only woman in her graduating class.

This is my first novel, and while I'm not familiar with the legal world, since I'm not a lawyer, I find the subject fascinating and think readers will too. I've written a lot of short stories dealing with women's lives but they were much more romanticized than the story of Susan. Susan is someone you would know in real life. I've spent the last 20 years raising my children and think I have what it takes to become a successful writer.

I own the copyright on this book and would like to discuss possible advances and royalties with you sometime soon.

Thank you very much,

Donna Dudley

CONTACTING AGENTS

The Perfect Pitch

by Donald Maass

You have done it. Your breakout novel is complete. Your critique group raves; you have taken a leap in your writing, they say. You think so, too. This one was more work, a lot more. You are proud. You are also nervous. Will the folks in New York publishing recognize what you have accomplished?

Are you even sure yourself?

Whether or not you have written your breakout novel is a major question. Riding on the answer is years of work, lots of hope, perhaps the only shot you feel that you will ever have at the top of your publisher's list. You probably believe that this is *it*: the make-or-break book. If this doesn't work, you certainly are not going to go to this much trouble ever again!

So, who or what decides whether this is indeed your breakout novel? Your agent? Your editor? His editorial board? An auction? Catalog position? The media in 20 cities? The sales force? The bookstore chains? I have some good news and some bad news, and they are the same: The jury that will decide whether or not you have written your breakout novel is the public.

That is bad news because publication is a year or more away; plus, there are so many other factors that influence a book's success in the retail marketplace: cover, promo, season, timing, competition.

The good news is that if you have indeed written your breakout novel, chances are some people along the road to publication are going to think so, too.

THE PITCH

Query letter, fax, phone call, e-mail? The guidebooks (like *Guide to Literary Agents*) will tell you what each agent prefers. Generally speaking, skip fax and e-mail. The first feels arrogant (I don't know why but it does), and the second is too casual. If you have an offer from a publisher in hand, a phone call is appropriate, if a little nerve-wracking.

With no offer in hand, a query letter with SASE (that is, a self-addressed stamped envelope with sufficient postage to return to you the agent's reply and/or your material) is a business-like way to make your first approach.

Do not be intimidated by the legendary volume of agents' query mail, the so-called "slush pile." A well-written letter and a solid premise always stand out.

DONALD MAASS is president of the Donald Maass Literary Agency in New York, which he founded in 1980. Excerpted from *Writing the Breakout Novel* copyright © 2002 by Donald Maass. Used with permission of Writer's Digest Books, an imprint of F+W Publications, Inc. Visit your local bookseller or call 1-800-754-2912 to obtain your copy.

Now, the pitch: Why are novelists so bad at selling their own stories? Never mind, I know why. This is the crucial moment, though, when it pays to practice the art of the pitch. A good query letter has four components: introduction, summary, credentials, closing. The first and last should be, and usually are, short. It is the middle two that give people problems.

The summary

How to sum up your long, layered breakout novel in 100 to 200 words? It is a challenge, but there are guidelines. First, remember the purpose of your query letter is not to tell the whole plot or to convince me you are the hottest new writer since last week. Rather, the purpose of your query is simply to get me to read your manuscript. With that in mind, a summary gets easier.

The setting, protagonist, and problem

There are only three things you need to get me, or anybody, hooked on a story: setting, protagonist, problem. Deliver those briefly and with punch, and you have a basic pitch. Conveying some of your story's layers is a tougher challenge. My advice is to be brief and to focus on the elements that lend your story plausibility (its real-world inspiration, briefly stated, can help), inherent conflict, originality, and gut emotional appeal.

Things to avoid in your pitch

No-no's to avoid are adjectives, superlatives, and anything more than a word or two on your theme.

Also, skip all that junk about the size of the audience for your novel. Your ambition, years of effort, professional attitude, willingness to promote, etc., are also unnecessary. You are ahead of yourself. What matters at this stage is your story.

Items you may want to include in your pitch

Publishing credentials can be helpful to include. Prior novel publications always make me sit up and take notice, although self-publication has the opposite effect—unless it resulted in an Edgar Award nomination, or similar. Short story sales to recognized magazines are also good. Journalistic experience, professional articles, ad writing and the like are nice but do not imply skill as a novelist.

What if you have never been published? What if this is your first piece of writing? No doubt about it, you may have a tough time persuading any top agent that your book is worth a look. The novel is a vastly complicated art form that takes years to master. For that reason, I am happier to hear that the offered manuscript is the author's third or fourth. That said, the right first novel pitched well can be a big winner.

There are other things that get my attention, too. A M.F.A. in writing or study with a reputable teacher are pluses. So are referrals from published novelists. The best recommendation of all, needless to say, is a novel that sounds dynamite. Work on your pitch. Mention your models. If your premise is good, your approach professional, and your skill evident, it is entirely possible to interest even a top New York agent.

The Art of the Synopsis

by Evan Marshall

Many new writers think that when their manuscripts are finished, their work is done. Wrong! Nowadays agents and editors are likely to ask to see a synopsis as well as your manuscript. As a marketing tool, the synopsis is even more important than the query letter—though if your query letter isn't just right, you won't reach the synopsis stage at all.

Too often at my agency I hear something to the effect of, "Why should I have to write a synopsis of my novel? I've already written the novel!" Or, "By the time I finish the synopsis, I could have half the novel written!"

Unfortunately, the synopsis is a necessary tool you're going to have to learn to master if you want to make it as a novelist. It's something agents need; very often, in response to a query letter, they will ask to see a synopsis and the first three chapters of your novel, or they may ask to see the synopsis alone. Everyone works differently.

Editors, too, need a synopsis. They often request that a writer or agent include one with the manuscript. Why? Editors are extremely overworked and must plow through mountains of material. A simple way to find out whether a novel is worth spending a lot of time on is to read the sample chapters, and if the writing is appealing, read the synopsis to see if the writer also knows how to plot a good story. Those are the two factors agents and editors look for in their hunt for new talent: good writing and good storytelling.

SYNOPSIS BASICS

So what, exactly, *is* a synopsis? It's a summary of your novel, written in a way that conveys the excitement of the novel itself.

The synopsis is always written in the present tense. In the synopsis, you tell your *whole* story. You do not—even in the case of a mystery—leave out the solution in an attempt to induce an agent or editor to request the manuscript. Nor do you pick up where your sample chapters leave off. As mentioned above, your synopsis is your novel—your entire novel—in miniature.

See Also

There's no hard-and-fast rule about how long a synopsis should be, but most agents and editors agree that a too-long synopsis defeats its own purpose. Some agents and editors request extremely short synopses (see The Short Synopsis on page 63), which aren't really

EVAN MARSHALL is a successful literary agent and author with nearly 30 years of publishing experience. Excerpted from *The Marshall Plan for Getting Your Novel Published* Visit your local bookseller or call 1-800-754-2912 to obtain your copy.

synopses at all, but more like jacket or cover copy, or what Hollywood calls "coverage." As a rule, I like to aim for a page of synopsis for every 25 pages of manuscript. This would mean a 400-page manuscript gets a synopsis of about 16 pages. But this rule is often broken, depending on the novel itself. A mystery, for example, may require a longer synopsis because of the level of detail that must be presented. Eventually, you'll find yourself allowing your synopses to seek their own length, and that they'll almost always come out about right.

To achieve such conciseness, you must write as clean and tight as you know how. Don't do what many writers do and try to keep boiling down your actual novel until it's short enough. Instead, learn to write in a synoptic style—read a section or chapter of your novel and simply retell it, as you might describe a great book or movie to a friend.

Leaving out unnecessary adverbs and adjectives, focus on your story's essential points. Much must be left out, such as inconsequential specifics of a particular incident.

Actual dialogue from your novel is rarely needed, though a few chosen lines can be effective. Remember, overall, that whereas in a novel you should *show* rather than *tell*, in a synopsis you *should* tell. Here, it's OK simply to write: *Yvette is furious*, though you would not write that in your novel, you would show us how Yvette's anger manifests itself.

Write your synopsis as one unified narrative. Don't divide it into sections or chapters. Use paragraphing and short transitions to signify these breaks.

Professional novelists know how to put together a synopsis that makes agents and editors sit up and take notice—and ask for the manuscript.

SYNOPSIS SPECIFICS

The hook

To create an arresting hook for your synopsis, start with your story's lead character and the crisis that has befallen him—the crisis that begins the story. Then explain what your lead must do in order to remedy the crisis; in other words, what is his story goal? For example:

> RHONDA STERN has always considered herself immune to the danger and unpleasantness of the outside world, quietly creating tapestries in the house she occupies alone on lush, secluded Bainbridge Island, Washington. But the world intrudes in a horrible way when one morning a desperate criminal breaks into Rhonda's home and takes her hostage, threatening to kill her if she doesn't help him get off the island. Now Rhonda must fight to save her life while at the same time trying not to help a man she knows is guilty of murder.

The back-up

Right after your hook paragraph, back up a little to give some further background that makes the situation clearer. This is where you should also make sure you've covered the basics: your lead's age, occupation, marital status (if you haven't already given us this information in the hook); the time (past—if so, when?—present, or future); and the place.

The meat

Now move on to the action of your story. Give us not only the things that happen to make up your plot, but also how your lead character feels about them or is affected by them.

So many synopses are dull because the author has left out the emotional component. Remember that people read novels primarily to be moved emotionally; they want to live the story through the lead. The only way they can do that is to know how the lead feels. In other words, emotions and feelings are plot; they are as important as the things that happen.

Words are precious in the synopsis, so pick the best ones you can! Use strong action words, and keep the action crisp, clean, and clear.

Formatting Your Synopsis

Type your real name (not a pseudonym if you are using one).

Your novel's genre.

Double space twice.

Type your name (or pseudonym if you are using one).

Indent first paragraph and start text of synopsis.

Use sluglines as shown.

Your name
Your street address
City, State ZIP code
Day and evening phone numbers
E-mail address

Mystery

TOASTING TINA

by

Evan Marshall

RHONDA STERN has always considered herself immune to the danger and unpleasantness of the outside world, quietly creating tapestries in the house she occupies alone on lush, secluded Bainbridge Island, Washington. But the world intrudes in a horrible way when one morning a desperate criminal breaks into Rhonda's home and takes her hostage, threatening to kill her if she doesn't help him get off the island. Now Rhonda must fight to save her life while at the same time trying not to help a man she knows is guilty of murder.

Rhonda, a blonde, ethereally beautiful 24-year-old, has heard about

Marshall/TOASTING TINA/Synopsis2

a string of murders on the island, but the authorities believe the killer has already escaped to the mainland. But he's here, in her house, and now Rhonda finds herself wishing she hadn't asked her husband to move out only two weeks ago.

The intruder, who introduces himself as RYDER CANNON, barricades himself and Rhonda in her workroom, allowing her to leave only to get him some food. He is limping and she soon discovers why: He has an ugly gash in his upper thigh—the work, he says, of a neighbor's vicious dog. He's bleeding profusely. He tells Rhonda to bring him some rags to wrap around the wound, and as she watches him her heart goes out to him, in spite of what she believes he's done, for under his

Think miniature

Very often in a novel, there are secrets and other information that must at some point be revealed. For some reason, many writers believe that in a synopsis they must reveal all of this information right up front. Not so. In your synopsis, reveal secrets and other surprising information in exactly the same spots where you have done so (or intend to do so) in the novel itself.

Stay out of it

Don't let your scaffolding show. By this I mean don't use devices that suggest the mechanical aspects of your story. This is another reason you shouldn't run character sketches at the beginning of the synopsis, or use headings within the synopsis such as *Background* or *Setting*. Work these elements smoothly into the synopsis; give us background when it's necessary for the reader to understand something.

Pace it right

As you near the end of your story, indicate its quickened pace by using shorter paragraphs that give a speeded-up, staccato effect. For example:

> Rhonda stands at the edge of the bridge, her gaze locked on Ryder as he slips deeper into the water. At the other end of the bridge, Denis cries out to her, begging her to believe he's not the killer.

The Short Synopsis

Here are some tips for writing a short synopsis:

- Use the present tense.
- Lead off with a strong hook sentence—anything that will grab the attention of your reader.
- Paragraph only for broad transitions in your story.
- Use no dialogue.
- Quickly introduce your lead, the opposition, the romantic interest, and any other important characters, while setting up the story in terms of place and time.
- Quickly state the conflict between your lead and the opposition; then state the lead's story goal.
- Stick to the high points of your lead's main story line.
- Do not include any subplots.
- Move smoothly from one event to another; avoid the choppiness often seen in beginners' short synopses—a result of having whittled down a longer synopsis without regard for smoothness of reading.
- Use powerful verbs and few, if any, adverbs and adjectives.
- Tell the entire story.

Maximum drama

This is your novel in miniature, and you want to leave the reader of your synopsis with the same great feeling he'll have after reading your book. The way to do that is to slow down a little at the novel's end, after the story has resolved itself, and really bear down on the emotional elements. These are what produce that goose-bumps-at-the-back-of-the-neck feeling when we finish a wonderful novel. Go into more detail here; give us a line of dialogue if that's appropriate.

Polish it

The editing of your synopsis is, in a way, more important than the editing of your book—though I would never tell you it's OK to do less than your best work on either.

Because a synopsis is more brief than a novel, errors stand out more clearly. Make yours as close to perfect as you can, even if that means several rounds of editing. Check for misspelled words, awkward sentence structure, confusing writing, grammatical errors, and typographical errors. Be consistent in referring to your characters: don't write *Ryder* in one place and *Gannon* in another. Stick with one name for each character to avoid confusion.

Make it your business to master the synopsis. Don't be one of those writers who says, "I just can't write a synopsis." They're usually the writers who get the poorer deals or no deal at all.

The synopsis is a necessary tool for a novelist, as, say, the preliminary study is for many painters. Once you get the technique down, you'll probably even find synopsis writing fun.

Professional Proposals

Creating a Nonfiction Proposal

by Michael Larsen

Some writers find it easier to write a book than a proposal. For others, writing the proposal is the most creative part of producing a book. Why? Because you have the freedom to plan the book in the way that excites you most without bearing the responsibility for writing it, changing your vision to suit your publisher's needs, or being pressured by the deadline that comes with a contract.

Even one of the following 10 hot buttons can excite editors enough to buy your book:

1. Your idea
2. Your title
3. Your writing
4. Your credentials
5. Your book's timing
6. Your ability to promote your book
7. The size of the markets for your book
8. Your book's subsidiary-rights potential
9. Your book's potential for bulk sales to businesses
10. Your book's potential as a series of books that sell each other

Your job: Push as many hot buttons as you can.

As competitive books prove, there is not just one way to write a proposal any more than there is just one way to write a book. My approach has evolved over the last three decades, and it continues to evolve as editors' needs change.

Most proposals range from 30 to 50 pages. Your proposal will have three parts (the introduction, the outline, and the sample chapter) in a logical sequence, each of which has a goal. Your goal is to impress agents and editors enough with each part of your proposal to convince them to go on to the next.

THE INTRODUCTION

Your introduction should prove that you have a marketable, practical idea and that you are the right person to write about it and promote it. The introduction has three parts: the

---

MICHAEL LARSEN is a literary agent in San Francisco. In 1972, Larsen and his wife Elizabeth started Michael Larsen/Elizabeth Pomada Literary Agents. Excerpted from *How to Write a Book Proposal, 3rd ed.* copyright © 2003 by Michael Larsen. Used with permission of Writer's Digest Books, an imprint of F+W Publications, Inc. Visit your local bookseller or call 1-800-754-2912 to obtain your copy.

Preparing Your Proposal

DO type on one side of 8 1/2 x 11, 20-pound bond paper.

DO number pages consecutively, not by section or chapter.

DO use a standard 12-point typeface (like Times New Roman).

DO type 25, 10-word, 60-character lines, about 250 words on a page.

DON'T leave "widows"— a subhead at the bottom of a page, or the last line of a chapter at the top.

DO use running headers as shown.

DON'T justify the right margin.

DON'T add extra spaces between paragraphs.

1

FINDING A LITERARY AGENT

by

Jane Writer

An agent represents a writer's work to buyers, negotiates contracts, follows up to see that contracts are fulfilled, and generally handles a writer's business affairs, leaving the writer free to write. Effective agents are valued for their contacts in the publishing industry, their savvy about which publishers and editors to approach with which ideas, their ability to guide an author's career, and their business sense.

While many book publishers publish books by unagented writers, some of the larger houses are reluctant to consider unagented submissions.

PROFESSIONALISM AND COURTESY

Writer/FINDING AGENT 2

An editor's time is precious. Between struggling to meet deadlines, maintain budgets, and deal with hundreds of submissions on a daily basis, it's only natural that an editor's communication with writers is limited.

To help advance your communication with editors and receive professional communication in return, there are a few things you can do. Keep all correspondence, whether written or spoken, short and to the point. Don't hound an editor with follow up e-mails, letters, or phone calls to find out the status of your submission. Honor all agree-

"overview," "resources needed to complete the book," and "about the author." They give you the opportunity to provide as much ammunition about you and your book as you can muster.

The Overview

The overview consists of 12 parts, 9 of which are optional:

Your subject hook: This is the most exciting, compelling thing that you can write in as few words as possible that justifies the existence of your book. Use a quote, event, fact, trend, anecdote, statistic, idea, or joke. For example, your subject hook could be an anecdote about someone using your advice to solve a problem followed by a statistic about the number of people with the problem.

Your book hook: This includes your title, your selling handle, and the length of your book:

- **Your title:** The titles for most books have to tell and sell. Make sure yours says what your book is and gives browsers an irresistible reason to buy it.
- **Your selling handle:** This is a sentence that ideally says, "[*Your book's title*] will be the first book to . . ." You can also use Hollywood shorthand by comparing your book to one or two successful books: "[*Your book's title*] is *Seabiscuit* meets *What to Expect When You're Expecting*."
- **The length of your book (and number of illustrations, if it will have them):** Provide a page or word count for your manuscript that you determine by outlining your book and estimating the length of your chapters and back matter.

Markets for your book: List the groups of people who will buy your book and the channels through which it can be sold, starting with the largest ones.

Your book's special features (Optional): This includes humor, structure, anecdotes, checklists, exercises, sidebars, the tone and style of your book, and anything you will do to give the text visual appeal. Use competitive books as models.

A foreword by a well-known authority (Optional): Find someone who will give your book credibility and salability in 50 states 2 years from now to write a foreword. If getting a foreword isn't possible, write: "The author will contact [names of three potential authorities] for a foreword."

Answers to technical or legal questions (Optional): If your book's on a specialized subject, name the expert who has reviewed it. If your book may present legal problems, name the intellectual-property attorney who has reviewed it.

Your back matter (Optional): Check competitive books to see if your book needs an appendix, a glossary, a resource directory, a bibliography, or footnotes.

Your book's subsidiary-rights possibilities (Optional): Start with the most commercial category, whether it's movie rights, foreign rights, book club rights, or even merchandising rights (for products like T-shirts), which usually require a book to be a bestseller before manufacturers will be interested.

Spin-offs (Optional): If your book can be a series or lend itself to sequels, mention up to five of them in descending order of their commercial appeal.

A mission statement (Optional): If you feel a sense of mission about writing and promoting your book, describe it in one, first-person paragraph.

Your platform (Optional): In descending order of impressiveness, list what you have done and are doing to promote your work and yourself.

Your promotion plan (Optional): List in descending order of importance what you will do to promote your book when and after it's published. If you're writing a reference book or a gift book, you may not need a promotion plan. Also, small and medium-sized houses

A Professional Presentation

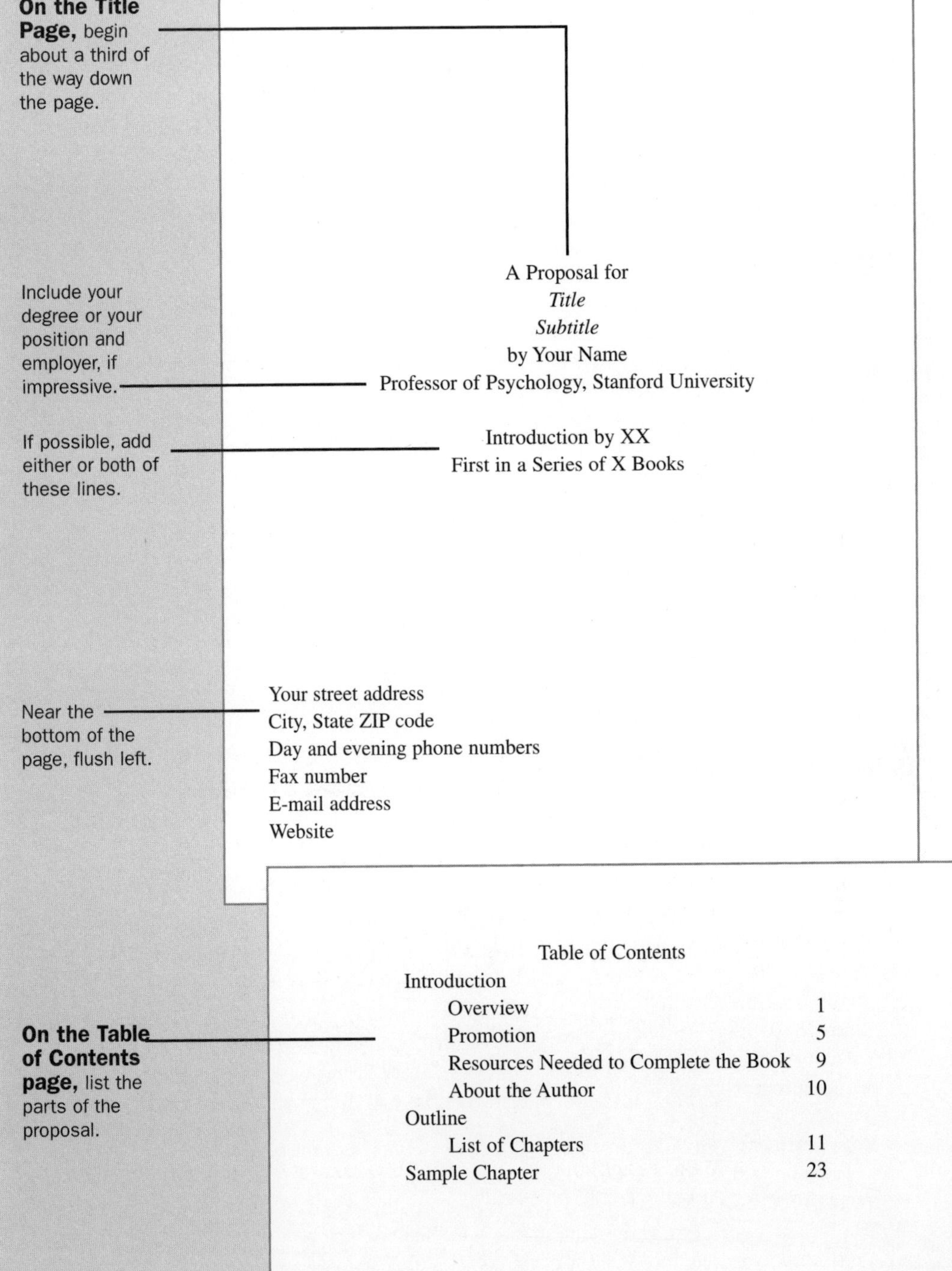

outside of New York don't need the promotional ammunition big publishers do. At the beginning of your career, or if your idea or your ability to promote your book isn't as strong as it needs to be to excite Big Apple publishers, you may find small and medium-sized publishers more receptive to your work.

Also list books that will compete with and complement yours. Provide basic information on the half-dozen most important titles.

Resources needed to complete the book

Starting with the largest expense, list out-of-pocket expenses of $500 or more for a foreword, permissions, travel, or illustrations (not for office expenses). Use a round figure for how much each will cost and give the total. (You may decide not to include the dollar amounts when submitting your proposal, but you do have to know what they are because they affect the money you need to write your book as well as the negotiation of your contract.)

About the author

Include everything not mentioned in your platform that you want editors to know about you in descending order of relevance and importance.

THE OUTLINE

Your outline is a paragraph to a page of prose outlining your chapters to prove that there's a book's worth of information in your idea and that you have devised the best structure for organizing it. Aim for about one line of outline for every page of text you guesstimate; for example, 19 lines of outline for a 19-page chapter. To help make your outlines enjoyable to read, start each one with the strongest anecdote or slice of copy from each chapter, then outline it.

SAMPLE CHAPTER

Include the one sample chapter that best shows how you will make your book as enjoyable to read as it is informative.

Tips for Proofreading and Submitting

- **Read aloud,** and follow along with your index finger under each word.
- **Proofread back to front,** so you can concentrate on the words and not be seduced into reading the proposal.
- **Submit without staples.** Always submit your work without any form of binding. Paper clips are acceptable, but they leave indentations.
- **Use paper portfolios.** Insert your proposal in the right-side of a double-pocket portfolio. You can use the left pocket for writing samples, illustrations, supporting documents, and your business card if the left flap is scored. Put a self-adhesive label on the front of the folder with your book's title and your name.
- **Make everything 8 1/2 × 11.** This makes it easy to reproduce and submit via mail or e-mail.

BEFORE YOU SIGN

Scam Alert!

Avoid Learning the Hard Way

If you were going into business with another person, you'd make sure you knew him, felt comfortable with him, had the same vision as he did—and that he'd never had trouble with the law or a history of bankruptcy, wouldn't you? As obvious as this sounds, many writers take for granted that any agent who expresses interest in their work is trustworthy. They'll sign a contract before asking any questions, cross their fingers for luck, and simply hope everything will turn out OK.

Don't fall into this trap. Doing a little research ahead of time can save you a lot of frustration later. So, how do you check up on an agent? How do you spot a scam before you're already taken in by it?

BEFORE YOU SUBMIT

First, research the agency itself. What kind of reputation does it have? If it's a well-established literary agency and all the agents are members of the Association of Authors' Representatives (AAR), you should be safe from scams.

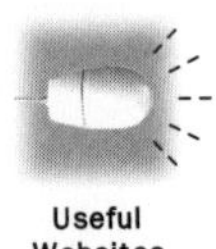

Useful Websites

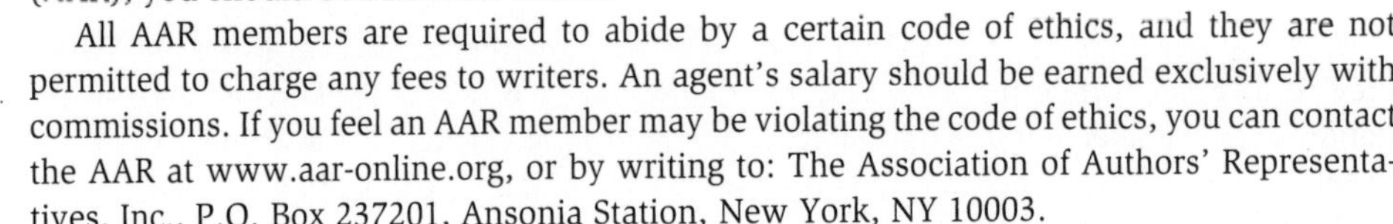

All AAR members are required to abide by a certain code of ethics, and they are not permitted to charge any fees to writers. An agent's salary should be earned exclusively with commissions. If you feel an AAR member may be violating the code of ethics, you can contact the AAR at www.aar-online.org, or by writing to: The Association of Authors' Representatives, Inc., P.O. Box 237201, Ansonia Station, New York, NY 10003.

A writer should never pay any fees to an agent, including reading fees, retainers, marketing fees, or submission fees. And rather than paying an agent for a critique service, join a writer's group. Invest your time instead of your money. Give feedback to others in exchange for their feedback to you.

BEFORE YOU SIGN

If you have any concerns about the agency's practices, ask the agent about them before you sign. Once an agent is interested in representing you, she should be willing to answer any questions or concerns that you have. If the agent is rude or unresponsive or tries to tell you that information is confidential or classified, the agent is uncommunicative at best and, at worst, is already trying to hide something from you.

An agent should be willing to discuss her recent sales with you: how many, what type of books, and to what publishers. If it's a new agent without a track record, be aware that you're taking more of a risk signing with that agent than with a more established agent. However, even a new agent should not be new to publishing. Many agents were editors before they were agents, or they worked at an agency as an assistant. This experience in publishing is crucial for making contacts in the publishing industry and learning about rights and contracts. So, ask the agent how long she's been an agent and what she did before becoming an agent. Ask the agent to name a few editors off the top of her head who she thinks may be interested in your work and why they sprang to mind. Has she sold to them before? Do they publish books in your genre?

If an agent has no contacts in the business, she has no more clout than you do. Without publishing prowess, the agent's just an expensive mailing service. Anyone can make photocopies, slide them into an envelope, and address them to "Editor." Unfortunately, without a contact name and a familiar return address on the envelope or a phone call from a trusted colleague letting an editor know a wonderful submission is on its way, your work will land in the slush pile with all the other submissions that don't have representation. And you can do your own mailings with higher priority than such an agent could.

Occasionally, an agent will charge for the cost of photocopies, postage, and long-distance phone calls made on your behalf. This is acceptable, so long as she keeps an itemized account of the expenses, and you've agreed on a ceiling cost. Be sure to talk over any expenses you don't understand until you have a clear grasp of what you're paying for.

Other times, an agent will recognize the value of the content of your work but will recommend hiring an editor to revise it before she will submit it to publishers. In this case, the agent may suggest an editor (someone with references you'll check) who understands your subject matter or genre and has some experience getting manuscripts into shape. Occasionally, if your story is exceptional or your ideas and credentials are marketable but your writing needs help, you will work with a ghostwriter or co-author who will share a percentage of your commission, or work with you at an agreed upon cost per hour.

Important

An agent may refer you to editors she knows, or you may choose an editor in your area. Many editors do freelance work and would be happy to help you with your writing project. Of course, before entering into an agreement, make sure you know what you'll be getting for your money. Ask the editor for writing samples, references, or critiques she's done in the past. Make sure you feel comfortable working with him before you give him your business.

An honest agent will not make any money for referring you to an editor.

Some agents claim that charging a reading fee cuts down on the number of submissions they receive, and while that is a very real possibility, we recommend writers work with nonfee-charging agents if at all possible. Nonfee-charging agents have a stronger incentive to sell your work. After all, until they make a sale, they don't make a dime.

Agencies who charge fees don't have the same urgency to sell your work. If you do the math, you can see how much money they're bringing in without selling anything: If an agency has 300 clients, each sending in quarterly marketing fees of $100, the agent is making $400 a year from each client. That's $120,000 a year—and that doesn't include the reading fees or any other fees they collect.

AFTER YOU'VE SIGNED

Periodically, you should ask your agent for a full report of where your manuscript has been sent, including the names of the publishing houses and editors. Then, contact a few of the editors/publishers on the list to see if they know your agent and have a strong working relationship with him.

If the agent has ever successfully sold anything to the editor before (or at least sent the editor some promising work before), the editor should remember her name. It's a small world in publishing, and news of an agent's reputation spreads very fast.

But this industry is all about contacts, and if you can't find a worthy agent to make contacts for you, it's entirely possible to do it yourself. Think about it: The agent was once an unknown too. She made first contact by knocking on doors or schmoozing at conferences.

You can do this too. The doors aren't locked to outsiders; they're just harder to find.

It might seem like making toast before baking the bread, but if you can find an interested editor, publisher, or producer at a conference or by referral, she can probably recommend an agent to you. If you mention a credible person interested in your work, many agents would be delighted to take over the contract negotiations for you. And letting a legitimate agent haggle over your contract instead of going at it yourself will help you keep your rights and negotiate the best advance.

Not everyone has this gift for making contacts, so many writers must rely on agents for the agents' pre-existing contacts. The trouble is, unless you know an agent's track record, you're taking the agent's word for it that she indeed has these contacts. If she doesn't, even if she lives right there in New York, she's no more able to sell your work for you than you are, even if you're living in Massachusetts. So check the agent's references and make sure she's made recent sales with legitimate publishers or production companies.

As a side note, agents should return clients' phone calls or e-mails quickly and keep the clients informed about prospects. An agent should also consult clients about any offers before accepting or rejecting them.

IF YOU'VE BEEN SCAMMED

If you have trouble with your agent and you've already tried to resolve it yourself to no avail, it may be time to call for help. Please alert the writing community to protect others. If you find agents online, in directories, or in this book who aren't living up to their promises or

If You've Been Scammed . . .

For More Info

. . . or if you're trying to prevent a scam, the following resources should be of help. You can contact:

- **The Federal Trade Commission, Bureau of Consumer Protection** (CRC-240, Washington DC 20580, 1-877-382-4357). While they won't resolve individual consumer problems, the FTC depends on your complaints to help them investigate fraud, and your speaking up may even lead to law enforcement action. Contact the FTC by mail or phone, or visit their website at www.ftc.gov.
- **Volunteer Lawyers for the Arts** (1 E. 53rd St., 6th Floor, New York NY 10022) is a group of volunteers from the legal profession who assist with questions of law pertaining to the arts. You can phone their hotline at (212)319-2787, ext. 1, and have your questions answered for the price of the phone call. For more information visit their website at www.vlany.org.
- **The Better Business Bureau** (check local listings or visit www.bbb.org) is the organization to contact if you have a complaint or if you want to investigate a publisher, literary agent, or other business related to writing and writers.
- **Your State's Attorney General.** Don't know your attorney general's name? Go to www.attorneygeneral.gov/ags. This site provides a wealth of contact information, including a complete list of links to the attorney general's website for each state.

are charging you money when they're listed as nonfee-charging agents, please let the webmaster or editor of the publication know. Sometimes they can intervene for an author, and if no solution can be found, they can at the very least remove a listing from their directory so no other authors will be scammed in the future. All efforts are made to keep scam artists out, but in a world where agencies are bought and sold, a reputation can change overnight.

If you have complaints about any business, you can call the Better Business Bureau (BBB) to report them. The BBB will at least file your complaint, and that way, if anyone contacts the BBB before dealing with the business, the BBB will inform them of any unresolved complaints against the business. Their website is www.bbb.org, or you may send a written complaint to: The Council of Better Business Bureaus, 4200 Wilson Blvd., Suite 800, Arlington, VA 22203-1838.

Finally, legal action may seem like a drastic step, but sometimes people do it. You can file a suit with the Attorney General and try to find other writers who want to sue for fraud with you. The Science Fiction Writers of America's website, www.sfwa.org, offers sound advice on recourse you can take in these situations. For further details see: www.sfwa.org/beware/overview.html.

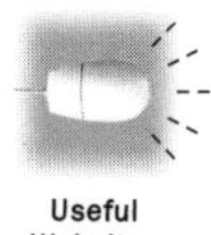

Useful Websites

If you live in the same state as your agent, it may be possible to settle the case in small claims court. This is a viable option for collecting smaller damages and a way to avoid lawyer fees. The jurisdiction of the small claims court includes cases in which the claim is $5,000

Warning Signs! Beware Of:

Important

- **Excessive typos or poor grammar** in an agent's correspondence.
- **A form letter accepting you as a client,** praising generic things about your book that could apply to any book. An agent should call or send a personalized letter. A good agent doesn't take on a new client very often, so when she does, it's a special occasion that warrants a personal note or phone call.
- **Unprofessional contracts** that ask you for money up front, contain clauses you haven't discussed, or are covered with amateur clip-art or silly borders.
- **Rudeness** when you inquire about any points you're unsure of. Don't employ any business partner who doesn't treat you with respect.
- **Pressure,** by way of threats, bullying, or bribes. A good agent is not desperate to represent more clients. She invites worthy authors but leaves the final decision up to them.
- **Promises of publication.** No agent can guarantee you a sale. Not even the top agents sell everything they choose to represent. They can only send your work to the most appropriate places, have it read with priority, and negotiate you a better contract if a sale does happen.
- **A print-on-demand book contract** or any contract offering you no advance. You can sell your own book to an e-publisher any time you wish without an agent's help. An agent should pursue traditional publishing routes with respectable advances.

or less. (This varies from state to state but should still cover the amount for which you're suing.) Keep in mind suing takes a lot of effort and time. You'll have to research all the necessary legal steps. If you have lawyers in your family, that could be a huge benefit if they'll agree to help you organize your case, but legal assistance is not necessary.

MOVING ON AND STARTING AGAIN

Above all, if you've been scammed, don't waste time blaming yourself. It's not your fault if someone lies to you. People who scam, cheat, lie, and steal—they'll get what's coming to them. Respect in the literary world is built on reputation, and word about bad agents gets around. Editors ignore their submissions. Writers begin to avoid them. Without clients or buyers, a swindling agent will find her business collapsing.

Meanwhile, you'll keep writing and believing in yourself. One day, you'll see your work in print, and you'll tell everyone what a rough road it was to get there but how you wouldn't trade it for anything in the world.

BEFORE YOU SIGN

What Should I Ask?

13 Questions to Ask an Agent

by The Association of Authors' Representatives

The following is a suggested list of topics for authors to discuss with literary agents who have offered to represent them. Please bear in mind that most agents are *not* going to be willing to spend the time answering these questions unless they have already read your material and wish to represent you.

1. Are you a member of the Association of Authors' Representatives?
2. How long have you been in business as an agent?
3. Do you have specialists at your agency who handle movie and television rights? Foreign rights?
4. Do you have subagents or corresponding agents in Hollywood and overseas?
5. Who in your agency will actually be handling my work? Will the other staff members be familiar with my work and the status of my business at your agency?
6. Will you oversee or at least keep me apprised of the work that your agency is doing on my behalf?
7. Do you issue an agent/author agreement? May I review the language of the agency clause that appears in contracts you negotiate for your clients?
8. How do you keep your clients informed of your activities on their behalf?
9. Do you consult with your clients on any and all offers?
10. What are your commission rates? What are your procedures and time frames for processing and disbursing client funds? Do you keep different bank accounts separating author funds from agency revenue? What are your policies about charging clients for expenses incurred by your agency?
11. When you issue 1099 tax forms at the end of each year, do you also furnish clients, upon request, with a detailed account of their financial activity, such as gross income, commissions and other deductions, and net income, for the past year?
12. In the event of your death or disability, what provisions exist for my continued representation?
13. If we should part company, what is your policy about handling any unsold subsidiary rights in my work?

BEFORE YOU SIGN

Know Your Rights

Most writers who want to be published envision their book in store fronts and on their friends' coffee tables. They imagine book signings and maybe even an interview on *Oprah*. Usually the dream ends there; having a book published seems exciting enough. In actuality, a whole world of opportunities exists for published writers beyond seeing their books in print. These opportunities are called "subsidiary rights."

Subsidiary rights, or sub-rights, are the additional ways that a book can be presented. Any time a book is made into a movie or excerpted in a magazine, a subsidiary right has been sold. If these additional rights to your book are properly "exploited," you'll not only see your book in a variety of forms, but you'll also make a lot more money than you would have made on book sales alone.

Unfortunately, the terminology of subsidiary rights can be confusing. Phrases like "secondary rights," "traditional splits," or "advance against royalty" could perplex any writer. And the thought of negotiating the terms of these rights with a publisher can be daunting.

Although there are many advantages to working with agents, the ability to negotiate sub-rights is one of an agent's most beneficial attributes. Through experience, an agent knows which publishing houses have great sub-rights departments. If the agent knows a house can make money with a right, the agent will grant that right to the publisher when the contract is negotiated. Otherwise, the agent will keep, or "retain," certain rights for her clients, which she will try to exploit by selling them to her own connections. In an interview in a previous *Guide to Literary Agents*, writer Octavia Butler said that working with an agent, "is certainly a good thing if you don't know the business. It's a good way to hang onto your foreign and subsidiary rights and have somebody actively peddling those rights because there were years when I lived off subsidiary rights."

Important

If you want to work with an agent, you should have a basic understanding of sub-rights for two reasons. First, you'll want to be able to discuss these rights with your agent intelligently. (Although, you should feel comfortable asking your agent any question you have about sub-rights.) Second, different agents have more expertise in some sub-right areas than others. If you think your book would make a great movie, you should research the agents who have strong film connections. A knowledge of sub-rights can help you find the agent best suited to help you achieve your dreams.

An agent negotiates sub-rights with the publishing house at the same time a book is sold. In fact, the sale of certain sub-rights can even determine how much money the publisher offers for the book. But the author doesn't get paid immediately for these rights. Instead, the author is paid an "advance against royalties." An advance is a loan to the author that is paid back when the book starts earning money. Once the advance is paid, the author starts earning royalties, which are a pre-determined percentage of the book's profit.

The agent always keeps certain rights, the publisher always buys certain rights, and the others are negotiated. When an agent keeps a right, she is then free to sell it at will. If she does sell it, the money she receives from the purchasing company goes immediately to the author, minus the agent's commission. Usually the companies who purchase rights pay royalties instead of a one-time payment.

If the publisher keeps the right, any money that is made from it goes toward paying off the advance. Because the publisher kept the right, they will keep part of the money it makes. For most rights, half the money goes to the publisher and half goes to the writer, although for some rights the percentages are different. This separation of payment is called a "traditional split" because it has become standard over the years. And, of course, the agent takes her commission from the author's half.

Most agents have dealt with certain publishers so many times that they have pre-set, or "boilerplate," contracts, which means they've already agreed to the terms of certain rights, leaving only a few rights to negotiate. The following describes the main sub-rights and discusses what factors an agent takes into account when deciding whether or not to keep a right. As you read through this piece, carefully consider the many opportunities for your book, and encourage your agent and publisher to exploit these rights every chance they get.

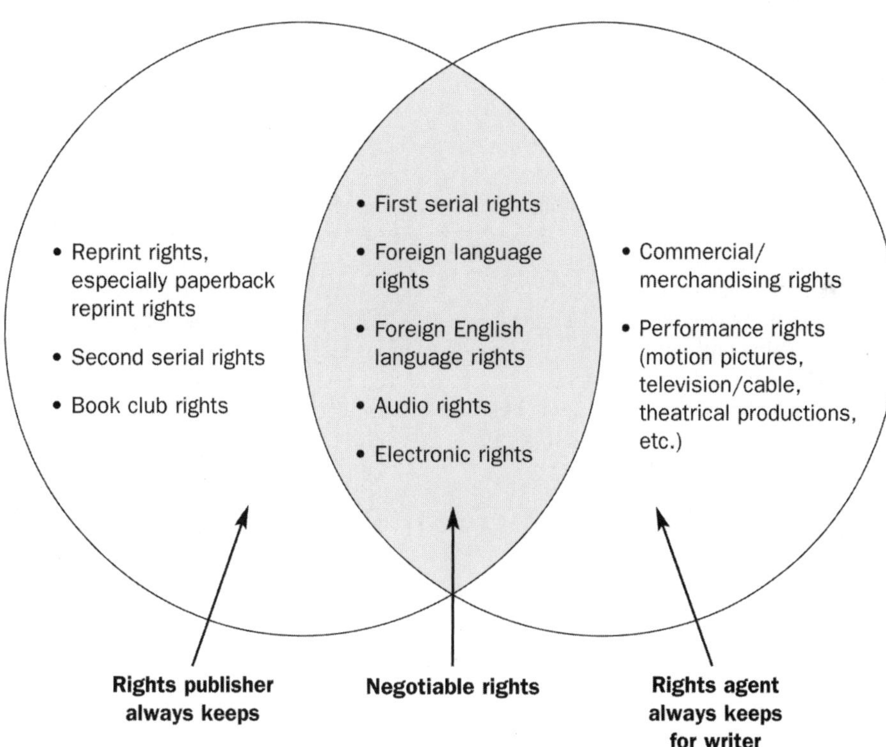

RIGHTS THE PUBLISHER ALWAYS KEEPS

The following sub-rights are always kept by the publisher and are often called "nonnegotiable rights." Money earned from these rights is split between the publisher and the author, and the author's share goes toward paying back the advance. Selling these rights helps repay the advance faster, which hopefully means the writer will receive royalty checks sooner.

Reprint rights

In publishing, a "reprint right" refers to the paperback edition of the book. When a hardcover book is reprinted in paperback, the reprint right has been used. According to Donald Maass of the Donald Maass Literary Agency, "In deals with major trade publishers, it's a long-standing practice to grant them control of reprint rights. However, in some cases—a small-press deal, for instance—we withhold these rights." Traditionally, if a hardcover book sold really well, paperback houses bought the rights to reprint the book in a more affordable version. Any money earned from the paperback was then split 50/50 between the publisher and writer. Paperback houses often paid substantial amounts of money for these reprint rights.

But the recent consolidation of publishing houses has changed the value of reprint rights. "In the old days, most books were hardcover, and paperbacks were cheap versions of the book," explains Maass. "Today so many paperback publishers have either merged with a hardcover publisher or begun their own hardcover publisher that the business of selling reprint rights has diminished." Now many publishers make what is called a "hard/soft deal," meaning the house will first print the book in hardcover and, if the book sells well, they reprint the book in paperback. This type of deal can still benefit writers because they no longer have to split the money earned from reprint with the publisher. Instead, the writer earns royalties from both the hardcover and paperback versions.

Book club rights

These days it seems that a book club exists for every possible interest. There are the traditional book clubs, like Book-of-the-Month and its paperback counterpart, the Quality Paperback Book Club. But there are also mystery book clubs, New Age book clubs, book clubs for writers and artists, and even online book clubs. Most book clubs are very selective, and you should be flattered if your book is chosen. Like reprint rights, any money made from book club rights is split 50/50 between the publisher and the writer. If an agent believes a book will appeal to a certain book club's audience, the agent will target the manuscript to publishers who have good relationships with—or who own—that book club.

Serial rights

A serial is an excerpt of the book that appears in a magazine or in another book. To have your book serialized is wonderful because excerpts not only make additional money for you, but they also provide wonderful publicity for your book. There are actually two types of serial rights: first serial and second serial. First serial means the excerpt of the book is available before the book is printed. A second serial is an excerpt that appears after the book is already in bookstores. First serial rights are actually negotiable; sometimes the right to use them is kept by the agent. Usually an agent's decision is based upon her knowledge of the publications available in the book's subject. If she doesn't know the various magazines, she will let the publisher have this right. Second serial rights, however, are almost always granted to the publisher.

Nonfiction books are more commonly excerpted than fiction. Nonfiction excerpts usually stand alone well, and magazines are eager to use these excerpts because they usually cost less than hiring a freelancer to write original material. Recently, though, serialized fiction has regained popularity. A few years ago, John Grisham's *A Painted House* (Doubleday, 2001) made a giant splash by appearing in six installments in *The Oxford American*.

RIGHTS NEGOTIATED BETWEEN THE AGENT AND PUBLISHER

The owner of these sub-rights is always determined when the book is sold. Often an agent and editor must compromise for these rights. In other words, an agent may agree to sell foreign rights if she can keep electronic rights. Or, an editor will offer more money if he can obtain the audio rights to a book.

Foreign language rights

If your book might appeal to audiences in a non-English-speaking country, then you'll want an agent who has good connections with foreign co-agents. According to James Vines of The Vines Agency, Inc., a "foreign co-agent is someone who specializes in the sales of foreign publishing rights and who has good relationships with the heads of publishing houses throughout the world. These agents work on behalf of a New York City agency and approach the foreign publishers with manuscripts and proposals. They will typically have appointments booked at big trade shows like Frankfurt Book Fair, London Book Fair, and BookExpo America. That's where a lot of the big foreign deals happen." Usually an agent charges a 20 percent commission when a foreign co-agent is used, and the two split the earnings.

"All of my clients have benefited from the sale of foreign rights," continues Vines. "For example, *Kokology* (Fireside, 2003), by Tadahiko Nagao and Isamu Saito started as a big phenomenon in Japan, selling more than 4 million copies. A game you play about psychology, it's one of those ideas that crosses all languages and cultural boundaries because it's uniquely human. We all want to know more about ourselves." Vines sold the book to Simon & Schuster, and then worked with a co-agent to sell it all over the world.

When agents are considering how a book will do abroad, they must be aware of trends in other countries. "Most agents try to stay on top of the foreign markets as much as possible and listen to what foreign co-agents have to say," says Vines. "Trends vary from territory to territory, and I try to keep those trends in mind." Vines also points out that writers can benefit from different sub-rights over a period of time depending on how well a sub-right is selling.

Many publishing houses have foreign counterparts, and often an agent will grant the publisher these rights if she knows the book can be printed by one of these foreign houses. If the publisher has foreign language rights, the author receives an average of 75 percent of any money made when the book is sold to a foreign publisher.

British rights

Like foreign language rights, the owner of a book's British rights can sell the book to publishers in England. Australia was once included in these rights, but Australian publishers are becoming more independent. If an agent keeps these rights, she will use a co-agent in England and the two will likely split a 20 percent commission. If a publisher has these rights, the traditional split is 80/20 with the author receiving the larger share.

Electronic rights

A few years ago, Stephen King caused a big commotion in the publishing world first by using an electronic publisher for his book, *Riding the Bullet*, and then by self-publishing his serialized novel, *The Plant*. Many publishing professionals worried that King would start a trend drawing writers away from publishers, while others claimed only high-profile writers like King could ever compete successfully against the vast amounts of information on the Web. Regardless, King's achievement showed that readers are paying attention to the Internet.

Basically, electronic rights refer to the hand-held electronic, Internet, and print-on-demand versions of a book. This right is currently one of the hottest points of contention between agents and publishers because the potential for these rights is unknown—it is quite possible that electronic versions of a book will make a lot of money one day.

This area of publishing is changing so rapidly that both agents and editors struggle with how to handle electronic rights. Many publishers believe any version of a book is the same material as the printed book, and, therefore, they should own the rights. Agents worry, however, that if the publisher lets the book go out of print, the rights to the book will never be returned to the author.

Audio rights

Before people feared that the Internet would cause the end of traditional book publishing, people worried that audio versions of books would erase the need to have printed books. In actuality, audio books have complimented their printed counterparts and have proved to be a fantastic source of additional income for the person who owns the rights to produce the book in audio form—whether through cassette tape or compact disc.

Many publishers own audio imprints and even audio book clubs, and if they are successful with these ventures, an agent will likely grant the audio rights to the publisher. The traditional split is 50/50. Otherwise, the agent will try to save this right and sell it to a company that can turn it into a profit.

RIGHTS THE WRITER ALWAYS KEEPS

When a book is sold, an agent always reserves two rights for her authors: performance and merchandising. Some books are naturally more conducive to being made into films or products, and when they do, there's usually a lot of money to be made. A smart agent can quickly identify when a book will be successful in these areas.

Important

Performance rights

Many writers fantasize about seeing their book on the big screen. And a lot of times, agents share this dream—especially for best-selling titles. If your agent feels your book will work well as a movie, or even as a television show or video game, she will sell these rights to someone in the entertainment industry. This industry works fairly differently than the publishing industry. Usually a producer "options" the right to make your book into a movie. An option means the producer can only make the movie during a specific amount of time, like a year. If the movie isn't made during that time period, the rights revert back to the writer. You can actually option these rights over and over—making money for every option—without the book ever being made into a movie.

As with foreign rights, agents usually work with another agent to sell performance rights. Usually these agents live in Los Angeles and have the connections to producers that agents outside California just don't have. Agents normally take a 20 percent commission from any money made from performance rights. That 20 percent will be split if two agents partner to sell the rights.

Merchandising rights

Merchandising rights create products—like calendars, cards, action figures, stickers, dolls, and so on—that are based on characters or other elements of your book. Few books transfer well into such products, but they can be successful when they do. Keep in mind that if a producer options the performance rights to your book, the merchandising rights are usually included in the deal.

For example, several years ago agent Steven Malk, of Writers House, made wonderful use of these two rights for his client Elise Primavera and her book, *Auntie Claus* (Silver Whistle/ Harcourt, 1999). According to Malk, "When I first read the manuscript of *Auntie Claus* and saw a couple of Primavera's sample illustrations, I immediately knew the book had a lot of possibilities in the sub-rights realm. First of all, the character of Auntie Claus is extremely memorable and unique, and from a visual standpoint, she's stunning. Also, the basic concept

Listing Policy and Complaint Procedure

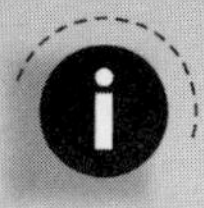
For More Info

Listings in *Guide to Literary Agents* are compiled from detailed questionnaires, phone interviews, and information provided by agents. The industry is volatile, and agencies change frequently. We rely on our readers for information on their dealings with agents and changes in policies or fees that differ from what has been reported to the editor of this book. Write to us (*Guide to Literary Agents*, 4700 E. Galbraith Rd., Cincinnati, OH 45236) or e-mail us (literaryagent@fwpubs.com) if you have new information, questions, or problems dealing with the agencies listed.

Listings are published free of charge and are not advertisements. Although the information is as accurate as possible, the listings are not endorsed or guaranteed by the editor or publisher of *Guide to Literary Agents*. If you feel you have not been treated fairly by an agent or representative listed in *Guide to Literary Agents*, we advise you to take the following steps:

- Try to contact the agency. Sometimes one phone call or a letter can clear up the matter.
- Document all your correspondence with the agency. When you write to us with a complaint, provide the name of your manuscript, the date of your first contact with the agency, and the nature of your subsequent correspondence.

We will enter your letter into our files and attempt to contact the agency. The number, frequency, and severity of complaints will be considered in our decision whether or not to delete the listing from the next edition. *Guide to Literary Agents* reserves the right to exclude any agency for any reason.

of the book is completely fresh and original, which is very hard to accomplish with a Christmas book.

"The first thing I did was to approach Saks Fifth Avenue with the idea of featuring *Auntie Claus* in their Christmas windows. In addition to using the book as the theme for their window displays, they created some merchandise that was sold through Saks. It's a perfect project for them; the character of Auntie Claus is so sophisticated and refined, and it seemed ideal for their windows. Shortly after that, the movie rights were optioned by Nickelodeon."

Like Malk did for Primavera, many agents successfully exploit subsidiary rights every day. If you want the most for your book, look for an agent who has the know-how and connections to take your publishing dream to its fullest potential. Use the information in this article to help your agent make the most of your subsidiary rights.

Literary Agents

Agents listed in this section generate 98 to 100 percent of their income from commission on sales. They do not charge for reading, critiquing, or editing your manuscript or book proposal. It's the goal of an agent to find salable manuscripts: Her income depends on finding the best publisher for your manuscript.

Because an agent's time is better spent meeting with editors, she will have little or no time to critique your writing. Agents who don't charge fees must be selective and often prefer to work with established authors, celebrities, or those with professional credentials in a particular field.

Some agents in this section may charge clients for office expenses such as photocopying, foreign postage, long-distance phone calls, or Express Mail services. Make sure you have a clear understanding of what these expenses are before signing any agency agreement. While most agents deduct expenses from the advance or royalties a book earns, a few agents included in this section charge their clients a one-time up-front, "marketing" or "handling" fee.

Canadian and international agents are included in this section. Canadian agents have a 🍁 icon preceding their listing, and international agents have a 🌐 icon preceding their listing. Remember to include an International Reply Coupon (IRC) with your self-addressed envelope when contacting Canadian and international agents.

SUBHEADS

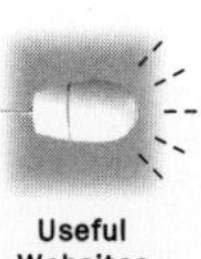

Each agent/agency listing is broken down into specific subheads to make locating information within the listing easier. In the first section, you'll find contact information for each agency. You'll also learn if the agents within the agency belong to any professional organizations; membership in these organizations can tell you a lot about an agency. For example, members of the Association of Authors' Representatives (AAR) are prohibited from charging reading or evaluating fees. This book contains contact information for all agents who are currently registered with the AAR (www.aar-online.org). Additional information in this section includes the size of each agency, its willingness to work with new or previously unpublished writers, and its general areas of interest.

Member Agents: Agencies comprised of more than one agent list member agents and their individual specialties. This information will help you determine the appropriate person to whom you should send your query letter.

Represents: This section allows agencies to specify what nonfiction and fiction subjects they represent. Make sure you query only those agents who represent the type of material you write. To help narrow your search, check the **Literary Agents Specialties Index** in the back of the book.

O→ Look for the key icon to quickly learn an agent's areas of specialization. In this portion of the listing, agents mention the specific subject areas they're currently seeking, as well as those subjects they do not want to receive.

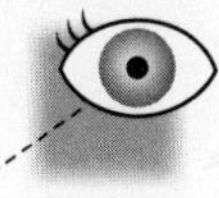

How to Contact: Most agents open to submissions initially prefer to receive a query letter briefly describing your work (see How to Write a Query Letter on page 51). While some agents may ask for an outline and a specific number of sample chapters, most don't. You should send these items only if the agent requests them. In this section, agents also mention if they accept queries by fax or e-mail; if they consider simultaneous submissions; and how they prefer to solicit new clients.

Recent Sales: To give you a sense of the types of material they represent, the agents list specific titles they've sold, as well as a sampling of clients' names. However, it is important to note that some agents consider their client list confidential and may only share client names once they agree to represent you.

Terms: Provided here are details of an agent's commission; whether a contract is offered and for how long; and what additional office expenses you might have to pay if the agent agrees to represent you. Standard commissions range from 10 to 15 percent for domestic sales, and 15 to 20 percent for foreign or dramatic sales (with the difference going to the co-agent who places the work).

Writers' Conferences: A great way to meet an agent is at a writers' conference. Here agents list the conferences they usually attend. For more information about a specific conference, check the **Writers' Conferences** section starting on page 245.

Tips: In this section, agents offer advice and additional instructions for writers.

ANDREA BROWN LITERARY AGENCY, INC.
1076 Eagle Dr., Salinas CA 93905. (831)422-5925. Fax: (831)422-5915. E-mail: andrea@andreabrownlit.com. Website: www.andreabrownlit.com. **Contact** Andrea Brown, president. Estab. 1981. 10% of clients are new/unpublished writers. Currently handles: 95% juvenile nonfiction books; 5% adult nonfiction and fiction.

• Prior to opening her agency, Ms. Brown served as an editorial assistant at Random House and Dell Publishing and as an editor with Alfred A. Knopf.

Member Agents Andrea Brown, Laura Rennert, Caryn Wiseman, Jennifer Jaeger, Robert Welsh.

Represents Nonfiction books (juvenile). **Considers these nonfiction areas:** Animals; anthropology/archaeology; art/architecture/design; biography/autobiography; current affairs; ethnic/cultural interests; history; how-to; juvenile nonfiction; nature/environment; photography; popular culture; science/technology; sociology; sports. All nonfiction subjects for juveniles and adults.

O→ This agency specializes in "all kinds of children's books—illustrators and authors." Considers all juvenile fiction areas; all genres of nonfiction.

How to Contact Query with SASE. Accepts e-mail queries. No fax queries. Considers simultaneous queries. Obtains most new clients through recommendations from others, referrals from editors, clients, and agents.

Terms Agent receives 15% commission on domestic sales; 20% commission on foreign sales. Offers written contract. Charges clients for shipping costs.

2006 GUIDE TO LITERARY AGENTS KEY TO SYMBOLS

 market new to this edition

 Canadian agency

 agency located outside of the U.S. and Canada

 newer agency actively seeking clients

 agency seeks both new and established writers

 agency prefers to work with established writers, mostly obtains new clients through referrals

 agency handling only certain types of work or work by writers under certain circumstances

 agency not currently seeking new clients

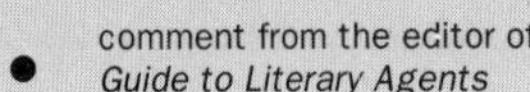

● comment from the editor of *Guide to Literary Agents*

O-т agency's specializations

ms, mss manuscript(s)

SASE self-addressed, stamped envelope

SAE self-addressed envelope

IRC International Reply Coupon, for use in countries other than your own

(For definitions of words and expressions used throughout the book, see the Glossary. For translations of acronyms of organizations connected with agenting or writing, refer to the Table of Acronyms.)

Find a pull-out bookmark, a quick reference to the icons used in this book, right inside the front cover.

SPECIAL INDEXES TO REFINE YOUR SEARCH

Literary Agents Specialties Index: In the back of the book on page 284 is an index which organizes agencies according to the subjects they are interested in receiving. This index should help you compose a list of agents specializing in your areas. Cross-referencing categories and concentrating on agents interested in two or more aspects of your manuscript might increase your chances of success.

Agencies Indexed by Openness to Submissions: This index lists agencies according to how receptive they are to new clients.

Geographic Index: For writers looking for an agent close to home, this index lists agents according to the state in which they are located.

Agents Index: Often you will read about an agent who is an employee of a larger agency, and you may not be able to locate her contact information. Starting on page 345 is a list of agents' names in alphabetical order along with the name of the agency for which they work. Find the name of the person you would like to contact, and then check the agency listing.

General Index: This index lists all agencies, independent publicists, production companies, script contests, and writers' conferences appearing in the book.

DOMINICK ABEL LITERARY AGENCY, INC.

146 W. 82nd St., #1B, New York NY 10024. Fax: (212)595-3133. E-mail: agency@dalainc.com. Estab. 1975. Member of AAR. Represents 100 clients. Currently handles: adult nonfiction books; adult novels.

How to Contact Query with SASE by mail.

Terms Agent receives 15% commission on domestic sales; 20% commission on foreign sales.

CAROLE ABEL LITERARY AGENT

160 W. 87th St., #7D, New York NY 10024. Fax: (212)724-1384. E-mail: caroleabel@aol.com. 50% of clients are new/unpublished writers. Currently handles: nonfiction books.

How to Contact Query with SASE by mail, e-mail or fax.

Recent Sales *Instant Self Hypnosis*, by Forbes Blair (Sourcebooks); *Word Play*, by L. Myers/L. Goodman (McGraw Hill).

ACACIA HOUSE PUBLISHING SERVICES, LTD.

51 Acacia Rd., Toronto ON M4S 2K6 Canada. (416)484-8356. Fax: (416)484-8356. E-mail: fhanna.acacia@rogers.com. **Contact:** (Ms.) Frances Hanna. Estab. 1985. Represents 100 clients. Currently handles: 30% nonfiction books; 70% novels.

- Ms. Hanna has been in the publishing business for 30 years, first in London (UK) as a fiction editor with Barrie & Jenkins and Pan Books, and as a senior editor with a packager of mainly illustrated books. She was condensed books editor for 6 years for *Reader's Digest* in Montreal, senior editor and foreign rights manager for (the then) William Collins & Sons (now HarperCollins) in Toronto. Her husband, vice president Bill Hanna, has over 40 years experience in the publishing business.

Member Agents Bill Hanna, vice president (business, self-help, modern history).

Represents Nonfiction books, novels. **Considers these nonfiction areas:** Animals; biography/autobiography; language/literature/criticism; memoirs; military/war; music/dance; nature/environment; theater/film; travel. **Considers these fiction areas:** Action/adventure; detective/police/crime; literary; mainstream/contemporary; mystery/suspense; thriller.

This agency specializes in contemporary fiction: literary or commercial. Actively seeking "outstanding first novels with literary merit." Does not want to receive horror, occult, science fiction.

How to Contact Query with outline and SASE. *No unsolicited mss.* No e-mail or fax queries. Responds in 6 weeks to queries. Returns materials only with SASE.

Recent Sales Sold over 75 titles in the last year. Also made numerous international rights sales. This agency prefers not to share information on specific sales or clients.

Terms Agent receives 15% commission on English language sales, 20% on dramatic sales, 25% commission on foreign sales. Charges clients for photocopying, postage, and courier, as necessary.

Tips "We prefer that writers be previously published, with at least a few short stories or articles to their credit. Strongest consideration will be given to those with 3 or more published books. However, we would take on an unpublished writer of outstanding talent."

N ADAMS LITERARY

295 Greenwich St., #260, New York NY 10007. (212)786-9140. Fax: (212)786-9170. E-mail: info@adamsliterary.com. Website: www.adamsliterary.com. **Contact:** Tracey Adams. Estab. 2004. Member of AAR.

- Prior to becoming an agent, Ms. Adams worked in the marketing and editorial departments of Greenwillow Books and Margaret K. McElderry Books.

Adams Literary is a full-service literary agency exclusively representing children's book authors and artists. "Although we remain absolutely dedicated to finding new talent, we must announce that until further notice we can no longer accept unsolicited manuscripts. We also cannot accept queries or submissions via e-mail."

BRET ADAMS LTD. AGENCY

448 W. 44th St., New York NY 10036. (212)765-5630. **Contact:** Bruce Ostler. Member of AAR.

- Query before submitting.

AGENTS INK!

(formerly Agents, Inc., For Medical and Mental Health Professionals), P.O. Box 4956, Fresno CA 93744. (559)438-8289. **Contact:** Sydney H. Harriet, Ph.D., Psy. D., director. Estab. 1987. Member of APA. Represents 20 clients. 70% of clients are new/unpublished writers. Currently handles: 80% nonfiction books; 20% novels; multimedia.

- Prior to opening his agency, Dr. Harriet was a psychologist, radio and television reporter, and professor of English. Dinah McNichols has a B.A. in classical Greek and an M.A. in classics. She has more than 20 years of experience as an editor for daily and alternative newspapers, major syndicates and independent authors.

Member Agents Sydney Harriet, Ph.D., director; Dinah McNichols.

Represents Nonfiction books, novels. **Considers these nonfiction areas:** Animals; cooking/foods/nutrition; government/politics/law; health/medicine (mind-body healing); history; language/literature/criticism; psychology; science/technology; self-help/personal improvement; sociology; sports (medicine, psychology); Foreign affairs, international topics. **Considers these fiction areas:** *Currently representing previously published novelists only.*

O- This agency specializes in writers who have education experience in the business, legal and health professions. It is helpful if the writer is licensed, but not necessary. Prior nonfiction book publication not necessary. For fiction, previously published fiction is a prerequisite for representation. Does not want memoirs, autobiographies, stories about overcoming an illness, science fiction, fantasy, religious materials, and children's books.

How to Contact Query with SASE. Considers simultaneous queries. Responds in 1 month.

Recent Sales Sold 5 titles in the last year. *Infantry Soldier*, by George Neil (University of Oklahoma Press); *SAMe, The European Arthritis and Depression Breakthrough*, by Sol Grazi, M.D. and Maria Costa (Prima); *What to Eat if You Have Diabetes*, by Danielle Chase M.S. (Contemporary); *How to Turn Your Fat Husband Into a Lean Lover*, by Maureen Keane (Random House).

Terms Agent receives 15% commission on domestic sales; 20% commission on foreign sales. Offers written contract, binding for 6-12 months (negotiable).

Writers' Conferences "Scheduled as a speaker at a number of conferences across the country. Contact agency to book authors and agents for conferences."

Tips "Remember, query first. Do not call to pitch an idea. The only way we can judge the quality of your idea is to see how you write. Please, unsolicited manuscripts will not be read if they arrive without a SASE. Currently, we are receving more than 200 query letters and proposals each month. Send complete proposal/manuscript only if requested. Please, ask yourself why someone would be compelled to buy your book. If you think the idea is unique, spend the time to create a query and then a proposal where every word counts. Fiction writers need to understand that the craft is just as important as the idea. 99% of the fiction is rejected because of sloppy, overwritten dialogue, wooden characters, predictable plotting, and lifeless narrative. Once you finish your novel, put it away and let it percolate, then take it out and work on fine-tuning it some more. A novel is never finished until you stop working on it. Would love to represent more fiction writers and probably will when we read a manuscript that has gone through a dozen or more drafts. Because of rising costs, we no longer can respond to queries, proposals, and/or complete manuscripts without receiving a return envelope and sufficient postage."

THE AHEARN AGENCY, INC.

2021 Pine St., New Orleans LA 70118-5456. (504)861-8395. Fax: (504)866-6434. E-mail: pahearn@aol.com. **Contact:** Pamela G. Ahearn. Estab. 1992. Member of MWA. Represents 25 clients. 20% of clients are new/unpublished writers. Currently handles: 10% nonfiction books; 90% novels.

- Prior to opening her agency, Ms. Ahearn was an agent for 8 years and an editor with Bantam Books.

Represents Nonfiction books, novels, short story collections (if stories previously published). **Considers these nonfiction areas:** Animals; child guidance/parenting; current affairs; ethnic/cultural interests; gay/lesbian issues; health/medicine; history; music/dance; popular culture; self-help/personal improvement; theater/film; true crime/investigative; women's issues/studies. **Considers these fiction areas:** Action/adventure; contemporary issues; detective/police/crime; ethnic; family saga; feminist; gay/lesbian; glitz; historical; humor/satire; literary; mainstream/contemporary; mystery/suspense; psychic/supernatural; regional; romance; thriller.

O- This agency specializes in historical romance and is also very interested in mysteries and suspense fiction. Does not want to receive category romance, science fiction, or fantasy.

How to Contact Query with SASE. Accepts e-mail queries, no attachments. Considers simultaneous queries. Responds in 8 weeks to queries; 10 weeks to mss. Obtains most new clients through recommendations from others, solicitations, conferences.

Recent Sales *The Perfumed Sleeve*, by Laura Joh Rowland (St. Martin's); *To Pleasure a Prince*, by Sabrina Jeffries (Pocket).

Terms Agent receives 15% commission on domestic sales; 20% commission on foreign sales. Offers written contract, binding for 1 year; renewable by mutual consent.

Writers' Conferences Moonlight & Magnolias; RWA National Conference (Orlando); Virginia Romance Writers (Williamsburg VA); Florida Romance Writers (Ft. Lauderdale FL); Golden Triangle Writers Conference; Bouchercon (Monterey, November); Malice Domestic (DC, May).

Tips "Be professional! Always send in exactly what an agent/editor asks for, no more, no less. Keep query letters brief and to the point, giving your writing credentials and a very brief summary of your book. If one agent rejects you, keep trying—there are a lot of us out there!"

ALIVE COMMUNICATIONS, INC.

7680 Goddard St., Suite 200, Colorado Springs CO 80920. (719)260-7080. Fax: (719)260-8223. Website: www.alivecom.com. Estab. 1989. Member of CBA, Authors Guild. Represents 200+ clients. 5% of clients are new/unpublished writers. Currently handles: 50% nonfiction books; 35% novels; 5% novellas; 10% juvenile books.

Member Agents Rick Christian, president (blockbusters, bestsellers); Jerry "Chip" MacGregor (popular/commercial nonfiction and fiction, new authors with breakout potential); Beth Jusino (thoughtful/inspirational nonfiction, women's fiction/nonfiction, Christian living); Lee Hough (popular/commercial nonfiction and fiction, thoughtful spirituality, children's).

Represents Nonfiction books, novels, short story collections, novellas. **Considers these nonfiction areas:** Biography/autobiography; business/economics; child guidance/parenting; how-to; memoirs; religious/inspirational; self-help/personal improvement; women's issues/studies. **Considers these fiction areas:** Action/adventure; contemporary issues; detective/police/crime; family saga; historical; humor/satire; literary; mainstream/contemporary; mystery/suspense; religious/inspirational; thriller.

O→ This agency specializes in fiction, Christian living, how-to, and commercial nonfiction. Actively seeking inspirational/literary/mainstream fiction and work from authors with established track record and platforms. Does not want poetry, young adult paperback, scripts, dark themes.

How to Contact Works primarily with well-established, bestselling, and career authors. Returns materials only with SASE. Obtains most new clients through recommendations from others. "On rare occasions accepts new clients through referrals."

Recent Sales Sold 300+ titles in the last year. Left Behind Series, by Tim LaHaye and Jerry B. Jenkins (Tyndale); *Let's Roll*, by Lisa Beamer (Tyndale); *The Message*, by Eugene Peterson (NavPress); Every Man Series, by Stephen Arterburn (Waterbrook); *One Tuesday Morning*, by Karen Kingsbury (Zondervan).

Terms Agent receives 15% commission on domestic sales; 15% commission on foreign sales. Offers written contract; 2-month written notice must be given to terminate contract.

Tips "Rewrite and polish until the words on the page shine. Endorsements and great connections may help, provided you can write with power and passion. Network with publishing professionals by making contacts, joining critique groups, and attending writers' conferences in order to make personal connections in publishing and to get feedback. Alive Communications, Inc., has established itself as a premiere literary agency. Based in Colorado Springs, we serve an elite group of authors who are critically acclaimed and commercially successful in both Christian and general markets."

ALTAIR LITERARY AGENCY, LLC

P.O. Box 11656, Washington DC 20008. (202)237-8282. Website: www.altairliteraryagency.com. Estab. 1996. Member of AAR. Represents 50 clients. 20% of clients are new/unpublished writers. Currently handles: 95% nonfiction books; 5% novels.

Member Agents Andrea Pedolsky, partner; Nicholas Smith, partner.

Represents Nonfiction books. **Considers these nonfiction areas:** History; popular culture; sports; science (history of); illustrated; current events/contemporary issues; museum; organization; and corporate-brand books. **Considers these fiction areas:** Historical (pre-20th century mysteries only).

O→ This agency specializes in nonfiction with an emphasis on authors who have credentials and professional recognition for their topic, and a high level of public exposure. Actively seeking solid, well-informed authors who have a public platform for the subject specialty.

How to Contact Query with SASE; or see website for more specific query information and to send an online query. Considers simultaneous queries. Responds in 2-4 weeks to queries; 1 month to mss. Obtains most new clients through recommendations from others, solicitations, author queries.

Recent Sales *Performance Nutrition for Runners*, by Matt Fitzgerald (Rodale); *Online Roots*, by Pamela Porter, CGRS, CGL and Amy Johnson Crow (Rutledge Hill Press); *How Herbs Work*, by Suzette Holly Phaneuf (Marlowe/Avalon Publshing); *You Can Sell It!*, by Frank McNair (Sourcebooks); *That Might Be Useful*, by Naton Leslie (Lyons Press); *Good Catholic Girls*, by Angela Bonavoglia (ReganBooks/HarperCollins); *Life's a Bitch and Then You Change Careers*, by Andrea Kay (Stewart/Tabori & Chang).

Terms Agent receives 15% commission on domestic sales; 20% commission on foreign sales. Offers written contract, binding for 1 year; 2-month notice must be given to terminate contract. Charges clients for postage, copying, messengers and FedEx and UPS.

MIRIAM ALTSHULER LITERARY AGENCY

53 Old Post Rd. N., Red Hook NY 12571. (845)758-9408. **Contact:** Miriam Altshuler. Estab. 1994. Member of AAR. Represents 40 clients. Currently handles: 45% nonfiction books; 45% novels; 5% story collections; 5% juvenile books.

- Ms. Altshuler has been an agent since 1982.

Represents Nonfiction books, novels, short story collections, juvenile books. **Considers these nonfiction areas:** Biography/autobiography; ethnic/cultural interests; history; language/literature/criticism; memoirs; multicultural; music/dance; nature/environment; popular culture; psychology; sociology; theater/film; women's issues/studies. **Considers these fiction areas:** Literary; mainstream/contemporary; multicultural.

O→ Does not want self-help, mystery, how-to, romance, horror, spiritual, fantasy, poetry, screenplays, science fiction, techno-thriller.

How to Contact Query with SASE. Prefers to read materials exclusively. If no SASE is included, no response will be sent. No unsolicited mss. No e-mail or fax queries. Considers simultaneous queries. Responds in 2 weeks to queries; 3 weeks to mss. Returns materials only with SASE. Obtains most new clients through recommendations from others.

Terms Agent receives 15% commission on domestic sales; 20% commission on foreign sales. Charges clients for overseas mailing, photocopies, overnight mail when requested by author.

Writers' Conferences Bread Loaf Writers' Conference (Middlebury VT, August); Washington Independent Writers Conference (Washington DC, June), North Carolina Writers Network Conference (Carrboro NC, October).

BETSY AMSTER LITERARY ENTERPRISES

P.O. Box 27788, Los Angeles CA 90027-0788. **Contact:** Betsy Amster. Estab. 1992. Member of AAR. Represents over 65 clients. 35% of clients are new/unpublished writers. Currently handles: 65% nonfiction books; 35% novels.

- Prior to opening her agency, Ms. Amster was an editor at Pantheon and Vintage for 10 years, and served as editorial director for the Globe Pequot Press for 2 years. "This experience gives me a wider perspective on the business and the ability to give focused editorial feedback to my clients."

Represents Nonfiction books, novels. **Considers these nonfiction areas:** Biography/autobiography; child guidance/parenting; ethnic/cultural interests; gardening; health/medicine; history; money/finance; psychology; sociology; women's issues/studies; career. **Considers these fiction areas:** Ethnic; literary; mystery/suspense (quirky); thriller (quirky); women's (high quality).

O→ Actively seeking "strong narrative nonfiction, particularly by journalists; outstanding literary fiction (the next Michael Chabon or Jhumpa Lahiri); witty, intelligent, commercial women's fiction (the next Elinor Lipman or Jennifer Weiner); and high-profile self-help and psychology, preferably research based." Does not want to receive poetry, children's books, romances, westerns, science fiction, action/adventure.

How to Contact For fiction, send query, first 3 pages, and SASE. For nonfiction, send query or proposal with SASE. No e-mail or fax queries. Considers simultaneous queries. Responds in 1 month to queries; 2 months to mss. Obtains most new clients through recommendations from others, solicitations, conferences.

Recent Sales *González & Daughter Trucking Co.*, by María Amparo Escandón (Crown); *The Modern Jewish Girl's Guide to Guilt*, edited by Ruth Andrew Ellenson (Dutton); *Rejuvenile: How a New Species of Reluctant Adults is Redefining Maturity*, by Christopher Nixon (Crown); *The Reluctant Tuscan*, by Phil Doran (Gotham). Other clients include Dwight Allen, Dr. Elaine N. Aron, Barbara DeMarco-Barrett, Dr. Helene Brenner, Robin Chotzinoff, Frank Clifford, Rob Cohen & David Wollock, Jan DeBlieu, Margaret Lobenstine, Paul Mandelbaum, Wendy Mogel, Sharon Montrose, Joy Nicholson, Katie Singer, R.J. Smith, Louise Steinman.

Terms Agent receives 15% commission on domestic sales; 20% commission on foreign sales. Offers written contract, binding for 1 year; 3-month notice must be given to terminate contract. Charges for photocopying, postage, long distance phone calls, messengers, and galleys and books used in submissions to foreign and film agents and to magazines for first serial rights.

Writers' Conferences Squaw Valley; San Diego Writers Conference; UCLA Extension Writer's Program; The Loft Literary Center (Minneapolis).

MARCIA AMSTERDAM AGENCY

41 W. 82nd St., New York NY 10024-5613. (212)873-4945. **Contact:** Marcia Amsterdam. Estab. 1970. Signatory of WGA. Currently handles: 15% nonfiction books; 70% novels; 5% movie scripts; 10% TV scripts.

- Prior to opening her agency, Ms. Amsterdam was an editor.

Represents Novels, feature film, TV movie of the week, sitcom. **Considers these fiction areas:** Action/adventure; detective/police/crime; horror; mainstream/contemporary; mystery/suspense; romance (contemporary, historical); science fiction; thriller; young adult. **Considers these script subject areas:** Comedy; mainstream; mystery/suspense; romantic comedy; romantic drama.

How to Contact Submit outline, 3 sample chapters, SASE. Responds in 1 month to queries.
Recent Sales *Rosey in the Present Tense*, by Louise Hawes (Walker); *Flash Factor*, by William H. Lovejoy (Kensington); *Lucky Leonardo*, by Jonathan Canter (Landmark); *Hidden Child*, by Isaac Millman (Frances Foster Books, FSG).
Terms Agent receives 15% commission on domestic sales; 20% commission on foreign sales; 10% commission on dramatic rights sales. Offers written contract, binding for 1 year. Charges clients for extra office expenses, foreign postage, copying, legal fees (when agreed upon).
Tips "We are always looking for interesting literary voices."

BART ANDREWS & ASSOCIATES

7510 Sunset Blvd., Suite 100, Los Angeles CA 90046. (310)271-9916. **Contact:** Bart Andrews. Estab. 1982. Represents 25 clients. 25% of clients are new/unpublished writers. Currently handles: 100% nonfiction books.
Represents Nonfiction books. **Considers these nonfiction areas:** Biography/autobiography; music/dance; theater/film; TV.

- This agency specializes in nonfiction only, and in the general category of entertainment (movies, TV, biographies, autobiographies).

How to Contact Query with SASE. Considers simultaneous queries. Responds in 1 week to queries; 1 month to mss.
Recent Sales Sold 25 titles in the last year. *Roseanne*, by J. Randy Taraborrelli (G.P. Putnam's Sons); *Out of the Madness*, by Rose Books packaging firm (HarperCollins).
Terms Agent receives 15% commission on domestic sales; 15% (after subagent takes his 10%) commission on foreign sales. Offers written contract. Charges clients for all photocopying, mailing, phone calls, postage, etc.
Writers' Conferences Frequently lectures at UCLA in Los Angeles.
Tips "Recommendations from existing clients or professionals are best, although I find a lot of new clients by seeking them out myself. I rarely find a new client through the mail. Spend time writing a query letter. Sell yourself like a product. The bottom line is writing ability, and then the idea itself. It takes a lot to convince me. I've seen it all! I hear from too many first-time authors who don't do their homework. They're trying to get a book published, and they haven't the faintest idea what is required of them. There are plenty of good books on the subject and, in my opinion, it's their responsibility—not mine—to educate themselves before they try to find an agent to represent their work. When I ask an author to see a manuscript or even a partial manuscript, I really must be convinced I want to read it—based on a strong query letter—because of wasting my time reading just for the fun of it."

APPLESEEDS MANAGEMENT

200 E. 30th St., Suite 302, San Bernardino CA 92404. (909)882-1667. **Contact:** S. James Foiles. Estab. 1988. 40% of clients are new/unpublished writers. Currently handles: 15% nonfiction books; 85% novels.
Represents Nonfiction books, novels. **Considers these nonfiction areas:** True crime/investigative. **Considers these fiction areas:** Detective/police/crime; mystery/suspense.
How to Contact Query with SASE. Responds in 2 weeks to queries; 2 months to mss.
Recent Sales This agency prefers not to share information on specific sales.
Terms Agent receives 10-15% commission on domestic sales; 20% commission on foreign sales. Offers written contract, binding for 1-7 years.
Tips "Appleseeds specializes in mysteries with a detective who could be in a continuing series because readership of mysteries is expanding."

ARCADIA

31 Lake Place N., Danbury CT 06810. E-mail: arcadialit@att.net. **Contact:** Victoria Gould Pryor. Member of AAR.
Represents Nonfiction books (readable, serious), literary and commercial fiction. **Considers these nonfiction areas:** Biography/autobiography; business/economics; current affairs; history; memoirs; psychology; science/technology; true crime/investigative; women's issues/studies; medicine; investigative journalism; culture; classical music; life transforming self-help.

- "I'm a very hands-on agent, necessary in this competitive marketplace. I work with authors on revisions until whatever we present to publishers is as perfect as it can be. I represent talented, dedicated, intelligent, and ambitious writers who are looking for a long-term relationship based on professional success and mutual respect." No science fiction/fantasy, or children's/YA. "We are only able to read fiction submissions from previously published authors."

How to Contact Query with SASE. E-mail queries accepted without attachments.
Recent Sales This agency prefers not to share information on specific sales.

AUTHENTIC CREATIONS LITERARY AGENCY

875 Lawrenceville-Suwanee Rd., Suite 310-306, Lawrenceville GA 30043. (770)339-3774. Fax: (770)339-7126. E-mail: ron@authenticcreations.com. Website: www.authenticcreations.com. **Contact:** Mary Lee Laitsch. Estab. 1993. Member of AAR, Authors Guild. Represents 70 clients. 30% of clients are new/unpublished writers. Currently handles: 60% nonfiction books; 40% novels.

- Prior to becoming an agent, Ms. Laitsch was a librarian and elementary school teacher; Mr. Laitsch was an attorney and a writer.

Member Agents Mary Lee Laitsch; Ronald Laitsch; Jason Laitsch.

Represents Nonfiction books, novels, scholarly books. **Considers these nonfiction areas:** Anthropology/archaeology; biography/autobiography; child guidance/parenting; crafts/hobbies; current affairs; history; how-to; science/technology; self-help/personal improvement; sports; true crime/investigative; women's issues/studies. **Considers these fiction areas:** Action/adventure; contemporary issues; detective/police/crime; family saga; literary; mainstream/contemporary; mystery/suspense; romance; sports; thriller.

How to Contact Query with SASE. No e-mail or fax queries. Considers simultaneous queries. Responds in 2 weeks to queries; 2 months to mss.

Recent Sales Sold 20 titles in the last year. *Secret Agent*, by Robyn Spizman and Mark Johnston (Simon & Schuster); *Beauchamp Beseiged*, by Elaine Knighton (Harlequin); *Visible Differences*, by Dominic Pulera (Continuum).

Terms Agent receives 15% commission on domestic sales; 15% commission on foreign sales. Charges clients for photocopying.

Tips "We thoroughly enjoy what we do. What makes being an agent so satisfying for us is having the opportunity to work with authors who are as excited about the works they write as we are about representing them."

THE AXELROD AGENCY

55 Main St., P.O. Box 357, Chatham NY 12037. (518)392-2100. Fax: (518)392-2944. E-mail: steve@axelrodagency.com. **Contact:** Steven Axelrod. Estab. 1983. Member of AAR. Represents 20-30 clients. 1% of clients are new/unpublished writers. Currently handles: 5% nonfiction books; 95% novels.

- Prior to becoming an agent, Mr. Axelrod was a book club editor.

Represents Nonfiction books, novels. **Considers these fiction areas:** Mystery/suspense; romance; women's.

How to Contact Query with SASE. Considers simultaneous queries. Responds in 3 weeks to queries; 6 weeks to mss. Returns materials only with SASE. Obtains most new clients through recommendations from others.

Recent Sales This agency prefers not to share information on specific sales.

Terms Agent receives 15% commission on domestic sales; 20% commission on foreign sales. No written contract.

Writers' Conferences Romance Writers of America (July).

BALKIN AGENCY, INC.

P.O. Box 222, Amherst MA 01004. (413)548-9835. Fax: (413)548-9836. **Contact:** Rick Balkin, president. Estab. 1972. Member of AAR. Represents 50 clients. 10% of clients are new/unpublished writers. Currently handles: 85% nonfiction books; 5% scholarly books; 5% textbooks; 5% reference books.

- Prior to opening his agency, Mr. Balkin served as executive editor with Bobbs-Merrill Company.

Represents Nonfiction books, scholarly books, textbooks. **Considers these nonfiction areas:** Animals; anthropology/archaeology; biography/autobiography; current affairs; health/medicine; history; how-to; language/literature/criticism; music/dance; nature/environment; popular culture; science/technology; sociology; translation; travel; true crime/investigative.

- This agency specializes in adult nonfiction. Does not want to receive fiction, poetry, screenplays, computer books.

How to Contact Query with SASE, proposal package, outline. No e-mail or fax queries. Responds in 1 week to queries; 2 weeks to mss. Returns materials only with SASE. Obtains most new clients through recommendations from others.

Recent Sales Sold 30 titles in the last year. *The Liar's Tale* (W.W. Norton Co.); *Adolescent Depression* (Henry Holt); *Eliz. Van Lew: A Union Spy in the Heart of the Confederacy* (Oxford U.P.).

Terms Agent receives 15% commission on domestic sales; 20% commission on foreign sales. Offers written contract, binding for 1 year. Charges clients for photocopying and express or foreign mail.

Tips "I do not take on books described as bestsellers or potential bestsellers. Any nonfiction work that is either unique, paradigmatic, a contribution, truly witty, or a labor of love is grist for my mill."

BARER LITERARY, LLC

156 Fifth Ave., Suite 1134, New York NY 10010. **Contact:** Julie Barer. Member of AAR.

- Query before submitting.

LORETTA BARRETT BOOKS, INC.

101 Fifth Ave., New York NY 10003. (212)242-3420. Fax: (212)807-9579. E-mail: mail@lorettabarrettbooks.com. **Contact:** Loretta A. Barrett or Nick Mullendore. Estab. 1990. Member of AAR. Currently handles: 60% nonfiction books; 40% novels.

- Prior to opening her agency, Ms. Barrett was vice president and executive editor at Doubleday and editor-in-chief of Anchor Books.

Represents Nonfiction books, novels. **Considers these nonfiction areas:** Biography/autobiography; business/economics; child guidance/parenting; creative nonfiction; current affairs; ethnic/cultural interests; gay/lesbian issues; government/politics/law; health/medicine; history; language/literature/criticism; memoirs; money/finance; multicultural; nature/environment; philosophy; popular culture; psychology; religious/inspirational; science/technology; self-help/personal improvement; sociology; spirituality; sports; women's issues/studies; nutrition. **Considers these fiction areas:** Action/adventure; contemporary issues; detective/police/crime; ethnic; family saga; historical; literary; mainstream/contemporary; mystery/suspense; psychic/supernatural; thriller.

O→ This agency specializes in general interest books. No children's, juvenile, science fiction or fantasy.

How to Contact Query with SASE. No e-mail or fax queries. Considers simultaneous queries. Responds in 6 weeks to queries. Returns materials only with SASE.

Recent Sales *Fantastic Voyage*, by Ray Kurzweil and Terry Grossman (Rodale); *The Singularity Is Near*, by Ray Kurzweil (Viking); *Invisible Heroes*, by Belleruth Naparstek (Bantam); *Islands of the Mind*, by John Gillis (Palgrave); *Letters to a Young Catholic* and *Cathedral and the Cube*, by George Weigel (Basic Books); *Talk to the Mirror*, by Florine Mark (John Wiley & Co.); *The Meaning of the 21st Century*, by James Martin (Riverhead); *Unattended Sorrow*, by Steve Levine (Rodale).

Terms Agent receives 15% commission on domestic sales; 20% commission on foreign sales. Offers written contract. Charges clients for shipping and photocopying.

Writers' Conferences San Diego State University Writer's Conference; Pacific Northwest Writer's Association; SEAK Medical Writer's Conference.

BEACON ARTISTS AGENCY

208 W. 30th St., Suite 401, New York NY 10001. (212)736-6630. Fax: (212)868-1052. **Contact:** Patricia McLaughlin. Member of AAR.

Tips "We are not taking new clients at this time."

BERMAN, BOALS, & FLYNN, INC.

208 W. 30th St., Room 401, New York NY 10001. (212)868-1068. Fax: (212)868-1052. **Contact:** Judy Boals. Member of AAR.

- Query before submitting.

MEREDITH BERNSTEIN LITERARY AGENCY

2112 Broadway, Suite 503A, New York NY 10023. (212)799-1007. Fax: (212)799-1145. Estab. 1981. Member of AAR. Represents 85 clients. 20% of clients are new/unpublished writers. Currently handles: 50% nonfiction books; 50% fiction.

- Prior to opening her agency, Ms. Bernstein served in another agency for 5 years.

Member Agents Meredith Bernstein, Elizabeth Cavanaugh.

Represents Nonfiction books, fiction of all kinds. **Considers these nonfiction areas:** Any area of nonfiction in which the author has an established platform. **Considers these fiction areas:** Literary; mystery/suspense; romance; thriller; women's.

O→ This agency does not specialize. It is "very eclectic."

How to Contact Query with SASE. No e-mail or fax queries. Considers simultaneous queries. Obtains most new clients through recommendations from others, conferences, also develops and packages own ideas.

Recent Sales *Tripping the Prom Queen: Envy, Competition & Jealousy Among Women*, by Susan Shepiro Barash (St. Martin's Press); *Sleep on It*, by Carol Gordon (Hyperion); 3-book deal of contemporary romances by Sandra Hill to Warner Books; 6-book deal by *The New York Times* best-selling romance writer Sharon Sala (aka Dinah McCall) to Mira Books/Harlequin.

Terms Agent receives 15% commission on domestic sales; 20% commission on foreign sales. Charges clients $75 disbursement fee/year.

Writers' Conferences SouthWest Writers Conference (Albuquereque, August); Rocky Moutnain Writers' Conference (Denver, September); Golden Triangle (Beaumont TX, October); Pacific Northwest Writers Conference; Austin League Writers Conference; Willamette Writers Conference (Portland OR); Lafayette Writers Conference (Lafayette LA); Surrey Writers Conference (Surrey BC); San Diego State University Writers Conference (San Diego CA).

DANIEL BIAL AGENCY

41 W. 83rd St., Suite 5-C, New York NY 10024-5246. (212)721-1786. Fax: (309)213-0230. E-mail: dbialagency@juno.com. **Contact:** Daniel Bial. Estab. 1992. Represents under 50 clients. 15% of clients are new/unpublished writers. Currently handles: 95% nonfiction books; 5% novels.

- Prior to opening his agency, Mr. Bial was an editor for 15 years.

Represents Nonfiction books, novels. **Considers these nonfiction areas:** Animals; anthropology/archaeology; biography/autobiography; business/economics; child guidance/parenting; cooking/foods/nutrition; current affairs; ethnic/cultural interests; government/politics/law; history; how-to; humor/satire; language/literature/criticism; memoirs; military/war; money/finance; music/dance; nature/environment; New Age/metaphysics; popular culture; psychology; religious/inspirational; science/technology; self-help/personal improvement; sociology; spirituality; sports; theater/film; travel; true crime/investigative; women's issues/studies. **Considers these fiction areas:** Action/adventure; contemporary issues; detective/police/crime; erotica; ethnic; humor/satire; literary.

How to Contact Submit proposal package, outline. Responds in 2 weeks to queries. Returns materials only with SASE. Obtains most new clients through recommendations from others, solicitations, "good rolodex"

Recent Sales This agency recently had a No. 1 *New York Times* bestseller with *Osama Bin Ladin: The Man Who Delcared War on America*, by Yossef Bodansky.

Terms Agent receives 15% commission on domestic sales; 25% commission on foreign sales. Offers written contract, binding for 1 year with cancellation clause. Charges clients for overseas calls, overnight mailing, photocopying, messenger expenses.

Tips "Publishers want their authors to have platforms. In other words, they want the authors to have the ability to sell their work or get themselves in the media even before the book comes out. And successful agents get publishers what they want."

BIGSCORE PRODUCTIONS, INC.

P.O. Box 4575, Lancaster PA 17604. (717)293-0247. Fax: (717)293-1945. E-mail: bigscore@bigscoreproductions.com. Website: www.bigscoreproductions.com. **Contact:** David A. Robie, agent. Estab. 1995. Represents 50-75 clients. 25% of clients are new/unpublished writers.

Represents Nonfiction and fiction (see website for categories of interest).

- This agency specializes in inspirational and self-help nonfiction and fiction, and has over 20 years in the publishing and agenting business.

How to Contact See website for submission guidelines. Query by e-mail or mail. No fax queries. Considers simultaneous queries. Responds in 2 months to proposals.

Terms Agent receives 15% commission on domestic sales. Offers written contract, binding for 6 months. Charges clients for expedited shipping, ms photocopying and preparation, and books for subsidiary rights submissions.

Tips "Very open to taking on new clients. Submit a well-prepared proposal that will take minimal fine-tuning for presentation to publishers. Nonfiction writers must be highly marketable and media savvy—the more established in speaking or in your profession, the better. Bigscore Productions works with all major general and Christian publishers"

VICKY BIJUR LITERARY AGENCY

333 West End Ave., Apt. 5B, New York NY 10023. Member of AAR.

- Query before submitting.

DAVID BLACK LITERARY AGENCY

156 Fifth Ave., Suite 608, New York NY 10010-7002. (212)242-5080. Fax: (212)924-6609. **Contact:** David Black, owner. Estab. 1990. Member of AAR. Represents 150 clients. Currently handles: 90% nonfiction books; 10% novels.

Member Agents David Black; Susan Raihofer (general nonfiction to literary fiction); Gary Morris (commercial fiction to psychology); Joy E. Tutela (general nonfiction to literary fiction); Leigh Ann Eliseo.

Represents Nonfiction books, novels. **Considers these nonfiction areas:** Biography/autobiography; business/economics; government/politics/law; history; memoirs; military/war; money/finance; multicultural; sports. **Considers these fiction areas:** Literary; mainstream/contemporary; Commercial.

- This agency specializes in business, sports, politics, and novels.

How to Contact Query with SASE, outline. No e-mail or fax queries. Considers simultaneous queries. Responds in 2 months to queries. Returns materials only with SASE.

Recent Sales *Body for Life*, by Bill Phillips with Mike D'Orso (HarperCollins); *Devil in the White City*, by Erik Carson; The Don't Know Much About Series by Ken Davis.

Terms Agent receives 15% commission on domestic sales. Charges clients for photocopying and books purchased for sale of foreign rights.

BLEECKER STREET ASSOCIATES, INC.

532 LaGuardia Place, #617, New York NY 10012. (212)677-4492. Fax: (212)388-0001. **Contact:** Agnes Birnbaum. Estab. 1984. Member of AAR, RWA, MWA. Represents 60 clients. 20% of clients are new/unpublished writers. Currently handles: 75% nonfiction books; 25% novels.

- Prior to becoming an agent, Ms. Birnbaum was a senior editor at Simon & Schuster, Dutton/Signet, and other publishing houses.

Represents Nonfiction books, novels. **Considers these nonfiction areas:** Animals; biography/autobiography; business/economics; child guidance/parenting; computers/electronic; cooking/foods/nutrition; current affairs; ethnic/cultural interests; government/politics/law; health/medicine; history; how-to; memoirs; military/war; money/finance; nature/environment; New Age/metaphysics; popular culture; psychology; religious/inspirational; science/technology; self-help/personal improvement; sociology; sports; true crime/investigative; women's issues/studies. **Considers these fiction areas:** Ethnic; historical; literary; mystery/suspense; romance; thriller; women's interest.

"We're very hands-on and accessible. We try to be truly creative in our submission approaches. We've had especially good luck with first-time authors." Does not want to receive science fiction, westerns, poetry, children's books, academic/scholarly/professional books, plays, scripts, short stories.

How to Contact Query with SASE. No email, phone, or fax queries. Considers simultaneous queries. Responds in 2 weeks to queries; 1 month to mss. Returns materials only with SASE. Obtains most new clients through recommendations from others, solicitations, conferences, "plus, I will approach someone with a letter if his/her work impresses me."

Recent Sales Sold 20 titles in the last year. *How America Got It Right*, by Bevin Alexander (Crown); *The Dim Sum of All Things*, by Kim Wong Keltner (Morrow/Avon); *American Bee*, by James Maguire (Rodale); *Guide to the Galaxy*, by Pat Barnes-Svarney (Sterling); *Deal Breakers*, by Maia Dunkel (Doubleday).

Terms Agent receives 15% commission on domestic sales; 25% commission on foreign sales. Offers written contract; 1-month notice must be given to terminate contract. Charges for postage, long distance, fax, messengers, photocopies, not to exceed $200.

Tips "Keep query letters short and to the point; include only information pertaining to book or background as writer. Try to avoid superlatives in description. Work needs to stand on its own, so how much editing it may have received has no place in a query letter."

THE BLUMER LITERARY AGENCY, INC.

350 Seventh Ave., Suite 2003, New York NY 10001-5013. (212)947-3040. **Contact:** Ms. Olivia B. Blumer. Estab. 2002; Board member of AAR. Represents 34 clients. 60% of clients are new/unpublished writers. Currently handles: 67% nonfiction books; 33% novels.

- Prior to becoming an agent, Ms. Blumer spent 25 years in publishing-subsidiary rights, publicity, editorial.

Represents Nonfiction and fiction. **Considers these nonfiction areas:** Agriculture/horticulture; animals; anthropology/archaeology; art/architecture/design; biography/autobiography; business/economics; cooking/foods/nutrition; ethnic/cultural interests; health/medicine; how-to; humor/satire; language/literature/criticism; memoirs; money/finance; nature/environment; photography; popular culture; psychology; religious/inspirational; self-help/personal improvement; true crime/investigative; women's issues/studies; crafts/hobbies; interior design/decorating; New Age/metaphysics. **Considers these fiction areas:** Detective/police/crime; ethnic; family saga; feminist; historical; humor/satire; literary; mainstream/contemporary; mystery/suspense; regional; thriller.

Actively seeking quality fiction, practical nonfiction, memoir with a larger purpose.

How to Contact Query with SASE. No e-mail or fax queries. Responds in 2 weeks to queries; 4-6 weeks to mss. Returns materials only with SASE. Obtains most new clients through recommendations from others, but significant exceptions have come from slush pile.

Recent Sales *Almost French*, by Sarah Turnbull (Gotham/Penguin); *What Happened to Henry*, by Sharon Pywell (Putnam) Other clients include Joan Anderson, Marialisa Calta, Ellen Rolfes, Mark Forstater, Laura Karr, Liz McGregor, Constance Snow, Lauri Ward, Michelle Curry Wright, Susann Cokal, Dennis L. Smith.

Terms Agent receives 15% commission on domestic sales; 20% commission on foreign sales. Charges for photocopying, overseas shipping, and Fed Ex/UPS.

REID BOATES LITERARY AGENCY

69 Cooks Crossroad, Pittstown NJ 08867. (908)730-8523. Fax: (908)730-8931. E-mail: boatesliterary@att.net. **Contact:** Reid Boates. Estab. 1985. Represents 45 clients. 5% of clients are new/unpublished writers. Currently handles: 85% nonfiction books; 15% novels; very rarely story collections.

How to Contact No unsolicited queries of any kind. Obtains most new clients through recommendations from others, new clients by personal referral only.

Recent Sales Sold 20 titles in the last year. This agency prefers not to share information on specific sales.

Terms Agent receives 15% commission on domestic sales; 20% commission on foreign sales.

BOOK DEALS, INC.

244 Fifth Ave., Suite 2164, New York NY 10001-7604. (212)252-2701. Fax: (212)591-6211. **Contact:** Caroline Francis Carney. Estab. 1996. Member of AAR. Represents 40 clients. 15% of clients are new/unpublished writers. Currently handles: 85% nonfiction books; 15% novels.

- Prior to opening her agency, Ms. Carney was editorial director for a consumer book imprint within Times Mirror and held senior editorial positions in McGraw-Hill and NYIF/Simon & Schuster.

Represents Nonfiction books, novels (commercial and literary). **Considers these nonfiction areas:** Business/economics; child guidance/parenting; ethnic/cultural interests; health/medicine (nutrition); history; how-to; money/finance; multicultural; popular culture; psychology (popular); religious/inspirational; science/technology; self-help/personal improvement; spirituality. **Considers these fiction areas:** Ethnic; literary; mainstream/contemporary; women's (contemporary); urban literature.

O→ This agency specializes in highly commercial nonfiction and books for African-American readers and women. Actively seeking well-crafted fiction and nonfiction from authors with engaging voices and impeccable credentials.

How to Contact Query with SASE. Considers simultaneous queries.

Recent Sales *Eat Right for Your Personality Type*, by Dr. Robert Kushner & Nancy Kushner (St. Martin's Press); *Self-Proclaimed*, by Rochelle Shapiro (Simon & Schuster); *Par for the Course*, by Alice Dye and Mark Shaw (HarperCollins).

Terms Agent receives 15% commission on domestic sales; 20% commission on foreign sales. Offers written contract. Charges clients for photocopying and postage.

BOOKENDS, LLC

136 Long Hill Rd., Gillette NJ 07933. (908)362-0090. E-mail: editor@bookends-inc.com. Website: www.bookends-inc.com. **Contact:** Jessica Faust, Jacky Sach or Kim Lionetti. Estab. 1999. Represents 50+ clients. 20% of clients are new/unpublished writers. Currently handles: 50% nonfiction books; 50% novels.

- "Please review submission guidelines on our website before sending anything to BookEnds." Fiction areas of interest include mystery, romance, chick lit, suspense, women's fiction. Current nonfiction areas of interest include parenting, spirituality, business, finance, true crime, general self-help.

Represents Nonfiction books, novels. **Considers these nonfiction areas:** Business/economics; child guidance/parenting; ethnic/cultural interests; gay/lesbian issues; health/medicine; how-to; money/finance; New Age/metaphysics; psychology; religious/inspirational; self-help/personal improvement; women's issues/studies. **Considers these fiction areas:** Mainstream/contemporary; mystery/suspense; romance; thriller; detective/police/crime/cozies.

O→ BookEnds does not want to receive children's books, screenplays, science fiction, poetry, technical/military thrillers.

How to Contact Submit outline, 3 sample chapters (but no more than 50 pages).

BOOKS & SUCH

4788 Carissa Ave., Santa Rosa CA 95405. (707)538-4184. Fax: (707)538-3937. E-mail: janet@janetgrant.com. Website: janetgrant.com. **Contact:** Janet Kobobel Grant. Estab. 1996. Member of CBA (associate). Represents 60 clients. 5% of clients are new/unpublished writers. Currently handles: 49% nonfiction books; 50% novels; 1% children's picture books.

- Prior to becoming an agent, Ms. Grant was an editor for Zondervan and managing editor for *Focus on the Family*.

Represents Nonfiction books, novels, children's picture books. **Considers these nonfiction areas:** Child guidance/parenting; humor/satire; juvenile nonfiction; religious/inspirational; self-help/personal improvement; women's issues/studies. **Considers these fiction areas:** Contemporary issues; family saga; historical; juvenile; mainstream/contemporary; picture books; religious/inspirational; romance; African American adult.

O→ This agency specializes in "general and inspirational fiction, romance, and in the Christian booksellers market." Actively seeking "material appropriate to the Christian market."

How to Contact Query with SASE. Considers simultaneous queries. Responds in 1 month to queries; 2 months to mss. Returns materials only with SASE. Obtains most new clients through recommendations from others, conferences.

Recent Sales Sold 60 titles in the last year. *Boo Hiss*, by Renee Gutterridge; *Mozart's Sister*, by Nancy Moser; *The Fine China Plate*, by Robin Jones Gunn. Other clients include Joanna Weaver, Janet McHenry, Jane Orcutt, Gayle Roper, Stephanie Grace Whitson.

Terms Agent receives 15% commission on domestic sales; 15% commission on foreign sales. Offers written contract; 2-month notice must be given to terminate contract. Charges clients for postage, photocopying, telephone calls, fax, and express mail.

Writers' Conferences Mt. Hermon Writers Conference (Mt. Hermon CA, March); Wrangling Writers (Tucson AZ, January); Glorieta Writer's Conference (Glorieta NM, October).

Tips "The heart of my motivation is to develop relationships with the authors I serve, to do what I can to shine the light of success on them, and to help be a caretaker of their gifts and time."

GEORGES BORCHARDT, INC.

136 E. 57th St., New York NY 10022. (212)753-5785. Fax: (212)838-6518. Estab. 1967. Member of AAR. Represents 200 clients. 10% of clients are new/unpublished writers. Currently handles: 60% nonfiction books; 37% novels; 1% novellas; 1% juvenile books; 1% poetry.

Member Agents Anne Borchardt; Georges Borchardt; Valerie Borchardt.

Represents Nonfiction books, novels. **Considers these nonfiction areas:** Anthropology/archaeology; biography/autobiography; current affairs; history; memoirs; travel; women's issues/studies. **Considers these fiction areas:** Literary.

O-- This agency specializes in literary fiction and outstanding nonfiction.

How to Contact Responds in 1 week to queries; 1 month to mss. Obtains most new clients through recommendations from others.

Recent Sales Sold 80 titles in the last year. *Tooth and Claw*, by T. Coraghessan Boyle (Viking/Penguin); *Saturday*, by Ian McEwan (Nan Talese/Doubleday); *Where Shall I Wander*, by John Ashbery (HarperCollins); *Anti-Intellectual Tradition*, by Susan Jacoby (Pantheon); *Anti Civilization*, by Anne Applebaum (Doubleday).

Terms Agent receives 15% commission on domestic sales; 20% commission on foreign sales. Offers written contract. "We charge clients cost of outside photocopying and shipping manuscripts or books overseas."

THE BARBARA BOVA LITERARY AGENCY

3951 Gulfshore Blvd. N., PH1-B, Naples FL 34103. (941)649-7237. Fax: (239)649-7263. Website: www.barbarabovaliteraryagency.com. **Contact:** Barbara Bova. Estab. 1974. Represents 30 clients. Currently handles: 20% nonfiction books; 80% novels.

Represents Nonfiction books, novels. **Considers these nonfiction areas:** Biography/autobiography; science/technology; self-help/personal improvement; true crime/investigative; women's issues/studies; social sciences. **Considers these fiction areas:** Action/adventure; detective/police/crime; glitz; mystery/suspense; science fiction; thriller; women's; chick lit; teen lit.

O-- This agency specializes in fiction and nonfiction, hard and soft science.

How to Contact Query through website. Obtains most new clients through recommendations from others.

Recent Sales Sold 6 titles in the last year. *Mercury*, by Ben Bova; *Magic Street*, by Orson Scott Card; *Malpractice*, by Aaron Johnston; *Walks on Shadows*, by Joyce Henderson; *Inuit*, by M. Shayne Bell.

Terms Agent receives 15% commission on domestic sales; 20% commission on foreign sales.

Tips This agency also handles foreign rights, movies, television, audio.

BRANDT & HOCHMAN LITERARY AGENTS, INC.

1501 Broadway, Suite 2310, New York NY 10036. (212)840-5760. Fax: (212)840-5776. **Contact:** Carl Brandt; Gail Hochman; Marianne Merola; Charles Schlessiger. Estab. 1913. Member of AAR. Represents 200 clients.

Represents Nonfiction books, novels, short story collections, juvenile books, journalism. **Considers these nonfiction areas:** Biography/autobiography; current affairs; ethnic/cultural interests; government/politics/law; history; women's issues/studies. **Considers these fiction areas:** Contemporary issues; ethnic; historical; literary; mainstream/contemporary; mystery/suspense; romance; thriller; young adult.

How to Contact Query with SASE. No e-mail or fax queries. Considers simultaneous queries. Responds in 1 month to queries. Returns materials only with SASE. Obtains most new clients through recommendations from others.

Recent Sales This agency prefers not to share information on specific sales. Clients include Scott Turow, Carlos Fuentes, Ursula Hegi, Michael Cunningham, Mary Pope Osborne, Julia Glass.

Terms Agent receives 15% commission on domestic sales; 20% commission on foreign sales. Charges clients for "manuscript duplication or other special expenses agreed to in advance."

Tips "Write a letter which will give the agent a sense of you as a professional writer, your long-term interests as well as a short description of the work at hand."

THE HELEN BRANN AGENCY, INC.

94 Curtis Rd., Bridgewater CT 06752. Member of AAR.

- Query before submitting.

BARBARA BRAUN ASSOCIATES, INC.

104 Fifth Ave., 7th Floor, New York NY 10011. Fax: (212)604-9041. E-mail: barbarabraun@earthlink.net. Website: www.barbarabraunagency.com. **Contact:** Barbara Braun. Member of AAR.

Member Agents Barbara Braun; John F. Baker.

Represents Nonfiction books, novels.

"Our fiction is strong on stories for women, historical and multicultural stories, as well as mysteries and thrillers. We're interested in narrative nonfiction and books by journalists. We do not represent poetry, science fiction, fantasy, horror, or screenplays." Look online for more details.

How to Contact Query with SASE. Accepts e-mail queries.

Recent Sales *The Forest Lover*, by Susan Vreeland (Viking/Penguin); *The Lost Van Gogh*, by A.J. Zerries (Tor/Forge); *Sakharov: Science and Freedom*, by Gennady Gorelik and Antonina Bouis (Oxford University Press).

Terms Agent receives 15% commission on domestic sales; 20% commission on foreign sales.

BRICK HOUSE LITERARY AGENTS

80 Fifth Ave., Suite 1101, New York NY 10011. Website: www.brickhouselit.com. **Contact:** Wofford-Girand Sally. Member of AAR.

- Query before submitting.

M. COURTNEY BRIGGS

100 N. Broadway Ave., 28th Floor, Oklahoma City OK 73102-8806. **Contact:** M. Courtney Briggs. Estab. 1994. 25% of clients are new/unpublished writers. Currently handles: 5% nonfiction books; 10% novels; 80% juvenile books; 5% multimedia.

- Prior to becoming an agent, Ms. Briggs was in subsidiary rights at Random House for 3 years; an associate agent and film rights associate with Curtis Brown, Ltd; also an attorney for 12 years.

Represents Nonfiction books, novels, juvenile books. **Considers these nonfiction areas:** Animals; biography/autobiography; health/medicine; juvenile nonfiction; self-help/personal improvement; young adult. **Considers these fiction areas:** Juvenile; mainstream/contemporary; picture books; young adult.

M. Courtney Briggs is an agent and attorney. "I work primarily, but not exclusively, with children's book authors and illustrators. I will also consult or review a contract on an hourly basis." Actively seeking children's fiction, children's picture books (illustrations and text), young adult novels, fiction, nonfiction.

How to Contact Query with SASE. No e-mail or fax queries. Responds in 2 weeks to queries; 6 weeks to mss. Returns materials only with SASE. Obtains most new clients through recommendations from others.

Recent Sales This agency prefers not to share information on specific sales.

Terms Agent receives 15% commission on domestic sales; 25% commission on foreign sales. Offers written contract; 60-day notice must be given to terminate contract.

Writers' Conferences National Conference on Writing & Illustrating for Children (August).

RICK BROADHEAD & ASSOCIATES LITERARY AGENCY

501-47 St. Clair Ave. W., Toronto ON M4V 3A5 Canada. (416)929-0516. Fax: (416)927-8732. E-mail: rickb@rbaliterary.com. Website: www.rbaliterary.com. **Contact:** Rick Broadhead, president. Estab. 2002. Member of The Authors Guild. Represents 20 clients. 50% of clients are new/unpublished writers. Currently handles: 85% nonfiction books; 5% novels; 10% juvenile books.

- Mr. Broadhead discovered his passion for books when he co-authored his first bestseller at the age of 23. His vast knowledge of the publishing industry, both as an author and an agent, and his relationships with American publishers have allowed the agency to consistently negotiate excellent deals for its clients. Mr. Broadhead brings a passion, tenacity, and energy to agenting that his clients love.

Member Agents Rick Broadhead (all genres, primarily nonfiction).

Represents Nonfiction books, novels, juvenile books. **Considers these nonfiction areas:** Animals; anthropology/archaeology; art/architecture/design; biography/autobiography; business/economics; child guidance/parenting; computers/electronic; cooking/foods/nutrition; crafts/hobbies; current affairs; education; ethnic/cultural interests; government/politics/law; health/medicine; history; how-to; humor/satire; language/literature/criticism; memoirs; military/war; money/finance; music/dance; nature/environment; popular culture; psychology; religious/inspirational; science/technology; self-help/personal improvement; sociology; sports; true crime/investigative; women's issues/studies; interior design/decorating, juvenile nonfiction. **Considers these fiction areas:** Action/adventure; detective/police/crime; humor/satire; juvenile; literary; mainstream/contemporary; mystery/suspense; picture books; thriller.

O→ This established agency represents American authors to American and foreign publishers in a wide variety of genres, including business, self-help, gift books, parenting, memoir, reference, history/politics, current affairs, health/medicine, pop culture, and humor. The agency is deliberately small, which allows clients to receive personalized service to maximize the success of their book projects and brands. The agency sells projects directly to foreign publishers (United Kingdom, Australia/New Zealand) and in partnership with co-agents. Actively seeking compelling nonfiction proposals, especially from authors with an established media platform (television, radio, print exposure). Does not want television or movie scripts, or poetry.

How to Contact If sending by mail, include a complete proposal and 1-2 sample chapters. Agency will reply only to projects of interest. E-mail queries preferred. Considers simultaneous queries. Responds in 1-2 weeks to queries; 4 weeks to mss. Obtains most new clients through solicitations, e-mail queries, referrals from existing clients.

Recent Sales Sold 9 titles in the last year. *Confessions of a Military Housewife*, by Sarah Smiley (Penguin); *The Full-Flavor Diet*, by David Katz, MD (Rodale); *Corporate Canaries: How to Avoid Business Disasters with a Coalminer's Secrets*, by Gary Sutton (Thomas Nelson Business Books). Other clients include Mat Connolley, Marianne Szymanski, Michelle Schoffro Cook, Al Heavens, Terence Denman, George Lorenzo, Kim Danger.

Terms Agent receives 15% commission on domestic sales; 20-25% commission on foreign sales. Offers written contract.

Tips "The agency has excellent relationships with New York publishers and most of the agency's clients are American authors. The agency welcomes queries by e-mail."

BROADWAY PLAY PUBLISHING

56 E. 81st St., New York NY 10028-0202. (212)772-8334. Fax: (212)772-8358. E-mail: bppi@broadwayplaypubl.com. Website: www.broadwayplaypubl.com. Member of AAR.

- Query before submitting.

Member Agents Christopher Gould.

MARIE BROWN ASSOCIATES, INC.

412 W. 154th St., New York NY 10032. (212)939-9725. Fax: (212)939-9728. E-mail: mbrownlit@aol.com. **Contact:** Marie Brown. Estab. 1984. Represents 60 clients. Currently handles: 75% nonfiction books; 10% juvenile books; 15% other.

Member Agents Janell Walden Agyeman (Miami, Florida).

Represents Nonfiction books, juvenile books. **Considers these nonfiction areas:** Art/architecture/design; biography/autobiography; business/economics; ethnic/cultural interests; history; juvenile nonfiction; music/dance; religious/inspirational; self-help/personal improvement; theater/film; women's issues/studies. **Considers these fiction areas:** Contemporary issues; ethnic; juvenile; literary; mainstream/contemporary.

O→ This agency specializes in multicultural and African-American writers.

How to Contact Query with SASE. Prefers to read materials exclusively. Responds in 6-10 to queries. Obtains most new clients through recommendations from others.

Recent Sales *We Shall Overcome*, by Herb Boyd; *When the Spirits Dance Mambo*, by Marta Moreno Vega; *Trapped*, by A. Faison & A. Tyehimbu; *Black Adam*, by Jeffrey Stewart.

Terms Agent receives 15% commission on domestic sales; 20% commission on foreign sales. Offers written contract.

CURTIS BROWN, LTD.

10 Astor Place, New York NY 10003-6935. (212)473-5400. Also Peter Ginsberg, President at CBEF: 1750 Montgomery St., San Fancisco CA 94111. (415)954-8566. Member of AAR; signatory of WGA.

Member Agents Laura Blake Peterson; Ellen Geiger; Emilie Jacobson, senior vice president; Maureen Walters, senior vice president; Ginger Knowlton, vice president (adult, children's); Timothy Knowlton, CEO (film, screenplays); Ed Wintle; Mitchell Waters; Elizabeth Harding; Kirsten Manges; Dave Barbor (translation rights).

Represents Nonfiction books, novels, short story collections, novellas, juvenile books, poetry books, movie scripts, feature film, TV movie of the week. **Considers these nonfiction areas:** Agriculture/horticulture; americana; animals; anthropology/archaeology; art/architecture/design; biography/autobiography; business/economics; child guidance/parenting; computers/electronic; cooking/foods/nutrition; crafts/hobbies; creative nonfiction; current affairs; education; ethnic/cultural interests; gardening; gay/lesbian issues; government/politics/law; health/medicine; history; how-to; humor/satire; interior design/decorating; juvenile nonfiction;

language/literature/criticism; memoirs; military/war; money/finance; multicultural; music/dance; nature/environment; New Age/metaphysics; philosophy; photography; popular culture; psychology; recreation; regional; religious/inspirational; science/technology; self-help/personal improvement; sex; sociology; software; spirituality; sports; theater/film; translation; travel; true crime/investigative; women's issues/studies; young adult. **Considers these fiction areas:** Action/adventure; comic books/cartoon; confession; contemporary issues; detective/police/crime; erotica; ethnic; experimental; family saga; fantasy; feminist; gay/lesbian; glitz; gothic; hi-lo; historical; horror; humor/satire; juvenile; literary; mainstream/contemporary; military/war; multicultural; multimedia; mystery/suspense; New Age; occult; picture books; plays; poetry; poetry in translation; psychic/supernatural; regional; religious/inspirational; romance; science fiction; short story collections; spiritual; sports; thriller; translation; westerns/frontier; young adult; women's.

How to Contact Query individual agent with SASE. Prefers to read materials exclusively. *No unsolicited mss.* No e-mail or fax queries. Responds in 3 weeks to queries; 5 weeks to mss. Obtains most new clients through recommendations from others, solicitations, conferences.

Recent Sales This agency prefers not to share information on specific sales.

Terms Offers written contract. Charges for photocopying, some postage.

ANDREA BROWN LITERARY AGENCY, INC.

1076 Eagle Dr., Salinas CA 93905. (831)422-5925. Fax: (831)422-5915. E-mail: andrea@andreabrownlit.com. Website: www.andreabrownlit.com. **Contact:** Andrea Brown, president. Estab. 1981. 10% of clients are new/unpublished writers. Currently handles: 95% juvenile nonfiction nonfiction books; 5% adult nonfiction and fiction.

- Prior to opening her agency, Ms. Brown served as an editorial assistant at Random House and Dell Publishing and as an editor with Alfred A. Knopf.

Member Agents Andrea Brown, Laura Rennert, Caryn Wiseman, Jennifer Jaeger, Robert Welsh.

Represents Nonfiction books (juvenile). **Considers these nonfiction areas:** Animals; anthropology/archaeology; art/architecture/design; biography/autobiography; current affairs; ethnic/cultural interests; history; how-to; juvenile nonfiction; nature/environment; photography; popular culture; science/technology; sociology; sports; All nonfiction subjects for juveniles and adults. **Considers these fiction areas:** Juvenile; young adult; All fiction genres for juveniles; some adult fiction but not genre fiction.

This agency specializes in "all kinds of children's books—illustrators and authors." Considers all juvenile fiction areas; all genres of nonfiction.

How to Contact Query with SASE. Accepts e-mail queries. No fax queries. Considers simultaneous queries. Obtains most new clients through recommendations from others, referrals from editors, clients, and agents.

Recent Sales *Chloe*, by Catherine Ryan Hyde (Knopf); *Sasha Cohen Autobiography* (HarperCollins); *The Five Ancestors*, by Jeff Stone (Random House).

Terms Agent receives 15% commission on domestic sales; 20% commission on foreign sales. Offers written contract. Charges clients for shipping costs.

Writers' Conferences Austin Writers League; SCBWI, Orange County Conferences; Mills College Childrens Literature Conference (Oakland CA); Asilomar (Pacific Grove CA); Maui Writers Conference; Southwest Writers Conference; San Diego State University Writer's Conference; Big Sur Children's Writing Workshop (Director); William Saroyan Conference; Columbus Writers Conference; Willamette Writers Conference.

Tips "Query first—so many submissions come in it takes 3-4 months to get a response. Taking on very few picture books. Must be unique—no rhyme, no anthropomorphism. Handling some adult historical fiction."

BROWNE & MILLER LITERARY ASSOCIATES

410 S. Michigan Ave., Suite 460, Chicago IL 60605-1465. (312)922-3063. E-mail: mail@browneandmiller.com. **Contact:** Danielle Egan-Miller. Estab. 1971. Member of AAR, RWA, MWA, Author's Guild. Represents 150 clients. 2% of clients are new/unpublished writers. Currently handles: 40% nonfiction books; 60% novels.

Member Agents Danielle Egan-Miller.

Represents Nonfiction books, novels. **Considers these nonfiction areas:** Agriculture/horticulture; animals; anthropology/archaeology; biography/autobiography; business/economics; child guidance/parenting; cooking/foods/nutrition; crafts/hobbies; creative nonfiction; current affairs; ethnic/cultural interests; health/medicine; how-to; humor/satire; juvenile nonfiction; memoirs; money/finance; nature/environment; popular culture; psychology; religious/inspirational; science/technology; self-help/personal improvement; sociology; sports; true crime/investigative; women's issues/studies. **Considers these fiction areas:** Contemporary issues; detective/police/crime; ethnic; family saga; glitz; historical; juvenile; literary; mainstream/contemporary; mystery/suspense; religious/inspirational; romance (contemporary, gothic, historical, regency); sports; thriller.

"We are generalists looking for professional writers with finely honed skills in writing. We are partial to authors with promotion savvy. We work closely with our authors through the whole publishing process, from proposal to after publication." Actively seeking highly commercial mainstream fiction

and nonfiction. Does not represent poetry, short stories, plays, screenplays, articles, children's books.
How to Contact Query by mail, SASE required. *No unsolicited mss.* Prefers to read material exclusively. Responds in 1 month to queries. Returns materials only with SASE. Obtains most new clients through "referrals, queries by professional, marketable authors."
Terms Agent receives 15% commission on domestic sales; 20% commission on foreign sales. Offers written contract, binding for 2 years. Charges clients for photocopying, overseas postage, faxes, phone calls.
Writers' Conferences BEA (June); Frankfurt Book Fair (October); RWA (July); CBA (July); London International Book Fair (March); Boucheron (October).
Tips "If interested in agency representation, be well informed."

PEMA BROWNE, LTD.

11 Tena Place, Valley Cottage NY 10989. Website: www.pemabrowneltd.com. **Contact:** Perry Browne or Pema Browne. Estab. 1966. Signatory of WGA. Represents 30 clients. Currently handles: 40% nonfiction books; 30% novels & romance novels; 25% juvenile books.

- Prior to opening their agency, Mr. Browne was a radio and TV performer; Ms. Browne was a fine artist and art buyer.

Member Agents Pema Browne (children's fiction and nonfiction, adult fiction and nonfiction).
Represents Nonfiction books, novels, juvenile books, reference books. **Considers these nonfiction areas:** Business/economics; child guidance/parenting; cooking/foods/nutrition; ethnic/cultural interests; gay/lesbian issues; health/medicine; how-to; juvenile nonfiction; military/war; money/finance; nature/environment; New Age/metaphysics; popular culture; psychology; religious/inspirational; self-help/personal improvement; spirituality; sports; true crime/investigative; women's issues/studies; reference. **Considers these fiction areas:** Action/adventure; contemporary issues; detective/police/crime; feminist; gay/lesbian; glitz; historical; humor/satire; juvenile; literary; mainstream/contemporary (commercial); mystery/suspense; picture books; psychic/supernatural; religious/inspirational; romance (contemporary, gothic, historical, regency); young adult.

"We are not accepting any new projects or authors until further notice." Seeking adult nonfiction, romance, juvenile, middle grade, some young adult, picture books, novelty books.

How to Contact Query with SASE. No e-mail or fax queries. Responds in 6 weeks to queries; 6-8 weeks to mss. Returns materials only with SASE. Obtains most new clients through "editors, authors, *LMP, Guide to Literary Agents* and as a result of longevity!"
Recent Sales *The Savior,* by Faye Snowden (Dafina/Kensington); *Salvation,* by Susan Scott Cora (Verlag); *Point Horror-Dark I and II,* by Linda Cargill (Scholastic UK).
Terms Agent receives 15% commission on domestic sales; 20% commission on foreign sales.
Tips "We do not review manuscripts that have been sent out to publishers. If writing romance, be sure to receive guidelines from various romance publishers. In nonfiction, one must have credentials to lend credence to a proposal. Make sure of margins, double-space and use clean, dark type."

KNOX BURGER ASSOCIATES, LTD.

10 W. 15th St., Suite 1914, New York NY 10011. Member of AAR.
Tips "We are not taking on new clients at this time."

SHEREE BYKOFSKY ASSOCIATES, INC.

16 W. 36th St., 13th Floor, New York NY 10018. E-mail: shereebee@aol.com. Website: www.shereebee.com. **Contact:** Sheree Bykofsky. Estab. 1984, incorporated 1991. Member of AAR, ASJA, WNBA. Currently handles: 80% nonfiction books; 20% novels.

- Prior to opening her agency, Ms. Bykofsky served as executive editor of The Stonesong Press and managing editor of Chiron Press. She is also the author or co-author of more than 17 books, including *The Complete Idiot's Guide to Getting Published.* Ms. Bykofsky teaches publishing at NYU and The 92nd St. Y.

Member Agents Janet Rosen, associate; Megan Buckley, associate.
Represents Nonfiction books, novels. **Considers these nonfiction areas:** Americana; animals; art/architecture/design; biography/autobiography; business/economics; child guidance/parenting; cooking/foods/nutrition; crafts/hobbies; creative nonfiction; current affairs; education; ethnic/cultural interests; gardening; gay/lesbian issues; government/politics/law; health/medicine; history; how-to; humor/satire; interior design/decorating; language/literature/criticism; memoirs; military/war; money/finance (personal finance); multicultural; music/dance; nature/environment; New Age/metaphysics; philosophy; photography; popular culture; psychology; recreation; regional; religious/inspirational; science/technology; self-help/personal improvement; sex; sociology; spirituality; sports; theater/film; translation; travel; true crime/investigative; women's issues/studies; anthropolgy. **Considers these fiction areas:** Literary; mainstream/contemporary; mystery/suspense.

This agency specializes in popular reference nonfiction, commercial fiction with a literary quality, and mysteries. "I have wide-ranging interests, but it really depends on quality of writing, originality, and

Literary Agents

how a particular project appeals to me (or not). I take on fiction when I completely love it—it doesn't matter what area or genre." Does not want to receive poetry, material for children, screenplays, westerns, horror, science fiction, or fantasy.

How to Contact Query with SASE. No unsolicited mss or phone calls. Considers simultaneous queries. Responds in 1 week to queries with SASE. Responds in 1 month to requested mss. Returns materials only with SASE. Obtains most new clients through recommendations from others.

Recent Sales Sold 100 titles in the last year. *10 Sure Signs a Movie Character Is Doomed and Other Surprising Movie Lists*, by Richard Roeper (Hyperion); *What Is Love?*, by Taro Gold (Andrews & McMeel); *How to Make Someone Love You in 90 Minutes or Less—And Make it Last Forever*, by Nick Boothman.

Terms Agent receives 15% commission on domestic sales; 20% commission on foreign sales. Offers written contract, binding for 1 year. Charges for postage, photocopying and fax.

Writers' Conferences ASJA (New York City); Asilomar (Pacific Grove CA); St. Petersburg; Whidbey Island; Jacksonville; Albuquerque; Austin; Columbus; Southwestern Writers; Willamette (Portland); Dorothy Canfield Fisher (San Diego); Writers Union (Maui); Pacific NW; IWWG; and many others.

Tips "Read the agent listing carefully, and comply with guidelines."

THE JOHN CAMPBELL AGENCY

11 Island Ave., Suite 1107, Miami Beach FL 33139. E-mail: litraryagt@aol.com. **Contact:** John Campbell. Estab. 1985. Currently handles: 90% nonfiction books; 10% novels.

Represents Nonfiction books, novels. **Considers these nonfiction areas:** Art/architecture/design; biography/autobiography; ethnic/cultural interests; health/medicine; history; how-to; interior design/decorating; language/literature/criticism; photography; popular culture; psychology; self-help/personal improvement. **Considers these fiction areas:** Action/adventure; literary; thriller.

- This agency specializes in high-quality nonfiction, illustrated, reference, how-to and entertainment books. Does not want to receive poetry, memoir, children's fiction, category fiction, romance, science fiction, or horror.

How to Contact Submit proposal package, outline, SASE. Prefers to read materials exclusively. Accepts e-mail queries. No fax queries. Responds in 5 days to queries; 2 weeks to mss. Obtains most new clients through recommendations from others, solicitations.

Recent Sales Sold 38 titles in the last year. *In Character*, by Howard Schatz (Bulfinch); *The Essential Dale Chihuly* (Abrams); *Faces of Africa*, by Angela Carol/Fisher Beckwith (National Geographic); *Line of Beauty* (Rizzoli); *The New Garden Paradise* (Norton/House & Garden).

Terms Agent receives 15% commission on domestic sales. Offers written contract; 1- to 2-month notice must be given to terminate contract. Offers criticism service, included in 15% commission. Charges clients for photocopying, long-distance telephone, overnight express-mail, messengering.

Tips "We welcome submissions from new authors, but proposals must be unique, of high commercial interest, and well written. Follow your talent. Write with passion. Know your market. Submit polished work instead of apologizing for its mistakes, typos, incompleteness, etc. We want to see your best work."

N CYNTHIA CANNELL LITERARY AGENCY

833 Madison Ave., New York NY 10021. **Contact:** Cynthia Cannell. Member of AAR.

- Query before submitting.

CANTON SMITH AGENCY

194 Broadway, Amityville NY 11701. (631)842-9476 or (701)483-0153. E-mail: bookhold2@yahoo.com. Address Other: 538 1st St. E., Dickinson ND 58601. **Contact:** Eric Smith, senior partner; Chamein Canton, partner; M. Kessler, administrative assistant. Estab. 2001. Represents 22 clients. 100% of clients are new/unpublished writers.

- Prior to becoming agents, Mr. Smith was in advertising and bookstore retail; Ms. Canton was a writer and a paralegal.

Member Agents Eric Smith (science fiction, fantasy, sports, literature); Chamein Canton (how-to, reference, literary, women's, multicultural, ethnic, crafts, cooking, health).

Represents Nonfiction books, juvenile books, scholarly books, textbooks, movie scripts. **Considers these nonfiction areas:** Art/architecture/design; business/economics; child guidance/parenting; cooking/foods/nutrition; education; ethnic/cultural interests; health/medicine; history; how-to; humor/satire; language/literature/criticism; military/war; music/dance; photography; psychology; sports; translation; women's issues/studies. **Considers these script subject areas:** Action/adventure; comedy; romantic comedy; romantic drama; science fiction.

- "We specialize in helping new and established writers expand their marketing potential for prospective publishers." Actively seeking well-written and researched nonfiction (all genres)—cooking, women's studies, humor, health, how-to. "We are not actively seeking fiction (all genres) until further notice."

How to Contact Query with SASE, submit e-mail query with synopsis (preferred); include the title and genre in the subject line. Send nonfiction snail mail to Chamein Canton at New York address. Send all other snail mail queries to Eric Smith at North Dakota address. Considers simultaneous queries. Responds in 3 weeks to queries; 6 weeks to mss. Obtains most new clients through recommendations from others.

Recent Sales Sold 4 titles in the last year. Clients include Robert Koger, Olivia, Jennifer DeWit, Sheila Smestad, James Weil, Jaime Nava, JC Miller, Diana Smith, Robert Beers, Marcy Gannon, Keith Maxwell, Dawn Jackson, Jeannine Carney, Mark Barlow, Robert Marsocci, Anita Ballard Jones, Deb Mohr, Seth Ahonen, Melissa Graf, Robert Zavala, Cliff Webb, John & Carolyn Osborne.

Terms Agent receives 15% commission on domestic sales; 20% commission on foreign sales. Offers written contract; 2-months notice must be given to terminate contract.

Tips "Know your market. Agents, as well as publishers, are keenly interested in writers with their finger on the pulse of their said market. We're currently changing our focus to nonfiction (all subjects may query)."

MARIA CARVAINIS AGENCY, INC.

1350 Avenue of the Americas, Suite 2905, New York NY 10019. (212)245-6365. Fax: (212)245-7196. E-mail: mca@mariacarvainisagency.com. **Contact:** Maria Carvainis, president; Donna Bagdasarian, literary agent. Estab. 1977. Member of AAR, Authors Guild, Women's Media Group, ABA, MWA, RWA; signatory of WGA. Represents 75 clients. 10% of clients are new/unpublished writers. Currently handles: 34% nonfiction books; 65% novels; 1% poetry.

- Prior to opening her agency, Ms. Carvainis spent more than 10 years in the publishing industry as a senior editor with Macmillan Publishing, Basic Books, Avon Books, and Crown Publishers. Ms. Carvainis has served as a member of the AAR Board of Directors and AAR Treasurer, as well as serving as chair of the AAR Contracts Committee. She presently serves on the AAR Royalty Committee. Donna Bagdasarian began her career as an academic at Boston University, then spent 5 years with Addison Wesley Longman as an acquisitions editor before joining the William Morris Agency in 1998. She has represented a breadth of projects, ranging from literary fiction to celebrity memoir.

Member Agents Moira Sullivan, literary associate; Daniel Listwa, literary associate; Anna Parrinello, contracts manager.

Represents Nonfiction books, novels. **Considers these nonfiction areas:** Biography/autobiography; business/economics; history; memoirs; science/technology (pop science); women's issues/studies. **Considers these fiction areas:** Historical; literary; mainstream/contemporary; mystery/suspense; thriller; women's; middle grade and young adult.

O→ Does not want to receive science fiction or children's picture books.

How to Contact Query with SASE. Responds in 1 week to queries; 3 months to mss. Obtains most new clients through recommendations from others, conferences; 60% from conferences/referrals, 40% from query letters.

Recent Sales *Simply Unforgettable*, by Mary Balogh (Delacorte); *The Mourning Sexton*, by Michael Baron (Doubleday); *In the Shadow of Fame*, by Sue Erikson Bloland (Viking); *Chill Factor*, by Sandra Brown (Simon & Schuster); *An Unexpected Pleasure*, by Candace Camp (MIRA); *The Grail Bird*, by Tim Gallagher (Houghton Mifflin); *The Edge & The Limit*, by Cindy Gerard (St. Martin's Press); *The Perfect Hero*, by Samantha Jones (Avon); *A Killing Rain*, by P.J. Parrish (Kensington); *To Kingdom Come*, by Will Thomas (Touchstone Fireside). Other clients include Elisabeth Brink, Greg Chandler, Pam Conrad, Tim Cummings, S.V. Date, Michael G. Downs, Phillip DePoy, Carlos Dews, Tyler Dilts, John Faunce, Stan Goldberg, Kristan Higgins, Dorothy Love, Staton Rabin, Kristine Rolofson, Christine Sneed.

Terms Agent receives 15% commission on domestic sales; 20% commission on foreign sales. Offers written contract, binding for 2 years on a book-by-book basis. Charges clients for foreign postage, bulk copying.

Writers' Conferences BEA; Frankfurt Book Fair; London Book Fair.

CASTIGLIA LITERARY AGENCY

1155 Camino Del Mar, Suite 510, Del Mar CA 92014. (858)755-8761. Fax: (858)755-7063. **Contact:** All agents. Estab. 1993. Member of AAR, PEN. Represents 50 clients. Currently handles: 55% nonfiction books; 45% novels.

Member Agents Julie Castiglia, Winifred Golden, Sally Van Haitsma.

Represents Nonfiction books, novels. **Considers these nonfiction areas:** Animals; anthropology/archaeology; biography/autobiography; business/economics; child guidance/parenting; cooking/foods/nutrition; current affairs; ethnic/cultural interests; health/medicine; history; language/literature/criticism; money/finance; nature/environment; New Age/metaphysics; psychology; religious/inspirational; science/technology; self-help/personal improvement; sociology; women's issues/studies. **Considers these fiction areas:** Contemporary issues; ethnic; literary; mainstream/contemporary; mystery/suspense; women's (especially).

Literary Agents

O→ Does not want to receive horror, screenplays, or academic nonfiction.

How to Contact Query with SASE. No fax queries. Responds in 2 months to mss. Returns materials only with SASE. Obtains most new clients through recommendations from others, solicitations, conferences.

Recent Sales Sold 25 titles in the last year. *Imaginary Men*, by Anjali Banerjee (Pocket Books/Simon & Schuster); *Courtyards*, by Douglas Keister (Gibbs Smith); *Historic English Arts & Crafts Homes*, by Brian Coleman (Gibbs Smith); *The New Vegan: Fresh, Fabulous and Fun*, by Janet Hudson (Thorsons/HarperCollins); *Will He Really Leave Her for Me*, by Rona Subotnik (Adams Media).

Terms Agent receives 15% commission on domestic sales; 25% commission on foreign sales. Offers written contract; 6-week notice must be given to terminate contract. Charges clients for Fed Ex or Messenger.

Writers' Conferences Southwestern Writers Conference (Albuquerque NM, August); National Writers Conference; Willamette Writers Conference (OR); San Diego State University (CA); Writers at Work (UT); Austin Conference (TX).

Tips "Be professional with submissions. Attend workshops and conferences before you approach an agent."

JANE CHELIUS LITERARY AGENCY

548 Second St., Brooklyn NY 11215. Website: www.janechelius.com. Member of AAR.

O→ "We accept all genres except for young adult, children's, scripts/screenplays and poetry."

How to Contact Query first with the first 3 chapters and synopsis. No unsolicted mss.

⊘ LINDA CHESTER AND ASSOCIATES

630 Fifth Ave., Suite 2036, New York NY 10111. (212)218-3350. E-mail: lcassoc@mindspring.com. Website: www.lindachester.com. Member of AAR.

- Unsolicited queries are not being accepted at this time, and any unsolicited query or ms received will not be acknowledged.

Member Agents Linda Chester, Laurie Fox, Gary Jaffe.

Recent Sales *First Man: The Life of Neil A. Armstrong*, by James R. Hansen (Simon & Schuster); *Easier Than You Think*, by Richard Carlson (HarperSanFrancisco).

⊘ CINE/LIT REPRESENTATION

P.O. Box 802918, Santa Clarita CA 91380-2918. **Contact:** Mary Alice Kier. Member of AAR.

- Query before submitting.

WM CLARK ASSOCIATES

355 W. 22nd St., New York NY 10011. (212)675-2784. Fax: (646)349-1658. E-mail: query@wmclark.com. Website: www.wmclark.com. Estab. 1997. Member of AAR. 50% of clients are new/unpublished writers. Currently handles: 50% nonfiction books; 50% novels.

- Prior to opening WCA, Mr. Clark was an agent at the William Morris Agency.

Represents Nonfiction books, novels. **Considers these nonfiction areas:** Art/architecture/design; biography/autobiography; current affairs; ethnic/cultural interests; history; memoirs; music/dance; popular culture; religious/inspirational (Eastern philosophy only); science/technology; sociology; theater/film; translation. **Considers these fiction areas:** Contemporary issues; ethnic; historical; literary; mainstream/contemporary; Southern fiction.

O→ "Building on a reputation for moving quickly and strategically on behalf of his clients, and offering individual focus and a global presence, William Clark practices an agressive, innovative, and broad-ranged approach to the representation of content and the talent that creates it, ranging from authors of first fiction and award-winning bestselling narrative nonfiction, to international authors in translation, musicians, and artists."

How to Contact E-mail queries only. Prefers to read requested materials exclusively. Responds in 1-2 months to queries.

Recent Sales Sold 25 titles in the last year. *Fallingwater Rising: E.J. Kaufman and Frank Lloyd Wright Create the Most Exciting House in the World*, by Franklin Toker (Alfred A. Knopf); *The Balthazar Cookbook*, by Riad Nasr, Lee Hanson, and Keith McNally (Clarkson Potter); *The Book of 'Exodus': The Making and Meaning of Bob Marley's Album of the Century*, by Vivien Goldman (Crown/Three Rivers Press); *Hungry Ghost*, by Keith Kachtick (HarperCollins). Other clients include Russell Martin, Daye Haddon, Bjork, Mian Mian, Jonathan Stone, Jocko Weyland, Peter Hessler, Rev. Billy (aka Billy Talen).

Terms Agent receives 15% commission on domestic sales; 20% commission on foreign sales. Offers written contract.

Tips "WCA works on a reciprocal basis with Ed Victor Ltd. (UK) in representing select properties to the U.S. market and vice versa. Translation rights are sold directly in the German, Italian, Spanish, Portuguese, Latin American, French, Dutch, and Scandinavian territories in association with Andrew Nurnberg Associates Ltd.

(UK); through offices in China, Bulgaria, Czech Republic, Latvia, Poland, Hungary, and Russia; and through corresponding agents in Japan, Greece, Israel, Turkey, Korea, Taiwan, and Thailand.''

JOANNA LEWIS COLE, LITERARY AGENT

404 Riverside Dr., New York NY 10025. Member of AAR.

- Query before submitting.

FRANCES COLLIN, LITERARY AGENT

P.O. Box 33, Wayne PA 19087-0033. Website: www.francescollin.com. **Contact:** Frances Collin. Estab. 1948. Member of AAR. Represents 90 clients. 1% of clients are new/unpublished writers. Currently handles: 50% nonfiction books; 48% novels; 1% textbooks; 1% poetry.

Represents Nonfiction books, fiction.

- Almost no new clients, unless recommended by publishing professionals or clients. Does not want cookbooks, crafts, children's books, software, or original screenplays.

How to Contact Query with SASE and brief proposal. No phone, fax or e-mail inquiries. Enclose sufficient IRCs if outside the US. Considers simultaneous queries.

Terms Agent receives 15% commission on domestic sales; 20% commission on foreign sales. Offers written contract. Charges clients for overseas postage for books mailed to foreign agents; photocopying of mss, books, proposals; copyright registration fees; registered mail fees; passes along cost of any books purchased.

COLLINS MCCORMICK LITERARY AGENCY

30 Bond St., New York NY 10012. (212)219-2894. Fax: (212)219-2895. E-mail: info@collinsmccormick.com. Website: www.collinsmccormick.com. **Contact:** David McCormick or Nina Collins. Estab. 2002. Member of AAR. Represents 150 clients. 60% of clients are new/unpublished writers. Currently handles: 60% nonfiction books; 30% novels; 5% story collections; 5% poetry.

- Prior to becoming an agent, Mr. McCormick was an editor at *The New Yorker* and *Texas Monthly*; Ms. Collins was a book scout for foreign publishers and film and TV companies.

Member Agents Leslie Falk (literary fiction, narrative nonfiction); Matthew Elblonk (literary fiction, narrative nonfiction, pop culture); Amy Williams (literary fiction, narrative nonfiction); PJ Mark (literary fiction, narrative nonfiction, pop culture).

DON CONGDON ASSOCIATES INC.

156 Fifth Ave., Suite 625, New York NY 10010-7002. (212)645-1229. Fax: (212)727-2688. E-mail: dca@doncongdon.com. **Contact:** Don Congdon, Michael Congdon, Susan Ramer, Cristina Concepcion. Estab. 1983. Member of AAR. Represents 100 clients. Currently handles: 60% nonfiction books; 40% fiction.

Represents Nonfiction books, fiction. **Considers these nonfiction areas:** Anthropology/archaeology; biography/autobiography; child guidance/parenting; cooking/foods/nutrition; creative nonfiction; current affairs; ethnic/cultural interests; government/politics/law; health/medicine; history; humor/satire; language/literature/criticism; memoirs; military/war; multicultural; music/dance; nature/environment; popular culture; psychology; science/technology; sociology; theater/film; travel; true crime/investigative; women's issues/studies. **Considers these fiction areas:** Action/adventure; detective/police/crime; horror; humor/satire; literary (especially); mainstream/contemporary; multicultural; mystery/suspense; short story collections; thriller; women's.

How to Contact Query with SASE or via e-mail (material should be copied and pasted into e-mail). Responds in 1 week to queries; 1 month to mss. Obtains most new clients through recommendations from others.

Terms Agent receives 15% commission on domestic sales; 19% commission on foreign sales. Charges client for extra shipping costs, photocopying, copyright fees, and book purchases.

Tips ''Writing a query letter with a self-addressed stamped envelope is a must. No phone calls. We never download attachments to e-mail queries for security reasons, so please copy and paste material into your e-mail.''

N CONNOR LITERARY AGENCY

2911 W. 71st St., Minneapolis MN 55423. Phone/Fax: (612)866-1486. E-mail: coolmkc@aol.com. **Contact:** Marlene Connor Lynch. Estab. 1985. Represents 50 clients. 30% of clients are new/unpublished writers. Currently handles: 50% nonfiction books; 50% novels.

- Prior to opening her agency, Ms. Connor served at the Literary Guild of America, Simon & Schuster and Random House. She is author of *What is Cool: Understanding Black Manhood in America* (Crown).

Member Agents Deborah Coker (children's books)

Represents Nonfiction books, novels, especially with a minority slant. **Considers these nonfiction areas:** Child guidance/parenting; cooking/foods/nutrition; crafts/hobbies; current affairs; ethnic/cultural interests; government/politics/law; health/medicine; how-to; humor/satire; interior design/decorating; language/litera-

Literary Agents

ture/criticism; money/finance; photography; popular culture; self-help/personal improvement; sports; true crime/investigative; women's issues/studies; relationships. **Considers these fiction areas:** Historical; horror; literary; mainstream/contemporary; multicultural; thriller; women's; suspense.

How to Contact All unsolicited mss returned unopened. Obtains most new clients through recommendations from others, conferences, grapevine.

Recent Sales *Outrageous Commitments*, by Dr. Ronn Elmore (HarperCollins); *Seductions*, by Snow Starborn (Sourcebooks); *Simplicitys Simply the Best Sewing Book, Revised Edition.*

Terms Agent receives 15% commission on domestic sales; 25% commission on foreign sales. Offers written contract, binding for 1 year.

Writers' Conferences National Writers Union, Midwest Chapter; Agents, Agents, Agents; Texas Writer's Conference; Detroit Writer's Conference.

Tips "Seeking previously published writers with good sales records and new writers with real talent."

THE COOKE AGENCY

278 Bloor St. E., Suite 305, Toronto ON M4W 3M4 Canada. (416)406-3390. Fax: (416)406-3389. E-mail: agents@cookeagency.ca. Website: www.cookeagency.ca. **Contact:** Elizabeth Griffin. Estab. 1992. Represents 60 clients. 30% of clients are new/unpublished writers. Currently handles: 50% nonfiction books; 50% novels.

Represents Nonfiction books, literary novels. **Considers these nonfiction areas:** Biography/autobiography; business/economics; child guidance/parenting; current affairs; gay/lesbian issues; health/medicine; popular culture; science/technology; young adult. **Considers these fiction areas:** Literary.

The Cooke Agency represents some of the best Canadian writers in the world. "Through our contacts and sub-agents, we have built an international reputation for quality. Curtis Brown Canada is jointly owned by Dean Cooke and Curtis Brown New York. It represents Curtis Brown New York authors in Canada." Does not want to receive how-to, self-help, spirituality, genre fiction (science fiction, fantasy, mystery, thriller, horror).

How to Contact Query with SASE. Accepts e-mail and fax queries. Considers simultaneous queries. Responds in 6-8 weeks to queries. Returns materials only with SASE. Obtains most new clients through recommendations from others.

Recent Sales Sold 20 titles and sold 4 scripts in the last year. *Last Crossing*, by Guy Vanderhaeghe (Grove/Atlantic); *Adultery*, by Richard B. Wright (HarperCollins Canada, HarperAustralia, De Geus Holland); *Story House*, by Timothy Taylor (Knopf Canada); *Wrong Way; The Fall of Conrad Black*, by Jacque McNish and Sinclair Stewart (Penguin); *Possesing Genius: The Bizarre Odyssey of Einstein's Brain*, by Carolyn Abraham (Penguin Canada, St. Martin's Press, Icon Books UK). Other clients include Lauren B. Davis, Doug Hunter, Andrew Podnieks, Steven Hayward, Robertson Davies.

Terms Agent receives 15% commission on domestic sales; 20% commission on foreign sales. Offers written contract. Charges clients for postage, photocopying, courier.

Tips "Check our website for complete guidelines rather than calling for them."

THE DOE COOVER AGENCY

P.O. Box 668, Winchester MA 01890. (781)721-6000. Fax: (781)721-6727. Estab. 1985. Represents more than 100 clients. Currently handles: 80% nonfiction books; 20% novels.

Member Agents Doe Coover (general nonfiction, cooking); Colleen Mohyde (literary and commercial fiction, general and narrative nonfiction); Amanda Lewis (children's books); Frances Kennedy, associate.

This agency specializes in nonfiction, particularly books on history, biography, social issues and narrative nonfiction, as well as cooking and gardening and literary and commercial fiction. Does not want romance, fantasy, science fiction, poetry.

How to Contact Query with SASE, outline. No e-mail or fax queries. Considers simultaneous queries. Returns materials only with SASE. Obtains most new clients through recommendations from others, solicitations.

Recent Sales Sold 25-30 titles in the last year. *The Gourmet Cookbook*, by Gourmet Magazine (Houghton Mifflin); *Fast Food My Way*, by Jacques Pepin (Houghton Mifflin); *Seven Things Your Teenager Doesn't Want You to Know*, by Jennifer Lippincott and Robin Deutsch (Ballantine); *The Art of Civilized Conversation*, by Margaret Shepherd and Sharon Hogan (Broadway Books); *Portrait of My Mother Who Posed Nude in Wartime*, by Marjorie Sandor (Sarabande Books). Movie/TV MOW script optioned/sold: *Drinking: A Love Story*, by Caroline Knapp. Other clients include WGBH, Blue Balliett, Deborah Madison, Rick Bayless, Adria Bernardi, Suzanne Berne.

Terms Agent receives 15% commission on domestic sales; 10% on original advance commission on foreign sales.

CORNERSTONE LITERARY, INC.

4500 Wilshire Blvd., 3rd Floor, Los Angeles CA 90010. (323)930-6037. Fax: (323)930-0407. Website: www.cornerstoneliterary.com. **Contact:** Helen Breitwieser. Estab. 1998. Member of AAR; Author's Guild; MWA; RWA. Represents 40 clients. 30% of clients are new/unpublished writers.

- Prior to founding her own boutique agency, Ms. Breitwieser was a literary agent at The William Morris Agency.

Represents Nonfiction books, novels. **Considers these fiction areas:** Detective/police/crime; erotica; ethnic; family saga; glitz; historical; literary; mainstream/contemporary; multicultural; mystery/suspense; romance; thriller; women's.

O→ Actively seeking first fiction, literary. Does not want to receive science fiction, westerns, children's books, poetry, screenplays, fantasy, gay/lesbian, horror, self-help, psychology, business or diet.

How to Contact Query with SASE. Responds in 6-8 weeks to queries; 2 months to mss. Returns materials only with SASE. Obtains most new clients through recommendations from others.

Recent Sales Sold 38 titles in the last year. *How Was It For You*, by Carmen Reid (Pocket); *Sisters in Pink*, by Kayla Perrin (St. Martin's Press); *What Angels Fear*, by Candice Proctor (NAL). Other clients include Stan Diehl, Elaine Coffman, Danielle Girard, Rachel Lee, Marilyn Jaye Lewis, Carole Matthews.

Terms Agent receives 15% commission on domestic sales; 20% commission on foreign sales. Offers written contract, binding for 1 year; 2-month notice must be given to terminate contract.

Tips "Don't query about more than 1 manuscript. Do not e-mail queries/submissions."

CRAWFORD LITERARY AGENCY

92 Evans Rd., Barnstead NH 03218. (603)269-5851. Fax: (603)269-2533. E-mail: crawfordlit@att.net. Winter Office: 3920 Bayside Rd., Fort Myers Beach FL 33931. (239)463-4651. Fax: (239)463-0125. **Contact:** Susan Crawford. Estab. 1988. Represents 45 clients. 10% of clients are new/unpublished writers. Currently handles: 50% nonfiction books; 50% novels.

Member Agents Susan Crawford; Lorne Crawford (commercial fiction and nonfiction); Scott Neister (scientific/techno thrillers).

Represents Nonfiction books, novels. **Considers these nonfiction areas:** Psychology; religious/inspirational; self-help/personal improvement; women's issues/studies; celebrity/media. **Considers these fiction areas:** Action/adventure; mystery/suspense; thriller (medical).

O→ This agency specializes in celebrity and/or media-based books and authors. Actively seeking action/adventure stories, medical thrillers, self-help, inspirational, how-to, and women's issues. Does not want to receive short stories, poetry.

How to Contact Query with SASE. Considers simultaneous queries. Responds in 3 weeks to queries. Returns materials only with SASE. Obtains most new clients through recommendations from others, solicitations, conferences.

Recent Sales Sold 44 titles in the last year. *The Soul of a Butterfly*, by Muhammad Ali with Hana Ali (Simon & Schuster); *John Travolta's Autobiography* (Hyperion); *The Hormonally Vulnerable Woman*, by Geoffrey Redmond, MD (Regan Books); *Flashback*, by Gary Braver (Tor/Forge); *The Xeno Solution*, by Dr. Nelson Erlick (Tor/Forge); *What's a Parent to Do?*, by Henry Abraham, MD (New Horizon).

Terms Agent receives 15% commission on domestic sales; 20% commission on foreign sales. Offers written contract. 100% of business is derived from commissions on ms sales.

Writers' Conferences International Film & Television Workshops (Rockport ME); Maui Writers Conference.

Tips "Keep learning to improve your craft. Attend conferences and network."

THE CREATIVE CULTURE, INC.

72 Spring St., Suite 304, New York NY 10012. **Contact:** Debra Goldstein. Member of AAR.

- Query before submitting.

Member Agents Nicole Diamond Austin, Debra Goldstein, Mary Ann Naples.

N CREATIVE MEDIA AGENCY, INC.

240 W. 35th St., Suite 500, New York NY 10001. (212)560-0909. E-mail: assistantcma@aol.com. Website: www.thecmagency.com. **Contact:** Paige Wheeler, Lisa VanAuken, Nadia Cornier. Estab. 1998. Represents approximately 60 clients. 50% of clients are new/unpublished writers. Currently handles: 25% nonfiction books; 70% novels; 5% juvenile books.

- Paige Wheeler, president of Creative Media Agency, has worked as an agent in both a literary and entertainment capacity over the course of her career. She was an editor for Harlequin/Silhouette and for Euromoney Publications in London, and is an active member of Women in Publishing. Before becoming an agent, Lisa VanAuken fell into the real estate industry as both a title searcher and an acquisitions agent at an investment company. Before joining CMA, Nadia Cornier worked with award-winning and bestselling authors through her public relations firm Cornier & Associates.

Member Agents Paige Wheeler (romance, mysteries, thrillers, adventure, nonfiction); Lisa Van Auken (romance, thrillers, adventure, erotica, nonfiction); Nadia Cornier (young adult/juvenile, science fiction, fantasy).

Represents Nonfiction books, novels, novellas, juvenile books, scholarly books. **Considers these nonfiction areas:** Agriculture/horticulture; animals; anthropology/archaeology; art/architecture/design; biography/autobiography; business/economics; child guidance/parenting; cooking/foods/nutrition; crafts/hobbies; current affairs; education; ethnic/cultural interests; gay/lesbian issues; government/politics/law; health/medicine; history; how-to; juvenile nonfiction; language/literature/criticism; memoirs; military/war; money/finance; music/dance; nature/environment; New Age/metaphysics; popular culture; psychology; religious/inspirational; science/technology; self-help/personal improvement; sociology; sports; true crime/investigative; women's issues/studies. **Considers these fiction areas:** Action/adventure; confession; erotica; ethnic; experimental; family saga; feminist; gay/lesbian; historical; humor/satire; juvenile; literary; mainstream/contemporary; mystery/suspense; psychic/supernatural; regional; religious/inspirational; romance; sports; thriller; young adult.

O- CMA is committed to nurturing an open, communicative relationship with its clients. "We represent authors, not projects. We are enthusiastic about what we do. In other words, we strive never to become disenchanted, cynical, or closed-minded about new writers. We love books as much as you do, and we enjoy helping our clients make a living doing what they love to do."

How to Contact For snail mail only, send query, synopsis, first 50 pages. Accepts e-mail submissions (no attachments). Considers simultaneous queries. Responds in 2-4 weeks to queries; 3-8 weeks to mss.

Recent Sales Sold 60 titles in the last year.

Terms Agent receives 15% commission on domestic sales; 20% commission on foreign sales. Offers written contract. Charges for postage, copying.

Writers' Conferences RWA (Reno NV, July).

Tips "Whether your subject is small-town life or medieval Paris, or a man who runs a bakery, or a woman who strives to cure cancer, you must be able write about your subject as easily and comfortably as if you lived it. I'm eager to find talented writers who are scrupulously informed about their subject matter, and who fascinate and captivate readers using that knowledge."

RICHARD CURTIS ASSOCIATES, INC.

171 E. 74th St., New York NY 10021. (212)772-7363. Fax: (212)772-7393. Website: www.curtisagency.com. Estab. 1979. Member of RWA; MWA; WWA; SFWA; signatory of WGA. Represents 100 clients. 1% of clients are new/unpublished writers. Currently handles: 70% nonfiction books; 20% genre fiction, 10% fiction.

- Prior to opening his agency, Mr. Curtis was an agent with the Scott Meredith Literary Agency for 7 years and has authored over 50 published books.

Member Agents Richard Curtis; Pamela Valvera.

Represents Commercial nonfiction and fiction. **Considers these nonfiction areas:** Health/medicine; history; science/technology.

How to Contact One-page query letter, plus no more than a 1-page synopsis of proposed submission. No submission of ms unless specifically requested. If requested, submission must be accompanied by a SASE. No e-mail or fax queries. Returns materials only with SASE.

Recent Sales Sold 150 titles in the last year. *Olympos*, by Dan Simmons; *The Side-Effects Solution*, by Dr. Frederic Vagnini and Barry Fox; *Quantico*, by Greg Bear. Other clients include Janet Dailey, Jennifer Blake, Leonard Maltin, D.J. MacHale, John Altman, Beverly Barton, Earl Mindell, Barbara Parker.

Terms Agent receives 15% commission on domestic sales; 25% commission on foreign sales. Offers written contract, binding for book-by-book basis. Charges for photocopying, express, international freight, book orders.

Writers' Conferences Science Fiction Writers of America; Horror Writers of America; Romance Writers of America; World Fantasy Conference.

JAMES R. CYPHER, THE CYPHER AGENCY

816 Wolcott Ave., Beacon NY 12508-4261. Phone/Fax: (845)831-5677. E-mail: jimcypher@prodigy.net. Website: pages.prodigy.net/jimcypher/. **Contact:** James R. Cypher. Estab. 1993. Member of AAR, Authors Guild. Represents 30 clients. 35% of clients are new/unpublished writers. Currently handles: 100% nonfiction books.

- Prior to opening his agency, Mr. Cypher worked as a corporate public relations manager for a Fortune 500 multi-national computer company for 28 years.

Represents Nonfiction books. **Considers these nonfiction areas:** Biography/autobiography; current affairs; government/politics/law; health/medicine; popular culture; science/technology; self-help/personal improvement; sports; true crime/investigative.

O- Actively seeking a wide variety of topical nonfiction. Does not want to receive humor, pets, gardening, cookbooks, crafts, spiritual, religious, or New Age topics.

How to Contact Query with SASE, proposal package, outline, 2 sample chapters. Accepts e-mail and fax queries. Considers simultaneous queries. Responds in 2 weeks to queries; 6 weeks to mss. Obtains most new clients through recommendations from others, conferences, networking on online computer service.
Recent Sales Sold 9 titles in the last year. *The Man Who Predicts Earthquakes*, by Cal Orey (Sentient Publications); *No Cleansing Fire: A True Story of Jealousy, Deceit, Rage and Fiery Murder*, by Tom Basinski (Berkley Books); *True to the Roots: Excursions Off Country Music's Beaten Path*, by Monte Dutton (University of Nebraska Press); *Minds on Trial; 20 Great Cases in Forensic Psychology*, by Charles Patrick Ewing and Joseph T. McCann (Oxford University Press). Other clients include Walter Harvey, Mark Horner, Charles Hustmyre, Glenn Puit, Robert L. Snow.
Terms Agent receives 15% commission on domestic sales; 20% commission on foreign sales. Offers written contract; 1-month notice must be given to terminate contract. 100% of business is derived from commissions on ms sales. Charges clients for postage, photocopying, overseas phone calls and faxes.

LAURA DAIL LITERARY AGENCY, INC.

350 7th Ave., Suite 2003, New York NY 10010. (212)239-2861. Fax: (212)947-0460. E-mail: trcohen@ldlainc.com. Website: www.ldlainc.com. **Contact:** Laura Dail. Member of AAR.
Member Agents Talia Cohen, Laura Dail.
Represents Nonfiction books, novels.

- ''Due to the volume of queries and manuscripts received, we apologize for not answering every e-mail and letter.'' Specializes in commercial and literary fiction and nonfiction.

How to Contact Query with SASE.
Recent Sales *Bras & Broomsticks*, by Sarah Mlynowski (Delacorte); *Hide Yourself Away*, by Mary Jane Clark (St. Martin's Press); *Eating in the Raw*, by Carol Alt (Clarkson Potter).

DARHANSOFF, VERRILL, FELDMAN LITERARY AGENTS

236 W. 26th St., Suite 802, New York NY 10001. (917)305-1300. Fax: (917)305-1400. Estab. 1975. Member of AAR. Represents 120 clients. 10% of clients are new/unpublished writers. Currently handles: 25% nonfiction books; 60% novels; 15% story collections.
Member Agents Liz Darhansoff, Charles Verrill, Leigh Feldman.
Represents Nonfiction books, novels, short story collections.
How to Contact Obtains most new clients through recommendations from others.

LIZA DAWSON ASSOCIATES

240 W. 35th St., Suite 500, New York NY 10001. (212)465-9071. **Contact:** Liza Dawson, Caitlin Blasdell. Member of AAR, MWA, Women's Media Group. Represents 50 clients. 15% of clients are new/unpublished writers. Currently handles: 60% nonfiction books; 40% novels.

- Prior to becoming an agent, Ms. Dawson was an editor for 20 years, spending 11 years at William Morrow as vice president and 2 at Putnam as executive editor. Ms. Blasdell was a senior editor at HarperCollins and Avon.

Member Agents Liza Dawson, Caitlin Blasdell.
Represents Nonfiction books, novels. **Considers these nonfiction areas:** Biography/autobiography; health/medicine; history; memoirs; psychology; sociology; women's issues/studies; politics; business; parenting. **Considers these fiction areas:** Ethnic; family saga; historical; literary; mystery/suspense; regional; science fiction (Blasdell only); thriller.

- This agency specializes in readable literary fiction, thrillers, mainstream historicals, women's fiction, academics, historians, business, journalists and psychology. Does not want to receive westerns, sports, computers, juvenile.

How to Contact Query with SASE. Responds in 3 weeks to queries; 6 weeks to mss. Obtains most new clients through recommendations from others, conferences.
Recent Sales Sold 40 titles in the last year. *Going for It*, by Karen E. Quinones Miller (Warner); *Mayada: Daughter of Iraq*, by Jean Sasson (Dutton); *It's So Much Work to Be Your Friend: Social Skill Problems at Home and at School*, by Richard Lavoie (Touchstone); *WORDCRAFT: How to Write Like a Professional*, by Jack Hart (Pantheon); *. . . And a Time to Die: How Hospitals Shape the End of Life Experience*, by Dr. Sharon Kaufman (Scribner); *Zeus: A Biography*, by Tom Stone (Bloomsbury).
Terms Agent receives 15% commission on domestic sales; 20% commission on foreign sales. Offers written contract. Charges clients for photocopying and overseas postage.

DEFIORE & CO.

72 Spring St., Suite 304, New York NY 10012. (212)925-7744. Fax: (212)925-9803. E-mail: info@defioreandco.c om. Website: www.defioreandco.com. **Contact:** Brian DeFiore. Estab. 1999. Represents 55 clients. 50% of clients are new/unpublished writers. Currently handles: 70% nonfiction books; 30% novels.

• Prior to becoming an agent, Mr. DeFiore was Publisher of Villard Books 1997-1998; Editor-in-Chief of Hyperion 1992-1997; Editorial Director of Delacorte Press 1988-1992.

Member Agents Brian DeFiore (popular nonfiction, business, pop culture, parenting, commercial fiction); Laurie Abkemeier (nonfiction only—memoir, health, parenting, business, how-to/self-help, cooking, spirituality, popular science); Kate Garrick (literary fiction, crime, pop culture, politics, history, psychology, narrative nonfiction).

Represents Nonfiction books, novels. **Considers these nonfiction areas:** Biography/autobiography; business/economics; child guidance/parenting; cooking/foods/nutrition; health/medicine; money/finance; multicultural; popular culture; psychology; religious/inspirational; self-help/personal improvement; sports. **Considers these fiction areas:** Ethnic; literary; mainstream/contemporary; mystery/suspense; thriller.

How to Contact Query with SASE. Considers simultaneous queries. Responds in 3 weeks to queries; 2 months to mss. Returns materials only with SASE. Obtains most new clients through recommendations from others.

Recent Sales Sold 20 titles in the last year. *Food Forensics*, by Steve Ettlinger; *Marley and Me*, by John Grogan; *She's Got Issues*, by Stephanie Lessing; *This Is My Future*, by David Goodwillie; *All for a Few Perfect Waves*, by David Rensin. Other clients include Loretta LaRoche, Jason Starr, Joel Engel, Christopher Keane, Robin McMillan, Jessica Teich, Ronna Lichtenberg, Fran Sorin, Jimmy Lerner, Lou Manfredini, Bally's Total Fitness, Hilary Devries, Norm Green, Lisa Kusel.

Terms Agent receives 15% commission on domestic sales; 20% commission on foreign sales. Offers written contract; 10-day notice must be given to terminate contract. Charges clients for photocopying, overnight delivery (deducted only after a sale is made).

Writers' Conferences Maui Writers Conference (Maui HI, September); Pacific Northwest Writers Association Conference; North Carolina Writer's Network Conference.

DH LITERARY, INC.

P.O. Box 990, Nyack NY 10960-0990. (212)753-7942. E-mail: dhendin@aol.com. **Contact:** David Hendin. Estab. 1993. Member of AAR. Represents 5 clients. Currently handles: 80% nonfiction books; 10% novels; 10% scholarly books.

• Prior to opening his agency, Mr. Hendin served as president and publisher for Pharos Books/World Almanac as well as senior VP and COO at sister company United Feature Syndicate.

O→ "We are not accepting new clients."

Recent Sales *No Vulgar Hotel*, by Judith Martin (Norton); *Murder Between the Covers* (mystery series), by Elaine Viets (Penguin/Putnam); *Coined by God*, by Jeffrey McQuain and Stanley Malless (Norton).

Terms Agent receives 15% commission on domestic sales; 20% commission on foreign sales. Offers written contract, binding for 1 year. Charges for out-of-pocket expenses for overseas postage specifically related to sale. No other fees.

DHS LITERARY, INC.

10711 Preston Rd., Suite 100, Dallas TX 75230. (214)363-4422. Fax: (214)363-4423. E-mail: submissions@dhsliterary.com. Website: www.dhsliterary.com. **Contact:** David Hale Smith, president. Estab. 1994. Represents 35 clients. 15% of clients are new/unpublished writers. Currently handles: 60% nonfiction books; 40% novels.

• Prior to opening his agency, Mr. Smith was an editor at a newswire service.

Represents Nonfiction books, novels. **Considers these nonfiction areas:** Biography/autobiography; business/economics; child guidance/parenting; cooking/foods/nutrition; current affairs; ethnic/cultural interests; popular culture; sports; true crime/investigative. **Considers these fiction areas:** Detective/police/crime; ethnic; literary; mainstream/contemporary; mystery/suspense; thriller; westerns/frontier.

O→ This agency specializes in commercial fiction and nonfiction for the adult trade market. Actively seeking thrillers, mysteries, suspense, etc., and narrative nonfiction. Does not want to receive poetry, short fiction, children's books.

How to Contact Accepts new material by referral only. *No unsolicited mss.* Considers simultaneous queries. Responds in 1 month to queries. Obtains most new clients through recommendations from others.

Recent Sales Sold 35 titles in the last year. *The Curve of the World*, by Marcus Stevens (Algonquin); *No Mountain High Enough: Raising Lance, Raising Me*, by Linda Armstrong Kelly (Broadway).

Terms Agent receives 15% commission on domestic sales; 25% commission on foreign sales. Offers written contract; 10-day notice must be given to terminate contract. Charges for client expenses, i.e., postage, photocopying. 100% of business is derived from commissions on sales.

Tips "Remember to be courteous and professional, and to treat marketing your work and approaching an agent as you would any formal business matter. When in doubt, always query first via e-mail.Visit our website for more information."

SANDRA DIJKSTRA LITERARY AGENCY

1155 Camino del Mar, PMB 515, Del Mar CA 92014. (858)755-3115. Fax: (858)794-2822. E-mail: sdla@dijkstraagency.com. **Contact:** Elise Capron. Estab. 1981. Member of AAR, Authors Guild, PEN West, Poets and Editors, MWA. Represents 200 clients. 30% of clients are new/unpublished writers. Currently handles: 50% nonfiction books; 45% novels; 5% juvenile books.

- We specialize in a number of fields.

Member Agents Sandra Dijkstra.

Represents Nonfiction books, novels. **Considers these nonfiction areas:** Anthropology/archaeology; business/economics; child guidance/parenting; cooking/foods/nutrition; ethnic/cultural interests; government/politics/law; health/medicine; history; language/literature/criticism; military/war; money/finance; nature/environment; psychology; science/technology; sociology; women's issues/studies. **Considers these fiction areas:** Ethnic; literary; mainstream/contemporary; mystery/suspense; thriller.

How to Contact Submit proposal package, outline, sample chapters, author bio, SASE. No e-mail or fax queries. Responds in 1 month to queries; 6 weeks to mss. Obtains most new clients through recommendations from others, solicitations, conferences.

Recent Sales *The Hottentot Venus*, by Barbara Chase-Riboud (Doubleday); *The Lady, the Chef and the Lover*, by Marisol Konczal (Harper Collins); *End of Adolescence*, by Robert Epstein (Harcourt).

Terms Agent receives 15% commission on domestic sales; 20% commission on foreign sales. Offers written contract. Charges clients for expenses "to cover domestic costs so that we can spend time selling books instead of accounting expenses. We also charge for the photocopying of the full manuscript or nonfiction proposal and for foreign postage."

Writers' Conferences "Have attended Squaw Valley, Santa Barbara, Asilomar, Southern California Writers Conference, Rocky Mountain Fiction Writers, to name a few. We also speak regularly for writers groups such as PEN West and the Independent Writers Association."

Tips "Be professional and learn the standard procedures for submitting your work. Give full biographical information on yourself, especially for a nonfiction project. Send no more than 50 pages of your manuscript, a very brief synopsis, detailed author bio (awards, publications, accomplishments) and a SASE. We will not respond to submissions without a SASE. Nine-page letters telling us your life story, or your book's, are unprofessional and usually not read. Tell us about your book and write your query well. It's our first introduction to who you are and what you can do. Call if you don't hear within 6 weeks. Be a regular patron of bookstores, and study what kind of books are being published. Read. Check out your local library and bookstores—you'll find lots of books on writing and the publishing industry that will help you. At conferences, ask published writers about their agents. Don't believe the myth that an agent has to be in New York to be successful—we've already disproved it!"

THE JONATHAN DOLGER AGENCY

49 E. 96th St., Suite 9B, New York NY 10128. (212)427-1853. **Contact:** Herbert Erinmore; President: Jonathan Dolger. Estab. 1980. Member of AAR. Represents 70 clients. 25% of clients are new/unpublished writers.

- Query before submitting.

Represents Nonfiction books, novels, illustrated books.

O→ This agency specializes in adult trade fiction and nonfiction, and illustrated books.

How to Contact Query with SASE.

Recent Sales This agency prefers not to share information on specific sales.

Terms Agent receives 15% commission on domestic sales; 25% commission on foreign sales. Charges clients for "standard expenses."

Tips "Writer must have been previously published if submitting fiction. Prefers to work with published/established authors; works with a small number of new/previously unpublished writers."

DONADIO & ASHWORTH, INC.

121 W. 27th St., Suite 704, New York NY 10001. Member of AAR.

- Query before submitting.

Member Agents Neil Olson, Ira Silverberg.

JANIS A. DONNAUD & ASSOCIATES, INC.

525 Broadway, 2nd Floor, New York NY 10012. (212)431-2664. Fax: (212)431-2667. E-mail: jdonnaud@aol.com. **Contact:** Janis A. Donnaud. Member of AAR; signatory of WGA. Represents 40 clients. 5% of clients are new/unpublished writers. Currently handles: 100% nonfiction books.

- Prior to opening her agency, Ms. Donnaud was vice president, associate publisher of Random House Adult Trade Group.

Represents Nonfiction books. **Considers these nonfiction areas:** Biography/autobiography; child guidance/

Literary Agents

parenting; cooking/foods/nutrition; current affairs; health/medicine; humor/satire; psychology (pop); women's issues/studies; lifestyle.

O→ This agency specializes in health, medical, cooking, humor, pop psychology, narrative nonfiction, photography, biography, parenting and current affairs. "We give a lot of service and attention to clients." Actively seeking serious narrative nonfiction; cookbooks; health and medical all written by experts with an already established platform in their area of specialty. Does not want to receive fiction, poetry, mysteries, juvenile books, romances, science fiction, young adult, religious, fantasy.

How to Contact Query with SASE, description of book, and 2-3 pages of sample material. Prefers to read materials exclusively. Responds in 1 month to queries; 1 month to mss. Obtains most new clients through recommendations from others.

Recent Sales Sold 25 titles in the last year. *Southern Fried Divorce* and *Southern Fried Secrets*, by Judy Conner (Gotham); *The Little Pro*, by Eddie Merrins. Two cookbook deals for the No. 1 food network.

Terms Agent receives 15% commission on domestic sales; 20% commission on foreign sales; 20% commission on dramatic rights sales. Offers written contract; 1-month notice must be given to terminate contract. Charges clients for messengers, photocopying, purchase of books.

JIM DONOVAN LITERARY

4515 Prentice St., Suite 109, Dallas TX 75206. **Contact:** Jim Donovan, president; Kathryn Lindsey. Estab. 1993. Represents 30 clients. 20% of clients are new/unpublished writers. Currently handles: 65% nonfiction books; 35% novels.

Member Agents Jim Donovan (president); Kathryn Lindsey.

Represents Nonfiction books, novels. **Considers these nonfiction areas:** Biography/autobiography; business/economics; child guidance/parenting; current affairs; health/medicine; history; military/war; money/finance; music/dance; nature/environment; popular culture; sports; true crime/investigative. **Considers these fiction areas:** Action/adventure; detective/police/crime; historical; horror; literary; mainstream/contemporary; mystery/suspense; sports; thriller; westerns/frontier.

O→ This agency specializes in commercial fiction and nonfiction. Does not want to receive poetry, humor, short stories, juvenile, romance, or religious work.

How to Contact Query with SASE. For nonfiction, send query letter. For fiction, send 2- to 5-page outline and 3 sample chapters. No e-mail or fax queries. Considers simultaneous queries. Responds in 1 month to queries; 1 month to mss. Obtains most new clients through recommendations from others, solicitations.

Recent Sales Sold 24 titles in the last year. *Brotherhood of Heroes*, by Bill Sloan (Simon & Schuster); *Halfbreed*, by David Halaas and Andy Masich (Da Capo); *Given Up for Dead*, by Bill Sloan (Bantam); *Slam*, by Curt Sampson (Da Capo); *Streetcar: Blanche Dubois, Marlon Brando, and the Movie that Outraged America*, by Sam Staggs (St. Martin's); *Sea of Bones*, by Ron Faust (Bantam); *How Mrs. Claus Saved Christmas*, by Jeff Guinn (Tarcher).

Terms Agent receives 15% commission on domestic sales; 20% commission on foreign sales. Offers written contract, binding for 1 year; written notice must be given to terminate contract.

Tips "The vast majority of material I receive, particularly fiction, is not ready for publication. Do everything you can to get your fiction work in top shape before you try to find an agent. I've been in the book business since 1981, in retail (as a chain buyer), as an editor, and as a published author. I'm open to working with new writers if they're serious about their writing and are prepared to put in the work necessary—the rewriting—to become publishable."

DOYEN LITERARY SERVICES, INC.

1931 660th St., Newell IA 50568-7613. (712)272-3300. Website: www.barbaradoyen.com. **Contact:** (Ms.) B.J. Doyen, president. Estab. 1988. Represents over 100 clients. 20% of clients are new/unpublished writers. Currently handles: 95% nonfiction books; 5% novels.

• Prior to opening her agency, Ms. Doyen worked as a published author, teacher, guest speaker, and wrote and appeared in her own weekly TV show airing in 7 states. She is also the co-author of *The Everything Guide to Writing a Book Proposal* (Adams, 2005).

Represents Nonfiction books, novels. **Considers these nonfiction areas:** Agriculture/horticulture; americana; animals; anthropology/archaeology; art/architecture/design; biography/autobiography; business/economics; child guidance/parenting; computers/electronic; cooking/foods/nutrition; crafts/hobbies; creative nonfiction; current affairs; education; ethnic/cultural interests; gardening; government/politics/law; health/medicine; history; how-to; humor/satire; interior design/decorating; juvenile nonfiction; language/literature/criticism; memoirs; military/war; money/finance; multicultural; music/dance; nature/environment; New Age/metaphysics; philosophy; photography; popular culture; psychology; recreation; regional; religious/inspirational; science/technology; self-help/personal improvement; sex; sociology; software; spirituality; sports; theater/film; translation; travel; true crime/investigative; women's issues/studies; young adult. **Considers these fiction areas:**

Contemporary issues; family saga; historical; literary; mainstream/contemporary; occult; psychic/supernatural.

O→ This agency specializes in nonfiction and occasionally handles mainstream fiction for adults. Actively seeking business, health, how-to, self-help; all kinds of adult nonfiction suitable for the major trade publishers. Does not want to receive pornography, children's, poetry.

How to Contact Query with SASE. No e-mail or fax queries. Considers simultaneous queries. Responds in 3 weeks to mss. Responds immediately to queries. Returns materials only with SASE.

Recent Sales *The Birth Order Effect for Couples*, by Isaacson/Schneider (Fairwinds); *An Egg on Three Sticks*, by Fischer (St. Martin's Griffin).

Terms Agent receives 15% commission on domestic sales; 20% commission on foreign sales. Offers written contract, binding for 2 years.

Tips "Our authors receive personalized attention. We market aggressively, undeterred by rejection. We get the best possible publishing contracts. We are very interested in nonfiction book ideas at this time; will consider most topics. Many writers come to us from referrals, but we also get quite a few who initially approach us with query letters. Do not use phone queries unless you are successfully published or a celebrity. It is best if you do not collect editorial rejections prior to seeking an agent, but if you do, be up-front and honest about it. Do not submit your manuscript to more than 1 agent at a time—querying first can save you (and us) much time. We're open to established or beginning writers—just send us a terrific letter with SASE!"

DUNHAM LITERARY, INC.

156 Fifth Ave., Suite 625, New York NY 10010-7002. (212)929-0994. Website: www.dunhamlit.com. **Contact:** Jennie Dunham. Estab. 2000. Member of AAR. Represents 50 clients. 15% of clients are new/unpublished writers. Currently handles: 25% nonfiction books; 25% novels; 50% juvenile books.

- Prior to opening her agency, Ms. Dunham worked as a literary agent for Russell & Volkening. The Rhoda Weyr Agency is now a division of Dunham Literary, Inc.

Represents Nonfiction books, novels, short story collections, juvenile books. **Considers these nonfiction areas:** Anthropology/archaeology; biography/autobiography; ethnic/cultural interests; government/politics/law; health/medicine; history; language/literature/criticism; nature/environment; popular culture; psychology; science/technology; women's issues/studies. **Considers these fiction areas:** Ethnic; juvenile; literary; mainstream/contemporary; picture books; young adult.

How to Contact Query with SASE. No e-mail or fax queries. Responds in 1 week to queries; 2 months to mss. Obtains most new clients through recommendations from others, solicitations.

Recent Sales *America the Beautiful*, by Robert Sabuda; *Dahlia*, by Barbara McClintock; *Living Dead Girl*, by Tod Goldberg; *In My Mother's House*, by Margaret McMulla; *Black Hawk Down*, by Mark Bowden; *Look Back All the Green Valley*, by Fred Chappell; *Under a Wing*, by Reeve Lindbergh; *I Am Madame X*, by Gioia Diliberto.

Terms Agent receives 15% commission on domestic sales; 20% commission on foreign sales.

N DUNOW, CARLSON, & LERNER AGENCY

27 W. 20th St., Suite 1003, New York NY 10011. **Contact:** Rolph Blythe, Jennifer Carlson, Henry Dunow, Betsy Lerner. Member of AAR.

- Query before submitting.

DUPREE/MILLER AND ASSOCIATES INC. LITERARY

100 Highland Park Village, Suite 350, Dallas TX 75205. (214)559-BOOK. Fax: (214)559-PAGE. E-mail: dmabook @aol.com. **Contact:** Submissions Department. President: Jan Miller. Estab. 1984. Member of ABA. Represents 200 clients. 20% of clients are new/unpublished writers. Currently handles: 90% nonfiction books; 10% novels.

Member Agents Jan Miller; Michael Broussard; Shannon Miser-Marven (business affairs); Kym Wilson; Jennifer Holder; Annabelle Baxter (assistant to Jan Miller).

Represents Nonfiction books, novels, scholarly books, syndicated material. **Considers these nonfiction areas:** Americana; animals; anthropology/archaeology; art/architecture/design; biography/autobiography; business/economics; child guidance/parenting; cooking/foods/nutrition; crafts/hobbies; creative nonfiction; current affairs; education; ethnic/cultural interests; gardening; gay/lesbian issues; government/politics/law; health/medicine; history; how-to; humor/satire; interior design/decorating; language/literature/criticism; memoirs; money/finance; multicultural; music/dance; nature/environment; New Age/metaphysics; philosophy; photography; popular culture; psychology; recreation; regional; religious/inspirational; science/technology; self-help/personal improvement; sex; sociology; spirituality; sports; theater/film; translation; travel; true crime/investigative; women's issues/studies. **Considers these fiction areas:** Action/adventure; contemporary issues; detective/police/crime; ethnic; experimental; family saga; feminist; gay/lesbian; glitz; historical; humor/satire; literary; mainstream/contemporary; mystery/suspense; picture books; psychic/supernatural; religious/inspirational; sports; thriller.

O‑ This agency specializes in commercial fiction, nonfiction.

How to Contact Query with SASE, outline. Considers simultaneous queries. Responds in 3 months to mss. Obtains most new clients through recommendations from others, conferences, lectures and "very frequently through publisher's referrals."

Recent Sales Sold 30 titles in the last year. *Family First*, by Dr. Phil McGraw (Simon & Schuster); *The 8th Habit*, by Stephen Covey; *Kitchen Life*, by Art Smith; *Crucial Confrontations*, by Joseph Grenny. Other clients include Fantasia Barrino, Nicole Richie, Anthony Robbins.

Terms Agent receives 15% commission on domestic sales. Offers written contract.

Writers' Conferences Aspen Writers Foundation (Aspen CO).

Tips If interested in agency representation, "it is vital to have the material in the proper working format. As agents' policies differ, it is important to follow their guidelines. The best advice I can give is to work on establishing a strong proposal that provides sample chapters, an overall synopsis (fairly detailed), and some bio information on yourself. Do not send your proposal in pieces; it should be complete upon submission. Remember you are trying to sell your work, and it should be in its best condition."

DWYER & O'GRADY, INC.

P.O. Box 790, Cedar Key FL 32625. (352)543-9307. Website: www.dwyerogrady.com. **Contact:** Elizabeth O'Grady. Estab. 1990. Member of SCBWI. Represents 20 clients. Currently handles: 100% juvenile books.

- Prior to opening their agency, Mr. Dwyer and Ms. O'Grady were booksellers and publishers.

Member Agents Elizabeth O'Grady (children's books); Jeff Dwyer (children's books).

Represents Juvenile books. **Considers these nonfiction areas:** Juvenile nonfiction. **Considers these fiction areas:** Juvenile; picture books; young adult.

O‑ This agency represents only writers and illustrators of children's books. Does not want to receive submissions that are not for juvenile audiences.

How to Contact Not accepting new clients. *No unsolicited mss.* Obtains most new clients through recommendations from others, direct approach by agent to writer whose work they've read.

Recent Sales Sold 22 titles in the last year. Clients include Kim Ablon Whitney, Mary Azarian, Tom Bodett, Odds Bodkin, E.B. Lewis, Steve Schuch, Virginia Stroud, Natasha Tarpley, Zong-Zhou Wang, Rich Michelson, Barry Moser, Peter Sylvada, James Rumford, Clemence McLaren, Hat Tripp, Lita Judge, Goeffrey Horman.

Terms Agent receives 15% commission on domestic sales; 20% commission on foreign sales. Offers written contract; 1-month notice must be given to terminate contract. Charges clients for "photocopying of longer manuscripts or mutually agreed upon marketing expenses."

Writers' Conferences Book Expo; American Library Association; Society of Children's Book Writers & Illustrators.

DYSTEL & GODERICH LITERARY MANAGEMENT

1 Union Square W., Suite 904, New York NY 10003. (212)627-9100. Fax: (212)627-9313. E-mail: miriam@dystel.com. Website: www.dystel.com. **Contact:** Miriam Goderich. Estab. 1994. Member of AAR. Represents 300 clients. 50% of clients are new/unpublished writers. Currently handles: 65% nonfiction books; 25% novels; 10% cookbooks.

- Dystel & Goderich Literary Management recently acquired the client list of Bedford Book Works.

Member Agents Stacey Glick; Jane Dystel; Miriam Goderich; Michael Bourret; Leslie Josephs; Jim McCarthy.

Represents Nonfiction books, novels, cookbooks. **Considers these nonfiction areas:** Animals; anthropology/archaeology; biography/autobiography; business/economics; child guidance/parenting; cooking/foods/nutrition; current affairs; education; ethnic/cultural interests; gay/lesbian issues; government/politics/law; health/medicine; history; humor/satire; military/war; money/finance; New Age/metaphysics; popular culture; psychology; religious/inspirational; science/technology; true crime/investigative; women's issues/studies. **Considers these fiction areas:** Action/adventure; contemporary issues; detective/police/crime; ethnic; family saga; gay/lesbian; literary; mainstream/contemporary; mystery/suspense; thriller (especially).

O‑ This agency specializes in commercial and literary fiction and nonfiction, plus cookbooks.

How to Contact Query with SASE. Considers simultaneous queries. Responds in 1 month to queries; 6 weeks to mss. Obtains most new clients through recommendations from others, solicitations, conferences.

Terms Agent receives 15% commission on domestic sales; 19% commission on foreign sales. Offers written contract, binding for book-to-book basis. Charges for photocopying. Galley charges and book charges from the publisher are passed on to the author.

Writers' Conferences West Coast Writers Conference (Whidbey Island WA, Columbus Day weekend); University of Iowa Writer's Conference; Pacific Northwest Writer's Conference; Pike's Peak Writer's Conference; Santa Barbara Writer's Conference; Harriette Austin's Writer's Conference; Sandhills Writers Conference; ASU Writers Conference.

Tips "Work on sending professional, well-written queries that are concise and addressed to the specific agent the author is contacting. No dear Sirs/Madam."

ANNE EDELSTEIN LITERARY AGENCY

20 W. 22nd St., Suite 1603, New York NY 10010. Member of AAR.

- Query before submitting.

EDUCATIONAL DESIGN SERVICES, INC.

7238 Treviso Ln., Boynton Beach FL 33437-7338. (561)739-9402. **Contact:** Bertram L. Linder, president. Estab. 1979. Represents 17 clients. 70% of clients are new/unpublished writers. Currently handles: 100% textbooks.

Represents Scholarly books, textbooks. **Considers these nonfiction areas:** Anthropology/archaeology; business/economics; child guidance/parenting; current affairs; education; ethnic/cultural interests; government/politics/law; history; language/literature/criticism; military/war; money/finance; science/technology; sociology; women's issues/studies.

O→ This agency specializes in textual material for the educational (K-12) market.

How to Contact Query with SASE, proposal package, outline, 1-2 sample chapters. Considers simultaneous queries. Responds in 1 month to queries; 6 weeks to mss. Returns materials only with SASE. Obtains most new clients through recommendations from others, solicitations, conferences.

Recent Sales Sold 4 titles in the last year. *Minority Report*, by H. Gunn and J. Singh (Scarecrow Press); *Spreadsheets for School Administrators & Supervisors* (Scarecrow Press); *How to Solve the Word Problems in Arithmetic Grades 6-8*, by P. Pullman (McGraw-Hill/Schaum); *How to Solve Math Word Problems on Standardized Tests*, by D. Wayne (McGraw-Hill/Schaum); *First Principles of Cosmology*, by E.V. Linder (Addison-Wesley Longman).

Terms Agent receives 15% commission on domestic sales; 25% commission on foreign sales. Offers written contract. Charges clients for photocopying, actual postage/shipping costs.

LISA EKUS PUBLIC RELATIONS CO., LLC

57 North St., Hatfield MA 01038. (413)247-9325. Fax: (413)247-9873. E-mail: lisaekus@lisaekus.com. Website: www.lisaekus.com. **Contact:** Lisa Ekus. Estab. 1982. Member of AAR.

Represents Nonfiction books. **Considers these nonfiction areas:** Cooking/foods/nutrition.

How to Contact Submit a proposal with title page, proposal contents, concept, author bio, marketing and promotion, competition, TOC, chapter summaries, complete sample chapter.

Recent Sales *The Low-Carb Bartender*, by Bob Skilnik (Adams Media); *Kitchen of Light*, by Andreas Viestad (Artisan); *Simply Shellfish! No Bones About It*, by Leslie Glover Pendleton (HarperCollins).

ETHAN ELLENBERG LITERARY AGENCY

548 Broadway, #5-E, New York NY 10012. (212)431-4554. Fax: (212)941-4652. E-mail: agent@ethanellenberg.com. Website: www.ethanellenberg.com. **Contact:** Ethan Ellenberg. Estab. 1983. Represents 80 clients. 10% of clients are new/unpublished writers. Currently handles: 25% nonfiction books; 75% novels.

- Prior to opening his agency, Mr. Ellenberg was contracts manager of Berkley/Jove, and associate contracts manager for Bantam.

Member Agents Ethan Ellenberg.

Represents Nonfiction books, novels. **Considers these nonfiction areas:** Biography/autobiography; health/medicine; history; military/war; New Age/metaphysics; religious/inspirational; science/technology. **Considers these fiction areas:** Fantasy; romance; science fiction; thriller; women's.

O→ This agency specializes in commercial fiction, especially thrillers, romance/women's fiction and specialized nonfiction. "We also do a lot of children's books." Actively seeking commercial and literary fiction, children's books, break-through nonfiction. Does not want to receive poetry, short stories, westerns, autobiographies, screenplays.

How to Contact For fiction, send introductory letter (with credits, if any), outline, first 3 chapters, and SASE (stamps only, post office will not accept metered mail). For nonfiction: Send query letter and/or proposal, 1 sample chapter, if written, and SASE. For children's books: Send introductory letter (with credits, if any), up to 3 picture book mss, outline, first 3 chapters for longer projects, SASE. No fax queries. Accepts e-mail queries, no attachments. Will only respond to e-mail queries if interested. Considers simultaneous queries. Responds in 4-6 weeks to mss. Returns materials only with SASE.

Recent Sales Has sold over 100 titles in the last 3 years. *The Aide*, by Ward Carroll (Dutton); *The Lord of the Libraries*, by Mel Odom (Tor); *Mystic and Rider* and *The Thirteenth House*, by Sharon Shinn (Berkley); *Lethal Lies*, by Laurie Breton (Mira); *She, Myself and I*, by Whitney Gaskell (Bantam); *I Hunger for You*, by Susan Sizemore (Pocket); *What Einstein Told His Cook 2*, by Robert Wolke (Norton); *Clara and Asha*, by Eric Rohmann (Roaring Book Press).

Terms Agent receives 15% commission on domestic sales; 10% commission on foreign sales. Offers written

contract. Charges clients for "direct expenses only limited to photocopying, postage, by writer's consent only."
Writers' Conferences RWA National; Novelists, Inc; and other regional conferences.
Tips "We do consider new material from unsolicited authors. Write a good, clear letter with a succinct description of your book. We prefer the first 3 chapters when we consider fiction. For all submissions you must include a SASE for return or the material is discarded. It's always hard to break in, but talent will find a home. Check our website for complete submission guidelines. We continue to see natural storytellers and nonfiction writers with important books."

NICHOLAS ELLISON, INC.

Affiliated with Sanford J. Greenburger Associates, 55 Fifth Ave., 15th Floor, New York NY 10003. (212)206-6050. Fax: (212)463-8718. Website: www.greenburger.com. **Contact:** Nicholas Ellison. Estab. 1983. Represents 70 clients. Currently handles: 50% nonfiction books; 50% novels.

- Prior to becoming an agent, Mr. Ellison was an editor at Minerva Editions, Harper & Row, and editor-in-chief at Delacorte.

Member Agents Nicholas Ellison, Jennifer Cayea, Abigail Koons.
Represents Nonfiction books, novels. **Considers these nonfiction areas:** Considers most nonfiction areas. **Considers these fiction areas:** Literary; mainstream/contemporary.
How to Contact Query with SASE. Responds in 6 weeks to queries.
Recent Sales *Night Fall*, by Nelson DeMille (Warner); *The Big Love*, by Sarah Dunn (Little, Brown); *The Stupidest Angel*, by Christopher Moore (HarperCollins). Other clients include Olivia Goldsmith, P.T. Deutermann, Nancy Geary, Jeff Lindsay, Lee Gruenfeld, Thomas Christopher Greene, Bill Mason.
Terms Agent receives 15% commission on domestic sales; 20% commission on foreign sales.

ANN ELMO AGENCY, INC.

60 E. 42nd St., New York NY 10165. (212)661-2880, 2881. Fax: (212)661-2883. **Contact:** Lettie Lee. Estab. 1959. Member of AAR, MWA, Authors Guild.
Member Agents Lettie Lee; Mari Cronin (plays); A.L. Abecassis (nonfiction).
Represents Nonfiction books, novels. **Considers these nonfiction areas:** Biography/autobiography; current affairs; health/medicine; history; how-to; money/finance; music/dance; popular culture; psychology; science/technology; self-help/personal improvement; theater/film. **Considers these fiction areas:** Contemporary issues; ethnic; family saga; mainstream/contemporary; romance (contemporary, gothic, historical, regency); thriller; women's.
How to Contact Letter queries only with SASE. No fax queries. Responds in 3 months to queries. Obtains most new clients through recommendations from others.
Recent Sales This agency prefers not to share information on specific sales.
Terms Agent receives 15% commission on domestic sales; 20% commission on foreign sales. Offers written contract. Charges clients for "special mailings or shipping considerations or multiple international calls. No charge for usual cost of doing business."
Tips "Query first, and when asked only please send properly prepared manuscript. A double-spaced, readable manuscript is the best recommendation. Include SASE, of course."

ELAINE P. ENGLISH

Graybill & English, LLC, 1875 Connecticut Ave. NW, Suite 712, Washington DC 20009. (202)588-9798, ext. 143. Fax: (202)457-0662. E-mail: elaineengl@aol.com. Website: www.graybillandenglish.com. **Contact:** Elaine English. Member of AAR. Represents 18 clients. 50% of clients are new/unpublished writers. Currently handles: 100% novels.

- Ms. English is also an attorney specializing in media and publishing law.

Member Agents Elaine English (fiction, including women's fiction, romance, thrillers and mysteries).
Represents Novels. **Considers these fiction areas:** Historical; mainstream/contemporary; multicultural; mystery/suspense; romance (including single titles, historical, contemporary, romantic, suspense, chick lit, erotic); thriller; women's.

> "While not as an agent per se, I have been working in publishing for over 15 years. Also, I'm affiliated with other agents who represent a broad spectrum of projects." Actively seeking women's fiction, including single-title romances. Does not want to receive any science fiction or time travel.

How to Contact Submit synopsis and first 3 chapters, SASE. Responds in 6-12 weeks to queries; 6 months to requested ms. Returns materials only with SASE. Obtains most new clients through recommendations from others, solicitations, conferences.
Terms Agent receives 15% commission on domestic sales; 20% commission on foreign sales. Offers written contract; 30-day notice must be given to terminate contract. Charges only for expenses directly related to sales of manuscript (long distance, postage, copying).

Writers' Conferences RWA Nationals (July); SEAK Medical Fiction Writing for Physcians (Cape Cod, September); Emerald City (Seattle WA, October); Novelists, Inc. (New York, April).

FELICIA ETH LITERARY REPRESENTATION

555 Bryant St., Suite 350, Palo Alto CA 94301-1700. (650)375-1276. Fax: (650)401-8892. E-mail: feliciaeth@aol.com. **Contact:** Felicia Eth. Estab. 1988. Member of AAR. Represents 25-35 clients. Currently handles: 85% nonfiction books; 15% adult novels.

Represents Nonfiction books, novels. **Considers these nonfiction areas:** Animals; anthropology/archaeology; biography/autobiography; business/economics; child guidance/parenting; current affairs; ethnic/cultural interests; gay/lesbian issues; government/politics/law; health/medicine; history; nature/environment; popular culture; psychology; science/technology; sociology; true crime/investigative; women's issues/studies. **Considers these fiction areas:** Ethnic; feminist; gay/lesbian; literary; mainstream/contemporary; thriller.

This agency specializes in "provocative, intelligent, thoughtful nonfiction on a wide array of subjects which are commercial, and high-quality fiction—preferably mainstream and contemporary."

How to Contact Query with SASE, outline. Considers simultaneous queries. Responds in 3 weeks to queries; 4-6 weeks to mss.

Recent Sales Sold 7-10 titles in the last year. *Jane Austen in Boca*, by Paula Marantz Cohen (St. Martin's Press); *Beyond Pink and Blue*, by Dr. Leonard Sax (Doubleday/Random House); *Lavendar Road to Success*, by Kirk Snyder (Ten Speed Press).

Terms Agent receives 15% commission on domestic sales; 20% commission on foreign sales; 20% commission on dramatic rights sales. Charges clients for photocopying, express mail service—extraordinary expenses.

Writers' Conferences Independent Writers of LA (Los Angeles); Conference of National Coalition of Independent Scholars (Berkley CA); Writers Guild.

Tips "For nonfiction, established expertise is certainly a plus, as is magazine publication—though not a prerequisite. I am highly dedicated to those projects I represent, but highly selective in what I choose."

MARY EVANS INC.

242 E. Fifth St., New York NY 10003. (212)979-0880. Member of AAR.

- Query before submitting.

Member Agents Mary Evans, Tanya McKinnon.

FARBER LITERARY AGENCY, INC.

14 E. 75th St., #2E, New York NY 10021. (212)861-7075. Fax: (212)861-7076. E-mail: farberlit@aol.com. Website: www.donaldfarber.com. **Contact:** Ann Farber; Dr. Seth Farber. Estab. 1989. Represents 40 clients. 50% of clients are new/unpublished writers. Currently handles: 25% nonfiction books; 15% scholarly books; 25% stage plays; 35% fiction books.

Member Agents Ann Farber (novels); Seth Farber (plays, scholarly books, novels); Donald C. Farber (attorney, all entertainment media).

Represents Nonfiction books, novels, juvenile books, textbooks, stage plays. **Considers these nonfiction areas:** Child guidance/parenting; cooking/foods/nutrition; music/dance; psychology; theater/film. **Considers these fiction areas:** Action/adventure; contemporary issues; humor/satire; juvenile; literary; mainstream/contemporary; mystery/suspense; thriller; young adult.

How to Contact Submit outline, 3 sample chapters, SASE. Prefers to read materials exclusively. Responds in 1 month to queries; 2 month to mss. Obtains most new clients through recommendations from others.

Terms Agent receives 15% commission on domestic sales; 20% commission on foreign sales. Offers written contract, binding for 1 year. Client must furnish copies of ms, treatments, and any other items for submission.

Tips "Our attorney, Donald C. Farber, is the author of many books. His services are available to the agency's clients as part of the agency service at no additional charge."

N FARRIS LITERARY AGENCY, INC.

P.O. Box 570069, Dallas TX 75357. (972)203-8804. E-mail: agent@farrisliterary.com. Website: www.farrisliterary.com. **Contact:** Mike Farris or Susan Morgan Farris. Estab. 2002. Represents 30 clients. 60% of clients are new/unpublished writers.

- Both Mike and Susan are attorneys.

Member Agents "We specialize in both fiction and nonfiction books. We are particularly interested in discovering unpublished authors. We adhere to AAR guidelines"

Represents Nonfiction books, novels. **Considers these nonfiction areas:** Biography/autobiography; business/economics; child guidance/parenting; cooking/foods/nutrition; current affairs; government/politics/law; health/medicine; history; how-to; humor/satire; memoirs; military/war; music/dance; popular culture; religious/inspirational; self-help/personal improvement; sports; women's issues/studies. **Considers these fiction**

areas: Action/adventure; detective/police/crime; historical; humor/satire; literary; mainstream/contemporary; mystery/suspense; religious/inspirational; romance; sports; thriller; westerns/frontier.

O→ Does not consider science fiction, fantasy, gay and lesbian, erotica, young adult, children's.

How to Contact Query with SASE. Considers simultaneous queries. Responds in 2-3 weeks to queries; 4-8 weeks to mss. Returns materials only with SASE. Obtains most new clients through recommendations from others, solicitations, conferences.

Recent Sales Sold 4 titles in the last year. *Detachment Fault*, by Susan Cummins Miller (Berkley); Untitled, by Susan Cummins Miller (Berkley); *Creed*, by Sheldon Russell (Oklahoma University Press); *How to Understand Autism: The Easy Way*, by Dr. Alexander Durig (Jessica Kingsley Publishers Ltd.).

Terms Agent receives 15% commission on domestic sales; 20% commission on foreign sales. Offers written contract, 30-day notice must be given to terminate contract. Postage and photocopying.

Writers' Conferences Oklahoma Writers Federation, Inc. (Oklahoma City OK); The Screenwriting Conference at Santa Fe (Sante Fe NM); Pikes Peak Writers Conference; Women Writing the West.

DIANA FINCH LITERARY AGENCY

116 W. 23rd St., Suite 500, New York NY 10011. (646)375-2081. E-mail: diana.finch@verizon.net. **Contact:** Diana Finch. Estab. 2003. Member of AAR. Represents 45 clients. 20% of clients are new/unpublished writers. Currently handles: 65% nonfiction books; 25% novels; 5% juvenile books; 5% multimedia.

• Prior to opening her agency, Ms. Finch was an agent with Ellen Levine Literary Agency for 18 years.

Represents Nonfiction books, novels, scholarly books. **Considers these nonfiction areas:** Biography/autobiography; business/economics; child guidance/parenting; computers/electronic; current affairs; ethnic/cultural interests; government/politics/law; health/medicine; history; how-to; humor/satire; memoirs; military/war; money/finance; music/dance; nature/environment; photography; popular culture; psychology; science/technology; self-help/personal improvement; sports; theater/film; translation; true crime/investigative; women's issues/studies; juvenile. **Considers these fiction areas:** Action/adventure; detective/police/crime; ethnic; historical; literary; mainstream/contemporary; thriller; young adult.

O→ Actively seeking narrative nonfiction, popular science, and health topics. Does not want romance, mysteries, or children's picture books.

How to Contact Query with SASE, or by e-mail (no attachments). No phone or fax queries. Considers simultaneous queries. Returns materials only with SASE. Obtains most new clients through recommendations from others.

Recent Sales Untitled nonfiction, by Greg Palast (Penguin US and UK); *Journey of the Magi*, by Tudor Parfitt (Farrar, Straus, & Giroux); *Sixth Grade*, by Susie Morgenstern (Viking Children's); *We Were There: African-American Vets*, by Yvonne Latty and Ron Tarver (HarperCollins); *Lipstick Jihad*, by Azadeh Moaveni (Public Affairs). Other clients include Keith Devlin, Daniel Duane, Thomas Goltz, Hugh Pope, Sebastian Matthews, Joan Lambert, Dr. Robert Marion.

Terms Agent receives 15% commission on domestic sales; 20% commission on foreign sales. Offers written contract. "I charge for photocopying, overseas postage, galleys, and books purchased, and try to recap these costs from earnings received for a client, rather than charging outright."

Tips "Do as much research as you can on agents before you query. Have someone critique your query letter before you send it. It should be only 1 page and describe your book clearly—and why you are writing it—but also demonstrate creativity and a sense of your writing style."

FLAMING STAR LITERARY ENTERPRISES

320 Riverside Dr., New York NY 10025. E-mail: flamingstarlit@aol.com. **Contact:** Joseph B. Vallely or Janis C. Vallely. Estab. 1985. Represents 100 clients. 25% of clients are new/unpublished writers. Currently handles: 100% nonfiction books.

• Prior to opening the agency, Joseph Vallely served as national sales manager for Dell; Janis Vallely was vice president of Doubleday.

Represents Nonfiction books. **Considers these nonfiction areas:** Current affairs; government/politics/law; health/medicine; nature/environment; science/technology; self-help/personal improvement; spirituality; sports.

O→ This agency specializes in upscale commercial nonfiction.

How to Contact E-mail only (no attachments). Obtains most new clients through recommendations from others, solicitations.

Terms Agent receives 15% commission on domestic sales; 20% commission on foreign sales. Offers written contract. Charges clients for photocopying, postage only.

FLANNERY LITERARY

1155 S. Washington St., Suite 202, Naperville IL 60540. (630)428-2682. Fax: (630)428-2683. **Contact:** Jennifer Flannery. Estab. 1992. Represents 33 clients. 90% of clients are new/unpublished writers. Currently handles: 100% juvenile books.

• Prior to opening her agency, Ms. Flannery was an editorial assistant.

Represents Juvenile books. **Considers these nonfiction areas:** Juvenile nonfiction; young adult. **Considers these fiction areas:** Juvenile; picture books; young adult.

O→ This agency specializes in children's and young adult/juvenile fiction and nonfiction.

How to Contact Query with SASE. No fax or e-mail queries, please. No e-mail or fax queries. Responds in 3 weeks to queries; 1 month to mss. Obtains most new clients through recommendations from others, submissions.

Recent Sales Sold 20 titles in the last year. This agency prefers not to share information on specific sales.

Terms Agent receives 15% commission on domestic sales; 20% commission on foreign sales. Offers written contract, binding for life of book in print; 1-month notice must be given to terminate contract. 100% of business is derived from commissions on ms sales.

Writers' Conferences SCBWI Summer Conference.

Tips "Write an engrossing, succinct query describing your work."

PETER FLEMING AGENCY

P.O. Box 458, Pacific Palisades CA 90272. (310)454-1373. **Contact:** Peter Fleming. Estab. 1962. Currently handles: 100% nonfiction books.

Represents Nonfiction books.

O→ This agency specializes in "nonfiction books that unearth innovative and uncomfortable truths with bestseller potential." Greatly interested in journalists in the free press (the internet).

How to Contact Query with SASE. Obtains most new clients through "through a different, one-of-a-kind idea for a book often backed by the writer's experience in that area of expertise."

Recent Sales *Rulers of Evil*, by F. Tupper Saussy (HarperCollins); *Why Is It Always About You—Saving Yourself from the Narcissists in Your Life*, by Sandy Hotchkiss (Free Press).

Terms Agent receives 15% commission on domestic sales; 25% commission on foreign sales. Offers written contract, binding for 1 year. Charges clients "only those fees agreed to in writing, i.e., NY-ABA expenses shared. We may ask for a TV contract, too."

Tips "You can begin by self-publishing, test marketing with direct sales, and starting your own website."

N FLETCHER & PARRY

The Carriage House, 121 E. 17th St., New York NY 10003. **Contact:** Christy Fletcher. Member of AAR.

• Query before submitting.

B.R. FLEURY AGENCY

P.O. Box 149352, Orlando FL 32814-9352. (407)895-8494. Fax: (407)898-3923 or (888)310-8142. E-mail: brfleuryagency@juno.com. **Contact:** Blanche or Margaret. Estab. 1994. Signatory of WGA.

Tips "We are not accepting queries until further notice."

THE FOGELMAN LITERARY AGENCY

7515 Greenville, Suite 712, Dallas TX 75231. (214)361-9956. Fax: (214)361-9553. E-mail: info@fogelman.com. Website: www.fogelman.com. Also: 415 Park Ave., New York NY 10022. (212)836-4803. **Contact:** Evan Fogelman. Estab. 1990. Member of AAR. Represents 100 clients. 2% of clients are new/unpublished writers. Currently handles: 40% nonfiction books; 40% novels; 10% scholarly books; 10% TV scripts.

• Prior to opening his agency, Mr. Fogelman was an entertainment lawyer. He is still active in the field and serves as chairman of the Texas Entertainment and Sports Lawyers Association.

Member Agents Evan Fogelman (nonfiction, women's fiction); Linda Kruger (women's fiction, nonfiction); Helen Brown (literary fiction/nonfiction).

Represents Nonfiction books, novels. **Considers these nonfiction areas:** Biography/autobiography; business/economics; child guidance/parenting; current affairs; education; ethnic/cultural interests; government/politics/law; health/medicine; popular culture; psychology; sports; true crime/investigative; women's issues/studies. **Considers these fiction areas:** Historical; literary; mainstream/contemporary; romance (all sub-genres).

O→ This agency specializes in women's fiction and nonfiction. "Zealous advocacy" makes this agency stand apart from others. Actively seeking "nonfiction of all types; romance fiction." Does not want to receive children's/juvenile.

How to Contact Query with SASE. Considers simultaneous queries. Responds in 3 months to mss. Returns materials only with SASE. Obtains most new clients through recommendations from others.

Recent Sales Sold 60 titles in the last year. *A Little Secret Between Friends*, by C.J. Carmichael (Harlequin Superromance); *The Good, the Bad and the Ugly Men I've Dated*, by Shane Bolks (Avon); *Caught in the Act*, by Pam McCutcheon (Kensington). Other clients include Caroline Hunt, Katherine Sutcliffe, Crystal Stovall.

Terms Agent receives 15% commission on domestic sales; 10% commission on foreign sales. Offers written contract, binding for project to project.
Writers' Conferences Romance Writers of America; Novelists, Inc.
Tips "Finish your manuscript, and see our website."

THE FOLEY LITERARY AGENCY

34 E. 38th St., New York NY 10016-2508. (212)686-6930. **Contact:** Joan Foley or Joseph Foley. Estab. 1961. Represents 10 clients. Currently handles: 75% nonfiction books; 25% novels.
Member Agents ICM (Ron Bernstein) handles TV/film rights.
Represents Nonfiction books, novels.
How to Contact Query with letter, brief outline, SASE. Responds promptly to queries. Obtains most new clients through recommendations from others, rarely taking on new clients.
Recent Sales This agency prefers not to share information on specific sales.
Terms Agent receives 10% commission on domestic sales; 15% commission on foreign sales. 100% of business is derived from commissions on ms sales.
Tips Desires brevity in querying.

FORT ROSS, INC., RUSSIAN-AMERICAN PUBLISHING PROJECTS

26 Arthur Place, Yonkers NY 10701-1703. (914)375-6448. Fax: (914)375-6439. E-mail: fort.ross@verizon.net. Website: www.fortross.net. **Contact:** Dr. Vladimir P. Kartsev. Estab. 1992. Represents about 100 clients. 2% of clients are new/unpublished writers. Currently handles: 50% nonfiction books; 40% novels; 10% juvenile books.
Member Agents Ms. Olga Borodyanskaya, St. Petersburg, Russia, phone: 7-812-1738607 (fiction, nonfiction); Mr. Konstantin Paltchikov, Moscow, Russia, phone: 7-095-2388272 (romance, science fiction, fantasy, thriller).
Represents Nonfiction books, novels, juvenile books. **Considers these nonfiction areas:** Biography/autobiography; history; memoirs; psychology; self-help/personal improvement; true crime/investigative. **Considers these fiction areas:** Action/adventure; detective/police/crime; fantasy; horror; juvenile; mystery/suspense; romance (contemporary, gothic, historical, regency); science fiction; thriller; young adult.

- This agency specializes in selling rights for Russian books and illustrations (covers) to American publishers; American books and illustrations for Europe; and Russian-English and English-Russian translations. Actively seeking adventure, fiction, mystery, romance, science fiction, thriller from established authors and illustrators for Russian and European markets.

How to Contact Send published book or galleys. Accepts e-mail and fax queries. Considers simultaneous queries. Returns materials only with SASE.
Recent Sales Sold 12 titles in the last year. *Mastering Judo with Vladimir Putin*, by Vladimir Putin et al (North Atlantic Books [USA]); *Max*, by Howard Fast (Baronet [Czech Republic]); *Kiss of Midas*, by George Vainer (Neri [Italy]); *Redemption*, by Howard Fast (Oram [Israel]); *A Suitcase*, by Sergey Doveatov (Amber [Poland]).
Terms Agent receives 10% commission on domestic sales; 20% commission on foreign sales. Offers written contract, binding for 2 years; 2-month notice must be given to terminate contract.
Tips "Established authors and book illustrators (especially cover art) are welcome for the following genres: romance, fantasy, science fiction, mystery, and adventure."

FOX CHASE AGENCY, INC.

701 Lee Rd., Suite 102, Chesterbrook Corporate Center, Chesterbrook PA 19087. Member of AAR.

- Query before submitting.

Member Agents A. L. Hart, Jo C. Hart.

LYNN C. FRANKLIN ASSOCIATES, LTD.

1350 Broadway, Suite 2015, New York NY 10018. (212)868-6311. Fax: (212)868-6312. E-mail: agency@fsainc.com. **Contact:** Lynn Franklin and Claudia Nys. Estab. 1987. Member of PEN America. Represents 30-35 clients. 50% of clients are new/unpublished writers. Currently handles: 90% nonfiction books; 10% novels.
Represents Nonfiction books, novels. **Considers these nonfiction areas:** Biography/autobiography; current affairs; health/medicine; history; memoirs; New Age/metaphysics; psychology; religious/inspirational (inspirational); self-help/personal improvement; spirituality. **Considers these fiction areas:** Literary; mainstream/contemporary (commercial).

- This agency specializes in general nonfiction with a special interest in health, biography, international affairs, and spirituality.

How to Contact Query with SASE. *No unsolicited mss*. Considers simultaneous queries. Responds in 2 weeks to queries; 6 weeks to mss. Obtains most new clients through recommendations from others, solicitations.
Recent Sales *God Has a Dream*, by Desmond Tutu (Doubleday); *Rabble-Rouser for Peace: The Authorized*

Biography of Desmond Tutu, by John Allen (The Free Press); *Alexander II: Russia Between Hope and Terror*, by Edvard Radzinsky (The Free Press); *The Tao of Poop: Growing Yourself While Growing Your Baby*, by Vivian Glyck (Shambala); *Healing Invisible Wounds*, by Richard Mollica (Harcourt).

Terms Agent receives 15% commission on domestic sales; 20% commission on foreign sales. Offers written contract; 100% of business is derived from commissions on ms sales. Charges clients for postage, photocopying, long distance telephone if significant.

FRANKLIN WEINRIB RUDELL VASSALLO

488 Madison Ave., New York NY 10022. (212)935-5500. Fax: (212)308-0642. E-mail: lawfirm@fwrv.com. Website: www.fwrv.com. **Contact:** Elliot Brown, Esq. Member of AAR.

- Query before submitting.

JEANNE FREDERICKS LITERARY AGENCY, INC.

221 Benedict Hill Rd., New Canaan CT 06840. (203)972-3011. Fax: (203)972-3011. E-mail: jfredrks@optonline.net. **Contact:** Jeanne Fredericks. Estab. 1997. Member of AAR, Authors Guild. Represents 90 clients. 10% of clients are new/unpublished writers. Currently handles: 100% nonfiction books.

- Prior to opening her agency, Ms. Fredericks was an agent and acting director with the Susan P. Urstadt, Inc. Agency. In an earlier career she held editorial positions in trade publishing, most recently as editorial director of Ziff-Davis Books.

Represents Quality adult nonfiction books by experts in their fields. **Considers these nonfiction areas:** Animals; biography/autobiography; child guidance/parenting; cooking/foods/nutrition; gardening; health/medicine (and alternative health); history; how-to; interior design/decorating; money/finance; nature/environment; photography; psychology; self-help/personal improvement; sports (not spectator sports); women's issues/studies.

O→ This agency specializes in quality adult nonfiction by authorities in their fields. No children's books or fiction.

How to Contact Query first with SASE, then send outline/proposal, 1-2 sample chapters and SASE. No fax queries. Accepts e-mail queries if short; no attachments. Considers simultaneous queries. Responds in 3-5 weeks to queries; 2-4 months to mss. Returns materials only with SASE. Obtains most new clients through recommendations from others, solicitations, conferences.

Recent Sales Sold 12 titles in the last year. *Lilias! Yoga Gets Better with Age*, by Lilias Folan (Rodale); *Homescaping*, by Anne Halpin (Rodale); *Stealing with Style*, by Emyl Jenkins (Algonquin); *Creating Optimism in Your Child*, by Bob Murray, Ph.D., and Alice Fortinberry, M.S. (McGraw-Hill); *Waking the Warrior Goddess*, by Christine Horner, M.D. (Basic Health); *Beyond the Blockage*, by Debra Braverman, M.D. (Celestial Arts); *Melanoma*, by Catherine Poole and Dupont Guerry, M.D. (Yale); *Bodywork*, by Thomas Claire (Basic Health); *Cowboys and Dragons: Achieving Successful American-Chinese Business Relations*, by Charles Lee (Dearborn).

Terms Agent receives 15% commission on domestic sales; 25% commission on foreign sales with co-agent; without co-agent receives 20% commission on foreign sales. Offers written contract, binding for 9 months; 2 months notice must be given to terminate contract. Charges client for photocopying of whole proposals and mss, overseas postage, priority mail, and express mail services.

Writers' Conferences PEN Women Conference (Williamsburg VA, February); Connecticut Press Club Biennial Writer's Conference (Stamford CT, April); ASJA Annual Writers' Conference East (New York NY, May); BEA (New York, June); Garden Writers of America Conference (New York, November).

Tips "Be sure to research the competition for your work and be able to justify why there's a need for it. I enjoy building an author's career, particularly if s(he) is professional, hardworking, and courteous. Aside from 14 years of agenting experience, I've had 10 years of editorial experience in adult trade book publishing that enables me to help an author polish a proposal so that it's more appealing to prospective editors. My MBA in marketing also distinguishes me from other agents."

ROBERT A. FREEDMAN DRAMATIC AGENCY, INC.

1501 Broadway, Suite 2310, New York NY 10036. (212)840-5760. Fax: (212)840-5776. Member of AAR.

- Query before submitting.

Member Agents Robert Freedman, Robin Kaver, Selma Luttinger, Marta Praeger.

CANDICE FUHRMAN LITERARY AGENCY

60 Greenwood Way, Mill Valley CA 94941. (415)383-6081. Fax: (415)384-0739. E-mail: candicef@pacbell.net. **Contact:** Candice Fuhrman. Estab. 1987. Member of AAR.

Member Agents Elsa Hurley.

Represents Nonfiction books (adult), novels (adult). **Considers these nonfiction areas:** Current affairs; health/medicine; popular culture; psychology; women's issues/studies; adventure, mind/body/spirit, lifestyle. **Considers these fiction areas:** Literary.

O┳ No children's category, no genre.

How to Contact *No unsolicited mss*. Please query first. Query with SASE and include e-mail address.

Terms Agent receives 15% commission on domestic sales; 20-30% commission on foreign sales.

MAX GARTENBERG, LITERARY AGENCY

12 Westminster Dr., Livingston NJ 07039-1414. Phone/Fax: (973)994-4457. E-mail: gartenbook@att.net. **Contact:** Max Gartenberg. Branch Office: 912 N. Pennsylvania Ave., Yardley PA 19067. (215)295-9230. Contact: Anne Devlin, agdevlin@aol.com; Will Devlin, wad411@hotmail.com. Estab. 1954. Represents 30 clients. 5% of clients are new/unpublished writers. Currently handles: 90% nonfiction books; 10% novels.

Represents Nonfiction books, novels. **Considers these nonfiction areas:** Agriculture/horticulture; animals; art/architecture/design; biography/autobiography; child guidance/parenting; current affairs; health/medicine; history; military/war; money/finance; music/dance; nature/environment; psychology; science/technology; self-help/personal improvement; sports; theater/film; true crime/investigative; women's issues/studies.

How to Contact Query with SASE. Considers simultaneous queries. Responds in 2 weeks to queries; 6 weeks to mss. Obtains most new clients through recommendations from others, occasionally by "following up on good query letters."

Recent Sales *What Patients Taught Me*, by Audrey Young, M.D. (Sasquatch Books); *Unorthodox Warfare: The Chinese Experience*, by Ralph D. Sawyer (Westview Press); *Encyclopedia of Earthquakes and Volcanoes*, by Alexander E. Gates (Facts on File).

Terms Agent receives 15% commission on first domestic sales; 10% subsequent commission on domestic sales; 15-20% commission on foreign sales.

Tips "This agency has recently expanded, with more access for new writers to the associate agents named above."

GELFMAN, SCHNEIDER, LITERARY AGENTS, INC.

250 W. 57th St., Suite 2515, New York NY 10107. (212)245-1993. Fax: (212)245-8678. **Contact:** Jane Gelfman, Deborah Schneider. Estab. 1981. Member of AAR. Represents 300+ clients. 10% of clients are new/unpublished writers.

Represents Nonfiction books, novels, **Considers these fiction areas:** Literary; mainstream/contemporary; mystery/suspense.

O┳ Does not want to receive romances, science fiction, westerns, or children's books.

How to Contact Query with SASE. No e-mail queries accepted. Responds in 1 month to queries; 2 months to mss. Obtains most new clients through recommendations from others.

Terms Agent receives 15% commission on domestic sales; 20% commission on foreign sales. Offers written contract. Charges clients for photocopying, messengers and couriers.

THE GERSH AGENCY

41 Madison Ave., 33rd Floor, New York NY 10010. (212)997-1818. Website: www.gershcomedy.com. Estab. 1949. Member of AAR.

- Query before submitting.

Member Agents John Buzzetti, Peter Franklin, Peter Hagan.

MARK GILROY COMMUNICATIONS, INC.

6528 E. 101st St., Suite 416, Tulsa OK 74133. (918)607-0069. Fax: (918)298-0041. E-mail: mark@markgilroy.com. Website: www.markgilroy.com. **Contact:** Mark K. Gilroy. Estab. 2001. Represents 10 clients. 50% of clients are new/unpublished writers. Currently handles: 90% nonfiction books; 10% novels.

- Prior to becoming an agent, Mr. Gilroy was executive vice president and publisher of a rapidly growing Christian publishing company that served Christian, general, mass, and special markets.

Represents Nonfiction books, novels. **Considers these nonfiction areas:** Current affairs; government/politics/law; religious/inspirational; self-help/personal improvement. **Considers these fiction areas:** Religious/inspirational.

O┳ Actively seeking Christian fiction, suitable for a general market, conservative political works that focus on values, and unique Christian nonfiction. Does not want autobiographical.

How to Contact Submit outline, 2 sample chapters. Considers simultaneous queries. Responds in 1 week to queries; 1 month to mss. Obtains most new clients through recommendations from others.

Recent Sales Sold 11 titles in the last year. *Entrepreneurial Faith*, by Kirbyjon Caldwell and Walt Kallestad (Waterbrook); *The Secret Blend*, by Stan Toler (Waterbrook); *Get Off My Honor!*, by Hans Zeiger (Broadman & Holman); *Desperate Dependence*, by Max Davis (Cook Communications).

Terms Agent receives 15% commission on domestic sales; 20% commission on foreign sales. Offers written contract, binding for 1 year. Charges up to $100 for postage.

THE GISLASON AGENCY

219 Main St. SE, Suite 506, Minneapolis MN 55414-2160. (612)331-8033. Fax: (612)331-8115. E-mail: gislasonbj@aol.com. Website: www.thegislasonagency.com. **Contact:** Barbara J. Gislason, literary agent. Estab. 1992. Member of Minnesota State Bar Association, American Bar Association, Art & Entertainment Law Section (former chair), Animal Law (section chair), Internet Committee, Minnesota Intellectual Property Law Association Copyright Committee (former chair); also a member of SFWA, MWA, Sisters in Crime, Icelandic Association of Minnesota (former president) and American Academy of Acupuncture and Oriental Medicine (advisory board member). 80% of clients are new/unpublished writers. Currently handles: 10% nonfiction books; 90% novels.

- Ms. Gislason became an attorney in 1980, and continues to practice Art & Entertainment Law. She has been nationally recognized as a Leading American Attorney and a Super Lawyer. She is also the owner of Blue Raven Press, which publishes fiction and nonfiction about animals.

Member Agents Deborah Sweeney (fantasy, science fiction); Kellie Hultgren (fantasy, science fiction); Lisa Higgs (mystery, literary fiction); Kris Olson (mystery); Kevin Hedman (fantasy, science fiction, mystery, literary fiction).

Represents Nonfiction books, novels. **Considers these nonfiction areas:** Animals (behavior/communications). **Considers these fiction areas:** Fantasy; literary; mystery/suspense; science fiction; thriller (legal).

O→ Do not send personal memoirs, poetry, short stories, screenplays, or children's books.

How to Contact For fiction, query with synopsis, first 3 chapters, and SASE. For nonfiction, query with proposal and sample chapters; published authors may submit complete ms. No e-mail or fax queries. Responds in 2 months to queries; 3 months to mss. Obtains most new clients through recommendations from others, conferences, *Guide to Literary Agents, Literary Market Place*, and other reference books.

Recent Sales *Historical Romance #4*, by Linda Cook (Kensington); *Dancing Dead*, by Deborah Woodworth (HarperCollins); *Owen Keane's Lonely Journey*, by Terence Faherty (Harlequin).

Terms Agent receives 15% commission on domestic sales; 20% commission on foreign sales. Offers written contract, binding for 1 year with option to renew. Charges clients for photocopying and postage.

Writers' Conferences SouthWest Writers; Willamette Writers; Wrangling with Writing. Also attends other state and regional writers conferences.

Tips "Cover letter should be well written and include a detailed synopsis (if fiction) or proposal (if nonfiction), the first 3 chapters, and author bio. Appropriate SASE required. We are looking for a great writer with a poetic, lyrical, or quirky writing style who can create intriguing ambiguities. We expect a well-researched, imaginative, and fresh plot that reflects a familiarity with the applicable genre. If submitting nonfiction work, explain how the submission differs from and adds to previously published works in the field. Scenes with sex and violence must be intrinsic to the plot. Remember to proofread. If the work was written with a specific publisher in mind, this should be communicated. In addition to owning an agency, Ms. Gislason practices law in the area of art and entertainment and has a broad spectrum of entertainment industry contacts."

N BARRY GOLDBLATT LITERARY AGENCY, INC.

320 7th Ave., #266, Brooklyn NY 11215. **Contact:** Barry Goldblatt. Member of AAR.

- Query before submitting.

GOLDFARB & ASSOCIATES

721 Gibbon St., Alexandria VA 22314. (202)466-3030. Fax: (703)836-5644. E-mail: rglawlit@aol.com. Website: www.ronaldgoldfarb.com. **Contact:** Ronald Goldfarb. Estab. 1966. Currently handles: 75% nonfiction books; 25% novels; roster of TV and movie projects is rapidly growing (works closely with MainStreet Media, a production company owned by Mr. Goldfarb).

Member Agents Ronald Goldfarb is an experienced trial lawyer and a veteran literary agent, as well as the author of 10 books and over 230 articles. Robbie Anna Hare, a native Australian currently residing in both Israel and the U.S., is a literary agent with experience as a reporter, writer and radio and television producer. Louise Wheatley, whose background is teaching English literature, is an editor who also works with new authors.

Represents Nonfiction books, novels, movie scripts, TV scripts.

O→ "Serious nonfiction is our must active area (with all publishing houses and editors), though we do handle fiction selectively. Our location in the nation's capital enables us to represent many well-known print journalists, TV correspondents, politicians, and policymakers in both fiction and nonfiction fields. But many of our clients come from all over this country and some from abroad."

How to Contact The firm is accepting select new projects, usually on the basis of personal referrals, or from existing clients.

Tips "We are a law firm and a literary agency. Through our work with writers' organizations, we are constantly adding new and talented writers to our list of literary clients, and matching collaborators with projects in need of authors or editors. We have found writers to develop book ideas at the request of publishers."

FRANCES GOLDIN LITERARY AGENCY, INC.

57 E. 11th St., Suite 5B, New York NY 10003. (212)777-0047. Fax: (212)228-1660. E-mail: agency@goldinlit.com. Website: www.goldinlit.com. Estab. 1977. Member of AAR. Represents over 100 clients.

Member Agents Francis Goldin, principal/agent; Sydelle Kramer, agent (works with established academics and young writers interested in breaking into mainstream); Matt McGowan, agent/rights director (innovative works of fiction and nonfiction); Sam Stoloff, agent (literary fiction, memoir, history, accessible sociology and philosophy, cultural studies, serious journalism, narrative and topical nonfiction with a progressive orientation); David Csontos, agent/office manager (literary fiction, biography, memoir, psychology, spirituality, gay and social studies and the arts).

Represents Nonfiction books, novels. **Considers these nonfiction areas:** Serious, controversial nonfiction with a progressive political orientation. **Considers these fiction areas:** Adult literary.

- "We are hands-on, and we work intensively with clients on proposal and manuscript development." Does not want anything that is racist, sexist, agist, homophobic, or pornographic. No screenplays, children's books, art books, cookbooks, business books, diet books, self-help, or genre fiction.

How to Contact Query with SASE. *No unsolicited mss*, or work previously submitted to publishers. No e-mail or fax queries. Responds in 4-6 weeks to queries.

Recent Sales *Skin Deep*, by Dalton Conley (Pantheon); *Conned: How Millions Have Lost the Right to Vote*, by Sasha Abramsky (New Press); *Wake-Up Calls*, by Bruce Grierson (Bloomsbury USA).

GOODMAN ASSOCIATES

500 West End Ave., New York NY 10024-4317. (212)873-4806. **Contact:** Elise Simon Goodman. Estab. 1976. Member of AAR. Represents 50 clients.

- Arnold Goodman is the former chair of the AAR Ethics Committee.

Member Agents Elise Simon Goodman; Arnold P. Goodman.

Represents Nonfiction books, novels. **Considers these nonfiction areas:** Americana; animals; anthropology/archaeology; biography/autobiography; business/economics; child guidance/parenting; cooking/foods/nutrition; creative nonfiction; current affairs; education; ethnic/cultural interests; government/politics/law; health/medicine; history; language/literature/criticism; memoirs; military/war; money/finance; multicultural; music/dance; nature/environment; philosophy; popular culture; psychology; recreation; regional; science/technology; sex; sociology; sports; theater/film; translation; travel; true crime/investigative; women's issues/studies. **Considers these fiction areas:** Action/adventure; contemporary issues; detective/police/crime; erotica; ethnic; family saga; historical; literary; mainstream/contemporary; military/war; multicultural; multimedia; mystery/suspense; regional; sports; thriller; translation.

- Accepting new clients by recommendation only. Does not want to receive poetry, articles, individual stories, children's, or YA material.

How to Contact Query with SASE. Responds in 10 days to queries; 1 month to mss.

Terms Agent receives 15% commission on domestic sales; 20% commission on foreign sales. Charges clients for certain expenses: faxes, toll calls, overseas postage, photocopying, book purchases.

N IRENE GOODMAN LITERARY AGENCY

80 Fifth Ave., Suite 1101, New York NY 10011. **Contact:** Irene Goodman. Member of AAR.

- Query before submitting.

THE THOMAS GRADY AGENCY

209 Bassett St., Petaluma CA 94952-2668. (707)765-6229. Fax: (707)765-6810. E-mail: tom@tgrady.com. Website: www.tgrady.com. **Contact:** Thomas Grady. Member of AAR. 10% of clients are new/unpublished writers.

How to Contact E-mail queries preferred.

THE GRAYBILL & ENGLISH LITERARY AGENCY

1875 Connecticut Ave. NW, Suite 712, Washington DC 20009. (202)956-5131. Fax: (202)457-0662. Website: www.graybillandenglish.com. **Contact:** See website for agents' interests and submission guidelines. Estab. 1997. Member of AAR. Represents 100 clients. 25-50% of clients are new/unpublished writers. Currently handles: 70% nonfiction books; 30% novels.

Member Agents Nina Graybill (serious and narrative nonfiction, literary and literary/commercial fiction); Elaine English (commercial women's fiction, including romance, thrillers and mysteries); Jeff Kleinman (narrative and practical nonfiction, literary and commercial fiction); Lynn Whittaker (sports, literary fiction, mystery/suspense); Kristen Auclair (practical and narrative nonfiction, literary fiction). See agents' individual listings on the website for guideline information.

Represents Adult nonfiction books and adult novels. **Considers these nonfiction areas:** Animals; anthropology/archaeology; biography/autobiography; business/economics; child guidance/parenting; cooking/foods/

nutrition; crafts/hobbies; current affairs; education; ethnic/cultural interests; government/politics/law; health/medicine; history; how-to; humor/satire; memoirs; military/war; nature/environment; popular culture; psychology; self-help/personal improvement; sociology; sports; true crime/investigative; women's issues/studies. **Considers these fiction areas:** Contemporary issues; detective/police/crime; ethnic; family saga; fantasy; feminist; glitz; historical; humor/satire; literary; mainstream/contemporary; mystery/suspense; romance; science fiction; sports; thriller.

O→ Actively seeking narrative, serious and practical nonfiction; literary fiction and well-written commercial (especially women's) fiction. Does not want novellas, short stories, poetry, children's, or young adult books. Very limited science fiction/fantasy.

How to Contact Query with SASE, submit outline/proposal. Considers simultaneous queries. Responds in 2-12 weeks to queries; 3-6 months to requested mss. Returns materials only with SASE. Obtains most new clients through recommendations from others, solicitations, conferences.

Recent Sales *Mansions of the Dead*, by Sarah Stewart Taylor (St. Martin's/Minotaur); *The Mind-Body Diabetes Revolution*, by Richard Surwit, Ph.D. (The Free Press); *The Memory of Running*, by Ron McLarty (Viking); *Open My Eyes, Open My Soul*, by Yolanda King and Elodia Tate (McGraw-Hill); *Mockingbird*, by Charles Shields (Holt); *Journey to the House of War*, by Geneive Abdo (Perseus); *The Butterfly House*, by Marcia Preston (Mira); *The River Devil*, by Diane Whiteside (Brava/Kensington); *Billy, Alfred and the General*, by William Pelfrey (Amacom); *Starmakers*, by Jane Jenkins and Janet Hirshenson (Harcourt).

Terms Agent receives 15% commission on domestic sales; 20% commission on foreign sales. Offers written contract; 1-month notice must be given to terminate contract. Minimal office expenses (copying, postage, phone).

Writers' Conferences Maui Writers Conference (Maui HI); Creative Nonfiction Conference (Baltimore MD); Words and Music Conference (New Orleans LA); Romance Writers of America (Dallas TX); Associated Writing Programs (Vancouver); Bouchercon (various cities); American Society of Writers and Journalists (New York NY); Novelists, Inc. (New York NY).

ASHLEY GRAYSON LITERARY AGENCY

1342 18th St., San Pedro CA 90732. Fax: (310)514-1148. E-mail: graysonagent@earthlink.net. Member of AAR. Represents 100 clients. 5% of clients are new/unpublished writers. Currently handles: 20% nonfiction books; 50% novels; 30% juvenile books.

Member Agents Ashley Grayson (commercial and literary fiction, historical novels, mysteries, science fiction, thrillers, young adult); Carolyn Grayson (mainstream commercial fiction, mainstream women's fiction, romance, crime fiction, suspense, thrillers, horror, true crime, young adult, science, medical, health, self-help, how-to, pop culture, creative nonfiction); Dan Hooker (commercial fiction, mysteries, thrillers, suspense, hard science fiction, contemporary and dark fantasy, horror, young adult and middle grade, popular subjects and treatment with high commercial potential, New Age by published professionals).

O→ "We prefer to work with published (traditional print publishing), established authors. We will give first consideration to authors who come recommended to us by our clients or other publishing professionals. We accept a very small number of new, previously unpublished authors."

How to Contact Submit query by regular post plus first 3 pages of ms or overview of the nonfiction proposal.

Recent Sales Sold more than 100 titles in the last year. *Dreaming Pachinko*, by Isaac Adamson (HarperCollins); *The Sky So Big and Black*, by John Barnes (Tor); *Move Your Stuff, Change Your Life*, by Karen Rauch Carter (Simon & Schuster).

Terms Agent receives 15% commission on domestic sales; 20% commission on foreign sales.

SANFORD J. GREENBURGER ASSOCIATES, INC.

55 Fifth Ave., New York NY 10003. (212)206-5600. Fax: (212)463-8718. Website: www.greenburger.com. **Contact:** Heide Lange. Estab. 1945. Member of AAR. Represents 500 clients.

Member Agents Heide Lange, Faith Hamlin, Dan Mandel, Peter McGuigan, Matthew Bialer.

Represents Nonfiction books, novels. **Considers these nonfiction areas:** Agriculture/horticulture; americana; animals; anthropology/archaeology; art/architecture/design; biography/autobiography; business/economics; child guidance/parenting; computers/electronic; cooking/foods/nutrition; crafts/hobbies; current affairs; education; ethnic/cultural interests; gardening; gay/lesbian issues; government/politics/law; health/medicine; history; how-to; humor/satire; interior design/decorating; juvenile nonfiction; language/literature/criticism; memoirs; military/war; money/finance; multicultural; music/dance; nature/environment; New Age/metaphysics; philosophy; photography; popular culture; psychology; recreation; regional; religious/inspirational; science/technology; self-help/personal improvement; sex; sociology; software; sports; theater/film; translation; travel; true crime/investigative; women's issues/studies; young adult. **Considers these fiction areas:** Action/adventure; contemporary issues; detective/police/crime; ethnic; family saga; feminist; gay/lesbian; glitz; historical;

humor/satire; literary; mainstream/contemporary; mystery/suspense; psychic/supernatural; regional; sports; thriller.

Does not want to receive romances or westerns.

How to Contact Submit query, first 3 chapters, synopsis, brief bio, SASE. Considers simultaneous queries. Responds in 2 months to queries and mss.

Recent Sales Sold 200 titles in the last year. This agency prefers not to share information on specific sales. Clients include Andrew Ross, Margaret Cuthbert, Nicholas Sparks, Mary Kurcinka, Linda Nichols, Edy Clarke, Brad Thor, Dan Brown, Sallie Bissell.

Terms Agent receives 15% commission on domestic sales; 20% commission on foreign sales. Charges for photocopying, books for foreign and subsidiary rights submissions.

GREGORY & CO. AUTHORS' AGENTS

3 Barb Mews, London W6 7PA England. 020-7610-4676. Fax: 020-7610-4686. E-mail: info@gregoryandcompany.co.uk. Website: www.gregoryandcompany.co.uk. **Contact:** Jane Gregory, sales; Anna Valdinger, editorial; Claire Morris, rights. Estab. 1987. Member of Association of Authors' Agents. Represents 60 clients. Currently handles: 10% nonfiction books; 90% novels.

- Prior to becoming an agent, Ms. Gregory was Rights Director for Chatto & Windus.

Represents Nonfiction books, and fiction books. **Considers these nonfiction areas:** Biography/autobiography; history. **Considers these fiction areas:** Detective/police/crime; historical; literary; mainstream/contemporary; thriller; contemporary women's fiction.

"Jane Gregory is successful at selling rights all over the world, including film and television rights. As a British agency we do not generally take on American authors." Actively seeking well-written, accessible modern novels. Does not want to receive horror, science fiction, fantasy, mind/body/spirit, children's books, screenplays and plays, short stories, poetry.

How to Contact Query with SASE, submit outline, 3 sample chapters, SASE. Considers simultaneous queries. Returns materials only with SASE. Obtains most new clients through recommendations from others, conferences.

Recent Sales Sold 100 titles in the last year. *Tokyo*, by Mo Hayder (Bantam UK/Gove Atlantic); *The Torment of Others*, by Val McDermid (HarperCollins UK/St. Martin's Press NY); *Disordered Minds*, by Minette Walters (MacMillan UK/Putnam USA); *The Lover*, by Laura Wilson (Orion UK/Bantam USA); *Gagged & Bound*, by Natasha Cooper (Simon & Schuster UK/St. Martin's Press USA); *Demon of the Air*, by Simon Levack (Simon & Schuster/St. Martin's USA).

Terms Agent receives 15% commission on domestic sales; 20% commission on foreign sales. Offers written contract; 3-month notice must be given to terminate contract. Charges clients for photocopying of whole typescripts and copies of book for submissions.

Writers' Conferences CWA Conference (United Kingdom, Spring); Dead on Deansgate (Manchester, Autumn); Harrogate Literary Festival (United Kingdom, Summer); Bouchercon (location varies, Autumn).

BLANCHE C. GREGORY, INC.

2 Tudor City Place, New York NY 10017. (212)697-0828. Member of AAR.

- Query before submitting.

Member Agents Gertrude Bregman, Merry Gregory Pantano.

MAXINE GROFFSKY LITERARY AGENCY

853 Broadway, Suite 708, New York NY 10003. (212)979-1500. Fax: (212)979-1405. Member of AAR.

- Query before submitting.

JILL GROSJEAN LITERARY AGENCY

1390 Millstone Rd., Sag Harbor NY 11963-2214. (631)725-7419. Fax: (631)725-8632. E-mail: jill6981@aol.com. Website: www.hometown.aol.com/jill6981/myhomepage/index.html. **Contact:** Jill Grosjean. Estab. 1999. Represents 27 clients. 100% of clients are new/unpublished writers. Currently handles: 100% novels.

- Prior to becoming an agent, Ms. Grosjean was manager of an independent bookstore. She also worked in publishing and advertising.

Represents Novels (exclusively). **Considers these fiction areas:** Contemporary issues; historical; literary; mainstream/contemporary; mystery/suspense; regional; romance.

This agency offers some editorial assistance (i.e., line-by-line edits). Actively seeking literary novels and mysteries.

How to Contact Query with SASE. No cold calls, please. Considers simultaneous queries. Responds in 1 week to queries; 1 month to mss. Returns materials only with SASE. Obtains most new clients through recommendations from others, solicitations.

Recent Sales *I Love You Like a Tomato*, by Marie Giordano (Forge Books); *Nectar*, by David C. Fickett (Forge Books); *Cycling* (Kensington), *Crooked Lines* (NavPress) and *Sanctuary* (Kensington), by Greg Garrett; *The Smoke*, by Tony Broadbent (St. Martin's/Minotaur); *Flights of Joy*, by Marie Bostwick (Kensington).

Terms Agent receives 15% commission on domestic sales; 20% commission on foreign sales. No written contract. Charges clients for photocopying, mailing expenses.

Writers' Conferences Book Passages Mystery Writer's Conference (Corte Madera CA, July); Writers' League of Texas Conference (Austin TX, July).

THE GROSVENOR LITERARY AGENCY

5510 Grosvenor Lane, Bethesda MD 20814. Fax: (301)581-9401. E-mail: dcgrosveno@aol.com. **Contact:** Deborah C. Grosvenor. Estab. 1996. Member of National Press Club. Represents 30 clients. 10% of clients are new/unpublished writers. Currently handles: 80% nonfiction books; 20% novels.

- Prior to opening her agency, Ms. Grosvenor was a book editor for 16 years.

Represents Nonfiction books, novels. **Considers these nonfiction areas:** Animals; anthropology/archaeology; art/architecture/design; biography/autobiography; business/economics; child guidance/parenting; current affairs; government/politics/law; health/medicine; history; how-to; language/literature/criticism; military/war; money/finance; music/dance; nature/environment; photography; popular culture; psychology; religious/inspirational; science/technology; self-help/personal improvement; sociology; spirituality; theater/film; translation; true crime/investigative; women's issues/studies. **Considers these fiction areas:** Contemporary issues; detective/police/crime; family saga; historical; literary; mainstream/contemporary; mystery/suspense; romance (contemporary, gothic, historical); thriller.

How to Contact Send outline/proposal for nonfiction; send query and 3 sample chapters for fiction. No fax queries. Responds in 1 month to queries; 2 months to mss. Returns materials only with SASE. Obtains most new clients through recommendations from others.

Terms Agent receives 15% commission on domestic sales; 20% commission on foreign sales. Offers written contract; 10-day notice must be given to terminate contract.

REECE HALSEY NORTH

98 Main St., Tiburon CA 94920. Fax: (310)652-7595. E-mail: info@reecehalseynorth.com. Website: www.reecehalseynorth.com. **Contact:** Kimberley Cameron (all queries) at Reece Halsey North. Estab. 1957 (Reece Halsey Agency); 1993 (Reech Halsey North). Member of AAR. Represents 40 clients. 30% of clients are new/unpublished writers. Currently handles: 25% nonfiction books; 75% fiction.

- The Reece Halsey Agency has an illustrious client list largely of established writers, including the estate of Aldous Huxley, and has represented Upton Sinclair, William Faulkner, and Henry Miller.

Member Agents Dorris Halsey, Reece Halsey Agency (Los Angeles); Kimberley Cameron, Reece Halsey North.

Represents Nonfiction books, novels. **Considers these nonfiction areas:** Biography/autobiography; current affairs; history; language/literature/criticism; popular culture; science/technology; true crime/investigative; women's issues/studies. **Considers these fiction areas:** Action/adventure; contemporary issues; detective/police/crime; ethnic; family saga; historical; literary; mainstream/contemporary; mystery/suspense; science fiction; thriller; women's.

"We are looking for a unique and heartfelt voice."

How to Contact Query with SASE, submit first 10 pages of novel. Please do not fax queries. Responds in 3-6 weeks to queries; 3 months to mss. Obtains most new clients through recommendations from others, solicitations.

Terms Agent receives 15% commission on domestic sales; 10% commission on dramatic rights sales. Offers written contract, binding for 1 year. Requests 6 copies of ms if representing an author.

Writers' Conferences Maui Writers Conference; Aspen; Willamette.

Tips "Always send a well-written query and include a SASE with it."

THE MITCHELL J. HAMILBURG AGENCY

149 S. Barrington Ave., #732, Los Angeles CA 90049-2930. (310)471-4024. Fax: (310)471-9588. **Contact:** Michael Hamilburg. Estab. 1937. Signatory of WGA. Represents 70 clients. Currently handles: 70% nonfiction books; 30% novels.

Represents Nonfiction books, novels. **Considers these nonfiction areas:** Anthropology/archaeology; biography/autobiography; business/economics; child guidance/parenting; cooking/foods/nutrition; creative nonfiction; current affairs; education; government/politics/law; health/medicine; history; memoirs; military/war; money/finance; psychology; recreation; regional; self-help/personal improvement; sex; sociology; spirituality; sports; travel; women's issues/studies; romance; architecture; inspirational; true crime. **Considers these fiction areas:** Action/adventure; experimental; feminist; glitz; humor/satire; military/war; mystery/suspense; New Age; occult; regional; religious/inspirational; romance; sports; thriller; crime; mainstream; psychic.

How to Contact Query with SASE, submit outline, 2 sample chapters. Responds in 1 month to mss. Obtains most new clients through recommendations from others, conferences, personal search.
Terms Agent receives 10-15% commission on domestic sales.

THE JOY HARRIS LITERARY AGENCY, INC.

156 Fifth Ave., Suite 617, New York NY 10010. (212)924-6269. Fax: (212)924-6609. E-mail: gen.office@jhlitagent.com. **Contact:** Joy Harris. Member of AAR. Represents over 100 clients. Currently handles: 50% nonfiction books; 50% novels.
Member Agents Leslie Daniels; Stéphanie Abou; Sara Lustg.
Represents Nonfiction books, novels. **Considers these fiction areas:** Contemporary issues; ethnic; experimental; family saga; feminist; gay/lesbian; glitz; hi-lo; historical; humor/satire; literary; mainstream/contemporary; multicultural; multimedia; mystery/suspense; picture books; regional; short story collections; spiritual; translation; women's.

O→ Does not want to receive screenplays.

How to Contact Query with sample chapter, outline/proposal, SASE. Considers simultaneous queries. Responds in 2 months to queries. Obtains most new clients through recommendations from clients and editors.
Recent Sales This agency prefers not to share information on specific sales.
Terms Agent receives 15% commission on domestic sales; 20% commission on foreign sales. Charges clients for some office expenses.

HARTLINE LITERARY AGENCY

123 Queenston Dr., Pittsburgh PA 15235-5429. (412)829-2495 or 2483. Fax: (412)829-2450. E-mail: joyce@hartlineliterary.com. Website: www.hartlineliterary.com. **Contact:** Joyce A. Hart. Estab. 1990. Represents 40 clients. 30% of clients are new/unpublished writers. Currently handles: 40% nonfiction books; 60% novels.
Member Agents Joyce A. Hart, principal agent; Janet Benrey; Tamela Hancock Murray; Andrea Boeshaar and James D. Hart.
Represents Nonfiction books, novels. **Considers these nonfiction areas:** Business/economics; child guidance/parenting; cooking/foods/nutrition; money/finance; religious/inspirational; self-help/personal improvement; women's issues/studies. **Considers these fiction areas:** Action/adventure; contemporary issues; family saga; historical; literary; mystery/suspense (amateur sleuth, cozy); regional; religious/inspirational; romance (contemporary, gothic, historical, regency); thriller.

O→ This agency specializes in the Christian bookseller market. Actively seeking adult fiction, self-help, nutritional books, devotional, business. Does not want to receive science fiction, erotica, gay/lesbian, fantasy, horror, etc.

How to Contact Submit outline, 3 sample chapters. Accepts e-mail and fax queries. Considers simultaneous queries. Responds in 2 months to queries; 3 months to mss. Returns materials only with SASE. Obtains most new clients through recommendations from others.
Recent Sales *Vanished*, by Ward Tanneberg (Kregel); *Hosea's Bride, Unless Two Agree, Beauty for Ashes* and *Joy for Mourning*, by Dorothy Clark (Steeple Hill); *Dead as a Scone* and *The Final Crumpet*, by Ron and Janet Benrey (Barbour Publishing); *Overcoming the Top Ten Reasons Singles Stay Single*, by Drs. Tom and Beverly Rodgers (NavPress); *A Land of Sheltered Promise* and *Homestead*, by Jane Kirkpatrick (Waterbrook); *An Act of Murder*, by Linda Rosencrance (Kensington); *When Skylarks Fall*, by John Robinson (Riveroak); *Some Welcome Home*, by Sharon Wildwind (Five Star); *Beauty Queens and Front Porch Princesses*, by Kathryn Springer (Steeple Hill); *Sahm I Am*, by Meredith Efken (Steeple Hill); *Disturbing Behavior*, by Lee Virkich and Steve Vandergriff.
Terms Agent receives 15% commission on domestic sales. Offers written contract.

JOHN HAWKINS & ASSOCIATES, INC.

71 W. 23rd St., Suite 1600, New York NY 10010. (212)807-7040. Fax: (212)807-9555. E-mail: jha@jhalit.com. Website: jhaliterary.com. **Contact:** John Hawkins, William Reiss. Estab. 1893. Member of AAR. Represents over 100 clients. 5-10% of clients are new/unpublished writers. Currently handles: 40% nonfiction books; 40% novels; 20% juvenile books.
Member Agents Moses Cardona; Warren Frazier; Anne Hawkins; John Hawkins; William Reiss.
Represents Nonfiction books, novels, juvenile books. **Considers these nonfiction areas:** Agriculture/horticulture; americana; anthropology/archaeology; art/architecture/design; biography/autobiography; business/economics; creative nonfiction; current affairs; education; ethnic/cultural interests; gardening; gay/lesbian issues; government/politics/law; health/medicine; history; how-to; interior design/decorating; language/literature/criticism; memoirs; money/finance; multicultural; nature/environment; philosophy; popular culture; psychology; recreation; science/technology; self-help/personal improvement; sex; sociology; software; theater/film; travel; true crime/investigative; young adult; music. **Considers these fiction areas:** Action/adventure; contem-

porary issues; detective/police/crime; ethnic; experimental; family saga; feminist; gay/lesbian; glitz; gothic; hi-lo; historical; literary; mainstream/contemporary; military/war; multicultural; multimedia; mystery/suspense; psychic/supernatural; religious/inspirational; short story collections; sports; thriller; translation; westerns/frontier; young adult; women's.

How to Contact Query with SASE, submit proposal package, outline. Considers simultaneous queries. Responds in 1 month to queries. Returns materials only with SASE. Obtains most new clients through recommendations from others.

Recent Sales *The Last Shot*, by Lynn Schooler; *Joplin's Ghost*, by Tananarive Due.

Terms Agent receives 15% commission on domestic sales; 20% commission on foreign sales. Charges clients for photocopying.

RICHARD HENSHAW GROUP

127 W. 24th St., 4th Floor, New York NY 10011. (212)414-1172. Fax: (212)414-1182. E-mail: submissions@henshaw.com. Website: www.rich.henshaw.com. **Contact:** Rich Henshaw. Estab. 1995. Member of AAR, SinC, MWA, HWA, SFWA, RWA. Represents 35 clients. 20% of clients are new/unpublished writers. Currently handles: 30% nonfiction books; 70% novels.

- Prior to opening his agency, Mr. Henshaw served as an agent with Richard Curtis Associates, Inc.

Represents Nonfiction books, novels. **Considers these nonfiction areas:** Animals; biography/autobiography; business/economics; child guidance/parenting; computers/electronic; cooking/foods/nutrition; current affairs; gay/lesbian issues; government/politics/law; health/medicine; how-to; humor/satire; military/war; money/finance; music/dance; nature/environment; New Age/metaphysics; popular culture; psychology; science/technology; self-help/personal improvement; sociology; sports; true crime/investigative; women's issues/studies. **Considers these fiction areas:** Action/adventure; detective/police/crime; ethnic; family saga; fantasy; glitz; historical; horror; humor/satire; literary; mainstream/contemporary; mystery/suspense; psychic/supernatural; romance; science fiction; sports; thriller.

O‑ This agency specializes in thrillers, mysteries, science fiction, fantasy, and horror.

How to Contact Query with SASE. Responds in 3 weeks to queries; 6 weeks to mss. Obtains most new clients through recommendations from others, solicitations, conferences.

Recent Sales *A Taint in the Blood*, by Dana Stabenow (St. Martin's); *Wife of Moon*, by Margaret Coel (Berkely); *The Well-Educated Mind*, by Susan Wise Bauer (Norton); *The Witch's Tongue*, by James D. Doss (St. Martin's); *How to Box Like the Pros*, by Joe Frazier and William Dettloff (HarperCollins). Other clients include Jessie Wise, Peter van Dijk, Jay Caselberg, Judith Laik.

Terms Agent receives 15% commission on domestic sales; 20% commission on foreign sales. No written contract. 100% of business is derived from commissions on ms sales. Charges clients for photocopying mss and book orders.

Tips "While we do not have any reason to believe that our submission guidelines will change in the near future, writers can find up-to-date submission policy information on our website. Always include a SASE with correct return postage."

THE JEFF HERMAN AGENCY, LLC

P.O. Box 1522, Stockbridge MA 01262. (413)298-0077. Fax: (413)298-8188. E-mail: jeff@jeffherman.com. Website: www.jeffherman.com. **Contact:** Jeffrey H. Herman. Estab. 1985. Represents 100 clients. 10% of clients are new/unpublished writers. Currently handles: 85% nonfiction books; 5% scholarly books; 5% textbooks.

- Prior to opening his agency, Mr. Herman served as a public relations executive.

Member Agents Deborah Levine (vice president, nonfiction book doctor); Jeff Herman.

Represents Nonfiction books. **Considers these nonfiction areas:** Business/economics; government/politics/law; health/medicine (and recovery issues); history; how-to; psychology (pop); self-help/personal improvement; spirituality; popular reference, technology.

O‑ This agency specializes in adult nonfiction.

How to Contact Query with SASE. Accepts e-mail and fax queries. Considers simultaneous queries.

Recent Sales Sold 35 titles in the last year. This agency prefers not to share information on specific sales.

Terms Agent receives 15% commission on domestic sales. Offers written contract. Charges clients for copying, postage.

SUSAN HERNER RIGHTS AGENCY

P.O. Box 57, Pound Ridge NY 10576. (914)234-2864. Fax: (914)234-2866. E-mail: sherneragency@optonline.net. **Contact:** Susan Herner. Estab. 1987. Represents 100 clients. 30% of clients are new/unpublished writers. Currently handles: 60% nonfiction books; 40% novels.

Member Agents Susan Herner, president (nonfiction, thriller, mystery, strong women's fiction).

Represents Nonfiction books (adult), novels (adult). **Considers these nonfiction areas:** Anthropology/archaeology; child guidance/parenting; current affairs; ethnic/cultural interests; gay/lesbian issues; government/politics/law; health/medicine; history; how-to; language/literature/criticism; nature/environment; New Age/metaphysics; popular culture; psychology; religious/inspirational; science/technology; self-help/personal improvement; sociology; spirituality; true crime/investigative; women's issues/studies; biography. **Considers these fiction areas:** Action/adventure; contemporary issues; detective/police/crime; ethnic; feminist; glitz; literary; mainstream/contemporary; mystery/suspense; thriller.

O‑ "I'm particularly looking for strong women's fiction and thrillers. I'm particularly interested in women's issues, popular science, and feminist spirituality."

How to Contact Query with SASE, outline, sample chapters, or query by e-mail (no attachments). Considers simultaneous queries. Responds in 1 month to queries. Returns materials only with SASE.

Recent Sales *Heartwood*, by Barbara Campbell (Daw Books); *Our Improbable Universe*, by Michael Mallary (4 Walls 8 Windows); *Everything You Need to Know About Latino History*, by Himilce Novas (Plume).

Terms Agent receives 15% commission on domestic sales; 20% commission on foreign sales; 20% commission on dramatic rights sales. Charges clients for extraordinary postage and photocopying. "Agency has 2 divisions: one represents writers on a commission-only basis; the other represents the rights for small publishers and packagers who do not have in-house subsidiary rights representation. Percentage of income derived from each division is currently 80-20."

Literary Agents

FREDERICK HILL BONNIE NADELL, INC.

1842 Union St., San Francisco CA 94123. (415)921-2910. Fax: (415)921-2802. **Contact:** Irene Moore. Estab. 1979. Represents 100 clients.

Member Agents Fred Hill (president); Bonnie Nadell (vice president); Irene Moore (associate).

Represents Nonfiction books, novels. **Considers these nonfiction areas:** Current affairs; language/literature/criticism; nature/environment; biography; government/politics. **Considers these fiction areas:** Literary; mainstream/contemporary.

How to Contact Query with SASE. No e-mail or fax queries. Considers simultaneous queries. Returns materials only with SASE.

Recent Sales *Field Guide to Getting Lost*, by Rebecca Solnit; *All That Matters*, by Senator Barbara Boxer; *Cancer Made Me a Shallower Person*, by Miriam Enjelberg.

Terms Agent receives 15% commission on domestic sales; 20% commission on foreign sales; 15% commission on dramatic rights sales. Charges clients for photocopying.

JOHN L. HOCHMANN BOOKS

320 E. 58th St., New York NY 10022-2220. (212)319-0505. **Contact:** Theadora Eagle. Director: John L. Hochmann. Estab. 1976. Member of PEN. Represents 23 clients. Currently handles: 100% nonfiction books.

Member Agents Theodora Eagle (popular medical and nutrition books).

Represents Nonfiction books, textbooks (college). **Considers these nonfiction areas:** Anthropology/archaeology; art/architecture/design; biography/autobiography; cooking/foods/nutrition; current affairs; gay/lesbian issues; government/politics/law; health/medicine; history; military/war; music/dance; sociology; theater/film.

O‑ This agency specializes in nonfiction books. "Writers must have demonstrable eminence in field or previous publications."

How to Contact Query first with detailed chapter outline, titles, and sample reviews of previously published books. Responds in 1 week to queries. Responds in 1 month to solicited mss. Obtains most new clients through recommendations from authors and editors.

Recent Sales Sold 6 titles in the last year. *Granite and Rainbow: The Life of Virginia Woolf*, by Mitchell Leaska (Farrar, Straus & Giroux); *Manuel Puig and the Spider Woman*, by Suzanne Jill Levine (Farrar, Straus & Giroux); *Part-Time Vegetarian*, by Louise Lambert-Lagasse (Stoddart).

Terms Agent receives 15% commission on domestic sales.

Tips "Detailed outlines are read carefully; letters and proposals written like flap copy get chucked. We make multiple submissions to editors, but we do not accept multiple submissions from authors. Why? Editors are on salary, but we work for commission, and do not have time to read manuscripts on spec."

BARBARA HOGENSON AGENCY

165 West End Ave., Suite 19-C, New York NY 10023. (212)874-8084. Fax: (212)362-3011. **Contact:** Barbara Hogenson. Member of AAR.

- Query before submitting.

HOPKINS LITERARY ASSOCIATES

2117 Buffalo Rd., Suite 327, Rochester NY 14624-1507. (585)352-6268. **Contact:** Pam Hopkins. Estab. 1996. Member of AAR, RWA. Represents 30 clients. 5% of clients are new/unpublished writers. Currently handles: 100% novels.

Represents Novels. **Considers these fiction areas:** Historical; mainstream/contemporary; romance; women's.

O→ This agency specializes in women's fiction, particularly historical, contemporary, and category romance, as well as mainstream work.

How to Contact Submit outline, 3 sample chapters. No e-mail or fax queries. Considers simultaneous queries. Responds in 2 weeks to queries; 1 month to mss. Returns materials only with SASE. Obtains most new clients through recommendations from others, solicitations, conferences.

Recent Sales Sold 50 titles in the last year. *The First Mistake*, by Merline Lovelace (Mira); *The Romantic*, by Madeline Hunter (Bantam); *The Damsel in this Dress*, by Marianne Stillings (Avon).

Terms Agent receives 15% commission on domestic sales; 20% commission on foreign sales. No written contract.

Writers' Conferences Romance Writers of America.

HORNFISCHER LITERARY MANAGEMENT, INC.

P.O. Box 50544, Austin TX 78763. E-mail: jim@hornfischerlit.com. Website: www.hornfischerlit.com. **Contact:** James D. Hornfischer, president. Estab. 2001. Represents 45 clients. 20% of clients are new/unpublished writers. Currently handles: 100% nonfiction books.

- Prior to opening his agency, Mr. Hornfischer was an agent with Literary Group International and held editorial positions at HarperCollins and McGraw-Hill. "I work hard to make an author's first trip to market a successful one. That means closely working with my clients prior to submission to produce the strongest possible book proposal or manuscript. My New York editorial background, at HarperCollins and McGraw-Hill, where I worked on books by a variety of best-selling authors such as Erma Bombeck, Jared Diamond, and Erica Jong among others, is useful in this regard. In 13 years as an agent I've handled 4 No. 1 *New York Times* nonfiction bestsellers."

Represents Nonfiction books. **Considers these nonfiction areas:** Anthropology/archaeology; biography/autobiography; business/economics; child guidance/parenting; current affairs; government/politics/law; health/medicine; history; how-to; humor/satire; memoirs; military/war; money/finance; multicultural; nature/environment; popular culture; psychology; religious/inspirational; science/technology; self-help/personal improvement; sociology; sports; true crime/investigative.

O→ Actively seeking the best work of terrific writers. Does not want poetry, fiction.

How to Contact Submit proposal package, outline, 2 sample chapters. Considers simultaneous queries. Responds in 6-8 weeks to queries. Returns materials only with SASE. Obtains most new clients through referrals from clients; reading books and magazines; pursuing ideas with New York editors.

Recent Sales See website for sales information.

Terms Agent receives 15% commission on domestic sales; 25% commission on foreign sales. Offers written contract. Reasonable expenses deducted from proceeds after book is sold.

Tips "When you query agents and send out proposals, present yourself as someone who's in command of his material and comfortable in his own skin. Too many writers have a palpable sense of anxiety and insecurity. Take a deep breath and realize that—if you're good—someone in the publishing world will want you."

IMPRINT AGENCY, INC.

5 W. 101 St., Suite 8B, New York NY 10025. E-mail: imprintagency@earthlink.net. **Contact:** Stephany Evans. Member of AAR.

- Query before submitting.

INKWELL MANAGEMENT, LLC

521 Fifth Ave., 26th Floor, New York NY 10175. (212)922-3500. Fax: (212)922-0535. E-mail: contact@inkwellmanagement.com. Estab. 2004. Represents 500 clients. Currently handles: 60% nonfiction books; 40% novels.

Member Agents Michael Carlisle; Richard Pine; Kimberly Witherspoon; George Lucas; Catherine Drayton; Matthew Guma.

Represents Nonfiction books, novels. **Considers these nonfiction areas:** Business/economics; current affairs; health/medicine; money/finance; psychology; self-help/personal improvement. **Considers these fiction areas:** Detective/police/crime; family saga; historical; literary; mainstream/contemporary; thriller.

How to Contact Query with SASE. Prefers to read materials exclusively. No e-mail or fax queries. Responds in 1 month to queries. Obtains most new clients through recommendations from others.

Recent Sales Sold 100 titles in the last year.

Terms Agent receives 15% commission on domestic sales; 15% commission on foreign sales. Offers written contract.

Tips "Our agency will consider exclusive submissions only. All submissions must be accompanied by postage or SASE. We will not read manuscripts before receiving a letter of inquiry."

INTERNATIONAL CREATIVE MANAGEMENT

40 W. 57th St., New York NY 10019. (212)556-5600. Fax: (212)556-5665. **Contact:** Literary Department. Member of AAR; signatory of WGA.

Member Agents Esther Newberg and Amanda Urban, department heads; Richard Abate; Lisa Bankoff; Kristine Dahl; Mitch Douglas; Sloan Harris; Jennifer Joel; Liz Farrell; Heather Schroder.

How to Contact Not currently accepting submissions. Obtains most new clients through recommendations from others.

Terms Agent receives 15% commission on domestic sales; 20% commission on foreign sales.

J DE S ASSOCIATES, INC.

9 Shagbark Rd., Wilson Point, South Norwalk CT 06854. (203)838-7571. **Contact:** Jacques de Spoelberch. Estab. 1975. Represents 50 clients. Currently handles: 50% nonfiction books; 50% novels.

- Prior to opening his agency, Mr. de Spoelberch was an editor with Houghton Mifflin.

Represents Nonfiction books, novels. **Considers these nonfiction areas:** Biography/autobiography; business/economics; current affairs; ethnic/cultural interests; government/politics/law; health/medicine; history; military/war; New Age/metaphysics; self-help/personal improvement; sociology; sports; translation. **Considers these fiction areas:** Detective/police/crime; historical; juvenile; literary; mainstream/contemporary; mystery/suspense; New Age; westerns/frontier; young adult.

How to Contact Query with SASE. Responds in 2 months to queries. Obtains most new clients through recommendations from authors and other clients.

Terms Agent receives 15% commission on domestic sales; 20% commission on foreign sales. Charges clients for foreign postage and photocopying.

JABBERWOCKY LITERARY AGENCY

P.O. Box 4558, Sunnyside NY 11104-0558. (718)392-5985. Website: awfulagent.com. **Contact:** Joshua Bilmes. Estab. 1994. Member of SFWA. Represents 40 clients. 15% of clients are new/unpublished writers. Currently handles: 15% nonfiction books; 75% novels; 5% scholarly books; 5% other.

Represents Nonfiction books, novels, scholarly books. **Considers these nonfiction areas:** Biography/autobiography; business/economics; cooking/foods/nutrition; current affairs; gay/lesbian issues; government/politics/law; health/medicine; history; humor/satire; language/literature/criticism; military/war; money/finance; nature/environment; popular culture; science/technology; sociology; sports; theater/film; true crime/investigative; women's issues/studies. **Considers these fiction areas:** Action/adventure; contemporary issues; detective/police/crime; ethnic; family saga; fantasy; gay/lesbian; glitz; historical; horror; humor/satire; literary; mainstream/contemporary; psychic/supernatural; regional; science fiction; sports; thriller.

O→ This agency represents quite a lot of genre fiction and is actively seeking to increase the amount of nonfiction projects. It does not handle juvenile or young adult. Book-length material only; no poetry, articles, or short fiction.

How to Contact Query with SASE. No mss unless requested. No e-mail or fax queries. Considers simultaneous queries. Responds in 2 weeks to queries. Returns materials only with SASE. Obtains most new clients through solicitations, recommendation by current clients.

Recent Sales Sold 20 titles in the last year. *Dead as a Doornail*, by Charlaine Harris (ACE); *Marque & Reprisal*, by Elizabeth Moon (Del Rey); *Elantris*, by Brandon Sanderson (Tor). Other clients include Simon Green, Tanya Huff and "Hot Blood and "Dark Delicacies" anthology series.

Terms Agent receives 15% commission on domestic sales; 20% commission on foreign sales. Offers written contract, binding for 1 year. Charges clients for book purchases, photocopying, international book/ms mailing.

Writers' Conferences Malice Domestic (Washington DC, May); World SF Convention (Los Angeles, August); Icon (Stony Brook NY, April).

Tips "In approaching with a query, the most important things to me are your credits and your biographical background to the extent it's relevant to your work. I (and most agents) will ignore the adjectives you may choose to describe your own work."

JAMES PETER ASSOCIATES, INC.

P.O. Box 358, New Canaan CT 06840. (203)972-1070. E-mail: gene_brissie@msn.com. **Contact:** Gene Brissie. Estab. 1971. Represents 75 individual and 6 corporate clients. 15% of clients are new/unpublished writers. Currently handles: 100% nonfiction books.

Represents Nonfiction books. **Considers these nonfiction areas:** Anthropology/archaeology; art/architecture/design; biography/autobiography; business/economics; child guidance/parenting; current affairs; ethnic/cultural interests; gay/lesbian issues; government/politics/law; health/medicine; history; language/literature/criticism; memoirs (political or business); military/war; money/finance; music/dance; popular culture; psychology; self-help/personal improvement; theater/film; travel; women's issues/studies.

O→ This agency specializes in all categories of nonfiction. "We are especially interested in general, trade, and reference." Actively seeking "good ideas in all areas of adult nonfiction." Does not want to receive "children's and young adult books, poetry, fiction."

How to Contact Submit proposal package, outline, SASE. Prefers to read materials exclusively. No e-mail or fax queries. Responds in 1 month to queries. Returns materials only with SASE. Obtains most new clients through recommendations from others, solicitations, contact "with people who are doing interesting things."

Recent Sales Sold 50 titles in the last year. *Nothing to Fear*, by Dr. Alan Axelrod (Prentice-Hall); *The Right Way*, by Mark Smith, Esq. (Regnery); *Churchill's Folly*, by Christopher Catherwood (Carroll & Graf); *The Encyclopedia of Cancer*, by Carol Turkington (Facts on File); *The Lazy Person's Guide to Investing*, by Paul Farrell (Warner Books); *The Subject Is Left-Handed*, by Barney Rosset (Algonquin Books); *It's OK to Be Neurotic*, by Dr. Frank Bruno (Adams Media).

Terms Agent receives 15% commission on domestic sales; 20% commission on foreign sales. Offers written contract.

JANKLOW & NESBIT ASSOCIATES

445 Park Ave., New York NY 10022. (212)421-1700. Fax: (212)980-3671. **Contact:** Morton L. Janklow; Lynn Nesbit. Estab. 1989. Member of AAR.

Member Agents Tina Bennett; Luke Janklow; Richard Morris; Eric Simonoff; Anne Sibbald; Cullen Stanley; Rebecca Gradinger.

Represents Nonfiction books (commerical and literary), novels (commercial and literary).

JCA LITERARY AGENCY

174 Sullivan St., New York NY 10012. (212)807-0888. E-mail: tom@jcalit.com. Website: www.jcalit.com. **Contact:** Tom Cushman. Estab. 1978. Member of AAR. Represents 100 clients. 10% of clients are new/unpublished writers. Currently handles: 20% nonfiction books; 75% novels; 5% scholarly books.

Member Agents Tom Cushman, Melanie Meyers Cushman, Tony Outhwaite.

Represents Nonfiction books, novels. **Considers these nonfiction areas:** Biography/autobiography; business/economics; current affairs; government/politics/law; history; language/literature/criticism; memoirs; military/war; money/finance; nature/environment; popular culture; science/technology; sociology; sports; theater/film; translation; true crime/investigative. **Considers these fiction areas:** Action/adventure; contemporary issues; detective/police/crime; family saga; historical; literary; mainstream/contemporary; mystery/suspense; sports; thriller.

O→ Does not want to receive screenplays, poetry, children's books, science fiction/fantasy, genre romance.

How to Contact Query with SASE. No e-mail or fax queries. Considers simultaneous queries. Responds in 2 weeks to queries; 10 weeks to mss. Returns materials only with SASE. Obtains most new clients through recommendations from others, solicitations, conferences.

Recent Sales *Jury of One*, by David Ellis (Putnam); *The Heaven of Mercury*, by Brad Watson (Norton); *The Rope Eater*, by Ben Jones; *The Circus in Winter*, by Cathy Dial. Other clients include Ernest J. Gaines, Gwen Hunter.

Terms Agent receives 15% commission on domestic sales; 20% commission on foreign sales. No written contract. "We work with our clients on a handshake basis." Charges for postage on overseas submissions, photocopying, mss for submission, books purchased for subrights submission, and bank charges, where applicable. "We deduct the cost from payments received from publishers."

Tips "We do not ourselves provide legal, accounting, or public relations services for our clients, although some of the advice we give falls somewhat into these realms. In cases where it seems necessary we will recommend obtaining outside advice or assistance in these areas from professionals who are not in any way connected to the agency."

N JELLINEK & MURRAY LITERARY AGENCY

2024 Muana Place, Honolulu HI 96822. (808)521-4057. Fax: (808)521-4058. E-mail: jellinek@lava.net. **Contact:** Roger Jellinek. Estab. 1995. Represents 75 clients. 90% of clients are new/unpublished writers. Currently handles: 70% nonfiction books; 30% novels.

- Prior to becoming an agent, Mr. Jellinek was deputy editor, *New York Times Book Review* (1966-74); Editor-in-Chief, New York Times Book Co. (1975-1981); editor/packager book/TV projects (1981-1995); Editorial Director, Inner Ocean Publishing (2000-2003).

Member Agents Roger Jellinek (general fiction, nonfiction); Eden Lee Murray (general fiction, nonfiction).

Represents Nonfiction books, novels, textbooks, movie scripts (from book clients), TV scripts (from book clients). **Considers these nonfiction areas:** Animals; anthropology/archaeology; art/architecture/design; biography/autobiography; business/economics; child guidance/parenting; computers/electronic; cooking/foods/nutrition; current affairs; ethnic/cultural interests; gay/lesbian issues; government/politics/law; health/medicine; history; how-to; memoirs; military/war; money/finance; nature/environment; New Age/metaphysics; popular culture; psychology; religious/inspirational; science/technology; self-help/personal improvement; travel; true crime/investigative; women's issues/studies. **Considers these fiction areas:** Action/adventure; confession; contemporary issues; detective/police/crime; erotica; ethnic; family saga; feminist; gay/lesbian; glitz; historical; horror; humor/satire; literary; mainstream/contemporary; multicultural; mystery/suspense; New Age; picture books; psychic/supernatural; regional (specific to Hawaii); thriller.

O→ This agency is the only literary agency in Hawaii. "Half our clients are based in Hawaii; half from all over the world. We prefer submissions (after query) via e-mail attachment. We only send out fully-edited proposals and manuscripts." Actively seeking first-rate writing.

How to Contact Query with SASE, submit outline, 2 sample chapters, author bio, credentials/platform. Accepts e-mail and fax queries. Considers simultaneous queries. Responds in 2-3 weeks to queries; 2 months to mss. Returns materials only with SASE. Obtains most new clients through recommendations from others, solicitations, conferences.

Recent Sales Sold 10 titles and sold 1 script in the last year.

Terms Agent receives 15% commission on domestic sales; 25% commission on foreign sales. Offers written contract, binding for indefinite period; 30-day notice must be given to terminate contract. Charges clients for photocopies and postage. May refer to editing services occasionally, if author asks for recommendation. "We have no income deriving from our referrals. Referrals to editors do not imply representation."

Writers' Conferences Mr. Jellinek manages the publishing program at the Maui Writers Conference.

Tips "Would-be authors should be well read and knowledgeable about their field and genre."

NATASHA KERN LITERARY AGENCY

P.O. Box 2908, Portland OR 97208-2908. (503)297-6190. Website: www.natashakern.com. **Contact:** Natasha Kern. Estab. 1986. Member of RWA, MWA, SinC.

- Prior to opening her agency, Ms. Kern worked as an editor and publicist for New York publishers (Simon & Schuster, Bantam, Ballantine). "This agency has sold over 600 books."

Represents Adult commercial nonfiction and fiction. **Considers these nonfiction areas:** Animals; anthropology/archaeology; business/economics; child guidance/parenting; current affairs; ethnic/cultural interests; gardening; health/medicine; nature/environment; New Age/metaphysics; popular culture; psychology; religious/inspirational; science/technology; self-help/personal improvement; spirituality; women's issues/studies; investigative journalism. **Considers these fiction areas:** Historical; mainstream/contemporary; multicultural; mystery/suspense; religious/inspirational; romance (contemporary, historical); thriller (medical, scientific, historical); chick lit; lady lit.

O→ This agency specializes in commercial fiction and nonfiction for adults. "We are a full-service agency." Does not represent sports, true crime, scholarly works, coffee table books, war memoirs, software, scripts, literary fiction, photography, poetry, short stories, children's, horror, fantasy, genre science fiction, stage plays, or traditional Westerns.

How to Contact Query with SASE, include submission history, writing credits, length of ms. Considers simultaneous queries. Responds in 3 weeks to queries.

Recent Sales Sold 53 titles in the last year. *Beyond the Shadows*, by Robin Lee Hatcher (Tyndale); *The Waiting Child*, by Cindy Champnella; *Perfect Killer*, by Lewis Perdue (TOR); *The Secret Lives of the Sushi Club*, by Christy Yorke; *Ride the Fire*, by Pamela Clare (Leisure).

Terms Agent receives 15% commission on domestic sales; 20% commission on foreign sales; 15% commission on dramatic rights sales.

Writers' Conferences RWA National Conference; MWA National Conference; and many regional conferences.

Tips "Your chances of being accepted for representation will be greatly enhanced by going to our website first. Our idea of a dream client is someone who participates in a mutually respectful business relationship, is clear about needs and goals, and communicates about career planning. If we know what you need and want, we can help you achieve it. A dream client has a storytelling gift, a commitment to a writing career, a desire to learn and grow, and a passion for excellence. We want clients who are expressing their own unique voice and truly have something of their own to communicate. This client understands that many people have to work together for a book to succeed and that everything in publishing takes far longer than one imagines. Trust and communication are truly essential."

KIRCHOFF/WOHLBERG, INC., AUTHORS' REPRESENTATION DIVISION

866 United Nations Plaza, #525, New York NY 10017. (212)644-2020. Fax: (212)223-4387. **Contact:** Liza Pulitzer Voges. Director of Operations: John R. Whitman. Estab. 1930s. Member of AAR, AAP, Society of Illustrators, SPAR, Bookbuilders of Boston, New York Bookbinders' Guild, AIGA. Represents 50 clients. 10% of clients are new/unpublished writers. Currently handles: 5% nonfiction books; 25% novels; 5% young adult; 65% picture books.

• Kirchoff/Wohlberg has been in business for over 60 years.

Member Agents Liza Pulitzer Voges (juvenile and young adult authors).

O━ This agency specializes in only juvenile through young adult trade books.

How to Contact Query with SASE, outline, a few sample chapters, for novels. For picture book submissions, please send entire ms. SASE required. No e-mail or fax queries. Considers simultaneous queries. Responds in 1 month to queries; 2 months to mss. Returns materials only with SASE. Obtains most new clients through recommendations from authors, illustrators, and editors.

Recent Sales Sold over 50 titles in the last year. *Three Nasty Gnarlies*, by Keith Graves (Scholastic); *Chu Ju's House*, by Gloria Whelan (HarperCollins); My Weird School Series, by Dan Gutman (HarperCollins).

Terms Offers written contract, binding for no less than 1 year. Agent receives standard commission, "depending upon whether it is an author only, illustrator only, or an author/illustrator book."

☐ KISSED PUBLICATIONS & LITERARY AGENCY

P.O. Box 9819, Hampton VA 23670. (757)722-3031. Fax: (757)722-1301. E-mail: kissed@kissedpublications.com. Website: www.kissedpublications.com. **Contact:** Kimberly T. Matthews. Estab. 2003. Member of Better Business Bureau. Currently handles: 10% nonfiction books; 90% novels.

• Prior to becoming an agent, Ms. Matthews was an author and speaker.

Represents Nonfiction books, novels, short story collections. **Considers these nonfiction areas:** Religious/inspirational. **Considers these fiction areas:** Ethnic; mainstream/contemporary; religious/inspirational; young adult; inspirational.

O━ This agency specializes in African-American mainstream fiction and inspirational nonfiction. Actively seeking new, unpublished authors/clients.

How to Contact Query with SASE. Accepts e-mail queries. No fax queries. Considers simultaneous queries. Responds in 2 weeks to queries; 8 weeks to mss. Returns materials only with SASE.

Terms Agent receives 15% commission on domestic sales; 20% commission on foreign sales. Offers written contract. Charges authors for postage and photocopying.

Literary Agents

HARVEY KLINGER, INC.

301 W. 53rd St., Suite 21-A, New York NY 10019. (212)581-7068. Fax: (212)315-3823. E-mail: queries@harveyklinger.com. Website: www.harveyklinger.com. **Contact:** Harvey Klinger. Estab. 1977. Member of AAR. Represents 100 clients. 25% of clients are new/unpublished writers. Currently handles: 50% nonfiction books; 50% novels.

Member Agents David Dunton (popular culture, with a speciality in music-related books; literary fiction; crime novels; thrillers); Wendy Silbert (narrative nonfiction; historical narrative nonfiction; politics; history; biographies; memoir; literary ficiton; business books; culinary narratives); Sara Crowe (children's and young adult authors, some adult authors, foreign rights sales).

Represents Nonfiction books, novels. **Considers these nonfiction areas:** Biography/autobiography; cooking/foods/nutrition; health/medicine; psychology; science/technology; self-help/personal improvement; spirituality; sports; true crime/investigative; women's issues/studies. **Considers these fiction areas:** Action/adventure; detective/police/crime; family saga; glitz; literary; mainstream/contemporary; mystery/suspense; thriller.

O━ This agency specializes in "big, mainstream, contemporary fiction and nonfiction."

How to Contact Query with SASE. No phone queries. Accepts e-mail queries. No fax queries. Responds in 2 months to queries and mss. Obtains most new clients through recommendations from others.

Recent Sales *The Red Hat Society: Fun & Friendship After Fifty*, by Sue Ellen Cooper; *Wilco: Learning How to Die*, by Greg Kot; *A Window Across the River*, by Brian Morton; *The Sweet Potato Queen's Field Guide to Men: Every Man I Love Is Either Gay, Married, or Dead*, by Jill Conner Browne; *Get Your Share: A Guide to Striking it Rich in the Stock Market*, by Julie Stav; *Wink: The Incredible Life & Epic Journey of Jimmy Winkfield*, by Ed Hotaling. Other clients include Barbara Wood, Terry Kay, Barbara De Angelis, Jeremy Jackson.

Terms Agent receives 15% commission on domestic sales; 25% commission on foreign sales. Offers written contract. Charges for photocopying mss, overseas postage for mss.

THE KNIGHT AGENCY

577 S. Main St., Madison GA 30650. E-mail: submissions@knightagency.net. Website: www.knightagency.net. **Contact:** Judson Knight, ms coordinator. Estab. 1996. Member of AAR, RWA, Authors Guild. Represents 65 clients. 40% of clients are new/unpublished writers. Currently handles: 50% nonfiction books; 50% novels.

Member Agents Deidre Knight (president, agent); Pamela Harty (agent); Nephele Tempest.

Represents Nonfiction books, novels. **Considers these nonfiction areas:** Business/economics; child guidance/parenting; current affairs; ethnic/cultural interests; health/medicine; history; how-to; money/finance; popular culture; psychology; religious/inspirational; self-help/personal improvement; theater/film. **Considers these**

fiction areas: Literary; mainstream/contemporary (commercial); romance (contemporary, paranormal, romantic suspense, historical, inspirational); women's.

O-■ "We are looking for a wide variety of fiction and nonfiction. In the nonfiction area, we're particularly eager to find personal finance, business investment, pop culture, self-help/motivational and popular reference books. In fiction, we're always looking for romance; women's fiction; commercial fiction; literary and multicultural fiction." Does not want science fiction/fantasy, mysteries, action/adventure, horror, short story or poetry collections.

How to Contact Query with SASE. Accepts e-mail queries; no attachments. No phone queries, please. Considers simultaneous queries. Responds in 1-3 weeks to queries; 3 months to mss.

Recent Sales Sold approximately 65 titles in the last year. *Soul Journey*, by Jacquelin Thomas (BET/New Spirit); *Heart Duel*, by Robin Owens (Berkley); *Pink Slip Party*, by Cara Lockwood (Pocket Books/Downtown Press).

Terms Agent receives 15% commission on domestic sales; 20-25% commission on foreign sales. Offers written contract, binding for 1 year; 1-month notice must be given to terminate contract. Charges clients for photocopying, postage, overnight courier expenses. "These are deducted from the sale of the work, not billed upfront."

Tips "At the Knight Agency, a client usually ends up becoming a friend."

LINDA KONNER LITERARY AGENCY

10 W. 15th St., Suite 1918, New York NY 10011-6829. (212)691-3419. E-mail: ldkonner@cs.com. **Contact:** Linda Konner. Estab. 1996. Member of AAR, ASJA; signatory of WGA. Represents 85 clients. 30-35% of clients are new/unpublished writers. Currently handles: 100% nonfiction books.

Represents Nonfiction books (adult only). **Considers these nonfiction areas:** Gay/lesbian issues; health/medicine (diet/nutrition/fitness); how-to; money/finance (personal finance); popular culture; psychology; self-help/personal improvement; women's issues; African American and Latino issues; business; parenting; relationships.

O-■ This agency specializes in health, self-help and how-to books.

How to Contact Query with SASE, synopsis, author bio, sufficient return postage. Prefers to read materials exclusively for 2 weeks. Considers simultaneous queries. Obtains most new clients through recommendations from others, occasional solicitation among established authors/journalists.

Recent Sales Sold 26 titles in the last year. *The Ultimate Body*, by Liz Neporent (Ballantine); *Strength for Their Journey: The Five Disciplines Every African-American Parent Must Teach Her Child*, by Robert Johnson, M.D., and Paulette Stanford, M.D., (Doubleday).

Terms Agent receives 15% commission on domestic sales; 25% commission on foreign sales. Offers written contract. Charges $85 one-time fee for domestic expenses; additional expenses may be incurred for foreign sales.

Writers' Conferences American Society of Journalists and Authors (New York City, Spring).

ELAINE KOSTER LITERARY AGENCY, LLC

55 Central Park W., Suite 6, New York NY 10023. (212)362-9488. Fax: (212)712-0164. **Contact:** Elaine Koster, Stephanie Lehmann. Member of AAR, MWA. Represents 40 clients. 10% of clients are new/unpublished writers. Currently handles: 30% nonfiction books; 70% novels.

- Prior to opening her agency in 1998, Ms. Koster was president and publisher of Dutton NAL.

Represents Nonfiction books, novels. **Considers these nonfiction areas:** Biography/autobiography; business/economics; child guidance/parenting; cooking/foods/nutrition; current affairs; ethnic/cultural interests; health/medicine; history; how-to; money/finance; nature/environment; popular culture; psychology; self-help/personal improvement; spirituality; women's issues/studies. **Considers these fiction areas:** Contemporary issues; detective/police/crime; ethnic; family saga; feminist; historical; literary; mainstream/contemporary; mystery/suspense (amateur sleuth, cozy, culinary, malice domestic); regional; thriller; chick lit.

O-■ This agency specializes in quality fiction and nonfiction. Does not want to receive juvenile, screenplays, or science fiction.

How to Contact Query with SASE, outline, 3 sample chapters. Prefers to read materials exclusively. No e-mail or fax queries. Responds in 3 weeks to queries; 1 month to mss. Returns materials only with SASE. Obtains most new clients through recommendations from others.

Recent Sales Sold 42 titles in the last year. *Dreaming in Titanic City*, by Khaled Hosseini (Riverhead); *The Nineteenth Wife*, by David Ebershoff (Random House); *Run the Risk*, by Scott Frost (Putnam).

Terms Agent receives 15% commission on domestic sales. Bills back specific expenses incurred doing business for a client.

Tips "We prefer exclusive submissions. Don't e-mail or fax submissions. Please include biographical information and publishing history."

BARBARA S. KOUTS, LITERARY AGENT

P.O. Box 560, Bellport NY 11713. (631)286-1278. Fax: (631) 286-1538. **Contact:** Barbara Kouts. Estab. 1980. Member of AAR. Represents 50 clients. 10% of clients are new/unpublished writers. Currently handles: juvenile books.

Represents Juvenile books.

O→ This agency specializes in children's books.

How to Contact Query with SASE. Considers simultaneous queries. Responds in 1 week to queries; 2 months to mss. Obtains most new clients through recommendations from others, solicitations, conferences.

Terms Agent receives 10% commission on domestic sales; 20% commission on foreign sales. Charges clients for photocopying.

Tips "Write, do not call. Be professional in your writing."

KRAAS LITERARY AGENCY

13514 Winter Creek Ct., Houston TX 77077. (281)870-9770. Fax: (281)679-1655. **Contact:** Irene Kraas. Address Other: 3447 NE 23rd Ave., Portland OR 97212. (503)319-0900. **Contact:** Ashley Kraas. Estab. 1990. Represents 40 clients. 75% of clients are new/unpublished writers. Currently handles: 5% nonfiction books; 95% novels.

Member Agents Irene Kraas, principal (psychological thrillers, medical thrillers, mysteries, literary fiction); Ashley Kraas, associate (romance, women's fiction, historical fiction, memoirs, biographies, self-help, spiritual). Please send appropriate submissions to the correct address.

Represents Nonfiction books, novels, young adult.

O→ This agency specializes in adult fiction. Actively seeking "books that are well written with commercial potential." Does not want to receive short stories, plays, or poetry.

How to Contact Submit cover letter, first 50 pages of a completed ms, SASE; must include return postage and/or SASE. No e-mail or fax queries. Considers simultaneous queries. Returns materials only with SASE.

Recent Sales *Words to Die By*, by Kyra Davis (Harlequin); St. Germain Series (17&18), by Chelsea Quinn Yarbro (Tor); *Shriker*, by Janet Lee Carey (Atheneum); *Crazy Quilt*, by Paula Paul (UNH Pres); *The Sword, The Shield* and *The Crown*, a trilogy by Hilari Bell (Simon & Schuster).

Terms Agent receives 15% commission on domestic sales. Offers written contract. Charges clients for photocopying and postage.

Writers' Conferences Irene: Southwest Writers Conference (Albuquerque NM); Durango Writers Conference (Durango CO); Wrangling with Writing (Tucson AZ); Ashley: Surrey Writers Conference (Surrey BC); Wrangling with Writing (Tucson AZ); Schuwap Writers Conference (Schuwap BC); Willamette Writers Group (Portland OR).

Tips "Material by unpublished authors will be accepted in the above areas only. Published authors seeking representation may contact us regarding any material in any area except children's picture books and chapter books."

STUART KRICHEVSKY LITERARY AGENCY, INC.

381 Park Ave. S., Suite 914, New York NY 10016. Fax: (212)725-5275. E-mail: query@skagency.com. Member of AAR.

Represents Nonfiction books, novels.

How to Contact Prefers queries by e-mail (no attachments).

N THE LA LITERARY AGENCY

P.O. Box 46370, Los Angeles CA 90046. (323)654-5288. E-mail: laliteraryag@aol.com. **Contact:** Ann Cashman & Maureen Lasher. Estab. 1980.

- Prior to becoming an agent, Ms. Lasher worked in publishing in New York.

Represents Nonfiction books, novels. **Considers these nonfiction areas:** Animals; anthropology/archaeology; art/architecture/design; biography/autobiography; business/economics; child guidance/parenting; cooking/foods/nutrition; current affairs; ethnic/cultural interests; government/politics/law; health/medicine; history; how-to; nature/environment; popular culture; psychology; science/technology; self-help/personal improvement; sociology; sports; true crime/investigative; women's issues/studies; narrative nonfiction. **Considers these fiction areas:** Action/adventure; detective/police/crime; family saga; feminist; historical; literary; mainstream/contemporary; sports; thriller.

How to Contact Query with SASE, submit outline, 1 sample chapter. No e-mail or fax queries.

Recent Sales *Full Bloom, A Biography of Georgia O'Keeffe*, by Hunter Drohojowska-Philp (Norton); *And the Walls Came Tumbling Down*, by H. Caldwell (Scribner); *Italian Slow & Savory*, by Joyce Goldstein (Chronicle); *A Field Guide to Chocolate Chip Cookies*, by Dede Wilson (Harvard Common Press); *Teen Knitting Club* (Artisan); *The Framingham Heart Study*, by Dr. Daniel Levy (Knopf).

Terms This agency charges clients for copying and postage for FedEx.

PETER LAMPACK AGENCY, INC.

551 Fifth Ave., Suite 1613, New York NY 10176-0187. (212)687-9106. Fax: (212)687-9109. E-mail: alampack@verizon.net. **Contact:** Andrew Lampack. Estab. 1977. Represents 50 clients. 10% of clients are new/unpublished writers. Currently handles: 20% nonfiction books; 80% novels.

Member Agents Peter Lampack (psychological suspense, action/adventure, literary fiction, nonfiction, contemporary relationships); Rema Delanyan (foreign rights); Andrew Lampack (new writers).

Represents Nonfiction books, novels. **Considers these fiction areas:** Action/adventure; detective/police/crime; family saga; historical; literary; mainstream/contemporary; mystery/suspense; thriller; contemporary relationships.

- This agency specializes in commercial fiction and nonfiction by recognized experts. Actively seeking literary and commercial fiction, thrillers, mysteries, suspense, psychological thrillers. Does not want to receive horror, romance, science fiction, western, academic material.

How to Contact Query with SASE. *No unsolicited mss.* Accepts e-mail queries. No fax queries. Considers simultaneous queries. Responds in 2 months. Obtains most new clients through referrals made by clients.

Recent Sales *Slow Man*, by J.M. Coetzee; *Black Wind*, by Clive and Dirk Cussler; *Sacred Stone*, by Clive Cussler and Craig Dirgo; *Lost City*, by Clive Cussler with Paul Kemprecos.

Terms Agent receives 15% commission on domestic sales; 20% commission on foreign sales.

Writers' Conferences BEA (Chicago, June).

Tips "Submit only your best work for consideration. Have a very specific agenda of goals you wish your prospective agent to accomplish for you. Provide the agent with a comprehensive statement of your credentials: educational and professional."

THE LANTZ OFFICE

200 W. 57th St., Suite 503, New York NY 10019. **Contact:** Robert Lantz. Member of AAR.

- Query before submitting.

MICHAEL LARSEN/ELIZABETH POMADA, LITERARY AGENTS

1029 Jones St., San Francisco CA 94109-5023. (415)673-0939. E-mail: larsenpoma@aol.com. Website: www.larsen-pomada.com. **Contact:** Mike Larsen or Elizabeth Pomada. Estab. 1972. Member of AAR, Authors Guild, ASJA, PEN, WNBA, California Writers Club, National Speakers Association. Represents 100 clients. 40-45% of clients are new/unpublished writers. Currently handles: 70% nonfiction books; 30% novels.

- Prior to opening their agency, Mr. Larsen and Ms. Pomada were promotion executives for major publishing houses. Mr. Larsen worked for Morrow, Bantam, and Pyramid (now part of Berkley). Ms. Pomada worked at Holt, David McKay, and The Dial Press.

Member Agents Michael Larsen (nonfiction); Elizabeth Pomada (fiction, narrative nonfiction, nonfiction for women).

Represents Adult book-length fiction and nonfiction that will interest New York publishers or are so irresistibly written or conceived that it doesn't matter. **Considers these nonfiction areas:** Anthropology/archaeology; art/architecture/design; biography/autobiography; business/economics; cooking/foods/nutrition; current affairs; ethnic/cultural interests; gay/lesbian issues; government/politics/law; health/medicine; history; how-to; humor/satire; memoirs; money/finance; music/dance; nature/environment; New Age/metaphysics; popular culture; psychology; religious/inspirational; science/technology; self-help/personal improvement; sociology; sports; theater/film; travel; true crime/investigative; women's issues/studies; futurism. **Considers these fiction areas:** Action/adventure; contemporary issues; detective/police/crime; ethnic; experimental; family saga; fantasy; feminist; gay/lesbian; glitz; historical; humor/satire; literary; mainstream/contemporary; mystery/suspense; religious/inspirational; romance (contemporary, gothic, historical); chick lit.

- "We have diverse tastes. We look for fresh voices and new ideas. We handle literary, commercial, and genre fiction, and the full range of nonfiction books." Actively seeking commercial and literary fiction. Does not want to receive children's books, plays, short stories, screenplays, pornography, poetry, or stories of abuse.

How to Contact Query with SASE, first 10 pages of completed novel, and 2-page synopsis, SASE. For nonfiction, send title, promotion plan and proposal done according to our plan (please see our website). No e-mail or fax queries. Responds in 2 days to queries; 2 months to mss.

Recent Sales Sold at least 15 titles in the last year. *If Life Is a Game, These Are the Stories*; *How to Sleep With a Movie Star*; *To Love a Thief*; *Guerilla Marketing for Consultants*.

Terms Agent receives 15% commission on domestic sales; 20% (30% for Asia) commission on foreign sales. May charge for printing, postage for multiple submissions, foreign mail, foreign phone calls, galleys, books, and legal fees.

Writers' Conferences Book Expo America; Santa Barbara Writers Conference (Santa Barbara); Founders of the San Francisco Writers Conference (www.sanfranciscowritersconference.com).

Tips "If you can write books that meet the needs of the marketplace, and you can promote your books, now is the best time ever to be a writer. We must find new writers to make a living, so we are very eager to hear from new writers whose work will interest large houses, and nonfiction writers who can promote their books. For a list of recent sales, helpful info and three ways to make yourself irresistible to any publisher, please visit our website."

N ☐ THE STEVE LAUBE AGENCY

5501 N. 7th Ave., #502, Phoenix AZ 85013. (602)336-8910. Fax: (602)532-7123. E-mail: krichards@stevelaube.com. Website: www.stevelaube.com. **Contact:** Steve Laube. Estab. 2004. Member of CBA. Represents 50 clients. 20% of clients are new/unpublished writers. Currently handles: 48% nonfiction books; 48% novels; 2% novellas; 2% scholarly books.

- Prior to becoming an agent, Mr. Laube worked 11 years as a bookseller and 11 years as an editor with Bethany House Publishers as editorial director nonfiction.

Represents Nonfiction books, novels. **Considers these nonfiction areas:** Biography/autobiography; business/economics; child guidance/parenting; current affairs; education; how-to; humor/satire; military/war; money/finance; music/dance; popular culture; psychology; religious/inspirational; self-help/personal improvement; sports; theater/film; true crime/investigative; women's issues/studies; juvenile nonfiction. **Considers these fiction areas:** Action/adventure; detective/police/crime; fantasy; historical; humor/satire; literary; mainstream/contemporary; mystery/suspense; religious/inspirational; romance; science fiction; thriller; westerns/frontier.

"We primarily serve the Christian market (CBA). However, we have had success representing books in a variety of fields." Actively seeking fiction, nonfiction religious. Does not want children's picture books, poetry, or cookbooks.

How to Contact Submit proposal package, outline, 3 sample chapters, SASE. Considers simultaneous queries. Responds in 1 month to mss. Responds in 6-8 weeks. Returns materials only with SASE. Obtains most new clients through recommendations from others, solicitations, conferences.

Recent Sales Sold 50 titles in the last year. Clients include Deborah Raney, Bright Media, Allison Bottke, H. Norman Wright, Ellie Kay, Jack Cavanaugh, Karen Ball, Tracey Bateman, and Clint Kelly.

Terms Agent receives 15% commission on domestic sales; 20% commission on foreign sales. Offers written contract; 30-day notice must be given to terminate contract.

Writers' Conferences Mt. Hermon Christian Writers (Mt. Hermon CA); American Christian Fiction Writers; Glorieta Christian Writers Conference (Glorieta NM).

N LAZEAR AGENCY, INC.

431 2nd St., Suite 300, Hudson WI 54016. (715)531-0012. Fax: (715)531-0016. E-mail: info@lazear.com. Website: www.lazear.com. **Contact:** Editorial Board. Estab. 1984. Represents 250 clients. Currently handles: 60% nonfiction books; 30% novels; 10% juvenile books.

- The Lazear Agency opened a New York Office in September 1997.

Member Agents Jonathon Lazear; Christi Cardenas; Julie Mayo; Anne Blackstone.

Represents Nonfiction books, novels, juvenile books, licensing; new media with connection to book project. **Considers these nonfiction areas:** Agriculture/horticulture; americana; animals; anthropology/archaeology; art/architecture/design; biography/autobiography; business/economics; child guidance/parenting; computers/electronic; cooking/foods/nutrition; crafts/hobbies; creative nonfiction; current affairs; education; ethnic/cultural interests; gardening; gay/lesbian issues; government/politics/law; health/medicine; history; how-to; humor/satire; interior design/decorating; juvenile nonfiction; language/literature/criticism; memoirs; military/war; money/finance; multicultural; music/dance; nature/environment; New Age/metaphysics; philosophy; photography; popular culture; psychology; recreation; regional; religious/inspirational; science/technology; self-help/personal improvement; sex; sociology; software; spirituality; sports; theater/film; translation; travel; true crime/investigative; women's issues/studies; young adult. **Considers these fiction areas:** Action/adventure; comic books/cartoon; confession; contemporary issues; detective/police/crime; erotica; ethnic; experimental; family saga; fantasy; feminist; gay/lesbian; glitz; gothic; hi-lo; historical; horror; humor/satire; juvenile; literary; mainstream/contemporary; military/war; multicultural; multimedia; mystery/suspense; New Age; occult; picture books; plays; poetry; poetry in translation; psychic/supernatural; regional; religious/inspirational; romance; science fiction; short story collections; spiritual; sports; thriller; translation; westerns/frontier; young adult; women's.

How to Contact Query with SASE, outline/proposal. Highly selective. No phone calls or faxes. Responds in 3 weeks to queries; 1 month to mss. Returns materials only with SASE. Obtains most new clients through recommendations from others, "through the bestseller lists, word-of-mouth."

Recent Sales Sold over 50 titles in the last year. *Lies and the Lying Liars Who Tell Them*, by Al Franken (Dutton); *All I Did Was Ask*, by Terry Gross (Hyperion); *We Got Fired and It Was the Best Thing that Ever*

Happened to Us, by Harvey Mackay (Ballantine); *Father Joe*, by Tony Hendra (Random House); *You Ain't Got No Easter Clothes*, by Laura Love (Hyperion).

Terms Agent receives 15% commission on domestic sales; 20% commission on foreign sales. Offers written contract. Charges clients for photocopying, international express mail, bound galleys and finished books used for subsidiary rights sales. "No fees charged if book is not sold."

Tips "The writer should first view himself as a salesperson in order to obtain an agent. Sell yourself, your idea, your concept. Do your homework. Notice what is in the marketplace. Be sophisticated about the arena in which you are writing."

SARAH LAZIN BOOKS

126 Fifth Ave., Suite 300, New York NY 10011. (212)989-5757. Fax: (212)989-1393. Member of AAR.

- Query before submitting.

Member Agents Paula Balzer, Sarah Lazin.

THE NED LEAVITT AGENCY

70 Wooster St., Suite 4F, New York NY 10012. (212)334-0999. Website: www.nedleavittagency.com/agency.html. **Contact:** Ned Leavitt. Member of AAR.

Member Agents Ned Leavitt, Britta Alexander.

Represents Nonfiction books, novels.

How to Contact For fiction, submit cover letter, 1-2 chapters, brief synopsis, author bio, SASE. For nonfiction, submit cover letter, TOC, brief chapter synopsis or outline, 1-2 sample chapters, author bio, SASE.

Tips See website for more info on needs.

ROBERT LECKER AGENCY

4055 Melrose Ave., Montreal QC H4A 2S5 Canada. (514)830-4818. Fax: (514)483-1644. E-mail: leckerlink@aol.com. Website: www.leckeragency.com. **Contact:** Robert Lecker. Estab. 2004. Represents 15 clients. 20% of clients are new/unpublished writers. Currently handles: 80% nonfiction books; 10% novels; 10% scholarly books.

- Prior to becoming an agent, Mr. Lecker was the co-founder and publisher of ECW Press and professor of English literature at McGill University. Mr. Lecker has 30 years of experience in book and magazine publishing.

Member Agents Robert Lecker (popular culture, music); Mary Williams (travel, food, popular science).

Represents Nonfiction books, novels, scholarly books, syndicated material. **Considers these nonfiction areas:** Biography/autobiography; cooking/foods/nutrition; ethnic/cultural interests; how-to; language/literature/criticism; music/dance; popular culture; science/technology; theater/film. **Considers these fiction areas:** Action/adventure; detective/police/crime; erotica; literary; mainstream/contemporary; mystery/suspense; thriller.

RLA specializes in books about popular culture, music, entertainment, food and travel. The agency responds to articulate, innovative proposals within 2 weeks. Actively seeking original book mss only after receipt of outlines and proposals. Does not want unsolicited mss.

How to Contact Submit proposal package, outline. Accepts e-mail queries. No fax queries. Considers simultaneous queries. Responds in 2 weeks to queries; 1 month to mss. Obtains most new clients through recommendations from others, conferences, interest in website.

Terms Agent receives 15% commission on domestic sales; 15-20% commission on foreign sales. Offers written contract, binding for 1 year; 6-month notice must be given to terminate contract.

LESCHER & LESCHER, LTD.

47 E. 19th St., New York NY 10003. (212)529-1790. Fax: (212)529-2716. **Contact:** Robert Lescher, Susan Lescher. Estab. 1966. Member of AAR. Represents 150 clients. Currently handles: 80% nonfiction books; 20% novels.

Represents Nonfiction books, novels. **Considers these nonfiction areas:** Current affairs; history; memoirs; popular culture; biography; cookbooks and wines; law; contemporary issues; narrative nonfiction. **Considers these fiction areas:** Literary; mystery/suspense; commercial fiction.

Does not want to receive screenplays, science fiction, or romance.

How to Contact Query with SASE. Obtains most new clients through recommendations from others.

Recent Sales Sold 35 titles in the last year. This agency prefers not to share information on specific sales. Clients include Neil Sheehan, Madeleine L'Engle, Calvin Trillin, Judith Viorst, Thomas Perry, Anne Fadiman, Frances FitzGerald, Paula Fox and Robert M. Parker, Jr.

Terms Agent receives 15% commission on domestic sales; 20-25% commission on foreign sales.

LEVINE GREENBERG LITERARY AGENCY, INC.

307 7th Ave., Suite 1906, New York NY 10001. (212)337-0934. Fax: (212)337-0948. Website: www.levinegreenberg.com. Estab. 1989. Member of AAR. Represents 250 clients. 33% of clients are new/unpublished writers. Currently handles: 70% nonfiction books; 30% novels.

• Prior to opening his agency, Mr. Levine served as vice president of the Bank Street College of Education.

Member Agents James Levine; Arielle Eckstut; Daniel Greenberg; Stephanie Kip Roston; Jenoyne Adams.

Represents Nonfiction books, novels. **Considers these nonfiction areas:** Animals; art/architecture/design; biography/autobiography; business/economics; child guidance/parenting; computers/electronic; cooking/foods/nutrition; gardening; gay/lesbian issues; health/medicine; money/finance; nature/environment; New Age/metaphysics; psychology; religious/inspirational; science/technology; self-help/personal improvement; sociology; spirituality; sports; women's issues/studies. **Considers these fiction areas:** Contemporary issues; literary; mainstream/contemporary; mystery/suspense; thriller (psychological); women's.

This agency specializes in business, psychology, parenting, health/medicine, narrative nonfiction, psychology, spirituality, religion, women's issues, and commercial fiction.

How to Contact See website for full submission procedure. Prefers e-mail queries. Obtains most new clients through recommendations from others.

Recent Sales *The Onion: Our Dumb Century*; *Alternadad*, by Neal Pollack; *The Opposite of Death Is Love*, by Nando Parrado.

Terms Agent receives 15% commission on domestic sales; 20% commission on foreign sales. Offers written contract, binding for variable length of time. Charges clients for out-of-pocket expenses—telephone, fax, postage, and photocopying—directly connected to the project.

Writers' Conferences ASJA Annual Conference (New York City, May).

Tips "We work closely with clients on editorial development and promotion. We work to place our clients as magazine columnists and have created columnists for *McCall's* (renamed *Rosie's*) and *Child*. We work with clients to develop their projects across various media—video, software, and audio."

PAUL S. LEVINE LITERARY AGENCY

1054 Superba Ave., Venice CA 90291-3940. (310)450-6711. Fax: (310)450-0181. E-mail: pslevine@ix.netcom.com. Website: home.netcom.com/~pslevine/lawliterary.html. **Contact:** Paul S. Levine. Estab. 1996. Member of the State Bar of California. Represents over 100 clients. 75% of clients are new/unpublished writers. Currently handles: 30% nonfiction books; 30% novels; 10% movie scripts; 30% TV scripts.

Represents Nonfiction books, novels, movie scripts, feature film, TV scripts, TV movie of the week, episodic drama, sitcom, animation, documentary, miniseries, syndicated material. **Considers these nonfiction areas:** Art/architecture/design; biography/autobiography; business/economics; child guidance/parenting; computers/electronic; cooking/foods/nutrition; crafts/hobbies; creative nonfiction; current affairs; education; ethnic/cultural interests; gay/lesbian issues; government/politics/law; health/medicine; history; how-to; humor/satire; interior design/decorating; language/literature/criticism; memoirs; military/war; money/finance; music/dance; nature/environment; New Age/metaphysics; photography; popular culture; psychology; religious/inspirational; science/technology; self-help/personal improvement; sociology; sports; theater/film; true crime/investigative; women's issues/studies. **Considers these fiction areas:** Action/adventure; comic books/cartoon; confession; contemporary issues; detective/police/crime; erotica; ethnic; experimental; family saga; feminist; gay/lesbian; glitz; historical; humor/satire; literary; mainstream/contemporary; mystery/suspense; regional; religious/inspirational; romance; sports; thriller; westerns/frontier. **Considers these script subject areas:** Action/adventure; biography/autobiography; cartoon/animation; comedy; contemporary issues; detective/police/crime; erotica; ethnic; experimental; family saga; feminist; gay/lesbian; glitz; historical; horror; juvenile; mainstream; multimedia; mystery/suspense; religious/inspirational; romantic comedy; romantic drama; sports; teen; thriller; western/frontier.

Actively seeking commercial fiction and nonfiction. Also handles children's and young adult fiction and nonfiction. Does not want to receive science fiction, fantasy, or horror.

How to Contact Query with SASE. Accepts e-mail and fax queries. Considers simultaneous queries. Responds in 1 day to queries; 2 months to mss. Returns materials only with SASE. Obtains most new clients through conferences, referrals, listings on various websites and through listings in directories.

Recent Sales Sold 25 titles in the last year. This agency prefers not to share information on specific sales.

Terms Agent receives 15% commission on domestic sales; 20% commission on foreign sales. Offers written contract. Charges clients for messengers, long distance, postage. "Only when incurred. No advance payment necessary."

Writers' Conferences California Lawyers for the Arts (Los Angeles CA); National Writers Club (Los Angeles CA); "Selling to Hollywood" Writer's Connection (Glendale CA); "Spotlight on Craft" Willamette Writers Conference (Portland OR); Women in Animation (Los Angeles CA); and many others.

ROBERT LIEBERMAN ASSOCIATES

400 Nelson Rd., Ithaca NY 14850-9440. (607)273-8801. Fax: (801)749-9682. E-mail: rhl10@cornell.edu. Website: www.people.cornell.edu/pages/rhl10. **Contact:** Robert Lieberman. Estab. 1993. Represents 30 clients. 50% of clients are new/unpublished writers. Currently handles: 20% nonfiction books; 80% textbooks.

Represents Nonfiction books (trade), scholarly books, textbooks (college, high school, and middle school level). **Considers these nonfiction areas:** Agriculture/horticulture; anthropology/archaeology; art/architecture/design; business/economics; computers/electronic; education; health/medicine; memoirs (by authors with high public recognition); money/finance; music/dance; nature/environment; psychology; science/technology; sociology; theater/film.

- This agency specializes in university/college-level textbooks, CD-ROM/software and popular trade books in math, engineering, economics and other subjects. Does not want to receive fiction, self-help, or screenplays.

How to Contact Query with SASE or by e-mail. Prefers to read materials exclusively. Prefers e-mail queries. Responds in 2 weeks to queries; 1 month to mss. Returns materials only with SASE. Obtains most new clients through referrals.

Recent Sales Sold 15 titles in the last year. *The Standard Model and the Triumph of 20th Century Physics*, by Robert Oerter (Pi Press); *Fundamentals in Voice Quality Engineering in Wireless Networks*, by Avi Perry (Cambridge University Press); *C++ Programming*, by John Mason (Prentice Hall); *College Physics*, by Giambattist & Richardson (McGraw-Hill); *Conflict Resolution*, by Baltos and Weir (Cambridge University Press).

Terms Agent receives 15% commission on domestic sales; 20% commission on foreign sales. Offers written contract, binding for open-ended length of time; 1-month notice must be given to terminate contract. 100% of business is derived from commissions on ms sales. "Fees are sometimes charged to clients for shipping and when special reviewers are required."

Tips "The trade books we handle are by authors who are highly recognized in their fields of expertise. Client list includes Nobel Prize winners and others with high name recognition, either by the public or within a given area of expertise."

LIMELIGHT MANAGEMENT

33 Newman St., London W1T 1PY England. 0207 6372529. E-mail: limelight.management@virgin.net. Website: www.limelightmanagement.com. **Contact:** Fiona Lindsay. Estab. 1990. Member of Association of Authors' Agents. Represents 70 clients. Currently handles: 100% nonfiction books; multimedia.

- Prior to becoming an agent, Ms. Lindsay was a public relations manager of the Dorchester and was working on her law degree.

Represents Nonfiction books, lifestyle TV. **Considers these nonfiction areas:** Agriculture/horticulture; art/architecture/design; cooking/foods/nutrition; crafts/hobbies; gardening; health/medicine; interior design/decorating; nature/environment; New Age/metaphysics; photography; self-help/personal improvement; sports; travel.

- This agency specializes in lifestyle subject areas, especially celebrity chefs, gardeners and wine experts. Actively seeking health, cooking, gardening. Does not want to receive any subject not listed above.

How to Contact Query with SASE, or send outline/proposal; IRCs. Prefers to read materials exclusively. Accepts e-mail and fax queries. Responds in 1 week to queries. Returns materials only with SASE. Obtains most new clients through recommendations from others.

Recent Sales Sold 45 titles in the last year. This agency prefers not to share information on specific sales. Clients include Oz Clarke, Antony Worrall Thompson, David Stevens, David Joyce, John Bly.

Terms Agent receives 15% commission on domestic sales; 20% commission on foreign sales. Offers written contract; 2 months notice must be given to terminate contract.

LINDSEY'S LITERARY SERVICES

7502 Greenville Ave., Suite 500, Dallas TX 75231. (214)890-9262. Fax: (214)890-9295. E-mail: bonedges001@aol.com. **Contact:** Bonnie James; Emily Armenta. Estab. 2002. Represents 14 clients. 60% of clients are new/unpublished writers. Currently handles: 70% nonfiction books; 30% novels.

- Prior to becoming an agent, Ms. James was a drama instructor and magazine editor, and Ms. Armenta was an independent film editor and magazine editor.

Member Agents Bonnie James (nonfiction: New Age/metaphysics, self-help, psychology, women's issues; fiction: mystery/suspense, thriller, horror, literary, mainstream, romance); Emily Armenta (nonfiction: New Age/metaphysics, self-help, psychology, women's issues; fiction: mystery/suspense, thriller, horror, literary, mainstream, romance).

Represents Nonfiction books, novels. **Considers these nonfiction areas:** Animals; biography/autobiography; ethnic/cultural interests; gay/lesbian issues; health/medicine; history; memoirs; multicultural; New Age/metaphysics; psychology; self-help/personal improvement; true crime/investigative; women's issues/studies. **Con-**

siders these fiction areas: Action/adventure; detective/police/crime; ethnic; historical; horror; literary; mainstream/contemporary; multicultural; mystery/suspense; New Age; religious/inspirational; romance; science fiction; thriller.

"We are a new agency with a clear vision and will aggressively represent our clients." Actively seeking nonfiction self-help, metaphysical, psychology, and women's issues; for fiction, seeking exceptionally written books. Does not want poetry, children's books, text books.

How to Contact Query with SASE or by e-mail. For nonfiction, submit proposal package, writing sample, and brief bio (list credentials and platform details). For fiction, include first 3 chapters, synopsis, and brief bio. No phone calls, please. Considers simultaneous queries. Responds in 4-6 weeks to queries; 2-3 months to mss. Returns materials only with SASE. Obtains most new clients through recommendations from others, solicitations.

Recent Sales Sold 5 titles in the last year. *Crisis Pending*, by Stephen Cornell (Durban House); *Horizon's End*, by Andrew Lazarus (Gladden Books); *No Ordinary Terror*, by J. Brooks Van Dyke (Durban House).

Terms Agent receives 15% commission on domestic sales; 20% commission on foreign sales. Offers written contract, binding for 1 year; cancelable by either party with 1-month written notice must be given to terminate contract.

Tips "Write a clear, concise query describing your project. Pay attention to the craft of writing. Provide complete package, including education, profession, writing credits, and what you want to accomplish."

WENDY LIPKIND AGENCY

120 E. 81st St., New York NY 10028. (212)628-9653. Fax: (212)585-1306. E-mail: lipkindag@aol.com. **Contact:** Wendy Lipkind. Estab. 1977. Member of AAR. Represents 60 clients. Currently handles: 90% nonfiction books; 10% novels.

Represents Nonfiction books, novels. **Considers these nonfiction areas:** Biography/autobiography; current affairs; health/medicine; history; science/technology; women's issues/studies; social history. **Considers these fiction areas:** Mainstream/contemporary; mystery/suspense (psychological suspense).

This agency specializes in adult nonfiction. Does not want to receive mass market originals.

How to Contact Prefers to read materials exclusively. Query by e-mail with query letter only. No attachments. Obtains most new clients through recommendations from others.

Recent Sales Sold 10 titles in the last year. *One Small Step*, by Robert Mauner (Workman); *In the Land of Lyme*, by Pamela Weintraub (Scribner).

Terms Agent receives 15% commission on domestic sales; 20% commission on foreign sales. Sometimes offers written contract. Charges clients for foreign postage, messenger service, photocopying, transatlantic calls, faxes.

Tips "Send intelligent query letter first. Let me know if you sent to other agents."

LITERARY & MEDIA REPRESENTATION

240 W. 35th St., Suite 500, New York NY 10001. **Contact:** Nancy Coffey. Member of AAR.

- Query before submitting.

LITERARY AND CREATIVE ARTISTS, INC.

3543 Albemarle St. NW, Washington DC 20008-4213. (202)362-4688. Fax: (202)362-8875. E-mail: lca9643@lcadc.com. Website: www.lcadc.com. **Contact:** Muriel Nellis. Estab. 1981. Member of AAR, Authors' Guild, the American Bar Association. Represents 75 clients. Currently handles: 70% nonfiction books; 15% novels.

Member Agents Muriel Nellis; Jane Roberts; Stephen Ruwe.

Represents Nonfiction books, novels. **Considers these nonfiction areas:** Biography/autobiography; business/economics; cooking/foods/nutrition; government/politics/law; health/medicine; how-to; memoirs; philosophy; human drama; lifestyle.

How to Contact Query with SASE. *No unsolicited mss.* Responds in 3 months to queries.

Recent Sales *How to Persuade People Who Don't Want to Be Persuaded*, by Joel Bauer and Mark Levy (John Wiley and Sons); *Goblins!*, by Brian Froud (Harry N. Abrams); *American Roulette*, by Richard Marcus (Thomas Dunne Books/St. Martin's Press).

Terms Agent receives 15% commission on domestic sales; 20% commission on foreign sales; 25% commission on dramatic rights sales. Charges clients for long-distance phone and fax, photocopying, shipping.

Tips "While we prefer published writers, it is not required if the proposed work has great merit."

THE LITERARY GROUP

270 Lafayette St., 1505, New York NY 10012. (212)274-1616. Fax: (212)274-9876. E-mail: fweimann@theliterarygroup.com. Website: www.theliterarygroup.com. **Contact:** Frank Weimann. Estab. 1985. 65% of clients are new/unpublished writers. Currently handles: 50% nonfiction books; 50% fiction.

Member Agents Frank Weimann (fiction, nonfiction); Ian Kleinert (fiction, nonfiction).

Represents Nonfiction books, and fiction books. **Considers these nonfiction areas:** Animals; anthropology/archaeology; biography/autobiography; business/economics; child guidance/parenting; crafts/hobbies; creative nonfiction; current affairs; education; ethnic/cultural interests; government/politics/law; health/medicine; history; how-to; humor/satire; juvenile nonfiction; language/literature/criticism; memoirs; military/war; money/finance; multicultural; music/dance; nature/environment; popular culture; psychology; religious/inspirational; science/technology; self-help/personal improvement; sociology; sports; theater/film; true crime/investigative; women's issues/studies. **Considers these fiction areas:** Action/adventure; contemporary issues; detective/police/crime; ethnic; family saga; fantasy; feminist; horror; humor/satire; mystery/suspense; psychic/supernatural; romance (contemporary, gothic, historical, regency); sports; thriller; westerns/frontier.

O→ This agency specializes in nonfiction (memoir, military, history, biography, sports, how-to).

How to Contact Query with SASE, outline, 3 sample chapters. Prefers to read materials exclusively. Responds in 1 week to queries; 1 month to mss. Returns materials only with SASE. Obtains most new clients through referrals, writers' conferences, query letters.

Recent Sales Sold 150 titles in the last year. *There and Back Again: An Actor's Tale*, by Sean Astin; *The Ambassador's Son*, by Homer Hickam; *Idiot*, by Johnny Damon; *Lemons Are Not Red*, by Laura Vaccaro Seeger; *The Good Guys*, by Bill Bonanno and Joe Pistone. Other clients include Robert Anderson, Michael Reagan, and J.L. King.

Terms Agent receives 15% commission on domestic sales; 20% commission on foreign sales. Offers written contract; 30-day notice must be given to terminate contract.

Writers' Conferences Detroit Women's Writers (MI); Kent State University (OH); San Diego Writers Conference (CA); Maui Writers Conference (HI); Austin Writers' Conference (TX).

Literary Agents

N ⊘ LITERARY MANAGERS AND DRAMATURGS OF THE AMERICAS

Box 728, Village Station, New York NY 10014. **Contact:** D.D. Kugler. Member of AAR.

- Query before submitting.

N ◙ JULIA LORD LITERARY MANAGEMENT

38 W. Ninth St., #4, New York NY 10011. (212)995-2333. Fax: (212)995-2332. **Contact:** Julia Lord. Estab. 1999. Member of AAR.

Represents Nonfiction books, novels. **Considers these nonfiction areas:** Biography/autobiography; history; sports; travel; lifestyle; African-American; narrative nonfiction. **Considers these fiction areas:** Action/adventure; historical; mainstream/contemporary; mystery/suspense.

How to Contact Query with SASE. Obtains most new clients through recommendations from others, solicitations.

◙ NANCY LOVE LITERARY AGENCY

250 E. 65th St., New York NY 10021-6614. (212)980-3499. Fax: (212)308-6405. E-mail: nloveag@aol.com. **Contact:** Nancy Love. Estab. 1984. Member of AAR. Represents 60-80 clients. 25% of clients are new/unpublished writers. Currently handles: 90% nonfiction books; 10% novels.

Member Agents Nancy Love; Miriam Tager.

Represents Nonfiction books, fiction. **Considers these nonfiction areas:** Biography/autobiography; child guidance/parenting; cooking/foods/nutrition; current affairs; ethnic/cultural interests; government/politics/law; health/medicine; history; how-to; nature/environment; New Age/metaphysics; popular culture; psychology; religious/inspirational; science/technology; self-help/personal improvement; sociology; spirituality; travel (armchair only, no how-to travel); true crime/investigative; women's issues/studies. **Considers these fiction areas:** Mystery/suspense; thriller.

O→ This agency specializes in adult nonfiction and mysteries. Actively seeking narrative nonfiction. Does not want to receive novels other than mysteries and thrillers.

How to Contact For nonfiction, send a proposal, chapter summary, and sample chapter. For fiction, query first. No e-mail or fax queries. Considers simultaneous queries. Responds in 3 weeks to queries; 6 weeks to mss. Returns materials only with SASE. Obtains most new clients through recommendations from others, solicitations.

Recent Sales Sold 18 titles in the last year. Book 5 in Blanco County Mystery Series, by Ben Rehder (St. Martin's Press); *Cutter Vaccine Incident*, by Paul Offit, M.D. (Yale U. Press); *Don't Panic*, by Stanton Peele, Ph.D. (Crown); *Regime Change*, by Steven Kinzer (Henry Holt).

Terms Agent receives 15% commission on domestic sales; 20% commission on foreign sales. Offers written contract. Charges clients for photocopying "if it runs over $20."

Tips "Nonfiction author and/or collaborator must be an authority in subject area and have a platform. Send a SASE if you want a response."

LOWENSTEIN-YOST ASSOCIATES

121 W. 27th St., Suite 601, New York NY 10001. (212)206-1630. Fax: (212)727-0280. **Contact:** President: Barbara Lowenstein. Estab. 1976. Member of AAR. Represents 150 clients. 20% of clients are new/unpublished writers. Currently handles: 60% nonfiction books; 40% novels.

Member Agents Barbara Lowenstein (president); Nancy Yost (vice president); Eileen Cope (agent); Norman Kurz (business affairs); Dorian Karchmar (agent); Julie Culver (foreign rights manager).

Represents Nonfiction books, novels. **Considers these nonfiction areas:** Animals; anthropology/archaeology; biography/autobiography; business/economics; child guidance/parenting; creative nonfiction; current affairs; education; ethnic/cultural interests; government/politics/law; health/medicine; history; how-to; language/literature/criticism; memoirs; money/finance; multicultural; nature/environment; popular culture; psychology; self-help/personal improvement; sociology; travel; women's issues/studies; music; narrative nonfiction; science; film. **Considers these fiction areas:** Contemporary issues; detective/police/crime; erotica; ethnic; feminist; historical; literary; mainstream/contemporary; mystery/suspense; romance (contemporary, historical, regency); thriller.

O→ This agency specializes in health, business, creative nonfiction, literary fiction, commercial fiction—especially suspense, crime and women's issues. "We are a full-service agency, handling domestic and foreign rights, film rights and audio rights to all of our books."

How to Contact Query with SASE. Prefers to read materials exclusively. For fiction, send outline and first chapter. No unsolicited mss. Responds in 6 weeks to queries. Returns materials only with SASE. Obtains most new clients through recommendations from others, solicitations, conferences.

Recent Sales Sold 75 titles in the last year. *6 Day Body Makeover*, by Michael Thurmond (Warner); *Hot Ice*, by Cherry Adair. Other clients include Ishmael Reed, Deborah Crombie, Leslie Glass, Jennifer Haigh, Stephanie Laurens, Grace Edwards, Kuwana Hausley, Perri O'Shaughnessy, Tim Cahill, Kevin Young.

Terms Agent receives 15% commission on domestic sales; 20% commission on foreign sales. Offers written contract. Charges for large photocopy batches, messenger service and international postage.

Writers' Conferences Malice Domestic; Bouchercon.

Tips "Know the genre you are working in and read!"

ANDREW LOWNIE LITERARY AGENCY, LTD.

17 Sutherland St., London SW1V4JU England. (0207)828 1274. Fax: (0207)828 7608. E-mail: lownie@globalnet.co.uk. Website: www.andrewlownie.co.uk. **Contact:** Andrew Lownie. Estab. 1988. Member of Association of Author's Agents. Represents 130 clients. 20% of clients are new/unpublished writers. Currently handles: 90% nonfiction books; 10% novels.

- Prior to becoming an agent, Mr. Lownie was a journalist, bookseller, publisher, author of 12 books, and previously a director of the Curtis Brown Agency.

Represents Nonfiction books. **Considers these nonfiction areas:** Biography/autobiography; current affairs; government/politics/law; history; memoirs; military/war; popular culture; true crime/investigative.

O→ This agent has wide publishing experience, extensive journalistic contacts, and a specialty in showbiz memoir and celebrities. Actively seeking showbiz memoirs, narrative histories, and biographies. Does not want to receive poetry, short stories, children's fiction, scripts, academic.

How to Contact Query with SASE and/or IRCs. Submit outline, 1 sample chapter. Accepts e-mail and fax queries. Considers simultaneous queries. Responds in 1 week to queries; 1 month to mss. Returns materials only with SASE. Obtains most new clients through recommendations from others.

Recent Sales Sold 50 titles in the last year. *Avenging Justice*, by David Stafford (Time Warner). Other clients include Norma Major, Guy Bellamy, Joyce Cary estate, Lawrence James, Juliet Barker, Patrick McNee, Sir John Mills, Peter Evans, Desmond Seward, Laurence Gardner, Richard Rudgley, Timothy Good, Tom Levine.

Terms Agent receives 15% commission on domestic sales; 15% commission on foreign sales. Offers written contract, binding until author chooses to break it but valid while book is in print; 30-day notice must be given to terminate contract. Charges clients for some copying, postage, copies of books for submission.

Tips "I prefer submissions in writing by letter."

DONALD MAASS LITERARY AGENCY

160 W. 95th St., Suite 1B, New York NY 10025. (212)866-8200. Website: www.maassagency.com. **Contact:** Donald Maass, Jennifer Jackson, Rachel Vater, Cameron McClure. Estab. 1980. Member of AAR, SFWA, MWA, RWA. Represents over 100 clients. 5% of clients are new/unpublished writers. Currently handles: 100% novels.

- Prior to opening his agency, Mr. Maass served as an editor at Dell Publishing (New York) and as a reader at Gollancz (London). He also served as the president of AAR.

Member Agents Donald Maass (mainstream, literary, mystery/suspense, science fiction); Jennifer Jackson (commercial fiction, especially romance, science fiction, fantasy, mystery/suspense); Rachel Vater (chick lit, mystery, thriller, fantasy, commercial, literary); Cameron McClure (literary, historical, mystery/suspense, fantasy, women's fiction, narrative nonfiction and projects with multicultural, international and environmental themes).

Represents Novels. **Considers these fiction areas:** Detective/police/crime; fantasy; historical; horror; literary; mainstream/contemporary; mystery/suspense; psychic/supernatural; romance (historical, paranormal, time travel); science fiction; thriller; women's.

- This agency specializes in commercial fiction, especially science fiction, fantasy, romance and suspense. Actively seeking "to expand the literary portion of our list and expand in women's fiction." Does not want to receive nonfiction, children's, or poetry.

How to Contact Query with SASE, synopsis, or first 5 pages. Returns material only with SASE. Considers simultaneous queries. Responds in 2 weeks to queries; 3 months to mss.

Recent Sales Sold over 100 titles in the last year. *The Shifting Tide*, by Anne Perry (Ballantine); *The Longest Night*, by Gregg Keizer (G.P. Putnam's Sons).

Terms Agent receives 15% commission on domestic sales; 20% commission on foreign sales.

Writers' Conferences *Donald Maass*: World Science Fiction Convention; Frankfurt Book Fair; Pacific Northwest Writers Conference; Bouchercon and others; *Jennifer Jackson*: World Science Fiction and Fantasy Convention; RWA National, and others; *Rachel Vater*: Pacific Northwest Writer's Conference, Pennwriters, and others.

Tips "We are fiction specialists, also noted for our innovative approach to career planning. Few new clients are accepted, but interested authors should query with SASE. Subagents in all principle foreign countries and Hollywood. No nonfiction or juvenile works considered."

GINA MACCOBY LITERARY AGENCY

P.O. Box 60, Chappaqua NY 10514. (914)238-5630. **Contact:** Gina Maccoby. Estab. 1986. Represents 25 clients. Currently handles: 33% nonfiction books; 33% novels; 33% juvenile books. Represents illustrators of children's books.

Represents Nonfiction books, novels, juvenile books. **Considers these nonfiction areas:** Biography/autobiography; current affairs; ethnic/cultural interests; history; juvenile nonfiction; popular culture; women's issues/studies. **Considers these fiction areas:** Juvenile; literary; mainstream/contemporary; mystery/suspense; thriller; young adult.

How to Contact Query with SASE. Considers simultaneous queries. Responds in 3 months to queries. Returns materials only with SASE. Obtains most new clients through recommendations from own clients and publishers.

Recent Sales Sold 21 titles in the last year.

Terms Agent receives 15% commission on domestic sales; 25% commission on foreign sales. Charges clients for photocopying. May recover certain costs such as the cost of shipping books by air to Europe or Japan or legal fees.

CAROL MANN AGENCY

55 Fifth Ave., New York NY 10003. (212)206-5635. Fax: (212)675-4809. E-mail: emily@carolmannagency.com. **Contact:** Emily Nurkin. Estab. 1977. Member of AAR. Represents 200 clients. 25% of clients are new/unpublished writers. Currently handles: 70% nonfiction books; 30% novels.

Member Agents Carol Mann (literary fiction, nonfiction); Emily Nurkin (fiction and nonfiction); Gareth Esersky.

Represents Nonfiction books, novels. **Considers these nonfiction areas:** Anthropology/archaeology; art/architecture/design; biography/autobiography; business/economics; child guidance/parenting; current affairs; ethnic/cultural interests; government/politics/law; health/medicine; history; money/finance; psychology; self-help/personal improvement; sociology; women's issues/studies. **Considers these fiction areas:** Literary; commercial.

- This agency specializes in current affairs; self-help; popular culture; psychology; parenting; history. Does not want to receive "genre fiction (romance, mystery, etc.)."

How to Contact Query with outline/proposal and SASE. Responds in 3 weeks to queries.

Recent Sales Clients include novelists Paul Auster and Marita Golden; journalists Tim Egan, Hannah Storm, Willow Bay, Pulitzer Prize-winner Fox Butterfield; best-selling essayist Shelby Steele; sociologist Dr. William Julius Wilson; economist Thomas Sowell; best-selling diet doctors Mary Dan and Michael Eades; ACLU president Nadine Strossen; pundit Mona Charen; memoirist Lauren Winner; photography project editors Rick Smolan and David Cohen (*America 24/7*); and Kevin Liles, president of Def Jam Records.

Terms Agent receives 15% commission on domestic sales; 20% commission on foreign sales. Offers written contract.

MANUS & ASSOCIATES LITERARY AGENCY, INC.

425 Sherman Ave., Suite 200, Palo Alto CA 94306. (650)470-5151. Fax: (650)470-5159. E-mail: manuslit@manuslit.com. Website: www.manuslit.com. **Contact:** Jillian Manus, Jandy Nelson, Stephanie Lee, Donna Levin, Penny Nelson. Also: 445 Park Ave., New York NY 10022. (212)644-8020. Fax (212)644-3374. **Contact**: Janet

Manus. Estab. 1985. Member of AAR. Represents 75 clients. 30% of clients are new/unpublished writers. Currently handles: 70% nonfiction books; 30% novels.

- Prior to becoming an agent, Jillian Manus was associate publisher of two national magazines and director of development at Warner Bros. and Universal Studios; Janet Manus has been a literary agent for 20 years.

Member Agents Jandy Nelson (self-help, health, memoirs, narrative nonfiction, women's fiction, literary fiction, multicultural fiction, thrillers); Stephanie Lee (self-help, narrative nonfiction, commercial literary fiction, quirky/edgy fiction, pop culture, pop science); Jillian Manus (political, memoirs, self-help, history, sports, women's issues, Latin fiction and nonfiction, thrillers); Donna Levin (mysteries, memoirs, self-help, nonfiction); Penny Nelson (memoirs, self-help, sports, nonfiction).

Represents Nonfiction books, novels. **Considers these nonfiction areas:** Biography/autobiography; business/economics; child guidance/parenting; creative nonfiction; current affairs; ethnic/cultural interests; health/medicine; how-to; memoirs; money/finance; nature/environment; popular culture; psychology; science/technology; self-help/personal improvement; women's issues/studies; Gen X and Gen Y issues. **Considers these fiction areas:** Literary; mainstream/contemporary; multicultural; mystery/suspense; thriller; women's; quirky/edgy fiction.

O╖ This agency specializes in commercial literary fiction, narrative nonfiction, thrillers, health, pop psychology, women's empowerment. "Our agency is unique in the way that we not only sell the material, but we edit, develop concepts, and participate in the marketing effort. We specialize in large, conceptual fiction and nonfiction, and always value a project that can be sold in the TV/feature film market." Actively seeking high-concept thrillers, commercial literary fiction, women's fiction, celebrity biographies, memoirs, multicultural fiction, popular health, women's empowerment, mysteries. Does not want to receive horror, romance, science fiction/fantasy, westerns, young adult, children's, poetry, cookbooks, magazine articles. Usually obtains new clients through recommendations from editors, clients and others, conferences, and unsolicited materials.

How to Contact Query with SASE. If requested, submit outline, 2-3 sample chapters. No faxes, please. All queries should be sent to California office. Accepts e-mail queries. No fax queries. Considers simultaneous queries. Responds in 3 months to queries; 3 months to mss. Returns materials only with SASE. Obtains most new clients through recommendations from others, solicitations, conferences.

Recent Sales *Nothing Down for the 2000's* and *Multiple Streams of Income for the 2000's*, by Robert Allen; *Missed Fortune* and *Missed Fortune 101*, by Doug Andrew; *Cracking the Millionaire Code*, by Mark Victor Hansen and Robert Allen; *Stress Free for Good*, by Dr. Fred Luskin and Dr. Ken Pelletier; *The Mercy of Thin Air*, by Ronlyn Domangue; *The Fine Art of Small Talk*, by Debra Fine; *Bone Man of Bonares*, by Terry Tarnoff. Other clients include Dr. Lorraine Zappart, Marcus Allen, Carlton Stowers, Alan Jacobson, Ann Brandt, Dr. Richard Marrs, Mary LoVerde, Lisa Huang Fleishman, Judy Carter, Daryl Ott Underhill, Glen Kleier, Andrew X. Pham, Alexander Sanger, Lalita Tademy, Frank Baldwin, Katy Robinson, K.M. Soehnlein, Joelle Fraser, James Rogan, Jim Schutze, Deborah Santana, Karen Neuburger, Mira Tweti, Newt Gingrich, William Forstchen, Ken Walsh, Doug Wead, Nadine Schiff, Deborah Santana, Tom Dolby, Laurie Lynn Drummond, Christine Wicker, Wendy Dale, Mineko Iwasaki, Dorothy Ferebee.

Terms Agent receives 15% commission on domestic sales; 20-25% commission on foreign sales. Offers written contract, binding for 2 years; 60 days notice must be given to terminate contract. Charges for photocopying and postage/UPS.

Writers' Conferences Maui Writers Conference (Maui HI, Labor Day); San Diego Writer's Conference (San Diego CA, January); Willamette Writers Conference (Willamette OR, July); BEA; MEGA Book Marketing University.

Tips "Research agents using a variety of sources, including *LMP*, guides, *Publishers Weekly*, conferences, and even acknowledgements in books similar in tone to yours."

MARCH TENTH, INC.

4 Myrtle St., Haworth NJ 07641-1740. (201)387-6551. Fax: (201)387-6552. E-mail: hchoron@aol.com. Website: www.marchtenthinc.com. **Contact:** Harry Choron, vice president. Estab. 1982. Represents 40 clients. 30% of clients are new/unpublished writers. Currently handles: 75% nonfiction books; 25% novels.

Represents Nonfiction books, novels. **Considers these nonfiction areas:** Biography/autobiography; current affairs; health/medicine; history; humor/satire; language/literature/criticism; music/dance; popular culture; theater/film. **Considers these fiction areas:** Confession; ethnic; family saga; historical; humor/satire; literary; mainstream/contemporary.

O╖ Writers must have professional expertise in their field. "We prefer to work with published/established writers."

How to Contact Query with SASE. Considers simultaneous queries. Responds in 1 month to queries. Returns materials only with SASE.

Recent Sales Sold 12 titles in the last year. *The Case for Zionism*, by Rabbi Arthur Hertzberg; *Learning Sickness*, by James Lang; *The 100 Simple Secrets of Happy Families*, by David Niven.

Terms Agent receives 15% commission on domestic sales; 20% commission on foreign sales; 20% commission on dramatic rights sales. Charges clients for postage, photocopying, overseas phone expenses. "Does not require expense money upfront."

THE DENISE MARCIL LITERARY AGENCY, INC.

156 Fifth Ave., Suite 625, New York NY 10010. (212)337-3402. Fax: (212)727-2688. **Contact:** Denise Marcil, president; Maura Kye, agent. Estab. 1977. Member of AAR. Represents 50 clients. 10% of clients are new/unpublished writers. Currently handles: Commercial fiction and nonfiction.

- Prior to opening her agency, Ms. Marcil served as an editorial assistant with Avon Books, and as an assistant editor with Simon & Schuster.

Represents Commercial fiction and nonfiction books.

O→ Denise Marcil specializes in thrillers, suspense, women's commercial fiction, popular reference, how-to, self-help, health, buesiness and parenting. "I am looking for fresh, new voices in commercial women's fiction: chick lit, mom lit, stories that capture women's experiences today—as well as historical fiction." Maura Kye is seeking narrative nonfiction (adventure, women's issues, humor, and memoir) and fiction (multicultural, paranormal, suspense, chick lit, and well-written novels with an edgy voice, quirky characters and/or unique plots and settings. "I'm particularly interested in representing books that would appeal to 20- and 30-year-olds."

How to Contact Query with SASE.

Recent Sales Sold 43 titles in the last year. *Fatal Flaw*, by Ginna Gray (Mira); *The Back-Up Plan*, by Sherryl Woods (Mira); *Silent Wager*, by Anita Bunkley (Dafina/Kensington); *10 Questions Every Leader Should Ask to Stay on Top of the Game*, by Graham Alexander (Nelson Business); *Going Visual: Using Images to Enhance Productivity and Profit*, by Alexis Gerard and Robert Goldstein (Wiley); *The Complete Book of Women Saints*, by Sarah Gallick (Harper San Francisco); *When Someone You Love is Angry*, by W. Doyle Gentry, Ph.D. (Berkley); *You Want Me to Work With Who?*, by Julie Janson (Penguin); *Death's Little Helpers*, by Peter Spiegelman (Knopf); *Lost: A Photo Expedition's Desperate Battle for Survival in the Amazon Jungle*, by Marlo and Stephen Kirkpatrick (W).

Terms Agent receives 15% commission on domestic sales; 20% commission on foreign sales. Offers written contract, binding for 2 years; 100% of business is derived from commissions on ms sales. Charges $100/year for postage, photocopying, long-distance calls, etc.

Writers' Conferences Pacific Northwest Writers Conference; RWA.

THE EVAN MARSHALL AGENCY

Six Tristam Place, Pine Brook NJ 07058-9445. (973)882-1122. Fax: (973)882-3099. E-mail: evanmarshall@thenovelist.com. Website: www.thenovelist.com. **Contact:** Evan Marshall. Estab. 1987. Member of AAR, MWA, RWA, Sisters in Crime, American Crime Writers League. Currently handles: 100% novels.

- Prior to opening his agency, Mr. Marshall served as an editor with Houghton Mifflin, New American Library, Everest House, and Dodd, Mead & Co., and then worked as a literary agent at The Sterling Lord Agency.

Represents Novels. **Considers these fiction areas:** Action/adventure; erotica; ethnic; historical; horror; humor/satire; literary; mainstream/contemporary; mystery/suspense; religious/inspirational; romance (contemporary, gothic, historical, Regency); science fiction; westerns/frontier.

How to Contact Query first with SASE; do not enclose material. No e-mail queries. Responds in 1 week to queries; 3 months to mss. Obtains most new clients through recommendations from others.

Recent Sales *Killer Take All*, by Erica Spindler (Mira); *Flaming Luau of Death*, by Jerrilyn Farmer (Morrow); *Haven*, by Bobbi Smith (Dorchester).

Terms Agent receives 15% commission on domestic sales; 20% commission on foreign sales. Offers written contract.

MARTIN LITERARY MANAGEMENT

17328 Ventura Blvd., Suite 138, Encino CA 91316. (818)595-1130. Fax: (818)715-0418. E-mail: sharlene@martinliterarymanagement.com. Website: www.martinliterarymanagement.com. **Contact:** Sharlene Martin. Estab. 2002. 75% of clients are new/unpublished writers. Currently handles: 100% nonfiction books.

- Prior to becoming an agent, Ms. Martin worked in film/TV production and acquisitions.

Represents Nonfiction books. **Considers these nonfiction areas:** Biography/autobiography; business/economics; child guidance/parenting; current affairs; health/medicine; history; how-to; humor/satire; memoirs; popular culture; psychology; religious/inspirational; self-help/personal improvement; true crime/investigative; women's issues/studies.

O→ This agency has strong ties to film/TV. Actively seeking nonfiction that is highly commercial and that can be adapted to film.

How to Contact Query with SASE, submit outline, 2 sample chapters. Accepts e-mail queries. No fax queries. Considers simultaneous queries. Responds in 1 week to queries; 3-4 weeks to mss. Returns materials only with SASE. Obtains most new clients through recommendations from others.

Terms Agent receives 15% commission on domestic sales; 25% commission on foreign sales. Offers written contract, binding for 1 year; 1-month notice must be given to terminate contract. Charges author for postage and copying if material is not sent electronically.

Tips "Have a strong platform for nonfiction. Don't call, use e-mail. I gladly welcome e-mail. Do your homework prior to submission, and only submit your best efforts."

⊘ HAROLD MATSON CO. INC.

276 Fifth Ave., New York NY 10001. (212)679-4490. **Contact:** Jonathan Matson. Member of AAR.

- Query before submitting.

Member Agents Jonathan Matson (literary, adult); Ben Camardi (literary, adult, dramatic).

⊘ JED MATTES, INC.

2095 Broadway, Suite 302, New York NY 10023-2895. (212)595-5228. Fax: (212)595-5232. E-mail: agency@jedmattes.com. **Contact:** Fred Morris. Member of AAR.

- Query before submitting.

MARGRET MCBRIDE LITERARY AGENCY

7744 Fay Ave., Suite 201, La Jolla CA 92037. (858)454-1550. Fax: (858)454-2156. E-mail: staff@mcbridelit.com. Website: www.mcbrideliterary.com. **Contact:** Michael Daley, submissions manager. Estab. 1980. Member of AAR, Authors Guild.

- Prior to opening her agency, Ms. McBride worked at Random House, Ballantine Books, and Warner Books.

Represents Nonfiction books, novels. **Considers these nonfiction areas:** Biography/autobiography; business/economics; cooking/foods/nutrition; current affairs; ethnic/cultural interests; government/politics/law; health/medicine; history; how-to; money/finance; music/dance; popular culture; psychology; science/technology; self-help/personal improvement; sociology; women's issues/studies; style. **Considers these fiction areas:** Action/adventure; detective/police/crime; ethnic; historical; humor/satire; literary; mainstream/contemporary; mystery/suspense; thriller; westerns/frontier.

O→ This agency specializes in mainstream fiction and nonfiction. Does not want to receive screenplays. Does not represent romance, poetry, or children's/young adult.

How to Contact Query with synopsis or outline and SASE. Visit website for complete submission guidelines. Will not respond/read e-mail queries. Considers simultaneous queries. Responds in 2 months to queries. Returns materials only with SASE.

Recent Sales Sold 22 titles in the last year. *Kingdomality*, by Sheldon Bowles, Richard Silvano and Susan Silvano (Hyperion); *Up from Orchard Street*, by Eleanor Widmer (Bantam); *The Confession*, by Sheldon Siegel (Putnam).

Terms Agent receives 15% commission on domestic sales; 25% commission on foreign sales. Charges for overnight delivery and photocopying.

THE MCCARTHY AGENCY, LLC

7 Allen St., Rumson NJ 07660. Phone/Fax: (732)741-3065. E-mail: mccarthylit@aol.com. **Contact:** Shawna McCarthy. Estab. 1999. Member of AAR. Currently handles: 25% nonfiction books; 75% novels.

Member Agents Shawna McCarthy, Nahvae Frost (ntfrost@hotmail.com).

Represents Nonfiction books, novels. **Considers these nonfiction areas:** Biography/autobiography; history; science/technology. **Considers these fiction areas:** Fantasy; mystery/suspense; romance; science fiction; general.

How to Contact Query via e-mail or regular mail.

⊘ GERARD MCCAULEY

P.O. Box 844, Katonah NY 10536. (914)232-5700. Fax: (914)232-1506. Estab. 1970. Member of AAR. Represents 60 clients. Currently handles: nonfiction books.

O→ This agency specializes in history, biography and general nonfiction.

How to Contact Obtains most new clients through recommendations from others.

Recent Sales Sold 30 titles in the last year. *Private Lives*, by Lawrence Friedman; *Heavens & Earth*, by Walter McDougall (HarperCollins); *Unfogivable Blackness*, by Ken Burns (Knopf); *At War at Sea*, by Ronald Spector (Viking).

Terms Agent receives 15% commission on domestic sales; 20% commission on foreign sales.

ANITA D. MCCLELLAN ASSOCIATES

50 Stearns St., Cambridge MA 02138. (617)576-6950. Fax: (617)576-6951. **Contact:** Anita McClellan. Member of AAR.

- Query before submitting.

HELEN MCGRATH

1406 Idaho Ct., Concord CA 94521. (925)672-6211. Fax: (925)672-6383. E-mail: hmcgrath_lit@yahoo.com. **Contact:** Helen McGrath. Estab. 1977. Currently handles: 50% nonfiction books; 50% novels.

Represents Nonfiction books, novels. **Considers these nonfiction areas:** Biography/autobiography; business/economics; current affairs; health/medicine; history; how-to; military/war; psychology; self-help/personal improvement; sports; women's issues/studies. **Considers these fiction areas:** Contemporary issues; detective/police/crime; literary; mainstream/contemporary; mystery/suspense; psychic/supernatural; romance; science fiction; thriller.

How to Contact Submit proposal with SASE. *No unsolicited mss.* Responds in 2 months to queries. Obtains most new clients through recommendations from others.

Terms Agent receives 15% commission on domestic sales. Offers written contract. Charges clients for photocopying.

MCHUGH LITERARY AGENCY

1033 Lyon Rd., Moscow ID 83843-9167. (208)882-0107. Fax: (603)688-6437. E-mail: elisabetmch@turbonet.com. **Contact:** Elisabet McHugh. Estab. 1994. Represents 42 clients. 30% of clients are new/unpublished writers. Currently handles: 30% nonfiction books; 70% fiction. **Considers these nonfiction areas:** Open to most subjects, except business. **Considers these fiction areas:** Historical; mainstream/contemporary; mystery/suspense; romance; thriller (psychological).

O→ Does not handle children's books, poetry, science fiction, fantasy, horror, westerns.

How to Contact Query first by e-mail. Do not send material unless asked for. Returns materials only with SASE.

Recent Sales *The Complete RV Handbook: Making the Most of Your Life on the Road* (Ragged Mountain Press/McGraw-Hill); *Dead Wrong* (Bantam); *Puppy Love* (Harlequin).

Terms Agent receives 15% commission on domestic sales; 20% commission on foreign sales. Does not charge any upfront fees. Offers written contract. "Client must provide all copies needed for submissions."

MCINTOSH & OTIS

353 Lexington Ave., 15th Floor, New York NY 10016. Member of AAR.

- Query before submitting.

Member Agents Samuel L. Pinkus (associate member); Elizabeth A. Winick (associate member); Eugene Winick (associate member).

SALLY HILL MCMILLAN & ASSOCIATES, INC.

429 E. Kingston Ave., Charlotte NC 28203. (704)334-0897. Fax: (704)334-1897. **Contact:** Sally Hill McMillan. Member of AAR.

- Query before submitting.

MENDEL MEDIA GROUP LLC

205 St. John's Place, Brooklyn NY 11217. (646)239-9896. Fax: (718)230-0887. E-mail: webmaster@mendelmedia.com (do not use for submissions). Website: www.mendelmedia.com. Estab. 2002. Member of AAR. Represents 40-60 clients.

- Prior to becoming an agent, Mr. Mendel was an academic. "I taught American literature, Yiddish, Jewish studies, and literary theory at the University of Chicago and at the University of Illinois at Chicago while working on my Ph.D. in English. I also worked as a freelance technical writer and, for a time, as the managing editor of a health care magazine. In 1998, I began working for the late Jane Jordan Browne, a long-time agent in the book publishing world."

Represents Nonfiction books, novels, scholarly books (if have potential for a broad, popular appeal). **Considers these nonfiction areas:** Americana; animals; anthropology/archaeology; art/architecture/design; biography/autobiography; business/economics; child guidance/parenting; cooking/foods/nutrition; creative nonfiction; current affairs; education; ethnic/cultural interests; gardening; gay/lesbian issues; government/politics/law; health/medicine; history; how-to; humor/satire; language/literature/criticism; memoirs; military/war; money/finance; multicultural; music/dance; nature/environment; philosophy; popular culture; psychology; recreation; regional; religious/inspirational; science/technology; self-help/personal improvement; sex; sociology; software; spirituality; sports; true crime/investigative; women's issues/studies; Jewish topics. **Considers these fiction areas:** Action/adventure; detective/police/crime; erotica; ethnic; feminist; gay/lesbian; historical; humor/satire; juvenile; literary; mainstream/contemporary; mystery/suspense; picture books; religious/inspirational; romance; sports; thriller; young adult; contemporary issues; glitz; Jewish fiction.

O→ "I am interested in major works of history, current affairs, biography, business, politics, economics, science, major memoirs, narrative nonfiction, and other sorts of general nonfiction." Actively seeking "new, major or definitive work on a subject of broad interest, or a controversial, but authoritative, new book on a subject that affects many people's lives. I also represent more light-hearted nonfiction projects, such as gift or novelty books, when they suit the market particularly well." Does not want queries about projects written years ago and that were unsuccessfully shopped to a long list of trade publishers by either the author or another agent. "I am specifically not interested in reading short, category romances (Regency, time travel, paranormal, etc.), horror novels, supernatural stories, poetry, original plays, or film scripts."

How to Contact Send query via regular mail. Do not e-mail or fax queries. For nonfiction, include a complete, fully-edited book proposal with sample chapters. For fiction, include a complete synopsis and no more than 20 pages of sample text. Responds in 2 weeks to queries; 4-6 weeks to mss. Returns materials only with SASE. Obtains most new clients through recommendations from others.

Terms Agent receives 15% commission on domestic sales; 20% commission on foreign sales. Offers written contract, binding for 2 years (renews automatically at the end of the 3rd year if not terminated by either party). In the 3rd year, 1-month notice must be given to terminate contract. Charges clients for ms duplication, expedited delivery services (when necessary), and any overseas shipping, telephone calls and faxes necessary for marketing the author's foreign rights.

Writers' Conferences Book Expo America; Frankfurt Book Fair; London International Book Fair; Romance Writers of America annual conference; Modern Language Association's annual conference, Jerusalem Book Fair.

Tips "While I am not interested in being flattered by a prospective client, it does matter to me that she knows why she is writing to me in the first place. Is one of my clients a colleague of hers? Has she read a book by one of my clients that led her to believe I might be interested in her work? Authors of descriptive nonfiction should have real credentials and expertise in their subject areas, either as academics or journalists or policy experts, and authors of prescriptive nonfiction should have a legitimate expertise and considerable experience communicating their ideas in seminars, workshops, in a successful business, through the media, etc."

MENZA-BARRON AGENCY

(formerly Claudia Menza Literary Agency), 1170 Broadway, Suite 807, New York NY 10001. (212)889-6850. **Contact:** Claudia Menza, Manie Barron. Estab. 1983. Member of AAR. Represents 100 clients. 50% of clients are new/unpublished writers.

Represents Nonfiction books, novels. **Considers these nonfiction areas:** Current affairs; education; ethnic/cultural interests (especially African-American); health/medicine; history; multicultural; music/dance; photography; psychology; theater/film.

O→ This agency specializes in African-American fiction and nonfiction, and editorial assistance.

How to Contact Query with SASE. Responds in 2-4 weeks to queries; 2-4 months to mss. Returns materials only with SASE.

Recent Sales This agency prefers not to share information on specific sales.

Terms Agent receives 15% commission on domestic sales; 20% (if co-agent is used) commission on foreign sales; 20% commission on dramatic rights sales. Offers written contract.

DORIS S. MICHAELS LITERARY AGENCY, INC.

1841 Broadway, Suite 903, New York NY 10023. (212)265-9474. Fax: (212)265-9480. E-mail: query@dsmagency.com. Website: www.dsmagency.com. **Contact:** Doris S. Michaels, president. Estab. 1994. Member of AAR, WNBA.

Represents Novels. **Considers these fiction areas:** Literary (with commercial appeal and strong screen potential).

How to Contact Query by e-mail; see submission guidelines on website. Obtains most new clients through recommendations from others, conferences.

Recent Sales Sold over 30 titles in the last year. *Cycles: How We'll Live, Work and Buy*, by Maddy Dychtwald (The Free Press); *In the River Sweet*, by Patricia Henley (Knopf); *Healing Conversations: What to Say When You Don't Know What to Say*, by Nance Guilmartin (Jossey-Bass); *The Mushroom Man*, by Sophie Powell (Peguin Putnam); *How to Become a Marketing Superstar*, by Jeff Fox (Hyperion).

Terms Agent receives 15% commission on domestic sales; 20% commission on foreign sales. Offers written contract, binding for 1 year; 1-month notice must be given to terminate contract. 100% of business is derived from commissions on ms sales. Charges clients for office expenses, not to exceed $150 without written permission.

Writers' Conferences BEA; Frankfurt Book Fair (Germany, October); London Book Fair; Maui Writers Conference.

MARTHA MILLARD LITERARY AGENCY

50 W. 67th St., #1G, New York NY 10023. (212)787-7769. Fax: (212)787-7867. E-mail: marmillink@aol.com. **Contact:** Martha Millard. Estab. 1980. Member of AAR, SFWA. Represents 50 clients. Currently handles: 25% nonfiction books; 65% novels; 10% story collections.

- Prior to becoming an agent, Ms. Millard worked in editorial departments of several publishers and was vice president at another agency for four and a half years.

Represents Nonfiction books, novels. **Considers these nonfiction areas:** Art/architecture/design; biography/autobiography; business/economics; child guidance/parenting; cooking/foods/nutrition; current affairs; education; ethnic/cultural interests; health/medicine; history; how-to; juvenile nonfiction; memoirs; money/finance; music/dance; New Age/metaphysics; photography; popular culture; psychology; self-help/personal improvement; theater/film; true crime/investigative; women's issues/studies. **Considers these fiction areas:** Considers fiction depending on writer's credits and skills.

How to Contact No unsolicited queries. No e-mail or fax queries. Returns materials only with SASE. Obtains most new clients through recommendations from others.

Recent Sales *Backfire*, by Peter Burrows (Wiley); *Fallen Star*, by Nancy Herkness (Berkley Sensation); *The Rosetta Codex*, by Richard Paul Russ (Penguin).

Terms Agent receives 15% commission on domestic sales; 20% commission on foreign sales. Offers written contract.

THE MILLER AGENCY

1 Sheridan Square, 7B, #32, New York NY 10014. (212) 206-0913. Fax: (212) 206-1473. E-mail: angela@milleragency.net. Website: www.milleragency.net. **Contact:** Angela Miller. Estab. 1990. Represents 100 clients. 5% of clients are new/unpublished writers.

Represents Nonfiction books. **Considers these nonfiction areas:** Anthropology/archaeology; art/architecture/design; biography/autobiography; business/economics; child guidance/parenting; cooking/foods/nutrition; current affairs; ethnic/cultural interests; gay/lesbian issues; health/medicine; language/literature/criticism; New Age/metaphysics; psychology; self-help/personal improvement; sports; women's issues/studies.

O‑ This agency specializes in nonfiction, multicultural arts, psychology, self-help, cookbooks, biography, travel, memoir, sports. Fiction considered selectively.

How to Contact Query with SASE, submit outline, a few sample chapters. Considers simultaneous queries. Responds in 1 week to queries. Obtains most new clients through referrals.

Recent Sales Sold 25 titles in the last year.

Terms Agent receives 15% commission on domestic sales; 20-25% commission on foreign sales. Offers written contract, binding for 2 years; 2-month notice must be given to terminate contract. 100% of business from commissions on ms sales. Charges clients for postage (express mail or messenger services) and photocopying.

MOORE LITERARY AGENCY

10 State St., Newburyport MA 01950. (978)465-9015. Fax: (978)465-8817. E-mail: cmoore@moorelit.com; dmckenna@moorelit.com. **Contact:** Claudette Moore, Deborah McKenna. Estab. 1989. 10% of clients are new/unpublished writers. Currently handles: 100% nonfiction books.

Represents Nonfiction books. **Considers these nonfiction areas:** Computers/electronic; technology.

O‑ This agency specializes in trade computer books (90% of titles).

How to Contact Submit outline. Obtains most new clients through recommendations from others, conferences.

Recent Sales *Windows XP Timesaving Techniques for Dummies*, by Woody Leonhard (Wiley); *Expert One-on-One Microsoft Access Application Development*, by Helen Feddema (Wiley); *Thinking in C++, Volume 2*, by Bruce Eckel and Chuck Allison (Prentice Hall); *Microsoft Windows XP Inside Out, Second Edition*, by Ed Bolt, Carl Siechert, and Craig Stinson (Microsoft Press).

Terms Agent receives 15% commission on domestic sales; 15% commission on foreign sales; 15% commission on dramatic rights sales. Offers written contract.

N PATRICIA MOOSBRUGGER LITERARY AGENCY

165 Bennet Ave., #6M, New York NY 10040. **Contact:** Patricia Moosbrugger. Member of AAR.

- Query before submitting.

MAUREEN MORAN AGENCY

P.O. Box 20191, Park West Station, New York NY 10025-1518. (212)222-3838. Fax: (212)531-3464. E-mail: maureenm@erols.com. **Contact:** Maureen Moran. Represents 30 clients. Currently handles: 100% novels.

Represents Novels. **Considers these fiction areas:** Women's.

O→ This agency specializes in women's fiction, principally romance and mystery. Does not want to receive science fiction, fantasy, or juvenile books.

How to Contact Query with SASE. Will accept e-mail query without attachments. *No unsolicited mss*. Considers simultaneous queries. Responds in 1 week to queries. Returns materials only with SASE.

Recent Sales *Alpine Quilt*, by Mary Daheim; *Death By Thunder*, by Gretchen Sprague; *Jeremy's Daddy*, by Julianna Morris.

Terms Agent receives 10% commission on domestic sales; 15-20% commission on foreign sales. Charges clients for extraordinary expenses such as courier, messenger and bank wire fees by prior arrangement.

Tips "This agency does not handle unpublished writers."

HOWARD MORHAIM LITERARY AGENCY

11 John St., Suite 407, New York NY 10038-4067. (212)529-4433. Fax: (212)995-1112. Member of AAR.

- Query before submitting.

WILLIAM MORRIS AGENCY, INC.

1325 Avenue of the Americas, New York NY 10019. (212)586-5100. Fax: (212)246-3583. Website: www.wma.com. California office: One William Morris Place, Beverly Hills CA 90212. (310)859-4000. Fax: (310)859-4462. Member of AAR.

Member Agents Owen Laster, Jennifer Rudolph Walsh, Suzanne Gluck, Joni Evans, Tracy Fisher, Mel Berger, Jay Mandel, Manie Barron.

Represents Nonfiction books, novels.

How to Contact Query with SASE. Considers simultaneous queries.

Recent Sales This agency prefers not to share information on specific sales.

Terms Agent receives 15% commission on domestic sales; 20% commission on foreign sales.

HENRY MORRISON, INC.

105 S. Bedford Rd., Suite 306A, Mt. Kisco NY 10549. (914)666-3500. Fax: (914)241-7846. **Contact:** Henry Morrison. Estab. 1965. Signatory of WGA. Represents 51 clients. 5% of clients are new/unpublished writers. Currently handles: 5% nonfiction books; 95% novels.

Represents Nonfiction books, novels. **Considers these nonfiction areas:** Anthropology/archaeology; biography/autobiography; government/politics/law; history. **Considers these fiction areas:** Action/adventure; detective/police/crime; family saga; historical.

How to Contact Query with SASE. Responds in 2 weeks to queries; 3 months to mss. Obtains most new clients through recommendations from others.

Recent Sales Sold 18 titles in the last year. *The Moscow Vector*, by Robert Ludlum and Patrick Larkin (St. Martin's Press); *The Bourne Legacy*, by Eric Van Lustbader (St. Martin's Press); *Doublecross Blind*, by Joel Ross (Doubleday); *Michelangelo's Notebook*, by Christopher Hyde (Signet Books); *The Last Spymaster*, by Gayle Lynds (St. Martin's Press); *Office Superman*, by Alan Axelrod (Running Press); *The Glass Tiger*, by Joe Gores (Penzler Books/Harcourt); *Native Sons*, by James Baldwin and Sol Stein (Ballantine Books); *Enemy of My Enemy*, by Allan Topol (Signet Books); *Kingdom Come*, by Beverly Swerling (Simon & Schuster); *The Coil*, by Gayle Lynds (St. Martin's Press). Other clients include Samuel R. Delany, Molly Katz, Daniel Cohen, Brian Garfield, Joe Gores.

Terms Agent receives 15% commission on domestic sales; 25% commission on foreign sales. Charges clients for ms copies, bound galleys, and finished books for submissions to publishers, movie producers, foreign publishers.

DEE MURA LITERARY

269 West Shore Dr., Massapequa NY 11758-8225. (516)795-1616. Fax: (516)795-8797. E-mail: samurai5@ix.netcom.com. **Contact:** Dee Mura, Karen Roberts, Frank Nakamura, Brian Hertler, Kimiko Nakamura. Estab. 1987. Signatory of WGA. 50% of clients are new/unpublished writers.

- Prior to opening her agency, Ms. Mura was a public relations executive with a roster of film and entertainment clients; and worked in editorial for major weekly news magazines.

Represents Nonfiction books, juvenile books, scholarly books, feature film, TV scripts, episodic drama, sitcom, animation, documentary, miniseries, variety show, fiction books. **Considers these nonfiction areas:** Agriculture/horticulture; animals; anthropology/archaeology; biography/autobiography; business/economics; child guidance/parenting; computers/electronic; current affairs; education; ethnic/cultural interests; gay/lesbian issues; government/politics/law; health/medicine; history; how-to; humor/satire; juvenile nonfiction; memoirs; military/war; money/finance; nature/environment; science/technology; self-help/personal improvement; sociology; sports; travel; true crime/investigative; women's issues/studies. **Considers these fiction areas:** Action/

adventure; contemporary issues; detective/police/crime; ethnic; experimental; family saga; fantasy; feminist; gay/lesbian; glitz; historical; humor/satire; juvenile; literary; mainstream/contemporary; mystery/suspense; psychic/supernatural; regional; romance (contemporary, gothic, historical, regency); science fiction; sports; thriller; westerns/frontier; young adult; espionage; political. **Considers these script subject areas:** Action/adventure; cartoon/animation; comedy; contemporary issues; detective/police/crime; family saga; fantasy; feminist; gay/lesbian; glitz; historical; horror; juvenile; mainstream; mystery/suspense; psychic/supernatural; religious/inspirational; romantic comedy; romantic drama; science fiction; sports; teen; thriller; western/frontier.

O-π "We work on everything, but are especially interested in literary fiction, commercial fiction and nonfiction, thrillers and espionage, humor and drama (we love to laugh and cry), self-help, inspirational, medical, scholarly, true life stories, true crime, women's stories and issues." Actively seeking "unique nonfiction manuscripts and proposals; novelists who are great storytellers; contemporary writers with distinct voices and passion." Does not want to receive "ideas for sitcoms, novels, films, etc., or queries without SASEs."

How to Contact Query with SASE. No fax queries. Accepts queries by e-mail without attachments. Considers simultaneous queries. Responds in 2 weeks to queries (depending on mail load). Returns materials only with SASE. Obtains most new clients through recommendations from others, and queries.

Recent Sales Sold over 40 titles and sold 35 scripts in the last year.

Terms Agent receives 15% commission on domestic sales; 20% commission on foreign sales. Offers written contract. Charges clients for photocopying, mailing expenses, overseas and long distance phone calls and faxes.

Tips "Please include a paragraph on the writer's background, even if the writer has no literary background,. and a brief synopsis of the project. We enjoy well-written query letters that tell us about the project and the author."

ERIN MURPHY LITERARY AGENCY

2700 Woodlands Village, #300-458, Flagstaff AZ 86001-7172. (928)525-2056. Fax: (928)525-2480. **Contact:** Erin Murphy. Member of AAR.

O-π This agency represents only children's books.

How to Contact "We do not accept unsolicited manuscripts or queries, but consider new clients by referral or personal contact (such as at conferences) only."

JEAN V. NAGGAR LITERARY AGENCY, INC.

216 E. 75th St., Suite 1E, New York NY 10021. (212)794-1082. **Contact:** Jean Naggar. Estab. 1978. Member of AAR, PEN, Women's Media Group, and Women's Forum. Represents 80 clients. 20% of clients are new/unpublished writers. Currently handles: 35% nonfiction books; 45% novels; 15% juvenile books; 5% scholarly books.

- Ms. Naggar served as president of AAR.

Member Agents Alice Tasman, senior agent (narrative nonfiction, commercial/literary fiction, thrillers); Anne Engel (academic-based nonfiction for general readership); Jennifer Weltz, director, subsidiary rights (also represents children's books and YA); Mollie Glick, agent (serious nonfiction, literary and commercial fiction).

Represents Nonfiction books, novels. **Considers these nonfiction areas:** Biography/autobiography; child guidance/parenting; current affairs; government/politics/law; health/medicine; history; juvenile nonfiction; memoirs; New Age/metaphysics; psychology; religious/inspirational; self-help/personal improvement; sociology; travel; women's issues/studies. **Considers these fiction areas:** Action/adventure; contemporary issues; detective/police/crime; ethnic; family saga; feminist; historical; literary; mainstream/contemporary; mystery/suspense; psychic/supernatural; thriller.

O-π This agency specializes in mainstream fiction and nonfiction, and literary fiction with commercial potential.

How to Contact Query with SASE. Prefers to read materials exclusively. No e-mail or fax queries. Responds in 1 day to queries; 2 months to mss. Returns materials only with SASE. Obtains most new clients through recommendations from others, solicitations, conferences.

Recent Sales *Leaving Ireland*, by Ann Moore (NAL); *The Associate*, by Phillip Margolin (HarperCollins); *Quantico Rules*, by Gene Riehl (St. Martin's Press). Other clients include Jean M. Auel, Robert Pollack, Mary McGarry Morris, Lily Prior, Susan Fromberg Schaeffer, David Ball, Elizabeth Crane, Maud Casey.

Terms Agent receives 15% commission on domestic sales; 20% commission on foreign sales. Offers written contract. Charges for overseas mailing; messenger services; book purchases; long-distance telephone; photocopying. "These are deductible from royalties received."

Writers' Conferences Willamette Writers Conference; Pacific Northwest Writers Conference; Breadloaf Writers Conference; Virginia Women's Press Conference (Richmond VA); Marymount Manhattan Writers Conference; SEAK Conference, New York is Book Country: Get Published.

Tips "Use a professional presentation. Because of the avalanche of unsolicited queries that flood the agency every week, we have had to modify our policy. We will now only guarantee to read and respond to queries from writers who come recommended by someone we know. Our areas are general fiction and nonfiction, no children's books by unpublished writers, no multimedia, no screenplays, no formula fiction, no mysteries by unpublished writers. We recommend patience and fortitude: The courage to be true to your own vision, the fortitude to finish a novel and polish and polish again before sending it out, and the patience to accept rejection gracefully and wait for the stars to align themselves appropriately for success."

KAREN NAZOR LITERARY AGENCY

3 Minot Ave., Acton MA 01720. Fax: (978)263-6230. E-mail: query@nazor.org. **Contact:** Karen Nazor. Estab. 1991. Represents 35 clients. 15% of clients are new/unpublished writers. Currently handles: 75% nonfiction books; 10% novels.

- Prior to opening her agency, Ms. Nazor served a brief apprenticeship with Raines & Raines and was assistant to Peter Ginsberg, president of Curtis Brown, Ltd.

Represents Nonfiction books, novels, novellas. **Considers these nonfiction areas:** Biography/autobiography; business/economics; child guidance/parenting; computers/electronic; current affairs; ethnic/cultural interests; government/politics/law; history; how-to; music/dance; nature/environment; photography; popular culture; science/technology; sociology; sports; travel; women's issues/studies. **Considers these fiction areas:** Feminist; literary; multicultural; regional; women's.

This agency specializes in "good writers! Mostly nonfiction—arts, culture, politics, technology, civil rights, etc."

How to Contact Query (preferred) or send outline/proposal (accepted). No unsolicited mss. Responds in 2 weeks to queries; 2 months to mss. Returns materials only with SASE.

Recent Sales Sold 12 titles in the last year. *The Secret Life of Dust*, by Hannah Holmes (John Wiley & Sons); *Childhood and Adolescent Obsessive Compulsive Disorder*, by Mitzi Waltz (O'Reilly).

Terms Agent receives 15% commission on domestic sales; 20% commission on foreign sales. Offers written contract. Charges clients for express mail services, photocopying costs.

Tips "I'm interested in good writers who want a long term, long haul relationship. Not a one-book writer, but a writer who has many ideas, is productive, professional, passionate and meets deadlines!"

CRAIG NELSON CO.

77 Bleecker St., Suite 527, New York NY 10012. (212)929-3242. Fax: (212)929-3667. **Contact:** Craig Nelson. Member of AAR.

- Query before submitting.

NELSON LITERARY AGENCY

1020 15th St., Suite 26L, Denver CO 80202. (303)463-5301. E-mail: query@nelsonagency.com. Website: www.nelsonagency.com. **Contact:** Kristin Nelson. Estab. 2002. Member of AAR.

- Prior to opening her own agency, Ms. Nelson worked as a literary scout and subrights agent for literary agent Jody Rein.

Represents Nonfiction books, novels. **Considers these nonfiction areas:** Biography/autobiography; business/economics; history; memoirs; popular culture; sports; women's issues/studies; narrative nonfiction; investigative journalism. **Considers these fiction areas:** Fantasy (with romantic elements); literary; mainstream/contemporary; romance; science fiction (literary); women's; chick lit.

NLA specializes in representing commercial fiction and high caliber literary fiction. Actively seeking Latina writers who tackle contemporary issues in a modern voice (think *Dirty Girls Social Club*). Does not want short story collections, mysteries, thrillers, Christian, horror, young adult, children.

How to Contact Query by e-mail only.

Recent Sales *Dress Rehearsal*, by Jennifer O'Connell (NAL/Penguin Group); *Nobody's Saint*, by Paula Reed (Kensington); *Enchanted Inc.*, by Shanna Swendson (Ballantine). Other clients include Ally Carter, Mike Freeman, Bobby "The Brain" Heenan, Jack McCallum, Cheryl Sawyer, Linnea Sinclair.

NEW BRAND AGENCY GROUP, LLC

E-mail: mark@literaryagent.net. Website: www.literaryagent.net. **Contact:** Mark Ryan. Estab. 1994. Represents 3 clients. Currently handles: 33% nonfiction books; 33% novels; 33% juvenile books.

- New Brand Agency is currently closed to submissions. Check website for more details.

Member Agents Mark Ryan handles fiction and nonfiction with bestseller and/or high commercial potential.

Represents Nonfiction books, novels, juvenile books (books for younger readers). **Considers these nonfiction areas:** Biography/autobiography; business/economics; juvenile nonfiction; memoirs; popular culture; psychology; religious/inspirational; self-help/personal improvement; sex; spirituality; women's issues/studies; body and soul, health, humor, family, finance, fitness, gift/novelty, leadership, men's issues, parenting, relationships, success. **Considers these fiction areas:** Fantasy; historical; horror; juvenile; literary; mainstream/contemporary; romance (mainstream); science fiction; thriller; cross-genre, mystery, magical realism, supernatural, suspense.

O→ "We only work with authors we are passionate about." Actively seeking the story and voice that no one else can share but you.

How to Contact Accepts e-mail queries only; submit electronic query online at website. Responds in 1 week to mss. Responds in 48 hours to queries if interested. Obtains most new clients through queries.

Recent Sales *Black Valley*, by Jim Brown (Ballantine); *The Marriage Plan*, by Aggie Jordan, Ph.D. (Broadway/Bantam); *Mother to Daughter*, by Harry Harrison (Workman); *The She*, by Carol Plum-Ucci (Harcourt).

Terms Agent receives 15% commission on domestic sales. Offers written contract, binding for 6 months; 1-month notice must be given to terminate contract. 20% commission for subsidiary rights. Charges for postage and phone costs after sale of the project.

NEW ENGLAND PUBLISHING ASSOCIATES, INC.

P.O. Box 5, Chester CT 06412-0645. (860)345-READ or (860)345-4976. Fax: (860)345-3660. E-mail: nepa@nepa.com. Website: www.nepa.com. **Contact:** Elizabeth Frost-Knappman, Edward W. Knappman, Kristine Schiavi, Ron Formica, or Victoria Harlow. Estab. 1983. Member of AAR, ASJA, Authors Guild, Connecticut Press Club. Represents 125-150 clients. 15% of clients are new/unpublished writers.

Member Agents Elizabeth Frost-Knappman; Edward W. Knappman; Kristine Schiavi; Ron Formica; Victoria Harlow.

Represents Nonfiction books. **Considers these nonfiction areas:** Biography/autobiography; business/economics; child guidance/parenting; government/politics/law; health/medicine; history; language/literature/criticism; military/war; money/finance; nature/environment; psychology; science/technology; self-help/personal improvement; sports; true crime/investigative; women's issues/studies; reference.

O→ This agency specializes in adult nonfiction of serious purpose.

How to Contact Send outline/proposal, SASE. Accepts e-mail and fax queries. Considers simultaneous queries. Responds in 1 month to queries; 5 weeks to mss. Returns materials only with SASE.

Recent Sales Sold over 60 titles in the last year. *Hot Button Marketing*, by Barry Feig (Adams Media); *Elizabeth I & Philip II*, by Ben Patterson (St. Martin's Press); *The Story of French*, by Jean-Benoit Nadeua and Julie Barlow (St. Martin's Press/Knopf Canada); *The Joys of Mathematics*, by George Szpiro (Joseph Henry Press); *The New Breastfeeding Diet*, by Melissa Block and Richard Rountree, M.D. (McGraw-Hill); *Crash-Proof Your Kids*, by Tim Smith (Touchstone/Fireside).

Terms Agent receives 15% commission on domestic sales; 20% commission on foreign sales. Offers written contract, binding for 6 months. Charges clients for copying.

Writers' Conferences BEA and London Book Fair

Tips "Send us a well-written proposal that clearly identifies your audience—who will buy this book and why. Check our website for tips on proposals and advice on how to market your books. Revise, revise, revise, but never give up. We don't."

NINE MUSES AND APOLLO, INC.

525 Broadway, Suite 201, New York NY 10012. (212)431-2665. **Contact:** Ling Lucas. Estab. 1991. Represents 50 clients. 10% of clients are new/unpublished writers. Currently handles: 90% nonfiction books; 10% novels.

• Ms. Lucas formerly served as vice president, sales & marketing director, and associate publisher of Warner Books.

Represents Nonfiction books. **Considers these nonfiction areas:** Animals; biography/autobiography; business/economics; current affairs; ethnic/cultural interests; health/medicine; language/literature/criticism; psychology; spirituality; women's issues/studies. **Considers these fiction areas:** Ethnic; literary; mainstream/contemporary (commercial).

O→ This agency specializes in nonfiction. Does not want to receive children's and young adult material.

How to Contact Submit outline, 2 sample chapters, SASE. Prefers to read materials exclusively. Responds in 1 month to mss.

Recent Sales *My Daddy Is a Pretzel*, by Baron Baptiste (Barefoot Books); *The Twelve Gifts of Healing*, by Charlene Costanzo (HarperCollins); *The Twelve Gifts of Marriage*, by C. Costanzo (HarperCollins); *Once Upon a Time in China*, by Jeff Yang (Atria).

Terms Agent receives 15% commission on domestic sales; 20-25% commission on foreign sales. Offers written contract. Charges clients for photocopying, postage.

Tips "Your outline should already be well developed, cogent, and reveal clarity of thought about the general structure and direction of your project."

HAROLD OBER ASSOCIATES

425 Madison Ave., New York NY 10017. (212)759-8600. Fax: (212)759-9428. Estab. 1929. Member of AAR. Represents 250 clients. 10% of clients are new/unpublished writers. Currently handles: 35% nonfiction books; 50% novels; 15% juvenile books.

Member Agents Phyllis Westberg; Pamela Malpas; Emma Sweeney; Knox Burger; Craig Tenney (not accepting new clients).

Represents Nonfiction books, novels, juvenile books. **Considers these nonfiction areas:** Considers all nonfiction areas. **Considers these fiction areas:** Considers all fiction subjects.

How to Contact Query letter only with SASE. No e-mail or fax queries. Responds as promptly as possible. Obtains most new clients through recommendations from others.

Terms Agent receives 15% commission on domestic sales; 20% commission on foreign sales. Charges clients for photocopying and express mail or package services.

FIFI OSCARD AGENCY, INC.

110 W. 40th St., 16th Floor, New York NY 10018. (212)764-1100. Fax: (212)840-5019. E-mail: agency@fifioscard.com. Website: www.fifioscard.com. **Contact:** Literary Department. Estab. 1956. Member of AAR; signatory of WGA. Represents 108 clients. 5% of clients are new/unpublished writers. Currently handles: 60% nonfiction books; 10% novels; 30% stage plays.

Member Agents Fifi Oscard; Peter Sawyer; Carmen La Via; Kevin McShane; Ivy Fischer Stone; Carolyn French; Jerry Rudes.

Represents Nonfiction books, novels, stage plays.

- This agency specializes in history, celebrity biography and autobiography, pop culture, travel/adventure, performing arts, fine arts/design.

How to Contact Query; submission form online. *No unsolicited mss.* Responds in 2 weeks to queries.

Recent Sales *My Father Had a Daughter: Judith Shakespeare's Tale*, by Grace Tiffany (Berkeley); *The Gospel According to Martin: The Spiritual Biography of Martin Luther King*, by Stewart Burns (Harper San Francisco); *Colored Lights*, by Kander and Ebb (Farrar, Strauss, & Giroux).

Terms Agent receives 15% commission on domestic sales; 20% commission on foreign sales; 10% commission on dramatic rights sales. Charges clients for photocopying expenses.

Tips "Writers must have screen credits if sending movie scripts."

PARAVIEW, INC.

40 Florence Circle, Bracey VA 23919. Phone/Fax: (434)636-4138. E-mail: lhagan@paraview.com. Website: www.paraview.com. **Contact:** Lisa Hagan. Estab. 1988. Represents 75 clients. 15% of clients are new/unpublished writers. Currently handles: 100% nonfiction books.

- Ms. Hagan has agented since 1995.

Member Agents Lisa Hagan (fiction and nonfiction self-help).

Represents Nonfiction books, novels (very few). **Considers these nonfiction areas:** Agriculture/horticulture; Americana; animals; anthropology/archaeology; art/architecture/design; biography/autobiography; business/economics; child guidance/parenting; computers/electronic; cooking/foods/nutrition; crafts/hobbies; creative nonfiction; current affairs; education; ethnic/cultural interests; gardening; gay/lesbian issues; government/politics/law; health/medicine; history; how-to; humor/satire; interior design/decorating; juvenile nonfiction; language/literature/criticism; memoirs; military/war; money/finance; multicultural; music/dance; nature/environment; New Age/metaphysics; philosophy; photography; popular culture; psychology; recreation; regional; religious/inspirational; science/technology; self-help/personal improvement; sex; sociology; software; spirituality; sports; theater/film; translation; travel; true crime/investigative; women's issues/studies; young adult. **Considers these fiction areas:** Action/adventure; contemporary issues; ethnic; feminist; literary; mainstream/contemporary; regional; romance; women's.

- This agency specializes in spiritual, New Age and self-help.

How to Contact Query via e-mail and include synopsis and author bio. Responds in 1 month to queries; 3 months to mss. Obtains most new clients through recommendations from editors and current clients.

Recent Sales Sold 40 titles in the last year. *Cause for Sucess*, by Christine Arena (New World Library); *Psychic Living*, by Stacey Wolf (Pocket Books); *Bedside Guide to Dreams*, by Stase Michaels (Random House); *Tarot Power*, by Lexa Rosean (Pocket Books); *Alien Rock*, by Michael Luckman (Pocket Books).

Terms Agent receives 15% commission on domestic sales; 20% commission on foreign sales.

Writers' Conferences BEA (Chicago, June); London Book Fair; E3—Electronic Entertainment Exposition.

Tips "New writers should have their work edited, critiqued, and carefully reworked prior to submission. First contact should be via e-mail."

THE RICHARD PARKS AGENCY

Box 693, Salem NY 12865. Website: www.richardparksagency.com. **Contact:** Richard Parks. Estab. 1988. Member of AAR. Currently handles: 55% nonfiction books; 40% novels; 5% story collections.

Represents Nonfiction books, novels. **Considers these nonfiction areas:** Animals; anthropology/archaeology; art/architecture/design; biography/autobiography; business/economics; child guidance/parenting; cooking/foods/nutrition; crafts/hobbies; current affairs; ethnic/cultural interests; gardening; gay/lesbian issues; government/politics/law; health/medicine; history; how-to; humor/satire; language/literature/criticism; memoirs; military/war; money/finance; music/dance; nature/environment; popular culture; psychology; science/technology; self-help/personal improvement; sociology; theater/film; travel; women's issues/studies. **Considers these fiction areas:** Considers fiction by referral only.

O→ Actively seeking nonfiction. Does not want to receive unsolicited material.

How to Contact Query by mail only with SASE. No e-mail or fax queries. Considers simultaneous queries Responds in 2 weeks to queries. Returns materials only with SASE. Obtains most new clients through recommendations and referrals.

Terms Agent receives 15% commission on domestic sales; 20% commission on foreign sales. Charges clients for photocopying or any unusual expense incurred at the writer's request.

KATHI J. PATON LITERARY AGENCY

19 W. 55th St., New York NY 10019-4907. (908)647-2117. E-mail: kjplitbiz@optonline.net. **Contact:** Kathi Paton. Estab. 1987. Currently handles: 65% nonfiction books; 35% fiction.

Represents Nonfiction books, novels, short story collections, book-based film rights. **Considers these nonfiction areas:** Business/economics; child guidance/parenting; money/finance (personal investing); nature/environment; psychology; religious/inspirational; women's issues/studies. **Considers these fiction areas:** Literary; mainstream/contemporary; short story collections.

O→ This agency specializes in adult nonfiction.

How to Contact Accepts e-mail queries. For nonfiction, send proposal, sample chapter, and SASE. For fiction, send first 40 pages, plot summary, or 3 short stories and SASE. Considers simultaneous queries. Obtains most new clients through recommendations from other clients.

Recent Sales *Future Wealth*, by McInerney and White (St. Martin's Press); *Unraveling the Mystery of Autism*, by Karyn Seroussi (Simon & Schuster).

Terms Agent receives 15% commission on domestic sales; 20% commission on foreign sales. Offers written contract. Charges clients for photocopying.

Writers' Conferences Attends major regional panels, seminars, and conferences.

L. PERKINS ASSOCIATES

16 W. 36 St., New York NY 10018. (212)279-6418. Fax: (718)543-5354. E-mail: lperkinsagency@yahoo.com. **Contact:** Lori Perkins or Amy Stout (astoutlperkinsagency@yahoo.com). Estab. 1990. Member of AAR. Represents 50 clients. 10% of clients are new/unpublished writers.

- Ms. Perkins has been an agent for 18 years. Her agency has an affiliate agency, Southern Literary Group. She is also the author of *The Insider's Guide to Getting an Agent* (Writer's Digest Books).

Represents Nonfiction books, novels. **Considers these nonfiction areas:** Popular culture. **Considers these fiction areas:** Fantasy; horror; literary (dark); science fiction.

O→ Most of Ms. Perkins' clients write both fiction and nonfiction. "This combination keeps my clients publishing for years. I am also a published author, so I know what it takes to write a good book." Actively seeking a Latino *Gone With the Wind* and *Waiting to Exhale,* and urban ethnic horror. Does not want to receive "anything outside of the above categories, i.e., westerns, romance."

How to Contact Query with SASE. Considers simultaneous queries. Responds in 6 weeks to queries; 3 months to mss. Returns materials only with SASE. Obtains most new clients through recommendations from others, solicitations, conferences.

Recent Sales Sold 100 titles in the last year. *How to Make Love Like a Porn Star: A Cautionary Tale,* by Jenna Jameson (Reagan Books); *Dear Mom, I Always Wanted You to Know,* by Lisa Delman (Perigee Books); *The Illustrated Ray Bradbury,* by Jerry Weist (Avon); *The Poet in Exile,* by Ray Manzarek (Avalon); *Behind Sad Eyes: The Life of George Harrison,* (St. Martin's Press).

Terms Agent receives 15% commission on domestic sales; 20% commission on foreign sales. No written contract. Charges clients for photocopying.

Writers' Conferences San Diego Writer's Conference; NECON; BEA; World Fantasy.

Tips "Research your field and contact professional writers' organizations to see who is looking for what. Finish your novel before querying agents. Read my book, *An Insider's Guide to Getting an Agent,* to get a sense of how agents operate."

STEPHEN PEVNER, INC.

382 Lafayette St., 8th Floor, New York NY 10003. (212)674-8403. Fax: (212)529-3692. E-mail: spevner@aol.com. **Contact:** Stephen Pevner.

Represents Nonfiction books, novels, feature film, TV scripts, TV movie of the week, episodic drama, animation, documentary, miniseries. **Considers these nonfiction areas:** Biography/autobiography; ethnic/cultural interests; gay/lesbian issues; history; humor/satire; language/literature/criticism; memoirs; music/dance; New Age/metaphysics; photography; popular culture; religious/inspirational; sociology; travel. **Considers these fiction areas:** Comic books/cartoon; contemporary issues; erotica; ethnic; experimental; gay/lesbian; glitz; horror; humor/satire; literary; mainstream/contemporary; psychic/supernatural; thriller; urban. **Considers these script subject areas:** Comedy; contemporary issues; detective/police/crime; gay/lesbian; glitz; horror; romantic comedy; romantic drama; thriller.

This agency specializes in motion pictures, novels, humor, pop culture, urban fiction, independent filmmakers. Actively seeking urban fiction, popular culture, screenplays, and film proposals.

How to Contact Query with SASE, outline/proposal. Prefers to read materials exclusively. No e-mail or fax queries. Responds in 2 weeks to queries; 1 month to mss. Obtains most new clients through recommendations from others.

Recent Sales *In the Company of Men* and *Bash: Latterday Plays*, by Neil Labote; *The Vagina Monologues*, by Eve Ensler; *Guide to Life*, by The Five Lesbian Brothers; *Noise From Underground*, by Michael Levine. Other clients include Richard Linklater, Gregg Araki, Tom DiCillo, Genvieve Turner/Rose Troche, Todd Solondz, Neil LaBute.

Terms Agent receives 15% commission on domestic sales; 20% commission on foreign sales. Offers written contract, binding for 1 year; 6-week notice must be given to terminate contract. 100% of business is derived from commissions on ms sales.

Tips "Be persistent, but civilized."

ALISON J. PICARD, LITERARY AGENT

P.O. Box 2000, Cotuit MA 02635. (508)477-7192. Fax: (508)477-7192 (please contact before faxing). E-mail: ajpicard@aol.com. **Contact:** Alison Picard. Estab. 1985. Represents 48 clients. 30% of clients are new/unpublished writers. Currently handles: 40% nonfiction books; 40% novels; 20% juvenile books.

- Prior to becoming an agent, Ms. Picard was an assistant at an NYC literary agency.

Member Agents Alison Picard (mysteries/suspense/thriller, romance, literary fiction, adult nonfiction, juvenile books).

Represents Nonfiction books, novels, short story collections, novellas, juvenile books. **Considers these nonfiction areas:** Animals; anthropology/archaeology; art/architecture/design; biography/autobiography; business/economics; child guidance/parenting; cooking/foods/nutrition; current affairs; education; ethnic/cultural interests; gay/lesbian issues; government/politics/law; health/medicine; history; how-to; humor/satire; juvenile nonfiction; memoirs; military/war; money/finance; multicultural; music/dance; nature/environment; New Age/metaphysics; popular culture; psychology; religious/inspirational; science/technology; self-help/personal improvement; translation; travel; true crime/investigative; women's issues/studies; young adult. **Considers these fiction areas:** Action/adventure; contemporary issues; detective/police/crime; erotica; ethnic; experimental; family saga; feminist; gay/lesbian; glitz; historical; horror; humor/satire; juvenile; literary; mainstream/contemporary; multicultural; mystery/suspense; New Age; picture books; psychic/supernatural; regional; religious/inspirational; romance; sports; thriller; young adult.

"Many of my clients have come to me from big agencies, where they felt overlooked or ignored. I communicate freely with my clients and offer a lot of career advice, suggestions for revising manuscripts, etc. If I believe in a project, I will submit it to a dozen or more publishers, unlike some agents who give up after four or five rejections." Actively seeking commercial adult fiction and nonfiction, middle grade juvenile fiction. Does not want to receive science fiction/fantasy, westerns, poetry, plays, articles.

How to Contact Query with SASE. Considers simultaneous queries. Responds in 2 weeks to queries; 4 months to mss. Returns materials only with SASE. Obtains most new clients through recommendations from others, solicitations.

Recent Sales Sold 32 titles in the last year. *A Hard Ticket Home*, by David Housewright (St. Martin's Press); *Indigo Rose*, by Susan Miller (Bantam Books/Random House); *Fly Fishing & Funerals*, by Mary Bartek (Henry Holt & Co.); *Stage Fright*, by Dina Friedman (Farrar Straus & Giroux); *Fashion Slaves*, by Louise de Teliga (Kensington). Other clients include Osha Gray Davidson, Amy Dean, David Housewright, Nancy Means Wright.

Terms Agent receives 15% commission on domestic sales; 20% commission on foreign sales. Offers written contract, binding for 1 year; 1-week notice must be given to terminate contract.

Tips "Please don't send material without sending a query first via mail or e-mail. I don't accept phone or fax queries. Always enclose a SASE with a query."

PINDER LANE & GARON-BROOKE ASSOCIATES, LTD.

159 W. 53rd St., Suite 14C, New York NY 10019-6005. (212)489-0880. E-mail: pinderl@interport.net. **Contact:** Robert Thixton. Member of AAR; signatory of WGA. Represents 30 clients. 20% of clients are new/unpublished writers. Currently handles: 25% nonfiction books; 75% novels.

Member Agents Dick Duane, Robert Thixton.

Represents Nonfiction books, novels. **Considers these fiction areas:** Contemporary issues; detective/police/crime; family saga; fantasy; gay/lesbian; literary; mainstream/contemporary; mystery/suspense; romance; science fiction.

This agency specializes in mainstream fiction and nonfiction. Does not want to receive screenplays, TV series teleplays, or dramatic plays.

How to Contact Query with SASE. *No unsolicited mss.* Responds in 3 weeks to queries; 2 months to mss. Obtains most new clients through referrals, queries.

Recent Sales Sold 20 titles in the last year. *Diana & Jackie—Maidens, Mothers & Myths*, by Jay Mulvaney (St. Martin's Press); The Sixth Fleet series, by David Meadows (Berkley); *Dark Fires*, by Rosemary Rogers (Mira Books).

Terms Agent receives 15% commission on domestic sales; 30% commission on foreign sales. Offers written contract, binding for 3-5 years.

Tips "With our literary and media experience, our agency is uniquely positioned for the current and future direction publishing is taking. Send query letter first giving the essence of the manuscript, and a personal or career bio with SASE."

ALICKA PISTEK LITERARY AGENCY, LLC

302A W. 12th St., #124, New York NY 10014. E-mail: info@alickapistek.com. Website: www.alickapistek.com. **Contact:** Alicka Pistek. Estab. 2003. Represents 15 clients. 50% of clients are new/unpublished writers. Currently handles: 60% nonfiction books; 40% novels.

- Prior to opening her agency, Ms. Pistek worked at ICM, and as an agent at Nicholas Ellison, Inc.

Represents Nonfiction books, novels. **Considers these nonfiction areas:** Animals; anthropology/archaeology; biography/autobiography; business/economics; child guidance/parenting; cooking/foods/nutrition; creative nonfiction; current affairs; government/politics/law; health/medicine; history; how-to; language/literature/criticism; memoirs; military/war; money/finance; nature/environment; psychology; religious/inspirational; science/technology; self-help/personal improvement; translation; travel. **Considers these fiction areas:** Detective/police/crime; ethnic; family saga; historical; literary; mainstream/contemporary; mystery/suspense; romance; thriller.

Does not want to receive fantasy, science fiction, westerns.

How to Contact Query with SASE, submit outline, 2 sample chapters. Considers simultaneous queries. Responds in 2 months to queries; 8 weeks to mss. Returns materials only with SASE.

Recent Sales *Erin Grady*, by Marcelle Difalco and Jocelyn Herz. Other clients include Alan Levy, Belisa Vranich, Michael Christopher Carroll, Alex Boese.

Terms Agent receives 15% commission on domestic sales; 20% commission on foreign sales. Offers written contract. Charges for photocopying over 40 pages, international postage.

Writers' Conferences Frankfurt Book Fair.

Tips "Be sure you are familiar with the genre you are writing in, and learn standard procedures for submitting your work. A good query will go a long way."

JULIE POPKIN

15340 Albright St., #204, Pacific Palisades CA 90272-2520. (310)459-2834. Fax: (310)459-4128. **Contact:** Julie Popkin. Estab. 1989. Represents 35 clients. 30% of clients are new/unpublished writers. Currently handles: 70% nonfiction books; 30% novels.

- Prior to opening her agency, Ms. Popkin taught at the university level and did freelance editing and writing.

Member Agents Julie Popkin (fiction, memoirs, biography); Alyson Sena (nonfiction).

Represents Nonfiction books, novels, translations. **Considers these nonfiction areas:** Art/architecture/design; ethnic/cultural interests; government/politics/law; history; memoirs; philosophy; women's issues/studies (feminist); criticism. **Considers these fiction areas:** Literary; mainstream/contemporary; mystery/suspense.

This agency specializes in selling book-length mss including fiction and nonfiction. Especially interested in social issues, ethnic and minority subjects, Latin American authors. Does not want to receive New Age, spiritual, romance, science fiction.

How to Contact Query with SASE. No e-mail or fax queries. Responds in 1 month to queries; 2 months to mss. Obtains most new clients through "Mostly clients find me through guides and personal contacts."

Recent Sales *The Rainforest*, by Alicia Steimberg (University of Nebraska Press); *The King's English*, by Betsy

Burton (Gibbs Smith); *Violations: Love Stories by Latin American Women*, edited by Psiche Hughes (University of Nebraska Press); *In the Break*, by Jack Lopez (Little, Brown); *Stories*, by Edgar Brau (Michigan State University Press); *Death as a Side Effect*, by Ana Maria Shua (Wisconsin).

Terms Agent receives 15% commission on domestic sales; 20% commission on foreign sales; 10% commission on dramatic rights sales. Sometimes asks for fee if ms requires extensive copying and mailing.

Writers' Conferences BEA (June); Santa Barbara (June).

Tips "Keep your eyes on the current market. Publishing responds to changes very quickly and often works toward perceived and fresh subject matter. Historical fiction seems to be rising in interest after a long, quiet period."

HELEN F. PRATT INC.

1165 Fifth Ave., New York NY 10029. (212)722-5081. Fax: (212)722-8569. **Contact:** Helen F. Pratt. Member of AAR.

- Query before submitting.

Member Agents Helen F. Pratt, Seamus Mullarkey.

AARON M. PRIEST LITERARY AGENCY

708 Third Ave., 23rd Floor, New York NY 10017-4103. (212)818-0344. Fax: (212)573-9417. E-mail: lchilds@aaronpriest.com. **Contact:** Aaron Priest or Molly Friedrich. Estab. 1974. Member of AAR. Currently handles: 25% nonfiction books; 75% novels.

Member Agents Lisa Erbach Vance; Paul Cirone; Aaron Priest; Molly Friedrich; Lucy Childs.

Represents Nonfiction books, novels.

How to Contact No e-mail or fax queries. Considers simultaneous queries. If interested, will respond within 2 weeks

Recent Sales *She is Me*, by Kathleen Schine; *Killer Smile*, by Lisa Scottoline.

Terms Agent receives 15% commission on domestic sales. Charges for photocopying, foreign-postage expenses.

SUSAN ANN PROTTER, LITERARY AGENT

110 W. 40th St., Suite 1408, New York NY 10018. (212)840-0480. **Contact:** Susan Protter. Estab. 1971. Member of AAR, Authors' Guild. Represents 40 clients. 5% of clients are new/unpublished writers. Currently handles: 50% nonfiction books; 50% novels; occasional magazine article or short story (for established clients only).

- Prior to opening her agency, Ms. Protter was associate director of subsidiary rights at Harper & Row Publishers.

Represents Nonfiction books, novels. **Considers these nonfiction areas:** Biography/autobiography; current affairs; health/medicine; science/technology; international and Middle Eastern issues. **Considers these fiction areas:** Fantasy; mystery/suspense; science fiction; thriller; crime.

O→ Writers must have book-length project or ms that is ready to sell. Does not want westerns, romance, children's books, young adult novels, screenplays, plays, poetry, Star Wars, or Star Trek.

How to Contact Currently looking for limited number of new clients. Send short query by mail with SASE. *No unsolicited mss.* Responds in 3 weeks to queries; 2 months to mss.

Recent Sales *Beyond the Mirage: America's Fragile Partnership with Saudi Arabia*, by Thomas W. Lippman (Westview); *House of Storms*, by Ian R. MacLeod (Ace); *Einstein for Dummies*, by Carlos Calle, Ph.D. (Wiley).

Terms Agent receives 15% commission on domestic sales; 15% commission on dramatic rights sales. "If, after seeing your query, we request to see your manuscript, there will be a small shipping and handling fee requested to cover cost of returning materials should they not be suitable." Charges clients for photocopying, messenger, express mail, airmail and overseas shipping expenses.

Tips "Please send neat and professionally organized queries. Make sure to include a SASE, or we cannot reply. We receive approximately 200 queries a week and read them in the order they arrive. We usually reply within 2 weeks to any query. Please, do not call or e-mail queries. If you are sending a multiple query, make sure to note that in your letter. I am looking for work that stands out in a highly competitive and difficult market."

N MICHAEL PSALTIS

200 Bennett Ave., New York NY 10040. **Contact:** Michael Psaltis. Member of AAR.

- Query before submitting.

QUICKSILVER BOOKS—LITERARY AGENTS

508 Central Park Ave., #5101, Scarsdale NY 10583. (914)722-4664. Fax: (914)722-4664. Website: www.quicksilverbooks.com. **Contact:** Bob Silverstein. Estab. 1973 as packager; 1987 as literary agency. Represents 50 clients. 50% of clients are new/unpublished writers. Currently handles: 75% nonfiction books; 25% novels.

• Prior to opening his agency, Mr. Silverstein served as senior editor at Bantam Books and Dell Books/ Delacorte Press.

Represents Nonfiction books, novels. **Considers these nonfiction areas:** Anthropology/archaeology; biography/autobiography; business/economics; child guidance/parenting; cooking/foods/nutrition; current affairs; ethnic/cultural interests; health/medicine; history; how-to; language/literature/criticism; memoirs; nature/environment; New Age/metaphysics; popular culture; psychology; religious/inspirational; science/technology; self-help/personal improvement; sociology; sports; true crime/investigative; women's issues/studies. **Considers these fiction areas:** Action/adventure; glitz; mystery/suspense; thriller.

O→ This agency specializes in literary and commercial mainstream fiction and nonfiction (especially psychology, New Age, holistic healing, consciousness, ecology, environment, spirituality, reference, cookbooks, narrative nonfiction). Actively seeking commercial mainstream fiction and nonfiction in most categories. Does not want to receive science fiction, pornography, poetry, or single-spaced mss.

How to Contact Query with SASE. Authors are expected to supply SASE for return of ms and for query letter responses. No e-mail or fax queries. Considers simultaneous queries. Responds in 2 weeks to queries; 1 month to mss. Returns materials only with SASE. Obtains most new clients through recommendations, listings in sourcebooks, solicitations, workshop participation.

Recent Sales Sold over 20 titles in the last year. *Nice Girls Don't Get Rich*, by Lois P. Frankel, Ph.D. (Warner Books); *The Young Patriots*, by Charles Cerami (Sourcebooks); *The Coming of the Beatles*, by Martin Goldsmith (Wiley); *The Real Food Daily Cookbook*, by Ann Gentry (Ten Speed Press); *The Complete Book of Vinyasa Yoga*, by Srivatsa Ramaswami (Marlow & Co.).

Terms Agent receives 15% commission on domestic sales; 20% commission on foreign sales. Offers written contract.

Writers' Conferences National Writers Union Conference (Dobbs Ferry NY, April).

Tips "Write what you know. Write from the heart. Publishers print, authors sell."

RAINES & RAINES

103 Kenyon Rd., Medusa NY 12120. (518)239-8311. Fax: (518)239-6029. **Contact:** Theron Raines (member of AAR); Joan Raines; Keith Korman.

• Query before submitting.

CHARLOTTE CECIL RAYMOND, LITERARY AGENT

32 Bradlee Rd., Marblehead MA 01945. **Contact:** Charlotte Cecil Raymond. Estab. 1983. Currently handles: 90% nonfiction books; 10% novels.

Represents Nonfiction books. **Considers these nonfiction areas:** Current affairs; ethnic/cultural interests (cultural, gender interests); history; nature/environment; psychology; sociology; biography.

O→ Does not want to receive self-help/personal improvement, science fiction, fantasy, young adult, juvenile, poetry, screenplays.

How to Contact Query with SASE, submit proposal package, outline. Responds in 2 weeks to queries; 6 weeks to mss.

Terms Agent receives 15% commission on domestic sales. 100% of business is derived from commissions on ms sales.

HELEN REES LITERARY AGENCY

376 North St., Boston MA 02113-2013. (617)227-9014. Fax: (617)227-8762. E-mail: reesagency@reesagency.com (no unsolicited e-mail submissions). **Contact:** Joan Mazmanian, Ann Collette, Helen Rees, or Lorin Rees. Estab. 1983. Member of AAR, PEN. Represents 80 clients. 50% of clients are new/unpublished writers. Currently handles: 60% nonfiction books; 40% novels.

Member Agents Ann Collette (literary fiction, women's studies, health, biography, history); Helen Rees (business, money/finance/economics, government/politics/law, contemporary issues, literary fiction); Lorin Rees (business, money, finance, management, history, narrative nonfiction, science, literary fiction, memoir).

Represents Nonfiction books, novels. **Considers these nonfiction areas:** Biography/autobiography; business/economics; current affairs; government/politics/law; health/medicine; history; money/finance; women's issues/studies. **Considers these fiction areas:** Contemporary issues; historical; literary; mainstream/contemporary; mystery/suspense; thriller.

How to Contact Query with SASE, outline, 2 sample chapters. No e-mail or fax queries. Responds in 2-3 weeks to queries. Obtains most new clients through recommendations from others, solicitations, conferences.

Recent Sales Sold 30 titles in the last year. *Get Your Shipt Together*, by Capt. D. Michael Abrashoff; *Overpromise and Overdeliver*, by Rick Berrara; *MBA in a Box*, by Joel Kurtzman; *America the Broke*, by Gerald Swanson; *Murder at the B-School*, by Jeffrey Cruikshank; *Skin River*, by Steven Sidor; *Father Said*, by Hal Sirowitz.

Terms Agent receives 15% commission on domestic sales; 20% commission on foreign sales.

REGAL LITERARY AGENCY

1140 Broadway, Penthouse, New York NY 10001. (212)684-7900. Fax: (212)684-7906. E-mail: office@regal-literary.com. Website: www.regal-literary.com. **Contact:** Bess Reed, Lauren Schott. Estab. 2002. Member of AAR. Represents 70 clients. 20% of clients are new/unpublished writers. Currently handles: 48% nonfiction books; 46% novels; 2% story collections; 2% novellas; 2% poetry.

- Prior to becoming agents, Gordon Kato was a psychologist, Jospeph Regal was a musician, and Peter Steinberg and Lauren Schott were magazine editors.

Member Agents Gordon Kato (literary fiction, commercial fiction, pop culture); Joseph Regal (literary fiction, science, history, memoir); Peter Steinberg (literary and commercial fiction, history, humor, memoir, narrative nonfiction); Bess Reed (literary fiction, narrative nonfiction, self-help); Lauren Schott (literary fiction, commercial fiction, memoir, narrative nonfiction, thrillers, mysteries).

Represents Nonfiction books, novels, short story collections, novellas. **Considers these nonfiction areas:** Anthropology/archaeology; art/architecture/design; biography/autobiography; business/economics; cooking/foods/nutrition; current affairs; ethnic/cultural interests; gay/lesbian issues; government/politics/law; history; humor/satire; language/literature/criticism; memoirs; military/war; music/dance; nature/environment; photography; popular culture; psychology; religious/inspirational (includes inspirational); science/technology (includes technology); sports; translation; true crime/investigative; women's issues/studies. **Considers these fiction areas:** Comic books/cartoon; detective/police/crime; ethnic; historical; literary; mystery/suspense; thriller; contemporary.

"We have discovered more than a dozen successful literary novelists in the last 5 years. We are small, but are extraordinarily responsive to our writers. We are more like managers than agents, with an eye toward every aspect of our writers' careers, including publicity and other media." Actively seeking literary fiction and narrative nonfiction. Does not want romance, science fiction, horror, screenplays, or children's books.

How to Contact Query with SASE, submit 5-15 sample pages. No e-mail or fax queries. Considers simultaneous queries. Responds in 2-3 weeks to queries; 4-12 to mss. Returns materials only with SASE. Obtains most new clients through recommendations from others, unsolicited submissions.

Recent Sales Sold 30 titles in the last year. Clients include James Reston, Jr., Tim Winton, Tony Earley, Dennie Hughes, Mark Lee, Jake Page, Cheryl Bernard, Daniel Wallace, John Marks, Keith Scribner, Alex Abella, Audrey Niffenegger, Cathy Day, Alicia Erian, Gergory David Roberts, Dallas Hudgens, John Twelve Hawks.

Terms Agent receives 15% commission on domestic sales; 20% commission on foreign sales. No written contract. Charges clients for typical, major office expenses, such as photocopying and foreign postage.

JODY REIN BOOKS, INC.

7741 S. Ash Court, Centennial CO 80122. (303)694-4430. Fax: (303)694-0687. Website: www.jodyreinbooks.com. **Contact:** Winnefred Dollar. Estab. 1994. Member of AAR, Authors' Guild. Currently handles: 70% nonfiction books; 30% novels.

- Prior to opening her agency, Jody Rein worked for 13 years as an acquisitions editor for Contemporary Books, Bantam/Doubleday/Dell (executive editor), and Morrow/Avon (executive editor).

Member Agents Jody Rein; Johnna Hietala.

Represents Nonfiction books (primarily narrative and commercial nonfiction), novels (select literary novels, commercial mainstream). **Considers these nonfiction areas:** Business/economics; child guidance/parenting; current affairs; ethnic/cultural interests; government/politics/law; history; humor/satire; music/dance; nature/environment; popular culture; psychology; science/technology; sociology; theater/film; women's issues/studies. **Considers these fiction areas:** Literary; mainstream/contemporary.

This agency specializes in commercial and narrative nonfiction, and literary/commercial fiction.

How to Contact Query with SASE. No e-mail or fax queries. Considers simultaneous queries. Responds in 6 weeks to queries; 2 months to mss. Obtains most new clients through recommendations from others, solicitations.

Recent Sales *8 Simple Rules for Dating My Teenage Daughter*, by Bruce Cameron (ABC/Disney); *Skeletons on the Zahara*, by Dean King (Little, Brown); *The Big Year*, by Mark Obmascik (The Free Press).

Terms Agent receives 15% commission on domestic sales; 25% commission on foreign sales; 20% commission on dramatic rights sales. Offers written contract. Charges clients for express mail, overseas expenses, photocopying ms.

Tips "Do your homework before submitting. Make sure you have a marketable topic and the credentials to write about it. Well-written books on fresh and original nonfiction topics that have broad appeal. Novels written by authors who have spent years developing their craft. Authors must be well established in their fields and have strong media experience."

JODIE RHODES LITERARY AGENCY

8840 Villa La Jolla Dr., Suite 315, La Jolla CA 92037-1957. **Contact:** Jodie Rhodes, president. Estab. 1998. Member of AAR. Represents 50 clients. 60% of clients are new/unpublished writers. Currently handles: 60% nonfiction books; 35% novels; 5% middle to young adult books.

- Prior to opening her agency, Ms. Rhodes was a university-level creative writing teacher, workshop director, published novelist, and Vice President Media Director at the N.W. Ayer Advertising Agency.

Member Agents Jodie Rhodes, president; Clark McCutcheon (fiction); Bob McCarter (nonfiction).

Represents Nonfiction books, novels, juvenile books. **Considers these nonfiction areas:** Biography/autobiography; child guidance/parenting; ethnic/cultural interests; government/politics/law; health/medicine; history; memoirs; military/war; science/technology; women's issues/studies. **Considers these fiction areas:** Contemporary issues; ethnic; family saga; historical; juvenile; literary; mainstream/contemporary; mystery/suspense; thriller; young adult; women's.

O➝ Actively seeking "writers passionate about their books with a talent for richly textured narrative, an eye for details, and a nose for research." Nonfiction writers must have recognized credentials and expert knowledge of their subject matter. Does not want to receive erotica, horror, fantasy, romance, science fiction, children's books, religious, or inspirational books.

How to Contact Query with brief synopsis, first 30-50 pages, and SASE. No e-mail or fax queries. Considers simultaneous queries. Responds in 10 days to queries. Returns materials only with SASE. Obtains most new clients through recommendations from others, agent sourcebooks.

Recent Sales Sold 32 titles in the last year. *The Village Bride in Beverly Hills*, by Kavita Daswani (Putnam US/HarperCollins UK); *Memory Matters*, by Scott Hagwood (Simon & Schuster); *Raising Healthy Eaters*, by Dr. Henry Legeres (Perseus/Da Capo Press); *The Anorexia Diaries*, by Linda and Tara Rio (Rodale); *Memoirs of a Dwarf in the Sun King's Court*, by Paul Weidner (University of Wisconsin Press); *Becoming Japanese*, by Karin Muller (Rodale); *Free Your Child from Asthma*, by Dr. Gary Rachelefsky (McGraw-Hill); *The Potty Myth*, by Jill Lekovic (Crown/3 Rivers Press); *Intimate Partner Violence*, by Dr. Connie Mitchell (Oxford University Press); *Our Fragile Planet*, by Dana Desonie (Facts on File); *Modern Babies*, by Dr. Daniel Potter (Marlowe & Co.); *Biology for a New Century*, by Dr. Stan Rice (John Wiley & Sons); *A Writer's Paris*, by Eric Maisel (Writer's Digest Books); *Post Adoption Blues*, by Karen Foli (Rodale).

Terms Agent receives 15% commission on domestic sales; 20% commission on foreign sales. Offers written contract; 1-month notice must be given to terminate contract. Charges clients for fax, photocopying, phone calls, and postage. "Charges are itemized and approved by writers upfront."

Tips "Think your book out before you write it. Do your research, know your subject matter intimately, write vivid specifics, not bland generalities. Care deeply about your book. Don't imitate other writers. Find your own voice. We never take on a book we don't believe in, and we go the extra mile for our writers. We welcome talented, new writers."

BARBARA RIFKIND LITERARY AGENCY

132 Perry St., 6th Floor, New York NY 10014. (212)229-0453. Fax: (212)229-0454. E-mail: barbara@barbararifkind.net. **Contact:** Barbara Rifkind. Estab. 2002. Member of AAR. Represents 20 clients. 50% of clients are new/unpublished writers. Currently handles: 80% nonfiction books; 10% scholarly books; 10% textbooks.

- Prior to becoming an agent, Ms. Rifkind was an acquisitions editor, editorial manager, and a general manager in educational publishing (Addison Wesley).

Represents Nonfiction books, scholarly books, textbooks. **Considers these nonfiction areas:** Anthropology/archaeology; art/architecture/design; biography/autobiography; business/economics; child guidance/parenting; current affairs; ethnic/cultural interests; government/politics/law; health/medicine; history; language/literature/criticism; money/finance; popular culture; psychology; science/technology; sociology; women's issues/studies.

O➝ "We represent writers of smart nonfiction—academics, journalists, scientists, thinkers, people who've done something real and have something to say—writing for general trade audiences and occassionally for trade scholarly or textbook markets. We like to work in the areas of history; science writing; business and economics; applications of social sciences to important issues; public affairs and current events; narrative nonfiction; women's issues and parenting from a discipline." Actively seeking smart nonfiction from credentialed thinkers or published writers in selected areas of interest. Does not want commercial or category fiction, juvenile, and other nonselected areas.

How to Contact Query with SASE, submit proposal package, outline. Accepts e-mail queries. No fax queries. Responds in 2 weeks to queries. Obtains most new clients through recommendations from others.

Recent Sales Clients include Zvi Bodie, Juan Enriquez, Nancy Folbre, Walter Friedman, James Hoopes, Herminia Ibarra, Milind Lele, Barry Nalebuff, Raghu Rajan, Steven Wall, Luigi Zingales, Ian Ayres, Greg Stone, Bill Hammack.

Terms Agent receives 15% commission on domestic sales; 10% commission on foreign sales. Offers written contract, binding for 6 months; immediate upon written notice to terminate contract.

RIGHTS UNLIMITED, INC.

101 W. 55th St., Suite 2D, New York NY 10019. (212)246-0900. **Contact:** Bernard Kurman. Member of AAR.

- Query before submitting.

ANGELA RINALDI LITERARY AGENCY

P.O. Box 7877, Beverly Hills CA 90212-7877. (310)842-7665. Fax: (310)837-8143. E-mail: mail@rinaldiliterary.com. Estab. 1994. Member of AAR. Represents 50 clients. Currently handles: 30% nonfiction books; 70% novels.

- Prior to opening her agency, Ms. Rinaldi was an editor at NAL/Signet, Pocket Books, and Bantam, and the Manager of Book Development for *The Los Angeles Times*.

Represents Nonfiction books, novels, TV and motion picture rights for clients only. **Considers these nonfiction areas:** Biography/autobiography; business/economics; health/medicine; money/finance; self-help/personal improvement; true crime/investigative; women's issues/studies; books by journalists and academics. **Considers these fiction areas:** Literary; commercial; upmarket women's fiction; suspense.

O→ Actively seeking commercial and literary fiction. Does not want to receive scripts, poetry, category romances, children's books, westerns, science fiction/fantasy, technothrillers, or cookbooks.

How to Contact For fiction, send the first 3 chapters, brief synopsis, SASE. For nonfiction, query with SASE first or send outline/proposal, SASE. Do not send certified mail. Do not send metered mail as SASE. Brief e-mail inquiries OK, no attachments. Considers simultaneous queries. Please advise if this is a multiple submission. Responds in 6 weeks to queries. Returns materials only with SASE.

Recent Sales *My First Crush*, by Linda Kaplan (Lyons Press); *Rescue Me*, by Megan Clark (Kensington); *The Blood Orange Tree*, by Drusilla Campbell (Kensington); *Some Writers Deserve to Starve: 31 Brutal Truths About the Publishing Industry*, by Elaura Niles (Writer's Digest Books); *Indivisible by Two: Great Tales of Twins, Triplets and Quads*, by Dr. Nancy Segal (Harvard University Press).

Terms Agent receives 15% commission on domestic sales; 20% commission on foreign sales. Offers written contract. Charges clients for photocopying if not provided by client.

ANN RITTENBERG LITERARY AGENCY, INC.

1201 Broadway, Suite 708, New York NY 10001. (212)684-6936. **Contact:** Ann Rittenberg, president. Estab. 1992. Member of AAR. Represents 35 clients. 40% of clients are new/unpublished writers. Currently handles: 50% nonfiction books; 50% novels.

Member Agents Ann Rittenberg, Ted Gideonse.

Represents Nonfiction books, novels. **Considers these nonfiction areas:** Biography/autobiography; gay/lesbian issues; history (social/cultural); memoirs; women's issues/studies. **Considers these fiction areas:** Literary.

O→ This agent specializes in literary fiction and literary nonfiction.

How to Contact Submit outline, 3 sample chapters, SASE. Considers simultaneous queries. Responds in 6 weeks to queries; 2 months to mss. Obtains most new clients through referrals from established writers and editors.

Recent Sales Sold 20 titles in the last year. *Bad Cat*, by Jim Edgar (Workman); *A Certain Slant of Light*, by Laura Whitcomb (Houghton Mifflin); *Cities of Weather*, by Matthew Fox (Cormorant Books); *Late & Soon*, by Bob Hughes (Carroll & Graf).

Terms Agent receives 15% commission on domestic sales; 20% commission on foreign sales. Offers written contract. Charges clients for photocopying only.

RIVERSIDE LITERARY AGENCY

41 Simon Keets Rd., Leyden MA 01337. (413)772-0067. Fax: (413)772-0969. E-mail: rivlit@sover.net. **Contact:** Susan Lee Cohen. Estab. 1990. Represents 40 clients. 20% of clients are new/unpublished writers.

Represents Nonfiction books (adult), novels (adult), very selective.

How to Contact Query with SASE, outline. Accepts e-mail queries. No fax queries. Considers simultaneous queries. Responds in 2 weeks to queries. Obtains most new clients through referrals.

Recent Sales *Writing to Change the World*, by Mary Pipher, Ph.D. (Riverhead/Penguin Putnam); *The Sociopath Next Door: The Ruthless Versus the Rest of Us*, by Dr. Martha Stout (Broadway); *Letting Go of the Person You Used to Be*, by Lama Surya Das (Doubleday Broadway); *Kindling*, by Mick Farren (Tor); *Pivot Points: The Power of Small Choices to Change Your Life*, by Dr. Carol Kauffman (M. Evans); *Right, Wrong and Risky: An American Usage Dictionary*, by Mark Davidson.

Terms Agent receives 15% commission on domestic sales. Offers written contract. Charges clients for foreign postage, photocopying large mss, express mail deliveries, etc.

RLR ASSOCIATES, LTD.

Literary Department, 7 W. 51st St., New York NY 10019. (212)541-8641. Fax: (212)541-6052. Website: www.rlrliterary.net. **Contact:** Jennifer Unter, Tara Mark. Represents 50 clients. 25% of clients are new/unpublished writers. Currently handles: 70% nonfiction books; 25% novels; 5% story collections.

Member Agents Jennifer Unter, Tara Mark.

Represents Nonfiction books, novels, short story collections, scholarly books. **Considers these nonfiction areas:** Animals; anthropology/archaeology; art/architecture/design; biography/autobiography; business/economics; child guidance/parenting; cooking/foods/nutrition; current affairs; education; ethnic/cultural interests; gay/lesbian issues; government/politics/law; health/medicine; history; humor/satire; interior design/decorating; language/literature/criticism; memoirs; money/finance; multicultural; music/dance; nature/environment; photography; popular culture; psychology; religious/inspirational; science/technology; self-help/personal improvement; sociology; sports; translation; travel; true crime/investigative; women's issues/studies. **Considers these fiction areas:** Action/adventure; comic books/cartoon; contemporary issues; detective/police/crime; ethnic; experimental; family saga; feminist; gay/lesbian; historical; horror; humor/satire; literary; mainstream/contemporary; multicultural; mystery/suspense; sports; thriller.

O→ "We provide a lot of editorial assistance to our clients and have connections." Actively seeking fiction (all types except for romance and fantasy), current affairs, history, art, popular culture, health, business. Does not want to receive romance or fantasy; screenplays.

How to Contact Query with SASE. Considers simultaneous queries. Responds in 5 weeks. Returns materials only with SASE. Obtains most new clients through recommendations from others.

Recent Sales Sold 20 titles in the last year. Clients include Shelby Foote, The Grief Recovery Institute, Don Wade, Don Zimmer, The Knot.com, David Plowden, PGA of America, Danny Peary, Goerge Kalinsky and Peter Hyman.

Terms Agent receives 15% commission on domestic sales; 20% commission on foreign sales. Offers written contract.

Tips "Please check out our website for more details on our agency. No e-mail submissions, please."

B.J. ROBBINS LITERARY AGENCY

5130 Bellaire Ave., North Hollywood CA 91607-2908. (818)760-6602. Fax: (818)760-6616. E-mail: robbinsliterary@aol.com. **Contact:** (Ms.) B.J. Robbins. Estab. 1992. Member of AAR. Represents 40 clients. 50% of clients are new/unpublished writers. Currently handles: 50% nonfiction books; 50% novels.

Member Agents Missy Pontious (YA).

Represents Nonfiction books, novels. **Considers these nonfiction areas:** Biography/autobiography; child guidance/parenting; current affairs; ethnic/cultural interests; health/medicine; how-to; humor/satire; memoirs; music/dance; popular culture; psychology; self-help/personal improvement; sociology; sports; theater/film; travel; true crime/investigative; women's issues/studies. **Considers these fiction areas:** Contemporary issues; detective/police/crime; ethnic; literary; mainstream/contemporary; mystery/suspense; sports; thriller; young adult.

How to Contact Submit 3 sample chapters, outline/proposal, SASE. E-mail queries OK; no attachments. No fax queries. Considers simultaneous queries. Responds in 2 weeks to queries; 6 weeks to mss. Returns materials only with SASE. Obtains most new clients through conferences, referrals.

Recent Sales Sold 15 titles in the last year. *The Sex Lives of Cannibals*, by J. Maarten Troost (Broadway); *Quickening*, by Laura Catherine Brown (Random House/Ballantine); *Snow Mountain Passage*, by James D. Houston (Knopf); *The Last Summer*, by John Hough, Jr. (Simon & Schuster); *Last Stand on the Little Bighorn*, by James M. Donovan (Little, Brown).

Terms Agent receives 15% commission on domestic sales; 20% commission on foreign sales. Offers written contract; 3-month notice must be given to terminate contract. 100% of business is derived from commissions on ms sales. Charges clients for postage and photocopying only. Writers charged for fees only after the sale of ms.

Writers' Conferences Squaw Valley Fiction Writers Workshop (Squaw Valley CA, August); SDSU Writers Conference (San Diego CA, January).

THE ROBBINS OFFICE, INC.

405 Park Ave., New York NY 10022. (212)223-0720. Fax: (212)223-2535. **Contact:** Kathy P. Robbins, owner.

Member Agents David Halpern, Teri Tobias (foreign rights).

Represents Nonfiction books, novels. **Considers these nonfiction areas:** Biography/autobiography; government/politics/law (political commentary); language/literature/criticism (criticism); memoirs; Investigative journalism. **Considers these fiction areas:** Literary; mainstream/contemporary (commercial); poetry.

O→ This agency specializes in selling serious nonfiction, commercial and literary fiction.

How to Contact Accepts submissions by referral only.

Recent Sales *Ask Not*, by Thurston Clarke (Holt); *The Sleeper*, by Christopher Dickey (Simon & Schuster); *Entering Hades*, by John Leake (Farrar Straus & Giroux); *Garlic and Sapphires*, by Ruth Reichl (Penguin); *French Women Don't Get Fat*, by Mireille Guiliano (Knopf).
Terms Agent receives 15% commission on domestic sales; 15% commission on foreign sales; 15% commission on dramatic rights sales. Bills back specific expenses incurred in doing business for a client.

LINDA ROGHAAR LITERARY AGENCY, INC.

133 High Point Dr., Amherst MA 01002. (413)256-1921. Fax: (413)256-2636. E-mail: contact@lindaroghaar.com. Website: www.lindaroghaar.com. **Contact:** Linda L. Roghaar. Estab. 1996. Represents 50 clients. 40% of clients are new/unpublished writers. Currently handles: 90% nonfiction books; 10% novels.

- Prior to opening her agency, Ms. Roghaar worked in retail bookselling for 5 years and as a publishers' sales rep for 15 years.

Represents Nonfiction books, novels. **Considers these nonfiction areas:** Animals; anthropology/archaeology; biography/autobiography; education; history; nature/environment; popular culture; religious/inspirational; self-help/personal improvement; women's issues/studies. **Considers these fiction areas:** Mystery/suspense (amateur sleuth, cozy, culinary, malice domestic).
How to Contact Query with SASE. Accepts e-mail queries. No fax queries. Considers simultaneous queries. Responds in 2 months to queries; 4 months to mss.
Recent Sales *Thieves Break In*, by Cristina Summers (Bantam); *Mindful Knitting*, by Tara Jon Manning (Tuttle).
Terms Agent receives 15% commission on domestic sales; negotiable commission on foreign sales. Offers written contract, binding for negotiable time.

THE ROSENBERG GROUP

23 Lincoln Ave., Marblehead MA 01945. (781)990-1341. Fax: (781)990-1344. Website: www.rosenberggroup.com. **Contact:** Barbara Collins Rosenberg. Estab. 1998. Member of AAR, recognized agent of the RWA. Represents 32 clients. 25% of clients are new/unpublished writers. Currently handles: 30% nonfiction books; 30% novels; 10% scholarly books; 30% textbooks.

- Prior to becoming an agent, Ms. Rosenberg was a senior editor for Harcourt.

Member Agents Barbara Collins Rosenberg.
Represents Nonfiction books, novels, textbooks. **Considers these nonfiction areas:** Current affairs; popular culture; psychology; sports; women's issues/studies; women's health; food/wine/beverages. **Considers these fiction areas:** Literary; romance; women's.

O→ Ms. Rosenberg is well-versed in the romance market (both category and single title). She is a frequent speaker at romance conferences. Actively seeking romance category or single title in contemporary chick lit, romantic suspense, and the historical sub-genres. Does not want to receive time-travel, paranormal, or inspirational/spiritual romances.

How to Contact Query with SASE. No e-mail or fax queries. Responds in 2 weeks to queries; 4-6 weeks to mss. Returns materials only with SASE. Obtains most new clients through recommendations from others, solicitations, conferences.
Recent Sales Sold 27 titles in the last year.
Terms Agent receives 15% commission on domestic sales; 15% commission on foreign sales. Offers written contract; 1-month notice must be given to terminate contract. Postage and photocopying limit of $350/year.
Writers' Conferences RWA Annual Conference (Reno NV); RT Booklovers Convention (St. Louis MO); BEA (New York).

RITA ROSENKRANZ LITERARY AGENCY

440 West End Ave., Suite 15D, New York NY 10024-5358. (212)873-6333. **Contact:** Rita Rosenkranz. Estab. 1990. Member of AAR. Represents 30 clients. 20% of clients are new/unpublished writers. Currently handles: 98% nonfiction books; 2% novels.

- Prior to opening her agency, Rita Rosenkranz worked as an editor in major New York publishing houses.

Represents Nonfiction books. **Considers these nonfiction areas:** Animals; anthropology/archaeology; art/architecture/design; biography/autobiography; business/economics; child guidance/parenting; computers/electronic; cooking/foods/nutrition; crafts/hobbies; current affairs; ethnic/cultural interests; gay/lesbian issues; government/politics/law; health/medicine; history; how-to; humor/satire; interior design/decorating; language/literature/criticism; military/war; money/finance; music/dance; nature/environment; New Age/metaphysics; photography; popular culture; psychology; religious/inspirational; science/technology; self-help/personal improvement; sports; theater/film; women's issues/studies.

O→ This agency focuses on adult nonfiction. Stresses strong editorial development and refinement before submitting to publishers, and brainstorms ideas with authors. Actively seeking authors "who are well paired with their subject, either for professional or personal reasons."

How to Contact Submit proposal package, outline, SASE. No e-mail or fax queries. Considers simultaneous queries. Responds in 2 weeks to queries. Obtains most new clients through solicitations, conferences, word of mouth.
Recent Sales Sold 35 titles in the last year. *Forbidden Fruit: True Love Stories from the Underground Railroad*, by Betty DeRamus (Atria Books); *Business Class: Etiquette Essentials for Success at Work*, by Jacqueline Whitmore (St. Martin's Press); *An Exaltation of Soups: The Soul-Satisfying Story of Soup, as Told in More Than 100 Recipes*, by Pat Solley (Three Rivers Press).
Terms Agent receives 15% commission on domestic sales; 20% commission on foreign sales. Offers written contract, binding for 3 years; 3-month written notice must be given to terminate contract. 100% of business is derived from commissions on ms sales. Charges clients for photocopying. Makes referrals to editing service.
Tips "Identify the current competition for your project to make sure the project is valid. A strong cover letter is very important."

ROSENSTONE/WENDER

38 E. 29th St., 10th Floor, New York NY 10016. (212)725-6445. Fax: (212)725-6447. Member of AAR.

- Query before submitting.

Member Agents Howard Rosenstone (literary, adult, dramatic); Phyllis Wender (literary, adult, dramatic); Sonia Pabley; Ronald Gwiazda (associate member).

THE GAIL ROSS LITERARY AGENCY

1666 Connecticut Ave. NW, #500, Washington DC 20009. (202)328-3282. Fax: (202)328-9162. E-mail: jennifer@gailross.com. Website: www.gailross.com. **Contact:** Jennifer Manguera. Estab. 1988. Member of AAR. Represents 200 clients. 75% of clients are new/unpublished writers. Currently handles: 95% nonfiction books.
Member Agents Gail Ross.
Represents Nonfiction books. **Considers these nonfiction areas:** Anthropology/archaeology; biography/autobiography; business/economics; education; ethnic/cultural interests; gay/lesbian issues; government/politics/law; health/medicine; money/finance; nature/environment; psychology; religious/inspirational; science/technology; self-help/personal improvement; sociology; sports; true crime/investigative.

O→ This agency specializes in adult trade nonfiction.

How to Contact Query with SASE. Considers simultaneous queries. Responds in 1 month to queries. Obtains most new clients through recommendations from others.
Recent Sales Sold 50 titles in the last year. This agency prefers not to share information on specific sales.
Terms Agent receives 15% commission on domestic sales; 25% commission on foreign sales. Charges for office expenses (i.e., postage, copying).

CAROL SUSAN ROTH, LITERARY AND CREATIVE

P.O. Box 620337, Woodside CA 94062. (650)323-3795. E-mail: carol@authorsbest.com. **Contact:** Carol Susan Roth. Estab. 1995. Represents 47 clients. 15% of clients are new/unpublished writers. Currently handles: 100% nonfiction books.

- Prior to becoming an agent, Ms. Roth was trained as a psychotherapist and worked as a motivational coach, conference producer, and promoter for best-selling authors (i.e., Scott Peck, Bernie Siegal, John Gray) and the 1987 Heart of Business conference (the first business and spirituality conference).

Represents Nonfiction books. **Considers these nonfiction areas:** Business/economics; money/finance (personal finance/investing); religious/inspirational; self-help/personal improvement; spirituality; wellness/health/medicine; yoga; Buddhism.

O→ This agency specializes in spirituality, health, personal growth, personal finance, business. Actively seeking previously published authors—experts in health, spirituality, personal growth, business with an established audience. Does not want to receive fiction.

How to Contact Submit proposal package, media kit, promotional video, SASE. Accepts e-mail queries, no attachments please. Considers simultaneous queries. Responds in 1 week to queries. Returns materials only with SASE. Obtains most new clients through recommendations from others, solicitations.
Recent Sales Sold 17 titles in the last year. *The Internship Advantage*, by Dario Bravo (Prentice Hall); *Mothers Dojo Wisdom*, by Jennifer Lawler (Viking); *Heart Smart*, by Matt Devane (Wiley); *Office Workout*, by Shirley Archer (Chronicle Books); *Chinese For Dummies*, by Wendy Abraham (Wiley); *Consumer Confidential*, by Michael Finney (Berrett-Koehler).
Terms Agent receives 15% commission on domestic sales; 15% commission on foreign sales. Offers written contract, binding for 3 years (only for work with the acquiring publisher only); 60-day notice must be given to terminate contract. This agency "asks the client to provide postage (Fed Ex airbills) and do copying." Refers out to book doctor for proposal development and publicity service on request.
Writers' Conferences MEGA Book Marketing University; Maui Writer's Conference (Maui HI, September).

Tips "Have charisma, content, and credentials—solve an old problem in a new way. I prefer experts with extensive seminar and media experience."

JANE ROTROSEN AGENCY LLC

318 E. 51st St., New York NY 10022. (212)593-4330. Fax: (212)935-6985. E-mail: firstinitiallastname@janerotrosen.com. Estab. 1974. Member of AAR, Authors Guild. Represents over 100 clients. Currently handles: 30% nonfiction books; 70% novels.

Member Agents Jane R. Berkey, Andrea Cirillo, Annelise Robey, Margaret Ruley, Perry Gordijn (director of translation rights).

Represents Nonfiction books, novels. **Considers these nonfiction areas:** Biography/autobiography; business/economics; child guidance/parenting; cooking/foods/nutrition; current affairs; health/medicine; how-to; humor/satire; money/finance; nature/environment; popular culture; psychology; self-help/personal improvement; sports; true crime/investigative; women's issues/studies. **Considers these fiction areas:** Action/adventure; detective/police/crime; family saga; historical; horror; mainstream/contemporary; mystery/suspense; romance; thriller; women's.

How to Contact Query with SASE. By referral only. No e-mail or fax queries. Responds in 2 months to mss. Responds in 2 weeks (to writers who have been referred by a client or colleague). Returns materials only with SASE.

Recent Sales This agency prefers not to share information on specific sales.

Terms Agent receives 15% commission on domestic sales; 20% commission on foreign sales. Offers written contract, binding for 3-5 years; 2-month notice must be given to terminate contract. Charges clients for photocopying, express mail, overseas postage, book purchase.

THE DAMARIS ROWLAND AGENCY

5 Cooper Rd., Apt. 13H, New York NY 10010. (212)475-8942. Fax: (212)358-9411. **Contact:** Damaris Rowland or Steve Axelrod. Estab. 1994. Member of AAR. Represents 50 clients. 10% of clients are new/unpublished writers. Currently handles: novels.

Represents Novels. **Considers these fiction areas:** Historical; literary; mainstream/contemporary; romance (contemporary, gothic, historical, regency); commercial.

This agency specializes in women's fiction.

How to Contact Submit query with SASE. Responds in 6 weeks to queries. Obtains most new clients through recommendations from others, solicitations, conferences.

Recent Sales *The Next Accident*, by Lisa Gardner; *To Trust a Stranger*, by Karen Robard; *Nursing Homes*, by Peter Silin.

Terms Agent receives 15% commission on domestic sales; 20% commission on foreign sales. Offers written contract; 1-month notice must be given to terminate contract. Charges only if extraordinary expenses have been incurred, i.e., photocopying and mailing 15 mss to Europe for a foreign sale.

Writers' Conferences Novelists, Inc. (Denver, October); RWA National (Texas, July); Pacific Northwest Writers Conference.

THE PETER RUBIE LITERARY AGENCY

240 W. 35th St., Suite 500, New York NY 10001. (212)279-1776. Fax: (212)279-0927. E-mail: peterrubie@prlit.com. Website: www.prlit.com. **Contact:** Peter Rubie or June Clark (pralit@aol.com). Estab. 2000. Member of AAR. Represents 130 clients. 20% of clients are new/unpublished writers.

- Prior to opening his agency, Mr. Rubie was a founding partner of another literary agency Perkins, Rubie & Associates, and the fiction editor at Walker and Co. Ms. Clark is the author of several books and plays, and previously worked in cable TV marketing and promotion.

Member Agents Peter Rubie (crime, science fiction, fantasy, literary fiction, thrillers, narrative/serious nonfiction, business, self-help, how-to, popular, food/wine, history, commercial science, music, education, parenting); June Clark (nonfiction consisting of celebrity biographies, parenting, pets, women's issues, teen nonfiction, how-to, self-help, offbeat business, food/wine, commercial New Age, pop culture, entertainment); Caren Johnson, assistant; Hanna Rubin, agent-at-large (hanna.rubin@prlit.com); Jodi Weiss, agent-at-large.

Represents Nonfiction books, novels. **Considers these nonfiction areas:** Business/economics; creative nonfiction; current affairs; ethnic/cultural interests; how-to; popular culture; science/technology; self-help/personal improvement; health/nutrition; cooking/food/wine; music; theater/film/television; prescriptive New Age; parenting/education; pets; commercial academic material; TV. **Considers these fiction areas:** Fantasy; historical; literary; science fiction; thriller.

How to Contact For fiction, submit short synopsis and first 30-40 pages. For nonfiction, submit 1-page overview of the book, TOC, outline, 1-2 sample chapters. Accepts e-mail queries. Responds in 2 months to queries; 3

months to mss. Returns materials only with SASE. Obtains most new clients through recommendations from others.

Recent Sales Sold 50 titles in the last year. *Walking Money*, by James Born (Putnam); *Finishing Business*, by Harlan Ullman (Naval Institute Press); *The Nouvelle Creole Cookbook*, by Joseph Carey (Taylor).

Terms Agent receives 15% commission on domestic sales; 20% commission on foreign sales. Offers written contract. Charges clients for photocopying and some foreign mailings.

Tips "We look for professional writers and writers who are experts, have a strong platform and reputation in their field, and have an outstanding prose style. Be professional and open-minded. Know your market and learn your craft. Go to our website for up-to-date information on clients and sales."

RUSSELL & VOLKENING

50 W. 29th St., #7E, New York NY 10001. (212)684-6050. Fax: (212)889-3026. **Contact:** Timothy Seldes, Kirsten Ringer. Estab. 1940. Member of AAR. Represents 140 clients. 20% of clients are new/unpublished writers. Currently handles: 45% nonfiction books; 50% novels; 3% story collections; 2% novellas.

Member Agents Timothy Seldes (nonfiction, literary fiction).

Represents Nonfiction books, novels, short story collections. **Considers these nonfiction areas:** Anthropology/archaeology; art/architecture/design; biography/autobiography; business/economics; cooking/foods/nutrition; creative nonfiction; current affairs; education; ethnic/cultural interests; gay/lesbian issues; government/politics/law; health/medicine; history; language/literature/criticism; military/war; money/finance; music/dance; nature/environment; photography; popular culture; psychology; science/technology; sociology; sports; theater/film; true crime/investigative; women's issues/studies. **Considers these fiction areas:** Action/adventure; detective/police/crime; ethnic; literary; mainstream/contemporary; mystery/suspense; picture books; sports; thriller.

O- This agency specializes in literary fiction and narrative nonfiction.

Recent Sales *The Amateur Marriage*, by Anne Tyler (Knopf); *Loot*, by Nadine Gardiner; *Flying Crows*, by Jim Lehrer (Random House).

Terms Agent receives 15% commission on domestic sales; 20% commission on foreign sales. Charges clients for "standard office expenses relating to the submission of materials of an author we represent, i.e., photocopying, postage."

Tips "If the query is cogent, well written, well presented, and is the type of book we'd represent, we'll ask to see the manuscript. From there, it depends purely on the quality of the work."

REGINA RYAN PUBLISHING ENTERPRISES, INC.

251 Central Park W., 7D, New York NY 10024. (212)787-5589. E-mail: queryreginaryanbooks@rcn.com. **Contact:** Regina Ryan. Estab. 1976. Currently handles: 100% nonfiction books.

- Prior to becoming an agent, Ms. Ryan was an editor at Alfred A. Knopf, editor-in-chief of Macmillan Adult Trade, and a book producer.

Represents Nonfiction books. **Considers these nonfiction areas:** Gardening; history; psychology; travel; women's issues/studies; narrative nonfiction, natural history (especially birds and birding), popular science, parenting, adventure, architecture.

How to Contact Query only by e-mail or mail with SASE. No telephone queries. Does not accept queries for juvenile or fiction. Considers simultaneous queries. Tries to respond in 1 month to queries. Returns materials only with SASE. Obtains most new clients through recommendations from others.

Recent Sales *Autopsy of a Suicidal Mind*, by Edwin Schneidman, Ph.D. (Oxford University Press); *Surviving Hitler*, by Andrea Warren (HarperCollins Books for Young Readers); *The Bomb in the Basement: The Israeli Nuclear Option*, by Michael Karpin (Simon & Schuster).

Terms Agent receives 15% commission on domestic sales; 15% commission on foreign sales. Offers written contract; 1 month, negotiable notice must be given to terminate contract. Charges clients for all out-of-pocket expenses, such as long distance, messengers, freight, copying, "if it's more than just a nominal amount."

Tips "An analysis of why your proposed book is different and better than the competition is essential; a sample chapter is helpful."

THE SAGALYN AGENCY

7201 Bethesda Ave., Suite 675, Bethesda MD 20814. (301)718-6440. Fax: (301)718-6444. E-mail: info@sagalyn.com. Website: sagalyn.com. **Contact:** Rebeca Sagalyn. Estab. 1980. Member of AAR. Currently handles: 85% nonfiction books; 5% novels; 10% scholarly books.

Member Agents Raphael Sagalyn, Rebeca Sagalyn.

Represents Nonfiction books (history, science, business).

O- Does not want to receive stage plays, screenplays, poetry, science fiction, romance, children's books, or young adult books.

How to Contact Please send e-mail queries only, no attachments. Include 1 of these words in subject line: Query, submission, inquiry. Response time depends on number of current queries, generally within 3 weeks.
Recent Sales See website for sales information.
Tips "We receive between 1,000-1,200 queries a year, which in turn lead to 2 or 3 new clients."

VICTORIA SANDERS & ASSOCIATES

241 Ave. of the Americas, Suite 11 H, New York NY 10014. (212)633-8811. Fax: (212)633-0525. E-mail: queriesvsa@hotmail.com. Website: www.victoriasanders.com. **Contact:** Victoria Sanders or Diane Dickensheid. Estab. 1993. Member of AAR; signatory of WGA. Represents 75 clients. 25% of clients are new/unpublished writers. Currently handles: 50% nonfiction books; 50% novels.
Member Agents Benee Knauer, assistant literary agent.
Represents Nonfiction books, novels. **Considers these nonfiction areas:** Biography/autobiography; current affairs; ethnic/cultural interests; gay/lesbian issues; government/politics/law; history; humor/satire; language/literature/criticism; music/dance; popular culture; psychology; theater/film; translation; women's issues/studies. **Considers these fiction areas:** Action/adventure; contemporary issues; ethnic; family saga; feminist; gay/lesbian; literary; thriller.
How to Contact Query by e-mail only.
Recent Sales Sold 20 titles in the last year. *Indelible*, by Karin Slaughter (Morrow); *When Love Calls, You Better Answer*, by Bertice Berry (Doubleday).
Terms Agent receives 15% commission on domestic sales; 20% commission on foreign sales. Offers written contract. Charges for photocopying, ms, messenger, express mail, and extraordinary fees. If in excess of $100, client approval is required.
Tips "Limit query to letter, no calls, and give it your best shot. A good query is going to get a good response."

SCHIAVONE LITERARY AGENCY, INC.

236 Trails End, West Palm Beach FL 33413-2135. (561)966-9294. Fax: (561)966-9294. E-mail: profschia@aol.com. Website: www.publishersmarketplace.com/members/profschia. **Contact:** James Schiavone, Ed.D. Estab. 1996. Member of National Education Association. Represents 60 clients. 2% of clients are new/unpublished writers. Currently handles: 50% nonfiction books; 49% novels; 1% textbooks.

- Prior to opening his agency, Dr. Schiavone was a full professor of developmental skills at the City University of New York and author of 5 trade books and 3 textbooks.

Represents Nonfiction books, novels, juvenile books, scholarly books, textbooks. **Considers these nonfiction areas:** Animals; anthropology/archaeology; biography/autobiography; child guidance/parenting; current affairs; education; ethnic/cultural interests; gay/lesbian issues; government/politics/law; health/medicine; history; how-to; humor/satire; juvenile nonfiction; language/literature/criticism; military/war; nature/environment; popular culture; psychology; science/technology; self-help/personal improvement; sociology; true crime/investigative. **Considers these fiction areas:** Contemporary issues; ethnic; family saga; historical; horror; humor/satire; juvenile; literary; mainstream/contemporary; science fiction; young adult.

O-π This agency specializes in celebrity biography and autobiography. Actively seeking serious nonfiction, literary fiction, and celebrity biography. Does not want to receive poetry.

How to Contact Query by letter only with SASE. One page e-mail queries with no attachments are accepted and encouraged for fastest response. Does not accept phone or fax queries. Considers simultaneous queries. Responds in 2 weeks to queries; 6 weeks to mss. Returns materials only with SASE. Obtains most new clients through recommendations from others, solicitations, conferences.
Terms Agent receives 15% commission on domestic sales; 20% commission on foreign sales. Offers written contract. Charges clients only for postage.
Writers' Conferences Key West Literary Seminar (Key West FL, January); South Florida Writer's Conference (Miami FL, May).
Tips "I prefer to work with established authors published by major houses in New York. I will consider marketable proposals from new/previously unpublished writers."

N Ø HAROLD SCHMIDT

415 W. 23rd St., #6F, New York NY 10011. **Contact:** Harold Schmidt. Member of AAR.

- Query before submitting.

✓ SUSAN SCHULMAN, A LITERARY AGENCY

454 W. 44th St., New York NY 10036-5205. (212)713-1633. Fax: (212)581-8830. E-mail: schulman@aol.com. Website: www.susanschulmanagency.com. **Contact:** Susan Schulman, president. Estab. 1979. Member of AAR, Dramatists Guild, Women's Media Group; signatory of WGA—East. 10-15% of clients are new/unpublished writers. Currently handles: 70% nonfiction books; 20% novels; 10% stage plays.

Literary Agents

Member Agents Susan Schulman (books for, by and about women and women's issues/interests, including self-help, health, business and spirituality); Linda Migalti (children's books, ecology, natural sciences, and business books); Emily Uhry (plays and pitches for films).

Represents Nonfiction books, novels. **Considers these nonfiction areas:** Anthropology/archaeology; biography/autobiography; child guidance/parenting; current affairs; education; ethnic/cultural interests; gay/lesbian issues; government/politics/law; health/medicine; history; how-to; juvenile nonfiction; money/finance; music/dance; nature/environment; popular culture; psychology; self-help/personal improvement; sociology; theater/film; translation; true crime/investigative; women's issues/studies. **Considers these fiction areas:** Contemporary issues; detective/police/crime; gay/lesbian; historical; literary; mainstream/contemporary; mystery/suspense; young adult. **Considers these script subject areas:** Comedy; contemporary issues; detective/police/crime; feminist; historical; mainstream; mystery/suspense; psychic/supernatural; teen.

O→ This agency specializes in books for, by and about women's issues, including family, careers, health and spiritual development, business, sociology, history and economics. Emphasizing contemporary women's fiction and nonfiction books of interest to women.

How to Contact Query with SASE, outline/proposal, SASE. Accepts e-mail and fax queries. Considers simultaneous queries. Responds in 1 week to queries; 6 weeks to mss. Returns materials only with SASE.

Recent Sales Sold 30 titles in the last year. *Prayers for a Non-Believer*, by Julia Cameron (Putnam); *The Half-Empty Heart*, by Alan Downs (St. Martin's Press); *The Walls Around Us*, by David Owen (Simon & Schuster); *Rise of the Creative Class*, by Richard Florida (Basic Books). Movie/TV MOW scripts optioned/sold: *In the Skin of a Lion*, by Michael Ondaatje (Serendipity Point Productions); *Holes*, by Louis Sachar (Disney); *Sideways Stories from Wayside School*, by Louis Sachar (Lin Oliver Productions); *Twirling at Ole Miss*, by Terry Southern (Blue Magic Pictures).

Terms Agent receives 15% commission on domestic sales; 7½-10% (plus 7½-10% to co-agent) commission on foreign sales; 10-20% commission on dramatic rights sales. Charges client for special messenger or copying services, foreign mail and any other service requested by client.

LAURENS R. SCHWARTZ AGENCY

5 E. 22nd St., Suite 15D, New York NY 10010-5325. (212)228-2614. **Contact:** Laurens R. Schwartz. Estab. 1984. Signatory of WGA. Represents 100 clients.

Represents Nonfiction books, novels, general mix of nonfiction and fiction. Also handles movie and TV tie-ins, licensing, and merchandising.

How to Contact Query with SASE. *No unsolicited mss.* Responds in 1 month to queries. "Have had 18 best-sellers."

Terms Agent receives 15% commission on domestic sales; 25% (WGA rates where applicable) commission on foreign sales. "No client fees except for photocopying, and that fee is avoided by an author providing necessary copies or, in certain instances, transferring files on diskette or by e-mail attachment." Where necessary to bring a project into publishing form, editorial work and some rewriting provided as part of service. Works with authors on long-term career goals and promotion.

Tips "I do not like receiving mass mailings sent to all agents. I am extremely selective—only take on 1-3 new clients a year. Do not send everything you have ever written. Choose 1 work and promote that. Always include an SASE. Never send your only copy. Always include a background sheet on yourself and a 1-page synopsis of the work (too many summaries end up being as long as the work)."

SCOVIL CHICHAK GALEN LITERARY AGENCY

381 Park Ave. S., Suite 1020, New York NY 10016. (212)679-8686. Fax: (212)679-6710. E-mail: mailroom@scglit.com. Website: www.scglit.com. **Contact:** Russell Galen. Estab. 1993. Member of AAR. Represents 300 clients. Currently handles: 70% nonfiction books; 30% novels.

Member Agents Russell Galen, Jack Scovil, Anna Ghosh.

How to Contact Accepts e-mail and fax queries. Considers simultaneous queries.

Recent Sales Sold 100 titles in the last year. *Across the Black Waters*, by Minai Hajratwala (Houghton Mifflin); *The Secret*, by Walter Anderson (HarperCollins); *Chainfire*, by Terry Goodkinf (Tor); *Lord John and the Private Matter*, by Diana Gabaldon; *The King of the Jews*, by Nick Tosches (Little, Brown).

Terms Charges clients for photocopying and postage.

N SCRIBBLERS HOUSE LLC LITERARY AGENCY

(formerly part of Clausen, Mays & Tahan), P.O. Box 1007, Cooper Station, New York NY 10276-1007. E-mail: query@scribblershouse.net. Website: www.scribblershouse.net. **Contact:** Stedman Mays, Garrett Gambino. Estab. 2003. 25% of clients are new/unpublished writers.

- Stedman Mays cofounded Clausen, Mays & Tahan in 1976.

Represents Mostly nonfiction and an occasional novel. **Considers these nonfiction areas:** Business/economics; health/medicine; history; how-to; language/literature/criticism; memoirs; popular culture; psychology; self-help/personal improvement; sex; spirituality; diet/nutrition; the brain; personal finance; biography; politics; writing books; relationships; gender issues; parenting. **Considers these fiction areas:** Historical; literary; women's; suspense; crime; thrillers.

How to Contact Query by e-mail. Put Nonfiction Query or Fiction Query in the subject line followed by the title of your project. Considers simultaneous queries. Responds in up to 1 month to queries.

Recent Sales *Perfect Balance: Dr. Robert Greene's Breakthrough Program for Getting the Hormone Health You Deserve*, by Robert Greene, M.D., and Leah Feldon (Clarkson Potter/Random House); *Age-Proof Your Mind*, by Zaldy Tan, M.D. (Warner); *The Okinawa Program* and *The Okinawa Diet Plan*, by Bradley Willcox, M.D., Craig Willcox, Ph.D., and Makoto Suzuki, M.D. (Clarkson Potter/Random House); *The Emotionally Abusive Relationship*, by Beverly Engel (Wiley); *Help Your Baby Talk*, by Dr. Robert Owens with Leah Feldon (Perigee).

Terms Agent receives 15% commission on domestic sales. Charges clients for postage, shipping and copying.

Tips "We prefer e-mail queries, but if you must send by snail mail, we will return material or respond to United States Postal Service-accepted SASE. (No international coupons or outdated mail strips, please.) Presentation means a lot. A well-written query letter with a brief author bio and your credentials is important. For query letter models, go to the bookstore or online and look at the cover copy and flap copy on other books in your general area of interest. Emulate what's best. Have an idea of other notable books that will be perceived as being in the same vein as yours. Know what's fresh or 'hooky' about your project and articulate it in as few words as possible. Consult our website for the most up-to-date information on submitting."

N ☐ SCRIBE AGENCY, LLC

5508 Joylynne Dr., Madison WI 53716. (608)249-0491. E-mail: queries@scribeagency.com. Website: www.scribeagency.com. **Contact:** Kris O'Higgins. Estab. 2004. Represents 1 client. 100% of clients are new/unpublished writers. Currently handles: 100% novels.

- "We worked as agency assitants at a literary agency, editorial assistants for a publishing company, and a copywriter in two marketing departments. Not only do we have previous experience working at a literary agency, but we also have editorial and marketing experience. We also love books as much or more than anyone you know."

Member Agents Kris O'Higgins and Jesse Vogel.

Represents Nonfiction books, novels, short story collections, novellas, juvenile books, poetry books. **Considers these nonfiction areas:** Cooking/foods/nutrition; crafts/hobbies; ethnic/cultural interests; gay/lesbian issues; how-to; humor/satire; memoirs; music/dance; New Age/metaphysics; photography; popular culture; science/technology; self-help/personal improvement; true crime/investigative; women's issues/studies. **Considers these fiction areas:** Action/adventure; comic books/cartoon; confession; detective/police/crime; erotica; ethnic; experimental; family saga; fantasy; feminist; gay/lesbian; historical; horror; humor/satire; juvenile; literary; mainstream/contemporary; mystery/suspense; picture books; regional; science fiction; thriller; young adult; psychic/supernatural.

O→ Actively seeking excellent writers with ideas and stories to tell. Does not want cat mysteries and anything not listed above.

How to Contact Query with SASE. Responds in 2 weeks to queries; 1-2 months to mss. Returns materials only with SASE.

Recent Sales Sold 2 titles in the last year.

Terms Agent receives 17% commission on domestic sales; 25% commission on foreign sales. Offers written contract. Charges for postage and photocopying.

Writers' Conferences WisCon, Wisconsin Book Festival, World Fantasy Convention (all in Madison WI).

SEDGEBAND LITERARY ASSOCIATES, INC.

7312 Martha Lane, Fort Worth TX 76112. (817)496-3652. Fax: (425)952-9518. E-mail: queries@sedgeband.com. Website: www.sedgeband.com. **Contact:** David Duperre. Estab. 1997. 50% of clients are new/unpublished writers. Currently handles: 50% nonfiction books; 50% fiction novels.

Member Agents David Duperre (literary, scripts, mystery, suspense); Ginger Norton (romance, horror, nonfiction, mainstream/contemporary).

Represents Nonfiction books, novels. **Considers these nonfiction areas:** Biography/autobiography; ethnic/cultural interests; history; true crime/investigative. **Considers these fiction areas:** Action/adventure; fantasy; literary; mainstream/contemporary; mystery/suspense; romance; science fiction.

O→ This agency is looking for talented writers who have patience and are willing to work hard. Actively seeking new nonfiction writers, query for fiction.

How to Contact Use the online submission form on our website. Prefers queries via e-mail. No phone queries accepted. No full mss unless requested. Accepts e-mail queries with no attachments; responds in 2-4 weeks. Paper response in 2-3 months to written queries. Responds in 4 months to requested mss. Returns materials only with SASE. Obtains most new clients through queries, the Internet, referrals.

Recent Sales Sold 8 titles in the last year.
Terms Agent receives 15% commission on domestic sales; 20% commission on foreign sales. Offers written contract, binding for 1 year; 30-day written notice must be given to terminate contract. Charges clients for postage, photocopies, long-distance calls, etc. "We do not charge any reading or retainer fees."
Tips "We care about writers and books, not just money, but we care about the industry as well. We will not represent anyone who might hurt our clients or our reputation. We expect our writers to work hard and to be patient. Do not send a rude query; it will get you nowhere. If we ask to see your book, don't wait around to send it or ask a bunch of irrelevant questions about movie rights and so forth. *(At this point we haven't even offered to represent you!)* If you can't write a synopsis, don't bother to query us. The industry is based on the synopsis; sometimes it is all the editor ever sees. Don't handwrite your query or send us samples of your writing that are handwritten—we won't read them. Be professional and follow our guidelines when submitting. And don't believe everything you hear on the Internet about editors and publishers—it isn't always true."

LYNN SELIGMAN, LITERARY AGENT

400 Highland Ave., Upper Montclair NJ 07043. (973)783-3631. **Contact:** Lynn Seligman. Estab. 1985. Member of Women's Media Group. Represents 32 clients. 15% of clients are new/unpublished writers. Currently handles: 70% nonfiction books; 30% novels.

- Prior to opening her agency, Ms. Seligman worked in the subsidiary rights department of Doubleday and Simon & Schuster, and served as an agent with Julian Bach Literary Agency (now IMG Literary Agency).

Represents Nonfiction books, novels. **Considers these nonfiction areas:** Anthropology/archaeology; art/architecture/design; biography/autobiography; business/economics; child guidance/parenting; cooking/foods/nutrition; current affairs; education; ethnic/cultural interests; government/politics/law; health/medicine; history; how-to; humor/satire; interior design/decorating; language/literature/criticism; money/finance; music/dance; nature/environment; photography; popular culture; psychology; science/technology; self-help/personal improvement; sociology; theater/film; true crime/investigative; women's issues/studies. **Considers these fiction areas:** Detective/police/crime; ethnic; fantasy; feminist; gay/lesbian; historical; horror; humor/satire; literary; mainstream/contemporary; mystery/suspense; romance (contemporary, gothic, historical, regency); science fiction.

O→ This agency specializes in "general nonfiction and fiction. I also do illustrated and photography books and have represented several photographers for books." This agency does not handle children or young adult books.

How to Contact Query with SASE, sample chapters, outline/proposal. Prefers to read materials exclusively. No e-mail or fax queries. Considers simultaneous queries. Responds in 2 weeks to queries; 2 months to mss. Returns materials only with SASE. Obtains most new clients through referrals from other writers or editors.
Recent Sales Sold 15 titles in the last year. *My Father Before Me*, by Dr. Michael Diamond with Roberta Israeloff; *Grave Intent*, by Deborah Le Blanc.
Terms Agent receives 15% commission on domestic sales; 25% commission on foreign sales. Charges clients for photocopying, unusual postage, or telephone expenses (checking first with the author), express mail.

SERENDIPITY LITERARY AGENCY, LLC

732 Fulton St., Suite 3, Brooklyn NY 11238. (718)230-7689. Fax: (718)230-7829. E-mail: rbrooks@serendipitylit.com. Website: www.serendipitylit.com. **Contact:** Regina Brooks. Estab. 2000. Represents 30 clients. 20% of clients are new/unpublished writers. Currently handles: 60% nonfiction books; 40% novels.

- Prior to becoming an agent, Ms. Brooks was an acquisitions editor for John Wiley & Sons, Inc. and McGraw-Hill Companies.

Represents Nonfiction books, novels, juvenile books, scholarly books, textbooks, children's. **Considers these nonfiction areas:** Business/economics; computers/electronic; education; ethnic/cultural interests; how-to; juvenile nonfiction; memoirs; money/finance; multicultural; New Age/metaphysics; popular culture; psychology; religious/inspirational; science/technology; self-help/personal improvement; sports; women's issues/studies. **Considers these fiction areas:** Action/adventure; confession; ethnic; historical; juvenile; literary; multicultural; mystery/suspense; picture books; romance; thriller. **Considers these script subject areas:** Ethnic; fantasy; juvenile; multimedia; also interested in children's CD/video projects.

O→ Serendipity provides developmental editing. "We help build marketing plans for nontraditional outlets." Actively seeking African-American nonfiction, commercial fiction, computer books (nonfiction), YA novels with an urban flair, juvenile books. Does not want to receive poetry.

How to Contact Prefers to read materials exclusively. Nonfiction, submit outline, 1 sample chapter, SASE. Responds in 2 months to queries; 3 months to mss. Obtains most new clients through conferences, referrals.
Recent Sales This agency prefers not to share information on specific sales. Recent sales available upon request by prospective client.
Terms Agent receives 15% commission on domestic sales; 20% commission on foreign sales. Offers written

contract; 2-month notice must be given to terminate contract. Charges clients $200 upon signing for office fees, or office fees will be taken from any advance. Does not make referrals to editing services. "If author requests editing services, I can offer a list of potential services." 0% of business is derived from referral to editing services.

Tips "Looking for African-American children's and teen novels. We also represent illustrators."

THE SEYMOUR AGENCY

475 Miner St., Canton NY 13617. (315)386-1831. Fax: (315)386-1037. E-mail: marysue@slic.com. Website: www.theseymouragency.com. **Contact:** Mary Sue Seymour. Estab. 1992. Member of AAR, CBA, RWA and The Author's Guild. Represents 75 clients. 5% of clients are new/unpublished writers. Currently handles: 50% nonfiction books; 50% fiction.

- Ms. Seymour is a retired New York State certified teacher.

Represents Nonfiction books, novels (romance). **Considers these nonfiction areas:** Business/economics; health/medicine; how-to; self-help/personal improvement; Christian books; cookbooks; any well-written nonfiction that includes a proposal in standard format and 1 sample chapter. **Considers these fiction areas:** Literary; religious/inspirational (Christian books); romance (any type); westerns/frontier.

How to Contact Query with SASE, synopsis, first 50 pages for romance. Accepts e-mail queries. No fax queries. Considers simultaneous queries. Responds in 1 month to queries; 3 months to mss. Returns materials only with SASE.

Recent Sales Penny McCusker's 3 books to Harlequin/Silhouette; Emilee Hines' 2-book deal to Warner Books; Dr. Val Dmitriev's Vocabulary book to Adams Media Corp.

Terms Agent receives 12% (from authors' material whose books the agency sold) and 15% (on new clients) commission on domestic sales.

Writers' Conferences Desert Rose (Scottsdale AZ); Mountain Laurel (Knoxville TN); Romantic Times Convention (New York City); RWA National (Dallas); CBA (Atlanta); Put Your Heart in a Book (New Jersey).

THE ROBERT E. SHEPARD AGENCY

1608 Dwight Way, Berkeley CA 94703-1804. (510)849-3999. E-mail: mail@shepardagency.com. Website: www.shepardagency.com. **Contact:** Robert Shepard. Estab. 1994. Member of Authors Guild (associate). Represents 60 clients. 15% of clients are new/unpublished writers. Currently handles: 90% nonfiction books; 10% scholarly books.

- Prior to opening his agency, Mr. Shepard "was an editor and a sales and marketing manager in book publishing"; he now teaches courses for nonfiction authors, speaks at many writers' conferences, and "has been known to write," himself.

Represents Nonfiction books, scholarly books (appropriate for trade publishers). **Considers these nonfiction areas:** Business/economics; current affairs; ethnic/cultural interests; gay/lesbian issues; government/politics/law; history; money/finance; popular culture; science/technology; sociology; sports; narrative nonfiction; Judaica.

O→ This agency specializes in nonfiction, particularly key issues facing society and culture. Actively seeking "works by experts recognized in their fields whether or not they're well-known to the general public, and books that offer fresh perspectives or new information even when the subject is familiar." Does not want to receive autobiography, art books, fiction.

How to Contact Query with SASE. E-mail queries encouraged. Fax and phone queries strongly discouraged. Considers simultaneous queries. Responds in 2-3 weeks to queries; 6 weeks to proposals or mss. Returns materials only with SASE. Obtains most new clients through recommendations from others, solicitations.

Recent Sales Sold 10 titles in the last year. Recent titles include the best-selling *Night Draws Near*, by Anthony Shadid (Henry Holt); *Word Freak: Heartbreak, Triumph, Genius, and Obsession in the World of Competitive Scrabble Players*, by Stefan Fatsis (Houghton Mifflin HC, Penguin PB); *Wine & War: The French, the Nazis, and the Battle for France's Greatest Treasure*, by Don and Petie Kladstrup (Broadway Books); *Coal: A Human History*, by Barbara Freese (Perseus); *Leave the Office Earlier*, by Laura Stack (Broadway Books); *The Root of Wild Madder: Chasing the History, Mystery, and Lore of the Persian Carpet*, by Brian Murphy (Simon & Schuster).

Terms Agent receives 15% commission on domestic sales; 20% commission on foreign sales. Offers written contract, binding for term of project or until canceled; 30-day notice must be given to terminate contract. Charges clients "actual expenses for phone/fax, photocopying, and postage only if and when project sells, against advance."

Tips "We pay attention to detail. We believe in close working relationships between author and agent, and in building better relationships between author and editor. Please do your homework! There's no substitute for learning all you can about similar or directly competing books and presenting a well-reasoned competitive analysis in your proposal. Be sure to describe what's new and fresh about your work, why you are the best person to be writing on your subject, and how the book will serve the needs or interests of your intended readers. Don't work in a vacuum; visit bookstores, talk to other writers about their experiences, and let the information you gather inform the work that you do as an author."

WENDY SHERMAN ASSOCIATES, INC.

450 Seventh Ave., Suite 3004, New York NY 10123. (212)279-9027. Fax: (212)279-8863. Website: www.wsherman.com. **Contact:** Wendy Sherman. Estab. 1999. Member of AAR. Represents 50 clients. 30% of clients are new/unpublished writers. Currently handles: 50% nonfiction books; 50% novels.

- Prior to opening the agency, Ms. Sherman worked for The Aaron Priest agency and was vice president, executive director of Henry Holt, associate publisher, subsidary rights director, sales and marketing director.

Member Agents Tracy Brown, Wendy Sherman.

Represents Nonfiction books, novels. **Considers these nonfiction areas:** Psychology; narrative nonfiction, practical. **Considers these fiction areas:** Literary; women's (suspense).

"We specialize in developing new writers as well as working with more established writers. My experience as a publisher has proven to be a great asset to my clients."

How to Contact Query with SASE, or send outline/proposal, 1 sample chapter. No e-mail queries. Considers simultaneous queries. Responds in 1 month to queries. Returns materials only with SASE. Obtains most new clients through recommendations from others.

Recent Sales Clients include Fiction: William Lashner, Nani Power, DW Buffa, Howard Bahr, Suzanne Chazin, Sarah Stonich, Ad Hudler, Mary Sharratt, Libby Street, Heather Estay, Darri Stephens, Megan Desales; Nonfiction: Rabbi Mark Borovitz, Alan Eisenstock, Esther Perel, Clifton Leaf, Maggie Estep, Greg Baer, Martin Friedman, Lundy Bancroft, Alvin Ailey Dance, Lise Friedman, Liz Landers, Vicky Mainzer.

Terms Agent receives 15% commission on domestic sales; 20% commission on foreign sales. Offers written contract.

ROSALIE SIEGEL, INTERNATIONAL LITERARY AGENCY, INC.

1 Abey Dr., Pennington NJ 08543. (609)737-1007. Fax: (609)737-3708. **Contact:** Rosalie Siegel. Estab. 1977. Member of AAR. Represents 35 clients. 10% of clients are new/unpublished writers. Currently handles: 45% nonfiction books; 45% novels; 10% young adult books and short story collections for current clients.

Represents Nonfiction books, novels, short story collections, young adult books.

How to Contact Obtains most new clients through referrals from writers and friends.

Terms Agent receives 15% commission on domestic sales; 20% commission on foreign sales. Offers written contract; 2-month notice must be given to terminate contract. Charges clients for photocopying.

Tips "I'm not looking for new authors in an active way."

JEFFREY SIMMONS LITERARY AGENCY

15 Penn House, Mallory St., London NW8 8SX England. (020)7224 8917. E-mail: jas@london-inc.com. **Contact:** Jeffrey Simmons. Estab. 1978. Represents 43 clients. 40% of clients are new/unpublished writers. Currently handles: 60% nonfiction books; 40% novels.

- Prior to becoming an agent, Mr. Simmons was a publisher, and he is also an author.

Represents Nonfiction books, novels. **Considers these nonfiction areas:** Biography/autobiography; current affairs; government/politics/law; history; language/literature/criticism; memoirs; music/dance; popular culture; sociology; sports; theater/film; translation; true crime/investigative. **Considers these fiction areas:** Action/adventure; confession; detective/police/crime; family saga; literary; mainstream/contemporary; mystery/suspense; thriller.

This agency seeks to handle good books and promising young writers. "My long experience in publishing and as an author and ghostwriter means I can offer an excellent service all around, especially in terms of editorial experience where appropriate." Actively seeking quality fiction, biography, autobiography, showbiz, personality books, law, crime, politics, world affairs. Does not want to receive science fiction, horror, fantasy, juvenile, academic books, specialist subjects (i.e., cooking, gardening, religious).

How to Contact Submit sample chapter, outline/proposal, IRCs if necessary, SASE. Prefers to read materials exclusively. Responds in 1 week to queries; 1 month to mss. Obtains most new clients through recommendations from others, solicitations.

Recent Sales Sold 18 titles in the last year. *Decoding Sion*, by Picknett & Prince (Time Warner UK, Simon & Schuster US); *Complete Carry On*, by Webber (Random House).

Terms Agent receives 10-15% commission on domestic sales; 15% commission on foreign sales. Offers written contract, binding for lifetime of book in question or until it becomes out of print.

Tips "When contacting us with an outline/proposal, include a brief biographical note (listing any previous publications, with publishers and dates). Preferably tell us if the book has already been offered elsewhere."

BEVERLEY SLOPEN LITERARY AGENCY

131 Bloor St. W., Suite 711, Toronto ON M5S 1S3 Canada. (416)964-9598. Fax: (416)921-7726. E-mail: beverly@slopenagency.ca. Website: www.slopenagency.ca. **Contact:** Beverley Slopen. Estab. 1974. Represents 60 clients. 40% of clients are new/unpublished writers. Currently handles: 60% nonfiction books; 40% novels.

- Prior to opening her agency, Ms. Slopen worked in publishing and as a journalist.

Represents Nonfiction books, novels, scholarly books, textbooks (college). **Considers these nonfiction areas:** Anthropology/archaeology; biography/autobiography; business/economics; current affairs; psychology; sociology; true crime/investigative; women's issues/studies. **Considers these fiction areas:** Literary; mystery/suspense.

This agency has a "strong bent towards Canadian writers." Actively seeking "serious nonfiction that is accessible and appealing to the general reader." Does not want to receive fantasy, science fiction, or children's.

How to Contact Query with SAE and IRCs. Returns materials only with SASE (Canadian postage). Accepts short e-mail queries. Considers simultaneous queries. Responds in 2 months to queries.

Recent Sales Sold over 40 titles in the last year. *Court Lady* and *Country Wife*, by Lita-Rose Betcherman (HarperCollins Canada/Morrow/Wiley UK); *Vermeer's Hat*, by Timothy Brook (HarperCollins Canada); *Midnight Cab*, by James W. Nichol (Canongate US/Droemer/Germany); *Fatal Passage* and *Ancient Mariner*, by Ken McGoogan (Carroll & Graf US/Bantam Press UK); *Understanding Uncertainty*, by Jeffrey Rosenthal (HarperCollins Canada); *Damaged Angels*, by Bonnie Buxton (Carroll & Graf US); *Sea of Dreams*, by Adam Mayers (McClelland & Stewart Canada); *Hair Hat*, by Carrie Snyder (Penguin Canada). Other clients include Modris Eksteins, Michael Marrus, Robert Fulford, Donna Morrissey, Howard Engel, Morley Torgov, Elliott Leyton, Don Gutteridge, Joanna Goodman, Roberta Rich, Jennifer Welsh, Margaret Wente, Frank Wydra.

Terms Agent receives 15% commission on domestic sales; 10% commission on foreign sales. Offers written contract, binding for 2 years; 3-month notice must be given to terminate contract.

Tips "Please, no unsolicited manuscripts."

ROBERT SMITH LITERARY AGENCY, LTD.

12 Bridge Wharf, 156 Caledonian Rd., London NI 9UU England. (020) 7278 2444. Fax: (020) 7833 5680. E-mail: robertsmith.literaryagency@virgin.net. **Contact:** Robert Smith. Estab. 1997. Member of Association of Authors' Agents. Represents 25 clients. 10% of clients are new/unpublished writers. Currently handles: 80% nonfiction books; 20% syndicated material.

- Prior to becoming an agent, Mr. Smith was a book publisher.

Member Agents Robert Smith (all nonfiction).

Represents Nonfiction books, syndicated material. **Considers these nonfiction areas:** Biography/autobiography; cooking/foods/nutrition; health/medicine; memoirs; music/dance; New Age/metaphysics; popular culture; self-help/personal improvement; theater/film; true crime/investigative.

This agency offers clients full management service in all media. Clients are not necessarily book authors. "Our special expertise is in placing newspaper series internationally." Actively seeking autobiographies.

How to Contact Submit outline/proposal, IRCs if necessary, SASE. Prefers to read materials exclusively. Accepts e-mail and fax queries. Responds in 1 week to queries. Returns materials only with SASE. Obtains most new clients through recommendations from others, direct approaches to prospective authors.

Recent Sales Sold 25 titles in the last year. *Bill Hicks*, by Kevin Booth and Michael Bertin (HarperCollins); *For Better or Worse: Her Story*, by Christine Hamilton (Robson Books); *Warlord (Himmler)*, by Martin Allen (Constable and Robinson). Other clients include Stewart Evans, Neil & Christine Hamilton, James Haspiel, Geoffrey Guiliano, Robert Kray, Norman Parker, Mike Reid, Donald Rumbelow, Douglas Thompson.

Terms Agent receives 15% commission on domestic sales; 20% commission on foreign sales. Offers written contract, binding for 3 months; 3-month notice must be given to terminate contract. Charges clients for couriers, photocopying and postage, overseas mailings of mss, subject to client authorization.

MICHAEL SNELL LITERARY AGENCY

P.O. Box 1206, Truro MA 02666-1206. (508)349-3718. **Contact:** Michael Snell. Estab. 1978. Represents 200 clients. 25% of clients are new/unpublished writers. Currently handles: 90% nonfiction books; 10% novels.

- Prior to opening his agency, Mr. Snell served as an editor at Wadsworth and Addison-Wesley for 13 years.

Member Agents Michael Snell (business, pets, sports); Patricia Snell (pets, relationships, parenting, self-help, how-to).

Represents Nonfiction books. **Considers these nonfiction areas:** Agriculture/horticulture; animals (pets); anthropology/archaeology; art/architecture/design; business/economics; child guidance/parenting; computers/electronic; cooking/foods/nutrition; crafts/hobbies; creative nonfiction; current affairs; education; ethnic/cultural interests; gardening; gay/lesbian issues; government/politics/law; health/medicine; history; how-to; humor/satire; interior design/decorating; language/literature/criticism; military/war; money/finance; music/

Literary Agents

dance; nature/environment; New Age/metaphysics; photography; popular culture; psychology; recreation; religious/inspirational; science/technology; self-help/personal improvement; sex; spirituality; sports (fitness); theater/film; travel; true crime/investigative; women's issues/studies.

O→ This agency specializes in how-to, self-help and all types of business and computer books, from low-level how-to to professional and reference. Especially interested in business, health, law, medicine, psychology, science, women's issues. Actively seeking "strong book proposals in any nonfiction area where a clear need exists for a new book. Especially self-help, how-to books on all subjects, from business to personal well-being." Does not want to receive "complete manuscripts; considers proposals only. No fiction. No children's books."

How to Contact Query with SASE. Prefers to read materials exclusively. Responds in 1 week to queries; 2 weeks to mss. Obtains most new clients through unsolicited mss, word of mouth, *LMP* , and *Guide to Literary Agents*.
Recent Sales *The Complete Idiot's Guide to Intimacy*, by Paul Coleman (Macmillan Alpha); *Can-Do Kids*, by Brad Smart (Amacom); *Start a Million Dollar Business with Other People's Money*, by Don Debelak (Adams); *The Ultimate Real Estate Guide*, by Stu Rider (Entrepreneur Press).
Terms Agent receives 15% commission on domestic sales; 15% commission on foreign sales.
Tips "Send a half- to full-page query, with SASE. Brochure 'How to Write a Book Proposal' available on request and SASE. We suggest prospective clients read Michael Snell's book, *From Book Idea to Bestseller* (Prima, 1997)."

SPECTRUM LITERARY AGENCY

320 Central Park W., Suite 1-D, New York NY 10025. Website: www.spectrumliteraryagency.com. **Contact:** Eleanor Wood, president. Represents 90 clients. Currently handles: 10% nonfiction books; 90% novels.
Member Agents Lucienne Diver.
Represents Nonfiction books, novels. **Considers these nonfiction areas:** Considers select nonfiction. **Considers these fiction areas:** Contemporary issues; fantasy; historical; mainstream/contemporary; mystery/suspense; romance; science fiction.
How to Contact Query with SASE, include publishing credits and background information. No phone, e-mail, or fax queries. Responds in 1-3 months to queries. Obtains most new clients through recommendations from authors and others.
Recent Sales Sold over 100 titles in the last year. This agency prefers not to share information on specific sales.
Terms Agent receives 15% commission on domestic sales. Deducts for photocopying and book orders.

SPENCERHILL ASSOCIATES

P.O. Box 374, Chatham NY 12032. (518)392-9293. Fax: (518)392-9554. E-mail: ksolem@klsbooks.com. **Contact:** Karen Solem. Estab. 2001. Member of AAR. Represents 40 clients. 5% of clients are new/unpublished writers. Currently handles: 5% nonfiction books; 90% novels; 5% novellas.

- Ms. Solem is not taking on many new clients at the present time. Prior to becoming an agent, Ms. Solem was editor-in-chief at HarperCollins and associate publisher.

Represents Nonfiction books (Christian), novels. **Considers these nonfiction areas:** Animals; religious/inspirational. **Considers these fiction areas:** Detective/police/crime; historical; mainstream/contemporary; religious/inspirational; romance; thriller.

O→ "I handle mostly commercial women's fiction, romance, thrillers, and mysteries. I also represent Christian fiction and nonfiction." No poetry, science fiction, juvenile, or scripts.

How to Contact Query with SASE, submit proposal package, outline. Responds in 1 month to queries. Returns materials only with SASE.
Recent Sales Sold 110 titles in the last year.
Terms Agent receives 15% commission on domestic sales; 20% commission on foreign sales. Offers written contract; 3-months notice must be given to terminate contract.

THE SPIELER AGENCY

154 W. 57th St., 13th Floor, Room 135, New York NY 10019. **Contact:** Katya Balter. Estab. 1981. Represents 160 clients. 2% of clients are new/unpublished writers.

- Prior to opening his agency, Mr. Spieler was a magazine editor.

Member Agents Joe Spieler; John Thornton (nonfiction); Lisa M. Ross (fiction/nonfiction); Deirdre Mullane (nonfiction/fiction); Eric Myers (nonfiction/fiction). Spieler Agency West (Oakland, CA): Victoria Shoemaker.
Represents Nonfiction books, literary fiction, children's books. **Considers these nonfiction areas:** Biography/autobiography; business/economics; child guidance/parenting; current affairs; gay/lesbian issues; government/politics/law; history; memoirs; money/finance; music/dance; nature/environment (environmental issues); religious/inspirational; sociology; spirituality; theater/film; travel; women's issues/studies. **Considers these fiction areas:** Experimental; feminist; gay/lesbian; literary.

How to Contact Query with SASE. Prefers to read materials exclusively. Returns materials only with SASE; otherwise materials are discarded when rejected. No fax queries. Considers simultaneous queries. Responds in 2 weeks to queries; 5 weeks to mss. Obtains most new clients through recommendations and occasionally through listing in *Guide to Literary Agents*.
Recent Sales *What's the Matter with Kansas*, by Thomas Frank (Metropolitan/Holt); *Natural History of the Rich*, by Richard Conniff (W.W. Norton).
Terms Agent receives 15% commission on domestic sales. Charges clients for messenger bills, photocopying, postage.
Writers' Conferences London Bookfair.

PHILIP G. SPITZER LITERARY AGENCY

50 Talmage Farm Lane, East Hampton NY 11937. (631)329-3650. Fax: (631)329-3651. E-mail: spitzer516@aol.com. **Contact:** Philip Spitzer. Estab. 1969. Member of AAR. Represents 60 clients. 10% of clients are new/unpublished writers. Currently handles: 50% nonfiction books; 50% novels.

- Prior to opening his agency, Mr. Spitzer served at New York University Press, McGraw-Hill, and the John Cushman Associates literary agency.

Represents Nonfiction books, novels. **Considers these nonfiction areas:** Biography/autobiography; business/economics; current affairs; ethnic/cultural interests; government/politics/law; health/medicine; history; language/literature/criticism; military/war; music/dance; nature/environment; popular culture; psychology; sociology; sports; theater/film; true crime/investigative. **Considers these fiction areas:** Contemporary issues; detective/police/crime; literary; mainstream/contemporary; mystery/suspense; sports; thriller.

O→ This agency specializes in mystery/suspense, literary fiction, sports, general nonfiction (no how-to).

How to Contact Query with SASE, outline, 1 sample chapter. Responds in 1 week to queries; 6 weeks to mss. Obtains most new clients through recommendations from others.
Recent Sales *The Narrows*, by Michael Connelly; *Lost Light*, by Michael Connelly; *Shadow Man*, by Jonathon King; *Something's Down There*, by Mickey Spillane; *Missing Justice*, by Alafair Burke; *Last Car to Elysian Fields*, by James Lee Burke; *Shattered*, by Deborah Puglisi Sharp with Marjorie Perston.
Terms Agent receives 15% commission on domestic sales; 20% commission on foreign sales. Charges clients for photocopying.
Writers' Conferences BEA.

NANCY STAUFFER ASSOCIATES

P.O. Box 1203, Darien CT 06820. (203)655-3717. Fax: (203)655-3704. E-mail: nanstauf@optonline.net. **Contact:** Nancy Stauffer Cahoon. Estab. 1989. Member of the Authors Guild. 5% of clients are new/unpublished writers. Currently handles: 15% nonfiction books; 85% novels.
Represents Nonfiction books, novels. **Considers these nonfiction areas:** Creative nonfiction; current affairs; ethnic/cultural interests. **Considers these fiction areas:** Contemporary issues; literary; regional.
How to Contact Obtains most new clients through referrals from existing clients.
Recent Sales Untitled nonfiction and Richard Pryor biography by Sherman Alexie; *No Enemy But Time*, by William C. Harris (St. Martin's Press); *An Unfinished Life*, by Mark Spragg.
Terms Agent receives 15% commission on domestic sales; 20% commission on foreign sales; 15% commission on dramatic rights sales.

STEELE-PERKINS LITERARY AGENCY

26 Island Lane, Canandaigua NY 14424. (585)396-9290. Fax: (585)396-3579. E-mail: pattiesp@aol.com. **Contact:** Pattie Steele-Perkins. Member of AAR, RWA. Currently handles: 100% romance and mainstream women's fiction.
Represents Novels. **Considers these fiction areas:** Mainstream/contemporary; multicultural; romance (inspirational); women's.

O→ Actively seeking inspirational, romance, women's fiction, and multicultural works.

How to Contact Submit outline, 3 sample chapters, SASE. Considers simultaneous queries. Responds in 6 weeks to queries. Returns materials only with SASE. Obtains most new clients through recommendations from others, queries/solicitations.
Recent Sales This agency prefers not to share information on specific sales.
Terms Agent receives 15% commission on domestic sales. Offers written contract, binding for 1 year; 1-month notice must be given to terminate contract.
Writers' Conferences National Conference of Romance Writers of America; BookExpo America Writers' Conferences; CBA; Romance Slam Jam.
Tips "Be patient. E-mail rather than call. Make sure what you are sending is the best it can be."

STERLING LORD LITERISTIC, INC.

65 Bleecker St., 12th Floor, New York NY 10012. (212)780-6050. Fax: (212)780-6095. E-mail: info@sll.com. Website: www.sll.com. Estab. 1952. Member of AAR; signatory of WGA. Represents 600 clients. Currently handles: 50% nonfiction books; 50% novels.

Member Agents Philippa Brophy, Laurie Liss, Chris Calhoun, Peter Matson, Sterling Lord, Claudia Cross, Neeti Madan, George Nicholson, Jim Rutman, Charlotte Sheedy (affiliate); Douglas Stewart; Manuel Stoeckl; Paul Rodeen; Robert Guinsler.

Represents Nonfiction books, novels, literary value considered first.

How to Contact Query with SASE. Responds in 1 month to mss. Obtains most new clients through recommendations from others.

Recent Sales This agency prefers not to share information on specific sales. Clients include Kent Haruf, Dick Fancis, Mary Gordon, Sen. John McCain, Simon Winchester, James McBride, Billy Collins, Richard Paul Evans, Dave Pelzer.

Terms Agent receives 15% commission on domestic sales; 20% commission on foreign sales. Offers written contract. Charges clients for photocopying.

STERNIG & BYRNE LITERARY AGENCY

2370 S. 107th St., Apt. #4, Milwaukee WI 53227-2036. (414)328-8034. Fax: (414)328-8034. E-mail: jackbyrne@hotmail.com. Website: www.sff.net/people/jackbyrne. **Contact:** Jack Byrne. Estab. 1950s. Member of SFWA, MWA. Represents 30 clients. 10% of clients are new/unpublished writers. Currently handles: 5% nonfiction books; 85% novels; 10% juvenile books.

Member Agents Jack Byrne.

Represents Nonfiction books, novels, juvenile books. **Considers these fiction areas:** Fantasy; horror; mystery/suspense; science fiction.

- "Our client list is comfortably full and our current needs are therefore quite limited." Actively seeking science fiction/fantasy by established writers. Does not want to receive romance, poetry, textbooks, highly specialized nonfiction.

How to Contact Query with SASE. Accepts e-mail queries, no attachments. Responds in 3 weeks to queries; 3 months to mss. Returns materials only with SASE.

Recent Sales Sold 12 new titles and 30 reprints/foreign rights in the last year. *Beast Master's Quest*, by Andre Norton and Lyn McConchie; *Farthing*, by Jo Walton. Other clients include Jane Routley, Gerard Houarner, Betty Ren Wright, Moira Moore, John C. Wright, Naomi Kritzer, William Gagliani.

Terms Agent receives 15% commission on domestic sales; 20% commission on foreign sales. Offers written contract; 2-month notice must be given to terminate contract.

Tips "Don't send first drafts; have a professional presentation—including cover letter; know your field. Read what's been done—good and bad."

STIMOLA LITERARY STUDIO

308 Chase Court, Edgewater NJ 07020. Phone/Fax: (201)945-9353. E-mail: ltrystudio@aol.com. **Contact:** Rosemary B. Stimola. Member of AAR.

Member Agents Rosemary B. Stimola.

Represents Preschool through young adult fiction/nonfiction.

How to Contact Query with SASE, or via e-mail. Responds in 3 weeks to queries; 2 months to mss. Obtains most new clients through referrals from editors, agents and clients. Unsolicted submissions are still accepted.

Recent Sales *Gregor and the Prophecy of Bane*, by Suzanne Collins; *Black & White*, by Paul Volponi; *Queen of Twilight*, by Lisa Papademetriou; *A Raisin & A Grape*, by Tom Amico and James Proimos.

Terms Agent receives 15% commission on domestic sales; 20% (if subagents are employed) commission on foreign sales. Offers written contract, covering all children's literary work not previously published or under agreement.

Tips "No phone inquiries."

PAM STRICKLER AUTHOR MANAGEMENT

2760 Lucas Turnpike, P.O. Box 429, Accord NY 12404. (845)687-0186. **Contact:** Pamela Dean Strickler. Member of AAR.

- Query before submitting.

THE STROTHMAN AGENCY, LLC

One Faneuil Hall Marketplace, 3rd Floor, Boston MA 02109. (617)742-2011. Fax: (617)742-2014. **Contact:** Wendy Strothman or Dan O'Connell. Estab. 2003. Represents 45 clients. Currently handles: 60% nonfiction books; 15% novels; 5% juvenile books; 20% scholarly books.

• Prior to becoming an agent, Ms. Strothman was Executive Vice President and head of Houghton Mifflin's Trade & Reference Division, 1996-2002; head of Beacon Press, 1983-1995.

Member Agents John Ryden, Wendy Strothman, Dan O'Connell.

Represents Nonfiction books, novels, scholarly books. **Considers these nonfiction areas:** Current affairs; government/politics/law; history; language/literature/criticism; nature/environment. **Considers these fiction areas:** Literary.

"Because we are highly selective in the clients we represent, we increase the value publishers place on our properties. We seek out public figures, scholars, journalists, and other acknowledged and emerging experts in their fields. We specialize in narrative nonfiction, memoir, history, science and nature, arts and culture, literary travel, current affairs and some business. We have a highly selective practice in literary fiction and children's literature." Actively seeking scholarly nonfiction written to appeal to several audiences. Does not want commercial fiction, romance, science fiction, self-help.

How to Contact Query with SASE. Considers simultaneous queries. Responds in 3 weeks to queries; 1 month to mss. Returns materials only with SASE. Obtains most new clients through recommendations from others.

Recent Sales Sold 16 titles in the last year. Clients include Marlene Zuk, Peter Freund, Allan Gallay, Warren Goldstein, Paul Goldstein, Michael Graetz, Ian Shapiro, Doris Grumbach, David Blight, Martha Sandweiss, Susan Hirsch, Julian Houston, Gregory Katz, Kenn Kaufman, Moying Li, Thomas Rogers, Phil & Alice Shabecoff, Allison Wallace, Shirin Ebadi, Jessie Gruman.

Terms Agent receives 15% commission on domestic sales; 20% commission on foreign sales. Offers written contract; 30 days notice must be given to terminate contract.

THE SUSIJN AGENCY

3rd Floor, 64 Great Titchfield St., London W1W 7QH England. 0044 (207)580-6341. Fax: 0044 (207)580-8626. E-mail: info@thesusijnagency.com. Website: www.thesusijnagency.com. **Contact:** Laura Susijn, Charles Buchau. Estab. 1998. Currently handles: 15% nonfiction books; 85% novels.

• Prior to becoming an agent, Ms. Susijn was a rights director at Sheil Land Associates and at Fourth Estate, Ltd.

Member Agents Laura Susijn.

Represents Nonfiction books, novels. **Considers these nonfiction areas:** Biography/autobiography; memoirs; multicultural; popular culture; science/technology; travel. **Considers these fiction areas:** Literary.

This agency specializes in international works, selling world rights, representing non-English language writing as well as English. Emphasis on cross-cultural subjects. Does not want self-help, romance, sagas, science fiction, screenplays.

How to Contact Submit outline, 2 sample chapters. Considers simultaneous queries. Responds in 2 months to queries. Returns materials only with SASE. Obtains most new clients through recommendations from others, via publishers in Europe and beyond.

Recent Sales Sold 120 titles in the last year. *Trespassing*, by Uzma Aslam Khan (Flamingo UK); *Gone*, by Helena Echlin (Secker and Warburg, UK); *Daalder*, by Philibert Schogt (4 Walls 8 Windows); *The Memory Artists*, by Jeffrey Moore (Weidenfeld & Nicholson). Other clients include Vassallucci, Podium, Atlas, De Arbeiderspers, Tiderne Skifter, MB Agency, Van Oorschot

Terms Agent receives 15% commission on domestic sales; 15-20% commission on foreign sales. Offers written contract; 6 weeks notice must be given to terminate contract. Charges clients for photocopying, buying copies only if sale is made.

MARY M. TAHAN LITERARY, LLC

(formerly part of Clausen, Mays & Tahan Literary Agency), P.O. Box 1060 Gracie Station, New York NY 10028. E-mail: query.mary.tahan@earthlink.net. **Contact:** Mary M. Tahan. Member of AAR, Authors Guild.

Member Agents Mary M. Tahan and Jena H. Anderson.

Represents Nonfiction books, novels. **Considers these nonfiction areas:** Biography/autobiography; cooking/foods/nutrition; health/medicine; history; how-to; memoirs; money/finance; psychology; writing books; fashion/beauty/style; relationships; also rights for books optioned for TV movies and feature films.

How to Contact Send via regular mail or e-mail. For nonfiction, query or proposal package and outline with SASE. For fiction, brief (1-2 pages single-spaced) synopsis, first 3 chapters with SASE. Responds in 4 weeks to queries. Returns materials only with SASE.

Recent Sales *A Few Good Women: A History of the Rise of Women in the Military*, by Evelyn Monahan and Rosemary Neidel-Greenlee (Knopf); *The Siren of Solace Glen*, by Susan S. James (Berkley); *Finding the Right Words for the Holidays*, by J. Beverly Daniels (Pocket); *The Stinking Rose Restaurant Cookbook*, by Andrea Froncillo with Jennifer Jeffrey (Ten Speed Press).

Tips "For nonfiction, it's crucial to research how to write a proposal, especially how to analyze your book's competiting titles. For both fiction and nonfiction, do not send a full manuscript. Please do not phone or fax queries."

TALCOTT NOTCH LITERARY

276 Forest Rd., Milford CT 06460. (203)877-1146. Fax: (203)876-9517. E-mail: gpanettieri@talcottnotch.net or editorial@talcottnotch.net. Website: www.talcottnotch.net. **Contact:** Gina Panettieri. Estab. 2003. Represents 25 clients. 75% of clients are new/unpublished writers.

- Prior to becoming an agent, Ms. Panettieri was a freelance writers and editor.

Represents Nonfiction books, novels, juvenile books, scholarly books, textbooks. **Considers these nonfiction areas:** Agriculture/horticulture; animals; anthropology/archaeology; art/architecture/design; biography/autobiography; business/economics; child guidance/parenting; computers/electronic; cooking/foods/nutrition; current affairs; education; ethnic/cultural interests; gay/lesbian issues; government/politics/law; health/medicine; history; how-to; memoirs; military/war; money/finance; music/dance; nature/environment; popular culture; psychology; religious/inspirational; science/technology; self-help/personal improvement; sociology; sports; true crime/investigative; women's issues/studies; New Age/metaphysics, interior design/decorating, juvenile nonfiction. **Considers these fiction areas:** Action/adventure; detective/police/crime; erotica; ethnic; family saga; fantasy; feminist; gay/lesbian; historical; horror; juvenile; literary; mainstream/contemporary; mystery/suspense; religious/inspirational; romance; science fiction; thriller; westerns/frontier; young adult; psychic/supernatural, glitz.

Actively seeking nonfiction, mystery, and women's fiction. Does not want poetry or picture books.

How to Contact Query with SASE. Considers simultaneous queries. Responds in 1 week to queries; 2 weeks to mss. Returns materials only with SASE. "Most new clients are found through our listings with publishing-related websites or from writers seeing our sales listed in Publishers Marketplace."

Recent Sales Sold 9 titles in the last year. *Your Plus-Size Pregnancy*, by Dr. Bruce Rodgers and Brette Sember (Barricade Books); *Tactical Pistol Shooting*, by Erik Lawrence (Krause Publications); *A Happy Life*, by Charlotte Harris (Genesis Press). Other clients include Mark Ellis (writing as James Axler), Wayne Wilson, Richard Leahy.

Terms Agent receives 15% commission on domestic sales; 20% commission on foreign sales. Offers written contract, binding for 1 year.

Tips "Present your book or project effectively in your query. Don't include links to a webpage rather than use a traditional query, but take the time to prepare a thorough but brief synopsis of the material. Make th effort to prepare a thoughtful analysis of comparison titles. Why is your work different, yet would appeal to those same readers?"

ROSLYN TARG LITERARY AGENCY, INC.

105 W. 13th St., New York NY 10011. (212)206-9390. Fax: (212)989-6233. E-mail: roslyn@roslyntargagency.com. **Contact:** Roslyn Targ. Estab. 1945. Member of AAR. Represents 100 clients.

How to Contact Query with SASE, outline/proposal, curriculum vitae. Prefers to read materials exclusively. No mss without query first. Obtains most new clients through recommendations from others, solicitations.

Terms Agent receives 15% commission on domestic sales; 20% commission on foreign sales. Charges standard agency fees (bank charges, long distance, postage, photocopying, shipping of books, overseas long distance and shipping, etc.).

PATRICIA TEAL LITERARY AGENCY

2036 Vista Del Rosa, Fullerton CA 92831-1336. Phone/Fax: (714)738-8333. **Contact:** Patricia Teal. Estab. 1978. Member of AAR. Represents 20 clients. 10% of clients are new/unpublished writers. Currently handles: 10% nonfiction books; 90% fiction.

Represents Nonfiction books, novels. **Considers these nonfiction areas:** Animals; biography/autobiography; child guidance/parenting; health/medicine; how-to; psychology; self-help/personal improvement; true crime/investigative; women's issues/studies. **Considers these fiction areas:** Glitz; mainstream/contemporary; mystery/suspense; romance (contemporary, historical).

This agency specializes in women's fiction and commercial how-to and self-help nonfiction. Does not want to receive poetry, short stories, articles, science fiction, fantasy, regency romance.

How to Contact *Published authors only.* Query with SASE. No e-mail or fax queries. Considers simultaneous queries. Responds in 10 days to queries; 6 weeks to mss. Returns materials only with SASE. Obtains most new clients through conferences, recommendations from authors and editors.

Recent Sales Sold 20 titles in the last year. *Texas Rose*, by Marie Ferrarella (Silhouette); *Watch Your Language*, by Sterling Johnson (St. Martin's); *The Black Sheep's Baby*, by Kathleen Creighton (Silhouette); *Man with a Message*, by Muriel Jensen (Harlequin).

Terms Agent receives 10-15% commission on domestic sales; 20% commission on foreign sales. Offers written contract, binding for 1 year. Charges clients for postage.

Writers' Conferences Romance Writers of America conferences; Asilomar (California Writers Club); BEA; Bouchercon; Hawaii Writers Conference (Maui).
Tips "Include SASE with all correspondence. Taking on very few authors."

TESSLER LITERARY AGENCY, LLC

80 Fifth Ave., Suite 1503, New York NY 10011. (212)242-0466. Fax: (212)242-2366. Website: www.tessleragency.com. **Contact:** Michelle Tessler. Member of AAR.

- Prior to forming her own agency, Ms. Tessler worked 4 years as a senior agent at Carlisle & Co. She's also worked at the William Morris Agency and the Elaine Markson Literary Agency.

O→ The Tessler Agency is a full-service boutique agency that represents writers of high-quality nonfiction and literary and commercial fiction.

How to Contact Submit query through website only.
Recent Sales *The Post-Truth Era*, by Ralph Keyes (St. Martin's Press); *Jefferson's Demons*, by Michael Knox Beran (Free Press); *Sleep Toward Heaven*, by Amanda Eyre Ward (Perennial). Other clients include Scott Huler, Paul Collins, Andrea Rock, Jennifer Paddock, Leanne Ely.

THOTH LITERARY AGENCY

P.O. Box 620277, Littleton CO 80162-0277. (303)932-0277. E-mail: medulla@sprintmail.com. Website: www.hawaiianhulahips.com/thothliteraryagency/. **Contact:** Manulani Thelen. Estab. 2003. Represents 6 clients. 50% of clients are new/unpublished writers. Currently handles: 50% (YA) novels; 20% juvenile books; 10% crafts/hobbies; 20% horror.

- Prior to becoming an agent, Manulani Thelen was the artistic director of a 501(c)(3) nonprofit for 33 years. Thelen is also a composer, curriculum developer, educator, and professor of ethnology.

Member Agents Monica Lanie (cooking, crafts, animals, YA, theater/film, fantasy); Manulani Thelen (ethnic, juvenile, YA, music/dance, picture book).
Represents Nonfiction books, novels, novellas, juvenile books. **Considers these nonfiction areas:** Animals; cooking/foods/nutrition; ethnic/cultural interests; music/dance; crafts/hobbies, juvenile nonfiction.

O→ "We provide honest, customized feedback at no cost, not merely a vague note of rejection. We never charge reading or publisher search fees. Although we are not yet members of AAR, we abide by their Canon of Ethics." Actively seeking "well-written works in the areas of fiction (adventure, ethnic, fantasy, juvenile, picture book, young adult) and nonfiction (animals, cooking/food, crafts/hobbies, ethnic/cultural interests, juvenile nonfiction, music/dance/theater/film). Does not want to receive poetry, gore/slasher/psychopathic, romance, screenplays, self-help, westerns, science fiction, or detective/crime.

How to Contact Query with SASE, submit synopsis, 3 sample chapters, SASE. No e-mail or fax queries. Considers simultaneous queries. Responds in 3 weeks to queries; 6 weeks to mss. Returns materials only with SASE. Obtains most new clients through word of mouth and website.
Recent Sales Clients include Michael Oppenheim, Frank Laurence, Ph.D., Matthew Wayne Opal.
Terms Agent receives 10% commission on domestic sales; 15% commission on foreign sales. Offers written contract, binding for 1 year; 6-months notice must be given to terminate contract.
Writers' Conferences Highlights Foundation Writers Workshop (Chautauqua NY, July).
Tips "We are not interested in receiving poorly written submissions from authors with grandiose attitudes; don't compare yourself to Jane Austen, J.R.R. Tolkien, etc. Blackmail never works—don't tell us that you'll only send your manuscript to us if we can guarantee you will be published. Please always send a SASE or else we won't be able to contact you. Write stories that make sense; research everything down to the bone. Most importantly, be proud of your work; no self-deprecation."

3 SEAS LITERARY AGENCY

P.O. Box 7038, Madison WI 53708. (608)221-4306. E-mail: threeseaslit@aol.com. Website: www.threeseaslit.com. **Contact:** Michelle Grajkowski. Estab. 2000. Member of Romance Writers of America, Chicago Women in Publishing. Represents 40 clients. 15% of clients are new/unpublished writers. Currently handles: 5% nonfiction books; 80% novels; 15% juvenile books.

- Prior to becoming an agent, Ms. Grajkowski worked in both sales and in purchasing for a medical facility. She has a degree in journalism from the University of Wisconsin-Madison.

Represents Nonfiction books, novels, juvenile books, scholarly books.

O→ 3 Seas focuses on romance (including category, historicals, regencies, westerns, romantic suspense, paranormal), women's fiction, mysteries, nonfiction, young adult and children's stories. Does not want to receive poetry, screenplays, or short stories.

How to Contact For fiction, please query with first 3 chapters, a synopsis, your bio, and SASE. For nonfiction, please query with your complete proposal, first 3 chapters, number of words, a bio, and SASE. Considers

simultaneous queries. Responds in 1 month to queries. Responds in 3 months to partials. Returns materials only with SASE. Obtains most new clients through recommendations from others, conferences.
Recent Sales Sold 75 titles in the last year. *Fire Me Up, Sex, Lies & Vampires* and *Hard Day's Knight*, by Katie MacAlister; *Calendar Girl*, by Naomi Neale; *To Die For*, by Stephanie Rowe; *The Phantom in the Bathtub*, by Eugenia Riley; *The Unknown Daughter*, by Anna DeStefano. Other clients include Winnie Griggs, Diane Amos, Pat Pritchard, Barbara Jean Hicks, Carrie Weaver, Robin Popp, Kerrelyn Sparks, Sandra Madden.
Terms Agent receives 15% commission on domestic sales; 20% commission on foreign sales. Offers written contract, binding for 1 month.
Writers' Conferences RWA National Conference (July).

ANN TOBIAS—A LITERARY AGENCY FOR CHILDREN'S BOOKS

520 E. 84th St., Apt. 4L, New York NY 10028. **Contact:** Ann Tobias. Estab. 1988. Represents 25 clients. 50% of clients are new/unpublished writers. Currently handles: 100% juvenile books.

- Prior to opening her agency, Ms. Tobias worked as a children's book editor at Harper, William Morrow, Scholastic.

Represents Juvenile books. **Considers these nonfiction areas:** Juvenile nonfiction; young adult. **Considers these fiction areas:** Picture books; poetry (for children); young adult; illustrated mss; mid-level novels.

O→ This agency specializes in books for children. Actively seeking material for children.

How to Contact Send entire ms for picture books; 30 pages and synopsis for longer work, both fiction and nonfiction. No phone queries. All queries must be in writing and accompanied by a SASE. No overnight mail or mail by private carrier that requires a signature. No e-mail or fax queries. Considers simultaneous queries. Responds in 2 months to mss. Returns materials only with SASE. Obtains most new clients through recommendations from editors.
Recent Sales Sold 12 titles in the last year. This agency prefers not to share information on specific sales.
Terms Agent receives 15% commission on domestic sales; 20% commission on foreign sales. No written contract. Charges clients for photocopying, overnight mail, foreign postage, foreign telephone.
Tips "Read at least 200 children's books in the age group and genre in which you hope to be published. Follow this by reading another 100 children's books in other age groups and genres so you will have a feel for the field as a whole."

S©OTT TREIMEL NY

434 Lafayette St., New York NY 10003. (212)505-8353. Fax: (212)505-0664. E-mail: st.ny@verizon.net. Estab. 1995. Member of AAR, Authors Guild. Represents 43 clients. 15% of clients are new/unpublished writers. Currently handles: 100% juvenile books.

- Prior to becoming an agent, Mr. Treimel was an assistant at Curtis Brown, Ltd. (for Marilyn E. Marlow); a rights agent for Scholastic, Inc; a book packager and rights agent for United Feature Syndicate; a freelance editor, a rights consultant for HarperCollins Children's Books; and the founding director of Warner Bros. Worldwide Publishing.

Represents Children's book authors and illustrators.

O→ This agency specializes in tightly focused segments of the trade and institutional markets. Interested in seeing author-illustrators, first chapter books, middle-grade and teen fiction. Does not consider activity or coloring books.

How to Contact Two complete picture book texts may be submitted. For longer work, query with SASE and sample chapters. No multiple submissions. No fax queries.
Recent Sales Sold 19 titles in the last year. *Open Ice*, by Pat Hughes (Random House/Wendy Lamb Books); *Papa, Do You Love Me?*, by Barbara Joosse (Chronicle Books).
Terms Agent receives 15-20% commission on domestic sales; 20-25% commission on foreign sales. Offers verbal or written contract, "binding on a book, contract-by-contract basis." Charges clients for photocopying, express postage, messengers, and books ordered to sell foreign, film, etc. rights.
Writers' Conferences Can You Make a Living from Children's Books, Society of Children's Book Writers & Illustrators (Los Angeles, August); "Understanding Book Contracts," SCBWI (Watertown NY); "Creating Believable Teen Characters," SCBWI; Picture Book Judge for Tassie Walden Award; New Voices in Children's Literature; "Craft" SCBWI (North Carolina); "Understanding Book Contracts" SCBWI (North Dakota); The New School; The Professionals Panel; SouthWest Writers Workshop; Pike's Peak Writers Association; "How to Get the Right Agent" (Hawaii).
Tips "Keep cover letters short and do not pitch. Manuscripts and illustration samples received without a SASE are recycled on receipt."

TRIADA U.S. LITERARY AGENCY, INC.

P.O. Box 561, Sewickley PA 15143. (412)401-3376. E-mail: uwe@triadaus.com. Website: www.triadaus.com. **Contact:** Dr. Uwe Stender. Estab. 2004. Represents 27 clients. 74% of clients are new/unpublished writers.

Currently handles: 14% nonfiction books; 72% novels; 11% juvenile books; 3% scholarly books.

- Mr. Stender was a management consultant, acquisitions editor, technology director, teacher, coach, and university lecturer.

Member Agents Paul Hudson (science fiction, fantasy).

Represents Nonfiction books, novels, short story collections, juvenile books, scholarly books. **Considers these nonfiction areas:** Biography/autobiography; business/economics; child guidance/parenting; education; humor/satire; memoirs; popular culture; self-help/personal improvement; sports. **Considers these fiction areas:** Action/adventure; detective/police/crime; ethnic; fantasy; historical; horror; juvenile; literary; mainstream/contemporary; mystery/suspense; romance; science fiction; sports; thriller; young adult.

"We specialize in literary novels and suspense. Education, business, and narrative nonfiction are other strong suits. Our response time is fairly unique. We recognize that neither we nor the authors have time to waste, so we guarantee a 5-day response time. We usually respond within 24 hours." Actively seeking quality fiction and nonfiction.

How to Contact Query with SASE. Considers simultaneous queries. Responds in 1-5 weeks to queries; 2-4 weeks to mss. Returns materials only with SASE. Obtains most new clients through recommendations from others, conferences.

Terms Agent receives 10% commission on domestic sales; 15% commission on foreign sales. Offers written contract; 30-day notice must be given to terminate contract.

Tips "I comment on all requested manuscripts which I reject."

TRIDENT MEDIA GROUP

41 Madison Ave., 36th Floor, New York NY 10010. E-mail: levine.assistant@tridentmediagroup.com. Website: www.tridentmediagroup.com. **Contact:** Ellen Levine. Member of AAR.

Member Agents Jenny Bent; Scott Miller; Paul Fedarko; Alex Glass; Melissa Flashman.

Actively seeking new or established authors in a variety of genres both fiction and nonfiction.

How to Contact Query with SASE by regular mail or via e-mail. Check online for more details.

2M COMMUNICATIONS, LTD.

121 W. 27 St., #601, New York NY 10001. (212)741-1509. Fax: (212)691-4460. E-mail: morel@bookhaven.com. Website: www.2mcommunications.com. **Contact:** Madeleine Morel. Estab. 1982. Represents 50 clients. 20% of clients are new/unpublished writers. Currently handles: 100% nonfiction books.

- Prior to becoming an agent, Ms. Morel worked at a publishing company.

Represents Nonfiction books. **Considers these nonfiction areas:** Biography/autobiography; child guidance/parenting; ethnic/cultural interests; health/medicine; history; self-help/personal improvement; women's issues/studies; Music; cookbooks.

This agency specializes in adult nonfiction.

How to Contact Query with SASE, submit outline, 3 sample chapters. Considers simultaneous queries. Responds in 1 week to queries; 1 month to mss. Obtains most new clients through recommendations from others, solicitations.

Recent Sales Sold 25 titles in the last year. *How Do You Compare?*, by Andy Williams (Penguin Putnam); *Hormone Wisdom*, by Theresa Dale (John Wiley); *Irish Dessert Cookbook*, by Margaret Johnson (Chronicle).

Terms Agent receives 15% commission on domestic sales; 20% commission on foreign sales. Offers written contract, binding for 2 years. Charges clients for postage, photocopying, long-distance calls, faxes.

THE RICHARD R. VALCOURT AGENCY, INC.

177 E. 77th St., PHC, New York NY 10021-1934. Phone/Fax: (212)570-2340. **Contact:** Richard R. Valcourt, president. Estab. 1995. Represents 25 clients. 20% of clients are new/unpublished writers. Currently handles: 100% nonfiction books.

- Not accepting new clients at this time. Prior to opening his agency, Mr. Valcourt was a journalist, editor and college political science instructor. He is also editor-in-chief of the International Journal of Intelligence and faculty member at American Military University in West Virginia.

Represents Scholarly books.

This agency specializes in intelligence and other national security affairs. Represents exclusively academics, journalists and professionals in the categories listed.

How to Contact Query with SASE. Prefers to read materials exclusively. No e-mail or fax queries. Responds in 1 week to queries; 1 month to mss. Returns materials only with SASE. Obtains most new clients through recommendations from others.

Terms Agent receives 15% commission on domestic sales; 20% commission on foreign sales. Offers written contract. Charges clients for excessive photocopying, express mail, overseas telephone expenses.

VAN DER LEUN & ASSOCIATES

40 E. 89th St., New York NY 10128. (212)477-2033. E-mail: pvanderleun@earthlink.net. Website: www.publishersmarketplace.com/members/pvanderleun. **Contact:** Patricia Van der Leun, president. Estab. 1984. Represents 30 clients. Currently handles: 75% nonfiction books; 25% novels.

- Prior to becoming an agent, Ms. Van der Leun was a professor of Art History.

Represents Nonfiction books, novels, illustrated books. **Considers these nonfiction areas:** Art/architecture/design (art history); biography/autobiography; cooking/foods/nutrition (food and wine, cookbooks); creative nonfiction; current affairs; ethnic/cultural interests; gardening; history; memoirs; religious/inspirational; spirituality; sports; travel. **Considers these fiction areas:** Comic books/cartoon; contemporary issues; humor/satire; literary; mainstream/contemporary; multicultural; multimedia; picture books; short story collections; translation; women's.

This agency specializes in fiction, art history, food and wine, gardening, biography.

How to Contact Query with letter only, include author bio and SASE. Considers simultaneous queries. Responds in 2 weeks to queries.

Recent Sales Sold 15 titles in the last year. *De Kooning's Bicycle*, by Robert Long (Farrar, Straus & Giroux, Inc.); *The Perfect $100,000 House*, by Karrie Jacobs (Viking); *Buddhist Meditation Straight Up*, by Alan Wallace (John Wiley).

Terms Agent receives 15% commission on domestic sales; 25% commission on foreign sales. Offers written contract. Charges clients for postage and photocopying of ms.

VENTURE LITERARY

8895 Towne Centre Dr., Suite 105, #141, San Diego CA 92122. (619)807-1887. Fax: (772)365-8321. E-mail: submissions@ventureliterary.com. Website: www.ventureliterary.com. **Contact:** Frank R. Scatoni. Estab. 1999. Represents 30 clients. 50% of clients are new/unpublished writers. Currently handles: 95% nonfiction books; 5% novels.

- Prior to becoming an agent, Mr. Scatoni worked as an editor at Simon & Schuster.

Member Agents Frank R. Scatoni (general nonfiction, including biography, memoir, narrative nonfiction, sports and serious nonfiction); Greg Dinkin (general nonfiction/business, gambling).

Represents Nonfiction books, novels. **Considers these nonfiction areas:** Animals; anthropology/archaeology; biography/autobiography; business/economics; current affairs; ethnic/cultural interests; government/politics/law; history; memoirs; military/war; money/finance; multicultural; music/dance; nature/environment; popular culture; psychology; science/technology; sports; true crime/investigative; gambling. **Considers these fiction areas:** Action/adventure; detective/police/crime; literary; mainstream/contemporary; mystery/suspense; sports; thriller.

Specializes in nonfiction, sports, business, natural history, biography, gambling. Actively seeking nonfiction.

How to Contact Considers e-mail queries only. *No unsolicited mss.* Responds in 3-6 months to queries; 6 months to mss. Returns materials only with SASE. Obtains most new clients through recommendations from others.

Recent Sales *Hunting Fish*, by Jay Greenspan (St. Martin's Press); *Dead Heat*, by William Murray (Eclipse Press); *Shuffle Up and Deal*, by Jonathan Grotenstein and Storms Reback (Thomas Dunne Books).

Terms Agent receives 15% commission on domestic sales; 20% commission on foreign sales. Offers written contract.

N VERITAS LITERARY AGENCY

1157 Valencia, Suite 4, San Francisco CA 94110. **Contact:** Katherine Boyle. Member of AAR.

- Query before submitting.

RALPH VICINANZA, LTD.

303 W. 18th St., New York NY 10011. (212)924-7090. Fax: (212)691-9644. Member of AAR. Represents 120 clients. 5% of clients are new/unpublished writers.

- Query before submitting.

Member Agents Ralph M. Vicinanza, Chris Lotts, Chris Schelling.

Represents Nonfiction books, novels. **Considers these nonfiction areas:** Biography/autobiography; business/economics; history; popular culture; religious/inspirational; science/technology. **Considers these fiction areas:** Fantasy; literary; mainstream/contemporary (popular fiction); multicultural; science fiction; thriller; women's.

This agency specializes in foreign rights.

How to Contact Agency takes on new clients by professional recommendation only.

Recent Sales This agency prefers not to share information on specific sales.

Terms Agent receives 15% commission on domestic sales; 20% commission on foreign sales.

DAVID VIGLIANO LITERARY AGENCY

584 Broadway, Suite 809, New York NY 10012. (212)226-7800. Fax: (212)226-5508. Member of AAR.

- Query before submitting.

Member Agents Donna Bagdasarian, Michael Harriot.

THE VINES AGENCY, INC.

648 Broadway, Suite 901, New York NY 10012. (212)777-5522. Fax: (212)777-5978. E-mail: jv@vinesagency.com. Website: www.vinesagency.com. **Contact:** James C. Vines, Ali Ryan, Gary Neuwirth, Alexis Caldwell. Estab. 1995. Signatory of WGA; Author's Guild. Represents 52 clients. 20% of clients are new/unpublished writers. Currently handles: 50% nonfiction books; 50% novels.

- Prior to opening his agency, Mr. Vines served as an agent with the Virginia Barber Literary Agency.

Member Agents James C. Vines (quality and commercial fiction and nonfiction); Gary Neuwirth; Alexis Caldwell (women's fiction, ethnic fiction, quality nonfiction); Ali Ryan (women's fiction and nonfiction, mainstream).

Represents Nonfiction books, novels, feature film. **Considers these nonfiction areas:** Biography/autobiography; business/economics; current affairs; ethnic/cultural interests; history; how-to; humor/satire; memoirs; military/war; money/finance; nature/environment; New Age/metaphysics; photography; popular culture; psychology; religious/inspirational; science/technology; self-help/personal improvement; sociology; spirituality; sports; translation; travel; true crime/investigative; women's issues/studies. **Considers these fiction areas:** Action/adventure; contemporary issues; detective/police/crime; ethnic; experimental; family saga; feminist; gay/lesbian; historical; horror; humor/satire; literary; mainstream/contemporary; mystery/suspense; occult; psychic/supernatural; regional; romance (contemporary, historical); science fiction; sports; thriller; westerns/frontier; women's. **Considers these script subject areas:** Action/adventure; comedy; detective/police/crime; ethnic; experimental; feminist; gay/lesbian; historical; horror; mainstream; mystery/suspense; romantic comedy; romantic drama; science fiction; teen; thriller; western/frontier.

O→ This agency specializes in mystery, suspense, science fiction, women's fiction, ethnic fiction, mainstream novels, screenplays, teleplays.

How to Contact Submit outline, 3 sample chapters, SASE. Considers simultaneous queries. Responds in 2 weeks to queries; 1 month to mss. Returns materials only with SASE. Obtains most new clients through query letters, recommendations from others, reading short stories in magazines, soliciting conferences.

Recent Sales Sold 48 titles and sold 5 scripts in the last year. *Sunset and Sawdust*, by Joe R. Lansdale; *Camilla's Rose*, by Bernice McFadden; *Ecstasy*, by Beth Saulnier.

Terms Agent receives 15% commission on domestic sales; 25% commission on foreign sales. Offers written contract, binding for 1 year; 1-month notice must be given to terminate contract. 100% of business is derived from commissions on ms sales. Charges clients for foreign postage, messenger services, photocopying.

Writers' Conferences Maui Writer's Conference.

Tips "Do not follow up on submissions with phone calls to the agency. The agency will read and respond by mail only. Do not pack your manuscript in plastic 'peanuts' that will make us have to vacuum the office after opening the package containing your manuscript. Always enclose return postage."

MARY JACK WALD ASSOCIATES, INC.

111 E. 14th St., New York NY 10003. (212)254-7842. **Contact:** Danis Sher. Estab. 1985. Member of AAR, Authors' Guild, SCBWI. Represents 35 clients. 5% of clients are new/unpublished writers. Currently handles: nonfiction books; novels; story collections; novellas; juvenile books.

- This agency is not accepting mss at this time.

Member Agents Mary Jack Wald, Danis Sher, Lynne Rabinoff Agency (association who represents foreign rights); Alvin Wald.

Represents Nonfiction books, novels, short story collections, novellas, juvenile books, movie and TV scripts by our authors. **Considers these nonfiction areas:** Biography/autobiography; current affairs; ethnic/cultural interests; history; juvenile nonfiction; language/literature/criticism; music/dance; nature/environment; photography; sociology; theater/film; translation; true crime/investigative. **Considers these fiction areas:** Action/adventure; contemporary issues; detective/police/crime; ethnic; experimental; family saga; feminist; gay/lesbian; glitz; historical; juvenile; literary; mainstream/contemporary; mystery/suspense; picture books; thriller; young adult; satire.

O→ This agency specializes in literary works and juvenile works.

How to Contact Not accepting new clients at this time.

Recent Sales *The Secret of Castle Cant*, by K.P. Bath; *Summer at Ma Dear's House*, by Denise Lewis Patnick.

Terms Agent receives 15% commission on domestic sales; 15-30% commission on foreign sales. Offers written contract, binding for 1 year.

WALES LITERARY AGENCY, INC.

P.O. Box 9428, Seattle WA 98109-0428. (206)284-7114. E-mail: waleslit@waleslit.com. Website: www.waleslit.com. **Contact:** Elizabeth Wales, Josie di Bernardo. Estab. 1988. Member of AAR, Book Publishers' Northwest, Pacific Northwest Booksellers Association, PEN. Represents 65 clients. 10% of clients are new/unpublished writers. Currently handles: 60% nonfiction books; 40% fiction.

- Prior to becoming an agent, Ms. Wales worked at Oxford University Press and Viking Penguin.

Member Agents Elizabeth Wales, Adrienne Reed.

O→ This agency specializes in narrative nonfiction and quality mainstream and literary fiction. Does not handle screenplays, children's literature, genre fiction or most category nonfiction.

How to Contact Query with cover letter, writing sample (approx. 30 pages), and SASE. No phone or fax queries. Prefers regular mail queries, but accepts 1-page e-mail queries with no attachments. Considers simultaneous queries. Responds in 3 weeks to queries; 6 weeks to mss. Returns materials only with SASE.

Recent Sales *Breaking Ranks*, by Norman H. Stamper (Nation Books); *Birds of Central Park*, photographs by Cal Vornberger (Abrams); *Against Gravity*, by Farnoosh Moshiri (Penguin).

Terms Agent receives 15% commission on domestic sales; 20% commission on foreign sales.

Writers' Conferences Pacific NW Writers Conference (Seattle); Writers at Work (Salt Lake City); Writing Rendezvous (Anchorage); Willamette Writers (Portland).

Tips "Especially interested in work that espouses a progressive cultural or political view, projects a new voice, or simply shares an important, compelling story. Encourages writers living in the Pacific Northwest, West Coast, Alaska, and Pacific Rim countries, and writers from historically underrepresented groups, such as gay and lesbian writers and writers of color, to submit work (but does not discourage writers outside these areas). Most importantly, whether in fiction or nonfiction, the agency is looking for talented storytellers."

JOHN A. WARE LITERARY AGENCY

392 Central Park W., New York NY 10025-5801. (212)866-4733. Fax: (212)866-4734. **Contact:** John Ware. Estab. 1978. Represents 60 clients. 40% of clients are new/unpublished writers. Currently handles: 75% nonfiction books; 25% novels.

- Prior to opening his agency, Mr. Ware served as a literary agency with James Brown Associates/Curtis Brown, Ltd., and as an editor for Doubleday & Co.

Represents Nonfiction books, novels. **Considers these nonfiction areas:** Anthropology/archaeology; biography/autobiography; current affairs; health/medicine (academic credentials reqired); history (including oral history, Americana and folklore); language/literature/criticism; music/dance; nature/environment; popular culture; psychology (academic credentials reqired); science/technology; sports; true crime/investigative; women's issues/studies; social commentary; investigative journalism; 'bird's eye' views of phenomena. **Considers these fiction areas:** Detective/police/crime; mystery/suspense; thriller; accessible literary noncategory fiction.

O→ Does not want personal memoirs.

How to Contact Query first by letter only, including SASE. No e-mail or fax queries. Considers simultaneous queries. Responds in 2 weeks to queries.

Recent Sales *Hawking the Empire: Inside the National Security Syndicate*, by Tim Shorrock (Simon & Schuster); *The Pledge (of Allegiance)*, by Jeffrey Owen Jones (Thomas Dunne Books/St. Martin's); *Rise of the Cajun Mariner: The Race for Big Oil*, by Woody Falgoux (Pelican); *Jedburgh: The Mobilization of the French Resistance*, by Will Irwin (PublicAffairs); *Chain Lightning: The True Legend of Man o' War*, by Dorothy Ours (St. Martin's); *The Traveller: A Biography of John Ledyard*, by Bill Gifford (Harcourt).

Terms Agent receives 15% commission on domestic sales; 20% commission on foreign sales; 15% commission on dramatic rights sales. Charges clients for messenger service, photocopying.

Tips "Writers must have appropriate credentials for authorship of proposal (nonfiction) or manuscript (fiction); no publishing track record required. Open to good writing and interesting ideas by new or veteran writers."

HARRIET WASSERMAN LITERARY AGENCY

137 E. 36th St., New York NY 10016. (212)689-3257. E-mail: hwlainc@aol.com. **Contact:** Harriet Wasserman. Member of AAR.

How to Contact Query before submitting. Full-length mss only on exclusive submission.

WATERSIDE PRODUCTIONS, INC.

2187 Newcastle Ave., #204, Cardiff-by-the-Sea CA 92007. (760)632-9190. Fax: (760)632-9295. Website: www.waterside.com. **Contact:** Matt Wagner, Margot Maley, David Fugate. President: Bill Gladstone. Estab. 1982. Represents 300 clients. 20% of clients are new/unpublished writers. Currently handles: 100% nonfiction books.

Member Agents Bill Gladstone (trade computer titles, business); Margot Maley Hutchison (trade computer titles, nonfiction); Matthew Wagner (trade computer titles, nonfiction); Carole McClendon (trade computer titles); David Fugate (trade computer titles, business, general nonfiction, sports books); Christian Crumlish (trade computer titles); Neil Gudovitz, William E. Brown, Craig Wiley, Ming Russell.

Represents Nonfiction books. **Considers these nonfiction areas:** Art/architecture/design; biography/autobiography; business/economics; child guidance/parenting; computers/electronic; ethnic/cultural interests; health/medicine; humor/satire; money/finance; nature/environment; popular culture; psychology; sociology; sports.

How to Contact Prefers to read materials exclusively. Query via online form. See website for more information. Considers simultaneous queries. Responds in 2 weeks to queries; 2 months to mss. Obtains most new clients through recommendations from others.

Recent Sales Sold 300 titles in the last year. *Dan Gookin's Naked Windows*, by Dan Gookin (Sybex); *Battlebots: The Official Guide*, by Mark Clarkson (Osborne McGraw-Hill); *The Art of Deception*, by Kevin Mitnick and William Simon (Wiley); *Just for Fun*, by Linus Torvalds and David Diamond (HarperCollins).

Terms Agent receives 15% commission on domestic sales; 25% commission on foreign sales. Offers written contract. Charges clients for photocopying and other unusual expenses.

Writers' Conferences "We host the Waterside Publishing Conference each spring. Please check our website for details."

Tips "For new writers, a quality proposal and a strong knowledge of the market you're writing for goes a long way toward helping us turn you into a published author."

WATKINS LOOMIS AGENCY, INC.

133 E. 35th St., Suite 1, New York NY 10016. (212)532-0080. Fax: (212)889-0506. **Contact:** Katherine Fausset. Estab. 1908. Represents 150 clients.

Member Agents Gloria Loomis (president); Katherine Fausset (agent).

Represents Nonfiction books, novels, short story collections. **Considers these nonfiction areas:** Art/architecture/design; biography/autobiography; current affairs; ethnic/cultural interests; history; nature/environment; popular culture; science/technology; true crime/investigative; journalism. **Considers these fiction areas:** Literary.

O→ This agency specializes in literary fiction, nonfiction.

How to Contact Query with SASE, by standard mail only. Responds in 1 month to queries.

Recent Sales This agency prefers not to share information on specific sales. Clients include Walter Mosley and Cornel West.

Terms Agent receives 15% commission on domestic sales; 20% commission on foreign sales.

WAXMAN LITERARY AGENCY, INC.

80 Fifth Ave., Suite 1101, New York NY 10011. Website: www.waxmanagency.com. Estab. 1997. Represents 60 clients. 50% of clients are new/unpublished writers. Currently handles: 60% nonfiction books; 40% novels.

• Prior to opening his agency, Mr. Waxman was editor for five years at HarperCollins.

Member Agents Scott Waxman (all categories of nonfiction, commercial fiction).

Represents Nonfiction books, novels. **Considers these nonfiction areas:** Narrative nonfiction. **Considers these fiction areas:** Literary.

O→ "Looking for serious journalists and novelists with published works."

How to Contact Query through website. All unsolicited mss returned unopened. Considers simultaneous queries. Responds in 2 weeks to queries; 6 weeks to mss. Returns materials only with SASE. Obtains most new clients through recommendations from others, solicitations, conferences.

Terms Agent receives 15% commission on domestic sales; 25% commission on foreign sales. Offers written contract; 2-month notice must be given to terminate contract.

THE WENDY WEIL AGENCY, INC.

232 Madison Ave., Suite 1300, New York NY 10016. (212)685-0030. Fax: (212)685-0765. E-mail: wweil@wendyweil.com. Website: www.wendyweil.com. Member of AAR.

• Query before submitting.

Member Agents Wendy Weil, Emily Forland, Emma Patterson.

CHERRY WEINER LITERARY AGENCY

28 Kipling Way, Manalapan NJ 07726-3711. (732)446-2096. Fax: (732)792-0506. E-mail: cherry8486@aol.com. **Contact:** Cherry Weiner. Estab. 1977. Represents 40 clients. 10% of clients are new/unpublished writers. Currently handles: 10-20% nonfiction books; 80-90% novels.

• This agency is currently not looking for new clients except by referral or by personal contact at writers' conferences.

Represents Nonfiction books, novels. **Considers these nonfiction areas:** Self-help/personal improvement. **Considers these fiction areas:** Action/adventure; contemporary issues; detective/police/crime; family saga;

fantasy; historical; mainstream/contemporary; mystery/suspense; psychic/supernatural; romance; science fiction; thriller; westerns/frontier.

O→ This agency specializes in fantasy, science fiction, westerns, mysteries (both contemporary and historical), historical novels, Native American works, mainstream, all genre romances.

How to Contact Query with SASE. Prefers to read materials exclusively. No fax queries. Responds in 1 week to queries; 2 months to mss. Returns materials only with SASE.

Recent Sales Sold 75 titles in the last year.

Terms Agent receives 15% commission on domestic sales; 15% commission on foreign sales. Offers written contract. Charges clients for extra copies of mss "but would prefer author do it"; 1st-Class postage for author's copies of books; Express Mail for important document/mss.

Writers' Conferences Western writers conventions; science fiction conventions; fantasy conventions; romance conventions.

Tips "Meet agents and publishers at conferences. Establish a relationship, then get in touch with them reminding them of meetings and conference."

THE WEINGEL-FIDEL AGENCY

310 E. 46th St., 21E, New York NY 10017. (212)599-2959. **Contact:** Loretta Weingel-Fidel. Estab. 1989. Currently handles: 75% nonfiction books; 25% novels.

- Prior to opening her agency, Ms. Weingel-Fidel was a psychoeducational diagnostician.

Represents Nonfiction books, novels. **Considers these nonfiction areas:** Art/architecture/design; biography/autobiography; memoirs; music/dance; psychology; science/technology; sociology; women's issues/studies; Investigative. **Considers these fiction areas:** Literary; mainstream/contemporary.

O→ This agency specializes in commercial, literary fiction and nonfiction. Actively seeking investigative journalism. Does not want to receive genre fiction, self-help, science fiction, fantasy.

How to Contact Referred writers only. *No unsolicited mss.* Obtains most new clients through referrals.

Terms Agent receives 15% commission on domestic sales; 20% commission on foreign sales. Offers written contract, binding for 1 year; automatic renewal. Bills sent back to clients all reasonable expenses such as UPS, express mail, photocopying, etc.

Tips "A very small, selective list enables me to work very closely with my clients to develop and nurture talent. I only take on projects and writers about which I am extremely enthusiastic."

TED WEINSTEIN LITERARY MANAGEMENT

35 Stillman St., Suite 203, San Francisco CA 94107. Website: www.twliterary.com. **Contact:** Ted Weinstein. Estab. 2001. Member of AAR. Represents 50 clients. 75% of clients are new/unpublished writers. Currently handles: 100% nonfiction books.

Represents Nonfiction books. **Considers these nonfiction areas:** Biography/autobiography; business/economics; current affairs; government/politics/law; health/medicine; history; popular culture; science/technology; self-help/personal improvement; travel; environment, lifestyle.

How to Contact Accepts e-mail or paper submissions with SASE. Please visit website for detailed submission guidelines before submitting. Considers simultaneous queries. Responds in 3 weeks to queries.

Terms Agent receives 15% commission on domestic sales; 20-30% commission on foreign sales. Offers written contract, binding for 1 year. Charges clients for photocopying and express shipping.

LYNN WHITTAKER, LITERARY AGENT

Graybill & English, LLC, 1875 Connecticut Ave. NW, Suite 712, Washington DC 20009. (202)588-9798, ext. 127. Fax: (202)457-0662. E-mail: lynnwhittaker@aol.com. Website: www.graybillandenglish.com. **Contact:** Lynn Whittaker. Estab. 1998. Member of AAR. Represents 24 clients. 10% of clients are new/unpublished writers. Currently handles: 80% nonfiction books; 20% novels.

- Prior to becoming an agent, Ms. Whittaker was an editor, owner of a small press, and taught at the college level.

Represents Nonfiction books, novels. **Considers these nonfiction areas:** Animals; biography/autobiography; current affairs; ethnic/cultural interests; health/medicine; history; memoirs; money/finance; multicultural; nature/environment; popular culture; science/technology; sports; women's issues/studies. **Considers these fiction areas:** Detective/police/crime; ethnic; historical; literary; multicultural; mystery/suspense; sports.

O→ "As a former editor, I especially enjoy working closely with writers to polish their proposals and manuscripts." Actively seeking literary fiction, sports, history, mystery/suspense. Does not want to receive romance/women's commercial fiction, children's/young adult, religious, fantasy/horror.

How to Contact Query with SASE. Responds in 2 weeks to queries; 1 month to mss. Returns materials only with SASE. Obtains most new clients through recommendations from others.

Terms Agent receives 15% commission on domestic sales; 20% commission on foreign sales. Offers written

contract; 1-month notice must be given to terminate contract. Direct expenses for photocopying of proposals and mss, UPS/FedEx.

WIESER & ELWELL, INC.

80 Fifth Ave., Suite 1101, New York NY 10011. (212)260-0860. **Contact:** Jake Elwell. Estab. 1975. 30% of clients are new/unpublished writers. Currently handles: 50% nonfiction books; 50% novels.

Member Agents Jake Elwell (history, military, mysteries, romance, sports, thrillers, psychology, fiction, pop medical).

Represents Nonfiction books, novels. **Considers these nonfiction areas:** Business/economics; cooking/foods/nutrition; current affairs; health/medicine; history; money/finance; nature/environment; psychology; sports; true crime/investigative. **Considers these fiction areas:** Contemporary issues; detective/police/crime; historical; literary; mainstream/contemporary; mystery/suspense; romance; thriller.

This agency specializes in mainstream fiction and nonfiction.

How to Contact Query with outline/proposal and SASE. Responds in 2 weeks to queries. Obtains most new clients through queries, authors' recommendations and industry professionals.

Recent Sales *Honored*, by Roberta Kells Dorr (Revell); *History's Greatest Conspiracies*, by H. Paul Jeffers (Lyons); *Havoc's Sword*, by Dewey Lambdin (St. Martin's Press); *The Voyage of the Hunley*, by Edwin P. Hoyt (Burford Books); *Threat Level Black*, by Jim DeFelice (Pocket); *Street Hungry*, by Bill Kent.

Terms Agent receives 15% commission on domestic sales; 20% commission on foreign sales. Offers written contract. Charges clients for photocopying and overseas mailing.

Writers' Conferences BEA; Frankfurt Book Fair.

WILLIAMS LITERARY AGENCY

909 Knox Rd., Kosciusko MS 39090. (662)290-0617. E-mail: submissions@williamsliteraryagency.com. Website: williamsliteraryagency.com. **Contact:** Sheri Williams. Estab. 1997. Represents 35 clients.

- Prior to becoming an agent, Sheri Homan Williams was a freelance writer and literary assistant.

Represents Nonfiction books, novels, movie scripts, feature film.

Prefers published authors. "Looks for well-written books with a strong plot and consistency throughout."

How to Contact Short queries only by mail or e-mail. No unsolicited phone calls.

AUDREY A. WOLF LITERARY AGENCY

2510 Virginia Ave. NW, #702N, Washington DC 20037. Member of AAR.

- Query before submitting.

WORDSERVE LITERARY GROUP

10152 S. Knoll Circle, Highlands Ranch CO 80130. (303)471-6675. Fax: (303)471-1297. E-mail: greg@wordserveliterary.com. Website: www.wordserveliterary.com. **Contact:** Greg Johnson. Estab. 2003. Represents 20 clients. 25% of clients are new/unpublished writers. Currently handles: 30% nonfiction books; 40% novels; 10% story collections; 5% novellas; 10% juvenile books; 5% multimedia.

- Prior to becoming an agent in 1994, Mr. Johnson was a magazine editor and freelance writer of more than 20 books and 200 articles.

Represents Primarily religious books in these categories: nonfiction books, novels, short story collections, novellas, juvenile books. **Considers these nonfiction areas:** Biography/autobiography; business/economics; child guidance/parenting; current affairs; how-to; humor/satire; memoirs; religious/inspirational; self-help/personal improvement; sports. **Considers these fiction areas:** Action/adventure; detective/police/crime; family saga; historical; humor/satire; juvenile; religious/inspirational; romance; sports; thriller.

How to Contact Query with SASE, submit proposal package, outline, 2-3 sample chapters. Considers simultaneous queries. Responds in 1 week to queries; 1 month to mss. Returns materials only with SASE. Obtains most new clients through recommendations from others, solicitations.

Recent Sales Sold 1,300 titles in the last 10 years. Clients include Gilbert Morris, Calvin Miller, Robert Wise, Jim Burns, Ed Young Sr., Wayne Cordeiro, Denise George, Jordan Robin, Susie Shellenberger, Tim Smith, Joe Wheeler.

Terms Agent receives 15% commission on domestic sales; 10-15% commission on foreign sales. Offers written contract; 30-60 days notice must be given to terminate contract.

Tips "We are looking for good proposals, great writing, and authors willing to market their books, as appropriate."

WRITERS HOUSE

21 W. 26th St., New York NY 10010. (212)685-2400. Fax: (212)685-1781. Estab. 1974. Member of AAR. Represents 440 clients. 50% of clients are new/unpublished writers. Currently handles: 25% nonfiction books; 40% novels; 35% juvenile books.

Member Agents Albert Zuckerman (major novels, thrillers, women's fiction, important nonfiction); Amy Berkower (major juvenile authors, women's fiction, art and decorating, psychology); Merrilee Heifetz (quality children's fiction, science fiction and fantasy, popular culture, literary fiction); Susan Cohen (juvenile and YA fiction and nonfiction, Judaism, women's issues); Susan Ginsburg (serious and popular fiction, true crime, narrative nonfiction, personality books, cookbooks); Michele Rubin (serious nonfiction); Robin Rue (commercial fiction and nonfiction, YA fiction); Jennifer Lyons (literary, commercial fiction, international fiction, nonfiction, and illustrated); Jodi Reamer (juvenile and YA fiction and nonfiction, adult commercial fiction, popular culture); Simon Lipskar (literary and commercial fiction, narrative nonfiction); Nicole Pitesa (juvenile and YA fiction, literary fiction); Steven Malk (juvenile and YA fiction and nonfiction).

Represents Nonfiction books, novels, juvenile books. **Considers these nonfiction areas:** Animals; art/architecture/design; biography/autobiography; business/economics; child guidance/parenting; cooking/foods/nutrition; health/medicine; history; interior design/decorating; juvenile nonfiction; military/war; money/finance; music/dance; nature/environment; psychology; science/technology; self-help/personal improvement; theater/film; true crime/investigative; women's issues/studies. **Considers these fiction areas:** Action/adventure; contemporary issues; detective/police/crime; erotica; ethnic; family saga; fantasy; feminist; gay/lesbian; gothic; hi-lo; historical; horror; humor/satire; juvenile; literary; mainstream/contemporary; military/war; multicultural; mystery/suspense; New Age; occult; picture books; psychic/supernatural; regional; romance; science fiction; short story collections; spiritual; sports; thriller; translation; westerns/frontier; young adult; women's; cartoon.

> This agency specializes in all types of popular fiction and nonfiction. Does not want to receive scholarly, professional, poetry, plays, or screenplays.

How to Contact Query with SASE. No e-mail or fax queries. Responds in 1 month to queries. Obtains most new clients through recommendations from others.

Recent Sales Sold 200-300 titles in the last year. *Moneyball*, by Michael Lewis (Norton); *Cut and Run*, by Ridley Pearson (Hyperion); *Report from Ground Zero*, by Dennis Smith (Viking); *Northern Lights*, by Nora Roberts (Penguin/Putnam); Captain Underpants series, by Dav Pilkey (Scholastic); Junie B. Jones series, by Barbara Park (Random House). Other clients include Francine Pascal, Ken Follett, Stephen Hawking, Linda Howard, F. Paul Wilson, Neil Gaiman, Laurel Hamilton, V.C. Andrews, Lisa Jackson, Michael Fruber, Chris Paolini, Barbara Delinsky, Ann Martin.

Terms Agent receives 15% commission on domestic sales; 20% commission on foreign sales. Offers written contract, binding for 1 year. Agency charges fees for copying mss and proposals, and overseas airmail of books.

Tips "Do not send manuscripts. Write a compelling letter. If you do, we'll ask to see your work."

WRITERS' REPRESENTATIVES, INC.

116 W. 14th St., 11th Floor, New York NY 10011-7305. Phone/Fax: (212)620-0023. E-mail: transom@writersreps.com. Website: www.writersreps.com. **Contact:** Glen Hartley or Lynn Chu. Estab. 1985. Represents 130 clients. 5% of clients are new/unpublished writers. Currently handles: 90% nonfiction books; 10% novels.

- Prior to becoming agents, Ms. Chu was a lawyer, and Mr. Hartley worked at Simon & Schuster, Harper & Row, and Cornell University Press.

Member Agents Lynn Chu, Glen Hartley, Catharine Sprinkel.

Represents Nonfiction books, novels. **Considers these fiction areas:** Literary.

> This agency specializes in serious nonfiction. Actively seeking serious nonfiction and quality fiction. Does not want to receive motion picture/television screenplays.

How to Contact Query with SASE. Prefers to read materials exclusively. Considers simultaneous queries, but must be informed at time of submission. Obtains most new clients through "reading"

Recent Sales Sold 30 titles in the last year. *Where Shall Wisdom Be Found?*, by Harold Bloom; *War Like No Other*, by Victor Davis Hanson; *Call of the Mall*, by Paco Underhill; *The Language of Police*, by Diane Ravitch.

Terms Agent receives 15% commission on domestic sales; 20% commission on foreign sales.

Tips "Always include a SASE—that will ensure a response from the agent and the return of material submitted."

WYLIE-MERRICK LITERARY AGENCY

1138 S. Webster St., Kokomo IN 46902-6357. (765)459-8258. E-mail: smartin@wylie-merrick.com; rbrown@wylie-merrick.com. Website: www.wylie-merrick.com. **Contact:** S.A. Martin, Robert Brown. Estab. 1999. Member of SCBWI. Currently handles: 10% nonfiction books; 50% novels; 40% juvenile books.

- Ms. Martin holds a master's degree in Language Education and is a writing and technology curriculum specialist.

Member Agents S.A. Martin (juvenile/picture books/young adult); Robert Brown (adult fiction/nonfiction, young adult).

Represents Nonfiction books (adult and juvenile), novels (adult and juvenile), juvenile books. **Considers these nonfiction areas:** Biography/autobiography; juvenile nonfiction. **Considers these fiction areas:** Mystery/suspense; picture books; religious/inspirational; romance; young adult; women's; chick lit, high-level mainstream.

O-→ This agency specializes in children's and young adult literary as well as genre adult fiction.

How to Contact Obtains most new clients through recommendations from others, conferences.

Recent Sales *How I Fell in Love and Learned to Shoot Free Throws*, by Jon Ripslinger (Roaring Brook); *Red Polka Dot in a World Full of Plaid*, by Varian Johnson; *Death for Dessert*, by Dawn Richard; *Secret War*, by Regina Silsby.

Terms Agent receives 15% commission on domestic sales; 20% commission on foreign sales; 20% commission on dramatic rights sales. Offers written contract. Charges clients for postage, photocopying, handling.

Writers' Conferences Pike's Peak (CO); Willamette (Portland OR).

Tips "We no longer accept queries from writers unless we have met with them at a writing conference or they've been referred to us by an editor or another agent we've worked with in the past. Any queries we receive that don't meet these criteria will be deleted or recycled unread."

ZACHARY SHUSTER HARMSWORTH

1776 Broadway, Suite 1405, New York NY 10019. (212)765-6900. Fax: (212)765-6490. E-mail: sshagat@zshliterary.com. Website: www.zshliterary.com. Boston Office: 535 Boylston St., 11th Floor. (617)262-2400. Fax: (617)262-2468. **Contact:** Sandra Shagat. Estab. 1996. Represents 125 clients. 20% of clients are new/unpublished writers. Currently handles: 45% nonfiction books; 45% novels; 5% story collections; 5% scholarly books.

- "Our principals include 2 former publishing and entertainment lawyers, a journalist and an editor/agent." Lane Zachary was an editor at Random House before becoming an agent.

Member Agents Esmond Harmsworth (commercial mysteries and literary fiction, history, science, adventure, business); Todd Shuster (narrative and prescriptive nonfiction, biography, memoirs); Lane Zachary (biography, memoirs, literary fiction); Jennifer Gates (literary fiction, nonfiction).

Represents Nonfiction books, novels. **Considers these nonfiction areas:** Animals; biography/autobiography; business/economics; current affairs; gay/lesbian issues; government/politics/law; health/medicine; history; how-to; language/literature/criticism; memoirs; money/finance; music/dance; psychology; science/technology; self-help/personal improvement; sports; true crime/investigative; women's issues/studies. **Considers these fiction areas:** Contemporary issues; detective/police/crime; ethnic; feminist; gay/lesbian; historical; literary; mainstream/contemporary; mystery/suspense; thriller.

O-→ This agency specializes in journalist-driven narrative nonfiction, literary and commercial fiction. Actively seeking narrative nonfiction, mystery, commercial and literary fiction, memoirs, history, biographies. Does not want to receive poetry.

How to Contact For fiction, submit query letter with 1-page synopsis, SASE. For nonfiction, submit letter explaining topic of proposed book, along with analysis of why book is needed and will be a commercial success for publisher. No e-mail or fax queries. Considers simultaneous queries. Responds in 3 months to mss. Obtains most new clients through recommendations from others, solicitations, conferences.

Recent Sales Sold 40-50 titles in the last year. *The Pentagon's New Map*, by Thomas Barnett (Putnam's); *A Carnivore's Inquiry*, by Sabina Murray (Grove); *War Trash*, by Ha Jin (Pantheon); *The Pennington Plan*, by Dr. Andrea Pennington (Avery); *Choke Point*, by James S. Mitchell (St. Martin's). Other clients include Leslie Epstein, David Mixner.

Terms Agent receives 15% commission on domestic sales; 20% commission on foreign sales. Offers written contract, binding for 1 work only; 30-days notice must be given to terminate contract. Charges clients for postage, copying, courier, telephone. "We only charge expenses if the manuscript is sold."

Tips "We work closely with all our clients on all editorial and promotional aspects of their works."

SUSAN ZECKENDORF ASSOC., INC.

171 W. 57th St., New York NY 10019. (212)245-2928. **Contact:** Susan Zeckendorf. Estab. 1979. Member of AAR. Represents 15 clients. 25% of clients are new/unpublished writers. Currently handles: 50% nonfiction books; 50% novels.

- Prior to opening her agency, Ms. Zeckendorf was a counseling psychologist.

Represents Nonfiction books, novels. **Considers these nonfiction areas:** Biography/autobiography; child guidance/parenting; health/medicine; history; music/dance; psychology; science/technology; sociology; women's issues/studies. **Considers these fiction areas:** Detective/police/crime; ethnic; historical; literary; mainstream/contemporary; mystery/suspense; thriller.

O-→ Actively seeking mysteries, literary fiction, mainstream fiction, thrillers, social history, parenting, classical music, biography. Does not want to receive science fiction, romance. "No children's books."

How to Contact Query with SASE. No e-mail or fax queries. Considers simultaneous queries. Responds in 10 days to queries; 3 weeks to mss. Returns materials only with SASE.
Recent Sales *How to Write a Damn Good Mystery*, by James N. Frey (St. Martin's); *Moment of Madness*, by Una-Mary Parker (Headline); *The Handscrabble Chronicles* (Berkley); *Something to Live For (The Susan McCorkle Story)* (Northeastern University Press).
Terms Agent receives 15% commission on domestic sales; 20% commission on foreign sales. Charges for photocopying, messenger services.
Writers' Conferences Central Valley Writers Conference; The Tucson Publishers Association Conference; Writer's Connection; Frontiers in Writing Conference (Amarillo TX); Golden Triangle Writers Conference (Beaumont TX); Oklahoma Festival of Books (Claremont OK); SMU Writers Conference (NYC).
Tips "We are a small agency giving lots of individual attention. We respond quickly to submissions."

MARKETS

Script Agents

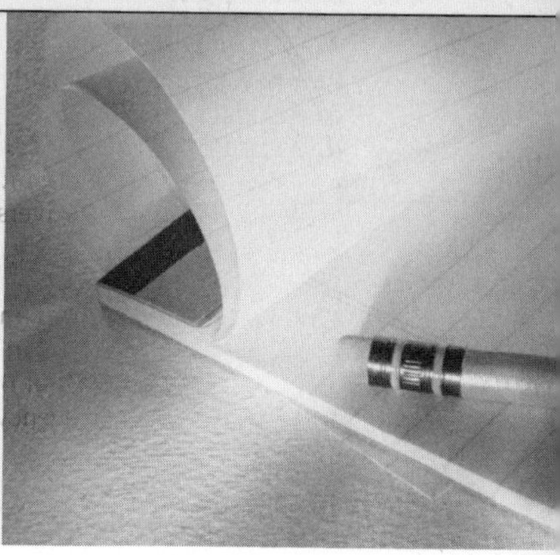

This section contains agents who sell feature film scripts, television scripts, and theatrical stage plays. A breakdown of the types of scripts each agency handles is included in the listing.

Many of the script agents listed here are signatories to the Writers Guild of America (WGA) Artists' Manager Basic Agreement. They have paid a membership fee and agree to abide by the WGA's standard code of behavior. Agents who are WGA signatories are not permitted to charge a reading fee to WGA members but are allowed to do so to nonmembers. They are permitted to charge for critiques and other services, but they may not refer you to a particular script doctor. Enforcement is uneven, however. Although a signatory can, theoretically, be stripped of its signatory status, this rarely happens.

A few of the listings in this section are actually management companies. The role of managers is quickly changing in Hollywood; they were once only used by actors, or ''talent,'' and the occasional writer. Now many managers are actually selling scripts to producers.

It's a good idea to register your script before sending it out, and the WGA offers a registration service to members and nonmembers alike. Membership in the WGA is earned through the accumulation of professional credits and carries a number of significant benefits. Write the WGA for more information on specific agencies, script registration, and membership requirements, or visit its website at www.wga.org.

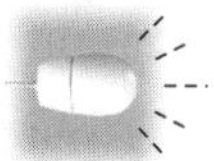

Useful Websites

Like the literary agents listed in this book, some script agencies ask that clients pay for some or all of the office fees accrued when sending out scripts. Some agents ask for a one-time ''handling'' fee up front, while others deduct office expenses after a script has been sold. Always have a clear understanding of any fee an agent asks you to pay.

Canadian and international agents are included in this section. Canadian agents have a 🍁 icon preceding their listing, while international agents have a 🌐 icon preceding their listing. Remember to include an International Reply Coupon (IRC) with your self-addressed envelope when contacting Canadian and international agents.

When reading through this section, keep in mind the following information specific to the script agent listings.

SUBHEADS

Each listing is broken down into subheads to make locating specific information easier. In the first section, you'll find contact information for each agency. You'll also learn if the agent is a WGA signatory or a member of any other professional organizations. (An explanation of all organizations' acronyms is available on page 278.) Further information is provided which indicates an agency's size, its willingness to work with a new or unpublished writer,

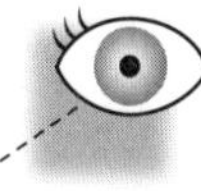

See Also

and a percentage breakdown of the general types of scripts the agency will consider.

Member Agents: Agencies comprised of more than one agent list member agents and their individual specialties to help you determine the most appropriate person for your query letter.

Represents: Make sure you query only agents who represent the type of material you write. To help you narrow your search, we've included a **Script Agents Specialties Index** and the **Script Agents Format Index** in the back of the book.

O➛ Look for the key icon to quickly learn an agent's areas of specializations and individual strengths. Here agents also mention what specific areas they are currently seeking, as well as subjects they do not wish to receive.

How to Contact: Most agents open to unsolicited submissions initially prefer to receive a query letter briefly describing your work. Script agents usually discard material sent without a SASE. Here agents also indicate if they accept queries by fax or e-mail; if they consider simultaneous submissions; and their preferred way of meeting new clients.

Recent Sales: Reflecting the different ways scriptwriters work, agents list scripts optioned or sold and scripting assignments procured for clients. The film industry is very secretive about sales, but you may be able to get a list of clients or other references upon request—especially if the agency is interested in representing your work.

Terms: Most agents' commissions range from 10 to 15 percent, and WGA signatories may not earn over 10 percent from WGA members.

Writers' Conferences: For screenwriters unable to move to Los Angeles, writers' conferences provide another venue for meeting agents. For more information about a specific conference, check the **Writers' Conferences** section starting on page 245.

Tips: Agents offer advice and additional instructions for writers looking for representation.

See Also

SPECIAL INDEXES TO REFINE YOUR SEARCH

Script Agents Specialties Index: In the back of the book on page 328 is an index divided into various subject areas specific to scripts, such as mystery, romantic comedy, and teen. This index should help you compose a list of agents specializing in your areas. Cross-referencing categories and concentrating on agents interested in two or more aspects of your manuscript might increase your chances of success. Agencies open to all categories are grouped under the subject heading "open."

Script Agents Format Index: Following the **Script Agents Specialties Index** is an index organizing agents according to the script types they consider, such as TV movie of the week (MOW), sitcom, or episodic drama.

Script Agents

Quick Reference Icons

At the beginning of some listings, you will find one or more of the following symbols for quick identification of features particular to that listing.

 Agency new to this edition.

 Canadian agency.

 International agency.

Agencies Indexed by Openness to Submissions: This index lists agencies according to how receptive they are to new clients.

Geographic Index: For writers looking for an agent close to home, this index lists agents by state.

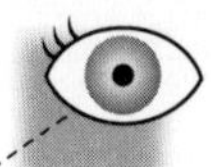
See Also

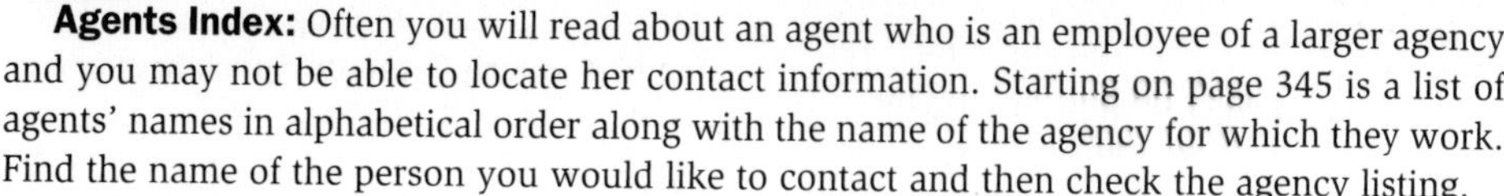

Agents Index: Often you will read about an agent who is an employee of a larger agency and you may not be able to locate her contact information. Starting on page 345 is a list of agents' names in alphabetical order along with the name of the agency for which they work. Find the name of the person you would like to contact and then check the agency listing.

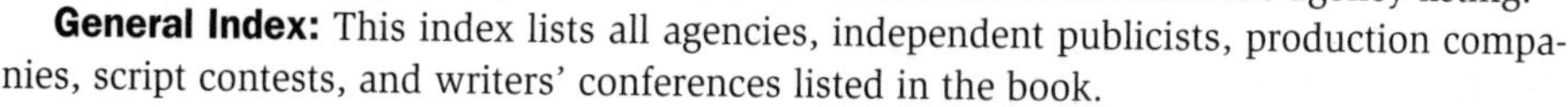

General Index: This index lists all agencies, independent publicists, production companies, script contests, and writers' conferences listed in the book.

Level of Openness

Each agency has an icon indicating its openness to submissions. Before contacting any agency, check the listing to make sure it's open to new clients.

- Newer agency actively seeking clients.
- Agency seeking both new and established writers.
- Agency prefers to work with established writers, mostly obtains new clients through referrals.
- Agency handling only certain types of work or work by writers under certain circumstances.
- Agency not currently seeking new clients. We include these agencies to inform you they are closed to new clients. *Unless you have a strong recommendation from someone well respected in the field, our advice is to avoid approaching these agents.*

For quick reference, a chart of these icons and their meanings is printed on the inside covers of this book.

ABRAMS ARTISTS AGENCY

275 Seventh Ave., 26th Floor, New York NY 10012. (646)486-4600. Fax: (646)486-2358.

Member Agents Maura E. Teitelbaum (film, TV, publishing, theater).

Represents Feature film, episodic drama, sitcom, animation (TV), soap opera, musical. **Considers these script subject areas:** Comedy; contemporary issues; mainstream; mystery/suspense; romantic comedy; romantic drama.

O→ This agency specializes in theater, film, TV, publishing.

How to Contact Query with SASE, outline. Returns material only with SASE.

Recent Sales This agency prefers not to share information on specific sales.

Terms Agent receives 10% commission on domestic sales; 10% commission on foreign sales; 10% commission on dramatic rights sales.

ACME TALENT & LITERARY

4727 Wilshire, #333, Los Angeles CA 90010. (323)954-2263. Fax: (323)954-2262. Other Address: 875 Avenue of the Americas, Suite 2108, New York NY 10001. (212)328-0388. Fax: (212)328-0391. **Contact:** Mickey Frieberg, head of literary division. Estab. 1993. Signatory of WGA. Represents 50 clients. Currently handles: movie scripts; TV scripts; video game rights.

Member Agents Mickey Freiberg (books, film scripts).

Represents Feature film. **Considers these script subject areas:** Action/adventure; biography/autobiography; cartoon/animation; comedy; contemporary issues; detective/police/crime; erotica; ethnic; experimental; family saga; fantasy; feminist; gay/lesbian; glitz; historical; horror; juvenile; mainstream; multicultural; multimedia; mystery/suspense; psychic/supernatural; regional; religious/inspirational; romantic comedy; romantic drama; science fiction; sports; teen; thriller; western/frontier.

O→ This agency specializes in "feature films, completed specs or pitches by established produced writers and new writers." Actively seeking great feature scripts. *No unsolicited material.*

How to Contact No e-mail or fax queries. Obtains most new clients through recommendations from established industry contacts, production companies of note, and reputable entertainment attorneys.

Terms Agent receives 10% commission on domestic sales; 15% commission on foreign sales. Offers written contract, binding for 2 years.

N MICHAEL AMATO AGENCY

1650 Broadway, Suite 307, New York NY 10019. (212)247-4456 or (212)247-4457. **Contact:** Michael Amato. Estab. 1970. Member of SAG, AFTRA. Represents 6 clients. 2% of clients are new/unpublished writers.

Represents Feature film, TV movie of the week, episodic drama, animation, documentary, miniseries. **Considers these script subject areas:** Action/adventure.

How to Contact Query with SASE. Responds in 1 month to queries. Obtains most new clients through recommendations from others.

Recent Sales This agency prefers not to share information on specific sales.

THE ARTISTS AGENCY

1180 S. Beverly, Suite 400, Los Angeles CA 90035. (310)277-7779. Fax: (310)785-9338. **Contact:** Richard Shepherd. Estab. 1974. Signatory of WGA. Represents 50 clients. 20% of clients are new/unpublished writers. Currently handles: 50% movie scripts; 50% TV scripts.

Represents Movie scripts (feature film), TV movie of the week. **Considers these script subject areas:** Action/adventure; comedy; contemporary issues; detective/police/crime; mystery/suspense; romantic comedy; romantic drama; thriller.

How to Contact Query with SASE. Responds in 2 weeks to queries. Obtains most new clients through recommendations from others.

Recent Sales This agency prefers not to share information on specific sales.

Terms Agent receives 10% commission on dramatic rights sales. Offers written contract, binding for 1-2 years, per WGA.

BEACON ARTISTS AGENCY

208 W. 30th St., Suite 401, New York NY 10001. (212)736-6630. **Contact:** Patricia McLaughlin. Member of AAR.

- *No unsolicited mss.* Prefers recommendations.

THE BOHRMAN AGENCY

8899 Beverly Blvd., Suite 811, Los Angeles CA 90048. (310)550-5444. **Contact:** Michael Hruska, Caren Bohrman. Signatory of WGA.

Script Agents

Represents Novels, feature film, TV scripts. **Considers these script subject areas:** Action/adventure; biography/autobiography; cartoon/animation; comedy; contemporary issues; detective/police/crime; erotica; ethnic; experimental; family saga; fantasy; feminist; gay/lesbian; glitz; historical; horror; juvenile; mainstream; multicultural; multimedia; mystery/suspense; psychic/supernatural; regional; religious/inspirational; romantic comedy; romantic drama; science fiction; sports; teen; thriller; western/frontier.
How to Contact Query with self-addressed postcard. *No unsolicited mss.* No phone calls. Obtains most new clients through recommendations from others.
Recent Sales This agency prefers not to share information on specific sales.

ALAN BRODIE REPRESENTATION

211 Piccadilly, London W1J 9HF England. 0207-917-2871. Fax: 0207-917-2872. E-mail: info@alanbrodie.com. Website: www.alanbrodie.com. **Contact:** Alan Brodie, Sarah McNair or Lisa Foster. Member of PMA. 10% of clients are new/unpublished writers.
Member Agents Alan Brodie; Sarah McNair; Lisa Foster.
This agency specializes in stage, film, TV and radio.
How to Contact Does not accept unsolicited mss. North American writers accepted only in exceptional circumstances. Accepts e-mail and fax queries. Obtains most new clients through recommendations from others.
Recent Sales This agency prefers not to share information on specific sales.
Terms Charges clients for photocopying.
Tips "Biographical details can be helpful. Generally only playwrights whose work has been performed will be considered, provided they come recommended by an industry professional."

DON BUCHWALD & ASSOCIATES, INC.

6500 Wilshire Blvd., 22nd Floor, Los Angeles CA 90048. (323)655-7400. Fax: (323)655-7470. Website: www.donbuchwald.com. Estab. 1977. Signatory of WGA. Represents 50 clients.
Represents Movie scripts, feature film, TV scripts, TV movie of the week, episodic drama, sitcom, documentary, miniseries.
This agency represents talent and literary clients.
How to Contact Query with SASE. Considers simultaneous queries. Obtains most new clients through recommendations from others.

CEDAR GROVE AGENCY ENTERTAINMENT

P.O. Box 1692, Issaquah WA 98027-0068. (425)837-1687. E-mail: cedargroveagency@juno.com. **Contact:** Samantha Powers. Estab. 1995. Member of Cinema Seattle. Represents 7 clients. 100% of clients are new/unpublished writers. Currently handles: 90% movie scripts; 10% TV scripts.

- Prior to becoming an agent, Ms. Taylor worked for the stock brokerage firm, Morgan Stanley Dean Witter. She is also a member of Bellevue Community College's Media Advisory Board. Ms. Powers was a customer service/office manager.

Member Agents Amy Taylor (senior vice president-motion picture division), Samantha Powers (executive vice president-motion picture division).
Represents Feature film, TV movie of the week, sitcom. **Considers these script subject areas:** Action/adventure; biography/autobiography; comedy; detective/police/crime; family saga; juvenile; mystery/suspense; romantic comedy; science fiction; sports; thriller; western/frontier.
Cedar Grove Agency Entertainment was formed in the Pacific Northwest to take advantage of the rich and diverse culture, as well as the many writers who reside there. Does not want period pieces, horror genres, children's scripts dealing with illness, or scripts with excessive substance abuse.
How to Contact Query with SASE, 1-page synopsis. No phone calls, please. Mail, e-mail, or fax. No attachments if e-mailed. Responds in 10 days to queries; 2 months to mss. Obtains most new clients through referrals and website.
Recent Sales This agency prefers not to share information on specific sales.
Terms Agent receives 10% commission on domestic sales. Offers written contract, binding for 6-12 months; 30-day notice must be given to terminate contract.
Tips "We focus on finding that rare gem, the undiscovered, multi-talented writer, no matter where they live. Write, write, write! Find time every day to write. Network with other writers when possible, and write what you know. Learn the craft through books. Read scripts of your favorite movies. Enjoy what you write!"

THE CHARACTERS TALENT AGENCY

8 Elm St., Toronto ON M3H 1Y9 Canada. (416)964-8522. Fax: (416)964-6349. E-mail: clib5@aol.com. **Contact:** Carl Liberman. Estab. 1968. Member of Signatory WGC. Represents 1,200 (includes writers, actors and directors) clients. 5% of clients are new/unpublished writers.

• Before becoming an agent, Mr. Liberman was an advertising executive, writer and actor.

Member Agents Glenn Cockburn (film/TV writers and publishers); Brent Sherman and Jeff Tsuji (film/TV writers and directors); Geoff Brooks (animation and children's writers); Ben Silverman (writers)

Represents Movie scripts, feature film, TV scripts, TV movie of the week, episodic drama, sitcom, animation, documentary, miniseries, soap opera, syndicated material. **Considers these script subject areas:** Action/adventure; biography/autobiography; cartoon/animation; comedy; contemporary issues; detective/police/crime; erotica (no porn); ethnic; family saga; fantasy; feminist; gay/lesbian; glitz; historical; horror; juvenile; mainstream; mystery/suspense; psychic/supernatural; romantic comedy; romantic drama; science fiction; sports; teen; thriller; western/frontier.

O╥ Actively seeking romantic comedy features, comedy features, strong female lead in thrillers MOW/features.

How to Contact Query with SASE. Accepts e-mail and fax queries. Considers simultaneous queries. Responds in 2 days to queries if by e-mail; 60 days to ms if query is accepted. Obtains most new clients through recommendations from others.

Recent Sales Sold 1 book/film rights; 1 TV series produced; 3 features in the last year. Movie/TV MOW scripts sold: *Ada*, by Ronalda Jones (Milagro Films); *13th Apostle*, by Paul Margolis (Stallion Films). Movie/TV MOW scripts in development: *CopyCat*, by Robert C. Cooper (New City Films); *Grounded in Eire*, by Ralph Keefer (Amaze Film & TV). Other clients include Tim Burns, Robert C. Cooper, Paul Margolis, Gerald Sanford.

Terms Agent receives 10% commission on domestic sales; 10% commission on foreign sales. No written contract.

Tips "To reach or get information about each individual agent, please call for e-mail address. Glen Cockburn is based in Los Angeles and Toronto; the rest are based in Toronto with one in Vancouver."

CIRCLE OF CONFUSION, LTD.

107-23 71st Rd., Suite 300, Forest Hills NY 11375. E-mail: queries@circleofconfusion.com. **Contact:** Shelly Narine and Nazia Boodram. Estab. 1990. Represents 30 clients. 40% of clients are new/unpublished writers. Currently handles: 95% movie scripts.

Member Agents Lawrence Mattis, David Mattis, Trisha Smith.

Represents Nonfiction books, novels, novellas, feature film, TV scripts. **Considers these nonfiction areas:** Biography/autobiography; current affairs; education; ethnic/cultural interests; gay/lesbian issues; government/politics/law; health/medicine; history; how-to; humor/satire; juvenile nonfiction; language/literature/criticism; memoirs; military/war; money/finance; multicultural; music/dance; nature/environment; New Age/metaphysics; philosophy; popular culture; psychology; recreation; regional; science/technology; self-help/personal improvement; sex; sociology; software; spirituality; sports; theater/film; translation; travel; true crime/investigative; women's issues/studies; young adult. **Considers these fiction areas:** Action/adventure; comic books/cartoon; confession; contemporary issues; detective/police/crime; erotica; ethnic; experimental; family saga; fantasy; feminist; gay/lesbian; glitz; gothic; hi-lo; historical; horror; humor/satire; juvenile; literary; mainstream/contemporary; military/war; multicultural; multimedia; mystery/suspense; New Age; occult; picture books; plays; poetry; poetry in translation; psychic/supernatural; regional; religious/inspirational; romance; science fiction; short story collections; spiritual; sports; thriller; translation; westerns/frontier; young adult; women's. **Considers these script subject areas:** Action/adventure; biography/autobiography; cartoon/animation; comedy; contemporary issues; detective/police/crime; erotica; ethnic; experimental; family saga; fantasy; feminist; gay/lesbian; glitz; historical; horror; juvenile; mainstream; multicultural; multimedia; mystery/suspense; psychic/supernatural; regional; religious/inspirational; romantic comedy; romantic drama; science fiction; sports; teen; thriller; western/frontier.

O╥ This agency specializes in screenplays for film and TV.

How to Contact Query with SASE. Responds in 1 month to queries; 2 months to mss. Obtains most new clients through recommendations from others, solicitations, writing contests, and queries.

Recent Sales Movie/TV MOW scripts optioned/sold: *The Matrix*, by Wachowski Brothers (Warner Brothers); *Reign of Fire*, by Chabot/Peterka (Dreamworks); *Mr. & Mrs. Smith*, by Simon Kinberg. Other clients include Jaswinki, Massa, Ferrer.

Terms Agent receives 10% commission on domestic sales; 10% commission on foreign sales. Offers written contract, binding for 1 year.

Tips "We look for writing that shows a unique voice, especially one which puts a fresh spin on commercial Hollywood genres."

COMMUNICATIONS AND ENTERTAINMENT, INC.

2851 S. Ocean Blvd., #5K, Boca Raton FL 33432-8407. (561)391-9575. Fax: (561)391-7922. E-mail: jlbearde@bellsouth.net. **Contact:** James L. Bearden. Estab. 1989. Represents 10 clients. 50% of clients are new/unpublished writers. Currently handles: 10% novels; 5% juvenile books; 40% movie scripts; 40% TV scripts.

- Prior to opening his agency, Mr. Bearden worked as a producer/director and an entertainment attorney.

Member Agents James Bearden (TV/film); Joyce Daniels (literary).

Represents Novels, juvenile books, movie scripts, TV scripts, syndicated material. **Considers these nonfiction areas:** History; music/dance; theater/film. **Considers these fiction areas:** Action/adventure; comic books/cartoon; fantasy; historical; mainstream/contemporary; science fiction; thriller.

How to Contact For scripts, query with SASE. For books, query with outline/proposal or send entire ms. Responds in 1 month to queries; 3 months to mss. Obtains most new clients through recommendations from others.

Recent Sales This agency prefers not to share information on specific sales.

Terms Agent receives 10% commission on domestic sales; 5% commission on foreign sales. Offers written contract.

Tips "Be patient."

THE CORE GROUP TALENT AGENCY, INC.

3 Church St., Suite #507, Toronto ON MSE 1M7 Canada. (416)955-0819. Fax: (416)955-0861. E-mail: literary@coregroupta.com. **Contact:** Charles Northcote, literary agent/co-owner. Estab. 1989. Member of WGC. Represents 60 clients. 10% of clients are new/unpublished writers. Currently handles: 25% movie scripts; 25% TV scripts; 50% stage plays.

Represents Movie scripts, feature film, TV scripts, TV movie of the week, episodic drama, sitcom, animation, documentary, miniseries, soap opera, stage plays. **Considers these script subject areas:** Action/adventure; biography/autobiography; cartoon/animation; comedy; contemporary issues; detective/police/crime; erotica; ethnic; experimental; family saga; fantasy; feminist; gay/lesbian; glitz; historical; horror; juvenile; mainstream; multicultural; mystery/suspense; psychic/supernatural; regional; romantic comedy; romantic drama; sports; teen; thriller; western/frontier.

- Seeks previously-produced writers with Canadian "status." Doesn't want international writers without Canadian "status."

How to Contact Query with SASE. Accepts e-mail queries. Responds in 1 week to queries. Returns materials only with SASE.

Terms Agent receives 10% commission on domestic sales. Offers written contract, binding for 1 year, renewable; 60-day notice must be given to terminate contract.

DOUGLAS & KOPELMAN ARTISTS, INC.

393 W. 49th St., Suite 5G, New York NY 10019. **Contact:** Sarah Douglas. Member of AAR.

Member Agents Sarah Douglas, Charles Kopelman.

Represents Stage plays. **Considers these script subject areas:** Action/adventure; biography/autobiography; cartoon/animation; comedy; contemporary issues; detective/police/crime; erotica; ethnic; experimental; family saga; fantasy; feminist; gay/lesbian; glitz; historical; horror; juvenile; mainstream; multicultural; multimedia; mystery/suspense; psychic/supernatural; regional; religious/inspirational; romantic comedy; romantic drama; science fiction; sports; teen; thriller; western/frontier.

- This agency specializes in musical stage plays.

How to Contact Query with SASE. Prefers to read materials exclusively. *No unsolicited mss.* No e-mail or fax queries.

THE E S AGENCY

6612 Pacheco Way, Citrus Heights CA 95610. (916)723-2794. Fax: (916)723-2796. E-mail: edley07@cs.com. **Contact:** Ed Silver, president. Estab. 1995. Represents 50-75 clients. 70% of clients are new/unpublished writers. Currently handles: 50% nonfiction books; 25% novels; 25% movie scripts.

- Prior to becoming an agent, Mr. Silver was an entertainment business manager.

Member Agents Ed Silver.

Represents Nonfiction books, novels, movie scripts, feature film, TV movie of the week. **Considers these nonfiction areas:** General nonfiction. **Considers these fiction areas:** Action/adventure; detective/police/crime; erotica; experimental; historical; humor/satire; literary; mainstream/contemporary; mystery/suspense; thriller; young adult. **Considers these script subject areas:** Action/adventure; comedy; contemporary issues; detective/police/crime; erotica; ethnic; experimental; family saga; mainstream; mystery/suspense; romantic comedy; romantic drama; sports; thriller.

- This agency specializes in theatrical screenplays, MOW, and miniseries. Actively seeking "anything unique and original."

How to Contact Query with SASE. Considers simultaneous queries. Returns materials only with SASE. Obtains most new clients through recommendations from others, queries from WGA agency list.

Recent Sales *Pet Loss and Children*, by Cheri Barton Ross; *Dutch Vacation*, by Steve Chase; *Laugh and Learn*, by Doni Tamblyn; *Ayurvedic Balancing*, by Joyce Bueker.
Terms Agent receives 15% commission on domestic sales; 20% commission on foreign sales; 10% commission on dramatic rights sales. Offers written contract; 30-day notice must be given to terminate contract.

EVATOPIA, INC.

400 S. Beverly Dr., Suite 214, Beverly Hills CA 90212. E-mail: submissions@evatopia.com. Website: www.evatopia.com. **Contact:** Margery Walshaw. Estab. 2004. Represents 15 clients. 85% of clients are new/unpublished writers. Currently handles: 100% movie scripts.

- Prior to becoming an agent, Ms. Walshaw was a writer and publicist for the entertainment industry.

Member Agents Mary Kay (story development); Stacy Glenn (story development); Jamie Davis (story assistant).
Represents Movie scripts. **Considers these script subject areas:** Action/adventure; biography/autobiography; cartoon/animation; comedy; contemporary issues; detective/police/crime; ethnic; family saga; fantasy; historical; horror; juvenile; mainstream; mystery/suspense; psychic/supernatural; romantic comedy; romantic drama; science fiction; sports; teen; thriller.

"We specialize in promoting and developing the careers of first-time screenwriters. All of our staff members have strong writing and entertainment backgrounds, making us sympathetic to the needs of our clients." Actively seeking dedicated and hard working writers.

How to Contact Submit via online submission form. Considers simultaneous queries. Responds in 2 weeks to queries; 3 weeks to mss. Returns materials only with SASE. Obtains most new clients through recommendations from others, solicitations.
Terms Agent receives 15% commission on domestic sales; 15% commission on foreign sales. Offers written contract, binding for up to 2 years; 30-day cancellation notice if not in active development of a project must be given to terminate contract.
Tips "Remember that you only have one chance to make that important first impression. Make your loglines original and your synopses concise. Don't rely on the cliche 'such and such' meets 'so and so.'"

FILMWRITERS LITERARY AGENCY

4932 Long Shadow Dr., Midlothian VA 23112. (804)744-1718. **Contact:** Helene Wagner. Signatory of WGA.

- Prior to opening her agency, Ms. Wagner was director of the Virginia Screenwriter's Forum for 7 years and taught college-level screenwriting classes. "As a writer myself, I have won or been a finalist in most major screenwriting competitions throughout the country and have a number of my screenplays optioned. Through the years, I have enjoyed helping and working with other writers. Some have gone on to have their movies made, their work optioned, and won national contests."

Represents Feature film, TV movie of the week, miniseries. **Considers these script subject areas:** Action/adventure; comedy; contemporary issues; detective/police/crime; historical; juvenile; mystery/suspense; psychic/supernatural; romantic comedy; romantic drama; teen; thriller.

This agency does not accept unsolicited queries. Currently not accepting new clients.

How to Contact No e-mail or fax queries. Obtains most new clients through recommendations from others.
Recent Sales Movie/TV MOW scripts optioned/sold: *Woman of His Dreams*, by Jeff Rubin (Ellenfreyer Productions).
Terms Agent receives 10% commission on domestic sales; 10% commission on foreign sales. Offers written contract. Clients supply photocopying and postage. Writers reimbursed for office fees after the sale of ms.
Tips "Professional writers should wait until they have at least 4 drafts done before they send out their work because they know it takes that much hard work to make a story and characters work. Show me something I haven't seen before with characters that I care about, that jump off the page. I not only look at a writer's work, I look at the writer's talent. If I believe in a writer, even though a piece may not sell, I'll stay with the writer and help nurture that talent, which a lot of the big agencies won't do."

FITZGERALD LITERARY MANAGEMENT

84 Monte Alto Rd., Santa Fe NM 87505. (505)466-1186. **Contact:** Lisa FitzGerald. Estab. 1994. Represents 12 clients. 75% of clients are new/unpublished writers. Currently handles: 15% film rights novels; 85% movie scripts.

- Ms. FitzGerald headed development at Universal Studios for Bruce Evans and Raynold Gideon, Oscar-nominated writer-producers. She also served as Executive Story Analyst at CBS, and held positions at Curtis Brown Agency in New York and Adams, Ray & Rosenberg Talent Agency in Los Angeles.

Represents Novels (film rights to), feature film, TV movie of the week. **Considers these fiction areas:** Mainstream/contemporary (novels with film potential). **Considers these script subject areas:** Action/adventure; biography/autobiography; comedy; contemporary issues; detective/police/crime; ethnic; family saga; fantasy;

historical; horror; mainstream; mystery/suspense; psychic/supernatural; romantic comedy; romantic drama; science fiction; sports; teen; thriller; western/frontier.

O→ This agency specializes in screenwriters and selling film rights to novels. Actively seeking mainstream feature film scripts. Does not want to receive true stories.

How to Contact We are not accepting new clients except by referral.
Recent Sales Sold 7 titles and sold 5 scripts in the last year.
Terms Agent receives 15% commission on domestic sales. Offers written contract, binding for 1-2 years. Charges clients for photocopying and postage.
Tips "Know your craft. Read produced screenplays. Enter screenplay contests. Educate yourself on the business in general (read *The Hollywood Reporter* or *Daily Variety*). Learn how to pitch. Keep writing and don't be afraid to get your work out there."

ROBERT A. FREEDMAN DRAMATIC AGENCY, INC.

1501 Broadway, Suite 2310, New York NY 10036. (212)840-5760. Fax: (212)840-5776. **Contact:** Robert A. Freedman. Estab. 1928. Member of AAR; signatory of WGA.

- Mr. Freedman has served as vice president of the dramatic division of AAR.

Member Agents Robert A. Freedman, president; Selma Luttinger, senior vice president; Robin Kaver, vice president (movie and TV scripts); Marta Praeger, associate (stage plays).
Represents Movie scripts, TV scripts, stage plays.

O→ This agency works with both established and new authors. Specializes in plays, movie and TV scripts.

How to Contact Query with SASE. All unsolicited mss returned unopened. Responds in 2 weeks to queries; 3 months to mss.
Recent Sales "We will speak directly with any prospective client concerning sales that are relevant to his/her specific script."
Terms Agent receives 10% commission on domestic sales. Charges clients for photocopying.

SAMUEL FRENCH, INC.

45 W. 25th St., New York NY 10010-2751. (212)206-8990. Fax: (212)206-1429. E-mail: samuelfrench@earthlink.net. Website: samuelfrench.com. **Contact:** Lawrence Harbison, senior editor. Estab. 1830. Member of AAR.
Member Agents Alleen Hussung, Brad Lohrenz, Charles R. Van Nostrand.
Represents Theatrical stage play, musicals. **Considers these script subject areas:** Comedy; contemporary issues; detective/police/crime; ethnic; fantasy; horror; mystery/suspense; thriller.

O→ This agency specializes in publishing plays which they also license for production.

How to Contact Query with SASE, or submit complete ms to Lawrence Harbison. Accepts e-mail and fax queries. Considers simultaneous queries. Responds in 2-8 months to mss. Responds immediately to queries.
Recent Sales This agency prefers not to share information on specific sales.
Terms Agent receives variable commission on domestic sales.

GRAHAM AGENCY

311 W. 43rd St., New York NY 10036. **Contact:** Earl Graham. Estab. 1971. Represents 40 clients. 30% of clients are new/unpublished writers. Currently handles: stage plays; musicals.
Represents Theatrical stage play, musicals.

O→ This agency specializes in playwrights. "We're interested in commercial material of quality." Does not want to receive one-acts or material for children.

How to Contact Query with SASE. No e-mail or fax queries. Responds in 3 months to queries; 6 weeks to mss. Obtains most new clients through recommendations from others, solicitations.
Recent Sales This agency prefers not to share information on specific sales.
Terms Agent receives 10% commission on dramatic rights sales.
Tips "Write a concise, intelligent letter giving the gist of what you are offering."

THE SUSAN GURMAN AGENCY, LLC

865 West End Ave., # 15A, New York NY 10025. (212)749-4618. Fax: (212)864-5055. E-mail: susan@gurmanagency.com. Website: www.gurmanagency.com. Estab. 1993. Signatory of WGA.
Represents Playwrights, screenwriters, directors, composers, and lyricists.
How to Contact No e-mail or fax queries. Responds in 2 weeks to queries.
Tips "Obtains new clients by referral only."

N HART LITERARY MANAGEMENT

5686 Antelope Trail, Orcutt CA 93455-6066. E-mail: hartliterary@verizon.net. Website: hartliterary.com. **Contact:** Susan Hart. Estab. 1997. Signatory of WGA. Represents 25 clients. 95% of clients are new/unpublished writers. Currently handles: 100% movie scripts.

Script Agents

- Prior to opening the agency, Ms. Hart was a screenwriter.

Represents Movie scripts, feature film, TV movie of the week, mostly PG-13. **Considers these script subject areas:** Action/adventure; comedy; science fiction; thriller; drama, family, true stories.

O— Screenplays must be set in the 1990s to present (or future, if sci-fi). "No animation or stories on folks in the biz."

How to Contact E-mail queries only. Paste 1-page synopsis in the e-mail. Considers simultaneous queries. Responds in 1 month to mss. Returns materials only with SASE. Obtains most new clients through solicitations.

Recent Sales *Encrypt*, by Richard Taylor (Sci-Fi Channel).

Terms Agent receives 10% domestic or worldwide sales on gross income written by any source from the screenplays commission. Offers written contract, binding for 1 year but may be cancelled at any time by both parties in writing. Charges clients for photocopies and postage; $7 domestic, $10 Canadian and $12 international (currently). This is the same as WGA requirement that screenwriters send copies of all screenplays to their agents and is cheaper than that in most cases.

Tips "I want a great story spell-checked, formatted, and typed in industry standard 12 point Courier or Courier New only, between 95-120 pages maximum. No overt gore, sex, violence. See website for genres I may look at."

N CAROLYN HODGES AGENCY

1980 Glenwood Dr., Boulder CO 80304-2329. (303)443-4636. Fax: (303)443-4636. E-mail: hodgesc@earthlink.net. **Contact:** Carolyn Hodges. Estab. 1989. Signatory of WGA. Represents 15 clients. 75% of clients are new/unpublished writers. Currently handles: 15% movie scripts; 45% TV scripts.

- Prior to opening her agency, Ms. Hodges was a freelance writer and founded the Writers in the Rockies Screenwriting Conference.

Represents Feature film, TV movie of the week. **Considers these script subject areas:** Comedy (light, black); romantic comedy; thriller (suspense, psychological).

O— This agency represents screenwriters for film and TV MOW. Does not want TV sitcom, drama or episodics.

How to Contact Query with SASE. Accepts e-mail and fax queries. Considers simultaneous queries. Responds in 1 week to queries; 10 weeks to mss. Returns materials only with SASE. Obtains most new clients through recommendations from others.

Recent Sales Available upon request.

Terms Agent receives 10% commission on domestic sales; 10% commission on foreign sales. Offers written contract. No charge for criticism. "I always try to offer concrete feedback, even when rejecting a piece of material."

Tips "Become proficient at your craft. Attend all workshops accessible to you. Read all the books applicable to your area of interest. Read as many 'produced' screenplays as possible. Live a full, vital and rewarding life so your writing will have something to say. Get involved in a writer's support group. Network with other writers. Receive 'critiques' from your peers and consider merit of suggestions. Don't be afraid to re-examine your perspective. Do yourself a favor and don't submit the 'first draft' of 'first script' to agents. Immature writing is obvious and will hurt your chance of later submissions."

BARBARA HOGENSON AGENCY

165 West End Ave., Suite 19-C, New York NY 10023. (212)874-8084. Fax: (212)362-3011. **Contact:** Barbara Hogenson. Estab. 1994. Member of AAR; signatory of WGA. Represents 60 clients. 5% of clients are new/unpublished writers. Currently handles: 35% nonfiction books; 15% novels; 50% stage plays.

- Prior to opening her agency, Ms. Hogenson was with the prestigious Lucy Kroll Agency for 10 years.

Represents Nonfiction books, novels, theatrical stage play. **Considers these nonfiction areas:** Biography/autobiography; history; interior design/decorating; music/dance; popular culture; theater/film. **Considers these fiction areas:** Detective/police/crime; ethnic; historical; humor/satire; literary; mainstream/contemporary; mystery/suspense; romance (contemporary); thriller.

How to Contact Query with SASE, outline. *No unsolicited mss.* Responds in 1 month to queries. Obtains most new clients through recommendations from others.

Recent Sales *On Grief and Grieving*, by Elisabeth Kubler-Ross and David Kessler; *The Songwriter Goes to War*, by Alan Anderson; *Wilder Biography*, by Penelope Niven.

Terms Agent receives 15% commission on domestic sales; 20% commission on foreign sales; 10% commission on dramatic rights sales. Offers written contract.

INTERNATIONAL LEONARDS CORP.

3612 N. Washington Blvd., Indianapolis IN 46205-3534. (317)926-7566. **Contact:** David Leonards. Estab. 1972. Signatory of WGA. Currently handles: 50% movie scripts; 50% TV scripts.

Represents Feature film, TV movie of the week, sitcom, animation, variety show. **Considers these script subject areas:** Action/adventure; cartoon/animation; comedy; contemporary issues; detective/police/crime; horror; mystery/suspense; romantic comedy; science fiction; sports; thriller.

How to Contact All unsolicited mss discarded.

Recent Sales This agency prefers not to share information on specific sales.

Terms Agent receives 10% commission on domestic sales; 10% commission on foreign sales. Offers written contract, binding for WGA standard terms, which vary.

CHARLENE KAY AGENCY

901 Beaudry St., Suite 6, St.Jean/Richelieu QC J3A 1C6 Canada. E-mail: lmchakay@hotmail.com. **Contact:** Louise Meyers, director of development. Estab. 1992. Member of BMI; signatory of WGA. 50% of clients are new/unpublished writers. Currently handles: 50% movie scripts; 50% TV scripts.

- Prior to opening her agency, Ms. Kay was a screenwriter.

Member Agents Louise Meyers; Karen Forsyth.

Represents Feature film, TV scripts, TV movie of the week, episodic drama, sitcom. **Considers these script subject areas:** Action/adventure; biography/autobiography; family saga; fantasy; psychic/supernatural; romantic comedy; romantic drama; science fiction.

O→ This agency specializes in teleplays and screenplays. "We seek stories that are out of the ordinary, something we don't see too often. A well-written and well-constructed script is important." Does not want to receive "thrillers or barbaric and erotic films. No novels, books, or manuscripts."

How to Contact Query with SASE, outline/proposal, IRCs for submissions outside of Canada. No e-mail or fax queries. Responds in 1 month to queries; 10 weeks to mss. Returns materials only with SASE.

Recent Sales This agency prefers not to share information on specific sales.

Terms Agent receives 10% commission on domestic sales; 10% commission on foreign sales. Offers written contract, binding for 1 year.

Tips "This agency is listed on the WGA lists, and query letters arrive by the dozens every week. As our present clients understand, success comes with patience. A sale rarely happens overnight, especially when you are dealing with totally unknown writers. We are not impressed by the credentials of a writer, amateur, or professional, or by his or her pitching techniques, but by his or her story ideas and ability to build a well-crafted script."

THE JOYCE KETAY AGENCY

630 Ninth Ave., Suite 706, New York NY 10036. (212)354-6825. Fax: (212)354-6732. **Contact:** Joyce Ketay, Carl Mulert. Signatory of WGA.

Member Agents Joyce Ketay, Carl Mulert.

Represents Feature film, TV movie of the week, episodic drama, sitcom, theatrical stage play. **Considers these script subject areas:** Comedy; contemporary issues; ethnic; experimental; feminist; gay/lesbian; historical; juvenile; mainstream; romantic comedy; romantic drama.

O→ This agency specializes in playwrights and screenwriters only. Does not want to receive novels.

Recent Sales This agency prefers not to share information on specific sales.

EDDIE KRITZER PRODUCTIONS

8484 Wilshire Blvd., Suite 205, Beverly Hills CA 90211. (323)655-5696. Fax: (323)655-5173. E-mail: producedby@aol.com. Website: www.eddiekritzer.com. **Contact:** Executive Story Editor. Estab. 1974.

Member Agents Eddie Kritzer (producer that also secures publishing agreements).

Represents Nonfiction books, movie scripts, feature film, TV scripts, TV movie of the week.

How to Contact Query with SASE. Prefers to read materials exclusively. Discards unwanted queries and mss. Obtains most new clients through recommendations from others, solicitations.

Recent Sales *Gmen & Gangsters* (Seven Locks Press); *The Practical Patient* (Seven Locks Press); *The Making of a Surgeon in the 21st Century*, by Dr. Craig Miller (Blue Dolphin Press); *Kids Say the Darndest Things*, by Art Linkletter (Ten Speed Press); *Live Ten Years Longer*, by Dr. Clarence Agrees (Ten Speed Press). Movie/TV MOW scripts optioned/sold: Currently producing a new version of *Kids Say the Darndest Things* on Nick @ Nite. *Gmen & Gangsters* in development at Mandeville Films. *Take Back a Scary Movie* currently at auction.

Terms Agent receives 15% commission on domestic sales; 20% commission on foreign sales. Offers written contract.

Writers' Conferences Michale Levine (Santa Monica, May).

Tips "I am only looking for the most compelling stories. Be succinct, but be compelling."

THE LANTZ OFFICE

200 W. 57th St., Suite 503, New York NY 10019. **Contact:** Robert Lantz. Member of AAR.

- Query before submitting.

LEGACIES...A LITERARY AGENCY

501 Woodstork Circle, Bradenton FL 34209-7393. **Contact:** MaryAnn Amato, executive director. Estab. 1992. Member of Licensed State of Florida Dept. of Business & Professional Regulations; registered WGA signatory. Currently handles: 90% movie scripts; 10% stage plays.

Represents Feature film. **Considers these script subject areas:** Comedy; contemporary issues; family saga; feminist; historical.

This agency specializes in screenplays.

How to Contact Referrals only. Not accepting new clients.

Recent Sales *Death's Parallel*, by Dr. Oakley Jordan (Rainbow Books). Movie/TV MOW scripts optioned/sold: *A Bench on Which to Rest*, by Maria Phillips; *Progress of the Sun*, by Patricia Friedberg; *Elsie Venner*, by Raleigh Marcell; *Glass House*, by Dan Guardino (adapted from *Glass House*, by Ari and Max Overton); *Dawn's Glory*, by Czerny Lee Miller.

Terms Agent receives 15% commission on domestic sales; 20% commission on foreign sales. Offers written contract.

THE LUEDTKE AGENCY

1674 Broadway, Suite 7A, New York NY 10019. (212)765-9564. Fax: (212)765-9582. **Contact:** Penny Luedtke. Represents 15 clients. 20% of clients are new/unpublished writers. Currently handles: 80% stage plays; 10% TV pilots/scripts; 10% film scripts.

- Prior to becoming an agent, Penny Luedtke was in classical music management.

Member Agents Penny Luedtke.

Represents Screenplays and stage plays of all lengths, TV pilots/scripts. **Considers these script subject areas:** Action/adventure; cartoon/animation; comedy; contemporary issues; detective/police/crime; ethnic; family saga; fantasy; feminist; gay/lesbian; historical; horror; juvenile; mainstream; multicultural; multimedia; mystery/suspense; psychic/supernatural; regional; romantic comedy; romantic drama; science fiction; teen; western/frontier.

Seeking well-written material with originality. Works closely with writers and offers editorial assistance, if desired. Does not want any project with graphic or explicit violence.

How to Contact Query with SASE. No e-mail or fax queries. Considers simultaneous queries. Responds in 1 month to queries; 6 months to mss. Returns materials only with SASE. Obtains most new clients through recommendations from others, and workshops.

Recent Sales This agency prefers not to share information on specific sales.

Terms Agent receives 10% commission on domestic sales; 15% commission on foreign sales. Offers written contract, binding for WGA standard terms.

THE MANAGEMENT CO.

1337 Ocean Ave., Suite F, Santa Monica CA 90401. (310)963-5670. **Contact:** Tom Klassen. Represents 15 clients.

- Prior to starting his agency Mr. Klassen was an agent with International Creative Management (ICM).

Member Agents Tom Klassen; Cindy Ware; Helene Taber; Paul Davis; Steve Gamber.

Represents Feature film (scripts), TV scripts, episodic drama, sitcom, miniseries.

Actively seeking "studio-quality, action-drama scripts and really good comedies." Does not want horror scripts.

How to Contact Submit query letter with synopsis. No e-mail or fax queries. Responds in 2-3 weeks to queries. Returns materials only with SASE. Obtains most new clients through recommendations from others, conferences.

Recent Sales Sold 11 scripts in the last year.

Terms Agent receives 10% commission on domestic sales; 10% commission on foreign sales. Offers written contract, binding for 2 years.

Writers' Conferences Sundance Film Festival; New York Film Festival; Telluride; Atlanta; Chicago; Minnesota.

Tips "We only accept query letters with a short, 1-page synopsis. We will request full manuscript with a SASE if interested. We rarely take on nonreferred material, but do review query letters and occasionally take on new writers. We have done very well with those we have taken on."

THE MARTON AGENCY, INC.

One Union Square W., Suite 612, New York NY 10003-3303. Fax: (212)691-9061. E-mail: info@martonagency.com. **Contact:** Tonda Marton. Member of AAR.

Member Agents Tonda Marton, Anne Reingold.

O→ This agency specializes in foreign-language licensing.

THE STUART M. MILLER CO.

11684 Ventura Blvd., #225, Studio City CA 91604-2699. (818)506-6067. Fax: (818)506-4079. E-mail: smmco@aol.com. **Contact:** Stuart Miller. Estab. 1977. Signatory of WGA; signatory of DGA. Currently handles: 50% movie scripts; 25% multimedia; 25% books.

Represents Nonfiction books, novels, movie scripts. **Considers these nonfiction areas:** Biography/autobiography; computers/electronic; current affairs; government/politics/law; health/medicine; history; how-to; memoirs; military/war; self-help/personal improvement; true crime/investigative. **Considers these fiction areas:** Action/adventure; detective/police/crime; historical; literary; mainstream/contemporary; mystery/suspense; science fiction; sports; thriller. **Considers these script subject areas:** Action/adventure; biography/autobiography; cartoon/animation; comedy; contemporary issues; detective/police/crime; family saga; historical; mainstream; multimedia; mystery/suspense; romantic comedy; romantic drama; science fiction; sports; teen; thriller.

How to Contact Query with SASE, 2-3 page narrative, and outline/proposal. Accepts e-mail and fax queries. Considers simultaneous queries. Responds in 3 days to queries; 6 weeks to mss. Returns materials only with SASE.

Recent Sales This agency prefers not to share information on specific sales.

Terms Agent receives 10% for movie/TV commission on domestic sales; 15-25% for books (includes domestic) commission on foreign sales. Offers written contract, binding for 2 years; WGA standard notice must be given to terminate contract.

Tips "Always include SASE, e-mail address, or fax number with query letters. Make it easy to respond."

MONTEIRO ROSE DRAVIS AGENCY

17514 Ventura Blvd., Suite 205, Encino CA 91316. (818)501-1177. Fax: (818)501-1194. Website: www.monteiro-rose.com. **Contact:** Candy Monteiro. Estab. 1987. Signatory of WGA. Represents 50 clients. Currently handles: 40% movie scripts; 20% TV scripts; 40% animation.

Member Agents Candace Monteiro (literary); Fredda Rose (literary); Jason Dravis (literary).

Represents Feature film, TV movie of the week, episodic drama, animation. **Considers these script subject areas:** Action/adventure; cartoon/animation; comedy; contemporary issues; detective/police/crime; ethnic; family saga; historical; juvenile; mainstream; mystery/suspense; psychic/supernatural; romantic comedy; romantic drama; science fiction; teen; thriller.

O→ This agency specializes in scripts for animation, TV and film.

How to Contact Query with SASE. Accepts e-mail and fax queries. Responds in 1 week to queries; 2 months to mss. Returns materials only with SASE. Obtains most new clients through recommendations from others, solicitations.

Recent Sales This agency prefers not to share information on specific sales.

Terms Agent receives 10% commission on domestic sales. Offers written contract, binding for 2 years; 3-month notice must be given to terminate contract. Charges for photocopying.

Tips "We prefer to receive inquiries by e-mail, although by mail is OK with a SASE. We do not return manuscripts. We suggest that all feature manuscripts be no longer than 120 pages."

NIAD MANAGEMENT

15030 Ventura Blvd., #19-860, Sherman Oaks CA 91423. (818)981-2505. Fax: (818)386-2082. E-mail: queries@niadmanagement.com. Website: www.niadmanagement.com. Estab. 1997. Represents 20 clients. 2% of clients are new/unpublished writers. Currently handles: 1% novels; 98% movie scripts; 1% stage plays.

Represents Movie scripts, feature film, TV movie of the week, miniseries, stage plays. **Considers these nonfiction areas:** Biography/autobiography. **Considers these fiction areas:** Action/adventure; detective/police/crime; family saga; literary; mainstream/contemporary; multicultural; mystery/suspense; psychic/supernatural; romance; thriller. **Considers these script subject areas:** Action/adventure; biography/autobiography; comedy; contemporary issues; detective/police/crime; ethnic; family saga; historical; horror; mainstream; multicultural; mystery/suspense; psychic/supernatural; romantic comedy; romantic drama; sports; teen; thriller.

How to Contact Query with SASE. Accepts e-mail and fax queries. Considers simultaneous queries. Responds in 1 week to queries; 3 months to mss. Returns materials only with SASE. Obtains most new clients through recommendations from others.

Recent Sales *MacGyver the Feature Film*; *Five Dollars a Day*, by Neal and Tippi Dobrofsky (New Line); *Farnsworth*, by Neil Cohen (HBO); *Preying on Puritans*, by Josh Rebell. Other clients include Julian Grant, Susan Sandler, Michael Lazarou, Jim McGlynn, Don Most, Fernando Fragata.

Terms Agent receives 15% commission on domestic sales. Offers written contract, binding for 1 year; 30-day notice must be given to terminate contract.

OMNIQUEST ENTERTAINMENT

1416 N. La Brae Ave., Hollywood CA 90028. (323)802-1630. Fax: (303)802-1633. E-mail: mk@omniquestmedia.com. Website: www.omniquestmedia.com. **Contact:** Michael Kaliski. Estab. 1997. Currently handles: 5% novels; 5% juvenile books; 40% movie scripts; 20% TV scripts; 10% multimedia; 15% stage plays.

Member Agents Michael Kaliski; Traci Belushi.

Represents Novels, short story collections, novellas, movie scripts, feature film, TV scripts, TV movie of the week, episodic drama, sitcom, miniseries, syndicated material, stage plays. **Considers these fiction areas:** Action/adventure; detective/police/crime; experimental; family saga; fantasy; literary; psychic/supernatural; romance; science fiction; thriller. **Considers these script subject areas:** Action/adventure; biography/autobiography; comedy; contemporary issues; detective/police/crime; experimental; family saga; fantasy; historical; mainstream; multimedia; mystery/suspense; psychic/supernatural; romantic comedy; romantic drama; science fiction; thriller.

O-ᵣ Actively seeking books that can be adapted for film and scripts.

How to Contact Query with SASE, or send outline and 2-3 sample chapters. Accepts e-mail and fax queries. Considers simultaneous queries. Returns materials only with SASE. Obtains most new clients through recommendations from others.

Recent Sales This agency prefers not to share information on specific sales.

Terms Agent receives 15% commission on domestic sales; 15% commission on foreign sales. Offers written contract.

DOROTHY PALMER

235 W. 56 St., New York NY 10019. (212)765-4280. Fax: (212)977-9801. Estab. 1968 (talent agency); 1990 (literary agency). Signatory of WGA. Represents 12 clients. 0% of clients are new/unpublished writers. Currently handles: 70% movie scripts; 30% TV scripts.

- In addition to being a literary agent, Ms. Palmer has also worked as a talent agent for 36 years.

Represents Feature film, TV movie of the week, episodic drama, sitcom, miniseries. **Considers these script subject areas:** Action/adventure; comedy; contemporary issues; detective/police/crime; family saga; feminist; mainstream; mystery/suspense; romantic comedy; romantic drama; thriller.

O-ᵣ This agency specializes in screenplays and TV. Actively seeking successful, published writers (screenplays only). Does not want to receive work from new or unpublished writers.

How to Contact Query with SASE. Prefers to read materials exclusively. Published writers only. Returns materials only with SASE. Obtains most new clients through recommendations from others.

Recent Sales This agency prefers not to share information on specific sales.

Terms Agent receives 10% commission on domestic sales; 10% commission on foreign sales. Offers written contract, binding for 1 year. Charges clients for postage, photocopies.

Tips "Do not telephone. When I find a script that interests me, I call the writer. Calls to me are a turn-off because they cut into my reading time. The only ones who can call are serious investors of independent films."

BARRY PERELMAN AGENCY

1155 N. La Cienega Blvd., Suite 412, W. Hollywood CA 90069. (310)659-1122. Fax: (310)659-1122. Estab. 1982. Member of DGA; signatory of WGA. Represents 40 clients. 15% of clients are new/unpublished writers. Currently handles: 100% movie scripts.

Member Agents Barry Perelman (motion picture/packaging).

Represents Movie scripts, TV scripts, reality shows. **Considers these script subject areas:** Action/adventure; biography/autobiography; contemporary issues; detective/police/crime; historical; horror; mystery/suspense; romantic comedy; romantic drama; science fiction; thriller.

O-ᵣ This agency specializes in motion pictures/packaging.

How to Contact Query with SASE, proposal package, outline. Responds in 1 month to queries. Obtains most new clients through recommendations from others, solicitations.

Recent Sales This agency prefers not to share information on specific sales.

Terms Agent receives 10% commission on domestic sales; 10% commission on foreign sales. Offers written contract, binding for 1-2 years. Charges clients for postage and photocopying.

PREFERRED ARTISTS TALENT AGENCY

16633 Ventura Blvd., Suite 1421, Encino CA 91436. (818)990-0305. Fax: (818)990-2736. **Contact:** Kimber Wheeler. Estab. 1985. Signatory of WGA. 90% of clients are new/unpublished writers. Currently handles: 10% novels; 90% movie scripts.

Represents Novels, movie scripts. **Considers these script subject areas:** Action/adventure; biography/autobiography; cartoon/animation; comedy; contemporary issues; detective/police/crime; ethnic; family saga; fan-

tasy; feminist; gay/lesbian; horror; mystery/suspense; psychic/supernatural; romantic comedy; romantic drama; science fiction; sports; thriller.
How to Contact Query with SASE, submit proposal package, outline.
Recent Sales This agency prefers not to share information on specific sales.
Terms Agent receives 10% commission on domestic sales. Offers written contract, binding for 1 year.
Tips "A good query letter is important. Use any relationship you have in the business to get your material read."

THE QUILLCO AGENCY

3104 W. Cumberland Court, Westlake Village CA 91362. (805)495-8436. Fax: (805)373-9868. E-mail: quillco2@aol.com. **Contact:** Sandy Mackey (owner). Estab. 1993. Signatory of WGA. Represents 7 client.
Represents Feature film, TV movie of the week, animation, documentary.
How to Contact Prefers to read materials exclusively. Not accepting query letters at this time. Returns materials only with SASE.
Recent Sales This agency prefers not to share information on specific sales.
Terms Agent receives 10% commission on domestic sales; 10% commission on foreign sales.

MICHAEL D. ROBINS & ASSOCIATES

23241 Ventura Blvd., #300, Woodland Hills CA 91364. (818)343-1755. Fax: (818)343-7355. E-mail: mdr2@msn.com. **Contact:** Michael D. Robins. Estab. 1991. Member of DGA; signatory of WGA. 10% of clients are new/unpublished writers. Currently handles: 5% nonfiction books; 5% novels; 20% movie scripts; 60% TV scripts; 10% syndicated material.

- Prior to opening his agency, Mr. Robins was a literary agent at a mid-sized agency.

Represents Nonfiction books, novels, movie scripts, feature film, TV scripts, TV movie of the week, episodic drama, animation, miniseries, syndicated material, stage plays. **Considers these nonfiction areas:** History; humor/satire; memoirs; military/war; popular culture; science/technology; true crime/investigative; urban lifestyle. **Considers these fiction areas:** Action/adventure; comic books/cartoon; detective/police/crime; family saga; fantasy; gay/lesbian; mainstream/contemporary; westerns/frontier; young adult. **Considers these script subject areas:** Action/adventure; biography/autobiography; cartoon/animation; comedy; contemporary issues; detective/police/crime; erotica; ethnic; experimental; family saga; fantasy; feminist; gay/lesbian; glitz; historical; horror; juvenile; mainstream; multicultural; multimedia; mystery/suspense; psychic/supernatural; regional; religious/inspirational; romantic comedy; romantic drama; science fiction; sports; teen; thriller; western/frontier.
How to Contact Query with SASE. Accepts e-mail and fax queries. Considers simultaneous queries. Responds in 1 week to queries; 1 month to mss. Obtains most new clients through recommendations from others.
Recent Sales This agency prefers not to share information on specific sales.
Terms Agent receives 10% commission on domestic sales; 10% commission on foreign sales. Offers written contract, binding for 2 years; 4-month notice must be given to terminate contract.

KEN SHERMAN & ASSOCIATES

9507 Santa Monica Blvd., Beverly Hills CA 90210. (310)273-3840. Fax: (310)271-2875. E-mail: kjassociates@earthlink.net. **Contact:** Ken Sherman. Estab. 1989. Member of BAFTA; PEN Int'l; signatory of WGA; DGA. Represents approximately 50 clients. 10% of clients are new/unpublished writers. Currently handles: juvenile books; movie scripts; TV scripts; fiction and nonfiction books; screenplays; teleplays; life rights; film and TV rights to books; video games/fiction.

- Prior to opening his agency, Mr. Sherman was with The William Morris Agency, The Lantz Office, and Paul Kohner, Inc.

Represents Nonfiction books, novels, movie scripts, TV scripts, film, television and life rights to books. **Considers these nonfiction areas:** Agriculture/horticulture; americana; animals; anthropology/archaeology; art/architecture/design; biography/autobiography; business/economics; child guidance/parenting; computers/electronic; cooking/foods/nutrition; crafts/hobbies; creative nonfiction; current affairs; education; ethnic/cultural interests; gardening; gay/lesbian issues; government/politics/law; health/medicine; history; how-to; humor/satire; interior design/decorating; juvenile nonfiction; language/literature/criticism; memoirs; military/war; money/finance; multicultural; music/dance; nature/environment; New Age/metaphysics; philosophy; photography; popular culture; psychology; recreation; regional; religious/inspirational; science/technology; self-help/personal improvement; sex; sociology; software; spirituality; sports; theater/film; translation; travel; true crime/investigative; women's issues/studies; young adult. **Considers these fiction areas:** Action/adventure; comic books/cartoon; confession; contemporary issues; detective/police/crime; erotica; ethnic; experimental; family saga; fantasy; feminist; gay/lesbian; glitz; gothic; hi-lo; historical; horror; humor/satire; juvenile; literary; mainstream/contemporary; military/war; multicultural; multimedia; mystery/suspense; New Age; occult; picture books; plays; poetry; poetry in translation; psychic/supernatural; regional; religious/inspirational; romance; science fiction; short story collections; spiritual; sports; thriller; translation; westerns/frontier; young adult. **Considers these script subject areas:** Action/adventure; biography/autobiography; cartoon/animation; comedy; contemporary issues; detective/police/crime; erotica; ethnic; experimental; family saga; fantasy; feminist; gay/lesbian; glitz; historical; horror; juvenile; mainstream; multicultural; multimedia; mystery/suspense; psychic/supernatural; regional; religious/inspirational; romantic comedy; romantic drama; science fiction; sports; teen; thriller; western/frontier.

O→ This agency specializes in solid writers for film, TV, books, and film and television rights to books.

How to Contact Contact by referral only please. Responds in 1 month to mss. Obtains most new clients through recommendations from others.

Recent Sales Sold over 20 scripts in the last year. *Back Roads*, by Tawni O'Dell (to Dreamworks); *Priscilla Salyers Story*, produced by Andrea Baynes (ABC); *Toys of Glass*, by Martin Booth (ABC/Saban Ent.); *Brazil*, by John Updike (film rights to Glaucia Carmagos); *Fifth Sacred Thing*, by Starhawk (Bantam); *Questions From Dad*, by Dwight Twilly (Tuttle); *Snow Falling on Cedars*, by David Guterson (Universal Pictures); *The Witches of Eastwick—The Musical*, by John Updike (Cameron Macintosh, Ltd.).

Terms Agent receives 15% commission on domestic sales; 15% commission on foreign sales; 15% (10% for WGA scripts) commission on dramatic rights sales. Offers written contract. Charges clients for reasonable office expenses, postage, photocopying, and other negotiable expenses.

Writers' Conferences Maui; Squaw Valley; Santa Barbara; Santa Fe; Aspen Institute; Aspen Writers Foundation, etc.

SILVER SCREEN PLACEMENTS

602 65th St., Downers Grove IL 60516-3020. (630)963-2124. Fax: (630)963-1998. E-mail: silverscreen11@yahoo.com. **Contact:** William Levin. Estab. 1989. Signatory of WGA. Represents 12 clients. 80% of clients are new/unpublished writers.

- Prior to opening his agency, Mr. Levin did product placement for motion pictures/TV.

Member Agents Bernadette LaHaie, Jeff Dudley.

Represents Novels, movie and feature film scripts. No TV. **Considers these nonfiction areas:** All genres. **Considers these fiction areas:** All genres. **Considers these script subject areas:** All genres except religious, x-rated, and horror.

How to Contact Be brief. Accepts e-mail queries. No fax queries. Responds ASAP to queries. Obtains most new clients through recommendations from others, listings with WGA, and *Guide to Literary Agents*.

Recent Sales Sold 2 titles and sold 3 scripts in the last year. This agency prefers not to share information on specific sales. Clients include C. Geier, M. Derosa, P. Sands, N. Melamed, R. Melley, N. Russell, D. Huganin and R. Rando.

Terms Agent receives 15% (ms) commission on domestic sales; 10% (screenplay) commission on dramatic rights sales. May make referrals to freelance editors. Use of said editors does not ensure representation.

Tips "No cute queries, please."

N STONE MANNERS AGENCY

6500 Wilshire Blvd., Suite 550, Los Angeles CA 90048. (323)655-1313. **Contact:** Tim Stone. Estab. 1982. Signatory of WGA. Represents 25 clients.

Represents Movie scripts, TV scripts. **Considers these script subject areas:** Action/adventure; biography/autobiography; cartoon/animation; comedy; contemporary issues; detective/police/crime; erotica; ethnic; experimental; family saga; fantasy; feminist; gay/lesbian; glitz; historical; horror; juvenile; mainstream; multicultural; multimedia; mystery/suspense; psychic/supernatural; regional; religious/inspirational; romantic comedy; romantic drama; science fiction; sports; teen; thriller; western/frontier.

How to Contact Not considering scripts at this time.

Recent Sales This agency prefers not to share information on specific sales.

Terms Agent receives 10% commission on domestic sales; 10% commission on foreign sales.

N MARK CHRISTIAN SUBIAS AGENCY

331 W. 57th St., #462, New York NY 10019. (212)445-1091. E-mail: marksubias@earthlink.net. **Contact:** Mark Subias. Estab. 2002. Represents 12 clients. Currently handles: movie scripts; stage plays.

How to Contact Query with SASE.

SUITE A MANAGEMENT TALENT & LITERARY AGENCY

120 El Camino Dr., Suite 202, Beverly Hills CA 90212. (310)278-0801. Fax: (310)278-0807. E-mail: suite-A@juno.com. **Contact:** Lloyd Robinson. Estab. 1996. Member of DGA; signatory of WGA. Represents 76 clients. 10%

of clients are new/unpublished writers. Currently handles: 15% novels; 40% movie scripts; 40% TV scripts; 5% stage plays.

- Prior to becoming an agent, Mr. Robinson worked as a manager.

Member Agents Lloyd Robinson (adaptation of books and plays for development as features or TV MOW); Kevin Douglas (scripts for film and TV); Judy Jacobs (feature development).

Represents Feature film, TV movie of the week, episodic drama, documentary, miniseries, variety show, stage plays, CD-ROM. **Considers these script subject areas:** Action/adventure; cartoon/animation; comedy; contemporary issues; detective/police/crime; erotica; ethnic; experimental; family saga; fantasy; mainstream; mystery/suspense; psychic/supernatural; religious/inspirational; romantic comedy; romantic drama; science fiction; sports; teen; thriller; western/frontier.

O→ "We represent screenwriters, playwrights, novelists, producers and directors."

How to Contact Submit synopsis, outline/proposal, log line. Obtains most new clients through recommendations from others.

Recent Sales This agency prefers not to share information on specific sales or client names.

Terms Agent receives 10% commission on domestic sales; 10% commission on foreign sales. Offers written contract, binding for 1 year minimum. Charges clients for photocopying, messenger, FedEx, and postage when required.

Tips "We are a talent agency specializing in the copyright business. Fifty percent of our clients generate copyright—screenwriters, playwrights, and novelists. Fifty percent of our clients service copyright—producers and directors. We represent produced, published, and/or WGA writers who are eligible for staff TV positions as well as novelists and playwrights whose works may be adapted for film on television."

TALENT SOURCE

1711 Dean Forest Rd., Suite H, Savannah GA 31408. (912)963-0941. Fax: (912)963-0944. E-mail: michael@talentsource.com. Website: www.talentsource.com. **Contact:** Michael L. Shortt. Estab. 1991. Signatory of WGA. 35% of clients are new/unpublished writers. Currently handles: 85% movie scripts; 15% TV scripts.

- Prior to becoming an agent, Mr. Shortt was a TV program producer/director.

Represents Feature film, TV movie of the week, episodic drama, sitcom. **Considers these script subject areas:** Comedy; contemporary issues; detective/police/crime; erotica; family saga; juvenile; mainstream; mystery/suspense; romantic comedy; romantic drama; teen.

O→ Actively seeking "character-driven stories (i.e., *Sling Blade*; *Sex, Lies, and Videotape*)." Does not want to receive "big budget special effects, or science fiction."

How to Contact Query with SASE, Must include a proper synopsis. No e-mail or fax queries. Responds in 10 weeks to queries. Obtains most new clients through recommendations from others.

Recent Sales This agency prefers not to share information on specific sales.

Terms Agent receives 10% commission on domestic sales; 15% commission on foreign sales. Offers written contract.

Tips "See the literary button on our website for complete submission details. No exceptions."

N TALENT WORKS

3500 W. Olive Ave., Suite 1400, Burbank CA 91505. (818)972-4300. Fax: (818)972-4313. **Contact:** Kimber Wheeler. Estab. 1985. Signatory of WGA. 60% of clients are new/unpublished writers. Currently handles: 90% movie scripts; 10% TV scripts.

Represents Movie scripts, TV scripts. **Considers these script subject areas:** Action/adventure; biography/autobiography; comedy; contemporary issues; detective/police/crime; ethnic; family saga; fantasy; feminist; gay/lesbian; mystery/suspense; psychic/supernatural; romantic comedy; romantic drama; science fiction; sports; thriller.

How to Contact Query with SASE, outline/proposal.

Recent Sales This agency prefers not to share information on specific sales.

Terms Agent receives 10% commission on domestic sales. Offers written contract, binding for 1 year; WGA rules on termination apply.

Tips "A good query letter is important. Use any relationship you have in the business to get your material read."

ANNETTE VAN DUREN AGENCY

11684 Ventura Blvd., #235, Studio City CA 91604. (818)752-6000. Fax: (818)752-6985. **Contact:** Annette Van Duren. Estab. 1985. Signatory of WGA. Represents 12 clients. 0% of clients are new/unpublished writers. Currently handles: 10% novels; 50% movie scripts; 40% TV scripts.

Represents Feature film, TV movie of the week, episodic drama, sitcom, animation.

How to Contact Not accepting new clients. Obtains most new clients through recommendations from others.

Recent Sales This agency prefers not to share information about specific sales.
Terms Agent receives 10% commission on domestic sales. Offers written contract, binding for 2 years.

N ◙ DONNA WAUHOB AGENCY

5280 S. Eastern Ave., Suite A3, Las Vegas NV 89119. (702)795-1523. Fax: (702)795-0696. E-mail: dwauhob@aol.com. **Contact:** Donna Wauhob. Represents 15 clients. Currently handles: 30% juvenile books; 50% movie scripts; 10% TV scripts; 10% animation.

- Prior to opening her agency, Ms. Wauhob was a model and secretary. She is now SAG franchised, AF of M franchised (since 1968), and WGA Signatory (''the only one in the state of Nevada'').

Represents Nonfiction books, novels, short story collections, juvenile books, poetry books, movie scripts, feature film, TV scripts, TV movie of the week, episodic drama, sitcom, animation, miniseries, soap opera, variety show. **Considers these nonfiction areas:** Animals; child guidance/parenting; cooking/foods/nutrition. **Considers these script subject areas:** Action/adventure; cartoon/animation; comedy; detective/police/crime; family saga; juvenile; romantic comedy; romantic drama; teen; thriller; western/frontier.

O→ Actively seeking film and TV scripts, juvenile, teen action, cartoon, comedy, family.

How to Contact Accepts e-mail and fax queries. Considers simultaneous queries. Responds in 2 months to queries.
Recent Sales This agency prefers not to share information on specific sales.
Terms Agent receives 10% commission on domestic sales; 10% commission on foreign sales. Offers written contract; 6-month notice must be given to terminate contract.

N ◙ PEREGRINE WHITTLESEY AGENCY

279 Central Park W., New York NY 10024. (212)787-1802. Fax: (212)787-4985. E-mail: pwwagy@aol.com. **Contact:** Peregrine Whittlesey. Estab. 1986. Signatory of WGA. Represents 30 clients. 50% of clients are new/unpublished writers. Currently handles: 2% movie scripts; 98% stage plays.
Represents Feature film, stage plays.

O→ This agency specializes in playwrights who also write for screen and TV.

How to Contact Query with SASE. Prefers to read materials exclusively. Accepts e-mail and fax queries. Responds in 1 week to queries; 1 month to mss. Obtains most new clients through recommendations from others.
Recent Sales Sold 20 scripts in the last year. *Christmas Movie*, by Darrah Cloud (CBS). Productions at Arena Stage in Washington, New Theatre in Miami, La Jolla Playhouse, Seattle Rep., Oregon Shakespeare Festival, South Coast Rep.
Terms Agent receives 10% commission on domestic sales; 15% commission on foreign sales. Offers written contract, binding for 2 years.

MARKETS

Production Companies

This section contains independent producers who buy feature-film scripts. These are smaller production companies with limited budgets who produce more character-driven stories. So, understand that if you have a science fiction script requiring a lot of special effects or an action movie with many locations or special props, your work may not be appropriate for this market.

Very few producers will accept unsolicited script submissions, but many are willing to consider a query letter. Your query letter should be no more than one page, including a one-paragraph summary of your story and a paragraph to list your credentials as they relate to the subject matter of the script or your writing experience.

Because of the large bulk of mail that producers receive, expect that the production company will likely respond only if it is interested in your script. If it does request to see your work, it will most likely send you a release form to sign and submit along with your script. This is a standard practice in the industry, and you should be willing to comply without worries that someone will steal your idea.

However, you should register your script before you send it out, just as you would when submitting to agents. The Writers Guild of America (WGA) offers a registration service to members and nonmembers alike. Write the WGA for more information on specific agencies, script registration, and membership requirements, or visit them online at www.wga.org.

Include either a self-addressed, stamped envelope (SASE) with enough room and postage for your script if you want it returned to you, or a smaller envelope with First-Class postage if you only want a reply. Allow six weeks from receipt of your manuscript before writing a follow-up letter.

Before you send a query letter, you should have your script written in proper screenplay format. Remember: Keep the binding simple—two or three brass brads with a plain black or white cover.

It's a good idea to visit the production company's website before submitting a query or a script to get a better feel for the kinds of films it's produced, its current movie or movies in production, and what scripts it's interested in producing next.

Many independent production companies are willing to work with new writers, and these venues present some of the best opportunities for writers to break into the film industry and get their screenplays produced.

The following listings are for low- to midsized-budget feature film producers. When reading through this section, keep in mind the following information specific to the independent producer listings.

SUBHEADS

Each listing is broken down into subheads to make locating specific information easier. In the first section, you'll find contact information for each producer. Further information is provided that indicates the producers' specialties, the type of work they want, and how you should approach them.

Needs: Look here to quickly learn producers' specializations and individual strengths. Producers also mention what specific areas they are currently seeking, as well as subjects they do not wish to receive.

How to Contact: Most producers open to submissions prefer to receive a query letter briefly describing your work. Producers usually discard material sent without a SASE. They also indicate in this section if they accept queries by fax or e-mail.

Tips: Producers offer advice and additional instructions for writers hoping to break into the film industry.

SPECIAL INDEX

General Index: This index lists all producers, agencies, independent publicists, script contests, and writers' conferences listed in the book.

ALLIANCE FILMWORKS
9595 Wilshire Blvd., Suite 900, Beverly Hills CA 90212. E-mail: submissions@alliancefilmworks.com. Website: www.alliancefilmworks.com. **Contact:** Greg Zanfardino, president. Estab. 2001. Produces 3 movies/year.
How to Contact Send query and synopsis via e-mail. Responds if interested in the material/e-mail pitch. Pays option, makes outright purchase. Include SASE for return of submissions.
Needs Produces all genres. Budgets are $1.5 million plus.

AXIAL ENTERTAINMENT
20 W. 21st St., 8th Floor, New York NY 10010. E-mail: submissions@axialentertainment.com. Website: www.axialentertainment.com. **Executive Producer:** Riaz Patel, CEO. **Contact:** Nora Francescani, director of development (film/theater); David Garfield, director of development (film/TV).
Needs "Axial is a New York-based production and management company with an unusual model: loosely based on the 'hot house' studio environment of the 1940s, Axial takes writers and film executives—2 parties that are often separated by distance and large, heavy, insurmountable barriers—and places them in the same work space. By incubating the development process before it gets to the studios, networks, or producers, Axial is exactly the place where chances can be taken on a new writer or a completely original idea. Axial's dynamic creative process is anchored in the weekly Tc (the Tuesday Think Tank meeting). Writers and executives gather together to discuss new story ideas, assess the gaps and gluts in the current marketplace, brainstorm current script roadblocks, and work to make each choice in every story as smart as possible. What are specific studios, networks, and theater companies looking for? What kinds of projects are considered out-of-date this month? What are some other ways of getting a character from point A to point B?"
How to Contact "Unfortunately, Axial Entertainment does not accept any unsolicited materials. If you are interested in submitting, please send an e-mail containing a brief (1 page or less) summary of your material to submissions@axialentertainment.com."
Tips "Axial is not for every writer. The writers who thrive in our environment not only have great talent and express themselves in exciting and dynamic voices, but are highly motivated, prolific, generous with their intelligence, and ego-free about their writing process. At Axial, we specialize in finding original voices (both established and emerging), creating and developing strong, marketable material, and championing that material the entire way from conception to production."

CODIKOW FILMS
8899 Beverly Blvd., Suite 501, Los Angeles CA 90048. (310)246-9388. Fax: (310)246-9877. E-mail: joinpowerup@aol.com. Website: www.codikowfilms.com. **Executive Producer:** Stacy Codikow. **Contact:** Codikow Story Department.
Needs Accepts material for all genres. "Currently searching for a romantic comedy. Codikow Films has been involved in the production of 10 feature films, including *Hollywood Heartbreak* and *Fatal Instinct*. Presently, the company is producing *In Search of Holden Caulfield*. We have an active development slate of projects, ranging from independent to studio features."
How to Contact "Submit a short pitch or synopsis (no more than one $8\frac{1}{2} \times 11$ page). Make sure you include your contact information (name, address, phone, fax, and e-mail) as well as the title, genre, and logline for your project. Pitches are reviewed each week by the Codikow Story Department. Because of the volume of material we receive, we can only respond to ideas we are interested in pursuing further. If we find a project interesting, a request for the screenplay will be made by e-mail or phone."
Tips Stacy Codikow is a member of the Producers Guild of America, the Writers Guild of America, Women in Film, USC Cinema Alumni Association, Cinewoman, AFI 3rd Decade Council, IFP West, and has been included in articles written for *The Wall Street Journal, The New York Times*, Movieline, *Premiere* magazine, *Scene at the Movies, Hollywood Reporter, The Daily Variety, Screen International, The Los Angeles Times, Daily News, Film & Video,* and *Entertainment Today*. She has been featured on the television shows Entertainment Tonight (ET), E!, HBO News, Extra, and Showbiz News (CNN).

LEE DANIELS ENTERTAINMENT
39 W. 131st St., Suite 2, New York NY 10037. (646)548-0930. Fax: (646)548-9883. E-mail: info@leedanielsentertainment.com. Website: www.leedanielsentertainment.com. **Executive Producer:** Lee Daniels.
Needs "We work with all aspects of entertainment, including film, television, and theater."
How to Contact "All scripts should be registered (WGA, etc.) or copyrighted for your own protection. All scripts should be in standard screenplay format. Include a synopsis, logline, and character breakdown (including lead and supporting roles). Do not send any extraneous materials."
Tips Lee Daniels produced *Monster's Ball*. Client list includes Wes Bently (*American Beauty*) and supermodel/actress Amber Valletta. Past clients include Marianne Jean-Baptiste and Morgan Freeman.

ENERGY ENTERTAINMENT

Website: www.energyentertainment.net. **Executive Producer:** Brooklyn Weaver. Estab. 2001.

How to Contact Submit query via website. "Energy Entertainment is only accepting electronic query letters, and will not accept unsolicited scripts."

GREY LINE ENTERTAINMENT, INC.

115 W. California Blvd., #310, Pasadena CA 91105-3005. E-mail: submissions@greyline.net. Website: www.greyline.net. **Contact:** Sara Miller, submissions coordinator.

Needs "Grey Line Entertainment is a full-service motion picture production and literary management company. We offer direct management of all services associated with the exploitation of stories. When our clients' motion picture screenplays are ready for the marketplace, Grey Line Entertainment places them directly with studios or with major co-producers who can assist in packaging cast and/or director before approaching financiers (like Warner Bros., New Line, Fox, or Disney), or broadcasters (HBO, Showtime, etc.)."

How to Contact Query via e-mail only to submissions@greyline.net. "Please review our submissions guidelines available at our website before querying." No attachments. Unsolicited queries OK. "E-mail queries for novels, nonfiction book proposals, screenplays, and treatments should consist of a compelling and business-like letter giving us a brief overview of your story—and a 1-sentence pitch. Be sure to include your return address, and a telephone number. Also include relevant background on yourself, including previous publication or production. Allow 2 weeks for consideration of initial query. No multiple submissions. Treatments and screenplays submitted without a completed and signed Grey Line Submission Form will be discarded. Include SASE for our reply. Submissions without SASE will be discarded. We recommend you register screenplays and treatments with the Copyright Office and/or the Writers Guild of America before submitting your query."

Tips "Your work must be finished and properly edited before seeking our representation (meaning proofread, spell-checked, and rewritten until it's perfect)."

MAINLINE RELEASING

A Film & TV Production and Distribution Co., 301 Arizona Ave., 4th Floor, Santa Monica CA 90401. (310)255-1200. Fax: (310)255-1201. E-mail: joe@mainlinereleasing.com. Website: www.mainlinereleasing.com. **Contact:** Joseph Dickstein, vice president of acquisitions. Estab. 1997.

Needs Produces family films, drama, thrillers, and erotic features.

NITE OWL PRODUCTIONS

126 Hall Rd., Aliquippa PA 15001. (724)775-1993. Fax: (801)881-3017. E-mail: niteowlprods@aol.com; mark@niteowlproductionsltd.com. Website: www.niteowlproductionsltd.com. **Contact:** Bridget Petrella. Estab. 2001.

Needs "We will be producing at least 5-10 feature films in the next 2-5 years. We are searching for polished, well-structured, well-written, and professional-looking screenplays that are ready for production. If your screenplay does not meet these standards, do not send us a query for that screenplay. All screenplays must be in English. Provide a working title for your screenplay. All screenplays must be in standard industry format."

How to Contact "For all submissions, send a 1-page query letter via e-mail or regular mail. The content of your query letter should be succinct and interesting enough to entice us to ask to see more of the project. Single-space your query letters. If our interest is piqued, we will request the completed synopsis and screenplay. Do not send the screenplay to us unless we specifically ask you to do so."

Tips "All submissions must include a dated and signed Submission Release Form or they will be discarded immediately. No exceptions. Page length varies according to the format you are submitting. Screenplays that are too long or short may be considered unprofessional. This is especially true for television because a show needs to squeeze into time slots. All full-length feature film screenplays must be between 80-130 pages in length. 1-hour television spec scripts need to be 55-65 pages in length. No less. No more. A common rule of thumb says 1 script page equals approximately 1 minute on television. Do not send us computer disks. One hard copy of your screenplay will suffice. Do not cheat on your margins. Stay within 1-1.25 inches on all sides. If you cheat, we will notice. The industry standard font style and size is Courier 11-12 point, but similar fonts are acceptable. Proofread your screenplay thoroughly before submitting to avoid senseless mistakes that might pull your reader's attention from the story, such as typos, punctuation, or grammatical errors. Be certain all of your pages are there and in order. Copyright your script with the U.S. Copyright Office before sending it to us or anyone else. Registration with The Writers Guild of America is also strongly suggested. All screenplays must be firmly bound with a cover page that states the title of work and the author(s) name, address, and contact information. Card stock covers are preferred. Send us a copy of your screenplay, as your materials will not be returned to you, regardless of enclosures. Copies will be disposed of properly."

RAINFOREST FILMS

2141 Powers Ferry Rd., Suite 300, Marrietta GA 30067. Fax: (770)953-0848. E-mail: staff@rainforest-films.com. Website: www.rainforestproductions.com.

Needs Rainforest's productions include *Pandora's Box, Chocolate City* and *Trois.* They have also produced a number of music videos for a variety of artists.
How to Contact Submit complete ms. "In order to submit a script, a detailed synopsis and signed release form must be included. Any material sent without the accompanying signed release form will be returned unread. Screenplays are sent to our development department where they are reviewed and discussed. Please allow 90 days for written confirmation and response to your work. All material should be marked 'Attn: Screenplay Submissions.'"

TRI-HUGHES ENTERTAINMENT GROUP

11601 Wilshire Blvd., 5th Floor, Los Angeles CA 90025. (818)592-6379. Fax: (310)575-1890. E-mail: info@trihughes.com. Website: www.trihughes.com. **Producer:** Patrick Hughes. **Contact:** Faye, creative executive. Estab. 2002. Produces 10 movies/year.
How to Contact Send query and synopsis, or submit complete ms; "mostly" agented submissions. Responds in 3 weeks. Does not return submissions.
Needs "Tri-Hughes looks to produce and develop feature-length screenplays, produced stage plays, novels (published only), well-developed pitches, and detailed treatments. Focus is on broad comedies, black comedies, socially smart comedies, family films (family adventure), and ground-breaking, abstract projects, and new writer/directors with an extremely unique and unparalleled point of view. Please do not send a script with, 'this can be made for under a million dollars.' If it can, we suggest you go make it. Don't focus on budget, cast, or locations. The 'story' is key to getting things done here."
Tips "Does not want to see talking-heads projects with no point in sight. Projects that scream, 'You've seen me before!' Projects that try too hard to be different. Dramas, biopics, and science fiction pics. Be yourself. Don't try to be different to get noticed. Never talk about budget and a star that's attached that pre-sold in Egypt for $100 million. We don't care. We care about a 'unique voice,' a filmmaker willing to take risks. Scripts that push the limits without trying for 'shock' value. We care about filmmakers here."

VALEO FILMS INC.

P.O. Box 5876, Longview TX 75644. (903)797-6489. Fax: (903)797-6806. Website: www.valeofilms.com. President: David Ulloa.
Needs Currently considering projects "that contain 1 or more of the following: character or story driven; identifies moral values; romance/love story; educational/documentary; presents the human condition; strong visual imagery; coming of age/learning; or intellectual drama/mystery."
How to Contact Query by e-mail or regular mail. "We require that you provide us with your name, phone number, address, the title of your work, and either a WGA registration number or a copyright number. After receiving this information, we will send you an 'Unsolicited Project Release Letter.' You must then sign and return it with a single copy of your screenplay and/or treatment."
Tips Does not want "projects that contain the following characteristics: one character saves the world; SFX based; highly action based; extreme and grotesque violence; high sexual content; or strong explicit language. Although we do have a vast array of production resources available to us, VFI is a relatively small production company who prefers to limit the number of projects we have in production. Consequently, we tend to be very selective when it comes to selecting new material."

VINTAGE ENTERTAINMENT

1045 Ocean Ave., Penthouse, Santa Monica CA 90403. E-mail: info@govintage.com. Website: www.govintage.com. **Producer/Manager:** Peter Scott. Estab. 1994. "Vintage Entertainment is a film production and boutique management company located in Santa Monica, California. The management side of the company includes motion picture and TV writers, directors, actors, novelists, and new media clientele."
Needs "Vintage Entertainment intends to find talented artists eager to create the Vintage classics of tomorrow. Artists who embrace change, push the envelope. Artists with unique voices who communicate by instinct, not by formula. We seek artists with talent, passion, and craft. We are a small shop."
How to Contact Writers who wish to be considered by Vintage Entertainment must first e-mail a succinct logline describing the screenplay they wish to have reviewed. If we have interest in reading your material, we will send you our submission release form via e-mail."
Tips "Approximately 5% of all artists who approach us get reviewed."

MARKETS

Script Contests

This section contains script contests for both playwrights and screenwriters. Besides cash awards or other prizes, winning a contest can give you credibility when querying an agent. Especially impressive to agents are winners of the more prestigious contests such as the Nicholl Fellowship in Screenwriting, the Chesterfield Writer's Film Project, or the writing-fellowship program sponsored by the Walt Disney Studios and ABC.

Contests can get you recognition from producers or catch the attention of other industry professionals who sponsor or judge the contests. Even making it to the final round of these contests can give you credibility as a screenwriter and should be mentioned in your query letter when you're ready to find an agent. Some contests may even lead directly to representation by an agency as part of the prize package.

Again, it's always a good idea to register your script before submitting it. The Writers Guild of America (WGA) offers a registration service to members and nonmembers alike. Write the WGA for more information on specific agencies, script registration, and membership requirements, or visit them online at www.wga.org.

See Also

Contest deadlines, entry fees, and rules may vary from year to year, so it's a good idea to visit the contest's website or send a SASE requesting its rules and regulations before submitting. (For more information on submitting a contest entry, see The Winning Checklist on page 217.) Contests often require a specific entry form that you may either request by mail or download from the contest's website. Some deadlines are extended at the last minute, so be sure you have the latest information available before sending your submission.

For more listings of script contests, see www.writersmarket.com, www.moviebytes.com, or www.scriptsales.com.

The Winning Checklist

1. **Understand the categories.** Carefully read the writing categories being considered in the contest to determine if it's a good fit for your writing. Select the category (or categories) you enter wisely. Choosing the wrong category can result in a poor—and perhaps unfair—evaluation of your work.

2. **Understand your rights.** Many contests buy one-time publication rights or first rights for manuscripts. Some ask (and may require) all rights, which means that your entry becomes the property of the contest sponsor. Giving up all rights to publish your work is only worth it when the prize or recognition is exceptional. Think twice before making this decision.

3. **Write your very best.** Revise your work multiple times. Edit very carefully.

4. **Follow the rules.** Stick to the word limit. In fact, leave yourself a little breathing room by staying 10-20 words under limit. If the rules say double-space your composition and put your name and address in the top right corner of the page, do it that way.

5. **Enter early.** Judges often read the first few entries with an enthusiasm and excitement that wanes by the 300th composition. Use this knowledge to your advantage; make sure your work is among the early arrivals.

6. **Send the right fee.** Double-check your math when calculating your entry fee. Make sure what you owe corresponds with the amount on the check you enclose.

7. **Arrival insurance.** You can make sure your manuscript arrives at the correct address on time by obtaining a receipt or postal number for tracking your package.

8. **Let it go.** If you realize there's a mistake in your manuscript after you've submitted it, do not send a revision or a new entry.

9. **Be patient.** Keep in mind that running a writing competition takes time. The contest sponsor will notify you as soon as results are available. You won't speed up the process by asking for progress reports by mail, e-mail, or phone calls.

10. **Different strokes.** Every judge looks for different qualities in a manuscript. Don't give in to defeat if your entry doesn't make the winners' list this time. All judging—especially of writing—is subjective. Keep trying.

—*Christine Mersch*

ALBERTA PLAYWRITING COMPETITION

Alberta Playwrights' Network, 2633 Hochwald Ave. SW, Calgary AB T3E 7K2 Canada. (403)269-8564 or (800)268-8564. Fax: (403)265-6773. E-mail: apn@nucleus.com. Website: www.nucleus.com/~apn. Offered annually for unproduced plays with full-length and Discovery categories. Discovery is open only to previously unproduced playwrights. Open only to residents of Alberta. **Deadline: January 15. Charges $40 fee (Canadian).** Prize: Full length: $3,500 (Canadian); Discovery: $1,500 (Canadian); written critique, workshop of winning play, reading of winning plays at a Showcase Conference.

ANNUAL INTERNATIONAL ONE-PAGE PLAY COMPETITION

Lamia Ink!, P.O. Box 202, Prince Street Station, New York NY 10012. Website: www.lamiaink.org. **Contact:** Cortland Jessup, founder/artistic director. Offered annually for previously published or unpublished 1-page plays. Acquires "the rights to publish in our magazine and to be read or performed at the prize awarding festival." Playwright retains copyright. **Deadline: March 15. Charges $2/play or $5 for 3 plays (maximum).** Prize: $200, staged reading, and publication of 12 finalists. There are 3 rounds of judging with invited judges that change from year to year. There are up to 12 judges for finalists round. Open to any writer.

ANNUAL NATIONAL PLAYWRITING CONTEST

Wichita State University, School of Performing Arts, 1845 Fairmount, Wichita KS 67260-0153. (316)978-3368. Fax: (316)978-3202. E-mail: steve.peters@wichita.edu. **Contact:** Dr. Steven J. Peters, contest director. Offered annually for full-length plays (minimum of 90 minutes playing time), or 2-3 short plays on related themes (minimum 90 minutes playing time). **Deadline: February 15.** Guidelines for SASE. Prize: Production by the Wichita State University Theatre. Winner announced April 15. No plays returned after February 15. Open to all undergraduate and graduate students enrolled at any college or university in the US (indicate school affiliation).

N ANNUAL ONE-ACT PLAYWRITING CONTEST

TADA!, 15 W. 28th St., 3rd Floor, New York NY 10001. (212)252-1619, ext. 17. Fax: (212)252-8763. E-mail: playcontest@tadatheater.com. Website: www.tadatheater.com. **Contact:** Emmanuel Wilson, literary manager. Offered annually to encourage playwrights to develop new plays for teen audiences ages 12-18. Call or e-mail for guidelines. Must address teen subjects and issues. Predominantly teen cast. **Deadline: January 4.** Prize: Cash award and staged readings.

N APPALACHIAN FESTIVAL OF PLAYS & PLAYWRIGHTS

Barter Theatre, Box 867, Abingdon VA 24212-0867. (276)619-3314. Fax: (276)619-3335. E-mail: apfestival@bartertheatre.com. Website: www.bartertheatre.com. **Contact:** Derek Davidson. "With the annual Appalachian Festival of New Plays & Playwrights, Barter Theatre wishes to celebrate new, previously unpublished/unproduced plays by playwrights from the Appalachian region (if the playwrights are not from Appalachia, the plays themselves must be about the region)." **Deadline: April 23.** Guidelines for SASE. Prize: $250, a staged reading performed at Barter's Stage II theater, and some transportation compensation and housing during the time of the Festival. There may be an additional award for the best staged readings. Judged by the Barter Theatre's artistic director and associate director.

AUSTIN HEART OF FILM FESTIVAL FEATURE LENGTH SCREENPLAY COMPETITION

1604 Nueces, Austin TX 78701. (512)478-4795. Fax: (512)478-6205. E-mail: info@austinfilmfestival.com. Website: www.austinfilmfestival.com. Offered annually for unpublished screenplays. The Austin Film Festival is looking for quality screenplays which will be read by industry professionals. 2 competitions: Adult/Family Category and Comedy Category. Guidelines for SASE or call (800)310-3378. The writer must hold the rights when submitted; it must be original work. The screenplay must be between 90 and 130 pages. It must be in standard screenplay format (industry standard). **Deadline: May 16. Charges $40 entry fee.** Prize: $5,000 in each category.

BAKER'S PLAYS HIGH SCHOOL PLAYWRITING CONTEST

Baker's Plays, P.O. Box 699222, Quincy MA 02269-9222. (617)745-0805. Fax: (617)745-9891. Website: www.bakersplays.com. **Contact:** Deirdre Shaw, managing editor. Offered annually for unpublished work by high school-age students. Plays can be about any subject, so long as the play can be reasonably produced on the high school stage. Plays may be of any length. Submissions must be accompanied by the signature of the sponsoring high school drama or English teacher, and it is recommended that the play receive a production or a public reading prior to the submission. Multiple submissions and co-authored scripts are welcome. Teachers may not submit a student's work. The ms must be firmly bound, typed, and come with SASE that includes enough postage to cover the return of the ms. Plays that do not come with a SASE will not be returned. Do not send originals; copies only. **Deadline: January 31.** Guidelines for SASE. Prize: 1st Place: $500, and publication by Baker's Plays; 2nd Place: $250; 3rd Place: $100.

N BAY AREA PLAYWRIGHTS FESTIVAL

Produced by Playwrights Foundation, 131 10th St., 3rd Floor, San Francisco CA 94103. (415)626-0453, ext. 106. E-mail: literary@playwrightsfoundation.org. Website: www.playwrightsfoundation.org. **Contact:** Amy Mueller, artistic director; Duca Knezevic, director of literary services. Offered annually for unpublished plays by established and emerging theater writers to support and encourage development of a new work. Unproduced full-length play only. **Deadline: January 15 (postmarked).** Prize: Small stipend and in-depth development process with dramaturg and director, and a professionally staged reading in San Francisco. Open to any writer.

N THE BEVERLY HILLS THEATRE GUILD-JULIE HARRIS PLAYWRIGHT AWARD COMPETITION

P.O. Box 39729, Los Angeles CA 90039-0729. **Contact:** Dick Dotterer. Estab. 1978. "The contest is a national event open to aspiring, emerging, and established playwrights in the United States. Playwrights must be U.S. citizens or legal residents. They may submit one unproduced playscript to the competition, accompanied by a signed application form. No one-acts, musicals or children's plays are eligible." **Deadline: August 1-November 1 (postmark accepted).** Prize: 1st: $3,500; 2nd: $2,500; 3rd: $1,500.

N BIENNIAL PROMISING PLAYWRIGHT CONTEST

Colonial Players, Inc., Box 2167, Annapolis MD 21404. (410)268-7373. **Contact:** Vice President. Offered every 2 years for unpublished full-length plays and adaptations. Open to any aspiring playwright residing in West Virginia, Washington DC, or any of the states descendant from the original 13 colonies (Connecticut, Delaware, Georgia, Maryland, Massachusetts, New Hampshire, New Jersey, New York, North Carolina, Pennsylvania, Rhode Island, South Carolina, and Virginia). Next contest runs September 1-December 1. Guidelines for SASE or online. Prize: $1,000 cash award, weekend workshop with playwright participation, and rehearsed reading.

N BIG BREAK INTERNATIONAL SCREENWRITING COMPETITION

Final Draft, Inc., 26707 W. Aguora Rd., Suite 205, Calabasas CA 91302. (800)231-4055. Fax: (818)995-4422. E-mail: bigbreak@finaldraft.com. Website: www.bigbreakcontest.com. **Contact:** Liz Alani, contest director. Estab. 2000. Annual global screenwriting competition designed to promote emerging creative talent. **Deadline: Febraury 15-June 15. Charges $40-60, depending on entry date.** Guidelines for SASE or online. Prize: Grand-prize winner is awarded $10,000, meetings with industry professionals and additional prizes worth over $5,000. Past winning scripts have been produced or optioned. The top 10 finalists will receive a copy of Final Draft scriptwriting software, Microsoft software, a screenwriting course from Gothan Writers' Workshop, a one-year subscription to *Fade In* and *Scr(i)pt* magazines, and a $50 gift certificate from The Writers Store. Judged by industry professionals. Open to any writer.

BUNTVILLE CREW'S AWARD BLUE

Buntville Crew, 118 N. Railroad Ave., Buckley IL 60918-0445. E-mail: buntville@yahoo.fr. **Contact:** Steven Packard, artistic director. Presented annually for the best unpublished/unproduced play script, under 15 pages, written by a student enrolled in any Illinois high school. Submit 1 copy of the script in standard play format, a brief biography, and a SASE (scripts will not be returned). Include name, address, telephone number, age, and name of school. **Deadline: May 31.** Guidelines for SASE. Prize: Cash prize, and possible productions in Buckley and/or New York City. Judged by panel selected by the theater.

BUNTVILLE CREW'S PRIX HORS PAIR

Buntville Crew, 118 N. Railroad Ave., Buckley IL 60918-0445. E-mail: buntville@yahoo.fr. **Contact:** Steven Packard, artistic director. Annual award for unpublished/unproduced play script under 15 pages. Plays may be in English, French, German, or Spanish (no translations, no adaptations). Submit 1 copy of the script in standard play format, a résumé, and a SASE (scripts will not be returned). Include name, address, and telephone number. **Deadline: May 31.** Guidelines for SASE. **Charges $8.** Prize: $200; possible production in Buckley and/or New York City. Judged by panel selected by the theater. Open to any writer.

CAA CAROL BOLT AWARD FOR DRAMA

Canadian Authors Association with the support of the Playwrights Guild of Canada and Playwrights Canada Press, 320 S. Shores Rd., P.O. Box 419, Campbellford ON K0L 1L0 Canada. (705)653-0323 or (866)216-6222. Fax: (705)653-0593. E-mail: admin@canauthors.org. Website: www.canauthors.org. **Contact:** Alec McEachern. Annual contest for the best English-language play for adults by an author who is Canadian or landed immigrant. Submissions should be previously published or performed in the year prior to the giving of the award. Open to Canadian citizens or landed immigrants. **Deadline: December 15, except for plays published or performed in December, in which case the deadline is January 15.** Guidelines for SASE. **Charges $35 (Canadian funds) fee.** Prize: $1,000, and a silver medal. Judged by a trustee for the award (appointed by the CAA). The trustee appoints up to 3 judges. The identities of the trustee and judges are confidential. Short lists are not made public. Decisions of the trustee and judges are final, and they may choose not to award a prize.

CALIFORNIA YOUNG PLAYWRIGHTS CONTEST

Playwrights Project, 450 B St., Suite 1020, San Diego CA 92101-8093. (619)239-8222. Fax: (619)239-8225. E-mail: write@playwrightsproject.com. Website: www.playwrightsproject.com. **Contact:** Cecelia Kouma, managing director. Offered annually for previously unpublished plays by young writers to stimulate young people to create dramatic works, and to nurture promising writers. Scripts must be a minimum of 10 standard typewritten pages; send 2 copies. Scripts will *not* be returned. All entrants receive detailed evaluation letter. Writers must be California residents under age 19 as of the deadline date. **Deadline: June 1.** Guidelines online. Prize: Professional production of 3-5 winning plays at the Old Globe in San Diego, plus royalty.

COE COLLEGE PLAYWRITING FESTIVAL

Coe College, 1220 First Ave. NE, Cedar Rapids IA 52402-5092. (319)399-8624. Fax: (319)399-8557. E-mail: swolvert@coe.edu. Website: www.public.coe.edu/departments/theatre/. **Contact:** Susan Wolverton. Estab. 1993. Offered biennially for unpublished work to provide a venue for new works for the stage. "There is usually a theme for the festival. We are interested in full-length productions, not one acts or musicals. There are no specific criteria although a current résumé and synopsis is requested." Open to any writer. **Deadline: November 1. Notification: January 15.** Guidelines for SASE. Prize: $325, plus 1-week residency as guest artist with airfare, room and board provided.

THE CUNNINGHAM COMMISSION FOR YOUTH THEATRE

The Theatre School, DePaul University, 2135 N. Kenmore, Chicago IL 60614-4111. (773)325-7938. Fax: (773)325-7920. E-mail: lgoetsch@depaul.edu. Website: theatreschool.depaul.edu/programs/prize.htm. **Contact:** Cunningham Commission Selection Committee. Chicago-area playwrights only. Commission will result in a play for younger audiences that "affirms the centrality of religion, broadly defined, and the human quest for meaning, truth, and community." **Deadline: December 1.** Guidelines for SASE or online. Prize: $5,000 ($2,000 when commission is contracted, $1,000 if script moves to workshop, $2,000 as royalty if script is produced by The Theatre School). Open to writers whose primary residence is in the Chicago area.

DAYTON PLAYHOUSE FUTUREFEST

The Dayton Playhouse, 1301 E. Siebenthaler Ave., Dayton OH 45414-5357. (937)333-7469. Website: www.daytonplayhouse.com. **Contact:** Dave Seyer, executive director. "Three plays selected for full productions, 3 for readings at July FutureFest weekend; the 6 authors will be given travel and lodging to attend the festival." Professionally adjudicated. Guidelines for SASE or online. **Deadline: October 30.** Prize: $1,000; and $100 to the other 5 playwrights.

DRURY UNIVERSITY ONE-ACT PLAY CONTEST

Drury University, 900 N. Benton Ave., Springfield MO 65802-3344. E-mail: msokol@drury.edu. **Contact:** Mick Sokol. Offered in even-numbered years for unpublished and professionally unproduced plays. One play/playwright. Guidelines for SASE or by e-mail. **Deadline: December 1.**

DUBUQUE FINE ARTS PLAYERS ANNUAL ONE-ACT PLAY CONTEST

Dubuque Fine Arts Players, 1686 Lawndale, Dubuque IA 52001. E-mail: gary.arms@clarke.edu. **Contact:** Gary Arms. "We select 3 one-act plays each year. We award cash prizes of up to $600 for a winning entry. We produce the winning plays in August." Offered annually for unpublished work. Guidelines and application form for SASE. **Deadline: January 31. Charges $10.** Prize: 1st Prize: $600; 2nd Prize: $300; 3rd Prize: $200. Judged by 3 groups who read all the plays; each play is read at least twice. Plays that score high enough enter the second round. The top 10 plays are read by a panel consisting of 3 directors and 2 other final judges. Open to any writer.

EMERGING PLAYWRIGHT'S AWARD

Urban Stages, 17 E. 47th St., New York NY 10017-1920. (212)421-1380. Fax: (212)421-1387. E-mail: tlreilly@urbanstages.org. Website: www.urbanstages.org. **Contact:** T.L. Reilly, producing director. Estab. 1986. Submissions required to be unproduced in New York City. Send script, letter of introduction, production history, author's name, résumé, and SASE. Submissions accepted year-round. Plays selected in August and January for award consideration. One submission/person. **Deadline: Ongoing. Charges $5.** Prize: $1,000 (in lieu of royalties), and a staged production of winning play in New York City. Open to US residents only.

ESSENTIAL THEATRE PLAYWRITING AWARD

The Essential Theatre, P.O. Box 8172, Atlanta GA 30306. (404)212-0815. E-mail: pmhardy@aol.com. Website: www.essentialtheatre.com. **Contact:** Peter Hardy. Offered annually for unproduced, full-length plays by Georgia writers. No limitations as to style or subject matter. **Deadline: January 13.** Prize: $400, and full production.

SHUBERT FENDRICH MEMORIAL PLAYWRITING CONTEST

Pioneer Drama Service, Inc., P.O. Box 4267, Englewood CO 80155. (303)779-4035. Fax: (303)779-4315. E-mail: playwrights@pioneerdrama.com. Website: www.pioneerdrama.com. **Contact:** Lori Conary, assistant editor. Offered annually for unpublished, but previously produced, submissions to encourage the development of quality theatrical material for educational and community theater. Rights acquired only if published. Authors already published by Pioneer Drama are not eligible. **Deadline: March 1 (postmarked).** Guidelines for SASE or online. Prize: $1,000 royalty advance, publication.

N FIREHOUSE THEATRE PROJECT NEW PLAY COMPETITION

The Firehouse Theatre Project, 1609 W. Broad St., Richmond VA 23220. (804)355-2001. E-mail: harry@firehousetheatre.org. Website: www.firehousetheatre.org. **Contact:** Literary Manager FTP. Calls for previously unpublished full-length works with non-musical and non-children's themes. Submissions must be in standard play format. Scripts should be accompanied by a letter of recommendation from a company or individual familiar with your work. Submissions must be unpublished. Visit website for complete submission guidelines. "We're receptive to unusual, but well-wrought works." **Deadline: August 31.** Prize: 1st Prize: $1,000; 2nd Prize: $500.

FULL-LENGTH PLAY COMPETITION

West Coast Ensemble, P.O. Box 38728, Los Angeles CA 90038. (323)876-9337. Fax: (323)876-8916. Website: www.wcensemble.org. **Contact:** Les Hanson, artistic director. Offered annually "to nurture, support, and encourage" unpublished playwrights. Permission to present the play is granted if work is selected as finalist. **Deadline: December 31.** Guidelines for SASE. Prize: $500, and presentation of play.

JOHN GASSNER MEMORIAL PLAYWRITING COMPETITION

New England Theatre Conference, PMB 502, 198 Tremont St., Boston MA 02116. E-mail: mail@netconline.org. Website: www.netconline.org. Offered annually to unpublished full-length plays and scripts. Open to New England residents and NETC members. Playwrights living outside New England may participate by joining NETC. **Deadline: April 15.** Guidelines for SASE. **Charges $10 fee.** Prize: 1st Place: $1,000; 2nd Place: $500.

GOVERNOR GENERAL'S LITERARY AWARD FOR DRAMA

Canada Council for the Arts, 350 Albert St., P.O. Box 1047, Ottawa ON K1P 5V8 Canada. (613)566-4414, ext. 5576. Fax: (613)566-4410. E-mail: joanne.larocque-poirier@canadacouncil.ca. Website: www.canadacouncil.ca/prizes/ggla. **Contact:** Joanne Larocque-Poirier. Offered for the best English-language and the best French-language work of drama by a Canadian. Submissions in English must be published between September 1, 2004 and September 30, 2005; submissions in French between July 1, 2004 and June 30, 2005. Publishers submit titles for consideration. **Deadline: March 15 or August 7, 2005, depending on the book's publication date.** Prize: Each laureate receives $15,000, and nonwinning finalists receive $1,000.

AURAND HARRIS MEMORIAL PLAYWRITING AWARD

The New England Theatre Conference, Inc., PMB 502, 198 Tremont St., Boston MA 02116-4750. (617)851-8535. E-mail: mail@netconline.org. Website: www.netconline.org. Offered annually for an unpublished full-length play for young audiences. Guidelines for SASE. "No phone calls, please." Open to New England residents and/or members of the New England Theatre Conference. **Deadline: May 1.** Guidelines for SASE. **Charges $20 fee.** Prize: 1st Place: $1,000; 2nd Place: $500. Open to any writer.

HENRICO THEATRE COMPANY ONE-ACT PLAYWRITING COMPETITION

Henrico Recreation & Parks, P.O. Box 27032, Richmond VA 23273. (804)501-5138. Fax: (804)501-5284. E-mail: per22@co.henrico.va.us. Website: www.co.henrico.va.us/rec. **Contact:** Amy A. Perdue. Offered annually for previously unpublished or unproduced plays or musicals to produce new dramatic works in one-act form. "Scripts with small casts and simpler sets given preference. Controversial themes and excessive language should be avoided." **Deadline: July 1.** Guidelines for SASE. Prize: $300; Runner-Up: $200. Winning entries may be produced; videotape sent to author.

N HOLLYWOOD SCREENPLAY AWARDS

433 N. Camden Dr., Suite 600, Beverly Hills CA 90210. (310)288-3040. Fax: (310)288-0060. E-mail: hollyinfo@hollywoodnetwork.com. Website: www.hollywoodawards.com. Annual contest that bridges the gap between writers and the established entertainment industry and provides winning screenwriters what they need most: access to key decision-makers. Only non-produced, non-optioned screenplays can be submitted. **Deadline: March 31.** Guidelines for SASE. **Charges $55 fee.** Prize: 1st Prize: $1,000; 2nd Prize: $500; 3rd Prize: $250. Scripts are also introduced to major studios and winners receive 2 VIP passes to the Hollywood Film Festival. Judged by reputable industry professionals (producers, development executives, story analysts). Open to any writer.

JEWEL BOX THEATRE PLAYWRIGHTING COMPETITION

Jewel Box Theatre, 3700 N. Walker, Oklahoma City OK 73118-7099. (405)521-1786. **Contact:** Charles Tweed, production director. Estab. 1982. Offered annually for full-length plays. Send SASE in October for guidelines. **Deadline: January 15.** Prize: $500.

N MARC A. KLEIN PLAYWRITING AWARD FOR STUDENTS

Dept. of Theater and Dance, Case Western Reserve University, 10900 Euclid Ave., Cleveland OH 44106-7077. (216)368-4868. Fax: (216)368-5184. E-mail: ksg@case.edu. Website: www.cwru.edu/artsci/thtr. **Contact:** Ron Wilson, reading committee chair. Estab. 1975. Offered annually for an unpublished, professionally unproduced full-length play, by a student at an American college or university. **Deadline: December 1.** Prize: $1,000, which includes $500 to cover residency expenses; production.

KUMU KAHUA/UHM THEATRE DEPARTMENT PLAYWRITING CONTEST

Kumu Kahua Theatre, Inc./University of Hawaii at Manoa, Dept. of Theatre and Dance, 46 Merchant St., Honolulu HI 96813. (808)536-4222. Fax: (808)536-4226. E-mail: kkt@pixi.com. Website: www.kumukahua.com. **Contact:** Harry Wong III, artistic director. Offered annually for unpublished work to honor full-length and short plays. Guidelines available every September. First 2 categories open to residents and nonresidents. For Hawaii Prize, plays must be set in Hawaii or deal with some aspect of the Hawaiian experience. For Pacific Rim prize, plays must deal with the Pacific Islands, Pacific Rim, or Pacific/Asian-American experience—short plays only considered in 3rd category. **Deadline: January 2.** Prize: $500 (Hawaii Prize); $400 (Pacific Rim); $200 (Resident).

L.A. DESIGNERS' THEATRE-COMMISSIONS

L.A. Designers' Theatre, P.O. Box 1883, Studio City CA 91614-0883. (323)650-9600 or (323)654-2700 T.D.D. Fax: (323)654-3210. E-mail: ladesigners@juno.com. **Contact:** Richard Niederberg, artistic director. Quarterly contest "to promote new work and push it onto the conveyor belt to filmed or videotaped entertainment." All submissions must be registered with copyright office and be unpublished. Material will not be returned. "Do not submit anything that will not fit in a #10 envelope. No rules, guidelines, fees, or entry forms. Just present an idea that can be commissioned into a full work." Proposals for uncompleted works are encouraged. Unpopular political, religious, social, or other themes are encouraged; 'street' language and nudity are acceptable. Open to any writer. **Deadline: March 15, June 15, September 15, December 15.** Prize: Production or publication of the work in the Los Angeles market. "We only want 'first refusal rights.'"

LOVE CREEK ANNUAL SHORT PLAY FESTIVAL

Love Creek Productions, % Granville, 162 Nesbit St., Weehawken NJ 07086-6817. E-mail: creekread@aol.com. **Contact:** Cynthia Granville-Callahan, festival manager. Estab. 1985. *E-mail address is for information only.* Annual festival for unpublished plays, unproduced in New York in the previous year. An author may submit no more than 2 English language scripts per submission packet, each not to exceed 40 minutes in length, except for monologues or any one-person plays, which should be 2-20 minutes in length. "We established the Festival as a playwriting competition in which scripts are judged on their merits in performance." All entries must specify "festival" on envelope and must include letter giving permission to produce script, if chosen, and stating whether equity showcase is acceptable. "We are giving strong preference to scripts featuring females in major roles in casts which are predominantly female." **Deadline: Ongoing.** Guidelines for SASE. Prize: Cash prize awarded to overall winner.

MAXIM MAZUMDAR NEW PLAY COMPETITION

Alleyway Theatre, One Curtain Up Alley, Buffalo NY 14202-1911. (716)852-2600. Fax: (716)852-2266. E-mail: email@alleyway.com. Website: alleyway.com. **Contact:** Literary Manager. Estab. 1990. Annual competition. Full Length: Not less than 90 minutes, no more than 10 performers. One-Act: Less than 20 minutes, no more than 6 performers. Children's plays. Musicals must be accompanied by audio tape. Finalists announced October 1.

"Playwrights may submit work directly. There is no entry form. Annual playwright's **fee $5**; may submit 1 in each category, but pay only 1 fee. Please specify if submission is to be included in competition. Alleyway Theatre must receive first production credit in subsequent printings and productions." **Deadline: July 1.** Prize: Full length: $400, production, and royalties; One-act: $100, production, plus royalties.

McKNIGHT ADVANCEMENT GRANT

The Playwrights' Center, 2301 Franklin Ave. E., Minneapolis MN 55406-1099. (612)332-7481, ext. 10. Fax: (612)332-6037. E-mail: info@pwcenter.org. Website: www.pwcenter.org. **Contact:** Kristen Gandrow, director of new play development. Offered annually for either published or unpublished playwrights to recognize those whose work demonstrates exceptional artistic merit and potential and whose primary residence is in the state of Minnesota. The grants are intended to significantly advance recipients' art and careers, and can be used to support a wide variety of expenses. Applications available December 1. Guidelines for SASE. Additional funds of up to $2,000 are available for workshops and readings. The Playwrights' Center evaluates each application and forwards finalists to a panel of 3 judges from the national theater community. Applicant must have been a citizen or permanent resident of the US and a legal resident of the state of Minnesota since July 1, 2004. (Residency must be maintained during fellowship year.) Applicant must have had a minimum of 1 work fully produced by a professional theater at the time of application. **Deadline: February 4.** Prize: $25,000 which can be used to support a wide variety of expenses, including writing time, artistic costs of residency at a theater or arts organization, travel and study, production, or presentation.

McLAREN MEMORIAL COMEDY PLAY WRITING COMPETITION

Midland Community Theatre, 2000 W. Wadley, Midland TX 79705. (432)682-2544. Fax: (432)682-6136. Website: www.mctmidland.org. **Contact:** Alathea Blischke, McLaren co-chair. Estab. 1990. Offered annually in 2 divisions: one-act and full-length. All entries must be comedies for adults, teens, or children; musical comedies accepted. Work must have never been professionally produced or published. See website for competition guidelines and required entry form. **Charges $15 fee/script.** Prize: $400 for winning full-length play; $200 for winning one-act play; staged readings for finalists in each category.

MOVING ARTS PREMIERE ONE-ACT COMPETITION

Moving Arts, 514 S. Spring St., Los Angeles CA 90013-2304. (213)622-8906. Fax: (213)622-8946. E-mail: treynichols@movingarts.org. Website: www.movingarts.org. **Contact:** Trey Nichols, literary director. Offered annually for unproduced one-act plays in the Los Angeles area and "is designed to foster the continued development of one-act plays." All playwrights are eligible except Moving Arts resident artists. Guidelines for SASE or by e-mail. **Deadline: February 1 (postmarked). Charges $10 fee/script.** Prize: 1st Place: $200, plus a full production with a 4-8 week run; 2nd and 3rd Place: Program mention and possible production.

N MOXIE FILMS/NEW CENTURY (PLAYWRITING)

New Century Writer, 107 Suffolk St., Studio #517, New York NY 10002. (212)982-5008. Fax: (212)353-3707. E-mail: stageplay@moxie-films.com. Website: www.moxie-films.com. Offered annually to discover and encourage emerging writers of stage plays and musicals. All genres. Guidelines/entry form on website. **Deadline: June 30. Charges $25 entry fee.** Prize: 1st Place: $1,500 and New York City production; 2nd Place: $500 and New York City reading; 3rd Place: $250 and New York City reading. Open to all playwrights, both nonproduced and those with a limited production history.

N MOXIE FILMS/NEW CENTURY (SCREENWRITING)

107 Suffolk St., Studio #517, New York NY 10002. (212)982-5008. Fax: (212)353-3707. E-mail: screenplay@moxie-films.com. Website: www.moxie-films.com. Offered annually to discover and encourage emerging writers of screenplays, TV scripts, TV movie scripts, and musicals. All genres, 75-130 pages. Guidelines/entry form available on website. **Deadline: September 30. Charges $25 entry fee.** Prize: 1st Place: $3,000 and option agreement; 2nd Place: $500 and public reading; 3rd Place: $250 and public reading. All winners receive management representation. Open to all writers, both nonproduced and those with limited production history.

MUSICAL STAIRS

West Coast Ensemble, P.O. Box 38728, Los Angeles CA 90038. (323)876-9337. Fax: (323)876-8916. **Contact:** Les Hanson. Offered annually for unpublished writers "to nurture, support, and encourage musical creators." Permission to present the musical is granted if work is selected as finalist. **Deadline: June 30.** Prize: $500, and presentation of musical.

NATIONAL AUDIO DRAMA SCRIPT COMPETITION

National Audio Theatre Festivals, 115 Dikeman St., Hempstead NY 11150. (516)483-8321. Fax: (516)538-7583. Website: www.natf.org. **Contact:** Sue Zizza. Offered annually for unpublished radio scripts. "NATF is particularly interested in stories that deserve to be told because they enlighten, intrigue, or simply make us laugh out loud. Contemporary scripts with strong female roles, multi-cultural casting, and diverse viewpoints will be favorably received." Preferred length is 25 minutes. Guidelines on website. Open to any writer. NATF will have the right to produce the scripts for the NATF Live Performance Workshop; however, NATF makes no commitment to produce any script. The authors will retain all other rights to their work. **Deadline: November 15. Charges $25 fee (US currency only).** Prize: $800 split between 2-4 authors, and free workshop production participation.

NATIONAL CANADIAN ONE-ACT PLAYWRITING COMPETITION

Ottawa Little Theatre, 400 King Edward Ave., Ottawa ON K1N 7M7 Canada. (613)233-8948. Fax: (613)233-8027. E-mail: olt@on-aibn.com. Website: www.o-l-t.com. **Contact:** Elizabeth Holden, office administrator. Estab. 1913. Purpose is "to encourage literary and dramatic talent in Canada." Guidelines for #10 SASE with Canadian postage or #10 SAE with 1 IRC. **Deadline: August 31.** Prize: 1st Place: $1,000; 2nd Place: $700; 3rd Place: $500.

NATIONAL CHILDREN'S THEATRE FESTIVAL

Actors' Playhouse at the Miracle Theatre, 280 Miracle Mile, Coral Gables FL 33134. (305)444-9293. Fax: (305)444-4181. E-mail: maulding@actorsplayhouse.org. Website: www.actorsplayhouse.org. **Contact:** Earl Maulding. Offered annually for unpublished musicals for young audiences. Target age is between 3-12. Script length should be 45-60 minutes. Maximum of 8 actors to play any number of roles. Settings which lend themselves to simplified scenery. Bilingual (English/Spanish) scripts are welcomed. Call or visit website for guidelines. Open to any writer. **Deadline: June 1. Charges $10 fee.** Prize: 1st Place: $500, and full production.

NATIONAL LATINO PLAYWRIGHTS AWARD

Arizona Theatre Co., 40 E. 14th St., Tucson AZ 85701. (520)884-8210, ext. 5510. Fax: (520)628-9129. E-mail: eromero@arizonatheatre.org. Website: www.arizonatheatre.org. **Contact:** Elaine Romero, playwright-in-residence. Offered annually for unproduced, unpublished plays over 50 pages in length. "The plays may be in English, bilingual, or in Spanish (with English translation). The award recognizes exceptional full-length plays by Latino playwrights on any subject." Open to Latino playwrights currently residing in the US, its territories, and/or Mexico. **Deadline: December 30.** Guidelines for SASE or via e-mail. Prize: $1,000.

NATIONAL ONE-ACT PLAYWRITING COMPETITION

Little Theatre of Alexandria, 600 Wolfe St., Alexandria VA 22314. Website: www.thelittletheatre.com/oneact. Estab. 1978. Offered annually to encourage original writing for theater. Submissions must be original, unpublished, unproduced, one-act stage plays. "We try to produce top 2 or 3 winners." Guidelines for SASE or on website. **Deadline: Submit scripts for contest from January 1-October 31. Charges $20/play; 2-play limit.** Prize: 1st Place: $350; 2nd Place: $250; 3rd Place: $150.

NATIONAL PLAYWRITING COMPETITION

Young Playwrights, Inc., 306 W. 38th St., Suite 300, New York NY 10018. (212)594-5440. Fax: (212)594-5441. E-mail: writeaplay@aol.com. Website: youngplaywrights.org. **Contact:** Literary Department. Offered annually for stage plays of any length (no musicals, screenplays, or adaptations). Writers ages 18 or younger (as of deadline) are invited to send scripts. **Deadline: December 1.** Prize: Invitation to week-long Writers' Conference in New York City (all expenses paid) and off-Broadway presentation.

NATIONAL TEN-MINUTE PLAY CONTEST

Actors Theatre of Louisville, 316 W. Main St., Louisville KY 40202-4218. (502)584-1265. E-mail: tpalmer@actorstheatre.org. Website: www.actorstheatre.org. **Contact:** Tanya Palmer, literary manager. Offered annually for previously (professionally) unproduced 10-minute plays (10 pages or less). "Entries must *not* have had an Equity or Equity-waiver production." One submission/playwright. Scripts are not returned. Please write or call for submission guidelines. Open to US residents. **Deadline: December 1 (postmarked).** Prize: $1,000.

DON AND GEE NICHOLL FELLOWSHIPS IN SCREENWRITING

Academy of Motion Picture Arts & Sciences, 1313 N. Vine St., Hollywood CA 90028-8107. (310)247-3010. E-mail: nicholl@oscars.org. Website: www.oscars.org/nicholl. **Contact:** Greg Beal, program coordinator. Estab. 1985. Offered annually for unproduced screenplays to identify talented new screenwriters. **Deadline: May 1. Charges $30 fee.** Prize: Up to five $30,000 fellowships awarded each year. Open to writers who have not earned more than $5,000 writing for films or TV.

OGLEBAY INSTITUTE TOWNGATE THEATRE PLAYWRITING CONTEST

Oglebay Institute, Stifel Fine Arts Center, 1330 National Rd., Wheeling WV 26003. (304)242-7700. Fax: (304)242-7747. Website: www.oionline.com. **Contact:** Kate H. Crosbie, director of performing arts. Estab. 1976. Offered annually for unpublished works. "All full-length nonmusical plays that have never been professionally produced or published are eligible." Open to any writer. **Deadline: January 1; winner announced May 31.** Guidelines for SASE. Prize: Run of play and cash award.

ONE ACT MARATHON

Attic Theatre Ensemble, 5429 W. Washington Blvd., Los Angeles CA 90016-1112. (323)525-0600. E-mail: info@attictheatre.org. Website: www.attictheatre.org. **Contact:** Literary Manager. Offered annually for unpublished and unproduced work. Scripts should be intended for mature audiences. Length should not exceed 45 minutes. Guidelines for SASE or online. **Deadline: December 31. Charges $15.** Prize: 1st Place: $250; 2nd Place: $100.

MILDRED & ALBERT PANOWSKI PLAYWRITING AWARD

Forest Roberts Theatre, Northern Michigan University, Marquette MI 49855-5364. (906)227-2559. Fax: (906)227-2567. Website: www.nmu.edu/theatre. **Contact:** David Hansen, award coordinator. Estab. 1977. Offered annually for unpublished, unproduced, full-length plays. Guidelines and application for SASE. **Deadline: August 15-November 15 (due at office on the 15th).** Prize: $2,000, a fully-mounted production, and transportation to Marquette to serve as Artist-in-Residence the week of the show.

PERISHABLE THEATRE'S WOMEN'S PLAYWRITING FESTIVAL

P.O. Box 23132, Providence RI 02903. (401)331-2695. Fax: (401)331-7811. E-mail: wpf@perishable.org. Website: www.perishable.org. **Contact:** Rebecca Wolff, festival coordinator. Offered annually for unproduced, one-act plays (up to 30 minutes in length when fully produced) to encourage women playwrights. **Deadline: October 15 (postmarked).** Guidelines for SASE. **Charges $5 fee/playwright (limit 2 plays/playwright).** Prize: $500, and travel to Providence. Judged blind by reading committee, the festival director, and the artistic director of the theater. Open to women playwrights exclusively.

PETERSON EMERGING PLAYWRIGHT COMPETITION

Catawba College Theatre Arts Department, 2300 W. Innes St., Salisbury NC 28144. (704)637-4440. Fax: (704)637-4207. E-mail: lfkesler@catawba.edu. Website: www.catawba.edu. **Contact:** Linda Kesler, theatre arts department staff. Offered annually for full-length unpublished work "to assist emerging playwrights in the development of new scripts, hopefully leading to professional production. Competition is open to all subject matter except children's plays. Musicals are accepted. Playwrights may submit more than 1 entry." Guidelines for SASE or by e-mail. **Deadline: December 1 (postmarked).** Prize: Production of the winning play at Catawba College; $2,000 cash award; transportation to and from Catawba College for workshop and performance; lodging and food while in residence; professional response to the performance of the play. Open to any writer.

ROBERT J. PICKERING AWARD FOR PLAYWRIGHTING EXCELLENCE

Coldwater Community Theater, % 89 Division, Coldwater MI 49036. (517)279-7963. Fax: (517)279-8095. **Contact:** J. Richard Colbeck, committee chairperson. Estab. 1982. Previously unproduced monetarily. "To encourage playwrights to submit their work, to present a previously unproduced play in full production." Submit script with SASE. "We reserve the right to produce winning script." **Deadline: December 31.** Guidelines for SASE. Prize: 1st Place: $300; 2nd Place: $100; 3rd Place: $50.

PLAYHOUSE ON THE SQUARE NEW PLAY COMPETITION

Playhouse on the Square, 51 S. Cooper, Memphis TN 38104. **Contact:** Jackie Nichols. Submissions required to be unproduced. **Deadline: April 1.** Guidelines for SASE. Prize: $500, and production.

N PLAYS FOR THE 21ST CENTURY

Playwrights Theater, 6732 Orangewood Dr., Dallas TX 75248-5024. E-mail: info@playwrightstheater.org. Website: www.playwrightstheater.org. **Contact:** Jack Marshall. Annual contest for unpublished or professionally unproduced plays (at time of submission). **Deadline: February 28. Charges $20.** Prize: $1,500 first prize; $500 each for second and third prizes. First prize receives a rehearsed reading. The judges decide on readings for second and third prizes. "Winners and their bios and contact info are posted on our website with a 15-page sample of the play (with playwright's permission)." Judged by an outside panel of 3 theater professionals. The judges are different each year. All rights remain with the author. Open to any writer.

PLAYWRIGHT DISCOVERY AWARD

VSA Arts, 1300 Connecticut Ave. NW, Suite 700, Washington DC 20036. (202)628-2800. Fax: (202)737-0725. E-mail: info@vsarts.org. Website: www.vsarts.org. **Contact:** Director, Performing Arts. Invites students with and without disabilities (grades 6-12) to submit a one-act play that explores the theme of disability. Recipients of the award will receive a scholarship and the opportunity to have their play produced at the John F. Kennedy Center for the Performing Arts in Washington, DC. **Deadline: April 15.**

PLAYWRIGHTS/SCREENWRITERS FELLOWSHIPS

NC Arts Council, Dept. of Cultural Resources, Raleigh NC 27699-4632. (919)715-1519. Fax: (919)733-4834. E-mail: debbie.mcgill@ncmail.net. Website: www.ncarts.org. **Contact:** Deborah McGill, literature director. Offered every even year for a play to support the development and creation of new work. **Deadline: November 1.** Guidelines online. Prize: $8,000 grant. Judged by a panel of film and theater professionals (playwrights, screenwriters, directors, producers, etc.). Artists must be current North Carolina residents who have lived in the state for at least 1 year as of the application deadline. Grant recipients must maintain their North Carolina status during the grant year and may not pursue academic or professional degrees during that period.

PRINCESS GRACE AWARDS PLAYWRIGHT FELLOWSHIP

Princess Grace Foundation—USA, 150 E. 58th St., 25th Floor, New York NY 10155. (212)317-1470. Fax: (212)317-1473. E-mail: pgfusa@pgfusa.com. Website: www.pgfusa.com. **Contact:** Christine Giancatarino, grants coordinator. Offered annually for unpublished, unproduced submissions to support playwright-through-residency program with New Dramatists, Inc., located in New York City. Entrants must be U.S. citizens or have permanent U.S. status. Guidelines for SASE or on website. **Deadline: March 31.** Prize: $7,500, plus residency with New Dramatists, Inc., in New York City, and representation/publication by Samuel French, Inc.

RICHARD RODGERS AWARDS IN MUSICAL THEATER

American Academy of Arts and Letters, 633 W. 155th St., New York NY 10032-7599. (212)368-5900. Fax: (212)491-4615. **Contact:** Lydia Kaim. Estab. 1978. The Richard Rodgers Awards subsidize full productions, studio productions, and staged readings by nonprofit theaters in New York City of works by composers and writers who are not already established in the field of musical theater. Authors must be citizens or permanent residents of the US. Guidelines and application for SASE. **Deadline: November 1.**

N MORTON R. SARETT NATIONAL PLAYWRITING COMPETITION

UNLV Fine Arts College/Theatre Dept., 4505 Maryland Pkwy., Las Vegas NV 89154-5036. (702)895-3666. Fax: (702)895-0833. E-mail: stacey.jansen@ccmail.nevada.edu. Website: www.theatre.unlv.edu. **Contact:** Dr. Jeffrey Koep, Dean of the College of Fine Arts at UNLV. Original, innovative, full-length plays on any subject in English (or musicals meeting the same standards) which have not been previously produced, adapted or published may be entered in this competition. Contest occurs every two years. **Deadline: February 1.** Guidelines for SASE. Prize: $3,000, plus travel and housing to attend rehearsals and the opening performance. The play will be produced by the Department of Theatre at UNLV. Manuscripts chosen from an initial screening will be submitted to a national panel of judges for the final reading and selection. An announced winner is not mandatory for every playwriting competition. The decision of the national judges will be final. Open to any writer.

SCRIPTAPALOOZA SCREENWRITING COMPETITION

Supported by Writers Guild of America and sponsored by Write Brothers, Inc., 7775 Sunset Blvd., PMB #200, Hollywood CA 90046. (323)654-5809. E-mail: info@scriptapalooza.com. Website: www.scriptapalooza.com. Annual contest open to unpublished scripts from any genre. Open to any writer, 18 or older. Submit 1 copy of a 90-130-page screenplay. Body pages must be numbered, and scripts must be in industry-standard format. All entered scripts will be read and judged by over 50 production companies. **Deadline: Early Deadline: January 5; Deadline: March 7; Late Deadline: April 15.** Guidelines for SASE. **Charges Early Deadline Fee: $40; Fee: $45; Late Deadline Fee: $50.** Prize: 1st Place: $10,000, and software package from Write Brothers, Inc; 2nd and 3rd Place, and 10 Runners-Up: Software package from Write Brothers, Inc. The top 13 scripts will be considered by over 50 production companies.

N REVA SHINER FULL-LENGTH PLAY CONTEST

Bloomington Playwrights Project, 312 S. Washington St., Bloomington IN 47401. (812)334-1188. E-mail: bppwrite@newplays.org. Website: www.newplays.org. **Contact:** Literary Manager. Annual award for unpublished/unproduced plays. The Bloomington Playwrights Project is a script-developing organization. Winning playwrights are expected to become part of the development process, working with the director in person or via long-distance. **Deadline: January 15.** Guidelines for SASE. **Charges $5 reading fee.** Prize: $500, a reading, and possible production. Judged by the literary committee of the BPP. Open to any writer.

SIENA COLLEGE INTERNATIONAL PLAYWRIGHTS COMPETITION

Siena College Theatre Program, 515 Loudon Rd., Loudonville NY 12211-1462. (518)783-2381. Fax: (518)783-2381. E-mail: maciag@siena.edu. Website: www.siena.edu/theatre. **Contact:** Gary Maciag, director. Offered every 2 years for unpublished plays "to allow students to explore production collaboration with the playwright. In addition, it provides the playwright an important development opportunity. Plays should be previously unproduced, unpublished, full-length, nonmusicals, and free of copyright and royalty restrictions. Plays should require unit set, or minimal changes, and be suitable for a college-age cast of 3-10. There is a required 4-6 week residency." Guidelines for SASE. Guidelines are available after November 1 in odd-numbered years. Winning playwright must agree that the Siena production will be the world premiere of the play. **Deadline: February 1-June 30 in even-numbered years.** Prize: $2,000 honorarium; up to $2,000 to cover expenses for required residency; full production of winning script.

DOROTHY SILVER PLAYWRITING COMPETITION

The Jewish Community Center of Cleveland, 26001 S. Woodland, Beachwood OH 44122. (216)831-0700. Fax: (216)831-7796. E-mail: dbobrow@clevejcc.org. Website: www.clevejcc.org. **Contact:** Deborah Bobrow, competition coordinator. Estab. 1948. All entries must be original works, not previously produced, suitable for a full-length presentation; directly concerned with the Jewish experience. **Deadline: May 1.** Prize: Cash award, plus staged reading.

N SOUTHEASTERN THEATRE CONFERENCE NEW PLAY PROJECT

P.O. Box 9868, Greensboro NC 27429. (336)272-3645. Fax: (336)272-8810. E-mail: setc@setc.org. Website: www.setc.org. **Contact:** Kenn Stilson. Offered annually for the discovery, development, and publicizing of worthy new unproduced plays and playwrights. Eligibility limited to members of 10-state SETC Region: Alabama, Florida, Georgia, Kentucky, Mississippi, North Carolina, South Carolina, Tennessee, Virginia, or West Virginia. Submissions accepted on disk only, in Microsoft Word format only. Check the SETC website for full submission details. No musicals or children's plays. **Deadline: March 1-June 1.** Guidelines for SASE. Prize: $1,000, staged reading at SETC Convention, and expenses paid trip to convention.

N SOUTHERN APPALACHIAN PLAYWRIGHTS CONFERENCE

Southern Appalachian Repertory Theatre, P.O. Box 1720, Mars Hill NC 28754. (828)689-1384. Fax: (828)689-1272. E-mail: sart@mhc.edu. Website: www.sartheatre.com. **Contact:** Andrew Reed, managing director. Offered annually for unpublished, unproduced, full-length plays to promote the development of new plays. All plays are considered for later production with honorarium provided for the winning playwright. **Deadline: October 31 (postmarked).** Guidelines for SASE. Prize: 4-5 playwrights are invited for staged readings in May, room and board provided.

SOUTHERN PLAYWRIGHTS COMPETITION

Jacksonville State University, 700 Pelham Rd. N., Jacksonville AL 36265-1602. (256)782-5414. Fax: (256)782-5441. E-mail: swhitton@jsucc.jsu.edu. Website: www.jsu.edu/depart/english/southpla.htm. **Contact:** Steven J. Whitton. Estab. 1988. Offered annually to identify and encourage the best of Southern playwriting. Playwrights must be a native or resident of Alabama, Arkansas, Florida, Georgia, Kentucky, Louisiana, Missouri, North Carolina, South Carolina, Tennessee, Texas, Virginia, or West Virginia. **Deadline: February 15.** Guidelines for SASE. Prize: $1,000, and production of the play.

SOUTHWEST THEATRE ASSOCIATION NATIONAL NEW PLAY CONTEST

Theatre Arts & Film Dept., University of Texas at El Paso, 500 W. University Ave., El Paso TX 79968. E-mail: cgordon@utep.edu. Website: www.southwest-theater.com. **Contact:** Chuck Gordon. Annual contest for unpublished, unproduced work to promote the writing and production of new one-act or full-length plays. No musicals, translations, adaptations of previously produced or published work, or children's plays. Guidelines for SASE or by e-mail. Open to writers who reside in the US. One entry/writer. **Deadline: March 15. Charges $10 (make check payable to SWTA).** Prize: $300 honorarium, a reading at the annual SWTA conference, complimentary registration at conference, 1-year membership in SWTA, and possibility of excerpt publication in the professional journal of SWTA.

STANLEY DRAMA AWARD

Dept. of Theatre Wagner College, One Campus Rd., Staten Island NY 10301. (718)390-3157. Fax: (718)390-3323. **Contact:** Dr. Felicia J. Ruff, director. Offered for original full-length stage plays, musicals, or one-act play sequences that have not been professionally produced or received trade book publication. **Deadline: October 1.** Guidelines for SASE. **Charges $10 submission fee.** Prize: $2,000.

N TELEPLAY COMPETITION

Austin Film Festival, 1604 Nueces, Austin TX 78701. (512)478-4795. Fax: (512)478-6205. E-mail: info@austinfilmfestival.con. Website: www.austinfilmfestival.com. Offered annually for unpublished work to discover talented television writers, and introduce their work to production companies. Categories: drama and sitcom (must be based on current television program). Contest open to writers who do not earn a living writing for television or film. **Deadline: June 1.** Guidelines for SASE. **Charges $30.** Prize: $1,000 in each category.

THEATRE BC'S ANNUAL CANADIAN NATIONAL PLAYWRITING COMPETITION

Theatre BC, P.O. Box 2031, Nanaimo BC V9R 6X6 Canada. (250)714-0203. Fax: (250)714-0213. E-mail: pwc@theatrebc.org. Website: www.theatrebc.org. **Contact:** Robb Mowbray, executive director. Offered annually to unpublished plays "to promote the development and production of previously unproduced new plays (no musicals) at all levels of theater. Categories: Full Length (75 minutes or longer); One Act (less than 75 minutes); and an open Special Merit (juror's discretion). Guidelines for SASE or on website. Production and publishing rights remain with the playwright. Open to Canadian residents. All submissions are made under pseudonyms. E-mail inquiries welcome. **Deadline: Fourth Monday in July. Charges $35/entry, and optional $25 for written critique.** Prize: Full Length: $1,000; One Act: $750; Special Merit: $500. Winners are also invited to New Play Festival: Up to 16 hours with a professional dramaturg, registrant actors, and a public reading in Kamloops (every Spring).

THEATRE CONSPIRACY ANNUAL NEW PLAY CONTEST

Theatre Conspiracy, 10091 McGregor Blvd., Ft. Myers FL 33919. (239)936-3239. Fax: (239)936-0510. E-mail: info@theatreconspiracy.org. **Contact:** Bill Taylor, award director. Offered annually for unproduced full-length plays with 8 or less characters and simple to moderate production demands. One entry per year. Send SASE for reply. **Deadline: March 30. Charges $5 fee.** Prize: $700, and full production. Open to any writer.

THEATREPEI NEW VOICES PLAYWRITING COMPETITION

P.O. Box 1573, Charlottetown PE C1A 7N3 Canada. (902)894-3558. Fax: (902)368-7180. E-mail: theatre@isn.net. **Contact:** Dawn Binkley, general manager. Offered annually. Open to individuals who have been residents of Prince Edward Island for 6 months preceding the deadline for entries. **Deadline: February 14.** Guidelines for SASE. **Charges $5 fee.** Prize: Monetary.

TRUSTUS PLAYWRIGHTS' FESTIVAL

Trustus Theatre, Box 11721, Columbia SC 29211-1721. (803)254-9732. Fax: (803)771-9153. E-mail: trustus@trustus.org. Website: www.trustus.org. **Contact:** Jon Tuttle, literary manager. Offered annually for professionally unproduced full-length plays; cast limit of 8; prefer challenging, innovative dramas and comedies; no musicals, plays for young audiences, or "hillbilly" southern shows. **Deadline: Applications received between December 1, 2005, and February 28, 2006, only.** Guidelines and application for SASE. Prize: Public staged-reading and $250, followed after a 1-year development period by full production, $500, plus travel/accommodations to attend opening.

UNICORN THEATRE NEW PLAY DEVELOPMENT

Unicorn Theatre, 3828 Main St., Kansas City MO 64111. (816)531-7529, ext. 15. Fax: (816)531-0421. Website: www.unicorntheatre.org. **Contact:** Herman Wilson, literary assistant. Offered annually to encourage and assist the development of an unpublished and unproduced play. Acquires 2% subsidiary rights of future productions for a 5-year period. **Deadline: Ongoing.** Guidelines for SASE. Prize: $1,000 royalty, and production.

VERMONT PLAYWRIGHT'S AWARD

The Valley Players, P.O. Box 441, Waitsfield VT 05673. (802)496-3751. E-mail: valleyplayers@madriver.com. Website: www.valleyplayers.com. **Contact:** Jennifer Howard, chair. Offered annually for unpublished, nonmusical, full-length plays suitable for production by a community theater group to encourage development of playwrights in Vermont, New Hampshire, and Maine. **Deadline: February 1.** Prize: $1,000.

THE HERMAN VOADEN NATIONAL PLAYWRITING COMPETITION

Drama Department, Queen's University, Kingston ON K7L 3N6 Canada. (613)533-2104. E-mail: hannaca@post.queensu.ca. Website: www.queensu.ca/drama. **Contact:** Carol Anne Hanna. Offered every 2 years for unpublished plays to discover and develop new Canadian plays. See website for deadlines, guidelines. Open to Canadian citizens or landed immigrants. **Charges $30 entry fee.** Prize: $3,000, $2,000, and 8 honorable mentions. 1st- and 2nd-prize winners are offered a 1-week workshop and public reading by professional director and cast. The 2 authors will be playwrights-in-residence for the rehearsal and reading period.

VSA ARTS PLAYWRIGHT DISCOVERY AWARD

VSA Arts, 1300 Connecticut Ave. NW, Suite 700, Washington DC 20036. (202)628-2800. Fax: (202)737-0725. Website: www.vsarts.org. **Contact:** Performing Arts Coordinator. The VSA Arts Playwright Discovery Award challenges students grades 6-12 of all abilities to express their views about disability by writing a one-act play. Two plays will be produced at The Kennedy Center in Washington, D.C. The Playwright Discovery Teacher Award honors teachers who bring disability awareness to the classroom through the art of playwriting. Recipient receives funds for playwriting resources, a scholarship, a trip to Washington, D.C., and national recognition. **Deadline: April 15.**

WEST COAST ENSEMBLE FULL-PLAY COMPETITION

West Coast Ensemble, P.O. Box 38728, Los Angeles CA 90038. (323)876-9337. Fax: (323)876-8916. **Contact:** Les Hanson, artistic director. Estab. 1982. Offered annually for unpublished plays in Southern California. No musicals or children's plays for full-play competition. No restrictions on subject matter. **Deadline: December 31.**

JACKIE WHITE MEMORIAL NATIONAL CHILDREN'S PLAYWRITING CONTEST

Columbia Entertainment Co., 309 Parkade, Columbia MO 65202. (573)874-5628. **Contact:** Betsy Phillips, director. Offered annually for unpublished plays. "Searching for good scripts, either adaptations or plays with original story lines, suitable for audiences of all ages." Script must include at least 7 well-developed roles. **Deadline: June 1.** Guidelines for SASE. **Charges $10 fee.** Prize: $500. Company reserves the right to grant prize money without production. All entrants receive written evaluation.

WRITE A PLAY! NYC

Young Playwrights, Inc., 306 W. 38th St., Suite 300, New York NY 10018. (212)594-5440. Fax: (212)594-5441. E-mail: writeaplay@aol.com. Website: youngplaywrights.org. **Contact:** Literary Department. Offered annually for plays by NYC elementary, middle, and high school students only. **Deadline: April 1.** Prize: Varies.

YEAR END SERIES (YES) NEW PLAY FESTIVAL

Dept. of Theatre, Nunn Dr., Northern Kentucky University, Highland Heights KY 41099-1007. (859)572-6362. Fax: (859)572-6057. E-mail: forman@nku.edu. **Contact:** Sandra Forman, project director. Receives submissions from May 1-October 31 in even-numbered years for the Festivals which occur in April of odd-numbered years. Open to all writers. **Deadline: October 31.** Guidelines for SASE. Prize: $500, and an expense-paid visit to Northern Kentucky University to see the play produced.

ANNA ZORNIO MEMORIAL CHILDREN'S THEATRE PLAYWRITING COMPETITION

University of New Hampshire, Dept. of Theatre and Dance, PCAC, 30 College Rd., Durham NH 03824-3538. (603)862-2919. Fax: (603)862-0298. E-mail: mike.wood@unh.edu. Website: www.unh.edu/theatre-dance/zornio.html. **Contact:** Michael Wood. Offered every 4 years for unpublished well-written plays or musicals appropriate for young audiences with a maximum length of 60 minutes. May submit more than 1 play, but not more than 3. All plays must be appropriate for children within the K-12 grades. **Deadline: March 3, 2008.** Guidelines and entry forms online. Prize: $1,000, and play produced and underwritten as part of the season by the UNH Department of Theatre and Dance. Winner will be notified in November 2008. Open to all playwrights in US and Canada. All ages are invited to participate.

MARKETS

Independent Publicists

You spent years writing your book, then several more months sending queries to agents. You finally find an agent who loves your work, but then you have to wait even more time as she submits your manuscript to editors. After a few months, your agent closes a great deal for your work with a publishing house you really admire. Now you can sit back and wait for the money to start rolling in, right?

If you've learned anything about publishing so far, you've learned that getting a book published takes a lot of work. And once you find a publisher, your work doesn't stop. You now have to focus on selling your book to make money and to ensure that publishing companies will work with you again. Industry experts estimate that 110,000 books are published each year in the United States. What can you do to ensure that your book succeeds with this amount of competition?

While most publishing houses do have in-house publicists, their time is often limited and priority is usually given to big-name authors who have already proved they will make money for the publisher. Often writers feel their books aren't getting the amount of publicity for which they had hoped. Because of this, many authors have decided to work with an independent publicist.

To help you market your book after publication, we've included a section of independent publicists in this book. Like agents, publicists view publishing as a business. And their business goal is to see that your book succeeds. Usually, publicists are more than happy to work in conjunction with your editor, your publisher, and your agent. Together, they can form a strong team that will help make you a publishing sensation.

What to look for in a publicist

When choosing an independent publicist, you'll want someone who has business savvy and experience in sales. And, of course, you'll want someone who is enthusiastic about you and your writing. When looking through the listings in this section, look at each person's experience both prior to and after becoming a publicist. The radio and television shows on which their clients have appeared can indicate the caliber of their contacts, and the recent promotions they have done for their clients' books can reveal their level of creativity.

You'll also want to look for a publicist who is interested in your subject area. Like agents and publishing houses, most independent publicists have specializations. By focusing on specific areas, publicists can actually do more for their clients. For example, if a publicist is interested in cookbooks, she can send her clients to contacts she has on Food Network shows, editors at gourmet cooking magazines, bookstores that have cafés, and culinary conferences. The more knowledge a publicist has about your subject, the more opportunities she will find to publicize your work.

How to make the initial contact

Contacting independent publicists should be much less stressful than the query process you've gone through to find an agent. Most publicists are open to a phone call, though some still prefer to receive a letter or an e-mail as the initial contact. Often you can receive a referral to a publicist through an agent, an editor, or even another writer. Because publicists do cost more out-of-pocket money than an agent, there isn't the same competition for their time. Of course, not every publicist you call will be the best fit for you. Be prepared to hear that the publicist already has a full client load or that she doesn't have the level of interest in your work that you want a publicist to have.

How much to spend

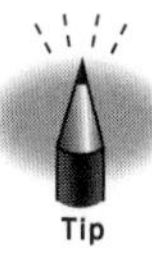

As you read over the listings of independent publicists, you'll quickly notice that many charge a substantial amount of money for their services. The cost of a publicist can be daunting, especially to a new writer. *You should only pay what you feel comfortable paying and what you can reasonably afford.* Keep in mind, however, that any money you spend on publicity will come back to you in the form of more books sold. A general rule of thumb is to budget one dollar for every copy of your book that is printed. For a print run of 10,000, you should expect to spend $10,000.

There are ways you can make working with a publicist less of a strain on your purse strings. If you received an advance for your book, you can use part of it to help with your marketing expenses. Some publishers will even agree to match the amount of money an author pays on outside publicity. If your publicist's bill is $2,000, you would pay half and your publisher would pay the other half. Be sure to ask your publishing house if this option is available to you. Most publicists are very willing to work with their clients on a marketing budget.

When reading through the listings of independent publicists, use the following listing breakdown to help you fully understand the information provided.

SUBHEADS

Each listing is broken down into subheads to make locating specific information easier. In this first paragraph, you'll find contact information for each independent publicist or publicity agency. Further information is provided that indicates the company's size and the publicist's experience in the publishing industry.

Members: To help you find a publicist who has a firm understanding of your book's subject and audience, we include the names of publicists and their specialties. The year the member joined the agency is also provided, indicating an individual's familiarity with book publicity.

Specializations: Similar to the agents listed in this book, most publicists have specific areas of interest. A publicist with knowledge of your book's subject will have contacts in your field and a solid sense of your audience.

Services: This subhead provides important details about what the publicist can do for you, including a list of services available for clients, book tour information, television shows on which clients have appeared, contents of media kits, and examples of recent promotions done by the publicist.

Look for the key icon to quickly learn the publicist's areas of specialization and specific marketing strengths.

How to Contact: Unlike literary agents, most independent publicists are open to phone calls, letters, and e-mail; check this subhead to see the individual publicist's preference. Also pay close attention to the time frame the publicist needs between your initial contact and your book's publication date.

Clients: To provide you with a better sense of their areas of interest, independent publicists list authors they have helped promote. Publicists also indicate here if they are willing to provide potential clients with references.

Costs: Specific details are provided on how much publicists charge their clients. Although the costs seem high, the payback in terms of books sold is usually worth the additional expense. Publicists indicate if they work with clients on a marketing budget, and if they offer a written contract.

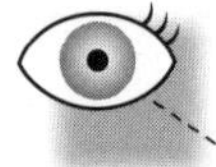

See Also

Writers' Conferences: A great way to meet and learn more about publicists is at writers' conferences. Here publicists list the writers' conferences they attend. For more information about a specific conference, check the Writers' Conferences section starting on page 245.

Tips: This section provides you with advice and additional instructions for working with an independent publicist.

Quick Reference Icons

At the beginning of some listings, you will find one or more of the following symbols for quick identification of features particular to that listing.

- N Independent publicist new to this edition.
- Newer independent publicist actively seeking clients.
- Independent publicist interested in working with both new and established writers.
- Independent publicist open only to established writers.
- Independent publicist who specializes in a specific type of work.
- Independent publicist not currently open to new clients.

SPECIAL INDEXES

Agencies Indexed by Openness to Submissions: This index, which also lists agents, lists publicists according to how open they are to accepting new clients.

Geographic Index: For writers looking for a publicist close to home, this index lists independent publicists by state.

Listing Index: This index lists all agencies, independent publicists, production companies, script contests, and writers' conferences listed in the book.

ACHESON-GREUB, INC.

P.O. Box 735, Friday Harbor WA 98250-0735. (360)378-2815. Fax: (360)378-2841. E-mail: aliceba@aol.com. **Contact:** Alice B. Acheson. Estab. 1981; specifically with books for 31 years. Currently works with 9 clients. 20% of clients are new/first-time writers.

- Prior to becoming a freelance publicist, Ms. Acheson was a trade book editor, associate publicity director (Simon & Schuster and Crown Publishers), and high school Spanish teacher.

Specializations Nonfiction, fiction, children's books. **Interested in these nonfiction areas:** Art/architecture/design, biography/autobiography, juvenile nonfiction, language/literature/criticism, memoirs, multicultural, music/dance/theater/film, nature/environment, photography. **Interested in these fiction areas:** Contemporary issues, historical, juvenile, literary, mainstream, multicultural, mystery/suspense.

Services Provides detailed outline of services provided, media training, market research, sends material to magazines/newspapers for reviews, brochures. Book tours include bookstores, radio interviews, TV interviews, newspaper interviews, magazine interviews. Assists in coordinating travel plans. Clients have appeared on CBS-TV, *Early Show*, CNN, and innumerable radio and TV shows nationwide. Media kit includes author's biography, testimonials, articles about author, basic information on book, professional photos, sample interview questions. Clients responsible for assisting with promotional material. Helps writer obtain endorsements.

"We mentor so writers can do the work on their own for their next projects."

How to Contact Call or e-mail. Send letter with SASE. Responds in 2 weeks, unless on teaching trip. Returns materials only with SASE. Obtains most new clients through recommendations from others and conferences. Contact 8 months prior to book's publication.

Clients *Africa*, by Art Wolfe (Wildlands Press); *Eating Heaven*, by Jennie Shortridge (NAL Accent/Penguin Group); *Great Lodges of the National Parks*, by Christine Barnes (W.W. West, Inc.). References and contact numbers available for potential clients.

Costs Clients charged hourly fee. Works with clients on marketing budget. Offers written contract. Contract can be terminated upon written notification.

AMERICAN BLACKGUARD, INC.

P.O. Box 680686, Franklin TN 37068-0686. (615)599-4032. E-mail: media@americanblackguard.com. Website: www.americanblackguard.com. **Contact:** Eddie Lightsey. Estab. 1977.

- Prior to becoming an independent publicist, Mr. Lightsey was the senior publicist for an award-winning country music PR firm.

Specializations Nonfiction, fiction, children's books. **Interested in these nonfiction areas:** Animals, art/architecture/design, biography/autobiography, cooking/food, history, how-to, interior design/decorating, music/dance/theater/film, nature/environment, popular culture, self-help/personal improvement, sports, travel. **Interested in these fiction areas:** Action/adventure, fantasy, historical, horror, mystery/suspense, science fiction, thriller/espionage, westerns/frontier. Other types of clients include publishers, record labels, theater companies, screenwriters, entertainment companies, financial institutions, physicians, nonprofits, and corporate.

Services Provides national publicity, creates and services press releases, sends material to magazines/newspapers for reviews. Book tours include bookstores, specialty stores, radio interviews, TV interviews, newspaper interviews, magazine interviews, speaking engagements. Clients have appeared on Discovery Channel, History Channel, ABC, CBS, NBC, PBS, and NPR. Media kit includes author's biography, testimonials, articles about author, basic information on book, professional photos. Clients responsible for assisting with promotional material.

How to Contact Call, e-mail, or fax. Responds in less than 1 week. Returns materials only with SASE. Obtains most new clients through recommendations from others and queries/solicitations. Contact 4 months prior to book's publication.

Clients *Queen of Diamonds*, by Carol Ann Rapp and Joseph Gregory (Providence House); *Genealogy 101*, by Barbara Ann Ranick (Rutledge Hill Press); *A Family Affair*, by Sandra Clunies (Rutledge Hill Press).

Costs Clients charged a monthly retainer. Offers a written contract binding for 3 months.

Writers' Conference(s) Council for the Written Word (Franklin TN).

Tips "American Blackguard will work on your behalf to handle all the promotional details of your career so you can focus on what you do best—being an author. We will be involved in your campaign as much or as little as you choose."

BRICKMAN MARKETING

395 Del Monte Center, #250, Monterey CA 93940. (831)633-4444. E-mail: brickman@redshift.net. Website: www.brickmanmarketing.com. **Contact:** Wendy Brickman. Estab. 1990; specifically with books for 15 years. Currently works with 30 clients. 10% of clients are new/first-time writers.

- Prior to becoming a freelance publicist, Ms. Brickman worked in public relations in the home video industries.

Specializations Nonfiction, children's book, academic. **Interested in these nonfiction areas:** Biography/autobiography; business; education; ethnic/cultural interests; health/medicine; history; how-to; interior design/decorating; music/dance/theater/film; nature/environment; New Age/metaphysics; popular culture; self-help/personal improvement; travel; women's issues/women's studies. **Interested in these fiction areas:** Children's. Other types of clients include home video producers and a wide variety of businesses.

Services Provides media training, market research, fax news releases, sends material to magazines/newspapers for reviews. Book tours include bookstores, specialty stores, radio interviews, TV interviews, newspaper interviews, magazine interviews, speaking engagements, conferences, libraries, schools, universities. Clients have appeared on *Howie Mandel*, CNN, Bloomberg TV, HGTV, Fox and Friends, more local TV, syndicated radio, and in hundreds of national and local magazines and newspapers. Media kit includes author's biography, testimonials, articles about author, basic information on book, professional photos, sample interview questions, book request information. Helps writer obtain endorsements.

O→ "My wide variety of clients and contacts makes me a valuable publicist."

How to Contact E-mail. Responds in 1 week. Discards unwanted queries and mss. Obtains most new clients through recommendations from others. Contact 4 months prior to book's publication.

Clients *What Do They Say When You Leave the Room*, by Brigid McGrath Massie (Eudemonia); *Diet for Allergies*, by Raphael Rethner; *Listening: It Will Change Your Life*, by Charles Page, attorney at law; *Writers and Artists Hideouts: Great Getaways for Seducing the Muse*, by Andrea Brown. Other clients include numerous special interest video producers.

Costs Clients charged hourly retainer fee or monthly retainer. No written contract.

BRODY PUBLIC RELATIONS

145 Route 519, Stockton NJ 08559-1711. (609)397-3737. Fax: (609)397-3666. E-mail: bebrody@aol.com. Website: www.brodypr.com. **Contact:** Beth Brody. Estab. 1988; specifically with books for 15 years. Currently works with 8-10 clients. 10% of clients are new/first-time writers.

Members Beth Brody (nonfiction, at firm for 15 years).

Specializations Nonfiction. **Interested in these nonfiction areas:** Business; child guidance/parenting; education; health/medicine; how-to; money/finance/economics; music/dance/theater/film; popular culture; psychology; self-help/personal improvement; travel. **Interested in these fiction areas:** Cartoons/comic. Other types of clients include musicians, artists, entertainment, healthcare.

Services Provides detailed outline of services provided, fax news releases, electronic news releases, sends material to magazines/newspapers for reviews, brochures, website assistance, website publicity. Book tours include bookstores, specialty stores, radio interviews, TV interviews, newspaper interviews, magazine interviews, speaking engagements, conferences, libraries, schools, universities. Assists in coordinating travel plans. Clients have appeared on *Oprah Winfrey Show*, *Good Morning America*. Media kit includes author's biography, testimonials, articles about author, basic information on book, sample interview questions, book request information. Helps writer obtain endorsements.

How to Contact Call or e-mail. Responds in 48 hours. Obtains most new clients through recommendations from others. Contact 6 months prior to book's publication.

Clients Music Sales Corporation, Crown Business, Random House, Berkeley Publishing, Free Spirit Publishing. Other clients include Dow Jones, Don & Bradstreet, Foundations Behaviorial Health, JVC Music, Mack Avenue Records, Magweb.com. References and contact numbers available for potential clients.

Costs Clients charged hourly fee or monthly retainer. Offers written contract.

Tips "Contact a publicist after you have secured a publisher and distributor."

EVENT MANAGEMENT SERVICES, INC.

519 Cleveland St., Suite 205, Clearwater FL 33757. (727)443-7115, ext. 208. E-mail: mfriedman@event-management.com. Website: www.event-management.com. **Contact:** Marsha Friedman. Estab. 1990; specifically with books for 11 years. Currently works with 38 clients. 20% of clients are new/first-time writers.

- Prior to becoming a freelance publicist, Ms. Friedman worked in PR and event management.

Members Rich Ghazarian (account manager); Joe Ullrich (business development); Lisa Gregory (business development); Jay Wilke (account manager); Cari Core (account manager).

Specializations Nonfiction. **Interested in these nonfiction areas:** Cooking/food/nutrition; current affairs; government/politics/law; health/natural; how-to; interior design/decorating; money/finance/economics; nature/environment; science/technology; sports; travel. Other types of clients include medical doctors, corporations in natural health industry, entertainment industry, and food industry.

Services Provides detailed outline of services provided. Book tours include bookstores, radio interviews, TV interviews, newspaper interviews, magazine interviews. Clients have appeared on *Good Morning America*, *Today*, *60 Minutes*, *CBS This Morning*, *Maury Povich*, *Montel*. Media kit includes author's biography, press release that gives the actual show idea or story.

O━ "We are paid on performance and our specialty is radio and TV. We book anywhere from 30-80 interviews per week!"

How to Contact Call, e-mail, or fax. Send letter with SASE. Responds in 2 weeks. Obtains most new clients through recommendations from others or an initial contact on our part. Contact 6 months prior to book's publication or after book's publication.

Clients *Anti Aging Bible*, by Dr. Earl Mindell (Simon & Schuster); *Slimdown For Life*, by Larry North (Kensington); *Special Trust*, by Robert McFarlane (Multi Media); *Selling Online*, by Jim Carrol and Rick Broadhead (Dearborn). Other clients include Jimmy Hoffa, Jr., Harry Browne, The Temptations. References and contact numbers available for potential clients.

Costs Clients charged on per placement basis ($165, radio and $5,000, national TV). Works with clients on marketing budget. Offers written contract.

Tips "Check references to see how much media they book every week/month. Find out if they have knowledge of your area of expertise."

N ☐ FIRSTWORD AGENCY

P.O. Box 521534, Salt Lake City UT 84152-1534. E-mail: info@firstwordagency.com. Website: www.firstwordagency.com. **Contact:** Stephanie Kallbacka, president. Estab. 2000; specifically with books for 2 years. Currently works with 10 clients. 75% of clients are new/first-time writers.

- Prior to becoming a freelance publicist, Ms. Kallbacka worked in public relations.

Members Stephanie Kallbacka (media relations, at firm for 2 years).

Specializations Nonfiction, fiction, children's book, academic. **Interested in these nonfiction areas:** art/architecture/design; biography/autobiography; business; child guidance/parenting; computers/electronics; cooking/food/nutrition; history; how-to; humor; language/literature/criticism; memoirs; military/war; music/dance/theater/film; New Age/metaphysics; popular culture; self-help/personal improvement; sports; travel; women's issues/women's studies; young adult. **Interested in these fiction areas:** action/adventure; detective/police/crime; experimental; historical; horror; humor/satire; juvenile; literary; mainstream; mystery/suspense; New Age/metaphysical; thriller/espionage; westerns/frontier; young adult. Other types of clients include music labels, film directories.

Services Provides detailed outline of services provided, media training, international publicity, if applicable, fax news releases, electronic news release, send material to magazines/newspapers for reviews, brochures, website assistance, website publicity. Book tours include bookstores, specialty stores, radio interviews, TV interviews, newspaper interviews, magazine interviews, speaking engagements, conferences, libraries, schools, universities. Assists in coordinating travel plans. Media kit includes résumé, author's biography, testimonials, articles about author, basic information on book, suggested story topics, professional photos, sample interview questions, book request information. Helps writer obtain endorsements.

O━ FirstWord Agency offers personal interaction with the author. "We help first-time authors gain media exposure through creative and unique publicity campaigns."

How to Contact E-mail, fax, send letter with 3 sample chapters with SASE. Responds in 2 months. Returns materials only with SASE. Obtains most new clients through recommendations from others, queries/solicitations. Contact 1-6 months prior to book's publication.

Clients *Hairdresser to the Stars*, by Ginger Blymyer (Xlibris); *The Sandscrapers*, by Griffin T. Garnett (Infinity Publishing); *Baseball's Greatest Players: The Saga Continues*, by David Shiner (Superior Books); *Hearing Footsteps*, by Edward Kallbacka (Infinity Publishing); *The Malco Polia Quartette*, by Gilbert Buchanan; *Novice of Souls*, by Kevin Holochwost; *Dawn of the New Man*, by eduard Pugovecki. Other clients include Talking Cloud Records. References and contact numbers available for potential clients.

Costs Clients charged flat fee $100-1,000/project; hourly retainer fee $20-60; monthly retainer $1,000-2,500. Works with clients on marketing budget. Offers written contract, usually binding for 3-12 months; negotiable. 1-month notice must be given to terminate contract.

Tips "At FirstWord Agency, it is important for both us and the author to be dedicated to the subject of our authors' work. We value close relationships with each of our clients and work together to achieve success on their behalf."

GARIS AGENCY—NATIONAL PUBLICISTS

100 E. San Marcos Blvd., Suite 400, San Marcos CA 92069. (760)471-4807. Fax: (760)454-1814. E-mail: publicists@garis-agency.com. Website: www.toppublicity.com. **Contact:** R.J. Garis. Estab. 1989; specifically with books since 1989. Currently works with 50 clients. 20% of clients are new/first-time writers.

- Prior to becoming a publicist, Mr Garis was a promoter and producer.

Members Taryn Roberts (associate national publicist, at firm since 1997); R.J. Garis.

Specializations Nonfiction, fiction, script. **Interested in these nonfiction areas:** Animals; biography/autobiography; business; child guidance/parenting; current affairs; gay/lesbian issues; government/politics/law; health/

medicine; how-to; humor; interior design/decorating; juvenile nonfiction; memoirs; military/war; money/finance/economics; multicultural; music/dance/theater/film; nature/environment; New Age/metaphysics; photography; popular culture; psychology; science/technology; self-help/personal improvement; sociology; sports; travel; true crime/investigative; women's issues/women's studies; young adult. **Interested in these fiction areas:** Action/adventure; cartoon/comic; contemporary issues; detective/police/crime; erotica; ethnic; family saga; fantasy; feminist; gay/lesbian; glitz; horror; humor/satire; juvenile; literary; mainstream; multicultural; mystery/suspense; New Age/metaphysical; picture book; psychic/supernatural; romance; science fiction; sports; thriller/espionage; westerns/frontier; young adult.

Services Provides media training, nationwide publicity, if applicable, fax news releases, electronic news release, material to magazines/newspapers for reviews, website assistance, website publicity. Book tours include bookstores, specialty stores, radio interviews, TV interviews, newspaper interviews, magazine interviews, speaking engagements, conferences. Assists in coordinating travel plans. Clients have appeared on *Oprah*, *Dateline*, *Larry King*, Fox, *Sally*, *Extra*, *48 Hours*, *Good Morning America*, *Montel*, *Inside Edition*, *20/20*, *Today*. Media kits include résumé, author's biography, testimonials, articles about author, basic infomation on book, professional photos, sample interview questions, book request information. Helps writer obtain endorsements. "We designed media information for author Missy Cummings (*Hornet's Nest*)—which resulted in TV interviews on *Extra*, *Inside Edition*, and a print feature in *The Star*."

O→ This company specializes in "quality media that works! Morning radio, national TV, regional TV, major newspapers, and national magazines. We currently book over 2,000 media interviews a year."

How to Contact E-mail. Responds in 3 days. Discards unwanted materials. Obtains most new clients through recommendations from others. Contact 3 months prior to book's publication.

Clients *Hornet's Nest*, by Missy Cummings (iUniverse); *Little Kids Big Questions*, by Dr. Judi Craig (Hearst Books); *There Are No Accidents*, by Robert Hopcke (Penguin Putnam); *Anger Work*, by Dr. Robert Puff (Vantage Press). References and contact numbers available for potential clients.

Costs Charges clients contract fee based on the project; monthly retainer. Offers written contract, binding for a minimum of 6 months. 1-month notice must be given to terminate contract.

Tips "Check references. Look for a publicist with a long history, it takes many years to establish powerful media contacts."

GREATER TALENT NETWORK, INC.

437 Fifth Ave., New York NY 10016-2205. (212)645-4200. Fax: (212)627-1471. E-mail: info@greatertalent.com. Website: www.gtnspeakers.com. **Contact:** Don Epstein. Estab. 1980; specifically with books for over 20 years. Currently works with more than 100 clients.

Members Don Epstein (corporate/literary, at firm over 20 years); Debra Greene (corporate/literary, at firm 21 years); Kenny Rahtz (corporate/associations, at firm 21 years); Barbara Solomon (health/hospitals/public relations, at firm 16 years); David Evenchick (Fortune 1000, at firm for 8 years); Josh Yablon (technology/corporate management, at firm for 9 years); Lisa Bransdorf (college/university, at firm for 7 years).

Specializations Nonfiction, fiction, academic. **Interested in these nonfiction areas:** Business, computers/electronics, current affairs, education, government/politics/law, humor, money/finance/economics, multicultural, popular culture, science/technology, sports, women's issues/women's studies. Other types of clients include government officials, athletes, CEO's, technology, media.

Services Provides detailed outline of services provided, international publicity, if applicable, fax news releases, brochures, website publicity. Book tours include radio interviews, TV interviews, newspaper interviews, speaking engagements. Assists in coordinating travel plans. Clients have appeared on all major networks. Media kit includes author's biography, testimonials, articles about author, professional photos, book request information.

O→ "We understand authors' needs and publishers' wants."

How to Contact Call, e-mail, fax. Discards unwanted queries and mss. Obtains most new clients through recommendations from others. Contact once a platform is started.

Clients *The CEO of the Sofa*, by P.J. O'Rourke (Atlantic Monthly Press); *Dude, Where's My Country*, by Michael Moore (Warner Books); *Hidden Power*, by Kati Marton (Pantheon); *The Travel Detective*, by Peter Greenberg (Villard); *American Gods*, by Neil Gaiman (Wm. Morrow). Other clients include Homer Hickman, Tom Wolfe, John Douglas, Christopher Buckley, Erica Jong, Michael Lewis. References and contact numbers available for potential clients.

Costs Clients charged variable commission. Offers written contract.

THE IDEA NETWORK

P.O. Box 38, Whippany NJ 07981. (973)560-0333. Fax: (973)560-0960. E-mail: esaxton@theideanetwork.net. Website: www.theideanetwork.net. **Contact:** Erin Saxton, founder. Estab. 2000, specifically with books for 5 years. Currently works with 15-20 clients. Less than 17 clients are new/first-time writers.

• Prior to starting her media/public relations firm, Ms. Saxton was a 4-time Emmy-nominated TV producer.

Members Jen Urezzio (vice president, media relations, at firm for 4 years); Allyson Klavens (senior account executive, at firm 2 years); Anders Bjornson (V.P. of business operations, at firm 2 years).

Specializations Nonfiction. **Interested in these nonfiction areas:** Child guidance/parenting, cooking/food/nutrition, crafts/hobbies, current affairs, health/medicine, how-to, interior design/decorating, money/finance/economics, psychology, women's issues/women's studies. "We don't work with many fiction writers and take them on a case-by-case system."

Services Full-service public relations agency. Every client's media and publicity plans differ. Call for more information. Book tours include radio interviews, TV interviews, newspaper interviews, magazine interviews. Clients have appeared on *The View*, *The Today Show*, Fox News Channel, *Good Morning America*, *The Early Show*, and *Ellen*.

O━ "This company is founded by a TV Producer and therefore knows what a producer is looking for in a 'pitch.' Because of our background, our clients have an advantage." Specializes in creating hooks that reporters, editors, ad producers find useful for their programs and outlets.

How to Contact Call, e-mail, fax. Responds in 1 week. Discards unwanted queries and mss. Obtains most new clients through recommendations from others, queries/solicitations, responses from press we've received. Contact 6 months prior to book's publication.

Clients *Chicken Soup for the Soul*, by Mark Victor Hansen and Jack Canfield (HCI Enterprises), and other notable authors.

Costs Clients charged monthly retainer ($3,500-10,000) and by project. Offers written contract. "We usually put dates within the contract." 1-month notice must be given to terminate contract.

KSB PROMOTIONS

(Specializes: general lifestyle books), 55 Honey Creek NE, Ada MI 49301-9768. (616)676-0758. Fax: (616)676-0759. E-mail: pr@ksbpromotions.com. Website: www.ksbpromotions.com. **Contact:** Kate Bandos. Estab. 1988; specifically with books since 1988. Currently works with 20-40 clients; 25% of clients are new/first-time writers.

• Prior to becoming a publicist, Ms. Bandos was a PR director for several publishers.

Members Kate Bandos (travel, cookbooks, at firm since 1988); Doug Bandos (radio/TV, at firm since 1989).

Specializations Nonfiction, children's books. **Interested in these nonfiction areas:** Child guidance/parenting; cooking/food/nutrition; health/medicine; travel; gardening; home/how-to; general lifestyle.

Services Provides detailed outline of services provided, sends material to magazines/newspapers for reviews. Book tours include radio interviews, TV interviews, newspaper interviews, magazine interviews. Clients have appeared on *Good Morning America*, CNN, *Business News Network*, *Parent's Journal*, and many regional shows. Media kit includes author's biography, testimonials, basic information on book, sample interview questions, book request information, recipes for cookbooks, other excerpts as appropriate. Helps writers obtain endorsements.

O━ This company specializes in cookbooks, travel guides, parenting books, and other general lifestyle books. "Our specialty has allowed us to build relationships with key media in these areas. We limit ourselves to those clients we can personally help."

How to Contact Call or e-mail. Responds in 2 weeks. Returns unwanted material only with SASE. Obtains most new clients through recommendations from others, conferences, listings in books on publishing. Contact 6-8 months prior to book's publication. Can do limited PR after book's publication.

Clients *The Home Depot 1-2-3 Series*, (Meredith Books); *Along Interstate 75*, by Dave Hunter (Mile Oak Publishing). Other clients include Bayou Publishing, PassPorter, Travel Guides, Barnesyard Books, and Dalmation Press. References and contact numbers available for potential clients.

Costs Client charged per service fee ($500 minimum). "Total of contracted services is divided into monthly payments." Offers written contract. 1-month notice must be given to terminate contract.

Writers' Conferences PMA University; BookExpo America.

Tips "Find a publicist who has done a lot with books in the same area of interest since they will know the key media, etc."

KT PUBLIC RELATIONS

1905 Cricklewood Cove, Fogelsville PA 18051-1509. (610)395-6298. Fax: (610)395-6299. E-mail: kt4pr@aol.com. Website: www.webbookstars.com. **Contact:** Kae Tienstra. Estab. 1993; specifically with books for 24 years. Currently works with 6 clients. 60% of clients are new/first-time writers.

• Prior to becoming a freelance publicist, Ms. Tienstra was publicity director for Rodale, Inc., and a freelance writer.

Members Kae Tienstra (writing, client contact, media relations, at firm 11 years); Jon Tienstra (editing, administration, at firm 8 years).

Specializations Nonfiction, fiction. **Interested in these nonfiction areas:** Agriculture/horticulture, animals, child guidance/parenting, cooking/food/nutrition, crafts/hobbies, health/medicine, how-to, interior design/

decorating, nature/environment, psychology, religious/inspirational, self-help/personal improvement, travel. **Interested in these fiction areas:** Mainstream, women's fiction. Other types of clients include nonprofit institutions, publishers.

Services Provides detailed outline of services provided, media training, sends material to magazines/newspapers for reviews, brochures. Book tours include bookstores, radio interviews, TV interviews, newspaper interviews, magazine interviews, speaking engagements, universities. Assists in coordinating travel plans. Clients have been interviewed by *Today*, CNN, CBS Radio, *Today Weekend Edition*, *New York Times*. Media kit includes author's biography, testimonials, articles about author, basic information on book, professional photos, sample interview questions, book request information, segment suggestions for TV, radio, pitch letter. Helps writer obtain endorsements.

O━ "Our personal, hands-on approach assures authors the 1-on-1 guidance they need. Our subsidiary service, WEBbookSTARS.com provides special, low-cost, self-paced author publicity service."

How to Contact Call, e-mail, or fax. Send letter with sample chapters and SASE. Responds in 1 week. Returns materials only with SASE. Obtains most new clients through recommendations from others and conferences. Contact 6 months prior to book's publication or after book's publication once a platform is started.

Clients *Are You Ready for Lasting Love*, by Paddy S. Welles, Ph.D. (Avalon Publisher); *The Witch Book*, by Raymond Buckland (Visible Ink Press); *Spiritual Training Wheels*, by Gloria Benish (Kensington Publishers); *Worry-Free Investing*, by Zvi Bodie (Financial Times Prentice Hall); *Crucial Confrontations* (McGraw-Hill). Other clients include Visible Ink Press, Better Homes & Gardens Books, Etruscan Press, Stillwater Publishing, Zone Labs, Lehigh University. References and contact numbers available for potential clients.

Costs Clients charged per service fee ($1,500); monthly retainer ($1,500). Works with clients on marketing budget. Offers written contract, binding for 3-6 months minimum. 1-month notice must be given to terminate contract.

Tips "We are a small, focused organization, designed to provide personal service. Authors who sign on with us work with us, not with junior staffers."

GAIL LEONDAR PUBLIC RELATIONS

21 Belknap St., Arlington MA 02474-6605. (781)648-1658. E-mail: gail@glprbooks.com. Website: www.glprbooks.com. **Contact:** Gail Leondar-Wright. Estab. 1992; specifically with books for 14 years. Currently works with 16 clients. 50% of clients are new/first-time writers.

- Prior to becoming a freelance publicist, Ms. Leondar-Wright directed theater.

Specializations Nonfiction, fiction, academic, any books on progressive social issues. **Interested in these nonfiction areas:** Biography/autobiography, current affairs, education, ethnic/cultural interests, gay/lesbian issues, government/politics/law, history, multicultural, music/dance/theater/film, sociology, women's issues/women's studies. **Interested in these fiction areas:** Feminist, gay/lesbian/transgender.

Services Provides detailed outline of services provided. Book tours include bookstores, radio interviews, TV interviews, newspaper interviews. Clients have appeared on *Fresh Air, Morning Edition*, *Weekend Edition*, CNN, C-SPAN. Media kit includes author's biography, testimonials, articles about author, basic information on book, professional photos, sample interview questions.

O━ GLPR promotes only books on progressive social issues. Our contacts give excellent interviews, primarily on noncommercial radio, including NPR.

How to Contact Call or e-mail. Responds in less than 1 week. Returns materials only with SASE. Obtains most new clients through recommendations from others. Contact 6 months prior to book's publication.

Clients *A Desperate Passion*, by Dr. Helen Caldicott (Norton); *The Good Heart*, by The Dalai Lama (Wisdom); *Love Canal*, by Lois Gibbs (New Society Publishers); *Gender Outlaw*, by Kate Bornstein (Routledge). References and contact numbers available for potential clients.

Costs Clients charged flat fee ($2,000-15,000). Works with clients on marketing budget. Offers written contract, binding for typically 3 months.

MARKETABILITY, INC.

6275 Simms St., Suite 207, Arvada CO 80004. (303)279-4349. Fax: (303)279-7950. E-mail: twist@marketability.com. Website: www.marketability.com. **Contact:** Kim Dushinski; Tami DePalma. Estab. 1989; specifically with books since 1995. Currently works with 20 clients. 50% of clients are new/first-time authors.

- Prior to becoming independent publicists, Ms. Dushinski and Ms. DePalma were in marketing/public relations for all types of companies.

Members Tami DePalma, partner (creative PR, at firm since 1993); Kim Dushinski, partner (strategic PR, at firm since 1989); Bradley James (lifestyle, gay/lesbian, at firm since 1998); Malea Melis (women, history, at firm since 1999).

Specializations Nonfiction. **Interested in these nonfiction areas:** business; child guidance/parenting; cooking/food/nutrition; crafts/hobbies; gay/lesbian issues; health/medicine; history; how-to; interior design/decorating;

money/finance/economics; self-help/personal improvement; travel; women's issues/women's studies. Other types of clients include publishers.

Services Provides detailed outline of services provided, fax news releases, electronic news release, material to magazines/newspapers for reviews. Book tours include radio interviews, TV interviews, newspaper interviews, magazine interviews. Media kit includes author's biography, basic information on book, professional photos, sample interview questions, book request information, other items as needed such as creative packaging/gimmicks. Helps writer obtain endorsements.

O→ "Not only can we be hired to do publicity, we also offer MAXIMUM EXPOSURE Marketing System—a book marketing training program for publishers and authors."

How to Contact Call, e-mail or fax. Responds in 3 weeks. Returns materials only with SASE. Obtains most new clients through recommendations from others. Contact 6 months prior to book's publication or anytime after book's publication.

Clients References and contact numbers available for potential clients.

Costs Charges clients per service fee ($2,000-3,000/monthly payment for 9-12 campaigns). "We have prices for each service we do and then we divide the total into monthly payments." Works with clients on marketing budget. Offers written contract. "We work on 9-12 month contracts typically." 30-day or for cause notice must be given to terminate contract.

Tips "Keep in mind that whether you are published by a publisher or independently publish your work, you will have to do marketing if you want your work to sell. We can help you do this marketing."

MEDIA MASTERS PUBLICITY

17600 S. Richmond Rd., Plainfield IL 60554. (815)254-7383. Fax: (815)254-1948. E-mail: tracey@mmpublicity.com. Website: www.mmpublicity.com. **Contact:** Tracey Daniels. Estab. 1998. Currently works with 10 clients. 10% of clients are new/first-time writers.

- Prior to becoming an independent publicist, Ms. Daniels worked in English Education—middle school and high school.

Members Karen Wadsworth (marketing, events, at firm since 2001).

Specializations Children's books, nonfiction. **Interested in these nonfiction areas:** Biography/autobiography; child guidance/parenting; cooking/food/nutrition; education; how-to; juvenile nonfiction; young adult. **Interested in these fiction areas:** Juvenile; picture book; young adult. Other types of clients include publishers.

Services Provides detailed outline of services provided, fax news releases, electronic news release, material to magazines/newspapers for reviews, brochures, website assistance, website publicity. Book tours include bookstores, specialty stores, radio interviews, TV interviews, newspaper interviews, magazine interviews, schools. Clients have appeared on CNN, *Talk America*, CBS, ABC, VOA, USA Radio Network, AP Radio Network, *20/20*. "Each media kit varies depending on focus, client needs, and budget." Helps writer obtain endorsements.

O→ "We have over 18 years of book publicity experience. Our company delivers 'publicity with personality'—we go beyond just covering the basics."

How to Contact E-mail or send letter with outline/proposal and sample chapters. Responds in 2 weeks. Returns materials only with SASE. Obtains most new clients through recommendations from others. Contact 3 months prior to book's publication.

Clients Clients include Roaring Brook, HarperCollins Children's Books, Kingfisher Books, NorthSouth Books, NorthWord Books for Young Readers, Boyds Mills Press, Sleeping Bear Press, plus individual authors. Reference and contact numbers available for potential clients.

Costs Charges for services depend on client's needs and budget. Offers written contract. 1-month notice must be given to terminate contract.

Writers' Conferences BEA, ALA.

PHENIX & PHENIX LITERARY PUBLICISTS, INC.

2100 Kramer Lane, Suite 300, Austin TX 78757. (512)478-2028. Fax: (512)478-2117. E-mail: info@bookpros.com. Website: www.bookpros.com. **Contact:** Andy Morales, director of client development. Estab. 1994; specifically with books since 1994. Currently works with 40 clients. 50% of clients are new/first-time writers.

Members Marika Flatt (director of publishers services); Elaine Krackau (publicist); Mike Odam (president); Steve Joiner (vice president).

Specializations Nonfiction, fiction, children's books, academic, coffee table books, biographies. **Interested in these nonfiction areas:** Animals; biography/autobiography; business; child guidance/parenting; computers/electronics; current affairs; health/medicine; money/finance/economics; multicultural; religious/inspirational; self-help/personal improvement; sports; travel; true crime/investigative; women's issues/women's studies; young adult. **Interested in these fiction areas:** Action/adventure; confessional; contemporary issues; detective/police/crime; family saga; historical; humor/satire; multicultural; mystery/suspense; regional; religious/inspirational; sports; young adult. Other types of clients include publishers.

Services Provides detailed outline of services provided, media training, fax news releases, electronic news releases, material to magazines/newspapers for reviews, brochures, website publicity. Book tours include bookstores, specialty stores, radio interviews, TV interviews, newspaper interviews, magazine interviews. Clients have appeared on *Oprah*, CNN, CNBC, Fox News Network, *Leeza*, *Montel*, *Good Morning America*, Talk America Radio Network, Business News Network, Westwood One Radio Network, UPI Radio Network. Media kit includes author's biography, testimonials, articles about author, basic information on book, professional photos, sample interview questions, book request information, press releases, excerpts. Recent promotions included video press releases, mystery contest, online publicity campaigns, creative angles for fiction positioning.
How to Contact Call, e-mail, fax, or send letter with entire ms. Responds in 5 days. Discards unwanted material. Obtains most new clients through recommendations from others, conferences, website. Contact 2-4 months prior to book's publication or after book's publication.
Clients *Kiss of God*, by Marshall Ball (Health Communications); *True Women/Hill Country*, by Janice Woods Windle (Longstreet Press); *Wizard of Ads*, by Roy Williams (Bard Press); *Faith on Trial*, by Pamela Ewen (Broadman & Holman). Other clients include Dr. Ivan Misner, Lisa Shaw-Brawley, Michele O'Donnell, Patrick Seaman (Timberwolf Press), Continuum Press. References and contact numbers available for potential clients.
Costs Charges clients monthly retainer ($2,500-6,500). Works with clients on a marketing budget. Offers written contract binding for 4-6 months.
Writers' Conferences Craft of Writing (Denton TX), BEA.
Tips "Find a publicist that will offer a guarantee. Educate yourself on the book/publicity process."

RAAB ASSOCIATES

345 Millwood Rd., Chappaqua NY 10514. (914)241-2117. Fax: (914)241-0050. E-mail: info@raabassociates.com. Website: www.raabassociates.com. **Contact:** Susan Salzman Raab. Estab. 1986; specifically with books since 1986. Currently works with 10 clients. 10% of clients are new/first-time writers.

- Prior to becoming an independent publicist, Ms. Salzman Raab worked on staff at major publishing houses in the children's book industry.

Members Susanna Reich (associate, at firm since 2000); Susan Salzman Raab (partner, at firm since 1986).
Specializations Children's books, parenting books and products. **Interested in these nonfiction areas:** Child guidance/parenting, juvenile nonfiction, young adult. **Interested in these fiction areas:** Juvenile, picture book, young adult, parenting. Other types of clients include publishers, toy companies, audio companies.
Services Provides detailed outline of services provided, market research, sends material to magazines/newspapers for review, website assistance, website development, extensive online publicity. Book tours include bookstores, specialty stores, radio interviews, TV interviews, newspaper interviews, magazine interviews, schools, and libraries. Can also assist in coordinating travel plans. Clients have appeared on NPR, CNN, C-SPAN, Radio-Disney, PRI. Media kit includes author's biography, testimonials, articles about author, basic information on book, sample interview questions, book request information. Helps writer obtain endorsements.

"We are the only PR agency to specialize in children's and parenting books."

How to Contact Call or e-mail. Responds in 2 weeks. Returns materials only with SASE. Obtains most new clients through recommendations from others, conferences. Contact 4 months prior to book's publication.
Costs Clients charged per-service fee. Offers written contract. 3-month notice must be given to terminate contract.
Writers' Conferences Society of Children's Book Writers & Illustrators (National and Mid-Winter); Society of Children's Book Writers & Illustrators (Regional Meeting); Book Expo America (New York, June); American Library Association (Chicago, June); Bologna Bookfair (April).

ROCKS-DEHART PUBLIC RELATIONS (BOOK PUBLICITY)

306 Marberry Dr., Pittsburgh PA 15215. (412)784-8811. Fax: (412)784-8610. E-mail: celiarocks@aol.com. Website: www.rdpr.com. **Contact:** Celia Rocks. Estab. 1993; specifically with books since 1993. Currently works with 10 clients; 20% of clients are new/first-time writers.

- Prior to becoming a publicist, Ms. Rocks was a publicity specialist at Burson Marsteller.

Members Dottie DeHart (principal, at firm since 1993); 8 other staff members.
Specializations Nonfiction, business, lifestyle. **Interested in these nonfiction areas:** Biography/autobiography; business; cooking/food/nutrition; current affairs; health/medicine; how-to; humor; popular culture; psychology; religious/inspirational; self-help/personal improvement; sociology; travel; women's issues/women's studies. Other types of clients include major publishing houses.
Services Provides detailed outline of services provided. Book tours include bookstores, specialty stores, radio interviews, TV interviews, newspaper interviews, magazine interviews, speaking engagements, conferences, libraries, schools, universities. Clients have appeared on *ABC World News*, *Oprah*, and others, as well as in *Time* and *Newsweek*. Media kit includes author's biography, testimonials, articles about author, basic information on book, professional photos, sample interview questions, book request information, breakthrough-plan materials,

and "any other pieces that are helpful." Helps writers obtain endorsements. Recent promotions included "taking a book like *Fishing for Dummies* and sending gummy worms with packages."

O- This company specializes in IDG "Dummies" Books, business, management, and lifestyle titles. "We are a highly creative firm that understands the best way to obtain maximum publicity."

How to Contact Call or e-mail. Responds in 1 day. Obtains most new clients through recommendations from others. Contact 2-4 months prior to book's publication.

Clients Clients include John Wiley & Sons, AAA Publishing, Dearborn, Jossey-Bass.

Costs Clients charged monthly retainer ($3,000-5,000). Works with clients on marketing budget. Offers written contract. 1-month notice must be given to terminate contract.

SHERRI ROSEN PUBLICITY

15 Park Row, Suite 25C, New York NY 10038. Phone/Fax: (212)587-0296. E-mail: sherri@sherrirosen.com. Website: www.sherrirosen.com. **Contact:** Sherri Rosen. Estab. 1997, specifically with books for 13 years. Currently works with 6 clients. 75% published authors, 25% self-published authors.

- Ms. Rosen's first client, Naura Hayden, was on *The New York Times* best-seller list for 63 weeks. The book made millions of dollars.

Specializations Sex, relationship, and spirituality. Likes to work on a book for at least 6 months. **Interested in these nonfiction areas:** Child guidance/parenting, cooking/food/nutrition, current affairs, education, ethnic/cultural interests, gay/lesbian issues, health/medicine, how-to, humor, juvenile nonfiction, memoirs, music/dance/theater/film, New Age/metaphysics, popular culture, psychology, religious/inspirational, self-help/personal improvement, travel, women's issues/women's studies, young adult. **Interested in these fiction areas:** Action/adventure, confessional, erotica, ethnic, experimental, family saga, fantasy, feminist, humor/satire, literary, mainstream, multicultural, New Age/metaphysical, psychic/supernatural, religious/inspirational, romance, young adult. Other types of clients include healers, business people.

Services Provides detailed outline of services provided, audio/video tapes, international publicity, if applicable, sends material to magazines/newspapers for reviews, brochures. Book tours include bookstores, radio interviews, TV interviews, newspaper interviews, magazine interviews, speaking engagements, conferences, libraries, schools, universities. Assists in coordinating travel plans. Clients have appeared on *Oprah*, *Montel*, *Politically Incorrect*, *Leeza*, *Men are from Mars*, *The Sally Show*, *The Other Half*, *Howard Stern*, 5-page spread in *Playboy* magazine. Media kit includes author's biography, testimonials, articles about author, basic information on book, professional photos, sample interview questions, book request information. Will write all of the promotional material or collaborate with client. Helps writer obtain endorsements.

O- "I work with eclectic clientele—sex books, spiritual books, personal inspirational, self-help books. What is distinct is I will only work with people I like, and I have to like and respect what they are doing."

How to Contact E-mail. Responds immediately. Discards unwanted queries or returns materials only with SASE. Obtains most new clients through recommendations from others, listings with other services in our industry. Contact 3 months prior to book's publication if possible; after book's publication once a platform is started.

Clients *How to Satisfy a Woman*, by Naura Hayden (self-published); *Men Who Can't Love*, by Steven Carten (HarperCollins); *Rebirth of the Goddess*, by Carol Christ (Addison-Wesley); *Buddhism Without Belief*, by Stephen Batchelor (Riverhead). Other clients include Eli Jaxon-Bear, Sandra Rothenberger, Elizabeth Ayres. References and contact numbers available for potential clients.

Costs Clients charged hourly retainer fee ($200); monthly retainer ($4,000-6,000). Flexible. Offers written contract. 1-month notice must be given to terminate contract.

Tips "Not only are contacts important, but make sure you like who you will be working with, because you work so closely."

ROYCE CARLTON, INC.

866 United Nations Plaza, Suite 587, New York, NY 10017. (212)355-7700. Fax: (212)888-8659. E-mail: info@roycecarlton.com. Website: www.roycecarlton.com. **Contact:** Carlton Sedgeley. Estab. 1968. Currently works with 71 clients.

- Royce Carlton, Inc., is a lecture agency and management firm for some 71 speakers who are available for lectures and speaking engagements.

Members Carlton S. Sedgeley, president (at firm since 1968); Lucy Lepage, executive vice president (at firm since 1968); Helen Churko, vice president (at firm since 1984).

Specializations Royce Carlton works with many different types of speakers. Other clients include celebrities, writers, journalists, scientists, etc.

Services Provides "full service for all our clients to lecture."

O- "Royce Carlton represents all speakers exclusively."

How to Contact Call, e-mail, or fax. Discards unwanted material. Obtains most new clients through recommendations or initiates contact directly.

Clients *Five People You Meet in Heaven*, by Mitch Albom; *House Made of Dawn*, by N. Scott Momaday. Other

clients include Joan Rivers, Elaine Pagels, Walter Mosley, David Halberstam, Tom Friedman, Fareed Zakaria, Susan Sontag. References and contact numbers available for potential clients.
Costs Client charged per placement; commission. Offers written contract. 1-month notice must be given to terminate contract.

SMITH PUBLICITY

431 S. Oxford Valley Rd., 2nd Floor, Fairless Hills PA 19030. (215)547-4778. Fax: (215)547-4785. E-mail: info@smithpublicity.com. Website: www.smithpublicity.com. **Contact:** Dan Smith, ext. 111. Estab. 1997; specifically with books for 4 years. Currently works with 10-12 clients. 70% of clients are new/first-time writers.

- Prior to starting Smith Publicity in 1997, Mr. Smith was a freelance public relations specialist and promotional writer.

Members Dan Smith (president, director of operations, campaign management, at firm 7 years); Deborah Ruriani (senior account executive, at firm 2 years); Erin MacDonald (account executive, at firm 1 year); Nikki Bowman (director of operations, at firm 2 years); Fran Rubin (director of marketing and business development, at firm 7 years).
Specializations Nonfiction, fiction. **Interested in these nonfiction areas:** Politics, how-to, humor, multicultural, New Age, popular culture, self-help, true crime/investigative. **Interested in these fiction areas:** Various genres. Other types of clients include entrepreneurs, businesses, and nonprofit organizations.
Services Provides detailed outline of services provided, media training, comprehensive publicity campaigns, specialized media pitching, press release distribution, book reviews, feature stories, radio/TV interviews, book tours, special events, seminars. Clients have appeared on *Today Show*, CNN, CNN International, Fox News, *Art Bell*, etc., *Montel*, *Sally*, *Good Morning America*, *Howard Stern*, *O'Reilly Factor*, *Mike Gallagher*, *Wall Street Journal*, *The New York Times*, *USA Today*, *People*, *The Philadelphia Inquirer*, *Details Magazine*, *Cosmopolitan*, and others. Media kit includes press releases, bio, sample questions, sell sheet, book information, excerpt, etc. Developed unorthodox publicity angles which transformed a local personality and author into a nationally known expert.

"We follow the Golden Rule: We give the media what they want . . . good story ideas and interview topics, while offering rates typically well below national averages, and unparalleled client service."

How to Contact Call, e-mail, mail, or fax. Responds in 1 week. Returns materials only with SASE. Obtains most new clients through referrals from current or previous clients. Contact 4 months prior to book's publication or after book's publication.
Clients *Conversations with Tom*, by Walda Woods (White Rose Publishing); *The Old Boys: The American Elite and the Origins of the Cat*, by Burton Hersh; *Emotionally Intelligent Parenting*, by Dr. Steven Tobias (Random House). Other clients include Rhys Bowen (author of *For the Love of Mike*); Barry Nadel (president of InfoLink Screening Services, Inc.); Angelo Paparelli (internationally recognized immigration attorney); Juliene Osborne-McKnight (author of *Bright Sword of Ireland*); Scott Kipp (author of Broadband Entertainment); Michael Johnston (author of *Brideshead Regained*). References available for potential clients.
Costs Clients charged monthly retainer (from $500-2,500/month; 4-6 month agreement), or flat fee. Offers written contract. 3-months notice must be given to terminate contract.
Writers' Conferences Book Expo America.
Tips "Ask questions and talk to at least 3 different publicists. Have fun with your project and enjoy the ride! Only the determined make it."

N THE SPIZMAN AGENCY

Atlanta GA 30327. (770)953-2040. Fax: (770)953-2172. E-mail: willy@spizmanagency.com. www.spizmanagency.com. **Contact:** Willy Spizman. Estab. 1981; specifically with books for 20 years. 50% of clients are new/first-time writers.
Specializations Nonfiction, fiction, children's book, academic. **Interested in these nonfiction areas:** business, child guidance/parenting, computers/electronics, cooking/food/nutrition, crafts/hobbies, current affairs, education, ethnic/cultural interests, health/medicine, history, how-to, humor, interior design/decorating, juvenile nonfiction, language/literature/criticism, memoirs, military/war, money/finance/economics, multicultural, music/dance/theater/film, nature/environment, New Age/metaphysics, photography, popular culture, psychology, religious/inspirational, science/technology, self-help/personal improvement, sociology, sports, travel, true crime/investigative, women's issues/women's studies, young adult. **Interested in these fiction areas:** contemporary issues, internet, mainstream, inspirational, young adult.
Services Provides detailed outline of services provided, media training, international publicity, if applicable, market research, fax news releases, electronic news releases, sends material to magazines/newspapers for reviews, brochures, websites assistance, website publicity. Book tours include bookstores, specialty stores, radio interviews, TV interviews, newspaper interviews, magazine interviews, satellite media tours, speaking engagements, conferences, libraries, schools, universities. Assists in coordinating travel plans. Clients have appeared on *Oprah*, CNN, *Today*, HGTV, *The Atlanta Journal-Constitution*. Media kit includes author's biogra-

phy, testimonials, articles about author, basic information on book, professional photos, sample interview questions, book request information. Helps writer obtain endorsements. Recent promotions included a 1-hour show on a client's book on CNN.

How to Contact E-mail. Responds in 1 week. Returns materials only with SASE. Obtains most new clients through recommendations from others. Contact 6 months prior to book's publication, once a platform is started.

Clients *11 Immutable Laws of the Internet*, by Al and Laura Ries (HarperCollins); *Live, Learn & Pass It On*, by H. Jackson Brown, Jr. (Rutledge Hill). Other clients include Turner Broadcasting, GlaxoSmithKline, Reproductive Biology Associates. References and contact numbers available for potential clients.

Costs Monthly retainer. Works with clients to help create a marketing budget. Offers written contract. 1-month notice must be given to terminate contract.

Tips "It gets down to one thing—who they know and what they know, plus years of successful clients. We score high on all counts."

WARWICK ASSOCIATES

18340 Sonoma Hwy., Sonoma CA 95476. (707)939-9212. Fax: (707)938-3515. E-mail: warwick@vom.com. Website: www.warwickassociates.net. **Contact:** Simon Warwick-Smith, president. Estab. 1983; specifically with books for 18 years. Currently works with 24 clients. 12% of clients are new/first-time writers.

- Prior to becoming a freelance publicist, Mr. Warwick-Smith was Senior Vice President of Marketing, Associated Publishers Group (books).

Members Cierra Trenery (celebrity, sports, at firm 6 years); Simon Warwick-Smith (metaphysics, business, at firm 18 years); Warren Misuraca (travel, writing, at firm 8 years).

Specializations Nonfiction, children's books, spirituality. **Interested in these nonfiction areas:** Biography/autobiography, business, child guidance/parenting, computers/electronics, cooking/food/nutrition, government/politics/law, health/medicine, how-to, New Age/metaphysics, psychology, religious/inspirational, self-help/personal improvement, sports, travel. Other types of clients include celebrity authors.

Services Provides media training, market research, fax news releases, electronic news releases, sends material to magazines/newspapers for reviews, brochures, website assistance, website publicity. Book tours include bookstores, specialty stores, radio interviews, TV interviews, newspaper interviews, magazine interviews, speaking engagements, online interviews. Assists in coordinating travel plans. Clients have appeared on *Larry King, Donahue, Oprah, Good Morning America*. Media kit includes résumé, author's biography, testimonials, articles about author, basic information on book, professional photos, sample interview questions, book request information. Helps writer obtain endorsements.

How to Contact See website. Responds in 2 weeks. Returns material only with SASE. Obtains most new clients through recommendations from others and on website. Contact 6 months prior to book's publication.

Clients References and contact numbers available for potential clients.

Costs Works with clients on marketing budget. Offers written contract binding for specific project.

WORLD CLASS SPEAKERS & ENTERTAINERS

5200 Kanan Rd., Suite 210, Aqoura Hills CA 91301. (818)991-5400. Fax: (818)991-2226. E-mail: wcse@speak.com. Website: www.speak.com. **Contact:** Joseph I. Kessler. Estab. 1965.

Specializations Nonfiction, academic. **Interested in these nonfiction areas:** Business; humor; money/finance/economics; psychology; science/technology; self-help/personal improvement; sociology; sports; women's issues/women's studies; high profile/famous writers. Other types of clients include experts in all fields.

Services Provides market research, sends material to magazines/newspapers for reviews, brochures, website publicity. Book tours include radio interviews, TV interviews, newspaper interviews, magazine interviews, speaking engagements, conferences, universities. Media kits include author's biography, testimonials, articles about author, professional photos. Helps writer obtain endorsements.

How to Contact Call, e-mail, or fax. Responds in 1 week. Discards unwanted materials. Obtains most new clients through recommendations from others. Contact prior to book's publication.

Costs Charges clients per placement basis ($1,500 minimum); 30% commission. Works with clients on marketing budget. Offers written contract. 2-3-month notice must be given to terminate contract.

THE WRITE PUBLICIST & CO.

1865 River Falls Dr., Roswell GA 30076. (770)998-9911. E-mail: thewritepublicist@earthlink.net. Website: www.thewritepublicist.com. **Contact:** Regina Lynch-Hudson. Estab. 1990; specifically with books for 10 years. Currently works with 5 clients. 50% of clients are new/first-time writers.

- Prior to becoming a publicist, Ms. Lynch-Hudson was public relations director for a 4-star resort.

Specializations Nonfiction, fiction, children's books, multicultural, ethnic and minority market books. **Interested in these nonfiction areas:** Biography/autobiography, business, education, ethnic/cultural interests, health/medicine, how-to, juvenile nonfiction, multicultural, religious/inspirational, women's issues/women's studies. **Interested in these fiction areas:** Confessional, contemporary issues, erotica, ethnic, family saga, humor/satire, mainstream, multicultural, religious/inspirational, romance, science fiction, sports. Other types of clients include physicians, lawyers, entertainers, artists.

Services Provides international publicity, if applicable, electronic news releases, sends material to magazines/newspapers for reviews, website publicity. Book tours include bookstores, radio interviews, TV interviews, newspaper interviews, magazine interviews, schools, universities. Assists in coordinating travel plans. Clients have appeared on *Oprah*, all national TV networks. Media kit includes author's biography, basic information on book, professional photos, book request information, propriety innovative enclosures that insure and increase the opportunity for publication. Helps writer obtain endorsements.

O‑ Twelve years experience publicizing people, places, products, performances. Owner of company was syndicated columnist to 215 newspapers, which solidified media contacts.

How to Contact E-mail. Send book or ms. Responds in 1 week. Returns materials only with SASE. Obtains most new clients through recommendations from others. "90% of our clients are referred nationally." Contact 1 month prior to book's publication or after book's publication.

Clients *Lifestyles for the 21st Century*, by Dr. Marcus Wells (Humanics Publishing); *Preconceived Notions*, by Robyn Williams (Noble Press); *Fed Up With the Fanny*, by Franklin White (Simon & Schuster). Other clients include Vernon Jones, CEO of DeKalb County; Atlanta Perinatal Associates; former NFLer-turned-sculptor George Nock. "Our clients' contracts state that they will not be solicited by prospective clients. Our website shows photos of clients who give their recommendation by consenting to be placed on our website."

Costs Clients charged flat fee ($9,500-15,000). Works with clients on marketing budget. Offers written contract. 3-day notice before our company has invested time interviewing the client and writing their release must be given to terminate a contract.

Tips "Does the publicist have a website that actually pictures clients? Our award-winning website ranks among top 10 of all major search engines as one of the few PR sites that actually depicts clients.

MERYL ZEGAREK PUBLIC RELATIONS, INC.

255 W. 108th St., Suite 9D1, New York NY 10025. (917)493-3601. Fax: (917)493-3598. E-mail: mz@mzpr.com. Website: www.mzpr.com. **Contact:** Meryl Zegarek. Worked specifically with books for 25 years.

- Prior to starting her publicity agency, Ms. Zegarek was a publicity director of 2 divisions of The Knopf Publishing Group, Pantheon/Schocken Books, Random House.

Specializations Nonfiction, fiction. **Interested in these nonfiction areas:** Animals, anthropology/archaeology, art/architecture/design, current affairs, ethnic/cultural interests, government/politics/law, health/medicine, history, how-to, humor, interior design/decorating, language/literature/criticism, multicultural, music/dance/theater/film, nature/environment, photography, popular culture, psychology, religious/inspirational, science/technology, self-help/personal improvement, sociology, travel, true crime/investigative, women's issues/women's studies. **Interested in these fiction areas:** Action/adventure, contemporary issues, detective/police/crime, ethnic, historical, literary, multicultural, mystery/suspense, religious/inspirational, science fiction, thriller/espionage. Other types of clients include theater, performance, nonprofits, human rights organizations, international publishers.

Services Provides detailed outline of services provided. Expertise in nationwide media campaigns, including print features, TV, radio, and World Wide Web exposure. Also does marketing campaigns, media training, and book tours with bookstore readings, and appearances in other local venues, interviews/features in newspapers, magazines, TV, and radio. Assists in coordinating travel plans. Clients have appeared on *Oprah*, *Good Morning America*, *Today*, Fox-News, *Fresh Air* (NPR), *Morning Edition* (NPR). Media kit includes résumé, author's biography, testimonials, articles about author, basic information on book, professional photos, sample interview questions, book request information. Plans nationwide print and radio campaigns with give-aways—with National Television and radio producing *New York Times* bestsellers.

O‑ Also has unique specialty in Jewish and nonreligious spiritual books and authors. "I have been a publicity director for 3 major publishing houses (Knopf, Bantam Doubleday, William Morrow) during a 25-year career in book publicity. I have experience in every genre of book with established contacts in TV, radio, and print—as well as bookstores and speaking venues."

How to Contact Call, e-mail, or fax. Send letter with entire ms or galley, outline/proposal, sample chapters with SASE. Responds in 2 weeks. Returns material only with SASE. Obtains most new clients through recommendations from others. Contact as early as possible, 4-5 months prior to book's publication, if possible.

Clients *The Piano Teacher*, by Elfriede Jelinek; *Lit From Within*, by Victoria Moran (Harper SF); *ETZ Hayim* (Jewish Publication Society); *The Zohar: Pritzker Edition* (Stanford University Press); *Mystics, Mavericks and Merrymakers: An Inside Journey Among Hasidic Girls*, by Stephanie Wellen Levine (NYU Press). Other clients include The Paulist Press, Harmony Books, Hidden Spring, Serpent's Tail, Continuum Books. References and contact numbers available for potential clients.

Costs Clients charged flat fee, hourly retainer fee for consultations, monthly retainer (divide up flat fee payable by month). Offers written contract. 1-month notice must be given to terminate contract.

Tips "Call early."

RESOURCES

Writers' Conferences

Attending a writers' conference that includes agents gives you both the opportunity to learn more about what agents do and the chance to show an agent your work. Ideally, a conference should include a panel or two with a number of agents to give writers a sense of the variety of personalities and tastes of different agents.

Not all agents are alike: Some are more personable, and sometimes you simply click better with one agent over another. When only one agent attends a conference there is tendency for every writer at that conference to think, "Ah, this is the agent I've been looking for!" When a larger number of agents is attending, you have a wider group from which to choose, and you may have less competition for the agent's time.

Besides including panels of agents discussing what representation means and how to go about securing it, many of these gatherings also include time, either scheduled or impromptu, to meet briefly with an agent to discuss your work.

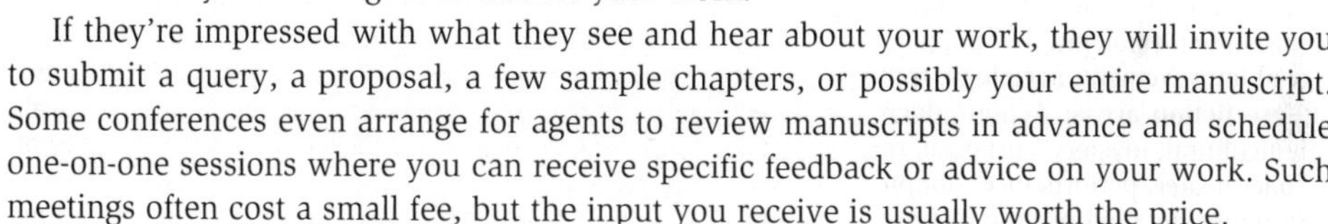

If they're impressed with what they see and hear about your work, they will invite you to submit a query, a proposal, a few sample chapters, or possibly your entire manuscript. Some conferences even arrange for agents to review manuscripts in advance and schedule one-on-one sessions where you can receive specific feedback or advice on your work. Such meetings often cost a small fee, but the input you receive is usually worth the price.

Ask writers who attend conferences and they'll tell you that at the very least you'll walk away with new knowledge about the industry. At the very best, you'll receive an invitation to send an agent your material!

Many writers try to make it to at least one conference a year, but cost and location can count as much as subject matter when determining which conference to attend. There are conferences in almost every state and province that can provide answers to your questions about writing and the publishing industry. Conferences also connect you with a community of other writers. Such connections help you learn about the pros and cons of different agents, and they also give you a renewed sense of purpose and direction in your own writing.

When reading through this section, keep in mind the following information to help you pick the best conference for your needs.

REGIONS

To make it easier for you to find a conference close to home—or to find one in an exotic locale to fit into your vacation plans—we've separated this section into geographical regions. The regions are as follows:

Northeast (pages 251-254): Connecticut, Maine, Massachusetts, New Hampshire, New York, Rhode Island, Vermont.

Get the Most from a Conference

Squeeze the most out of a conference by getting organized and staying involved. Follow these steps to ensure a worthwhile event.

Before you go:

- **Become familiar with all of the pre-conference literature,** particularly the agenda. Study the maps of the area, especially the locations of the rooms in which your meetings/events are scheduled.
- **Make a list of three to five objectives you'd like to attain,** e.g., who you want to meet, what you want to learn more about, what you want to improve on, how many new markets you want to find, etc.

At the conference:

- **Budget your time.** Label a map so you know ahead of time where, when, and how to get to each session. Note what you want to do most. Then, schedule time with agents and editors for critique sessions.
- **Don't be afraid to explore new areas.** You are there to learn. Pick one or two sessions you wouldn't typically attend. This is an education; keep your mind open to new ideas and advice.
- **Allow time for mingling.** Some of the best information is given after the session. Learn "frank truths" and inside scoops. Asking people what they've learned at the conference will trigger a conversation that may branch into areas you want to know more about but won't hear from the speakers.
- **Learn about agents, editors, and new markets.** Which are more open to new writers? Find a new contact in your area for future support.
- **Collect everything:** guidelines, sample issues, promotional fliers, and especially business cards. Make notes about the personalities of the people you meet on the back of business cards to remind you after the conference who to contact and who to avoid.
- **Find inspiration for future projects.** While you're away from home, people-watch, take a walk, ride a bike, or take a drive. You may even want to take pictures to enhance your memory.

After the conference:

- **Evaluate.** Write down the answers to these questions: Would I attend again? What were the pluses and minuses, e.g., speakers, location, food, topics, cost, lodging? What do I want to remember for next year? What should I try to do next time? Who would I like to meet?
- **Write a thank-you letter** to an agent or editor who was particularly helpful. They'll remember you when you later submit.

Midatlantic (pages 254-255): Washington D.C., Delaware, Maryland, New Jersey, Pennsylvania.

Midsouth (pages 255-257): North Carolina, South Carolina, Tennessee, Virginia, West Virginia.

Southeast (pages 257-258): Alabama, Arkansas, Florida, Georgia, Louisiana, Mississippi, Puerto Rico.

Midwest (pages 258-260): Illinois, Indiana, Kentucky, Michigan, Ohio.

North Central (page 260): Iowa, Minnesota, Nebraska, North Dakota, South Dakota, Wisconsin.

South Central (pages 260-264): Colorado, Kansas, Missouri, New Mexico, Oklahoma, Texas.

West (pages 264-268): Arizona, California, Hawaii, Nevada, Utah.

Northwest (pages 269-270): Alaska, Idaho, Montana, Oregon, Washington, Wyoming.

Canada (pages 270-272).

Quick Reference Icons

At the beginning of some listings, you will find one or more of the following symbols for quick identification of features particular to that listing.

N Conference new to this edition.

Canadian conference.

International conference.

CONFERENCE CALENDAR

To see which conferences are being held in the upcoming months, check the writers' conference calendar below. The calendar lists conferences alphabetically by the month in which they occur. It's often to your advantage to register for the conference you want to attend a few months in advance. This ensures you get the best prices and priority meeting slots available for consultations with the agents or editors. For screenwriters, some of the most popular conferences are UCLA Extension Writers' Program—Writers Studio (February), the ASA International Screenwriters Conference (August), and the Screenwriting Conference in Santa Fe (June).

For writers interested in screenplays or books, the San Diego State University Writers' Conference (January) and the Maui Writers' Conference (August) are popular choices not only for their beautiful locations, but also for the large number of high-quality industry professionals who lead workshops and meet one-on-one with attendees.

January

San Diego State University Writers' Conference (San Diego, CA)
Society of Southwestern Authors Writers' Conference—Wrangling with Writing (Tucson, AZ)

February

Florida Suncoast Writers' Conference (St. Petersburg, FL)
Society of Children's Book Writers & Illustrators Conference in Children's Literature, NYC (New York, NY)
UCLA Extension Writers' Program—Writers Studio (Los Angeles, CA)

March

Florida Christian Writers' Conference (Bradenton, FL)
Green River Writers' Novel-in-Progress Workshop (Louisville, KY)
IWWG Early Spring in California Conference (Santa Cruz, CA)
Kentucky Women Writers' Conference (Lexington, KY)
The Perspectives in Children's Literature Conference (Amherst, MA)
Tea with Eleanor Roosevelt (Hyde Park, NY)
Whidbey Island Writers' Conference (Langley, WA)
Writing Today (Birmingham, AL)

April

ASJA Writers' Conference (New York, NY)
IWWG Meet the Authors, Agents and Editors (New York, NY)
Mount Hermon Christian Writers' Conference (Mount Hermon, CA)
NETWO Writers' Roundup-Northeast Texas Writers Organization (Winfield, TX)
Norwescon (Seattle, WA)
Pikes Peak Writers' Conference (Colorado Springs, CO)
Society of Children's Book Writers and Illustrators/Hofstra Children's Literature Conference (Hemstead, NY)
Waterside Publishing Conference (Berkley, CA)

May

Florida First Coast Writers' Festival (Atlantic Beach, FL)
Midland Writers Conference (Midland, MI)
Pennwriters Annual Conference (Pittsburgh, PA)
Pima Writers' Workshop (Tucson, AZ)
Washington Independent Writers (WIW) Spring Writers Conference (Washington, DC)

June

Aspen Summer Words Writing Retreat (Aspen, CO)
Clarion West Writers' Workshop (Seattle, WA)
Frontiers in Writing (Amarillo, TX)
Great Lakes Writer's Workshop (Milwaukee, WI)
Heartland Writers' Conference (Sikeston, MO)
Highland Summer Conference (Radford, VA)
Indiana University Writers' Conference (Bloomington, IN)
Iowa Summer Writing Festival (Iowa City, IA)
Jackson Hole Writers' Conference (Laramie, WY)
Manhattanville Summer Writers' Week (Purchase, NY)
National Writers' Association Foundation Conference (Denver, CO)
The New Letters Weekend Writers' Conference (Kansas City, MO)
No Crime Unpublished™ Mystery Writers' Conference (Los Angeles, CA)
Pacific Northwest Writers Association (Edmonds, WA)
Remember the Magic 2006 (Saratoga Springs, NY)
Santa Barbara Writers' Conference (Montecito, CA)
Screenwriting Conference in Santa Fe (Santa Fe, NM)
Southern California Writers' Conference (San Diego, CA)
Wesleyan Writers' Conference (Middletown, CT)

July

Antioch Writers' Workshop (Yellow Springs, OH)
Festival of Words (Moose Jaw, SK, Canada)
Highlights Foundation Writers' Workshop (Chautauqua, NY)
Hofstra University Summer Writers' Conference (Hempstead, NY)
Maritime Writers' Workshop (Fredericton, NB, Canada)
New England Writers' Conference (Windsor, VT)
Romance Writers of America National Conference (various locations)
Sewanee Writers' Conference (Sewanee, TN)
Steamboat Springs Writers Conference (Steamboat Springs, CO)
Writers Workshop in Science Fiction (Lawrence, KS)

August

ASA International Screenwriters Conference (Los Angeles, CA)
Bread Loaf Writers' Conference (Ripton, VT)
The Columbus Writers' Conference (Columbus, OH)
The Festival of the Written Arts (Sechelt, BC, Canada)
Maui Writers' Conference (Kihei, HI)
Mendocino Coast Writers Conference (Fort Bragg, CA)
Sage Hill Writing Experience (Saskatoon, SK, Canada)
Society of Children's Book Writers and Illustrators/National Conference on Writing and Illustrating for Children (Los Angeles, CA)
Squaw Valley Community of Writers—Writers Workshop (Squaw Valley, CA)
Willamette Writers' Conference (Portland, OR)

September

Bouchercon 36 (Chicago, IL)
Last State Writers Conference (Greeneville, TN)
Winnipeg International Writers Festival (Winnipeg, MB, Canada)

October

Austin Film Festival & Heart of Film Screenwriters Conference (Austin, TX)
Central Ohio Fiction Writers Readers & Writers Holiday (Westerville, OH)
Flathead River Writers' Conference (Whitefish, MT)
Glorieta Christian Writers' Conference (Glorieta, NM)
IWWG Meet the Authors, Agents, and Editors (New York, NY)
New Jersey Romance Writers' Put Your Heart in a Book Conference (Somerset, NJ)
North Carolina Writers' Network Fall Conference (Carrboro, NC)
Rocky Mountain Fiction Writers Colorado Gold (Denver, CO)
Sandy Cove Christian Writers' Conference (North East, MD)
SIWC, Surrey International Writers' Conference (Surrey, BC, Canada)
The Vancouver International Writers Festival (Vancouver, BC, Canada)

November

Baltimore Writers' Alliance Conference (Riderwood, MD)
Police Writers Conference (Ashburn, VA)
Sage Hill Writing Experience (Saskatoon, SK, Canada)
Words & Music: A Literary Feast in New Orleans (New Orleans, LA)

SUBHEADS

Each listing is divided into subheads to make locating specific information easier. In the first section, you'll find contact information for each conference. This section also lists conference dates, the focus of the conference, and the average number of attendees. If a conference is small, you may receive more individual attention from speakers. If it is large, there may be a greater number and variety of agents in attendance. Finally, names of agents who will be speaking or have spoken in the past are listed along with details about their availability during the conference. Calling or e-mailing a conference director to verify the names of agents in attendance is always a good idea.

Costs: Looking at the price of events, plus room and board, may help writers on a tight budget narrow their choices.

Accommodations: Here conferences list overnight accommodations and travel information. Often conferences held in hotels will reserve rooms at a discount rate and may provide a shuttle to and from the local airport.

Additional Information: A range of features are provided here, including information on conference-sponsored contests, individual meetings, and the availability of brochures.

NORTHEAST (CT, MA, ME, NH, NY, RI, VT)

ASJA WRITERS CONFERENCE

American Society of Journalists and Authors, 1501 Broadway, Suite 302, New York NY 10036. (212)997-0947. Fax: (212)768-7414. E-mail: staff@asja.org. Website: www.asja.org. **Contact:** Brett Harvey, executive director. Estab. 1971. Annual. Conference held April. Conference duration: 2 days. Average attendance: 600. Nonfiction, screenwriting. Held at Grand Hyatt in New York. **Previous agents/speakers have included:** Dominick Dunne, James Brady, Dana Sobel. Agents will be speaking.

Costs $195-240, depending on when you sign up (includes lunch).

Accommodations "The hotel holding our conference always blocks out discounted rooms for attendees."

Additional Information Brochures available in February. Registration form on website. Inquiries by e-mail and fax OK.

BREAD LOAF WRITERS' CONFERENCE

Middlebury College, Middlebury VT 05753. (802)443-5286. Fax: (802)443-2087. E-mail: blwc@middlebury.edu. Website: www.middlebury.edu/blwc. **Contact:** Noreen Cargill, administrative manager. Estab. 1926. Annual. Conference held in late August. Conference duration: 11 days. Average attendance: 230. For fiction, nonfiction, and poetry. Held at the summer campus in Ripton, Vermont (belongs to Middlebury College).

Costs $2,081 (includes room/board) (2005).

Accommodations Accommodations are on campus in Ripton.

HIGHLIGHTS FOUNDATION WRITERS WORKSHOP AT CHAUTAUQUA

Dept. NM, 814 Court St., Honesdale PA 18431. (570)253-1192. Fax: (570)253-0179. E-mail: contact@highlightsfoundation.org. Website: www.highlightsfoundation.org. **Contact:** Kent Brown, executive director. Estab. 1985. Annual. Conference held in July. Average attendance: 100. "Writer workshops geared toward those who write for children—beginner, intermediate, advanced levels. Small group workshops, 1-to-1 interaction between faculty and participants plus panel sessions, lectures and large group meetings. Workshop site is the picturesque community of Chautauqua, New York." Classes offered include "Children's Interests," "Writing Dialogue," "Outline for the Novel," "Conflict and Developing Plot." **Previous agents/speakers have included:** Eve Bunting, James Cross Giblin, Walter Dean Myers, Jane Yolen, Patricia Gauch, Jerry Spinelli, Joy Cowley, and Ed Young.

Costs $2,100 conference fee. Fee includes all meals, conference supplies, gate pass to Chautauqua Institution.

Accommodations "We coordinate ground transportation to and from airports, trains, and bus stations in the Erie, Pennsylvania and Jamestown/Buffalo, New York area. We also coordinate accommodations for conference attendees."

Additional Information "We offer the opportunity for attendees to submit a manuscript for review at the conference." Workshop brochures/guidelines are available after January for SASE. Inquiries by fax OK.

HOFSTRA UNIVERSITY SUMMER WRITERS' CONFERENCE

250 Hofstra University, UCCE, Hempstead NY 11549-2500. (516)463-7600. Fax: (516)463-4833. E-mail: uccelibarts@hofstra.edu. Website: www.hofstra.edu/writers (includes details on dates, faculty, general description, tuition). **Contact:** Janet Kaplan, director of the summer writing workshops. Estab. 1972. Annual. Conference held July. Average attendance: 65. Conference offers workshops in short fiction, nonfiction, poetry, juvenile fiction, stage/screenwriting and, on occasion, 1 other genre such as detective fiction or science fiction. High school students welcome. Site is the university campus, a suburban setting, 25 miles from New York City. **Previous agent/speakers have incuded:** Roberta Allen, Ronald Bazarini, Carole Crowe, Brian Heinz and Rebecca Wolff. Agents will be speaking and available for meetings with attendees.

Costs Noncredit (2 meals, no room): approximately $335/workshop or $560/2 workshops. Credit available to undergraduate and graduate. See website for further information. Continental breakfast and lunch are provided daily; tuition also includes cost of banquet.

Accommodations Free bus operates between Hempstead Train Station and campus for those commuting from New York City. Dormitory rooms are available for approximately $450 for the 2-week conference.

Additional Information "All workshops include critiquing. Each participant is given 1-on-1 time for a half hour with workshop leader."

IWWG MEET THE AUTHORS, AGENTS AND EDITORS: THE BIG APPLE WORKSHOPS

% International Women's Writing Guild, P.O. Box 810, Gracie Station, New York NY 10028-0082. (212)737-7536. Fax: (212)737-9469. E-mail: iwwg@iwwg.org. Website: www.iwwg.org. **Contact:** Hannelore Hahn, executive director. Estab. 1980. Workshops held generally the third weekend in April and the second weekend in October. Average attendance: 200. Workshops to promote creative writing and professional success. Held midtown New York City. Saturday offers a 1-day writing workshop. Sunday morning: discussion with up to 10 recently published IWWG authors. Book fair during lunch. Sunday afternoon: Open house–Meet the Agents (up to 10 literary agents introduce themselves, and then members of the audience speak to the agents they wish to meet. Many as-yet-unpublished works have found publication in this manner). **Previous agents/speakers have included:** Meredith Bernstein, Rita Rosenkranz, and Jeff Herman.

Costs $110 for members for the weekend; $130 for nonmembers for the weekend; $70/80 for Saturday; $70/95 for Sunday.

Additional Information Information (including accommodations) given in brochure. Inquires by fax and e-mail OK. "A simple formula for success."

MANHATTANVILLE SUMMER WRITERS' WEEK

2900 Purchase St., Purchase NY 10577-0940. (914)694-3425. Fax: (914)694-0348. E-mail: gps@mville.edu. Website: www.mville.edu. **Contact:** Ruth Dowd, RSCJ, dean, graduate and professional studies. Estab. 1983. Annually. Conference held in late June/early July. Conference duration: 5 days. Average attendance: 100. Workshops in fiction, nonfiction, personal narrative, poetry, children's/young adult literature/playwriting. Held at suburban college campus 30 miles from New York City. Workshop sessions are held in a 19th century Norman Castle which serves as the college's administration building. **Speakers/agents have included:** Brian Morton, Valerie Martin, Ann Jones, Mark Matousek, Major Jackson, Linda Oatman High, Jeffrey Sweet, Alice Quinn (poetry editor, *The New Yorker*), Gerogia Jelatis Hoke (agent, McIntosh & Otis, Inc.), Paul Cirone (agent, Aaron Priest Literary Agency), Emily Sylvan Kim (Writer's House). Agents will be speaking and available for meetings with attendees.

Costs For noncredit: $650 (includes all workshops, craft seminars, readings, special keynote lecture by Amy Hempel). Program may also be taken for 2 graduate credits: $980. Participants may purchase meals in the college cafeteria or cafe.

Accommodations A list of hotels in the area is available upon request. Overnight accommodations are available in the college residence halls for $25/night.

Additional Information Brochures available for SASE or on website by end of February. Inquiries by e-mail and fax OK.

NEW ENGLAND WRITERS CONFERENCE

P.O. Box 5, Windsor VT 05089-0005. (802)674-2315. E-mail: newvtpoet@aol.com. Website: www.newengland writers.org. **Contact:** Dr. Frank and Susan Anthony, co-directors. Estab. 1986. Annually. Conference held third Saturday in July. Conference duration: 1 day. Average attendance: 100. Held at Old South Church, Windsor, Vermont. Seminars on publishing, agents, children's publishing, fiction, nonfiction, and poetry. **Previous agents/speakers have included:** John Talbot Agency, Tupelo Press, Dana Gioia, Wesley McNair, Michael C. White, and Rosanna Warren.

Costs $20 (includes panel-seminar sessions, open readings, contest ceremony, and refreshments).

Accommodations "Hotel list can be made available. There are many hotels in the area."

Additional Information "This annual conference continues our attempt to have a truly affordable writers conference that has as much as most 3-4 day events." Brochures available for SASE or on website. Inquiries by e-mail OK.

N THE PERSPECTIVES IN CHILDREN'S LITERATURE CONFERENCE

226 Furcolo Hall, School of Education, U-Mass, Amherst MA 01003-3035. Fax: (413)545-6130. E-mail: childlit@educ.umass.edu. Website: www.umass.edu/childlit/. **Contact:** Dr. Marsha Rudman, program director. Estab. 1970. Annual. Conference held in late March/early April. Conference duration: 1 day. Average attendance: 500. Conference focuses on various aspects of writing and illustrating children's books. Held at the University of Massachusetts School of Management. **Past agents/speakers attending included:** Jane Yolen, Jerry and Gloria Jean Pinkey, Patricia and Emily MacLachlan, Jan Cherpiko, Eric Carle, and Leslea Newman.

Costs $60-65 (includes light breakfast, lunch, freebies, snacks). For an additional fee, attendees can earn academic credit.

Additional Information "During lunch, authors, illustrators, and editors are assigned to a table giving participants an opportunity to converse and share experiences." Books available for sale. Inquiries by e-mail and fax OK.

REMEMBER THE MAGIC 2006

The 26th Annual International Women's Writing Guild Summer Conference, International Women's Writing Guild, P.O. Box 810, Gracie Station, New York NY 10028-0082. (212)737-7536. Fax: (212)737-9469. E-mail: iwwg@iwwg.org. Website: www.iwwg.org. **Contact:** Hannelore Hahn, executive director. Estab. 1979. Annual. Conference held third week in June. Average attendance: 500. Conference to promote creative writing and personal growth, professional know-how and contacts, networking. Site is the campus of Skidmore College in Saratoga Springs, New York (near Albany). Approximately 70 workshops are offered each day. Conferees have the freedom to make their own schedule. They come from all parts of the world; all ages and backgrounds represented.

Costs 7-day conference: $900 single/$790 double for members, $925 single/$815 double for nonmembers. These fees include program, room and board for the week. Rates for a 5-day stay and a weekend stay are also available, as well as commuter rates.

Additional Information Conference brochures/guidelines are available for SASE. Inquiries by e-mail and fax OK or view on web.

N SOCIETY OF CHILDREN'S BOOK WRITERS & ILLUSTRATORS CONFERENCE IN CHILDREN'S LITERATURE, NYC

P.O. Box 20233, Park West Finance Station, New York NY 10025. E-mail: conference@scbwi.org. Website: www.scbwi.org. Estab. 1975. Annual. Conference held in February. Average attendance: 350. Conference is to promote writing for children: picture books; fiction; nonfiction; middle grade and young adult; meet an editor; meet an agent; marketing your book; children's multimedia; etc. Conference held at Hilton New York.

Costs $290, members; $340 nonmembers.

Accommodations Write for information; hotel names will be supplied.

Additional Information Conference brochures/guidelines are available for SASE.

SOCIETY OF CHILDREN'S BOOK WRITERS & ILLUSTRATORS CONFERENCE/HOFSTRA CHILDREN'S LITERATURE CONFERENCE

University College for Continuing Education, 250 Hofstra University, Hempstead NY 11549-1090. (516)463-7600. Fax: (516)463-4833. E-mail: uccelibarts@hofstra.edu. Website: www.hofstra.edu/ucce. **Contact:** Marion Flomenhaft. Estab. 1985. Annual. Conference to be held in April. Average attendance: 200. Conference to encourage good writing for children. "The conference brings together writers, illustrators, librarians, agents, publishers, teachers and other professionals who are interested in writing for children. Each year we organize the program around a theme." The conference takes place at the Student Center Building of Hofstra University, located in Hempstead, Long Island. "We have two general sessions, five break-out groups, and a panel of children's book editors who critique randomly selected first-manuscript pages submitted by registrants. Agents will be speaking and available for meetings with attendees.

Costs (2004 rate) $77 members; $82 for nonmembers. Continental breakfast and full luncheon included.

TEA WITH ELEANOR ROOSEVELT

International Women's Writing Guild, P.O. Box 810, Gracie Station, New York NY 10028-0082. (212)737-7536. Fax: (212)737-9469. E-mail: iwwg@iwwg.org. Website: www.iwwg.org. **Contact:** Hannelore Hahn, executive director. Estab. 1980. Annual conference held in March. During Women's History Month, this is a traditional, annual visit to Mrs. Roosevelt's cozy retreat cottage. Conference duration: 1 day of writing. Average attendance: 50. Held at the Eleanor Roosevelt Center at Val-Kill in Hyde Park, New York. 2 hours from New York City in the Hudson Valley.

Costs $75 (includes lunch).

Additional Information Brochure/guidelines available for SASE. Inquiries by e-mail and fax OK.

WESLEYAN WRITERS CONFERENCE

Wesleyan University, Middletown CT 06459. (860)685-3604. Fax: (860)685-2441. E-mail: agreene@wesleyan.edu. Website: www.wesleyan.edu/writers. **Contact:** Anne Greene, director. Estab. 1956. Annual. Conference held the third week in June. Average attendance: 100. Fiction techniques, novel, short story, poetry, screenwriting, nonfiction, literary journalism, memoir. The conference is held on the campus of Wesleyan University, in the hills overlooking the Connecticut River. Features seminars and readings of new fiction, poetry, and nonfiction, and guest lectures on a range of topics including publishing. "Both new and experienced writers are welcome. Participants may attend seminars in all the genres." **Agents/speakers attending include:** Esmond Harmsworth (Zachary Schuster Agency); Daniel Mandel (Sanford J. Greenburger Associates); Dorian Karchmar; Amy Williams (ICM and Collins McCormick); Mary Sue Rucci (Simon & Schuster); Denise Roy (Simon & Schuster); John Kulka (Yale University Press); and many others. Participants are often successful in finding agents and publishers for their mss. Wesleyan participants are also frequently featured in the anthology, *Best New American Voices.* Agents will be speaking and available for meetings with attendees.

Costs In 2003, day rate $775 (includes meals); boarding students' rate $910 (includes meals and room for 5 nights).

Accommodations Meals and lodging are provided on campus.

Additional Information Ms critiques are available but are not required. Scholarships and teaching fellowships are available, including the Jakobson awards for fiction writers and poets and the Jon Davidoff Scholarships for journalists. Inquiries by e-mail, phone, and fax OK.

MIDATLANTIC (DC, DE, MD, NJ, PA)

BALTIMORE WRITERS' ALLIANCE CONFERENCE

P.O. Box 410, Riderwood MD 21139. (410)371-3515. E-mail: tmiller@towson.edu. Website: www.towson.edu/writersconference. **Contact:** Tracy Miller, coordinator. Estab. 1994. Annual. Conference held November. Conference duration: 1 day. Average attendance: 150-200. Writing and getting published—all areas. Held at Towson University. Topics have included: mystery, science fiction, poetry, children's writing, legal issues, grant funding, working with an agent, book and magazine panels. **Previous agents/speakers have included:** Nat Sobel (Sobel/Weber Associates); Nina Graybill (Graybill and English). Agents will be speaking.

Costs $80-100 (includes all-day conference, lunch, and snacks). Manuscript critiques for additional fee.

Accommodations Hotels close by, if required.

Additional Information Inquiries by e-mail OK. May register through BWA website.

BOUCHERCON 36

Detecto Mysterioso Books at Society Hill Playhouse, 507 S. Eighth St., Philadelphia PA 19147-1325. (215)923-0211. Fax: (215)923-1789. E-mail: shp@erols.com. Website: www.bouchercon.net. **Contact:** Deen Kogan, chairperson. Estab. 1970. Annual. Convention held in September. Average attendance: 1,500. Focus is on mystery, suspense, thriller, true crime novels, "an examination of the genre from many points of view." **Previous agents/speakers have included:** Lawrence Block, Jeremiah Healy, James Lee Burke, Ruth Rendell, Ian Rankin, Michael Connelly, Eileen Dreyer, Earl Emerson. Agents will be speaking and available for informal meetings with attendees.

Costs $175 registration fee.

Accommodations Attendees must make their own transportation arrangements. Special room rate available at convention hotel.

Additional Information "The Bookroom is a focal point of the convention. Forty specialty dealers are expected to exhibit, and collectables range from hot-off-the-press bestsellers to 1930s pulp; from fine editions to reading copies." Conference brochures/guidelines are available for SASE or by telephone. Inquiries by e-mail and fax OK.

NEW JERSEY ROMANCE WRITERS PUT YOUR HEART IN A BOOK CONFERENCE

2728 S. Colorado St., Philadelphia PA 19145. (732)625-1162 or (732)946-4044. E-mail: register2004njrwconf@hotmail.com. Website: www.njromancewriters.org. **Contact:** Lena Pinto. Estab. 1984. Annual. Conference held in October. Average attendance: 500. Conference concentrating on romance fiction. "Workshops offered on various topics for all writers of romance, from beginner to multi-published." Held at the Doubletree Hotel in Somerset New Jersey. **Previous agents/speakers have included:** Nora Roberts, Kathleen Woodiwiss, Patricia Gaffney, Jill Barnett, Kay Hooper.

Costs $170 (New Jersey Romance Writers members) and $195 (nonmembers).

Accommodations Special hotel rate available for conference attendees.

Additional Information Sponsors Put Your Heart in a Book Contest for unpublished writers and the Golden Leaf Contest for published members of Region One of RWA. Conference brochures, guidelines, and membership information are available for SASE. "Appointments offered for conference attendees, both published and unpublished, with editors and/or agents in the genre." Massive bookfair open to public with authors signing copies of their books; half of proceeds donated to literacy charities.

PENNWRITERS ANNUAL CONFERENCE

P.O. Box 63, Russell PA 16345. E-mail: conferenceco@pennwriters.org. Website: www.pennwriters.org. **Contact:** Carol Silvas, conference co-ordinator. Estab. 1987. Annually. Conference held third weekend of May. Conference duration: 3 days. Average attendance: 120. "We try to cover as many genres each year as we can." Held at the Wyndham Hotel Pittsburgh—spacious facility with most workshop rooms on 1 level. **Previous agents/speakers have included:** Evan Marshall, Nancy Martin. Agents will be speaking and available for meetings with attendees.

Costs $135 for members/$165 for nonmembers (includes all workshops and panels, as well as any editor or agent appointments). There is an additional charge for Friday's keynote dinner and Saturday night's dinner activity.

Accommodations "We have arranged a special rate with the hotel, and details will be in our brochure. Our rate for conference attendees is $73 plus tax/night. The hotel has a shuttle to and from the airport."

Additional Information "We are a multi-genre group encompassing the state of Pennsylvania and beyond." Brochures available February for SASE. Inquiries by e-mail OK. Visit website for current updates and details.

SANDY COVE CHRISTIAN WRITERS CONFERENCE

Sandy Cove Bible Conference, 60 Sandy Cove Rd., North East MD 21901. (410)287-5433. Fax: (410)287-3196. E-mail: info@sandycove.org. Website: www.sandycove.org. **Contact:** Jim Watkins, director. Estab. 1991. Annual. Conference begins first Sunday in October. Conference duration: 4 days (Sunday dinner through Thursday). Average attendance: 200. "There are major, continuing workshops in fiction, article writing, nonfiction books, and beginner's and advanced workshops. Twenty-eight 1-hour classes touch many topics. While Sandy Cove has a strong emphasis on available markets in Christian publishing, all writers are more than welcome. Sandy Cove is a full-service conference center located on the Chesapeake Bay. All the facilities are first class with suites, single or double rooms available." Handicap accessible. **Previous agents/speakers have included:** Francine Rivers (bestselling novelist); Lisa Bergen, Waterbrook Press; Ken Petersen (editor, Tyndale House); Linda Tomblin (editor, *Guideposts*); and Karen Ball (Zondervan).

Costs Call for rates.

Accommodations "Accommodations are available at Sandy Cove. Information available upon request." Cost is $418 double occupancy room and board, $519 single occupancy room and board for 4 nights and meals.

Additional Information Conference brochures/guidelines are available. "For exact dates, please visit our website."

WASHINGTON INDEPENDENT WRITERS (WIW) SPRING WRITERS CONFERENCE

733 15th St. NW, Suite 220, Washington DC 20005. (202)737-9500. Fax: (202)638-7800. E-mail: info@washwriter.org. Website: www.washwriter.org. **Contact:** Nicci Yang, membership manager. Estab. 1975. Annual. Conference held May 13-14. Conference duration: Friday and Saturday. Average attendance: 350. Fiction, nonfiction, screenwriting, poetry, children's, technical. "Gives participants a chance to hear from and talk with dozens of experts on book and magazine publishing as well as on the craft, tools,and business of writing." **Previous agents/speakers have included:** Erica Jong, John Barth, Kitty Kelley, Vanessa Leggett, Diana McLellan, and Stephen Hunter. New York and local agents at every conference.

Costs $185 members; $270 nonmembers; $285 membership and conference by May 17. $220 members; $265 nonmembers; $315 membership and conference after May 17.

Additional Information Brochures/guidelines available for SASE in mid-February.

MIDSOUTH (NC, SC, TN, VA, WV)

AMERICAN CHRISTIAN WRITERS CONFERENCES

P.O. Box 110390, Nashville TN 37222-0390. (800)21-WRITE. Fax: (615)834-7736. E-mail: acwriters@aol.com. Website: www.acwriters.com (includes schedule of cities). **Contact:** Reg Forder, director. Estab. 1981. Annual. Conference duration: 2 days. Average attendance: 60. Fiction, nonfiction, scriptwriting. To promote all forms of Christian writing. Conferences held throughout the year in 36 US cities.

Costs Approximately $169, plus meals and accommodations.

Accommodations Special rates available at host hotel. Usually located at a major hotel chain like Holiday Inn.

Additional Information Conference brochures/guidelines are available for SASE.

HIGHLAND SUMMER CONFERENCE

Box 7014, Radford University, Radford VA 24142-7014. (540)831-5366. Fax: (540)831-5951. E-mail: jasbury@radford.edu. Website: www.radford.edu/~arsc. **Contact:** JoAnn Asbury, assistant to director. Chair, Appalachian Studies Program: Dr. Grace Toney Edwards. Estab. 1978. Annual. Conference held in June. Conference duration: 14 days. Average attendance: 25. Fiction, nonfiction, poetry, screenwriting. **Previous speakers/agents have included:** Bill Brown, Robert Morgan, Sharyn McCrumb, Nikki Giovanni, Wilma Dykeman, Jim Wayne Miller.

Costs "The cost is based on current Radford tuition for 3 credit hours, plus an additional conference fee. On-campus meals and housing are available at additional cost. In 2004, conference tuition was $519 for in-state undergraduates, $1,401 for out-of-state undergraduates, $645 for in-state graduates, $1,191 for out-of-state graduates."

Accommodations "We do not have special rate arrangements with local hotels. We do offer accommodations on the Radford University Campus in a recently refurbished residence hall. (In 2004 cost was $24-33/night.)"

Additional Information "Conference leaders typically critique work done during the 2-week conference, but do not ask to have any writing submitted prior to the conference beginning." Conference brochures/guidelines are available after February for SASE. Inquiries by e-mail and fax OK.

LOST STATE WRITERS CONFERENCE

P.O. Box 1442, Greeneville TN 37744. (423)639-4031. E-mail: loststate@hotmail.com. Website: www.loststatewriters.xtn.net. **Contact:** Tamara Chapman, director. Estab. 1998. Annually. Conference held in September. Conference duration: 3 days. Average attendance: 300. Fiction, nonfiction, screenwriting, writing for children, poetry. Held at The General Morgan Inn & Conference Center, an historic hotel in Greeneville TN. Panels include fiction, nonfiction, and editor and agent panel, and a Southern writers panel. **Agents/speakers attending include:** Warren Frazier, Peter Steinberg. Agents will be speaking and available for meetings with attendees.

Costs $300 (includes all workshops and partial meals).

Accommodations List of area hotels on website and brochure. Cost for on-site accommodations: $69.

Additional Information Scholarships available. Brochures available for SASE. Inquiries by e-mail OK.

NORTH CAROLINA WRITERS' NETWORK FALL CONFERENCE

P.O. Box 954, Carrboro NC 27510-0954. (919)967-9540. Fax: (919)929-0535. E-mail: mail@ncwriters.org. Website: www.ncwriters.org (includes "history and information about the NC Writers' Network and our programs. Also has a links page to other writing-related websites"). **Contact:** Cynthia Barnett, executive director. Estab. 1985. Annual. "2004 Conference will be held in Research Triangle Park, October 29-31." Average attendance: 450. Keynote speaker every year including Gloria Naylor, Rick Bragg, and Andrei Codrescu. "The conference is a weekend full of classes, panels, book signings and readings, including open mic. We offer a variety of genres including fiction, poetry, creative nonfiction, journalism, children's book writing, screenwriting, and playwriting. We also offer craft, editing, and marketing classes. The conference moves out of the Research Triangle every other year to select locations in North Carolina in order to best serve our entire state. We hold the conference at a conference center with hotel rooms available." **Previous agents/speakers have included:** Donald Maass, Noah Lukeman, Joe Regal, Jeff Kleinman, and Evan Marshall. Some agents will be teaching classes and some are available for meetings with attendees.

Costs "Conference cost is approximately $250-350 and includes 2 meals."

Accommodations "Special conference hotel rates are available, but the individual makes his/her own reservations."

Additional Information Conference brochures/guidelines are available by sending street address to mail@ncwriters.org or on our website. Online secure registration is available.

POLICE WRITERS CONFERENCE

Police Writers Association, P.O. Box 738, Ashburn VA 20146. (703)723-4740. Fax: (703)723-4743. E-mail: leslye@policewriter.com. Website: www.policewriter.com. **Contact:** Leslyeann Rolik. Estab. 1996. Annual. Conference held in November. Conference duration: 2 days. Average attendance: 50. Related writing—both fiction and nonfiction. Focuses on police. Held in various hotels in various regions, determined annually. "Each year the conference focuses on helping club members get their work polished and published." **Previous agents/speakers have included:** Paul Bishop (novelist), Ed Dee (novelist), Roger Fulton (editor).

Costs $200-275 for members, depending on time of registration (includes all classes and seminars, fiction and nonfiction writing contest entries, and awards luncheons). Nonmembers add $75.

Accommodations Hotel arrangements, at special conference rates, are available.

Additional Information "Unpublished, police-genre writers are welcomed at the conference and as Police Writers Association Members." Brochures available on website. Inquiries by fax OK.

SEWANEE WRITERS' CONFERENCE

310 St. Luke's Hall, Sewanee TN 37383-1000. (931)598-1141. E-mail: cpeters@sewanee.edu. Website: www.sewaneewriters.org (includes general conference information and schedule of events). **Contact:** Cheri B. Peters, creative writing programs manager. Estab. 1990. Annual. Conference held in July. Conference duration: 12 days. Average attendance: 110. "We offer genre-based workshops (in fiction, poetry, and playwriting), not theme-based workshops. The Sewanee Writers' Conference uses the facilities of the University of the South. Physically, the University is a collection of ivy-covered Gothic-style buildings, located on the Cumberland Plateau in mid-Tennessee. Editors, publishers, and agents structure their own presentations, but there is always opportunity for questions from the audience." **2005 faculty members are:** Richard Bausch, Randall Kenan, Jill McCorkle, John Casey, Tony Earley, Daisy Foote, John Hollander, X.J. Kennedy, Brad Leithauser, Romulus Linney, Margot Livesey, Alice McDermott, Mary Jo Salter, and Mark Winegardner. **Visiting agents will include:** Gail Hochman and Georges Borchardt.

Costs Full conference fee is $1,470 (includes tuition, board, and basic room).

Accommodations Participants are housed in university dormitory rooms. Motel or B&B housing is available but not abundantly so. Dormitory housing costs are included in the full conference fee.

Additional Information Complimentary chartered bus service is available, on a limited basis, on the first and last days of the conference. "We offer each participant (excepting auditors) the opportunity for a private manuscript conference with a member of the faculty. These manuscripts are due 1 month before the conference begins.'' Conference brochures/guidelines are available, ''but no SASE is necessary. The conference has available a limited number of fellowships and scholarships; these are awarded on a competitive basis.''

N VIRGINIA ROMANCE WRITERS

P.O. Box 35, Midlothian VA 23113. E-mail: romancewriters@excite.com. Website: www.geocities.com/soho/museum/2164 (includes information about Virginia Romance Writers, authors, monthly meetings, workshops, conferences, contests). **Contact:** Annette Couch-Jareb, president. Fiction, nonfiction, scriptwriting.

SOUTHEAST (AL, AR, FL, GA, LA, MS, PUERTO RICO)

FLORIDA CHRISTIAN WRITERS CONFERENCE

2344 Armour Court, Titusville FL 32780. (321)269-5831. Website: www.flwriter.org. **Conference Director:** Billie Wilson. Estab. 1988. Annual. Conference held in March. Conference duration: 5 days. Average attendance: 200. To promote ''all areas of writing.'' Conference held at Christian Retreat Center in Brandenton, Florida. Editors will represent over 45 publications and publishing houses.

Costs Tuition is $400 (includes tuition, food); $500 (double occupancy); $775 (single occupancy).

Accommodations ''We provide shuttle from the Sarasota airport.''

Additional Information Critiques available. ''Each writer may submit 2 works for critique. We have specialists in every area of writing.'' Conference brochures/guidelines are available for SASE and on website.

FLORIDA FIRST COAST WRITERS' FESTIVAL

9911 Old Baymeadows Rd., Room C1301, FCCJ, Jacksonville FL 32256. (904)997-2669. Fax: (904)997-2746. E-mail: kclower@fccj.org. Website: www.fccj.org/wf (includes festival workshop speakers, contest information). **Contacts:** Kathy Clower and Howard Denson. Estab. 1985. Annual. Conference held in May. Held at Sea Turtle Inn, Atlantic Beach, Florida. Average attendance: 300. All areas: mainstream, plus genre. Fiction, nonfiction, scriptwriting, poetry, freelancing, etc. Offers seminars on narrative structure and plotting character development. **Confirmed agents/speakers include:** Andrei Codrescu, Gerald Hausman, Connie May Fowler, Leslie Schwartz, Larry Smith, Stella Suberman, Sophia Wadsworth, Amy Gash (editor), and agents David Hale Smith, Katharine Sands, Rita Rosenkranz, Jim McCarthy, David Poyer, Lenore Hart, Steve Berry, S.V. Date, and more to be announced. Agents will be speaking and available for meetings with attendees.

Costs (2005 rates) Early bird special: $185 (2 days with 2 meals); $230 (2 days with 2 meals and banquet).

Accommodations Sea Turtle Inn, (904)249-7402 or 1(800)874-6000, has a special festival rate.

Additional Information Conference brochures/guidelines are available for SASE. Sponsors a contest for short fiction, poetry, novels and plays. Novel judges are David Poyer and Lenore Hart. Entry fees: $30, novels; $10, short fiction; $5, poetry. Deadline: ''We offer 1-on-1 sessions at no additional costs for attendees to speak to selected writers, editors, agents on first-come, first served basis.'' Visit our website after January 1, 2005, for current festival updates and more details.

FLORIDA SUNCOAST WRITERS' CONFERENCE

University of South Florida, Division of Professional & Workforce Development, 4202 E. Fowler Ave., MHH-116, Tampa FL 33620-6610. (813)974-2403. Fax: (813)974-5421. E-mail: dcistaff@admin.usf.edu. Website: english.cas.usf.edu/fswc. Directors: Steve Rubin, Betty Moss, and Lagretta Lenkar. Estab. 1970. Annual. Held in February. Conference duration: 3 days. Average attendance: 400. Conference covers poetry, short story, novel, and nonfiction, including science fiction, detective, travel writing, drama, TV scripts, photojournalism, and juvenile. ''We do not focus on any one particular aspect of the writing profession, but instead offer a variety of writing-related topics. The conference is held on the picturesque university campus fronting the bay in St. Petersburg, Florida.'' Features panels with agents and editors. **Previous speakers/agents have included:** Lady P.D. James, William Styron, John Updike, Joyce Carol Oates, Francine Prose, Frank McCourt, David Guterson, and Jane Smiley.

Costs Call for information.

Accommodations Special rates available at area motels. ''All information is contained in our brochure.''

Additional Information Participants may submit work for critiquing. Extra fee charged for this service. Conference brochures/guidelines are available November 2004. Inquiries by e-mail and fax OK.

N WORDS & MUSIC: A LITERARY FEAST IN NEW ORLEANS

624 Pirates Alley, New Orleans LA 70116. (504)586-1609. Fax: (504)522-9725. E-mail: faulkhouse@aol.com. Website: www.wordsandmusic.org. Conference Director: Rosemary James DeSalvo. Estab. 1997. Annual. Conference held in November. Conference duration: 5 days. Average attendance: 350-400. Presenters include au-

thors, agents, editors and publishers. **Previous agents/speakers have included:** Deborah Grosvenor (Deborah Grosvenor Literary Agency); Jenny Bent (Harvey Klinger Agency); M.T. Caen. Agents will be speaking and available for meetings with attendees.

Costs $375 tuition fee.

Accommodations Hotel Monteleone in New Orleans.

Additional Information Write for additional information.

WRITING TODAY—BIRMINGHAM-SOUTHERN COLLEGE

Box 549003, Birmingham AL 35254. (205)226-4922. Fax: (205)226-4931. E-mail: agreen@bsc.edu. Website: www.writingtoday.org. **Contact:** Annie Greene. Estab. 1978. Annual. Conference held in March. Average attendance: 300-350. "This is a two-day conference with approximately 18 workshops, lectures and readings. We try to offer workshops in short fiction, novels, poetry, children's literature, magazine writing, songwriting, and general information of concern to aspiring writers such as publishing, agents, markets, and research. The conference is sponsored by Birmingham-Southern College and is held on the campus in classrooms and lecture halls." **Previous agents/speakers included:** Eudora Welty, Pat Conroy, Ernest Gaines, Ray Bradbury, Erskine Caldwell, John Barth, Galway Kinnell, Edward Albee.

Costs $120 for both days (includes lunches, reception, and morning coffee and rolls).

Accommodations Attendees must arrange own transporation. Local hotels and motels offer special rates, but participants must make their own reservations.

Additional Information "We usually offer a critique for interested writers. For those who request and send manuscripts by the deadline, we have had poetry and short story critiques. There is an additional charge for these critiques." Conference sponsors the Hackney Literary Competition Awards for poetry, short story, and novels. Brochures available for SASE.

MIDWEST (IL, IN, KY, MI, OH)

ANTIOCH WRITERS' WORKSHOP

P.O. Box 494, Yellow Springs OH 45387-0494. (937)475-7357. E-mail: info@antiochwritersworkshop.com. Website: www.antiochwritersworkshop.com. Director: Laura Carlson. Estab. 1984. Annual. Conference held in July. Average attendance: 80. Workshop concentration: poetry, nonfiction, fiction, mystery, and memoir. Workshop located on Antioch College campus in the Village of Yellow Springs. **Faculty in 2005 includes:** Sue Grafton, Mary Grimm, Lucrecia Guerrero, Jeff Gundy, Ralph Keyes, Michel Marriott, Sharon Short, Tim Waggoner, and Crystal Wilson Harris. Agents will be speaking and available for meetings with attendees.

Costs Tuition is $610 ($550 for locals and returning participants), $90 of which is a nonrefundable registration fee.

Accommodations Accommodations are available at local hotels and B&B's.

Additional Information Optional ms critique, $70. Phone or e-mail for a free brochure.

N CENTRAL OHIO FICTION WRITERS READERS & WRITERS HOLIDAY

A conference for book lovers, P.O. Box 1981, Westerville OH 43086-1981. Website: www.cofw.org. **Contact:** Katherine Helfrich, conference chair. Estab. 1991. Annually. Conference held in October. Conference duration: 1½ days. Average attendance: 100 attendees. Fiction, nonfiction, screenwriting, writing for children, poetry, etc. The conference is designed to address the needs of writers in all genres of fiction. The purpose of the conference is to explore fiction-writing trends, and discuss the business as well as the craft of writing. Central Ohio Fiction Writers's conference keynote speaker is usually a popular fiction author who can discuss writing trends. We also invite a publishing house editor and a literary agent to discuss the business side of writing. We offer a writing workshop. Attendees also are offered the opportunity to pitch their completed ms to the guest editor and/or agent. A continental breakfast and hearty lunch—complete with dessert—is part of the conference registration. The conference hosts a book fair with a number of popular fiction authors present to talk to readers and aspiring authors, as well as to autograph their books. Door prizes and raffles also are held. Held in a Columbus, Ohio-area hotel. The main events are held in a large ballroom. The workshop, book fair, editor and agent appointments are held in separate rooms.

Costs The agent appointment was $10 for non-Central Ohio Fiction Writers members; free for members. $65 for Central Ohio Fiction Writers members; $75 for non-Central Ohio Fiction Writers members. Fee includes conference registration, Friday night workshop, continental breakfast Saturday, writers' resource booklet and Saturday luncheon.

Accommodations As part of our contractual agreement with the hotel, Central Ohio Fiction Writers's conference attendees are given discounted hotel accommodations.

THE COLUMBUS WRITERS CONFERENCE

P.O. Box 20548, Columbus OH 43220. (614)451-3075. Fax: (614)451-0174. E-mail: angelapl28@aol.com. Website: creativevista.com. Director: Angela Palazzolo. Estab. 1993. Annual. Conference held in August. Average attendance: 350+. "In addition to consultations, the conference offers a wide variety of fiction and nonfiction topics presented by writers, editors, and literary agents. Writing topics have included novel, short story, children's, young adult, science fiction, fantasy, humor, mystery, playwriting, screenwriting, personal essay, travel, humor, cookbook, technical, magazine writing, query letter, corporate, educational, and greeting cards. Other topics for writers: finding and working with an agent, targeting markets, research, time management, obtaining grants, and writers' colonies." **Previous agents/writers/editors:** Donald Maass, Jeff Herman, Andrea Brown, Jennifer DeChiara, Jeff Kleinman, Nancy Ellis-Bell, Rita Rosenkranz, Simon Lipskar, Doris S. Michaels, Sheree Bykofsky, Lee K. Abbott, Lore Segal, Mike Harden, Oscar Collier, Maureen F. McHugh, Ralph Keyes, Nancy Zafris, Bonnie Pryor, Dennis L. McKiernan, Karen Harper, Melvin Helitzer, Susan Porter, Les Roberts, Tracey E. Dils, J. Patrick Lewis, Patrick Lubrutto, Brenda Copeland, Tracy Bernstein, and many other professionals in the writing field.

Costs For registration fees or to receive a brochure, available mid-summer, contact the conference by e-mail, phone, fax, or postal mail, or check out the website.

GREEN RIVER WRITERS NOVELS-IN-PROGRESS WORKSHOP

703 Eastbridge Court, Louisville KY 40223. (502)245-4902. E-mail: novelsinprogress@bellsouth.net. Website: greenriverwriters.org/nipw.html. Director: Jeff Yocom. Estab. 1991. Annual. Conference held 3rd week of March. Conference duration: 1 week. Average attendance: 55. Open to persons, college age and above, who have approximately 3 chapters (60 pages) or more of a novel. Mainstream and genre novels handled by individual instructors. Short fiction collections welcome. "Each novelist instructor works with a small group (5-7 people) for 5 days; then agents/editors are there for panels and appointments on the weekend." Site is The University of Louisville's Shelby Campus, suburban setting, graduate dorm housing (private rooms available with shared bath for each 2 rooms). "Meetings and classes held in nearby classroom building. Grounds available for walking, etc. Lovely setting, restaurants and shopping available nearby. Participants carpool to restaurants, etc. This year we are covering mystery, fantasy, mainstream/literary, suspense, historical."

Costs $299 for workshop basics; $449 for personal instruction. Discount given for early registration. Does not include meals.

Accommodations "We see that participants without cars have transportation to meals, etc. If participants would rather stay in hotel, we will make that information available." Graduate dormitory housing available for $119/week.

Additional Information Participants send 60 pages/3 chapters with synopsis and $150 deposit which applies to tuition. Conference brochures/guidelines are available for SASE. Visit website for additional details.

INDIANA UNIVERSITY WRITERS' CONFERENCE

464 Ballantine Hall, Bloomington IN 47405. (812)855-1877. Fax: (812)855-9535. E-mail: writecon@indiana.edu. Website: www.indiana.edu/~iuwc/. Director: Amy Locklin. Estab. 1940. Annual. Conference/workshops held in June. Average attendance: 100. "Conference to promote poetry and fiction." Located on the campus of Indiana University, Bloomington. "We emphasize an exploration of creativity through a variety of approaches, offering workshop-based craft discussions, classes focusing on technique, and talks about the careers and concerns of a writing life. Participants in the week-long conference join faculty-led workshops in fiction and poetry, take classes, engage in 1-on-1 consultations with authors, and attend a variety of reading and social events." **Previous speakers have included:** Raymond Carver, Mark Doty, Robert Olen Butler, Aimee Bender, Brenda Hillman, and Li-Young Lee.

Costs $350 for all classes only; $500 for all classes, plus 1 workshop (does not include food or housing). "We supply conferees with options for overnight accommodations. We offer special conference rates for both the hotel and dorm facilities on site."

Additional Information "In order to be accepted in a workshop, the writer must submit the work they would like critiqued. Work is evaluated before accepting applicant. Scholarships are available determined by an outside reader/writer, based on the quality of the manuscript." Conference brochures/guidelines available on website or for SASE in January. "We are the second oldest writer's conference in the country. We are in our 65th year."

KENTUCKY WOMEN WRITERS CONFERENCE

The W.T. Young Library, University of Kentucky, Lexington KY 40506. Fax: (859)257-8734. E-mail: kywwc@hotmail.com. Website: www.uky.edu/wwk. **Contact:** Rebecca Howell or Evie Russell. Annual. The Kentucky Women Writers Conference celebrated its 26th anniversary March 24-26, 2005 with an unprecedented collection of internationally renowned writers and up-and-coming talents. Faculty presenters include Candace Bushnell, Alexandra Robbins, Elaine Brown, Ann Telnaes, Beth Ann Fennelly, Patty Ann Friedmann, Neda Ulaby, Vijai

Nathan, Donna Hilbert, Neela VaSwani and Tift Merritt. Special Events will also include a screening with filmmaker Christine Fugate at the Kentucky Theater, The Nell Stuart Donovan Exhibit Series featuring a lecture by Carrie Mae Weems, and an evening with 2 of the most prominent poets of our time: recent U.S. Poet Laureate, Louise Glück and her apprentice, APR/Honickman prize recipient, Dana Levin.
Additional Information Please visit our website for further information and to register online.

MIDLAND WRITERS CONFERENCE

Grace A. Dow Memorial Library, 1710 W. St. Andrews, Midland MI 48640-2698. (989)837-3430. Fax: (989)837-3468. E-mail: ajarvis@midland-mi.org. Website: www.midland-mi.org/gracedowlibrary. **Contact:** Ann Jarvis, conference chair. Estab. 1980. Annual. Conference held in May. Average attendance: 100. Fiction, nonfiction, children's, and poetry. "The Conference is composed of a well-known keynote speaker and 6 workshops on a variety of subjects including poetry, children's writing, nonfiction, freelancing, agents, etc. The attendees are both published and unpublished authors. The Conference is held at the Grace A. Dow Memorial Library in the auditorium and conference rooms." **2004 speakers included:** Pete Hamill, Virginia Bailey Parker, Anniek Hivert-Carthew. Agents will be speaking.
Costs (2004 rates) Adult—$50; students, senior citizens and handicapped. Lunch is available. Costs are approximate until plans for upcoming conference are finalized.
Accommodations A list of area hotels is available.
Additional Information Conference brochures/guidelines are mailed mid-April. Call or write to be put on mailing list. Inquiries by e-mail and fax OK.

NORTH CENTRAL (IA, MN, NE, ND, SD, WI)

GREAT LAKES WRITER'S WORKSHOP

Alverno College, 3400 S. 43rd St., P.O. Box 343922, Milwaukee WI 53234-3922. (414)382-6176. Fax: (414)382-6332. Contact: Nancy Krase, Estab. 1985. Annual. Workshop held in June. Friday night will feature author Jacquelyn Mitchard. Average attendance: 100. "Workshop focuses on a variety of subjects including fiction, writing for magazines, freelance writing, writing for children, poetry, marketing, etc. Participants may select individual workshops or opt to attend the entire weekend session. The workshop is held in Milwaukee, Wisconsin at Alverno College."
Costs In 2003, cost was $115 for entire program.
Accommodations Attendees must make their own travel arrangments. Accommodations are available on campus; rooms are in residence halls. There are also hotels in the surrounding area. Call (414)382-6176 for information regarding overnight accommodations.
Additional Information Brochures are available for SASE after March. Inquiries by fax OK. Online brochure will be available at www.alverno.edu.

IOWA SUMMER WRITING FESTIVAL

100 Oakdale Campus, W310, University of Iowa, Iowa City IA 52242. (319)335-4160. Fax: (319)335-4039. E-mail: iswfestival@uiowa.edu. Website: www.uiowa.edu/~iswfest. **Contact:** Amy Margolis, director. Estab. 1987. Annual. Festival held in June and July. Workshops are 1 week or a weekend. Average attendance: limited to 12/class—over 1,500 participants throughout the summer. Held at University of Iowa campus. "We offer courses across the genres: novel, short story, essay, poetry, playwriting, screenwriting, humor, travel, writing for children, memoir, women's writing." **Previous agents/speakers have included:** Lee K. Abbott, Susan Power, Lan Samantha Chang, Gish Jen, Abraham Verghese, Robert Olen Butler, Ethan Canin, Clark Blaise, Gerald Stern, Donald Justice, Michael Dennis Browne, Marvin Bell, Hope Edelman. Guest speakers are undetermined at this time.
Costs $475-500/week; $225, weekend workshop. Housing and meals are separate.
Accommodations "We offer participants a choice of accommodations: dormitory, $40/night; Iowa House, $75/night; Sheraton, $75/night (rates subject to changes)."
Additional Information Brochure/guidelines are available in February. Inquiries by fax and e-mail OK.

SOUTH CENTRAL (CO, KS, MO, NM, OK, TX)

ASPEN SUMMER WORDS INTERNATIONAL LITERARY FESTIVAL & WRITING RETREAT

(formerly Aspen Summer Words Writing Retreat & Literary Festival), Aspen Writers' Foundation, 110 E. Hallam St., #116, Aspen CO 81611. (970)925-3122. Fax (970)920-5700. E-mail: info@aspenwriters.org. Website: www.aspenwriters.org. **Contact:** Jamie Abbott, operations manager. Estab. 1976. Annual. Conference held 4th week

Resources

of June. Conference duration: 5 days. Average attendance: 96 at writing retreat, 200 at literary festival. Retreat for fiction, poetry, creative nonfiction, personal essay, screenwriting, literature. Festival includes author readings, panel discussions with publishing industry insiders, professional consultations with editors and agents and social gatherings. **Previous agents/speakers have included:** Suzanne Gluck, Elizabeth Sheinkman and Jody Hotchkiss (agents); Jordan Pavlin and Hilary Black (editors); Pam Houston, Mark Salzman, Larry Watson and Anita Shreve (fiction); Harold Kushner, Ted Conover, Madeleine Blais, and Peter Stark (nonfiction); Jane Hirshfield, Mary Jo Salter, and J.D. McClatchy (poetry); Jan Greenberg (childen's literature); Gary Ferguson (personal essay); Laura Fraser and Daniel Glick (magazine writing); and many more.

Costs $375/retreat; $195/seminar; $200/festival.

Accommodations Rates for 2004: $65/night double; $110/night single.

Additional Information Deadline for admission is April 1. Mss to be submitted for review by admissions committee prior to conference. Conference brochures are available for SASE or on website.

AUSTIN FILM FESTIVAL & HEART OF FILM SCREENWRITERS CONFERENCE

1604 Nueces St., Austin TX 78701. (800)310-3378 or (512)478-5795. Fax:(512)478-6205. E-mail: info@austinfilmfestival.com. Website: www.austinfilmfestival.com. **Contact:** Megan Tunnell, office manager. Estab. 1994. Annual. Conference held in October. Conference duration: 4 days. Average attendance: 1,500. The Austin Film Festival & Heart of Film Screenwriters Conference is a nonprofit organization committed to furthering the art, craft, and business of screenwriters, and recognizing their contribution to the filmmaking industry. The 4-day Screenwriters Conference presents over 75 panels, roundtables, and workshops that address various aspects of screenwriting and filmmaking. Held at the Driskill and Stephen F. Austin Hotels, located in downtown Austin. **Agents/Speakers attenting include:** John August (*Charlie and the Chocolate Factory '05*), William Broyles, Jr. (*The Polar Express '04*), Philip Levens ("Smallville"), Thomas McCarthy (*The Station Agent*), Andrew Stanton (*Finding Nemo*), and Bill Wittliff (*The Perfect Storm*). Agents and production companies are in attendance each year.

Costs $325 before May 16 (2005 rate). Includes entrance to all panels, workshops and roundtables during the 4-day conference, as well as all films during the 8-night Film Exhibition, the Opening Night Party, and Closing Night Party. Please look at website for other offers.

Accommodations Discounted rates on hotel accommodations are available to conference attendees if the reservations are made through the Austin Film Festival office. Contact Austin Film Festival for holds, rates, and more information.

Additional Information "The Austin Film Festival is considered one of the most accessible festivals, and Austin is the premiere town for networking because when industry people are here, they are relaxed and friendly." The Austin Film Festival holds annual Screenplay/Teleplay and Film Competitions as well as a Young Filmmakers Program including Summer Camp. Informational brochures are available February 1 or check out the website. Inquiries by e-mail and fax are OK.

FRONTIERS IN WRITING

7221 Stagecoach Trail, Amarillo TX 79124. (806)383-4351. E-mail: fiw2005@yahoo.com. Website: www.panhandleprowriter.org. Estab. 1980. Annual. Conference held in June. Duration: 2 full days. Average attendance: 125. Nonfiction, poetry, and fiction (including mystery, romance, mainstream, science fiction, and fantasy). **Previous agents/speakers have included:** Devorah Cutler Rubenstein and Scott Rubenstein (editor/broker for screenplays); Andrea Brown (children's literary agent); Elsa Hurley (literary agent); Hillary Sears (editor with Kensington Books).

Costs 2005 conference: $100 early bird members; $130 early bird nonmembers; $150 nonmember, non early bird. Critique group extra.

Accommodations Special conference room rate.

Additional information Sponsors a contest. Guidelines available for SASE or on website.

GLORIETA CHRISTIAN WRITERS CONFERENCE

CLASServices, Inc., P.O. Box 66810, Albuquerque NM 87193. (800)433-6633. Fax: (505)899-9282. E-mail: info@classervices.com. Website: www.glorietacwc.com. **Contact:** Linda Jewell, executive director. Estab. 1997. Annually. Conference held in October. Conference duration: Wednesday afternoon through Sunday lunch. Average attendance: 330. Include programs for all types of writing. Conference held in the LifeWay Glorieta Conference Center. **Speakers attending include:** Agents, editors, and professional writers, who will be speaking and available for meetings with attendees.

Costs $350 early registration (1 month in advance); $390 program only. Critiques are available for an additional $35.

Accommodations Hotel rooms are available at the LifeWay Glorieta Conference Center. Sante Fe Shuttle offers service from the Albuquerque or Sante Fe airports to the conference center. Hotel rates vary.

Additional Information Brochures available April 1. Inquiries by phone, fax or, e-mail OK. Visit website for updates and current information.

HEARTLAND WRITERS CONFERENCE

P.O. Box 652. Kennett MO 63857. (573)297-3325. Fax: (573)297-3352. E-mail: hwg@heartlandwriters.org. Website: www.heartlandwriters.org. **Contact:** Harry Spiller, conference coordinator. Estab. 1990. Biennial (even years). Conference held in June. Conference duration: 3 days. Average attendance: 160. Popular fiction (all genres), nonfiction, children's, screenwriting, poetry. Held at the Best Western Coach House Inn in Sikeston, Missouri. Previous panels included Christopher Vogler's Myth Adventures: The Storytellers Journey. **Previous agents/speakers attending include:** Alice Orr, Jennifer Jackson, Ricia Mainhardt, Christy Fletcher, Sue Yuen, and Evan Marshall. Agents will be speaking and available for meetings with attendees. Evan Marshall was last year's keynote speaker.

Costs $215 for advance registration, $250 for general registration (includes lunch on Friday and Saturday, awards banquet Saturday, hospitality room, and get-acquainted mixer Thursday night).

Accommodations Blocks of rooms are available at a special conference rate at conference venue and at 2 nearby motels. Cost: $55-85/night (2002 price).

Additional Information Brochures available late January. Inquiries by e-mail and fax OK.

N NATIONAL WRITERS ASSOCIATION FOUNDATION CONFERENCE

P.O. Box 4187, Parker CO 80134. (303)841-0246. Fax: (303)841-2607. E-mail: sandywrter@aol.com. Website: www.nationalwriters.com. **Contact:** Sandy Whelchel, executive director. Estab. 1926. Annual. Conference held second week of June. Conference held in Denver, Colorado. Conference duration: 3 days. Average attendance: 200-300. General writing and marketing.

Costs $200 (approx.).

Additional Information Awards for previous contests will be presented at the conference. Conference brochures/guidelines are available via website or for SASE.

NETWO WRITERS ROUNDUP

Northeast Texas Writers Organization (NETWO), P.O. Box 411, Winfield TX 75493. (903)856-6724. E-mail: netwomail@netwo.org. Website: www.netwo.org. **Contact:** Georgia Henson, president. Estab. 1987. Annual. Conference held April. Conference duration: 2 days. Presenters include agents, writers, editors and publishers.

Costs (2004 rates) $60 (discount offered for early registration).

Additional Information Write for additional information. Conference is co-sponsored by Texas Commission on the Arts. See website for current updates and more information after November.

THE NEW LETTERS WEEKEND WRITERS CONFERENCE

University of Missouri-Kansas City, College of Arts and Sciences Continuing Education Division, 215 4825 Troost Bldg., 5100 Rockhill Rd., Kansas City MO 64110-2499. (816)235-2736. Fax: (816)235-2611. E-mail: newletters@umkc.edu. Website: www.newletters.org. **Contact:** Betsy Beasley or Sharon Seaton, administrative associates. Estab. in the mid-70s as The Longboat Key Writers Conference. Annual. Conference held in early June. Conference duration is 3 days over a weekend. Average attendance: 60. Fiction, nonfiction, scriptwriting, poetry, playwriting, journalism. "The New Letters Weekend Writers Conference brings together talented writers in many genres for lectures, seminars, readings, workshops, and individual conferences. The emphasis is on craft and the creative process in poetry, fiction, screenwriting, playwriting, and journalism; but the program also deals with matters of psychology, publications, and marketing. The conference is appropriate for both advanced and beginning writers. The conference meets at the beautiful Diastole conference center of The University of Missouri-Kansas City. 2- and 3-credit hour options are available by special permission of the instructor."

Costs Several options are available. Participants may choose to attend as a noncredit student or they may attend for 1 hour of college credit from the University of Missouri-Kansas City. Conference registration includes continental breakfasts, Saturday and Sunday lunch. For complete information, contact the University of Missouri-Kansas City.

Accommodations Registrants are responsible for their own transportation, but information on area accommodations is available.

Additional Information Those registering for college credit are required to submit a ms in advance. Ms reading and critique is included in the credit fee. Those attending the conference for noncredit also have the option of having their ms critiqued for an additional fee. Conference brochures/guidelines are available for SASE after March. Inquiries by e-mail and fax OK.

PIKES PEAK WRITERS CONFERENCE

4164 Austin Bluffs Pkwy., #246, Colorado Springs CO 80918. (719)531-5723. E-mail: info@ppwc.net. Website: www.pikespeakwriters.org. Estab. 1993. Annual. Conference held in April. Conference duration: 3 days. Average attendance: 400. Commercial fiction. Held at the Wyndham Hotel. "Workshops, presentations, and panels focus on writing and publishing genre fiction—romance, science fiction and fantasy, suspense thrillers, action adventure, mysteries. Agents and editors are available for meetings with attendees."

Costs $235-300 for PPW members; $260-325 for nonmembers, depending on when you register (includes all meals).

Accommodations Wyndham Colorado Springs holds a block of rooms for conference attendees until March 28 at a special $77 rate (1-800-996-3426).

Additional Information Readings with critique are available on Friday afternoon. 1-on-1 meetings with editors and agents available Saturday and Sunday. Brochures available in January. Inquiries by e-mail OK. Registration form available on website. Contest for unpublished writers; need not attend conference to enter contest.

N ROCKY MOUNTAIN FICTION WRITERS COLORADO GOLD

P.O. Box 260244, Denver CO 80226-0244. (303)331-2608. Website: www.rmfw.org (includes contest, membership, conference, critique). Estab. 1983. Annual. Conference held in September. Conference duration: 3 days. Average attendance: 250. For novel-length fiction. The conference will be held in Denver. Themes included general novel length fiction, genre fiction, contemporary romance, mystery, sf/f, mainstream, history. Guest speakers and panelists have included Terry Brooks, Dorothy Cannell, Patricia Gardner Evans, Diane Mott Davidson, Constance O'Day, Connie Willis, Clarissa Pinkola Estes and Michael Palmer; approximately 4 editors and 5 agents annually.

Costs $169-209, depending on when you sign up (includes conference, reception, banquet). Editor workshop $20-30 additional.

Accommodations Information on overnight hotel accommodations made available. The conference will be at the Renaissance Denver Hotel. Conference rates available.

Additional Information Editor conducted workshops are limited to 10 participants for critique with auditing available. Workshops in science fiction, mainstream, mystery, historical, contemporary romance. Sponsors a contest. For 20-page mss and 8-page synopsis; categories mentioned above. First rounds are done by qualified members, published and nonpublished, with editors doing the final ranking; 2 copies need to be submitted without author's name. $20 entry only, $40 entry and (one) critique. Guidelines available for SASE. Deadline June 1.

ROMANCE WRITERS OF AMERICA NATIONAL CONFERENCE

16000 Stuebner Airline Rd., Suite 140, Spring TX 77379. (832)717-5200. Fax: (832)717-5201. E-mail: jdetloff@rwanational.org. Website: www.rwanational.org. **Contact:** Chris Calhoon, communications manager. Executive Director: Allison Kelley. Estab. 1981. Annual. Conference held in late July or early August. Average attendance: 1,500. Fiction writers, scriptwriters. Over 100 workshops on writing, researching, and the business side of being a working writer. Publishing professionals attend and accept appointments. Keynote speaker is renowned romance writer. Conference has been held in Chicago, Washington DC, and Denver.

Costs $340-390/members; $415-465/nonmembers, depending on when you register.

Additional Information Annual RITA awards are presented for romance authors. Annual Golden Heart awards are presented for unpublished writers. Conference brochures/guidelines are available for SASE.

THE SCREENWRITING CONFERENCE IN SANTA FE

P.O. Box 29762, Santa Fe NM 87592. (866)424-1501. Fax: (505)424-8207. E-mail: writeon@scsfe.com. Website: www.scsfe.com. **Contact:** Larry N. Stouffer, founder. Estab. 1999. Annual. Conference held week following Memorial Day. Average attendance: 175. The Screenwriting Conference in Santa Fe is divided into 2 components: the screenwriting symposium, designed to teach the art and craft of screenwriting, and the producers seminar, which speaks to the business aspects of screenwriting. Held on the campus of the Institute of American Indian Arts, Santa Fe.

Costs $695 for the Symposium and $200 for the Producer's Seminar. Early discounts are available. Includes 9 hours of in-depth classroom instruction, over 30 workshops, panel discussions, live scene readings, social events, including the Outrageous Bonanza Creek Movie Ranch Barbeque Blowout and Wild West Fiesta.

Additional Information "More details available online."

SOUTHWEST WRITERS CONFERENCE MINI-CONFERENCE SERIES

3721 Morris St. NE, Suite A, Albuquerque NM 87111. (505)265-9485. Fax: (505)265-9483. E-mail: swriters@aol.com. Website: www.southwestwriters.org. Estab. 1983. Annual. Mini-conferences held throughout the year. Average attendance: 100/mini-conference. "Speakers include writers, editors, agents, publicists, and producers. All areas of writing, including screenwriting and poetry are represented. Preconference workshops and conference sessions are available for beginning or experienced writers."

Costs Fee includes conference sessions and lunch.

Accommodations Usually have official airline and hotel discount rates.

Additional Information Sponsors a contest judged by authors, editors, and agents from New York, Los Angeles, etc., and from major publishing houses. Twelve categories. Deadline: June 1. Entry fee is $25 (members) or $45 (nonmembers). Brochures/guidelines available on website or for SASE. Inquiries by e-mail and fax OK. "An appointment (10 minutes, 1-on-1) may be set up at the conference with the editor or agent of your choice on a first-registered/first-served basis."

STEAMBOAT SPRINGS WRITERS CONFERENCE

(formerly A Day for Writers), Box 774284, Steamboat Springs CO 80477. (970)879-8079. E-mail: sswriters@cs.com. Website: www.steamboatwriters.com. **Contact:** Harriet Freiberger, director. Estab. 1982. Annual. Conference held in mid-July. Conference duration: 1 day. Average attendance: 35. Featured areas of instruction change each year. Held at the restored train depot home of the Steamboat Springs Arts Council. **Previous agents/speakers have included:** Carl Brandt, Jim Fergus, Avi, Robert Greer, Renate Wood, Connie Willis, Margaret Coel.

Costs $35 prior to June 1; $45 after June 1 (includes seminars, catered luncheon). Pre-conference dinner also available. Limited enrollment.

Additional Information Brochures available in April for SASE. Inquiries by e-mail OK.

WRITERS' LEAGUE OF TEXAS

1501 W. Fifth St., Suite E-2, Austin TX 78703. (512)499-8914. Fax: (512)499-0441. E-mail: wlt@writersleague.org. Website: www.writersleague.org. **Contact:** Helen Ginger, executive director. Estab. 1982. Conference held in summer. Conference duration: Friday-Sunday. Average attendance 300. Fiction, nonfiction. **Agents/speakers have included:** Malaika Adero, Stacey Barney, Sha-shana Crichton, Jessica Faust, Dena Fischer, Mickey Freiberg, Jill Grosjean, Anne Hawkins, Jim Hornfischer, Jennifer Joel, David Hale Smith, and Elisabeth Weed. Agents will be speaking and available for meetings with attendees. Each summer the League holds its annual Agents & Editors Conference which provides writers with the opportunity to meet top literary agents and editors from New York and the West Coast. Topics include: Finding and working with agents and publishers; writing and marketing fiction and nonfiction; dialogue; characterization; voice; research; basic and advanced fiction writing/focus on the novel; business of writing; also workshops for genres.

Costs Conference: $220-275.

Additional Information Contests and awards programs are offered separately. Brochures/guidelines are available on request.

WRITERS WORKSHOP IN SCIENCE FICTION

English Department/University of Kansas, Lawrence KS 66045-2115. (785)864-3380. Fax: (785)864-1159. E-mail: jgunn@ku.edu. Website: www.ku.edu/~sfcenter/. **Contact:** James Gunn, professor. Estab. 1985. Annual. Conference held in July. Average attendance: 15. Conference for writing and marketing science fiction. "Classes meet in university housing on the University of Kansas campus. Workshop sessions operate informally in a lounge." **Previous agents/speakers have included:** Frederik Pohl, Kij Johnson, Chris McKitterick.

Costs Tuition: $400. Housing and meals are additional.

Accommodations Housing information available. Several airport shuttle services offer reasonable transportation from the Kansas City International Airport to Lawrence. During past conferences, students were housed in a student dormitory at $12.50/day double, $23.50/day single.

Additional Information "Admission to the workshop is by submission of an acceptable story. Two additional stories should be submitted by the middle of June. These 3 stories are copied and distributed to other participants for critiquing and are the basis for the first week of the workshop; 1 story is rewritten for the second week." Brochures/guidelines available for SASE. "The Writers Workshop in Science Fiction is intended for writers who have just started to sell work or need that extra bit of understanding or skill to become a published writer."

WEST (AZ, CA, HI, NV, UT)

ASA INTERNATIONAL SCREENWRITERS CONFERENCE

269 S. Beverly Dr., Suite 2600, Beverly Hills CA 90212-3807. Phone/Fax: (866)265-9091. E-mail: asa@goasa.com. Website: www.goasa.com. **Contact:** John Johnson, director. Estab. 1988. Annual. Conference held in August in LA area. Conference duration: 3 days. Average attendance: 275. "Conference targets scriptwriters and fiction writers, whose short stories, books, or scripts have strong feature film or TV potential, and who want to make valuable contacts in the industry. Full conference registrants receive a private consultation with the industry producer or professional of his/her choice who make up the faculty. Panels, workshops, pitching discussion groups and networking sessions include over 50 agents, professional film and TV scriptwriters, and

independent as well as studio and TV and feature film producers." **Agents/speakers attending include:** Michael Hauge, Linda Seger, Syd Field, Billy Mernit, Richard Walter, Heidi Wall, Lew Hunter.

Costs In 2004: full conference by May 31, $550; after May 31: $600. Includes some meals.

Accommodations $140/night (in LA) for private room; $70/shared room. Discount with designated conference airline.

Additional Information "This is the premier screenwriting conference of its kind in the world, unique in its offering of an industry-wide perspective from pros working in all echelons of the film industry. Great for making contacts." Conference brochure/guidelines available March; phone, e-mail, fax, or send written request.

DESERT DREAMS 2006

P.O. Box 40772, Mesa AZ 85274-0772. (480)821-1690. E-mail: desertdreams@desertroserwa.org. Website: desertroserwa.org. **Contact:** Cathi Lombardo, chapter president. Estab. 1986. Biannually. Conference held Spring 2006. Conference duration: 3 days. Average attendance: 250. Fiction, screenwriting, research. **Agents/speakers attending include:** Steven Axelrod, Irene Goodman, Christopher Vogler, Jill Barnett, Susan Elizabeth Phillips, Debbie Macomber, Linda Lael Miller, and editors from major publishing houses. Agents will be speaking and available for meetings with attendees.

Costs $150-225/members; $170-225/nonmembers, depending on when you sign up (includes meals, seminars, appointments with editors and agents).

Accommodations Discounted rates for conference attendees negotiated.

Additional Information Inquiries by e-mail OK. Visit website for updates and complete details.

IWWG EARLY SPRING IN CALIFORNIA CONFERENCE

International Women's Writing Guild, P.O. Box 810, Gracie Station, New York NY 10028-0082. (212)737-7536. Fax: (212)737-9469. E-mail: hirhahn@aol.com. Website: www.iwwg.org. **Contact:** Hannelore Hahn, executive director. Estab. 1982. Annual. Conference generally held on the 2nd weekend in March. Average attendance: 70-80. Conference to promote "creative writing, personal growth, and voice." Site is a redwood forest mountain retreat in Santa Cruz, California.

Costs $325 members/$345 nonmembers for weekend program with room and board, $150 for weekend program without room and board.

Accommodations All at conference site.

Additional Information Conference brochures/guidelines are available for SASE. Inquiries by e-mail and fax OK, or view on website.

MAUI WRITERS CONFERENCE

P.O. Box 1118, Kihei HI 96753. (808)879-0061 or (888)974-8373. Fax: (808)879-6233. E-mail: writers@mauiwriters.com. Website: www.mauiwriters.com (includes information covering all programs offered, writing competitions, presenters past and present, writers forum bulletin board, published attendees books, dates, price, hotel, and travel information). **Contact:** Shannon Tullius. Estab. 1993. Annual. Conference held at the end of August (Labor Day weekend). Conference duration: 5 days. Conference held at Wailea Marriott Resort. Average attendance: 800. For fiction, nonfiction, poetry, children's, young adult, horror, mystery, romance, science fiction, journalism, screenwriting. Manuscript Marketplace, held in June and October every year, is an online service where your book idea is reviewed by participating agents and editors. **Agents have included:** Andrea Brown (Andrea Brown Literary Agency); Kimberley Cameron (The Reece Halsey Agency); Susan Crawford (Crawford Literary Agency); Stephanie Lee (Manus & Associates Literary Agency), Jenny Bent (Trident Media Group), Barbara Bova (The Barbara Bova Literary Agency), Catherine Fowler (Redwood Agency), James D. Hornfischer (Hornfischer Literary Management), Debra Goldstein (The Creative Culture, Inc.). Many of these agents will be at the 2006 conference where they will be on panels discussing the business of publishing and will be available for 1-on-1 consultations with aspiring authors.

Additional Information "We offer a comprehensive view of the business of publishing, with over 2,000 consultation slots with industry agents, editors, and screenwriting professionals, as well as workshops and sessions covering writing instruction. Consider attending the MWC writers retreat immediately preceding the conference, or one of our writing cruises. Visit our website for current updates and full details on all of our upcoming programs." Write or call for additional information.

MENDOCINO COAST WRITERS CONFERENCE

1211 Del Mar Dr., Fort Bragg CA 95437. (707)964-7735. E-mail: info@mcwc.org. Website: www.mcwc.org. **Contact:** Virginia Wells, registrar. Estab. 1988. Annually. Conference held in August. Conference duration: 3 days. Average attendance: 90. All areas of writing covered. Provides workshops for fiction, nonfiction, scriptwriting, children's, mystery, writing for social change. Held at small community college campus on the northern Pacific Coast. **Agents/speakers attending include:** Jandy Nelson, John Dufresne, Dana Levin, John Lescroart,

Maxine Schur, and others. Agents will be speaking and available for meetings with attendees.

Costs $300-410 (includes 1 day intensive in 1 subject and 2 days of several short sessions; panels; meals; 2 socials with guest readers; 1 event open to the public.)

Accommodations Information on overnight accommodations is made available. Special conference attendee accommodations made in some cases. Shared rides from San Francisco Airport are available.

Additional Information Emphasis on writers who are also good teachers. Brochures available for SASE in January or on website. Inquiries by e-mail OK.

MOUNT HERMON CHRISTIAN WRITERS CONFERENCE

P.O. Box 413, Mount Hermon CA 95041-0413. (831)335-4466 or (888)MH-CAMPS. Fax: (831)335-9413. E-mail: dtalbott@mhcamps.org. Website: www.mounthermon.org/writers. **Contact:** David R. Talbott, director of adult ministries. Estab. 1970. Annual. Conference held Friday-Tuesday over Palm Sunday weekend, April 7-11, 2006. Average attendance: 450. "We are a broad-ranging conference for all areas of Christian writing, including fiction, children's, poetry, nonfiction, magazines, inspirational and devotional writing, books, educational curriculum, and radio and TV scriptwriting. This is a working, how-to conference, with many workshops within the conference involving on-site writing assignments. The conference is sponsored by and held at the 440-acre Mount Hermon Christian Conference Center near San Jose, California, in the heart of the coastal redwoods. The faculty/student ratio is about 1:6 or 7. The bulk of our more than 60 faculty are editors and publisher representatives from major Christian publishing houses nationwide." **Previous agents/speakers attending include:** Janet Kobobel Grant, Chip MacGregor, Karen Solem, T. Davis Bunn, Sally Suart, and others. Agents speaking and available for meetings with attendees.

Costs Registration fees include tuition, conference sessions, resource notebook, refreshment breaks, room and board, and vary from $660 (economy) to $990 (deluxe), double occupancy (2005 fees). Limited scholarship help is available by application over Internet.

Accommodations Registrants stay in hotel-style accommodations, and full board is provided as part of conference fees. Meals are taken family style, with faculty joining registrants. Airport shuttles are available from the San Jose International Airport. Housing is not required of registrants, but about 95% of our registrants use Mount Hermon's own housing facilities (hotel style double-occupancy rooms). Meals with the conference are required and are included in all fees.

Additional Information "The residential nature of our conference makes this a unique setting for 1-on-1 interaction with faculty/staff. There is also a decided inspirational flavor to the conference, and general sessions with well-known speakers are a highlight." Registrants may submit 2 works for critique in advance of the conference, then have personal interviews with critiquers during the conference. No advance work is required however. Conference brochures/guidelines are available December 1. All conference information and registration is now online only. Inquiries by e-mail and fax OK. Tapes of past conference workshops also available.

N NO CRIME UNPUBLISHED™ MYSTERY WRITERS' CONFERENCE

Sisters in Crime/Los Angeles, P.O. Box 251646, Los Angeles CA 90025. (213)694-2972. E-mail: sistersincrimela@yahoo.com. Website: www.sistersincrimela.com. Conference Coordinator: Jamie Wallace. Estab. 1995. Annual. Conference held in June. Conference duration: 1 day. Average attendance: 200. Conference on mystery and crime writing. Usually held in hotel near Los Angeles airport. 2-track program: Craft and forensic sessions; keynote speaker, luncheon speaker, agent panel, book signings.

Costs $99-125/members; $125-135/nonmembers, depending on when you sign up. Includes continental breakfast and lunch.

Accommodations Airport shuttle to hotel. Optional overnight stay available. Hotel conference rate $99/night at the LAX Hilton. Arrangements made directly with hotel.

Additional Information Conference brochure available for SASE.

PIMA WRITERS' WORKSHOP

Pima College, 2202 W. Anklam Rd., Tucson AZ 85709. (520)206-6974. Fax: (520)206-6020. E-mail: mfiles@pima.edu. **Contact:** Meg Files, director. Estab. 1988. Annual. Conference held in May. Conference duration: 3 days. Average attendance: 300. Fiction, nonfiction, poetry, scriptwriting. "For anyone interested in writing—beginning or experienced writer. The workshop offers sessions on writing short stories, novels, nonfiction articles and books, children's and juvenile stories, poetry, and screenplays." Sessions are held in the Center for the Arts on Pima Community College's West Campus. **Previous agents/speakers have included:** Michael Blake, Ron Carlson, Gregg Levoy, Nancy Mairs, Linda McCarriston, Larry McMurtry, Barbara Kingsolver, Jerome Stern, Connie Willis, Jack Heffron, Jeff Herman, Robert Morgan. Agents will be speaking and available for meetings with attendees.

Costs $70 (can include ms critique). Participants may attend for college credit, in which case fees are $104 for Arizona residents and $164 for out-of-state residents. Meals and accommodations not included.

Accommodations Information on local accommodations is made available, and special workshop rates are available, at a specified motel close to the workshop site (about $65/night).

Additional Information "The workshop atmosphere is casual, friendly, and supportive, and guest authors are very accessible. Readings and panel discussions are offered as well as talks and manuscript sessions." Participants may have up to 20 pages critiqued by the author of their choice. Manuscripts must be submitted 3 weeks before the workshop. Conference brochure/guidelines available for SASE. Inquiries by e-mail OK.

SAN DIEGO STATE UNIVERSITY WRITERS' CONFERENCE

SDSU College of Extended Studies, 5250 Campanile Dr., San Diego State University, San Diego CA 92182-1920. (619)594-2517. Fax: (619)594-0147. Website: www.ces.sdsu.edu/writers/index.html. **Contact:** Kevin Carter, coordinator, SDSU extension programs. Estab. 1984. Annual. Conference held in January. Conference duration: 2 days. Average attendance: approximately 375. Fiction, nonfiction, scriptwriting, e-books. Held at the Doubletree Hotel, Mission Valley. "Each year the SDSU Writers Conference offers a variety of workshops for the beginner and the advanced writer. This conference allows the individual writer to choose which workshop best suits his/her needs. In addition to the workshops, editor/agent appointments and office hours are provided so attendees may meet with speakers, editors and agents in small, personal groups to discuss specific questions. A reception is offered Saturday immediately following the workshops where attendees may socialize with the faculty in a relaxed atmosphere. Last year 18 agents attended in addition to editors and screenwriting experts." Agents will be speaking and available for meetings with attendees.

Costs Approximately $355-395 (includes all conference workshops and office hours, coffee and pastries in the morning, lunch and reception Saturday evening).

Accommodations Doubletree Hotel (800)222-TREE. Attendees must make their own travel arrangements.

Additional Information Editor/agent appointments are private, 1-on-1 opportunities to meet with editors and agents to discuss your submission. To receive information, e-mail, call, or write.

SANTA BARBARA WRITERS' CONFERENCE

280 Harvard Lane, Santa Barbara CA 93111. (805)967-8663. Fax: (805)684-7003. Website: www.sbwc.online.com. **Contact:** Marcia Meier, conference director. Estab. 1973. Annual. Conference held in June, at Westmont College in Montecito. Average attendance: 350. For poetry, fiction, nonfiction, journalism, playwriting, screenplays, travel writing, children's literature. **Previous agents/speakers have included:** Kenneth Atchity, Michael Larsen, Elizabeth Pomada, Linda Mead, Stuart Miller, Gloria Stern, Don Congdon, Mike Hamilburg, Sandra Dijkstra. Agents will be speaking and available for private meetings with attendees.

Accommodations Onsite accommodations available. Additional accommodations available at area hotels.

Additional Information Individual critiques are also available. Submit 1 ms of no more than 3,000 words in advance with SASE. Competitions with awards sponsored as part of the conference. Send SASE for brochure and registration forms.

SOCIETY OF CHILDREN'S BOOK WRITERS AND ILLUSTRATORS/NATIONAL CONFERENCE ON WRITING & ILLUSTRATING FOR CHILDREN

8271 Beverly Blvd., Los Angeles CA 90048-4515. (323)782-1010. Fax: (323)782-1892. E-mail: scbwi@scbwi.org. Website: www.scbwi.org. **Contact:** Stephen Mooser, president. Estab. 1972. Annual. Conference held in August. Conference duration: 4 days. Average attendance: 500. Writing and illustrating for children. Held at the Century Plaza Hotel in Los Angeles. **Previous agents/speakers have included:** Andrea Brown, Steven Malk, Scott Treimel (all agents), Ashley Bryan, Bruce Coville, Karen Hesse, Harry Mazer, Lucia Monfried, and Russell Freedman. Agents will be speaking and sometimes participate in ms critiques.

Costs Approx. $400. Cost does not include hotel room.

Accommodations Information on overnight accommodations made available.

Additional Information Ms and illustration critiques are available. Conference brochures/guidelines are available in June with SASE.

N SOCIETY OF SOUTHWESTERN AUTHORS WRITERS' CONFERENCE—WRANGLING WITH WRITING

P.O. Box 30355, Tucson AZ 85751-0355. (520)546-9382. Fax: (520)296-0409. E-mail: wporter202@aol.com and apetrillo@earthlink.net. Website: www.azstarnet.com/nonprofit/ssa. **Contact:** Penny Porter, conference chair. Estab. 1972. Annual. 2-day conference held in January. Maximum attendance: 400. Fiction, nonfiction, screenwriting, poetry. Conference offers 30 workshops covering all genres of writing; pre-scheduled 1-on-1 interviews with 30 agents, editors and publishers representing major book houses and magazines. **Keynote speakers for 2005 include:** William F. Nolan, Ben Bova, Lee Harris, Bruce Holland Rogers.

Costs $300 (general); $250 (member). Scholarships available.

Additional Information Conference brochures/guidelines are available via e-mail or by calling (520)296-5299.

Resources

SOUTHERN CALIFORNIA WRITERS' CONFERENCE

1010 University Ave., #54, San Diego CA 92103. Phone/Fax: (619)233-4651. E-mail: wewrite@writersconference.com. Website: www.writersconference.com. **Contact:** Michael Steven Gregory, executive director. Estab. 1986. Annually. Conference held in Februrary. Conference also held in Palm Springs, June 10-12 and in Los Angeles, October (dates to be announced). Conference duration: 3 days. Average attendance: 250. Fiction and nonfiction, with particular emphasis on reading and critiquing. "Extensive reading and critiquing workshops by working writers. Over 3 dozen daytime workshops and no time limit late-night sessions." Agents will be speaking and available for meetings with attendees.

Costs Depends on location.

Accommodations Depends on location.

Additional Information Late-night read and critique workshops run until 3 or 4 a.m. Brochures available for SASE or on website. Inquiries by e-mail and fax OK.

SQUAW VALLEY COMMUNITY OF WRITERS—WRITERS WORKSHOP

P.O. Box 1416. Nevada City CA 95959-1416. (530)470-8440. E-mail: info@squawvalleywriters.org. Website: www.squawvalleywriters.org. **Contact:** Ms. Brett Hall Jones, executive director. Estab. 1969. Annual. Conference held August. Conference duration: 1 week. Average attendance: 125. Fiction, nonfiction, memoir. Held in Squaw Valley, California—the site of the 1960 Winter Olympics. The workshops are held in a ski lodge at the foot of this spectacular ski area. **Previous agents/speakers have included:** Betsy Amster, Julie Barer, Michael Carlisle, Elyse Cheney, Mary Evans, Christy Fletcher, Theresa Park, B.J. Robbins, Peter Steinberg. Agents will be speaking and available for meetings with attendees.

Costs $750 (includes tuition, dinners). Housing is extra.

Accommodations Rooms available. Single: $550/week. Double: $350/week per person. Multiple room: $210/week per person. Airport shuttle available for additional cost. Contact conference for more information.

Additional Information Brochures available in March for SASE or on website. Inquiries by e-mail OK.

UCLA EXTENSION WRITERS' PROGRAM

10995 Le Conte Ave., #440, Los Angeles CA 90024. (310)825-9415 or (800)388-UCLA. Fax: (310)206-7382. E-mail: writers@uclaextension.edu. Website: www.uclaextension.org/writers. **Contact:** Cindy Lieberman, program manager. Estab. 1891. Courses held year-round with 1-day or intensive weekend workshops to 12-week courses. Writers Studio held in February. Fiction, nonfiction, scriptwriting. "The diverse offerings span introductory seminars to professional novel and script completion workshops. The annual Writers Studio and a number of 1-, 2- and 4-day intensive workshops are popular with out-of-town students due to their specific focus and the chance to work with industry professionals. The most comprehensive and diverse continuing education writing program in the country, offering over 500 courses a year including: screenwriting, fiction, writing for young people, poetry, nonfiction, playwriting, and publishing. Courses are offered in Los Angeles on the UCLA campus, as well as online over the Internet. Adult learners in the UCLA Extension Writers' Program study with professional screenwriters, fiction writers, playwrights, poets, and nonfiction writers who bring practical experience, theoretical knowledge, and a wide variety of teaching styles and philosophies to their classes." Online courses are also available. Call for details.

Costs Vary from $95 for a 1-day workshop to $485 for a 12-week course to $3,000 for 9-month Master Classes.

Accommodations Students make own arrangements. The program can provide assistance in locating local accommodations.

Additional Information "Some advanced-level classes have manuscript submittal requirements; instructions are always detailed in the quarterly UCLA Extension course catalog." Contact program for details. Studio brochures/guidelines are available in the Fall. Inquiries by e-mail and fax OK.

WATERSIDE PUBLISHING CONFERENCE

2187 Newcastle Ave., Suite 204, Cardiff CA 92007. (760)632-9190. Fax: (760)632-9295. E-mail: ming@waterside.com. Website: www.waterside.com. **Contact:** Ming Russell, conference coordinator. Estab. 1990 Annually. Conference held in April. Conference duration: 2-3 days. Average attendance: 200. Focused on computer and technology, books and their writers and publishers. Issues in the industry that affect the genre. Held at the Doubletree Berkeley Marina in Berkley, California. A bayside hotel with full amenities and beautiful view. Past themes: Digital Delivery; Ask the Buyer; Author Taxes, Branding, Contracts. **Previous agents/speakers have included:** Paul Hilts (*Publishers Weekly*); Carla Bayha (Borders Books); Bob Ipsen (John Wiley & Sons); Microsoft; Mighty Words.com. Agents will be speaking and available for meetings with attendees.

Costs In 2004: $500 general; $250 for authors (includes all sessions and parties, meals, coffee breaks). Conference attendees get a discounted room rate at the Doubletree.

Accommodations Other hotels are in the area if conference hotel is booked or too expensive.

Additional Information Brochures available via fax or e-mail, or call.

NORTHWEST (AK, ID, MT, OR, WA, WY)

CLARION WEST WRITERS' WORKSHOP

340 15th Ave. E., Suite 350, Seattle WA 98112-5156. (206)322-9083. E-mail: info@clarionwest.org. Website: www.clarionwest.org (includes critiquing, workshopping, names, dates). **Contact:** Leslie Howle, executive director. Workshop held mid-June to late July. Workshop duration: 6 weeks. Average attendance: 18. "Conference to prepare students for professional careers in science fiction and fantasy writing." Held near the University of Washington. Deadline for applications: April 1. Agents will be speaking and available for meetings with attendees.

Costs Workshop: $1,700 ($125 discount if application received by March 1). Dormitory housing: $1,200, some meals included.

Accommodations Students are strongly encouraged to stay on-site, in dormitory housing. Cost: $1,200, some meals included, for 6-week stay.

Additional Information "This is a critique-based workshop. Students are encouraged to write a story a week; the critique of student material produced at the workshop forms the principal activity of the workshop. Students and instructors critique manuscripts as a group." Limited scholarships are available, based on financial need. Students must submit 20-30 pages of ms to qualify for admission. Conference guidelines available for SASE. Visit website for updates and complete workshop details.

FLATHEAD RIVER WRITERS CONFERENCE

P.O. Box 7711, Kalispeil MT 59904-7711. E-mail: hows@centurytel.net. **Contact:** Jake How, director. Estab. 1990. Annual. Conference held in early October. Conference duration: 3 days. Average attendance: 100. "We provide several small, intense 3-day workshops before the general weekend conference on a wide variety of subjects every year, including fiction, nonfiction, screenwriting, and working with editors and agents." Held at Grouse Mountain Lodge. Workshops, panel discussions, and speakers focus on novels, nonfiction, screenwriting, short stories, magazine articles, and the writing industry. **Previous agents/speakers have included:** Donald Maass, Ann Rule, Cricket Pechstein, Marcela Landres, Amy Rennert, Ben Mikaelsen, Esmond Harmsworth, Linda McFall, Ron Carlson. Agents will be speaking and available for meetings with attendees.

Costs $150 (includes breakfast and lunch, but does not include lodging).

Accommodations Rooms available at discounted rates: $100/night. Whitefish is a resort town, and less expensive lodging can be arranged.

Additional Information "By limiting attendance to 100 people, we assure a quality experience and informal, easy access to the presentors and other attendees." Brochures available in June. Inquiries by e-mail OK.

JACKSON HOLE WRITERS CONFERENCE

University of Wyoming, Dept. 3972, 1000 E. University Ave., Laramie WY 82071. (877)733-3618, ext. 1. Fax: (307)766-3914. E-mail: jrieman@uwyo.edu. Website: jacksonholewriters.org. Conference Coordinator: Jerimiah Rieman. Estab. 1991. Annual. Conference held in June/July. Conference duration: 4 days. Average attendance: 70. For fiction, creative nonfiction, screenwriting. Offers critiques from authors, agents, and editors. Write for additional information or visit website.

N NORWESCON

P.O. Box 68547, Seattle WA 98168-9986. (206)270-7850. E-mail: info@norwescon.org. Website: www.norwescon.org. **Contact:** Programming Director. Estab. 1978. Annual. Conference held Easter weekend. Conference duration: Thursday-Sunday. Average attendance: 2,800. General multitrack programming convention focusing on science fiction and fantasy literature with wide spectrum coverage of other media. Held at Seatac Doubletree Hotel. Full Tracks of Science, Socio-Cultural, Literary, Publishing, Editing, Writing, Art, and other media of a science fiction/fantasy orientation. Agents will be speaking and available for meetings with attendees.

Costs See website for details. Membership includes admission to Norwescon, program book and membership privileges.

Accommodations Accommodations available, see website for details.

Additional Information "Please write ahead or make contact with programming director." Brochures available for SASE or on website. Inquiries by e-mail OK.

N PACIFIC NORTHWEST WRITERS ASSOCIATION

P.O. Box 2016, Edmonds WA 98020. (425)673-2665. E-mail: pnwa@pnwa.org. Website: www.pnwa.org. Estab. 1955. Annual. Conference held in July. Conference duration: 4 days. Information available in May. Average attendance: 400. Conference focuses on "fiction, nonfiction, poetry, film, drama, self-publishing, the creative process, critiques, core groups, advice from pros and networking." Site is Hilton Seattle Airport and Conference Center. "Editors and agents come from both coasts. They bring lore from the world of publishing. The PNWA provides opportunities for writers to get to know editors and agents. The literary contest provides feedback from professionals and possible fame for the winners." **Previous agents have included:** Sheree Bykofsky, Kimberley Cameron, Jennie Dunham, Donald Maass and Jandy Nelson.

Costs $350-400/members; $400-450/nonmembers. Meals and lodging are available at hotel.

Additional Information On-site critiques are available in small groups. Literary contest in these categories: Stella Cameron Romance, adult article/essay, adult genre novel, adult mainstream novel, adult short story, juvenile/young adult, screenwriting, nonfiction book, playwriting and poetry. Deadline: February 13. Over $9,000 awarded in prizes. Send SASE for guidelines.

WHIDBEY ISLAND WRITERS' CONFERENCE

P.O. Box 1289, Langley WA 98260. (360)331-6714. E-mail: writers@whidbey.com. Website: www.writeonwhidbey.org. **Contact:** Elizabeth Guss, director. Annual. Conference held in March. Conference duration: 3 days. Average attendance: 250. Fiction, nonfiction, screenwriting, writing for children, poetry, travel, and nature writing. Conference held at conference hall, and break-out fireside chats in local homes near sea. Panels include: "Writing the Perfect Proposal," "Police Procedures for the Mystery Writer." **Agents/speakers attending include:** Elizabeth George, Sabina Murray, Rita Rosenkranz, Larry Colt, Sharon Sala (aka Dina McCall), Andrea Hurst, and many more. Updated list on website.

Costs $325 before November 30, $375 after. Volunteer discounts available; early registration encouraged.

Additional Information Brochures available for SASE or on website. Inquiries by e-mail OK.

WILLAMETTE WRITERS CONFERENCE

9045 SW Barbur, Suite 5-A, Portland OR 97219. (503)452-1592. Fax: (503)452-0372. E-mail: wilwrite@willamettewriters.com. Website: www.willamettewriters.com. **Contact:** Bill Johnson. Estab. 1968. Annual. Conference held in August. Average attendance: 600. Fiction, nonfiction, scriptwriting. "Willamette Writers is open to all writers, and we plan our conference accordingly. We offer workshops on all aspects of fiction, nonfiction, marketing, scriptwriting, the creative process, etc. Also we invite top-notch inspirational speakers for keynote addresses. Recent theme was 'Writing Your Future.' We always include at least 1 agent or editor panel and offer a variety of topics of interest to both fiction, screenwriters, and nonfiction writers." **Previous agents/speakers have included:** Donald Maass, Kim Cameron, Bob Mecoy, Angela Rinaldi, Lisa Dicker, Richard Morris, Andrew Whelchel. Agents will be speaking and available for meetings with attendees.

Costs Cost for full conference including meals is $350 members; $375 nonmembers.

Accomodations If necessary, these can be made on an individual basis. Some years special rates are available.

Additional Information Conference brochures/guidelines are available for catalog-size SASE.

CANADA

THE FESTIVAL OF THE WRITTEN ARTS

Box 2299, Sechelt BC V0N 3A0 Canada. (800)565-9631 or (604)885-9631. Fax: (604)885-3967. E-mail: info@writersfestival.ca. Website: www.writersfestival.ca. **Contact:** Gail Bull, festival producer. Estab. 1983. Annual. Festival held in August. Average attendance: 3,500. To promote "all writing genres." Festival held at the Rockwood Centre. "The Centre overlooks the town of Sechelt on the Sunshine Coast. The lodge around which the Centre was organized was built in 1937 as a destination for holidayers arriving on the old Union Steamship Line; it has been preserved very much as it was in its heyday. A 12-bedroom annex was added in 1982, and in 1989 the Festival of the Written Arts constructed a 500-seat Pavilion for outdoor performances next to the annex. The festival does not have a theme. Instead, it showcases 25 or more Canadian writers in a wide variety of genres each year." **Previous agents/speakers have included:** Jane Urquhart, Sholagh Rogers, David Watmough, Zsuzsi Gartner, Gail Bowen, Charlotte Gray, Bill Richardson, P.K. Page, Richard B. Wright, Madeleine Thien, Ronald Wright, Michael Kusugak, Bob McDonald. Agents will be speaking.

Costs $12/event, or $175 for a 4-day pass (Canadian).

Accommodations Lists of hotels and bed/breakfast available.

Additional Information The festival runs contests during the 3½ days of the event. Prizes are books donated by publishers. Brochures/guidelines are available. "Visit our website for current updates and details."

FESTIVAL OF WORDS

217 Main St. N., Moose Jaw SK S6H 0W1 Canada. (306)691-0557. Fax: (306)693-2994. E-mail: word.festival@sasktel.net. Website: www.festivalofwords.com. **Contact:** Gary Hyland, coordinator; or Lori Dean, operations manager. Estab. 1997. Annual. Festival held in July. Festival duration: 4 days. The festival celebrates the imaginative uses of language, and features fiction and nonfiction writers, screenwriters, poets, children's authors, songwriters, dramatists, and film makers. Held at the Moose Jaw Public Library/Art Museum complex

and in Crescent Park. **Previous agents/speakers have included:** Alistair McLeaod, Roch Carrier, Jane Urquhart, Rohinton Mistry, Will Ferguson, Patrick Lane, Katherine Govier, Lynn Coady, Leon Rooke, Steven Heighton, Pamela Wallin, Bonnie Burnard, Erika Ritter, Wayson Choy, Koozma Tarasoff, Lorna Crozier, Sheree Fitch, Nino Ricci, Yann Martel, Connie Kaldor, The Arrogant Worms, Brent Butt.

Costs TBA (includes 3 meals).

Accommodations Motels, hotels, campgrounds, bed and breakfasts.

Additional Information "Our festival is an ideal meeting ground for people who love words to mingle, promote their books, and meet their fans." Brochures available for SASE. Inquiries by e-mail and fax OK.

MARITIME WRITERS' WORKSHOP

UNB College of Extended Learning, Box 4400, Fredericton NB E3B 5A3 Canada. Phone/Fax: (506)474-1144. E-mail: k4jc@unb.ca. Website: www.unb.ca/extend/writers. **Contact:** Rhona Sawlor, coordinator. Estab. 1976. Annual. Conference held in July. Average attendance: 50. "Workshops in 4 areas: fiction, poetry, nonfiction, writing for children." Site is University of New Brunswick, Fredericton campus.

Costs In 2003: $395, tuition; $160 meals; $150/double room; $170/single room (Canadian).

Accommodations On-campus accommodations and meals.

Additional Information "Participants must submit 10-20 manuscript pages which form a focus for workshop discussions." Must be at least 18 years old. Brochures are available after March. No SASE necessary. Inquiries by e-mail and fax OK.

SAGE HILL WRITING EXPERIENCE

Box 1731, Saskatoon SK S7K 2Z4 Canada. Phone/Fax: (306)652-7395. E-mail: sage.hill@sasktel.net. Website: www.sagehillwriting.ca (features complete program, including application and scholarship information). **Contact:** Steven Ross Smith, executive director. Annual. Workshops held in August and November. Workshop duration 10-14 days. Attendance: summer program limited to 40 total—6 groups of 5-6; fall program limited to 8 participants. "Sage Hill Writing Experience offers a special working and learning opportunity to writers at different stages of development. Top quality instruction, low instructor-student ratio, and the beautiful Sage Hill settings offer conditions ideal for the pursuit of excellence in the arts of fiction, nonfiction, poetry, and playwriting." The Sage Hill location features "individual accommodation, in-room writing area, lounges, meeting rooms, healthy meals, walking hills, and vistas in several directions." Seven classes are held: Introduction to Writing Fiction & Poetry; Fiction Workshop; Nonfiction Workshop; Writing Young Adult Fiction Workshop; Poetry Workshop; Poetry Colloquium; Fiction Colloquium; Novel ColloquiumPlaywriting Lab; Fall Poetry Colloquium. **Previous agents/authors speakers have included:** George Elliott Clarke, Sue Goyette, Phil Hall, Lynn Coady, Arthur Slade.

Costs Summer Program: $795 (Canadian) includes instruction, accommodation, meals, and all facilities. Fall Poetry Colloquium: $1,075.

Accommodations On-site, individual accommodations located at Lumsden, 45 kilometers outside Regina.

Additional Information For Introduction to Creative Writing: A 5-page sample of your writing or a statement of your interest in creative writing; list of courses taken required. For workshop and colloquium program: A résumé of your writing career, and a 12-page sample of your work, plus 5 pages of published work required. Guidelines are available for SASE. Inquiries by e-mail and fax OK. Scholarships and bursaries are available.

SIWC

Surrey International Writers' Conference, 10707 146th St., Surrey BC V3R 1T5 Canada. (604)589-2221. Fax: (604)588-9286. E-mail: n.sayre@siwc.ca. Website: www.siwc.ca. Estab. 1992. Annual. Conference held in October. Conference duration: 3 days. Average attendance: 600. Conference for fiction (romance/science fiction/fantasy/mystery—changes focus depending upon speakers and publishers scheduled), nonfiction, scriptwriting, and poetry. "For everyone from beginner to professional." Conference held at Sheraton Guildford Hotel. **Agent/speakers attending have included:** Donald Maass (Donald Maass Literary Agency), Meredith Bernstein (Meredith Bernstein Literary Agency), Charlotte Gusay (Charlotte Gusay Literary Agency), Denise Marcil (Denise Marcil Literary Agency), Anne Sheldon and Michael Vidor (The Hardy Agency). Agents will be speaking and available for 1-on-1 meetings with attendees.

Costs Approximately $399-449 (Canadian).

Accommodations Will provide information on hotels and B&Bs on request. Conference rate: $89. Attendee must make own arrangements for hotel and transportation. For accomodations, call (800)661-2818.

Additional Information Writer's contest entries must be submitted about 8 weeks early. Length: 3,500-5,000 words, storytellers; 1,500 words maximum, nonfiction; 36 lines, poetry. Cash prizes awarded ($1,000 top prize in each category). Contest is judged by a qualified panel of writers and educators. Write, call, or e-mail for additional information. See website for more details.

THE VANCOUVER INTERNATIONAL WRITERS FESTIVAL

202-1398 Cartwright St., Vancouver BC V6H 3R8 Canada. (604)681-6330. Fax: (604)681-8400. E-mail: viwf@writersfest.bc.ca. Website: www.writersfest.bc.ca (includes information on festival). **Contact:** Jane Davidson, general manager. Estab. 1988. Annual. Held in October. Average attendance: 11,000. "This is a festival for readers and writers. The program of events is diverse and includes readings, panel discussions, seminars. Lots of opportunities to interact with the writers who attend." Held on Granville Island—in the heart of Vancouver. Two professional theaters are used as well as Performance Works (an open space). "We try to avoid specific themes. Programming takes place between February and June each year and is by invitation." **Previous agents/speakers have included:** Margaret Atwood, Maeve Binchy, J.K. Rowling.

Accommodations Local tourist information can be provided when necessary and requested.

Additional Information Brochures/guidelines are available for SASE after August. Inquiries by e-mail and fax OK. "A reminder—this is a festival, a celebration, not a conference or workshop." See website for current updates and details.

WINNIPEG INTERNATIONAL WRITERS FESTIVAL

624-100 Arthur St., Winnipeg MB R3B 1H3 Canada. (204)927-7323. Fax: (204)927-7320. E-mail: info@winnipegwords.com. Website: www.winnipegwords.com. **Contact:** Charlene Diehl, artistic director. Estab. 1997. Annual. Festival held last week of September. Conference duration: 6 days. Average attendance: 10,000. Fiction, nonfiction, scriptwriting. All areas of written/spoken word. Previous themes: Words of Wisdom, Diverse Voices. **Previous speakers/agents have included:** Michael Ondaatje, George Elliot Clarke, Esta Spalding, Margaret Atwood, Douglas Copeland, Miriam Toews. Agents will be speaking.

Costs $10-30.

Additional Information Brochures available on website. Inquiries by e-mail and fax OK.

Resources

RESOURCES

Professional Organizations

ORGANIZATIONS FOR AGENTS

Association of Authors' Representatives (AAR), P.O. Box 237201, Ansonia Station, New York NY 10003. E-mail: info@aar-online.org. Website: www.aar-online.org.

Association of Authors' Agents, 62 Grafton Way, London W1P 5LD England. (011) 44 7387 2076. Website: www.agentsassoc.co.uk.

ORGANIZATIONS FOR WRITERS

The following professional organizations publish newsletters and hold conferences and meetings at which they often share information on agents. Organizations with an asterisk (*) have members who are liaisons to the AAR.

Academy of American Poets, 588 Broadway, Suite 604, New York NY 10012-3210. (212)274-0343. E-mail: academy@poets.org. Website: www.poets.org/index.cfm.

American Medical Writers Association, 40 W. Gude Dr., Suite 101, Rockville MD 20850-1192. (301)294-5303. E-mail: amwa@amwa.org. Website: www.amwa.org.

***American Society of Journalists & Authors**, 1501 Broadway, Suite 302, New York NY 10036. (212)997-0947. Website: www.asja.org.

American Translators Association, 225 Reinekers Lane, Suite 590, Alexandria VA 22314. (703)683-6100. E-mail: ata@atanet.org. Website: www.atanet.org.

Asian American Writers' Workshop, 16 W. 32nd St., Suite 10A, New York NY 10001. (212)494-0061. E-mail: desk@aaww.org. Website: www.aaww.org.

***The Association of Writers & Writing Programs**, Mail stop 1E3, George Mason University, Fairfax VA 22030. (703)993-4301. E-mail: awp@gmu.edu. Website: www.awpwriter.org.

***The Authors' Guild, Inc.**, 31 E. 28th St., 10th Floor, New York NY 10016. (212)563-5904. E-mail: staff@authorsguild.org. Website: www.authorsguild.org.

***The Dramatists Guild of America**, 1501 Broadway, Suite 701, New York NY 10036. (212)398-9366. E-mail: membership@dramatistsguild.com. Website: www.dramaguild.com.

Education Writers Association, 2122 P St. NW, Suite 201, Washington DC 20037. (202)452-9830. E-mail: ewa@ewa.org. Website: www.ewa.org.

***Horror Writers Association**, P.O. Box 50577, Palo Alto CA 94303. E-mail: hwa@horror.org. Website: www.horror.org.

The International Women's Writing Guild, P.O. Box 810, Gracie Station, New York NY 10028-0082. (212)737-7536. E-mail: dirhahn@aol.com. Website: www.iwwg.com.

***Mystery Writers of America**, 17 E. 47th St., 6th Floor, New York NY 10017. (212)888-8171. E-mail: mwa@mysterywriters.org. Website: www.mysterywriters.org.

National Association of Science Writers, P.O. Box 890, Hedgesville WV 25427. (304)754-5077. E-mail: info@nasw.org. Website: www.nasw.org.

National League of American Pen Women, 1300 17th St. NW, Washington DC 20036-1973. (202)785-1997. E-mail: info@americanpenwomen.org. Website: www.americanpenwomen.org.

***National Writers Union**, 113 University Place, 6th Floor, New York NY 10003. (212)254-0279. E-mail: nwu@nwu.org. Website: www.nwu.org.

***PEN American Center**, 588 Broadway, Suite 303, New York NY 10012. (212)334-1660. E-mail: pen@pen.org. Website: www.pen.org.

***Poets & Writers**, 72 Spring St., Suite 301, New York NY 10012. (212)226-3586. E-mail: admin@pw.org. Website: www.pw.org.

Poetry Society of America, 15 Gramercy Park, New York NY 10003. (212)254-9628. Website: www.poetrysociety.org.

***Romance Writers of America**, 16000 Stuebner Airline Rd., Suite 140, Spring TX 77379. (832)717-5200. E-mail: info@rwanational.org. Website: www.rwanational.com.

***Science Fiction and Fantasy Writers of America**, P.O. Box 877, Chestertown MD 21620. E-mail: execdir@sfwa.org. Website: www.sfwa.org.

Society of American Business Editors & Writers, University of Missouri, School of Journalism, 134 Neff Annex, Columbia MO 65211. (573)882-7862. E-mail: sabew@missouri.edu. Website: www.sabew.org.

Society of American Travel Writers, 1500 Sunday Dr., Suite 102, Raleigh NC 27607. (919)861-5586. E-mail: satw@satw.org. Website: www.satw.org.

***Society of Children's Book Writers & Illustrators**, 8271 Beverly Blvd., Los Angeles CA 90048. (323)782-1010. E-mail: scbwi@scbwi.org. Website: www.scbwi.org.

Volunteer Lawyers for the Arts, 1 E. 53rd St., 6th Floor, New York NY 10022. (212)319-2787. Website: www.vlany.org.

Washington Independent Writers, 220 Woodward Bldg., 733 15th St. NW, Washington DC 20005. (202)737-9500. E-mail: info@washwriter.org. Website: www.washwriter.org.

Western Writers of America, 1012 Fair St., Franklin TN 37064. (615)791-1444. Website: www.westernwriters.org.

Writers Guild of Alberta, 11759 Groat Rd., Edmonton, AB T5M 3K6 Canada. (780)422-8174. E-mail: mail@writersguild.ab.ca. Website: writersguild.ab.ca.

***Writers Guild of America—East**, 555 W. 57th St., Suite 1230, New York NY 10019. (212)767-7800. Website: www.wgaeast.org.

Writers Guild of America—West, 7000 W. Third St., Los Angeles CA 90048. (323)951-4000. Website: www.wga.org.

Websites of Interest

WRITING

Fiction Addiction (www.fictionaddiction.net)
This site features articles and listings of publishers, agents, workshops, and contests for fiction writers.

Writing-World.com (www.writing-world.com)
This site offers a free, biweekly newsletter for writers, as well as instructional articles.

AGENTS

Agent Research and Evaluation (www.agentresearch.com)
This is the website of AR&E, a company that specializes in keeping tabs on literary agents. For a fee you can order their varied services to learn more about a specific agent.

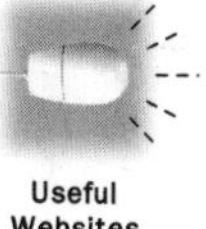
Useful Websites

Writer Beware (www.sfwa.org/beware)
The Science Fiction Writers of America's page of warnings about agents and subsidy publishers.

Writer's Market (www.writersmarket.com)
This searchable, subscription-based database is the online counterpart of *Writer's Market*, and includes contact information and submission guidelines for agents and publishers. This site also offers a free, biweekly e-newsletter.

WritersNet (www.writers.net)
This site includes a bulletin board where writers can discuss their experiences with agents.

SCRIPTWRITING

Done Deal (www.scriptsales.com)
The most useful features of this screenwriting site include descriptions of recently sold scripts, a list of script agents, and a list of production companies.

Samuel French, Inc. (www.samuelfrench.com/index.html)
This website for the play publisher Samuel French includes an index of authors and titles.

Hollywoodlitsales.com (www.hollywoodlitsales.com)
Find out what your fellow scribes are writing by reading their loglines on this website sponsored by two major Hollywood production companies.

Hollywood Creative Directory (www.hcdonline.com)
By joining this website, you'll have access to listings of legitimate players in the film, television, and new media industry.

MovieBytes (www.moviebytes.com)
Subscribe to *MovieBytes'* Who's Buying What for listings of the latest screenplay sales. Free access to one of the most comprehensive lists of screenplay contests is also offered on this site.

MARKETING AND PUBLICITY

Authorlink (www.authorlink.com)
"The news, information and marketing community for editors, literary agents, and writers." Showcases manuscripts of experienced and beginning writers.

BookTalk (www.booktalk.com)
This site "offers authors an opportunity to announce and market new releases to millions of viewers across the globe."

BookWire (www.bookwire.com)
BookWire bills itself as the book industry's most comprehensive online information source. The site includes industry news, features, reviews, fiction, events, interviews, and links to other book sites.

Useful Websites

Book Marketing Update (http://bookmarket.com)
This website by John Kremer, author of *1001 Ways to Market Your Book*, offers helpful tips for marketing books and many useful links to publishing websites. Also offers an e-newsletter so writers may share their marketing success stories.

Guerrilla Marketing (www.gmarketing.com)
The writers of *Guerrilla Marketing for Writers* provide many resources to help you successfully market your book.

Publishers Lunch (www.publisherslunch.com)
This site allows you to sign up for a free newsletter, which offers daily updates on what's going on in the wonderful world of publishing. It's a good way to keep on top of the market.

Publishers Weekly (www.publishersweekly.com)
Read the latest book publishing news on this electronic version of the popular print magazine.

Writer's Digest (www.writersdigest.com)
This site is the online counterpart of *Writer's Digest* magazine. It offers information on writing, as well as a complete bookstore of writing titles. This site also offers a free, biweekly e-newsletter.

ORGANIZATIONS

The Association of Authors' Representatives (www.aar-online.org)
This association page includes a list of member agents, a newsletter, and the organization's canon of ethics.

National Writer's Union (www.nwu.org)
Site of the National Writer's Union—the trade union for freelance writers of all genres publishing in the U.S.

PEN American Center (www.pen.org)

Site of the organization of writers and editors that seek to defend the freedom of expression and promote contemporary literature.

Writer's Guild of America (www.wga.org)

The WGA site includes advice and information on the art and craft of professional screenwriting for film, television, and interactive projects. This site offers script registration and a list of WGA signatory agencies.

Table of Acronyms

The organizations and their acronyms listed below are frequently referred to in the listings and are widely used in the industries of agenting and writing.

AAA	Association of Authors' Agents
AAP	American Association of Publishers
AAR	Association of Authors' Representatives
ABA	American Booksellers Association
ABWA	Associated Business Writers of America
AFTRA	American Federation of Television and Radio Artists
AGVA	American Guild of Variety Artists
AMWA	American Medical Writer's Association
ASJA	American Society of Journalists and Authors
ATA	Association of Talent Agents
AWA	Aviation/Space Writers Association
CAA	Canadian Authors Association
DGA	Director's Guild of America
GWAA	Garden Writers Association of America
HWA	Horror Writers of America
MWA	Mystery Writers of America, Inc.
NASW	National Association of Science Writers
NLAPW	National League of American Pen Women
NWA	National Writers Association
OWAA	Outdoor Writers Association of America, Inc.
RWA	Romance Writers of America
SAG	Screen Actor's Guild
SATW	Society of American Travel Writers
SCBWI	Society of Children's Book Writers & Illustrators
SFRA	Science Fiction Research Association
SFWA	Science Fiction and Fantasy Writers of America
WGA	Writers Guild of America
WIA	Women in the Arts Foundation, Inc.
WIF	Women in Film
WICI	Women in Communications, Inc.
WIW	Washington Independent Writers
WNBA	Women's National Book Association
WWA	Western Writers of America

Glossary

Above the line. A budgetary term for movies and TV. The line refers to money budgeted for creative talent, such as actors, writers, directors, and producers.

Advance. Money a publisher pays a writer prior to book publication, usually paid in installments, such as one-half upon signing the contract and one-half upon delivery of the complete, satisfactory manuscript. An advance is paid against the royalty money to be earned by the book. Agents take their percentage off the top of the advance, as well as from the royalties earned.

Auction. Publishers sometimes bid for the acquisition of a book manuscript with excellent sales prospects. The bids are for the amount of the author's advance, guaranteed dollar amounts, advertising and promotional expenses, royalty percentage, etc. Auctions are conducted by agents.

Backlist. Those books still in print from previous years' publication.

Backstory. The history of what has happened before the action in your script takes place, affecting a character's current behavior.

Below the line. A budgetary term for movies and TV referring to production costs, including production manager, cinematographer, editor, and crew members (gaffers, grips, set designers, make-up, etc.).

Bible. The collected background information on all characters and storylines of all existing episodes, as well as projections of future plots.

Bio. Brief (usually one page) background information about an artist, writer, or photographer. Includes work and educational experience.

Boilerplate. A standardized publishing contract. Most authors and agents make many changes to the boilerplate before accepting the contract.

Book club rights. Rights to sell a book through a book club.

Book packager. Draws elements of a book together, from the initial concept to writing and marketing strategies, and then sells the book package to a book publisher and/or movie producer. Also known as a book producer or book developer.

Business-size envelope. Also known as a #10 envelope.

Castable. A script with attractive roles for known actors.

Category fiction. A term used to include all various types of fiction. See *genre*.

Client. When referring to a literary or script agent, "client" is used to mean the writer whose work the agent is handling.

Clips. Samples, usually from newspapers or magazines, of your published work.

Commercial novels. Novels designed to appeal to a broad audience. These are often broken down into categories such as western, mystery, and romance. See *genre*.

Concept. A statement that summarizes a screenplay or teleplay—before the outline or treatment is written.

Contributor's copies. Copies of the author's book sent to the author. The number of contributor's copies is often negotiated in the publishing contract.

Co-agent. See *subagent*.

Co-publishing. Arrangement where the author and publisher share the publication costs and profits of a book. Also known as cooperative publishing.

Copyediting. Editing of a manuscript for writing style, grammar, punctuation, and factual accuracy.

Copyright. A means to protect an author's work.

Cover letter. A brief letter that accompanies the manuscript submitted to an agent or publisher.

Coverage. A brief synopsis and analysis of a script, provided by a reader to a buyer considering purchasing the work.

Critiquing service. A service offered by some agents in which writers pay a fee for comments on the salability or other qualities of their manuscript. Sometimes the critique includes suggestions on how to improve the work. Fees vary, as do the quality of the critiques. See *editing service*.

Curriculum vitae (cv). Short account of one's career or qualifications (i.e., résumé).

D person. Development person. Includes readers, story editors, and creative executives who work in development and acquisition of properties for TV and movies.

Deal memo. The memorandum of agreement between a publisher and author that precedes the actual contract and includes important issues such as royalty, advance, rights, distribution, and option clauses.

Development. The process where writers present ideas to producers who oversee the developing script through various stages to finished product.

Division. An unincorporated branch of a company.

Docudrama. A fictional film rendition of recent news-making events or people.

Editing service. A service offered by some agents in which writers pay a fee—either lump sum or per-page—to have their manuscript edited. The quality and extent of the editing varies from agency to agency. See *critiquing service*.

Electronic rights. Secondary or subsidiary rights dealing with electronic/multimedia formats (i.e., the Internet, CD-ROMs, electronic magazines).

Elements. Actors, directors, and producers attached to a project to make an attractive package.

El-hi. Elementary to high school. A term used to indicate reading or interest level.

Episodic drama. Hour-long, continuing TV show, often shown at 10 p.m.

Evaluation fees. Fees an agent may charge to evaluate material. The extent and quality of this evaluation varies, but comments usually concern the salability of the manuscript.

Exclusive. Offering a manuscript, usually for a set period of time, to just one agent and guaranteeing that agent is the only one looking at the manuscript.

Film rights. May be sold or optioned by an author to a person in the film industry, enabling the book to be made into a movie.

Flap copy. The text that appears on the inside covers of a published book and briefly explains the book's premise. Also called jacket copy.

Floor bid. If a publisher is very interested in a manuscript he may offer to enter a floor bid when the book goes to auction. The publisher sits out of the auction, but agrees to take the book by topping the highest bid by an agreed-upon percentage (usually 10 percent).

Foreign rights. Translation or reprint rights to be sold abroad.

Foreign rights agent. An agent who handles selling the rights to a country other than that of the first book agent. Usually an additional percentage (about 5 percent) will be added on to the first book agent's commission to cover the foreign rights agent.

Genre. Refers to either a general classification of writing, such as a novel, poem, or short story, or to the categories within those classifications, such as problem novels, or sonnets. Genre fiction is a term that covers various types of commercial novels, such as mystery, romance, western, science fiction, or horror.

Ghosting/ghostwriting. A writer puts into literary form the words, ideas, or knowledge of another person under that person's name. Some agents offer this service; others pair ghostwriters with celebrities or experts.

Half-hour. A 30-minute TV show, also known as a sitcom.

High concept. A story idea easily expressed in a quick, one-line description.

Hook. Aspect of the work that sets it apart from others.

Imprint. The name applied to a publisher's specific line of books.

IRC. International Reply Coupon. Buy at a post office to enclose with material sent outside your country to cover the cost of return postage. Recipients turn them in for stamps in their own country.

Log line. A one-line description of a plot as it might appear in *TV Guide.*

Long-form TV. Movies of the week (MOW) or miniseries.

Mainstream fiction. Fiction on subjects or trends that transcend popular novel categories like mystery or romance. Using conventional methods, this kind of fiction tells stories about people and their conflicts.

Marketing fee. Fee charged by some agents to cover marketing expenses. It may be used to cover postage, telephone calls, faxes, photocopying, or any other expense incurred in marketing a manuscript.

Mass market paperbacks. Softcover books, usually around 4×7, on a popular subject directed at a general audience and sold in groceries and drugstores, as well as bookstores.

MFTS. Made for TV series. A series developed for television. See *episodic drama.*

Middle reader. The general classification of books written for readers 9-11 years old.

Midlist. Those titles on a publisher's list expected to have limited sales. Midlist books are mainstream, not literary, scholarly, or genre, and are usually written by new or relatively unknown writers.

Miniseries. A limited dramatic series written for television, often based on a popular novel.

MOW. Movie of the week. A movie script written especially for television, usually seven acts with time for commercial breaks. Topics are often contemporary, sometimes controversial, fictional accounts. Also known as a made-for-TV movie.

Multiple contract. Book contract with an agreement for a future book(s).

Net receipts. One method of royalty payment based on the amount of money a book publisher receives on the sale of the book after the booksellers' discounts, special sales discounts, and returned copies.

Novelization. A novel created from the script of a popular movie, usually called a movie "tie-in" and published in paperback.

Novella. A short novel or long short story, usually 7,000 to 15,000 words. Also called a novelette.

One-time rights. This right allows a short story or portions of a fiction or nonfiction book to be published. The work can be printed again without violating the contract.

Option. Also known as a script option. Instead of buying a movie script outright, a producer buys the right to a script for a short period of time (usually six months to one year) for a small down payment. If the movie has not begun production and the producer does not wish to purchase the script at the end of the agreed time period, the rights revert back to the scriptwriter.

Option clause. A contract clause giving a publisher the right to publish an author's next book.

Outline. A summary of a book's contents in 5-15 double-spaced pages; often in the form of chapter headings with a descriptive sentence or two under each one to show the scope of the book. A script's outline is a scene-by-scene narrative description of the story (10-15 pages for a 1/2-hour teleplay; 15-25 pages for 1 hour; 25-40 pages for 90 minutes; and 40-60 pages for a 2-hour feature film or teleplay).

Packaging. The process of putting elements together, increasing the chances of a project being made. See *book packager*.

Platform. A writer's speaking experience, interview skills, website, and other abilities which help form a following of potential buyers for that author's book.

Picture book. A type of book aimed at the preschool to 8 year old that tells the story primarily or entirely with artwork. Agents and reps interested in selling to publishers of these books often handle both artists and writers.

Pitch. The process where a writer meets with a producer and briefly outlines ideas that could be developed if the writer is hired to write a script for the project.

Proofreading. Close reading and correction of a manuscript's typographical errors.

Property. Books or scripts forming the basis for a movie or TV project.

Proposal. An offer to an editor or publisher to write a specific work, usually a package consisting of an outline and sample chapters.

Prospectus. A preliminary, written description of a book, usually one page in length.

Query. A letter written to an agent or a potential market to elicit interest in a writer's work.

Reader. A person employed by an agent or buyer to go through the slush pile of manuscripts and scripts and select those worth considering.

Release. A statement that your idea is original, has never been sold to anyone else, and that you are selling negotiated rights to the idea upon payment.

Remainders. Leftover copies of an out-of-print or slow-selling book purchased from the publisher at a reduced rate. Depending on the contract, a reduced royalty or no royalty is paid on remaindered books.

Reporting time. The time it takes the agent to get back to you on your query or submission.

Reprint rights. The right to republish your book after its initial printing.

Royalties. A percentage of the retail price paid to the author for each copy of the book that is sold. Agents take their percentage from the royalties earned, as well as from the advance.

SASE. Self-addressed, stamped envelope; should be included with all correspondence.

Scholarly books. Books written for an academic or research audience. These are usually heavily researched, technical, and often contain terms used only within a specific field.

Screenplay. Script for a film intended to be shown in theaters.

Script. Broad term covering teleplay, screenplay, or stage play. Sometimes used as a shortened version of the word "manuscript" when referring to books.

Serial rights. The right for a newspaper or magazine to publish sections of a manuscript.

Simultaneous submission. Sending the same manuscript to several agents or publishers at the same time. Simultaneous queries are common; simultaneous submissions are unacceptable to many agents or publishers.

Sitcom. Situation comedy. Episodic comedy script for a television series. Term comes from the characters dealing with various situations with humorous results.

Slush pile. A stack of unsolicited submissions in the office of an editor, agent, or publisher.

Spec script. A script written on speculation without confirmation of a sale.

Standard commission. The commission an agent earns on the sales of a manuscript or script. For literary agents, this commission percentage (usually between 10 and 20 percent) is taken from the advance and royalties paid to the writer. For script agents, the commission is taken from script sales. If handling plays, agents take a percentage from the box office proceeds.

Story analyst. See *reader.*

Storyboards. Series of panels which illustrate a progressive sequence; graphics and story copy for a TV commercial, film, or filmstrip.

Subagent. An agent handling certain subsidiary rights, usually working in conjunction with the agent who handled the book rights. The percentage paid the book agent is increased to pay the subagent.

Subsidiary. An incorporated branch of a company or conglomerate (i.e., Alfred Knopf, Inc. is a subsidiary of Random House, Inc.).

Subsidiary rights. All rights other than book publishing rights included in a book publishing contract, such as paperback rights, book club rights, and movie rights. Part of an agent's job is to negotiate those rights and advise you on which to sell and which to keep.

Syndication rights. The right which allows a television station to rerun a sitcom or drama, even if the show originally appeared on a different network.

Synopsis. A brief summary of a story, novel, or play. As a part of a book proposal, it is a comprehensive summary condensed in a page or page and a half, single-spaced. See *outline.*

Tearsheet. Published samples of your work, usually pages torn from a magazine.

Teleplay. Script for television.

Terms. Financial provisions agreed upon in a contract.

Textbook. Book used in a classroom at the elementary, high school, or college level.

Trade book. Either a hardcover or softcover book; subject matter frequently concerns a special interest for a general audience; sold mainly in bookstores.

Trade paperback. A soft-bound volume, usually around 5×8, published and designed for the general public; available mainly in bookstores.

Translation rights. Sold to a foreign agent or foreign publisher.

Treatment. Synopsis of a television or film script (40-60 pages for a 2-hour feature film or teleplay).

Turnaround. When a script has been in development but has not been made in the time allotted, it can be put back on the market.

Unsolicited manuscript. An unrequested manuscript sent to an editor, agent, or publisher.

Young adult (YA). The general classification of books written for readers age 12-18.

Young reader. Books written for readers 5-8 years old, where artwork only supports the text.

Literary Agents Specialties Index

The subject index is divided into fiction and nonfiction subject categories. To find an agent interested in the type of manuscript you've written, see the appropriate sections under the subject headings that best describe your work.

FICTION

Action/Adventure

Comic Books/Cartoon

Confession

Contemporary Issues

Detective/Police/Crime

Specialties Index

Erotica

Ethnic

Experimental

Family Saga

Fantasy

Feminist

Gay/Lesbian

Glitz

Hi-Lo

Historical

Horror

Humor/Satire

Juvenile

Literary

Mainstream/ Contemporary

Military/War

Multicultural

Multimedia

Mystery/Suspense

Occult

Picture Books

Plays

Poetry

Poetry in Translation

Psychic/Supernatural

Regional

Religious/Inspirational

Romance

Science Fiction

Short Story Collections

Spiritual

Sports

Thriller

Translation

Westerns/Frontier

Women's

Young Adult

NONFICTION

Agriculture/Horticulture

Americana

Animals

Anthropology/Archaeology

Art/Architecture/Design

Biography/Autobiography

Business/Economics

Specialties Index

Child Guidance/ Parenting

Computers/Electronic

Cooking/Foods/Nutrition

Crafts/Hobbies

Creative Nonfiction

Current Affairs

Education

Ethnic/Cultural Interests

Gardening

Gay/Lesbian Issues

Government/Politics/Law

Health/Medicine

History

Specialties Index

How-To

Humor/Satire

Interior Design/ Decorating

Juvenile Nonfiction

Language/Literature/Criticism

Memoirs

Military/War

Money/Finance

Multicultural

Music/Dance

Nature/Environment

New Age/Metaphysics

Philosophy

Photography

Popular Culture

Psychology

Recreation

Regional

Religious/Inspirational

Science/Technology

Self-Help/Personal Improvement

Sex

Sociology

Software

Spirituality

Sports

Theater/Film

Translation

Travel

True Crime/ Investigative

Women's Issues/Studies

Young Adult

Script Agents Specialties Index

The subject index is divided into script subject categories. To find an agent interested in the type of screenplay you've written, see the appropriate sections under the subject headings that best describe your work.

Action/Adventure

Biography/Autobiography

Cartoon/Animation

Comedy

Contemporary Issues

Detective/Police/Crime

Erotica

Ethnic

Experimental

Family Saga

Fantasy

Feminist

Gay/Lesbian

Glitz

Historical

Horror

Juvenile

Mainstream

Multicultural

Multimedia

Mystery/Suspense

Psychic/Supernatural

Regional

Religious/Inspirational

Romantic Comedy

Romantic Drama

Science Fiction

Sports

Teen

Thriller

Western/Frontier

Script Agents Format Index

Soap Opera

Theatrical Stage Play

TV Movie Of The Week (TV MOW)

Variety Show

Agencies Indexed by Openness to Submissions

We've listed the literary and script agencies and independent publicists according to their openness to submissions. Check this index to find an agent or publicist who is appropriate for your level of experience. Some companies are listed under more than one category.

NEW AGENCY ACTIVELY SEEKING CLIENTS

Literary Agents

Publicists

AGENCIES SEEKING BOTH NEW AND ESTABLISHED WRITERS

Literary Agents

Script Agents

Publicists

AGENCIES PREFERRING TO WORK WITH ESTABLISHED WRITERS, MOSTLY OBTAIN NEW CLIENTS THROUGH REFERRALS

Literary Agents

Openness Index

Script Agents

Publicists

AGENCIES HANDLING ONLY CERTAIN TYPES OF WORK OR WORK BY WRITERS UNDER CERTAIN CIRCUMSTANCES

Literary Agents

Script Agents

Publicists

AGENCIES NOT CURRENTLY SEEKING NEW CLIENTS

Literary Agents

Script Agents

Geographic Index

Some writers prefer to work with an agent or independent publicist in their vicinity. If you're such a writer, this index offers you the opportunity to easily select agents who are close to home. Agencies and publicists are separated by state. We've also arranged them according to the sections in which they appear in the book (Literary Agents, Script Agents, or Independent Publicists).

ARIZONA

Literary Agents

CALIFORNIA

Literary Agents

Script Agents

Publicists

COLORADO

Literary Agents

Script Agents

Publicists

CONNECTICUT

Literary Agents

DISTRICT OF COLUMBIA

Literary Agents

FLORIDA

Literary Agents

Script Agents

Publicists

GEORGIA

Literary Agents

Script Agents

Publicists

HAWAII

Literary Agents

IDAHO

Literary Agents

ILLINOIS

Literary Agents

Script Agents

Publicists

INDIANA

Literary Agents

Script Agents

IOWA

Literary Agents

LOUISIANA

Literary Agents

MARYLAND

Literary Agents

MASSACHUSETTS

Literary Agents

Publicists

MICHIGAN

Publicists

MINNESOTA

Literary Agents

MISSISSIPPI

Literary Agents

NEVADA

Script Agents

NEW HAMPSHIRE

Literary Agents

NEW JERSEY

Literary Agents

Publicists

NEW MEXICO

Script Agents

NEW YORK

Literary Agents

Agents Index

This index of agent names can help you located agents you may have read or heard about even when you do not know the name of their agency. Agents names are listed with their agencies' names.

C

G

S

T

U

V

W

Y

Z

Agents Index

General Index

C

D

E

F

S

T

General Index